SCARLET CITADEL

Walking Shadow: Book One

Jack Fields

CONTENTS

<u>DEDICATION</u>

*For my mother, who moves mountains
while the rest of us struggle with hills.*

ACKNOWLEGMENTS

Whether you are listening during a June storm or thumbing through the pages
(digital or physical) on a pleasant afternoon, I feel both obliged and delighted
to inform you that this book would not have been realized without the support
of countless individuals, some of whom I shall thank by name here and some
who must regretfully accept a blanket (though heartfelt!) "thanks" from me.
To Jez, Chrissy, Geneva, Kristen, and the rest of The Legion Publisher family
at large, my deepest gratitude. Here's to the rest of the series, and thereafter,
gang.
Thanks also to my wonderful editors, Michelle Dunbar and Judy Roth, who lent
their incisive contributions to this first of three scarlet dreams.
Fellow authors Lars Machmüller, Rachel Ní Chuirc, and Brian J. Nordon
provided crucial advice that shaped this book's beginning.
Lastly, to family and to friends, thank you.
For everything.

ACT ONE

HUGHES

CHAPTER ONE

Through the thumping rains, the hot red sodium lamplight, the gabble, slurp, hiss, and splash of Corinth City's nighttime bazaar, three shadows ran—one terrified, the other two hunting.

The hunters were a man and a woman, and no one in their right mind would want to meet them in a dark alley at night. The woman was squat, cheerful-mouthed, and she had big wrists and bigger earrings of looped gold. Her companion was thin, sour-mouthed, and unnaturally tall. His hands were the gaunt hands of a piano player, only longer, stretched, and he wore a ring the color of smoke.

If you did happen to meet these two in a dark alley, and there was no moon to light it, then the hunters would light that alley themselves. Both man and woman shone, an eerie pale glitter that came from under their skin.

Stalking their quarry that early summer evening, they looked like diamond-dusted monsters that had escaped from the nightmare world of a child.

In the wild cramped trade hub where vendors ladled out soup with nutrient cubes bobbing like tofu-tasting marshmallows in the bowls, where bawdy laughter mixed with shouts and grunts and grumbles about noisy traffic congestion, where lentils and imitation beef broth scented the night, people made way for the man and the woman.

For here in Leonidas District in Corinth City, the pair had a reputation for the sort of trouble usually associated with plague, or natural disasters.

Their names were Miss Gleam and Mr. Glint.

The other shadow, the one the hunters were gaining on, gaining on *fast*, was not a remarkable person.

His hair was dark, and the pouches under his eyes were darker still. Cold puddle water soaked through his thin-soled shoes and squelched around his toes. Rain dripped from the tails of his long moth-gnawed coat. Ten thousand other people could claim to be wearing similar clothes in Leonidas District. It was a tatty place, as destitute a shamble of shacks, tenements, filthy apartments, and weed-stricken pavements as you could hope to find in the city. Its inhabitants could claim this swiftly running shadow's exhaustion, his doubt, even his poverty (although there was no one as afraid as he was just then, not even *close*).

What they couldn't claim was his face.

It was perhaps his one exceptional feature. At rest it was ordinary enough. The jaw was firm, and he had intelligent eyes like the eyes of a fox. But when his face expressed an emotion, every muscle, every line, every corner of that once ordinary face exploded with significance and energy. A hundred years ago, in the age of Corinth City theatre, a face that malleable—as pliant and shapeable as warm clay—would have been received with adulation and applause like stirring thunder.

In this day and age, it was worth shit.

The shadow risked a glance over one shoulder in time to see Glint shoving a party of late night drinkers aside. Gleam caught his eye and smiled with all her teeth. Even at this distance, he could see she had filed them into fangs.

The shadow felt panic wrap his guts like rancid snakeskin.

His name was Hughes.

***

To his left and right Hughes saw a blur of stalls set with plucked rotisserie pigeon, sizzling pans, steam-belching ovens tended by a girl with no eyes, only a single ocular implant in her forehead swiveling crazily, and over many stalls hung Yi-Shi paper lanterns adding their rich blue diffusion to the sodium-lit madness of the bazaar.

Splashing and elbowing his way through the densely packed crowd, Hughes snatched sight of a booth selling cracked night vision goggles, smooth black cattle prods repurposed as sex toys, and other weird sundries. The booth was moving right into his path on mechanical legs shaking so violently they might have belonged to a newborn foal. Sparks spat from the knee joints.

Coattails flapping, Hughes slowed, planted a boot in the weakest-looking joint, and applied pressure. A dozen worms of numbing voltage coursed up his shin. But the booth tilted, spilled some wares, then gave up the fight against gravity and tipped in a fantastic crash.

"Hey!" The booth's owner scrambled to gather up his merchandise. "Hey, what the fuck do you think you're—"

A streak in the damply murmuring dark, Hughes took off running helter-skelter, his elevated pulse throbbing in his temples.

What I need, he thought through the mist of fright. *What I need is a friendly streetbeater, a pot of the most soothing tea ever brewed, and a quiet place to drink it three-thousand miles away, in that order.*

Streetbeaters were Corinth City police. The chances of finding one in Leonidas District were pretty good this time of year. Cold snow-crisp winter kept the streetbeaters holed up in Ptolema or Nikandros Districts where fat wealthy citizens—keen to keep themselves fat and wealthy in a season of frostbitten desperates inclined to a little domestic robbery—turned on patio geothermals that made the air ripple and snowflakes evaporate against great invisible tongues of warmth. Quite the incentive for the police to guard the fat cats, leaving the rest of the city felines to duke it out for scraps in the pre-spring ice.

But summer?

Well, streetbeaters could be anywhere in summer.

Even Hughes' neck of the woods.

And the chances of them being friendly to him, a drenched, sweat-slicked nineteen-year-old kid without a single chipped credit to his name?

One step at a time, Hughes consoled himself, trying to ignore his lungs that felt like swollen bags full of boiling poison. *One step at a—*

Twenty strides behind him the angry hollering of the booth owner had changed.

"Asshole, what a... hey. Hey, do either of you two know that kid? He just wrecked my stall!"

Hughes looked back. The booth owner was getting in the way of Miss Gleam and Mr. Glint. "Hold up, I'm talking to you!"

Evidently he had not heard of Miss Gleam and Mr. Glint. He would not be making such a fuss if he had. Bazaar-goers and other people were giving the man a wide berth. Meanwhile both Gleam and Glint were looking at him the way wolves look at a sheep that has learned to growl.

"Black bird!" came the cry of an aviary boy in front of Hughes. The boy was advertising syringes of hallucinogens varying in intensity from softcore to explosive psychedelia from the cinched straps of a transparent briefcase. "Red hawk! Blue swallow! White robin! Get some Yellow raven in your veins, join the great rookery in the sky, man."

Hughes' overstimulated brain noted the constellation of track marks running along the boy's arms as quite suddenly there came a tremendous *crack* from behind him.

Hughes swallowed a yelp of alarm.

What the hell had that been? A whip? Sure sounded like one, but no. Even tonight, that would be a touch too absurd.

He turned to look, and too late, he jerked out of the way of a bodega merchant slopping out his bucket. The bucket had been filled to the brim with wine. Earlier that evening the wine was sipped, sloshed over diseased gums, and spat out again so the drinker could tell the bodega merchant, "Why, yes, that'll do."

Hughes was too worried about that terrible jarring *crack* to be overly bothered as a mixture of mulched grape and saliva splashed his right cheek, his neck, and a few warm sticky drops found his ear canal.

Okay, not a whip.

What then?

Kids popping snickerdrakes on the sidewalk for a giggle?

Hughes thought that a more likely explanation. He'd flung a few snickerdrakes in his time, and they did make a sound that would raise the hair on your neck.

That was when he heard the screams.

They were high-pitched, and puling, screams that hinted at pain so bad the brain could not even imagine it.

Of course, there was the possibility that the noise—the *crack*—was in fact something Glint or Gleam could do. Some nasty faculty at their disposal that could make someone (the affronted booth owner, probably) scream in that shrill, blood-curdling way...

Hughes ducked under a dripping rain-sagged awning. *What nasty faculty? What the hell am I thinking?*

Other than the telltale skin-glow that marked Glint and Gleam as agents of their employer, those two had no magic to call on.

Did they?

The screams went on and on, and Hughes realized he hadn't been seized by panic before. That greasy snakeskin nausea folding his belly wasn't panic.

It was dread.

This—the wheeling white pendulous thing swooping up and down his insides, *ticking ticking ticking* toward something, some absolute end, some catastrophe designed with special care for him and him alone, oh God, God, dear sweet fucking God—*THIS* was panic.

Bunching his leg muscles he leaped with a survivor's jacked-up athleticism over a lemon-yellow parasol hoisted above two elderly women without a single genuine tooth between them, their lined knotted hands twitching over a game of pavement poker.

He landed badly and scrambled up, skinning both palms in the process.

They stung.

The screaming faded. Silence spread at his heels.

That was Gleam and Glint closing in on him. The bazaar offered none of its wares to those two. It merely stepped aside with terrified politeness and let them get on with the night's dark business.

Lunging between two narrow-set stalls, Hughes redoubled his speed, achieved a sprint, and accelerated as he left the bazaar for the regular streets. Kiosks and stool-clustered counters were replaced with narrow garbage-smelling lanes. The hectic noise of the trade hub faded from his pounding eardrums, a concert played on the nerves rather than strings, receding, vanishing faster than he would have believed as the rains and the murky little side alleys of Leonidas welcomed their son Hughes as if he were prodigal. Street level windows peeped blindly at his passing. Rats squeaked in protest as his boots squashed their dissolving cardboard houses.

Quick breath hammered along the column of his raw throat.

Eddies of dirty water searching for sewer drains went *splish-splish-splash* under him. Somewhere close by, muffled through window glass, a shouting match between children, their voices' frantic tempo a cross between battle and melody.

No conscious thoughts occurred to Hughes, only a vague huge HOPE for escape and safety written across his brain in capitals as big as the night. The night, yes, the night he wished with all his soul would show him kindness, even mercy...

Wasn't he owed mercy after all he'd been through these past few weeks?

After Kim?

Ah, now *there* was a conscious thought piercing the panic. So conscious it shocked him into slowing for a precious second or two before he could recover himself and dash on.

Kim Kallaimon. He could almost see her face through the curtains of rain, the centerpiece of some beautiful stage play about to be revealed. But this was no time to think on her.

Swiftly turning from Porto Rosso Lane onto Agorippis Street, Hughes cut his eyes along it to check for potential hiding spots...

And stopped.

***

Ashimmer with rain, Agorippis Street wound before him like a slender animal, eventually reaching a cross section where bicycle bells tinkled and beggars sheltered under soggy news broadsheets and dirty magazines. Studied like that, the street seemed oddly dead. Aside from a few boarded up waxing houses, massage parlors, and replica dog purveyors, posters clung mummified to the lumpy uneven stone walls, and a single tenacious business advertised that Agorippis was, in point of fact, alive and kicking.

The sign was an eight-foot-high bullock, rendered in sickly green neon, one horn draped in a red cloak, the other skewering a dummy dressed to look like a matador, the puncture gushing light in a sort of funny, sort of vile simulation of blood at intervals.

Pamplona, the sign read. *All bulls are welcome. The hornier, the better!*

Insectile, the neon hummed under the *pitter-patter-plitter-simmer* of the rains.

Hughes had stopped because of the figure emerging from *Pamplona*—a man in his middle forties. A woman's arms snaked out of the dark of the whorehouse and scissored around the man's neck. He leaned in, his head vanishing from sight, and Hughes heard the woman giggle.

No cause for interest, sure. Except Hughes believed with a growing certainty that the armor the man wore was red. *Scarlet* red, no less.

Hughes broke into a jog, trying his best to look like an upstanding citizen.

"Uh, excuse me!" he called. "Scarlet Citadel, right?"

The armored man stiffened. He squinted at Hughes through the rain, his expression suspicious, and something else too (not scared, couldn't be). He reached up with big gauntleted hands, yanked the woman's arms loose, and said something to her that made her dart into *Pamplona* and slam the door shut. Then he strode away from Hughes as if the kid were carrying a special kind of leprosy.

Hughes didn't have time for this.

If this man was Scarlet Citadel, he was not a streetbeater cop or a common thug. He was, if the vids and city gossip about the Citadel were to be believed, a mixture between a celebrity and a warrior. That was good enough for Hughes. *More* than good enough.

Hughes picked up the pace, aware he was running on dwindling fumes now, and managed to clap the man on the shoulder.

"Hey," he said. "Look, I'm sorry to bother you, only I need some help."

The man turned to look at him, and Hughes felt the first prickle of foreboding. The man had a squashed often-broken nose, ruddy cheeks crusted in stubble, and beady piggish eyes that glared warily at Hughes from beneath a rat's nest of brown hair. Body odor wafted from his undershirt, and he must have been congested because he was breathing through his mouth, the lips dry and cracked.

That breath gave Hughes his second prickle.

It carried a sour whiff of cheap vodka.

Hughes hesitated. Not for long though, because in an instant he spotted what he'd been looking for. A small, carved *J* over the pectoral line of the man's breastplate.

J, short for *Jolene*, as in designed, forged, and fitted for this man by one of the brilliant artisans who bore that name. Who could believe a single engraved letter might inspire such incredible relief?

If he was wearing armor created by a Jolene, that meant this brothel-visiting drunk did indeed belong to that legendary organization known as the Scarlet Citadel. It meant he knew how to use the short-handled hatchet on his hip. Most important of all, it meant the hatchet was enchanted with magic.

Hughes felt his hope perk up again, vodka breath or no vodka breath.

"Didn't you hear me calling?" he asked. "I need help. There are people after me. They're going to hurt me if you don't stop them."

The man said nothing.

"Um. Hello?"

Nothing.

A third eerie prickling sensation, this one the strongest yet. "Do you understand me?"

The man's eyes flickered over Hughes' shoulder, and Hughes knew that Glint and Gleam were there, only sixty feet back, at the mouth of the street. He couldn't hear them. Still, they were there all right.

Glint would be shambling, his hat brim, gaunt cheekbones, and his pointed chin adrip with rain. Gleam would be sauntering as if she had all the time in the world, her smile like harvest moonlight capping the teeth of a werewolf.

If he let the swooping panic conquer him, if he spun around, Hughes would see the two of them poised exactly in that moving photograph, and his courage would shrivel like fruit in a drought.

So Hughes didn't turn.

He fixed the Scarlet Citadel man with a look that would arrest the most criminally distracted attention, dove deep inside himself, grabbed his Performance with steady determined fingers, and hauled it up to join them all in the ceaseless downpour and the imminent danger that would—at any moment—reach a terrible crescendo.

He summoned it as a Hortesian fakir summons his will to walk painlessly on hot coals, and in response Hughes' Performance shot through him like every drug that aviary boy in the bazaar had in his briefcase.

His Performance was, of course, only a very powerful feeling.

Hughes
Performance Level: 7
Influence the behavior of others using your physical and vocal performance, as well as your stage presence. **WARNING!** *Bad performances result in negative reception.*

Chance of Success: 27%	Next Level: +3% to Chance of Success
	Level 10 Secret Ability: ???

Hughes straightened. His shoulders squared. His head canted to one side just as his chin developed a forceful little jut, almost accusatory. He drew a deep breath, and when he spoke, his voice was different. It was strong, not loud exactly, but firm and unrelenting. The Performance had begun.

CHAPTER TWO

"**Y**ou look at me," said Hughes.

At last a reaction from the Scarlet Citadel man. Slowly, too slowly for Hughes' liking, the brows knit together.

"I'm looking," said the man.

"I bet you don't see much. Just some bothersome boy. Still, let me tell you why you're going to help me. I don't know much about the Citadel, but I do know they have a lot of status in the city. A status is built on reputation, and reputation is built on public opinion. That building, *Pamplona*, is a sex work residence, right?"

Hughes glanced at the building in question. So did the man, his face tightening in bewilderment. Hughes thought he also saw a flash of trepidation in those squinty bloodshot eyes.

"I wonder," said Hughes conversationally, "what your colleagues in the Scarlet Citadel would think if they knew where you were tonight. Do you think they'd be understanding? Sex work is perfectly legal in Corinth City. But, ah..." Hughes shrugged languidly. "There are social factors. Opinions are funny things. Sometimes they blow over us without issue. Other times, they're storms, much like the one drenching us tonight. Gossip tempests. Workplace murmurs like quiet thunder. Speculation fierce as lightning. I'm just a kid," Hughes added, "but I know opinions don't always blow over us. Sometimes they knock us on our ass.

"Now are you going to keep me safe from these people or not?"

How close were Gleam and Glint? Thirty feet? Twenty?

No matter. It was coming.

And here.

It.

Came.

With a rush of power Hughes pushed his Performance. He had used a combination of both physical and vocal theatrics, and now standing like some proud, intent gargoyle against a backdrop of rippling rain Hughes exerted his presence, completing the show that might save his skin if it worked.

The man's expression changed, as Hughes knew it would. It happened as quickly and as easily as you might turn off a light. One moment the man was guarded and hostile, the next he was slack from brow to jawbone, all the facial muscles loosening at once. He looked dumbly at Hughes with a cow's patient blandness.

The thing was, Hughes' little display was not something people were accustomed to. As far as everyone was concerned, those who had power (arcane power, mind you) commanded it through Strength, or Dexterity, or possibly Intelligence if they were feeling particularly adventurous. These feelings (we might call them "abilities") were the foundations on which the Scarlet Citadel was built. It was they and they alone who could make use of these abilities. Only they were legally able to wield magical weapons. Ordinary people were quite separate from the business of magic. The secrets of how to awaken someone's abilities, as well as the intricacies of enchanted objects, were just that—secret.

And so the Scarlet Citadel was an immensely important and gossip-worthy fixture of the city.

Which went a long way to say that Performance was not on anybody's radar. How could it be? Theatre and the power of words was dusty old stuff, a relic of different times. Not worse times, exactly, but different all the same.

Outmoded.

In fact as far as Hughes knew, he was the only one in the whole of Corinth City who used Performance like this, to influence people. Perhaps he was the only person who had *ever* been able to use it.

His eyes flickered over the man's face, searching.

Come on.

Testing Performance...

All at once Hughes was aware of footsteps.

Some jittery instinct made his ear twitch with warning.

There they were again, the footfalls! One set light, the other heavy. Both were behind him, so suddenly close that the patch of skin at the back of his neck began to crawl.

At his sides his hands were hooked into tense claws.

Come on you bastard.

Testing Performance...

Splish-splish, went Miss Gleam's shoes.

Splash, went Mr. Glint's.

Is this what a heart attack feels like? Hughes wondered. Under the rainfall he was drenched in sweat.

My heart. Fuck, but it hurts when it jumps like that.

Totally unaware he was doing it, he had bunched those hooked fingers of his into shivering fists.

Splish-splish.

Please.

Splash.

Please just let this work.

Registering Result...

His heart gave a terrific aching lurch...

... and then it froze. And his blood froze. Lastly his face froze in a locked look of absolute horror.

The whole thing, from the start of his Performance to the Result, seemed to take an agonizing length of time. In reality only about three or four seconds had passed. That was abilities for you. Fast and fickle.

Hughes was in a bad way just then. The Result was a feeling, like tiredness or hunger or love, just like the Performance was a feeling.

And as he felt it, it stunned him.

No, he thought numbly, even as Mr. Glint's long thin fingers slid like bone-stuffed eels up his back, closing tight around his shoulder. *No, that can't be right. Cannot be.*

But the sensation was like words in his head and heart.

Performance Failed

+1 Experience On A Failed Attempt

Congratulations!

***

I'm done for, he thought. *Done for. Done f—*

"Salutations and good evening to you, gentlemen," said Miss Gleam, her voice as sparkling and as cold as any star in a clear November sky. She approached, her padding gait like a tiger's as she passed by Mr. Glint whose hand was still tight on Hughes' shoulder. "We do hate to intrude, only we spied the pair of you malingering in this charming example of Leonidas District's perambulatory architecture—that is its *strutting space*, its *streets*, of course!—and could not help but feel a spike of envy. Why, this dank little corridor of dilapidation is so teeming with atmosphere, I feel I could slice off a corner of it and spread it on my toast. A veritable marmalade of decay."

She bared her gold-enameled fangs to show how happy this made her.

"Also," Gleam continued, "we noticed that one of your merry pair was in fact our long lost brother. Hughes, my dear fellow, how are you?"

She stepped close, grasped his chin, and proceeded to turn his head back and forth as if admiring something stuffed on a mantelpiece, or perhaps something she was merely considering stuffing after she had eaten the parts that were alive.

Congratulations, Hughes thought, who was so afraid he truly believed he would soon be as crazy as a loon. *+1 Experience. Congratulations. Why, thanks. Thank you so very much for that.*

This close, he could see Gleam was iridescent all over.

Her hair, blue as cobalt.

Her fingernails.

Her skin.

Even her eyeballs seemed to shine and might have been pretty were it not for the irises. Fascinated, he found that for love or money he simply could not take his eyes off those irises. They were hypnotic, black as a child's conception of the dark and all the hungry things that live there.

"Naturally we elected to join you," Gleam continued cheerfully. "Two birds, one stone, and so forth. Regardless, now that our family reunion has gotten off to an exciting start, we must keep the ball rolling and speak with our estranged sibling in private. You don't mind, do you?" She shot a coy glance at the man in the scarlet armor.

The man blinked. By now the rain had soaked his formerly dry hair. He pushed tangles of it from his face where it had plastered to his skin and looked from Hughes, to the short smiling Gleam, to the tall frowning Glint, and then back at Hughes again.

"He's your brother?" said the man doubtfully.

"Our *long lost* brother," Miss Gleam corrected. She snaked her arms around Hughes and planted a kiss on his cheek. "Oh, lost and found again! How wonderful it's going to be to have you all to ourselves."

"He's... your brother?" The man seemed to be sticking on this point.

"Yes," said Gleam. "Is there a problem?"

The man rasped a hand over his stubble. "Not much of a family resemblance," he said reluctantly. "What with ah... your um..."

"Ah. You are referring to our brother's unfortunate lack of luminosity. I grasp your confusion, sir." Gleam nodded sympathetically and fixed Hughes with a look of the deepest pity. "Indeed, our brother is not very bright in the flesh department. His mind is the same, more's the pity. He probably babbled all sorts of nonsense to you before we arrived. Isn't that so? Yes. Yes, I can imagine. He is a troubled boy. Still," she said, renewing the hug, "we do *adore* him so."

The man regarded her with the same flavor of suspicion he'd had for Hughes. Sometime in the past minute or so his hand had come to rest on the handle of his hatchet.

"He said there were people after him," said the man, and for a moment Hughes was more puzzled than frightened. The Performance had failed, hadn't it? "He said you were going to hurt him."

"*Us?* Hurt *him?*" Gleam's eyes widened at the effrontery of it all. "Do not be ridiculous. This is our flesh and blood. We take flesh and blood very seriously, do we not, Mr. Glint?"

"Yeah," Glint replied, and even though his voice was quiet like the crunch of gravel in a front yard, it seemed to fill the alley like the sound of a tomb door crashing shut. "Especially the stringy bits. Take them very serious-like, we do."

"There you have it!" declared Gleam. "Now, don't let us keep you..."

One last time the man looked at Hughes.

Draw your hatchet, Hughes begged the man with his expression, willing him desperately to do it. *Your hand's already there. It found the handle for a reason. Something in you knows this is all too strange to add up, so draw it now! Don't you see? How can you not? These people are deeply, extraordinarily wrong, and you, you fighter of the Scarlet Citadel have got to do what is right!*

The man took his hand off the hatchet. He snuffled, coughed, and croaked like a river toad. Something thick and wet hocked up from his lungs and into his mouth. Finally he spat, a great white-green gobbet of phlegmy spittle that skimmed Hughes' hand before splatting in the liquid flow of the pavement.

The Performance had indeed failed.

Hughes felt doomed.

"I'm off. You'd be as well off doing likewise. Weather like this doesn't bode well for your ah... *family reunion.* I'm off," the man repeated. "Take care."

"Oh, we will, sir," cooed Gleam as the man plodded away down Agorippis Street. "Most assuredly we will." She gave his retreating back a friendly wave, and then she turned her toothsome smile (which was not unlike a basket of gold-tipped darning needles) on Hughes, who shivered miserably.

"Alone at last," she said.

CHAPTER THREE

"I don't suppose..." Hughes swallowed drily. "I don't suppose it'd do any good if I said you don't have to do this?"

"That depends," said Gleam. "For you it would change absolutely nothing. For Mr. Glint and I, it would be quite funny, and therefore I encourage you to go ahead with this statement of yours."

"Right." Hughes sighed. "In that case, you don't have to do this. I don't have the money. Hurt me if you've got to, but I don't have a single credit on me. I'd give it to you. I will! Give it to you, that is. The full sum, all accounted for."

"When?" she said sweetly.

"Tonight."

Gleam's smile broadened. "Hughes. When I said your statement would be quite funny, only now, a moment ago? I could never—not *ever*—have predicted the shamelessly nude lies that would trip naked and coquettish off your tongue, could never have *dreamed* of the ensuing gush of utter bunk and scramble that would rattle out of that handsome weathercock you call a throat. You've led us a merry chase, and yet defeated at the finish line you had one final burst of jocularity in store for us." She seized his face, cupping it in her hands. "If I wore a skirt, I would twirl it. If I wore aluminum on the toes of my shoes, I would tap them. If I wore a corset, my very sides would now be splitting. In their absence, I am forced to improvise. Attend."

She reached into her jacket pocket and took out a pair of scissors. The blades were long and crooked as the teeth of a wolf. With a tensing of her fingers she closed them and opened them. The scissors made a horrible *snicker-snick.*

Gleam teased their edge along Hughes' jaw. "Hold him still, Mr. Glint."

Hughes felt Glint's hands tighten around him, impossibly strong.

"Now." Gleam took a lock of Hughes' hairs between her scintillating nails. "Where do you live?"

Hughes briefly considered lying to her. But why bother?

She knew.

"Leonidas District," he answered.

"That's very cute, Hughes. Name the building."

"The *Scriptorium and Flavored Tea Emporium*," he replied stiffly.

Snick.

A single lock of his dark hair wisped away.

Gleam held the scissors up for his inspection.

Before Hughes' gaze the blades deepened, their steel-gray exterior turning black as slate, black as Gleam's watchful eyes.

Hughes gave up on luck at that point. Obviously he and luck weren't meant for one another. He was a prisoner, his Performance had failed, and now at the end of his tether he was faced with the fact that Gleam did, in fact, wield a magic item.

He scowled bitterly as another lock was chosen.

Gleam said, "Did it make you happy, being caught by Mr. Glint and I?"

Hughes stared at her, dumbfounded. A sudden hysterical laugh boiled up his throat, but he capped it before it blasted out between his lips and got him killed. Even so, the absurdity of the question made him bold. "Certainly. It's made me all rosy inside."

Snick.

One more hair snatched away by the firm moist fingers of the rain.

But when Gleam held the scissors up for him to see, the blades did not turn black. Instead they bleached as white as bone.

"One thing you must know about me, my dear Hughes. I am not a woman who deals in gray areas. For me they do not offer a diversity of shades but rather one astonishingly stupid monochrome. I am, in point of fact, fatally opposed to grays. I tend to get upset by them. So I am a black and white sort of person. Large black truths." *Snick*, went the blades. "And little white lies." *Snicker-snick.*

"I like lies," said Mr. Glint.

Miss Gleam tittered. "They have their merits, old boy. That's true. And truths are very laudable, of course."

"I was only saying," clarified Glint for Hughes' benefit, "if you tell porky pies, that means we get to start hurting you right away. But if you spill your guts, well, then we got to hear you out. Sort of pro... Prol..."

"Prolongs," prompted Gleam kindly.

"Thanks, *prolongs* the job."

"My associate is quite right," Gleam announced to the street in general. "Alas, temporal considerations aside, things usually end up turning out the same. With flesh and blood, eh Mr. Glint?"

"Lovely stringy bits, Miss Gleam," agreed Glint.

His breath was warm, and it carried a whiff of decay. Hughes could only imagine what his teeth were like, and he did, much too vividly.

Meanwhile Gleam brandished the scissors and offered Hughes the look a deranged surgeon gives her strapped-down patient, a look that reassures you that in spite of all evidence to the contrary, this will not hurt a bit.

Well fuck me in the neon glow of Pamplona, thought Hughes. *She's got the world's sharpest lie-detector, and she's going to use it on me.*

An idea was beginning to form in his head. It was very young, only toddling and teething, but it was growing fast and before long it would be old enough for him to give it a voice.

"You are not—and you'll forgive me for being glib here, Hughes—a man of considerable means?" Gleam wanted to know. "You are, in actuality, poor?"

"Yes," he replied, and if his tone was rigid before it was stiff as wood now.

Snick.

The scissors went black: truth.

"You live with your father in his place of work?" she continued. "The *Scriptorium and Flavored Tea Emporium?*"

"Yeah."

Snick.

The scissors went black.

"Excellent," Gleam praised him. "It is our understanding, Hughes, that three months ago you entered into a formal arrangement with our employer, yes?"

"Yes."

Snick.

The scissors went black.

"Good. Now the arrangement was for a sizeable sum of credits, the repayment of which would be incremental, monthly, and with what I do not mind telling you amounts to a very reasonable rate of cumulative interest." Gleam tapped a claw-shaped fingernail thoughtfully on Hughes' cheekbone. "What did you use the money for, Hughes?"

"Does it matter?"

"Indulge me."

"I bought a car," said Hughes, and under that claw-shaped fingernail he felt his cheeks burn with hot shame. Not for buying the car but what had become of it.

Snick.

The scissors went black. But this time it was a washed-out black veering to gray, and Gleam glared at the blades with distaste.

"A half-truth at best," she said. "What else did you buy?"

"Lots of things. Dinners. Big screen vid tickets. A trip to the psychedelic jellyfish asylum. Maybe... a few hotel rooms. Oh," he added, "I rented an apartment near the Jamclaw Brewery Center in Nikandros District. But..." His mind forgot the idea it was forming, and for a few grueling moments it showed him memories of the day he'd woken to find the bed, the apartment, and his own heart empty. "I didn't keep the apartment very long."

Snick.

Another lock of Hughes' hair vanished and the scissors went pitch black.

"The car must have been expensive," Gleam pointed out. "The sum was very sizable, Hughes."

"It was an *Eschezmont*."

There was a moment's silence. Into the silence Miss Gleam gave a long, low whistle.

"That good?" asked Mr. Glint.

"My friend, it is not merely *good*, nor is it in fact *great*. The Escateline *Eschezmont* is without question the finest example of motor vehicular engineering ever to grace our fair city's streets." Gleam appraised Hughes anew, her scalpel-grin huge and girlish. "It is equipped with first-rate lane shifting boosters, exceptional fumigation, peerless internal atmosphere controls, and seats of the creakiest, shiniest Ikahaguan leather. It is a leopard barely contained within tungsten. An eagle flying among starlings. It is, simply put, a fabulous car. When business or leisure compels him to do so, our own *employer* is driven in an *Eschezmont*, Mr. Glint. Infer what you will from that! And where is yours now, Hughes?"

"Gone," he said simply.

"Gone?" That derailed Gleam completely. "What do you mean gone?"

"Departed. Vanished. Truant." Hughes tried to shrug and found he couldn't— Mr. Glint's hands were implacable. He settled for a thin-lipped smile. "Gone."

"Gone where?" Gleam demanded.

"I don't know."

"Stolen?"

"Yes."

"But the *Eschezmont* is equipped with the most comprehensive, the most baleful security system—"

"The person who stole it," Hughes cut in, "had the key."

For an instant she only frowned at him, uncomprehending.

"You all right?" said Mr. Glint.

"Who?" Gleam asked Hughes, ignoring her partner. "Who stole it?"

"Kim Kallaimon," he replied. "At least, I think her name was Kim Kallaimon. I never met any of her friends or family, and because I insisted on paying for everything she never had to produce ID, a credit chit, or anything like it. She um... was er... my girlfriend. Sort of my..." He hesitated. "Actually, no, we were seeing one another, but for me..."

"You borrowed money from our employer," said Gleam, and her voice seemed to scythe through the rainy summer dark and Hughes' flustered recollection in one single slice. "You purchased an *Eschezmont* you could not afford and had no intention of using in order to get courier work, or premium taxi work, or any kind of work for that matter. You became a lavish and imprudent spendthrift with credits sifting like sugar through your fingers... to please a *woman*?"

Hughes said nothing.

Then, quietly, so quietly that Mr. Glint and Miss Gleam had to strain to hear him over the humming sign of *Pamplona* and the somnolent rains, Hughes said:

"You didn't meet her."

***

Bike bells tinkled distantly along the nearby cross section. The breeze brought the tang of hashish from some recently opened window, and there was music too, seemingly sourceless, a bluesy guitar playing mellow tunes in azure and sapphire and cobalt.

"You didn't meet her," Hughes said again.

Kim had taken everything from him, cleaning out his bank account, bagging the clothes and jewelry he'd picked out with her in the spring sunshine, and driving off in his car while he slept and dreamed of her face, oval-curved and sweet as a frozen cherry cocktail. Her reasons for doing all of this eluded him, though Hughes had made his share of guesses before tonight.

And the strangest thing of all was that some part of him would do it again.

A dumb romantic part he was not proud of, but a part of him nonetheless.

"We have not, as yet, had the pleasure of meeting this woman of yours," affirmed Miss Gleam. "Inquiries will be made. That car she's nicked is rightfully the property of our employer. How do you spell Kallaimon, Hughes?"

"I don't know. I never saw it written down."

Snick.

The scissors turned black.

"Bugger," grumbled Gleam. Her demeanor changed, becoming pensive as she paced the puddly width of Agorippis Street. Clearly she had believed some of her employer's assets could be immediately recovered and hadn't anticipated Hughes' claim of penury to be completely accurate.

He really, truly, sincerely was bum-fuck broke.

"I won't lie to you, Hughes," Miss Gleam declared. "This is an absolutely deplorable state of affairs. What am I to tell our employer? That you are destitute and incapable of paying back even a fraction of his investment? That you cannot even conjure up the interest payment?"

"Could go to his house," suggested Mr. Glint. "People got stuff stashed all over, stuff maybe they don't even know about. Secret like."

That peeled snakeskin fear squeezed Hughes' insides. It rolled his belly back and forth in a greasy hammock.

They can't go to mine, he thought. *Dad will be there. And if he doesn't assess who they are, if he (God forbid) provokes them somehow, these two will...*

"Tempting," admitted Gleam. "Certainly it is a tempting idea, Mr. Glint. But no, I think that it would be a fruitless hunt. Honestly Hughes, couldn't you have demonstrated some care for us? For our labor and time? Is frugality something that simply happens to other people? Damn." She spread her hands in a gesture of infinite regret. "Oh well. Nothing for it. If you cannot keep up your end of the agreement, then we shall have to take you to our employer."

Hughes felt his relief squashed.

"What?" he croaked. "Your... your employer?"

"Indeed." Gleam folded away her scissors and put them in her coat. "He'll know what to do, I expect. Come along, Mr. Glint. We're on a schedule."

"Wait," Hughes protested.

"No more jocularities," warned Gleam. "The time for those has passed, my dear. Keep quiet now, or Mr. Glint will do something terrible to you."

"You can speak," confided Mr. Glint, and with his hideously strong hands he turned Hughes around as easily as you might turn the nozzle of a tap and began to march him back down Agorippis Street. "It won't be all that terrible, since you got to be able to walk."

"Most sagacious of you, old boy," said Gleam. "You *are* on form tonight."

"Socks."

Gleam paused. "Pardon?"

"Socks," said Mr. Glint. From his sallow mouth the usually soft word sounded about as comfortable as a cemetery. "I'm not on form. I'm on socks. Then shoes. Then street. Under that I think the city is built on loam."

"Oh," said Gleam meekly.

Glint nodded. "Heard that once."

"About the loam?"

"Yeah." The tall rakish man's face pinched with concentration. "A geographer told me about it."

"Really?" Gleam sounded thoroughly impressed. "He told you the city was built on loam?"

"Yeah."

"That's interesting. And he didn't scream at all?"

"Not at first. He didn't know why I'd come to visit him yet. Hold on a tick." Mr. Glint went very still. Then with an adder's speed he lunged into the shadows of Agorippis Street.

Hughes grunted in alarm and didn't have the wherewithal to attempt an escape—he was that scared.

In a moment one of Glint's hands was fastened once more around his arm. The other hand held a rat as large as a woodland hare in its sinuous fingers. The rat writhed, its pink tail flashing. Baring its dagger teeth it bit its captor right on the finger that bore the dark-stoned ring. Mr. Glint seemed not to notice.

Gleam gave a whooping cry, leaped up, and sent one of the deeper puddles splashing as if simulating applause. "Well seized, old boy!"

While all of this played out, Hughes had been aware of the idea occurring to him. It had matured rapidly: first waddling, then walking in balanced strides, and now running in a bright streak across his subconscious, looking for a way up into the sprinter's highway of his conscious mind.

When Miss Gleam planted both feet into the puddle, a spray of cool droplets struck him full in the face.

And just like that he had it.

He *had it*!

Oh, it was hair-brained and would require some of the very luck that had turned its face from him that night. But if he could pull it off, he would avoid being brought to Gleam and Glint's employer.

Even the prospect of that was dizzyingly awful.

Pitching his voice so it emerged with believability, a sort of syrupy cousin to honesty, and altering his face so it presented a mask behind which lay a variety of gorgeous and exciting things, Hughes flexed his Performance, sighed a vast melodramatic sigh, and said, "It's a shame, is all."

They looked at him, surprised.

"What's a shame?" said Glint.

"What?" Hughes' gaze returned from a long way away and focused on the pair. "Oh, nothing. I was just thinking about your payment."

"Yes, yes. As we've established you are free to discuss the matter with our employer—" Gleam began.

"No," said Hughes. "Not my loan payment. *Your* payment."

"Ours?"

"Well, think about it." Hughes made a concerted effort not to look at the rat squirming in Mr. Glint's hand and forced his lips into a winning smile. "You've been on my trail for, what, a few hours now? For people of your skillset a few hours represents a large investment. I'm thinking about your labor, Miss Gleam. Your time. I can't imagine your compensation will cover your expenses."

"Our compensation," said Gleam, "is none of your business, boy."

"It's mad, but you know, I think it *is* my business," said Hughes with more confidence than he himself would have believed possible. "As far as I can see, you don't want to take me to your employer any more than I want to go. Besides, I won't magically have more money to sate his anger. Who knows how intense that anger might be? Whom it might affect? I am only me." His eyes filled with a strange bright malice. "Once he's done with me he might have some rage left over. He might feel inclined to spread it around. I don't want that. What I want is for you both to be fairly compensated for services rendered. I want," he finished with a vocal flourish, "to avoid ambiguity. Miss Gleam, I don't like gray areas either. Let's be black and white together."

And with everything at stake, with Gleam's face abruptly loosening in that all-too familiar way, Hughes pushed his Performance.

***

Testing Performance...

No reaction whatsoever appeared on Gleam's face. As the world settled into that peculiar rhythm of rising tension, Hughes' heart rate climbed and climbed.

Dimly he registered a young woman standing up the street toward the cross section in the sheltered doorframe of the sex work bordello named *Pamplona*. He couldn't see her face, only a hand with long red nails clutched around a cigarette. The cigarette smoldered, and when she drew it into the shadowy dark and inhaled deeply, it winked like a demonic orange eye.

With his heartbeat ratcheting up into dangerous ribcage-whamming pain now, Hughes wondered if it was the same woman who had slept with the man in the scarlet armor. He wondered if her cigarette was a good omen, a bad omen, or something in between, a gray area where luck and destiny found themselves uncomfortable and lost and angry as Miss Gleam seemed in ambiguity.

Testing Performance...

Let it be a good omen, he hoped with everything he had. *Because this idea burning and winking in my head like a thousand cigarettes is wonderful. It's so goddamn wild and ridiculous and good. Only give me a chance.*

He had no idea where he was sending these thoughts to. Maybe the place where Strength, Dexterity, Intelligence, and his own weird Performance came from. The source of all magic.

Who knew where that was?

Not he.

Well, to hell with it.

He sent them anyway.

He sent those thoughts and his massive HOPE combined together, sent them out into the hammering rain and up into the blind thundercloud judgment of the night and—

Performance Success
Level Up!
7 → 8
Congratulations!
New Perk Gained: Criminal Eloquence

<table>
<tr><td colspan="2">Instead of using a Performance, you can force a criminal to reconsider their actions.
This Perk can only be used once.</td></tr>
<tr><td>Chance of Success: 30%</td><td>Next Level: +3% to Chance of Success
Level 10 Secret Ability: ???</td></tr>
</table>

Gleam tilted her face to the rippling wet sheets of rain. She blinked once. Twice. Hughes thought her face held such bewilderment in that moment she looked like someone who had ordered shellfish and been served deep-fried basking shark. Something happened behind those evil dark irises. Her expression firmed up. She looked at Hughes and smiled a sharp and wicked smile.

"Well, well, well," she said. "Color me every rotting shade of intrigued, Mr. Glint. I do believe we will hear you out, my dear Hughes. Regale us with your plan, and we will see."

"What?" said Glint.

"Sorry?" said Hughes, hardly believing it himself.

"Your plan." Miss Gleam approached him with a spring in her step. "You must have one. *Let's be black and white together,* wasn't that your phrase? Not an exotic choice of words, but a compelling one. Don't play coy with me, little Hughes. Lovestruck Hughes. Lubricious and loquacious Hughes! You've cooked up some scheme, some agenda you'd like to rope us into, so that myself and my partner are duly compensated for our efforts, and so our employer remains ignorant of your failures. Well? Here I am, attentive as a kitten." She slipped a hand beneath his coat and shirt and teased a razor-thin nail around his left nipple. Her tongue slid out, a pink slug oozing over her filed incisors. Hughes found that she did not resemble a kitten so much as a vampire from the grimmest fairy tale. "What did you have in mind?" she asked him.

Intimidated though he was, Hughes felt as if his chest would burst with relief. It worked! His Performance actually *worked,* by God!

He could have broken down and wept.

Impossible, of course.

Later, perhaps he would give in to the emotion closing his throat, but not now.

There were still some things to be done before he could call this a victory.

"Okay. You know I live in the *Scriptorium and Flavored Tea Emporium*, but here's the thing, I also work there. Recently we've had a customer who comes in. Big, really big. Covered in tattoos. I don't know how I didn't recognize what she was at first. I suppose it was too... um... sensational to believe."

"Go on," said Gleam. "Who's this giant mystery woman?"

"She's a Jolene."

Gleam cocked her head. "What's a Jolene doing in your scruffy little tea emporium, Hughes? Jolenes are important figures in the city, and it takes a lot to summon them away from their forges."

Hughes nodded. "Yeah, that's what delayed the realization I think. Just how odd it would be. But what I thought might explain it is my dad's tea. Probably she came for that. It has a reputation, you know?"

"Yes," said Gleam. She walked two nails down his soaked chest, down and down toward the spot where his shirt stuck wetly to his navel.

"Anyway," muttered Hughes. "This Jolene and I started talking. Turns out we have a lot in common. I don't mean to blow my own trumpet but she's really taken a..." He licked his lips nervously. "A liking to me. One day, this was only a week or two ago, she confessed that she has money trouble. Gambling, or something. She wouldn't tell me."

"Perhaps she fell in love with the wrong woman," suggested Gleam sweetly.

Eat shit, he thought inwardly.

Outwardly Hughes mirrored her plastic smile.

"Could be. Well we had one more thing to bond over: both myself and this Jolene needed money. Now she couldn't go forging magical items and doling them out on some kind of black market. The Jolenes keep tidy ledgers with every magic item listed, at least that's what this Jolene friend of mine told me," Hughes added, remembering Gleam's scissors, which were probably not accounted for in any ledger. He was inventing rapidly, lying enormous fantastic white lies, but Gleam seemed to be eating up his story and asking him for seconds with her eager eyes.

He went on before his newfound courage could abandon him. "There we were. The Jolene, desperate, and myself equally so. Here was our plan. I would get my hands on some raw material and she—the Jolene—would forge it into a magic weapon for me. Wielding that, I could join the Scarlet Citadel and go monster hunting in order to earn the credits we both needed."

"Raw materials?" Miss Gleam was not so eager anymore. Confusion scrunched her face, and then the confusion melted, and with gusto and joy she cackled. "*Raw materials?* Those *raw materials*, Hughes, are the guts of otherworldly creatures. They are the organs of the things that creep and scuttle and leap and bound across the wilderness of Iphigenia, a plane of existence much more dangerous than our own, which can only be reached through a portal. A portal you do not have access to, my dear." Gleam's fingers fluttered up and closed in his hair, tugging it just enough to hurt. The Performance may have worked, but she was still quite insane. "Furthermore," she continued, "say you *did* get your hands on said raw materials *and* a magic weapon to call your own. Do you honestly think the Scarlet Citadel would let you join their ranks? Just like that?"

"That man who was here before," Hughes said bitterly. "The one who skulked off rather than stand up to you. They let *him* join."

This sent Gleam into a fit of hysterics. She let go of Hughes and bent double, her shoulders juddering with laughter. Eventually she got herself under control, tears of amusement mingling with raindrops on her cheeks. "I think you have graduated from cute to adorable," she declared. "Well parried Hughes. I take your riposte and admit defeat. Yes, they did let that scallywag join, but the Citadel is not an impoverished Jolene to befriend in your tea house. It is a red dwarf star whose gravity has drawn in much of this city's genius. Combative genius. Strategic genius. If it were not so goody-goody, it would be an ideal spot for people like Mr. Glint and me. It is an *institution*, man. They do not engage in riffraff and hound-doggery, and they certainly do not offer charity to wayward street devils like yourself."

Hughes considered. After a while he shrugged. "I suppose I'll just have to be a genius, then," he said.

And saying that, he crammed his hands in the deep pockets of his coat, turned, and walked back toward the bazaar, and home.

***

Miss Gleam stared after him for a while, her arms crossed over one another like musing serpents.

"What was all that then?" asked Mr. Glint. "I thought we were gonna scrag him."

Gleam didn't answer.

Lightning strobed the dead street, much brighter than the nausea-green neon of *Pamplona*. Unseen, the omen smoker stubbed out her cigarette against the chipped brick and went inside.

Mr. Glint regarded his partner. "You all right?"

"Yes," Gleam replied, a bit too dreamily for Glint's liking.

"Only you're acting wonky."

"Oh?"

"Yeah. One moment we're taking this rangy twat Humbert—"

"Hughes."

"Yeah, right. One moment we're taking this Hughes bloke to face the music. Next moment you're letting him talk you out of it."

"Are you familiar with the expression, 'All good things come to those who wait,' Mr. Glint?"

"Here and there, yeah. One of them *province* things."

"I think you'll find the term is 'proverb,' old boy. And you are absolutely right," trilled Miss Gleam. "It is a proverb, and proverbs mean *wisdom*, Mr. Glint. They are wisdom passed like Tinfrost treats all wrapped in clever ribbon. Here's another one for you: Beggars cannot be choosers. That young man is our beggar, and he has chosen to pledge himself into collusion with us. It was his only choice."

"Right," said Glint uncertainly. He considered pointing out that they, on the other hand, had many choices, including knives, shards of broken glass, rusty-bladed chainsaws, and other methods of general scragging. They also might have chosen to go ahead and bring Hughes to their employer, as Gleam had said they would before her sudden change of heart. He considered these things, and then promptly forgot them. He was not, after all, the brains of the operation.

"So long as you're all right," he mumbled gravely.

Fifty feet away, Hughes was approaching the little side alleys of Leonidas. It was hard to see him now—the rain seemed, if anything, to have gotten heavier.

Lightning shivered up the street again.

Overhead, thunder began to play its solo on the rumbling old organ of the evening.

The sparkling woman smiled up at it (since she was a girl, Gleam had always loved the brooding fierceness of thunder). When she returned her gaze to Agorippis Street, Hughes was gone.

"I think," she said, "that we are going to have to keep an eye on our long lost brother, Mr. Glint."

There was an unexpected fretful sound, high-pitched and wretched, and she snapped her attention to the bushy wriggling thing clenched in her partner's hand.

"For shame, old boy," she chided gently. "You've gone and got yourself bitten to shreds."

Glint frowned at her. He followed her jabbing finger, and when his gaze settled on the enraged rat he was still holding, the frown cleared instantly.

"Thanks," he said. "I'd almost forgotten."

With a monstrous cracking sound Mr. Glint opened his jaws impossibly wide. It was the same *crack* Hughes had heard in the bazaar earlier that night. Incidentally, a good deal of the bazaar-goers had also heard the crack, including the affronted booth owner, who had just enough time to regret his decisions in life before Mr. Glint bit three of his fingers off at the knuckle. Which was why he'd shrieked so loud and so long, you see.

Mr. Glint's lips peeled back over his teeth, which were like rotted gray tombstones jutting out of gums the color of diseased earth. His eyes bulged. His sour mouth split and stretched until it seemed that if it grew any wider, it could swallow Agorippis Street whole.

He lifted his hand. The rat had the impression of being hoisted into a cave.

There was a brief, lonely squeak.

Then nothing.

Except, of course, for the chewing.

ACT TWO

CARNIVALS

CHAPTER FOUR

When Corinth City was built (on loam), it occupied the summit of a humpbacked slope that overlooked the countryside. Over years of complicated urban development the city spilled down the eastern side of the slope, devouring first the nearby hamlet of Casiobella and the royal town of Demeter before tucking in its bib and munching up acre after acre, forest after forest, until at last the city's great expansion was thwarted by stiff-necked farmers.

These blue-collar men were as wise and stubborn as haggard old crows. They refused the greasy proposals and the slimy threats of industrial tyrants, and they were willing to ruffle their feathers and peck if it came to that.

Obstinate and cunning as crows too, those farmers roosted on the most fertile swathe of land in the country, orchards so lush and blossoming you could lose yourself for days and nights. And if you did get lost, they were so beautiful you probably hoped never to be found.

It was good, honest land, as yet undigested by the never-full stomach of the electrical city.

And it was through that good, honest land, trundling and bumping on a strange indigo steam engine that laid tracks in front of itself, that the carnival arrived in Corinth City.

That was as spectacular an event as the people of Corinth had ever seen.

People came in their droves to see what was going to happen, for they had never hosted a carnival before, only parlor magicians and soothsayers and opportunists. Riffraff, in other words.

But Krys and The Mum's Rotbloom Carnival of Bright Oddments and Dark Delights did not seem like riffraff.

And that was proven when the carnies stopped in Symbarr Square, and with the crowd bunching and jostling and jabbing fingers, they revealed their venue.

In cargo hold number three of the train, the big top had lain folded up and spangled in rubbery bulbs. At the call of the Ringmaster, it inflated and sprang out with a huge hissing wallop! Fabric flapped. Bulbs fizzed to fabulous orange-gold life. The cheers began, first small and timid, then abruptly much larger than the whole square could accommodate, so that it seemed to burst with excitement as the immense tent was hoisted high.

Of course that was all thirteen years ago.

Things were very different by the time Hughes fell in love with a woman named Kim Kallaimon and got himself tangled up in the weeds with Miss Gleam and Mr. Glint.

An hour after Hughes succeeded his Performance against Gleam, huge charcoal clouds swarmed over the farms and up the humpbacked slope. Scattered purple-white lightning lit the clouds up from the inside like Yi-Shi lanterns. And how they *groaned*, those mighty drifters in the pouring darkness!

The storm seemed endless, almost apocalyptic, but here and there it showed a little mercy and chose merely to sprinkle the city. In those places only the softest bassy riffs of musical thunder could be distinguished from the whistle of the wind and the chuckle of the gutters.

***

This was one such place:

It was a cottage in the most forgotten corner of Leonidas District. It squatted near the rickety datalog library where you could find grainy vids, cinema reel, spools of cassette tape, even books (paper books were a rare sight in a city that had no use for them).

Hurrying by this particular cottage in the rain. you might not have noticed anything odd about it.

Perhaps you might wonder why it reminded you of an ancient cathedral instead of a shabby little cottage near some moldering fences, the main highway, and indeed, the datalog library with its grimy windows.

You might wonder why you were thinking about gargoyles.

And if you wondered that, you might turn back for another look.

Then you would see that, quite apart from the empty hanging baskets and the sad featureless garden of dead stalks and lumpy gray soil, the cottage was made out of the bones of a carousel.

The Painted Girl stood on the balcony, which was a hodgepodge of twisted poles, fiberglass seats, as well as horse muzzles, pony hooves, and staring glassy equine eyes.

Drizzle peppered her face, her bare arms, and the tattered hem of her dress.

"He's coming soon," she said.

Then she gripped the balcony railing (years ago this very railing was raised to allow children to flock onto the carousel), let it take her weight so she could leap up and waggle her feet happily before gravity pulled them down again, and at last gave a loud merry laugh. "He's coming to visit!"

She raced inside. Down the pinstriped stairs and into the warped living room she ran, and that was where she found the Ringmaster Woman.

"He's coming!" hooted the Painted Girl, as years ago the city crowds had hooted at her from the front rows all the way to the nosebleeds, hooted for more, for an *encore*. "And it is my firm belief that he shall be bringing a special prize." To show how much this pleased her she went up on her tippy-toes and let her momentum carry her in a spin. From her narrow hips her wrinkled unwashed skirt fanned out and drooped down as she completed her twirl and went to one knee next to the Woman.

"Isn't that wonderful?" the Painted Girl prompted.

From the depths of her chair, the Ringmaster Woman gave her an accusing look. "You were on the balcony again. You promised you wouldn't do that."

"Never mind that now," insisted the Painted Girl. She drew a breath to tell her companion everything, but all of a sudden her gaze was drawn to the table beside the Woman. On it were sheets of colored paper, much thicker than crêpe or the writing kind, and there were small iron bores to make holes in it and round the corners when it was cut, as well as a pair of snipping scissors to do the cutting. The Painted Girl's gaze drank all of these items up in less than a second, and quicker than a weasel her eyes darted to the interesting objects nestled in the Ringmaster Woman's lap.

The Painted Girl's eyes grew wider than wide.

"Oh wow! It's been so long," she said admiringly. "I thought you'd given up on making them."

The Ringmaster Woman snorted. "I had. Then you had to go and get it into your head that today was a good day for storm-sighting off the lip of our balcony. I don't know. You take the time mantling up a few rules, and then without a by-your-leave those rules get *dismantled*. That's flight and fancy for you. That's discipline." She rolled her rheumy eyes, as if hoping to find a saner world behind her lids. "Now here we are."

"They're lovely," said the Girl, still cherishing the experience of staring at the objects in the Woman's lap. "You've really outdone yourself. Lovely."

"*Rubbish*," corrected the Woman. "Mangled manky tripe. Don't try and convince me otherwise."

She held the objects up. With her warty fingers she'd crimped the colored paper into figures. Looming in shades of red, green, and caramel brown was a monster. Shrinking in shades of blue and orange was a child. The level of detailing for both figures was amazing.

With one tattooed finger the Painted Girl brushed the monster's paper flanks.

"I don't remember these two," she said, her happy mouth bowing in a frown. "What night did we show them?"

"Oh, some night or other. What's it matter?" The Ringmaster Woman snatched the figures away. With swift grouchy movements she opened the table drawer, whisked all the items back into it (including the paper monster and child she'd just crafted), and clicked it shut.

"There's remembering..." she said tartly.

And utterly crestfallen, the Painted Girl finished obediently, "And then there's remembering."

Seeing the slump in the Girl's shoulders, the Ringmaster Woman paused, debated, then gave in.

"Let's just forget it now. No harm done. Who is coming?" she asked kindly.

The Painted Girl gave her a puzzled look. "Hm?"

"Someone is coming."

"Are they?"

"You only said so now," said the Woman, a bit impatiently. "You said he'll be bringing a prize."

"Will he? That's nice." The Painted Girl smiled a faintly baffled smile. "Who are we talking about?"

And with that, the Ringmaster Woman's kindness evaporated.

She sighed. It was always like this when the Girl got the wanderlust for the balcony. She'd be scatterbrained for hours.

That's what came from messing about with the future.

The future was shy. It didn't like being seen any more than the crow-stubborn farmers in the countryside liked being gobbled up by urban sprawl.

And just like the farmers, and crotchety crows, the future pecked.

"You'd better put on the kettle," the Ringmaster Woman told the Girl. "In case *he* arrives."

The Girl sketched a bow. "At once."

And with a flourish she cartwheeled away, her skirts frumping and flowing around her.

A moment later her head popped back into the living room.

"In case who arrives?" she asked.

"Shut up," said the Ringmaster Woman.

***

On the opposite side of Leonidas District, another kettle began to belch steam from its spout like a tiny clay elephant sneezing mist.

Someone grunted nearby.

"Be with you in a moment," they told the kettle.

The grunt and the voice belonged to none other than Gormon Hughes.

He stood in the middle of his tea shop, his elbows working and his hands gripping a mortar and pestle, grinding tea leaves with a concentration and vigor that would make even a Jolene forgemaster pause.

And since Jolene forgemasters were renowned for their excellent focus, it was quite safe to say Mr. Gormon Hughes was concentrating very hard indeed.

The word "assiduous," which more learned men than he would know meant "taking great care in the doing of," could be employed to describe him. It was not how he would describe himself. As far as he was concerned, words like assiduous were well and good so long as the people who knew them kept language of that caliber to themselves and paid their tea tab without too much fuss.

Important to note as well—as far as he was concerned, fanciful "boujee language" (as Mr. Gormon Hughes called it) belonged at the tip of a pen rather than the tip of your tongue. But it did belong somewhere.

Patrons of his tea shop usually took one look at Gormon and concluded he was an unfortunate looking man in his early sixties. His posture was so bad you could balance cups on him. Stooped, weak-chinned, and touting that particular combover hairstyle common among a certain type of man that was more brave attempt than bold success, Gormon Hughes tended to put people in mind of a raggedy scarecrow who was only a few years away from being retired to the great harvest bonfire in the sky.

He lay aside the mortar and pestle he was using to grind tea with, whisked up the kettle, and set it on the counter to settle. The steam smelled pleasantly herbal and sweetly green, almost fresh-cut-grasslike. The aroma filled the tearoom, which was not like any other tearoom in all of Corinth City.

Walking in off the street, taking the squeaky, groaning steps in twos and threes as they zigzagged up the crumbling stone building with its rented apartments and windows with peeling shutters, you would see a door regularly and carefully painted a handsome strawberry red. A sign was hung by a frayed piece of string from the yellow doorknob.

The sign read: *Scriptorium and Flavored Tea Emporium.*

Pushing open the door and stepping inside (perhaps hesitating a moment or two as your feet crossed the threshold), you would see a room that against all odds looked to be made out of stories.

The walls were stuck with thousands upon thousands of manuscripts. Scripts clustered so densely they appeared to be leather-bound bricks. There were tables made out of theatre plays bound with elastic bands. Chairs of snipped and shaped and glued stories tucked up under the tables. Should your eyes be drawn over the sofa with its paper-stuffed cushions and the four masterwork collections of Mr. Arnold Wellington of Whitehall, which were stacked neatly under the sofa in place of legs, over the cheap Formica counter to the tea station where Gormon prepared his respectable and excellent teas, you would see all sorts of brewing equipment propped up on mounds of moldering paper, each sheaf carrying a library musk that mingled comfortably with the perfume of counterfeit herbs and spices.

Why would the herbs and spices be counterfeit?

Well, Gormon Hughes might have been unfortunate in appearance, true. But compared to the ugly state of his finances, he was absolutely gorgeous. Only very wealthy people could afford real herbs and spices nowadays.

Just then, sipping from a mug whose inscription read, *Yap All You Want, Just Don't Be Tea-dious,* he was thinking about his son.

Hughes Junior had shuffled in out of the rain only a few minutes ago.

"Here's the man himself," Gormon had barked.

He had been geared up to tell his son about the nice young college students who'd visited the *Emporium* earlier that day, about the things he was planning to buy with the money they'd brought in, but something in his boy's expression stopped him.

"Everything all right, son?"

The boy was drenched. He took off his coat and hung it on the hook just inside the door. Gormon thought he could use a hot bath and a drink of something toasty-warm, or maybe...

And suddenly his son was looking right at him.

There was no pain in Hughes' eyes, no stricken quality that might have indicated worry or sadness. The boy's eyes were vacant. There was no identifiable emotion in them at all, and Gormon Hughes found himself caught totally unawares by the bolts of fatherly outrage that rammed and splintered through his belly.

Something or (more likely) some*one* had passed his boy through the ringer tonight. They had given him a scare, or worse. Gormon Hughes did not know who, or why, and at that moment he did not particularly give a goddamn what the culprits called themselves or what their motivations were.

Right then he would have politely invited them in the door, gotten them quite comfortable. Then, very calmly, he would have upended a kettle's worth of scalding tea down the back of their shirts.

No one played silly buggers with his boy.

Not unless they wanted Trouble with a capital Tea.

"Junior..." Gormon said, his voice a husky croak. "What's happened to you?"

But if Hughes could hear his father, he showed no awareness of it.

Leaking rainwater like a skewered bucket, the boy squelched past the tea station and into the only other room they owned, a simple breadbox of a space where a mothy wardrobe accumulated dust and two smelly foam pallets lay on the floor trying their best to simulate beds.

Gormon listened with mounting anxiety as his son crawled into bed, wet clothes and all. He heard a rustle from the unlit bedroom. The Hughes family could not afford blankets, so they made do with plays full of earmarks and footnotes and musty annotated pages.

This little quirk of their impoverished sleeping arrangements meant that unique sayings emerged among the Hughes men.

Gormon liked to say the words of older, better times kept them snug in winter.

Whereas his son Hughes liked to say, "Ah crap. I've gone and torn the blankets again."

No other sound emerged from the back room. This struck Gormon as very odd. His boy was one of nature's snorers. If Hughes was asleep, it was a weird silent slumber. What could that mean?

Gormon Hughes, father and master of teas, had no clue.

He went and closed the front door (the boy had left it swinging on its hinge as he came in out of the sticky warm and almost unbearably damp night).

The door shut with a *snick*.

Gormon heard a sudden intake of breath and a rapid rustling from the back room, the sound of blanket-pages being disturbed.

He listened intently, his features crimped. For whatever reason the silence from the room his son occupied was now very tense.

Once more he heard the rustle. It was pensive, forlorn, and timid.

Then nothing.

Gormon Hughes clicked away the stiffness in his neck. Oh well. Never a dull moment for a parent nowadays. He was going to mull this over. Behind him and through the front door came the muffled, morose tap dance of the early June rains.

Strange as all that was, it was not the oddest thing that happened that night.

A little later, peering out through the grubby tearoom window, Gormon Hughes had pierced the fog sizzling up from the street with his eyes. Thunder whickered overhead like the stables in hell. The fog was not wispy or light. It conjured pale and thick like a magic trick pulled by the storm. On ghoulish milky fingers it crept through the street, which was eerily empty at that witching hour, except for...

Gormon's eyes narrowed.

Was he actually seeing this?

There, poised half in and half out of the streetlamp light, in the middle of the road and all on her own, stood a woman. He might have been mistaken—at this distance such a mistake would have been more than forgivable—but she seemed to be staring up at the building that housed the *Emporium*.

She could not have known he was watching her. Even so, she turned and met his gaze through the window, smiled a smile that made his pulse quicken in his throat, and faster than any magic trick she was gone, a specter lost in the foggy gloom.

That smile, he'd thought. *Sharp.*

Night became early morning.

Nursing his third mug, Gormon Hughes' mind had spun a full turn and was now focused on a point fixed squarely in the past. More specifically twenty-odd years ago, namely his gambling days in the *Duchess and Squirm Dice House* in Cleomenes District. He'd never been much of a bidder (even in his most prosperous days before the boy's mother left him for greener pastures), but Gormon had known some risk-takers and had even been friendly with some of them.

And while a handsome man Gormon Hughes was certainly not, he had over the years adopted the shrewdness of a fox who has lived a long time in a big city.

You developed particular instincts, got familiar with certain truisms.

You *always* knew a gambler by the expression on their face. On days during which they placed their bets, gamblers wore one of three.

First, he remembered a sort of vague hopefulness on the faces of his friends that said: *Hey, you win some, you lose some. I'm just here to lay credits and raise a little chaos, isn't that fantastic?*

Second were faces plastered with a huge giddy triumph, some distant cousin to the grin of a drunk after the first keg of the evening clangs hollowly under his knuckles. This version of the gambler's expression said: *Gentlemen, I have just won big. Isn't that fantastic?*

Third and most troubling, he recalled the haunted empty faces that said: *I have just lost every single credit I came in here with. That would be fine, absolutely fine. Only I also lost my watch, my gold-plated belt buckle, and oh yes, all of my life savings. Including the money I just inherited from my dead mother along with my kids' college fund. Now, if you'll kindly excuse me, I'm going to hang myself with my tie, or perhaps my buckleless belt, in my hotel room. Isn't that fantastic?*

Gormon Hughes sat on a stack of plays and compared this last look to the one worn by his son last night.

He did not like how closely they resembled one another.

Not one bit.

By the time mug number four was brewing in the small clay kettle, he'd reached a decision.

CHAPTER FIVE

Hughes dreamed he rode a carousel, high above the city.

It was not a merry-go-round of nuts and bolts and glossy polished steeds. Mules of cumulous clouds plodded; thin drifters of cirrus capered in the shapes of monkeys; crocodiles snapped their jaws and filled the starry night with thunder; hamsters flashed their feet on wheels of screw-top lightning; ponies pranced on molecules of water as easily as cobblestones; gorillas smashed the great sky cymbals; starlings and robins and hawks and gulls *chitter-cheeped* in a swirl of bending electrons; so it went! Round and round the menagerie of animals danced!

Hughes looked down and saw he was not on an animal.

He was (rather horrifyingly) atop Mr. Glint's shoulders.

"Hear that music?" said Glint.

Hughes did.

It was a fluting, a whistling, a splendid piping.

"That's a calliope," said Hughes wonderingly.

"Not my kind of instrument," Glint commented in his graveyard voice.

"No?"

"I always had a liking for violins." The gaunt man swung his legs over a tower of crackling white termites. "Cellos. Harps and the like. You know. The *stringy bits.*"

"I'm sorry?"

"The *stringy bits*, Brother Hughes."

"Hughes!" cried a new voice, sweet as swirled candy floss.

He whirled in his seat and saw a Painted Girl waving at him. Next to her stood a carbuncular woman in a suit of black and white stripes and a top hat almost as tall as Mr. Glint. The pair were taking tickets from a crowd eager to hop aboard the tempest carousel. Everyone in that throng was indistinct, more stratus clouds than human beings, apart from one figure at the very back of the line.

That figure was interesting. *Their eyes*, thought Hughes. *Something distinct about their eyes.*

Hughes could not make them out so well, not even when he craned his neck and squinted.

Maybe if he signaled the figure, he could—

"Step right up!" roared the carbuncular woman, who was called Ringmaster, though she had another name known only to a rare few. "Come through there, real good! Hopscotch and cross-stitch your way forward, folks. Form a disorderly line. Keep your asses and elbows inside reality. Come through, I say! Behold the Performance of a lifetime!"

The Painted Girl's fingers shredded a ticket.

A wave of dizziness struck Hughes. When he took his hand from his face, the scene had changed.

Now the distinct figure was in the middle of the line.

The Ringmaster threw up both hands, one locked around a cane. The head of the cane was clotted in blood and human hair. "Step right up and ride the lightning!"

Ticket fragments sprinkled like confetti.

Again that awful sickening dizziness hit him.

When he looked again Hughes saw the figure was three-quarters of the way up the line.

"All aboard, and make sure that you enjoy it!" the Ringmaster laughed. "Because you're never getting off. Not ever."

A hurricane of ticket stubs pinwheeled through the air. They sparkled in the cold starlight, bright as credits or the flesh of strange grinning women hunting you through bazaars out of space and time.

"Not *ever...*"

Hughes' head swam. His gut clenched itself into a hard slimy ball of nausea.

Wishing he did not have to look, knowing that he must, Hughes raised his eyes.

The figure was gone.

Only now he was aware of a noise. It rolled up out of the city, which was spread below the spinning carousel, and the rumble of that noise was so deep and powerful it made the jaws of crocodiles seem tame and charming by comparison.

"Hang on tight," said Mr. Glint under him. "This next bit's a trifle bumpy."

Rising up into the clouds was the most beautiful car Hughes had ever seen.

It was sleek and dark as a midnight cat. Its beams were burning yellow eyes. It was his. His *Eschezmont*. And behind the wheel, aiming that perfect machine at the carousel and at Hughes himself was Kim Kallaimon. Her fists were white knuckled on the wheel.

"Kim," he said.

"Who?" said Mr. Glint. "Who you talki—" He retched a gag.

Hughes looked down at him. "Are you all right, Mr. Glint?"

"Fine thanks. Just had something stuck in my—"

But before he could finish, Mr. Glint's eyes bulged, and the muscles in his neck stood out like cables, and with a sound like a balloon full of raspberry jam being dropped off a bridge, his head exploded.

Two hands burst from the bubbling neck stump. They got a firm purchase as Hughes fell, and with a tug the distinct figure from the crowd hauled himself out of the ruin of Mr. Glint. The figure glared down at Hughes with eyes of burning yellow.

Not sure what else he could say at a moment like this, Hughes said, "You've got eyes like my car. Only a bit more... reptilian."

Without a word the figure turned to examine something that clearly made him furiously angry.

Hughes followed that gaze to the ticket booth.

Amongst the wild shifting charcoal clouds the Painted Girl and the Ringmaster Woman were nowhere to be seen. In their place stood three bent crooked shapes with their backs to him. The shapes took tickets from the crowd with hands like twitching bloated spiders, and with a gesture they ushered the unsuspecting people onto the animal/storm carousel.

Hughes looked at the bloody figure now standing next to him.

"I don't understand," he said honestly.

A horn blared, exhaust pipe oozing steam scented like lawn grass in summertime.

The figure opened their mouth to speak...

***

Hughes woke up.

A bar of light the color of sadness pushed through the thin, sewn-paper curtains and drove a needle of ache through each eye.

He squeezed them shut, wiped the gum from them with the balls of his thumbs, and blinked into the silver-gray haze again.

Still not good, but a little better.

"What's that outside?" he asked the whole world groggily.

"Only rain," his dad replied. "Hey, now. Someone's jumpy."

"You startled me," Hughes grumbled. "What's this?"

"I see. Jumpy *and* slow. This, my son, is tea and toast." Gormon set a plate and mug down next to Hughes. The mug bore a small chubby cartoon face wearing a judge's fluffy white wig and wielding a gavel between its teeth. The inscription said: *Fine, I'm A Caffeine Addict.* And under that, in smaller letters, it said: *Guil-tea.*

Gormon gave his son a decidedly bemused look. "Do you ever look in the mirror and think about the fact that we are evolution's best effort?"

Hughes' eyebrows drew together. "What?"

"Perhaps only me then." His father sighed. "Eat. And get up out of those clothes. Then you can mop the floor for me."

"Right."

"Seeing as you nearly flooded the house last night with all that rain you dragged in."

"All right," said Hughes, more clipped than he'd intended. He slipped two fingers through the mug handle, lifted it, and swallowed a mouthful of soothing spicy warmth. "It's good."

His dad nodded. It was, of course, more than good. In terms of this tea's quality, "good" did not occupy the same neighborhood. It was Gormon Hughes' esteemed cardamom and fennel tea, and none, not in all of Corinth City, and perhaps the whole of the country and the wide world beyond, could brew finer.

What a night, Hughes thought. The dream had been incredibly vivid. It unnerved him, almost as much as his meeting with Miss Gleam and Mr. Glint. Hughes would be the first to admit he had a fruitful imagination, but unlike many creative young people who could fill their journals with detailed accounts from the Land of Nod, he and his dreams maintained a distant and healthy working relationship with one another. That arrangement had been fine by him until now. Evidently his dreams were developing different ideas. No longer content with melting away like morning mist as he rejoined the waking world, last night's dream clung to him as uncomfortably as the damp shirt clung to the small of his back.

That his dream had been a strange concoction of Mr. Glint, the Rotbloom Carnival, its Painted Girl and Ringmaster, violence, and bad weather, presented no great mystery for Hughes. His encounter with the sparkle-skinned pair in Agorippis Street had spooked him. No wonder it lingered as his consciousness slipped away.

During his hasty and inordinately soggy return home last night, he had also given thought to the carousel house tucked away in the fringe of Leonidas. Ditto the two ladies living there. He was going to visit them at the first opportunity he got.

That leaves those awful shapes conducting people onto the sky carousel.

Hughes wondered who they were.

What they were.

Thinking about it in the daytime offered no hint. Honestly he'd never seen anything like them.

And then there's that figure, he thought, feeling the fine hairs on the backs of his hands rise. *The one with the burning yellow eyes.*

"Junior?"

Hughes grunted, his reverie broken. "Hm?"

Leaning in the partition door with his arms folded, his father's face was impassive. Hughes thought he saw a twinkle of bemusement, but it was hard to tell.

"You were somewhere else entirely, son of mine," said Gormon. "What's on your mind?"

"Nothing," Hughes replied. "I'm going to pay Krys a visit."

"The carnival girl?"

Hughes nodded.

His dad stood up straight. "In that case I'll knock on Ernie Wilks' door, see if he can spare his tub for an hour. I know water is the last thing you want to see, but you need a bath like a snail needs a shell, especially when you're going to keep the company of a nice—if peculiar and verging on clinically insane—young woman."

A tub of water was, indeed, low on Hughes' list of desires.

However, his father was right.

Krys would wrinkle her nose at his smell. Her nose was even more sensitive than her disposition, which was very sensitive indeed. Not to mention The Mum. The Mum would have kittens if Hughes turned up at their door like some reeking, bedraggled zombie barely laced together in soggy boots.

"Thanks, Pops," he said. "Really."

His father shrugged as he left. It was no trouble.

Hughes hitched a deep breath, laid all the troubling and frankly scary images from his dream to one dark corner of his brain, and let the breath go. No time to ponder sleep when waking up had a laundry list of problems to solve.

That list contained the following:

1)   Get a magic item.
2)   Join the Scarlet Citadel.
3)   Pay back Gleam and Glint's employer.

It was not a list that inspired much hope.
Shit, he thought, and amended it.

1)   Get a magic item.
2)   Join the Scarlet Citadel.
3)   Pay back Gleam and Glint's employer.
4)   *Bathe.*

Well, at least he could handle that fourth one.

Hughes was no starry-eyed prodigy, but years of sitting on, being walled-in by, and sleeping underneath theatrical plays had given him ample opportunity to read them.

And read them he had.

Devour enough words, words with meaning and power that burn like black fire on the white forest of the page, and sooner or later the big wide fields of ignorance would be chewed up and replaced with tall towers of understanding, each windowpane agleam with wit and cleverness.

Now, sitting alone in the bedroom with its Spartan decoration, his clothes sopping and foul-smelling, and his survival instincts defining themselves into an arrow point somewhere deep within him, he brought whatever tactical thinking he had to bear.

And just as his Performance rose to answer his call, huge blueprints unfolded behind the dark portals of his eyes, the pupils of which began to dart and dilate as plots and plans began to take shape.

It was not, he knew, going to be easy.

He would need ideal circumstances, a little money, and a lot of luck.

"Is that all?" he said with a touch of sarcasm. "I'm sure I'll have it all sorted out by the weekend."

It was nine o'clock on Friday morning, and through the curtained window June pummeled the *Emporium* Hughes called home with cold wet fists.

A genius, he remembered suddenly. *That's what I told Gleam. Something about me becoming a genius of combat, or something.*

Now he thought about it, there was an implication that if he didn't become one, and fast, then horrible things would happen to him at the long-fingered hands of Mr. Glint and at the filed needle-sharp teeth of Miss Gleam.

"That's an affirmative on the bath!" his father called from the tearoom. "There'll be soap and everything. Good, eh? Um. One small update, son. You'll have to share it with Ernie's dog, Boochums."

Boochums was a Saint Bernard. He weighed two hundred pounds and was the shaggiest and most flatulent dog in Corinth City.

"I told Ernie you wouldn't mind," his father hollered. There was a moment's silence. "Erm. It's very good soap, mind. Sort of peachy."

Hughes pressed the heels of his hands to his temples, and wondered if his ex-girlfriend would run him over in real life as well as in his dreams.

CHAPTER SIX

Somewhere wicked, a telephone began to ring.

Miss Gleam and Mr. Glint had chosen their base of operations with the utmost care. In Miss Gleam's opinion, a pair of professionals so guileful, erudite, efficient, and reliable as they deserved nothing less than a *lair*.

Mr. Glint, for his part, wanted nothing so much as a place with a roof and a steady supply of things to eat. Wriggly squirming things that screamed when he bit down, for preference.

It seemed less than a few moon turns ago when they had stumbled upon the ruins of the leisure center.

Once it had been a place where children had run about zapping one another with laser-tag beams, where couples had congregated for a go at the bowling pins and a few kisses by the pool tables, and where a team of friendly smiling (and surprisingly well-paid) waiters and waitresses served (also surprisingly) delicious platters, all of which contained a serving of nachos with at least four different kinds of cheese melting over their crisp edges.

Now the leisure center was abandoned. Cobwebs and sinewy crawling spiders grown fat with darkness and the water from leaky sinks and toilets were the chief inhabitants. The green of the pool tables had withered to gray, and in their pockets the balls were filmed with dust. The kitchens and the restaurant were barren quiet places except for the occasional scutter and scratch of a mouse or a rat, or some other creature.

Even the venue's name had worn away upon its plaque above the lightless door, so much so that it bore no name at all.

The sparkling duo had chanced upon it one dark autumn evening. Miss Gleam had planted her hands on her not inconsiderable hips and declared in a loud and delighted voice, "Why Mr. Glint, I do believe it is *perfect.*"

In the desolate bowling alley, tucked on a podium next to moldering shoes with extra grip on the soles, the telephone rang.

And rang.

And—

"Good morning, sir," said Miss Gleam after plucking the phone out of its cradle. She spoke this introduction because it could only be one person. Only one person called them because only one person had their number. "How are you on this fine day in which the heavens themselves seem to ooze?"

She listened for a moment, then smiled hideously.

"That is marvelous to hear, sir. Me, sir? Hedonistic, sir. I am feeling everything, and everything is feeling me right back. What do I mean by everything? Just that. It is reciprocal, sir, and dare I say it—Zen."

She listened.

"Oh, sir is too kind. May I presume that you are calling us in pursuit of myself and my associate's particular brand of amenity? That is to say, you need someone taken care of, with all emphasis toward the barbaric and the gory and the spitefully cruel implied and explicit, sir?"

Meanwhile, Mr. Glint was looking for the mother spider. His search had taken him to this section of the leisure center where soft breezes tugged the strands of cobweb and made them flutter and shiver. Spiders abounded here, lovely big ones with thoraxes swollen with venom. Where there were big ones like this, there was a mother, he knew, a huge gnarly scarred fleshy lump of an arachnid, all clittering mandibles and milky eyes and bobbing belly. Bobbing *thorax*, rather.

He was particularly proud of this word.

Miss Gleam had taught it to him.

Now where was she, where was she. The case for the yummy mummy spider continued while over by the phone Miss Gleam's smile had frozen on her lips.

"Ah," she said. "Yes. Er. You see, sir, there was what you might call a shift in approach. A change of plan, if you will. The Hughes fellow is going to be an asset going forward, as I laid out with enviable clarity in my... in..."

She trailed off as the voice on the phone explained something of its own to her.

It explained its point in no uncertain terms, and the cold thin smile chilled a little more, and a little more, until it was an icy pouting thing bowing the corners of her mouth.

"But, *sir*," she complained bitterly. "As I explained in my correspondence with your secretary, my instincts tell me that Hughes will soon be a veritable feather in your cap, lining your pockets, and adorning your estimable person with his every wit and deed. Am I to deny those instincts, which have been well honed for many a—"

Again she was cut off as the voice on the line told her exactly what it thought of her well-honed instincts.

Without Gleam realizing it, the fingers of her right hand started to tug at a rancid shoelace dangling from the storage shelves.

"I see," she said quietly.

She listened.

"Perfectly, sir. My responsibility. Yes." Suddenly she perked up, if only the tiniest bit. "And now that this unfortunate bit of housekeeping has been concluded, might I inquire if indeed sir has some other task for myself and my associate to pursue. Sir?"

She held the phone away. She had not heard a click, which meant the voice was still on the other end of the line.

"Are you... still there, sir?"

The voice said four words.

Gleam heard them, and then she heard the click of the line going dead.

A shoe swung down off the shelf. She frowned, realizing she was holding its lace in between her forefinger and thumb.

Miss Gleam let go of the lace, walked around the dusty counter, and sat down in one of the hollow-drummed seats lining the bowling aisle, crossing her legs and resting her chin in her hand.

"Got her," said Mr. Glint, approaching. In his hands, he held the fattest, most malignant, most evil-looking spider Gleam had ever seen. It was easily the size of a small dog, perhaps a terrier. Its dishrag-gray and saggy flesh seemed busy somehow. Among the pins and ghostly machinery, the spider mother's bodyguards had fought to keep her from Mr. Glint's hands. The evidence of their rebellion showed on the tall man's boots, which were flecked with gobbets of gore. Spider legs spronged out from beneath the soles, and his fingernails were an awful sight to behold.

"Well done, old boy," said Miss Gleam.

"Here," her companion said. "You all right?"

Her radiant eyes found his and drifted away.

"Hm? Oh yes, dear man. Quite all right."

Swiftly, and without apparent effort, Mr. Glint squashed the mother spider between his palms, his plans for fun and games with the nasty eight-legged matriarch entirely forgotten. Her plump thorax burst with a truly gruesome sound halfway between a squish and a pop, and on a thousand skittering legs her babies crawled a quick escape across Mr. Glint's hands and forearms.

He stood in the oppressive bleakness of the doomed bowling alley, no sunlight finding him at all (for all the windows had been boarded up long before their arrival), his mouth pursed as if inside and nestled against his tongue were the sourest clutch of cut lemons.

"Time for lessons?" he said eventually.

The effect was immediate and encouraging.

Miss Gleam looked up, puzzled.

"Lessons, old boy? But it's Friday-of-the-long-weekend, and you know what that means, don't you?"

Mr. Glint nodded. "Means I get three days off from my education instead of two."

"Exactly," said his associate. "So what's this about lessons?"

"I have decided," said Mr. Glint philosophically, "that long weekends can stuff it."

His gambit paid off. Miss Gleam fairly beamed at him.

She leaped to her feet, her face like a terrible lantern sending out its glow, and threw her arms around him.

"General Linguistics or conceptualization?" she asked.

"Er." Unlike *thorax*, Mr. Glint was not familiar with either of these terms. "Erm. You pick, Miss Gleam."

"Conceptualization it is! And a cheer to that I say! Hip hip!"

"Hooray," finished Mr. Glint in his tombstone tones.

Miss Gleam set herself down. Her shoes clicked softly on the unswept pine floorboards. She cocked her head and grinned up at sour-mouthed Mr. Glint.

"First though, my eager pupil, I think you would be best served ridding yourself of your recent find's progeny."

"Eh?"

"The little ones, Mr. Glint. The spawn. The children. The progeny."

Mr. Glint regarded the baby spiders boiling in droves over his body.

"Right you are," he said.

He rolled out his long thick tongue and, in his way, tidied up.

Miss Gleam watched him, her face fond and glittering like the brightest penny in a noxious corrupted pond. Those four words stayed with her though, the ones their employer had spoken before the phone line went dead.

Sometimes you disappoint me, their employer had said.

Sometimes you disappoint me.

***

Hughes escaped through the bathroom and slammed it shut behind him.

Ernie Wilks cackled. "Boochums put the shits up you, huh?"

He was a fiery old codger with liver spots browning one hand and a wattle of loose skin at his throat that put Hughes in mind of a rooster. There was nothing roosterish about Ernie's cackle though, which was witchy and loud enough to rattle the cutlery soaking in the sink. The reason his left hand was not liver-spotted was this: it was made of a cleverly manufactured metal that twisted and gripped things, a prosthetic with the strength of a professional weightlifter's hand. Ernie's own had been crushed in a factory accident, and the company had paid for his new chrome-shiny digits, for this crummy apartment, and even a small claw-footed bath, an encounter with which Hughes had just about survived.

"Where are my clothes?" Hughes asked, ignoring Ernie's question. He was naked and in a pretty foul temper. Sharing a five-by-five bath with a two-hundred-pound dog will do that to you. Even if there are bubbles.

Until this summer he had habitually bathed in Sheila Kofatch's apartment. Sheila was a frazzled schoolteacher who always handed Hughes a dry towel with a blush creeping up her neck. He liked her. Earlier that spring Sheila had met a property realtor while out drinking with her girlfriends. In a whirlwind she became engaged, then married, and then her bags were packed for prettier pastures than Leonidas District quicker than you could say, "Congratulations."

The Hortesian family who moved into her apartment seemed polite enough, but they would have been less than pleased by the prospect of Hughes, a complete stranger, making monthly use of their bath.

Which left Hughes with Ernie and his sweet, stinky doggie, Boochums, whose breath could curl toenails, and the less said about Boochums' toenails the better.

All in all, the experience had been more comparable to germ warfare than bathing.

Hughes was not even sure he was clean. Awake, sure. By God, he was awake, more awake than if he'd drunk thirty pounds of ground coffee in a single swallow.

Clean? Well, that was a whole other matter.

"Got 'em here," said Ernie. He gestured to a rocking chair hung with Hughes' clothes, which to Hughes' surprise were not only dry but pleasantly warm to the touch.

Gray morning light filtered into Ernie's cluttered apartment. The windowsill was rusty, and raindrops raced one another down the pane of glass.

Hughes accepted the stiff, scratchy towel Ernie offered him, dried himself, and tugged on his underwear and trousers. He frowned. Patting his ass pocket, he found resistance where resistance ought not to have been. He fished in the pocket and produced an object.

Take a square of pink quartz crystal about the size of a Rubik's Cube. Pare away at it with a high-powered laser until it resembles the letter C.

That was what Hughes held.

It was about two-thirds of a complete credit chit, worth about as much as a decent acoustic guitar or a night in an expensive hotel room.

Hughes looked at Ernie. "What's this?"

Ernie shrugged two bony shoulders. "Don't ask me, kid. I just live here."

Ernie grinned toothlessly at the bathroom door, behind which Boochums was barking the happy bark of a dog who has driven off the foreign invader and claimed the country of bathdom for himself.

Meanwhile Hughes was turning the chit over in his hands.

On a hunch, he fished in the more obvious of his jacket pockets (Hughes' jacket was honeycombed with pockets, thanks to the local moth population) and was rewarded with a small scrap of note. He read it as Ernie shuffled off about his codgery day.

Junior,

> *You're in trouble. I'm not sure what kind, but I've got my suspicions.*
> *Think a minute before you run down here to the shop so we can talk about*
> *it. What good does talking do?*
> *Maybe a lot sometimes.*
> *But this isn't a time like that.*
> *Instead take this money and do something about it.*

Dad

P.S. Don't you ever call me "Pops" again.

Hughes read it again, his lips thinning, not hearing Ernie's witchy cackle as he flicked through comedy reels on his portable vid screen. Not hearing the rain or the sloshing sounds of Boochums causing sudsy bedlam in the bathroom, either.

Dad, he thought. *You didn't have to.*

Some inner voice replied, *Yes he did.* That was what good parents did. When their children went around breaking all the plates and cups in the porcelain shop, they only sighed, and scolded, and hoped their kids would be more careful next time and fetch the dustpan and broom. Because the good parents (the rare and best of them, really) remembered the days when it was them shattering everything they touched, their turn wreaking merry havoc with the plates and cups. They remembered those charming breathless days when cleaning up the mess was the farthest thing from their minds.

"Okay there?" called Ernie Wilks.

"Yes, thank you," said Hughes, who was crying, and trying to hide it as best he could. "I'm fine."

Ernie grunted and returned to his chuckle reels.

Hughes collected himself. He folded the note away and finished getting dressed. He armed and shouldered his way into his jacket. The credit chit vanished into one of its many secret pockets.

Well, he had successfully crossed item (4) off his checklist. That left:

1)   Get a magic item.
2)   Join the Scarlet Citadel.
3)   Pay back Gleam and Glint's employer.

Hughes looked around. "Where are my boots?"

"Corner by the door," Ernie told him. He looked at Hughes over the lip of his vid screen. "Boots like that you're like as not to catch cold. Take you ages to heel."

"Right."

"*Heel,*" Ernie prompted. "Get it?"

"Toe-tally."

Ernie bristled. "You keep yourself laced together out there."

"I'll keep on the right foot, I promise," said Hughes, tugging a boot on and hopping to keep his balance.

Ernie's eyes darted to-and-fro as his brain grasped for another good one. "Try the city on for size?"

"Not quite," said Hughes with a smile. "Needs more sole."

This set Ernie Wilks cackling like a storybook hag who has eaten all the handsome princes.

"Well played, kid!" he hooted.

Boochums gave a short bark of agreement.

"Ernie?" said Hughes, standing up with both boots tied and trusty.

"Yeah?"

"Your husband was a florist, right?"

"Sure was," Ernie said proudly. "Ran the finest stall in Corinth City before he died. Blooms so fresh and sweet, you'd give your arm just to hold one." He waggled his mechanical fingers and his pencil-thin eyebrows in tandem. "Course that was before the gangs figured out how low risk and high profit flowers were. The wealthy go wild for them in this city. *Once to blossom, soon to wither*, all that impermanence and shit. Some crime lord or other muscled in on my hubby, squeezed him for every chit he had. Ended up closing the stall. Then I had my accident. So we up and moved out of Nikandros to this grubby spot in Leonidas, me, hubby, and Boochums. Only two of us now, what with hubby gone to plant and pluck and sniff petals in whatever fifth season follows the four we got here on earth. He was a great one for puns. Would have liked you. Why'd you ask?"

"You wouldn't happen to know any other florists, would you?" Hughes asked hopefully. "Decent ones that won't cost me a leg and an..."

"Arm?"

"Um," said Hughes, embarrassed. "Yes."

Ernie gave him a sage look. "Now why would a fellow so down on his luck he just shared a bath with Boochums the Loud-Bottomed Wonder be interested in flower shopping? It's not exactly a cheap sport."

"Does it matter?" said Hughes.

"Well. I guess not." Ernie Wilks pondered a moment. "I know a few places. Decent ones, sure. Your best bet is *Amontillado's* on the corner of Whitewalls and Burst. Family run establishment. Big family, tough. No one could run them out of business, and they're honest and stubborn as weeds. Might be able to call ahead if you like, get you in with a slick haggling start on a bouquet or whatever you're fixing to buy. As for cost..." He trailed off meaningfully.

Hughes nodded. He understood perfectly.

Tucked into the complexities of his coat, the two-thirds of a credit chit seemed suddenly lighter.

It was not, in the grand scheme of things, a large amount.

Even so, it was going to have to go a long way or else the rest of his list would remain uncrossed, and Hughes would be reacquainted with Miss Gleam's scalpel teeth and Mr. Glint's unnaturally long fingers.

And maybe her scissors, too.

Snicker-snick.

No. No he would not think that way.

"I'd appreciate you making that call, Ernie."

"Okay then," the codger agreed. "Now put an egg in your shoe and beat it."

Hughes did just that.

As he walked down the zigzagging steps that clung to the building, his eyes fixed somewhere beyond the rise and fall of nearby buildings made hazy by the savage rains, the credit chit felt very light indeed.

And though it was also tucked snugly in his long-tailed coat, snippets of the note reread themselves in his mind over and over. They would occur to him all that day, and for many days thereafter.

You're in trouble. What good does talking do? Take this money, his father demanded. *Do something about it.*

Back in Ernie's, from behind the bathroom door there came a terrific splatter as Boochums wagged his wet, matted tail, and the sound of his contented doggie throat pitching in a whine. The sound was a little forlorn, but hopeful.

Hughes didn't hear it though.

He was off in search of something.

CHAPTER SEVEN

A brisk five-minute walk from the florist called *Amontillado's*, there wound a particularly long street. Walls ran along its sides, and these walls were covered in posters that moved. They each contained the animated face of William Keaton, a screen actor who made the difficult transition from theatre (which died) to screen (which thrived), and who had himself died in a traffic collision thirty years before Hughes' story began while high on a mixture of assorted methamphetamines and a few lines of extra-strength talcum powder. On any given day, these posters of the late William Keaton might turn to you as you walked by them, and with a smile that had lit up the red carpet for years, he would tell you about events near you: concerts; novelty attractions; fig eating contests; and other interesting things.

All the events were totally up to date. The company who owned this street of posters also owned William Keaton's likeness, and they retained the rights to dub him over, cementing their ability to keep investors happy in the knowledge that their products would be endorsed by the estimable, and extremely dead actor Mr. William Keaton Esquire, and therefore made lots of money, thus greasing the merry whirligigs of Corinth City capitalism forever.

Hughes, who had a huge respect for theatre and a middling appreciation for film, found the multitudes of Keatons immensely unsettling and would gladly have torn down every single poster had it not been a prosecutable offense to do so.

That day, a thousand wall-bound dead men turned to him and smiled an identical toothsome smile.

"Good day handsome," said the late William Keatons.

"Rainy day, Billy K."

"Sure is. A go-getter like you ought to take it easy. Why don't you make your way to The Hippodrome for a bit of enthralling gut-balling entertainment?"

"I can't just now, Billy," said Hughes. The posters eyes followed him as he hurried by like the eyes of paintings in creepy old TV shows. "I've too much to do."

"Oh, don't be like that," chided the late William Keatons. "Whet your appetite, can't I? It's going to be splendid. A little bedlam? Sure! A little blood? Yes! A little brut-al-it-y? Yessiree Momma!"

Reluctantly, Hughes slowed. "Okay. I'll humor you, Mr. Keaton. What's on at The Hippodrome?"

A thousand skilled, highly deceased smiles broadened before him.

"Let me tell you..."

***

Later, as Hughes pursued the recommendation of a dead actor, the storm capered and danced and played, a great circus of light and loud crashes as the air over the city found itself electrified and expanding with heat. Rain beaded the streetlamp glass. Windshield wipers lashed and sprayed fistfuls of crystal-clear water, and the wind carried that slightly alluring, slightly repulsing musky smell of city rain. For the second time that day Hughes was drenched, and this time there were no scented bubbles and no energetic dog to alleviate the harsh and absolute reality that he was wet as wet could be. The muggy moist sensation all over his skin, he could deal with. It was the state of his toes that rankled.

Hughes' shoes clung to his feet only with a concerted effort.

God, what he wouldn't give for a pair of hobnail boots with thick soles and wiggle room to keep his toes dry and free from pinching cramps, as well as some of the more interesting funguses that breed in soaked shoes.

He fixated on it so much his list gained another addition:

4. Have dry feet.

Before he knew it he'd reached the flat stone steps leading up to the entrance of The Hippodrome.

Presiding magnificently over the border between Leonidas and Cleomenes Districts, The Hippodrome was an arena of ochre-colored stone. There were spotlights and overpriced popcorn vendors, gougers selling bogus tickets and scratch cards, and the rainy smells were replaced with sticky fizzing soda, nostril-tickling cigarette smoke, and the tang of sweat. As Hughes stepped inside and paid his entrance fee, he felt a wave of giddiness mushroom up in his chest.

All around him everything was arches and turrets, busy promenades and glamorous advertisements.

This was a quirk of his personality, and not something he was altogether conscious of. The feeling of being born in the wrong time never occurred to Hughes. Nevertheless, some radiant part of his secret soul yearned for large spaces where entertainment ruled like some beautiful queen. Here in The Hippodrome, he felt his very veins sing in tongues of thespian splendor, crying *costumes!* and *makeup!* and *up with the curtain! Up! Up!*

Without knowing he was doing it, he began to hum a tune he'd invented a long time ago when he was small. It was a merry lilting tune that went along with a song he'd seen written down in a charming and adventurous play he loved above all other plays, which was called *A Summer Knight's Stroll.*

And, at least for a short while, he forgot about his tired, wet feet.

Hughes was early. He selected a seat, settled in, and waited for things to get rolling. Far below his spot in the gradually filling symposium of seats lay the field—a hairpin of closely cropped grass measuring one hundred feet lengthwise and about half that widthwise. Idly, he pondered whether or not it was real grass—now that would be a rare sight indeed in Corinth City where the greenest thing in abundance was envy. His was a greedy city where people scrounged and backbit, all in the hope of achieving some dream that was not designed for them.

Take Ernie Wilks. He and his husband had longed for peaceful suburbia together with their dog and their flowers. What they got was bereavement, one husband dead and the other alive to mourn him in poverty.

Ernie seemed happy enough nowadays, but Hughes believed some part of him just under the surface gasped and groped for the past. Envy for his former self, for better times.

As if I'm so far above that, he thought with alarming bitterness. *Remember Kim?*

Hughes did remember her. He simply wished he did not.

High above, The Hippodrome shutters were closed to ward off the afternoon rain. Spotlights threw their implacable light, making things vivid and stark, almost hyperreal. Under the heady synthwave thump of music pulsing from The Hippodrome's speakers, Hughes could hear the storm laying siege to the building. Flitting and twirling around the arena were a troupe of lusciously red moths, each one equipped with a lens beaming live footage along invisible cables to an equally invisible camera jockey tucked somewhere unobtrusive nearby.

The jockey pumped the footage to The Hippodrome's feed and the associated television networks. *Viewer numbers will be good today*, Hughes guessed with confidence.

For that day in early summer the Scarlet Citadel had scheduled a melee—a dangerous creature hauled to the city from another world in chains would face off against popular pageant fighter Tommy Fahrenheit.

Tommy was a member of the Citadel, famous for his skill, size, and sexual charisma. His curly autumnal hair caused quite a stir amongst a certain rather repressed subsection of middle-aged women who liked a large curly-haired man as much as they liked their afternoon tea.

Anyway, all across Corinth City people would be tuning in to watch on their home vidscreens, those screens cheap and brittle or huge and high-definition and wall-mounted.

Not Hughes though.

He would observe the show on a firsthand basis, feel the throb and gleeful delirium of the crowd, maybe enjoy himself, though entertainment was a secondary concern.

Primarily he was here for research.

How did the old saying go?

Failure to prepare, prepare to die horribly in unfortunate circumstances.

A grim expression brushed his lips. It faded as the show began.

Sandwiched elbow-tight between a very thin woman and a very large man, both of whom were busy on their portable vidscreens and not paying nearly as much attention as the spectacle warranted, Hughes watched with acute and childlike interest as Tommy Fahrenheit dismantled a scaly-skinned, gangling monster with his hands.

Those hands were wrapped in grooved black gloves—magical items fashioned to fit Tommy's deft fingers. A veritable giant, the man was an inch shy of seven feet, yet surprisingly lithe and quick. Never moving when he did not have to, Tommy Fahrenheit observed and bided his time, struck hard, retreated, then struck again with a speed that seemed to evoke flames rushing hungrily over a patch of crude oil, a quickness that produced a feeling of amazement in the spectator.

"That's so fast!" cooed a kid sitting nearby.

"Pretty fast," the kid's mother replied.

"Is he teleporting, Momma?"

"Yes, sweetie. See those gloves Mr. Fahrenheit is wearing?"

"Uh huh."

"Those give him something called *localized* teleportation. It shifts his body magically. Makes him very difficult to hit."

"He's so *fast*," the kid repeated happily.

Faster than the eye can follow, kid, Hughes thought. *My question is: what is it like to move that quickly?*

The question seemed to have no appreciable answer.

The ability Dexterity was certainly involved. Tommy was big, but he seemed to flow between stances like liquid mercury, which was not a Strength-based approach to combat. As he watched the melee play itself out, Hughes imagined inside Tommy Fahrenheit's mind, the magic felt something like this:

Testing Tommy Fahrenheit's Dexterity...

Success!

Tommy Fahrenheit has avoided a potentially fatal swipe, caught the monster's fingers, and he can now break the offending clawed hand, the wrist—hell! The whole arm!

Congratulations!

Hughes frowned as he speculated, for speculating was all he could do.

"Its arm!" the nearby kid cried as if they could hear him down in the field. "Snap its arm, Tommy! Get it! *GET IT GOOD!*"

The kid's mother saw Hughes looking and shot him a slightly embarrassed grin.

Hughes shrugged eloquently and returned to the problem of abilities.

As nuts went, it was a tough one to crack. Impossible perhaps, given his limited understanding of the subject.

He envied computer game characters who could assess their fictional threats with total clarity and a complete suite of insider knowledge. For himself, there was simply no codex of information to consult.

His Performance ability rose up in him when he called on it, but he had no idea how the abilities of Strength, Intelligence, or indeed Dexterity manifested in others.

If anyone did have an idea as to the truth, or could consult a codex of what was accurate and what was nonsense, it was the Scarlet Citadel.

As far as Corinth City was concerned, it was they and they alone who claimed abilities and wielded magic items. They alone controlled the largest slice of wealth and power.

Humiliatingly, excruciatingly, Hughes did not even know how you joined the Scarlet Citadel. He and the people of his class and background were *that* removed from wealth, *that* abstracted from power.

Sometimes he felt as if those with means and privileges were playing some fantastically complicated game, so grand in scope it spanned the city and all its culture and sociology and topography—its heart and soul.

If it was a game, what were the rules? How did things work?

Naturally he had some inklings because he was not an idiot and rumor was a rampant, wild, and uncontrollable thing.

But thinking of Gleam and her magic scissors, he really did envy those who could sort the large black truths from the little white lies.

Most of all, watching the carnage unfold below him, Hughes envied Tommy Fahrenheit's warrior prowess, his killing acumen. He wondered if the man's brain bristled with arrows and swords and spears instead of synaptic nerves.

He paused, the audience seething and rippling excitedly around him.

Did he envy that? Really?

No, of course not.

Hughes wiped at his brow with his hand and looked at it. The palm was wet. The heat and excitement were working him over. He felt encased in a clammy ball of sweat.

Course not, he thought.

Adventurous spirit aside, he did not relish the chance to hurt living things, even something as nasty as that monster in the arena.

What was it then?

I'm... he began, and almost at once had it.

I'm jealous of his surety. Tommy Fahrenheit knows exactly what he's doing down there, wading hip-deep in death. The only time I was sure about something was in the apartment I rented with Kim Kallaimon. I was sure that she loved me... Loved me enough that I could...

He suffocated the thought before it could complete itself.

Row upon row of spectators sprang to their feet in a wave that swept The Hippodrome as the battle reached its inevitable climax.

Slipping in its own blood, the creature gave an echoing grunt as Tommy Fahrenheit's gloved fist punched through its throat, bursting through its neck in an explosion of bright blood.

The creature shivered and went still.

Immediately upon death it began to dissolve—scaly skin and muscle and bone—as if it were made of sugar and someone was running a tap over it. After no time at all the only thing that remained of the creature was a single organ. It might have been a kidney, or a lung, or a malformed heart. It was difficult to tell.

Hughes squinted at the organ from his seat, wondering what it could be, and why it shone with a pale green light he found oddly comforting.

One of those, he thought with resolve. *I need to get my hands on one of those, and I'll be one step closer to my magic item. Because one thing rumors agree on is this: magic items aren't forged out of iron or steel or cogwheel alloys. They're forged out of the luminous green guts of monsters from another world— a world that is not like ours and is called Iphigenia.*

Tommy Fahrenheit picked the organ up and held it over his head.

The crowd roared.

On either side of him, Hughes was aware of the large man applauding and the thin woman whistling, her pinkies stuffed into her mouth so the whistle was extra shrill.

Well, why not?

Hell of a show.

Smiling a strained smile, and in spite of everything feeling quite inspired and only the teeniest bit terrified, Hughes rose to his feet with the rest of them and began to clap.

CHAPTER EIGHT

A few hours later, bundled in his coat and more than a little hungry, Hughes hurried through streets the storm had emptied as effectively as any government mandated curfew.

Not that such a curfew was likely. It was universally agreed by the general public that the members of Parliament were too busy arguing over where to order dinner from on any particular day to give much thought to the actual goings-on in Corinth City. Tabloid journalists with reliable insider information claimed the ruling outfit of the city were absolutely set against spicy curry dishes after the harrowing events of something called "The Two-For-One-Tuesday Vindaloo Incident," which resulted in several hospitalizations, and according to rumor, one death by extreme bowel instability.

"You there."

Hughes glanced away from the sidewalk (prolonged bouts of lashing rainfall gave the impression that the pavement under his boots was auditioning to become a river and was overall doing a sterling job of it) and found himself staring at nothing.

"Down here."

Hughes looked down. "Oh," he said. "Um. Good afternoon."

His unexpected company sneered. The man had a strange ratio of head-to-body size, a round face with a bulbous nose, and a sneer that seemed like a permanent fixture. Combined, the total sum of these qualities put Hughes in mind of a really irritated pin.

The pin man had stepped out of the shelter an awning provided, was now blocking Hughes' way, and as if to add insult to rude greeting, he snapped a big lilac umbrella open to ward off the rains, which thumped against the fabric like tiny fists on a door.

"Where you off to, Sunny Jim?" the pin man asked Hughes, who was soaked to his skin, busy besides, and not at all in the mood for a chat.

"Just on my way somewhere," Hughes replied.

"Where?"

"Out of this rain if I can help it."

"Yeah, good idea," said the pin man. He did not move out of the way. He stood there, dry under his umbrella and sneering truculently up at Hughes. "And where might that be, this place out of the rain?"

Hughes had had enough.

He went to step by the pin man. The pin man stuck out his arm and pushed an increasingly exasperated Hughes back in front of him. He reached into his coat and produced a wallet from his inside pocket. Flipping it open, he revealed a symbol that had been shaped by a skilled tanner into the firm brown leather.

"Know what that is?" the pin man asked Hughes.

"It's a boot," said Hughes accurately.

The pin man's eyes narrowed. "All right, Mr. Plucky, Mr. Sunny Jim, Mr. Clever Dick, unless you want my boot planted *ubi sol non lucet*, you'll just cooperate like a nice little vagrant. This boot on this here leather wallet is my seal of office. I am a streetbeater, my lad. A constable operating on behalf of the Parliament who happen to run this city. A man of the *Law*." The pin man pronounced the word as though he expected a peel of thunder to accompany it. When this did not happen, he drew himself up to his full height, which brought the top of his umbrella about on par with Hughes' chin. "Now you tell me where you're going, and if I don't like what I hear I'll box your ears and send you scurrying. Honestly, I don't know what this city's come to, what with young people roaming about full of cheek and bother. Besides, a fellow dressed like you walking around in this weather is bound to be up to no good!"

Hughes' lips were moving. "*Non lucet...* Where the sun doesn't shine?" he translated, his eyebrows drawing together.

"Well?" demanded the pin man. He prodded Hughes in the belly with a finger. "I'm waiting, Mr. Big Mouth."

Hughes supposed it couldn't hurt to tell him. "I'm on my way to see Krys and The Mum."

"Who?"

"They've got a cottage around here," Hughes explained. "It's got horses on it."

"Oh, the Painted Girl and the Ringmaster Woman." The pin man snorted. "What do you want with them freaks? Going to tell you your fortune?"

"I hope not," said Hughes, who knew that while Krys the Painted Girl might indeed know his future, she would rather eat a whole toad than tell him about it.

The pin man squared up to Hughes, his mouth crimping around his sneer. "Well, Mr. Freak Friend. I don't like you. I think I *shall* box your ears for you, even if I do believe you're just a lout in the road. Unless..." His eyes took on a new glimmer, one Hughes did not much like. "Unless, of course, you can get me a photograph of that Painted Girl."

For a moment Hughes wasn't sure he'd heard right. As the pin man talked on, it became clear that he had.

"I've got a camera I could give you. Small one. Tiny, really. You could get me a picture, and I could forget your cheekiness in a jiffy. Only... she is a pretty Painted Girl. Wouldn't you agree?"

Hughes regarded this quarrelsome and frankly horrible man for a moment. Hughes' hair was so wet it felt as if he'd been hung upside down and dipped in a duck pond. The rain was so pervasive it seemed to have a mind all its own—a cunning mind that knew where all the dry, cozy places in your clothes could be found, and find them it did, whereupon it soaked them with gusto.

He was, in short, quite finished with the storm, and this man with his belligerent sneer, and his booty seal of office, and his ugly interest in Krys the Painted Girl.

It was at that precise instant that the thunder chose to roll out, and with a shift in the wind that brought a reek of damp garbage from a nearby pile of busted bins spewing their bulging black bags onto the sidewalk, the rain intensified.

It chattered around Hughes and made the deep puddles ripple, and it slapped his skin and hair and clothes with a million carefully aimed droplets of warm anguish.

Hughes realized he was glaring up at the coal-dark sky, too dark for a quarter to three on a Friday afternoon. He turned back to the streetbeater.

The pin man, for his part, was fumbling with the clasp on a truly amazingly small camera shaped like an ordinary button.

"You can attach it to your shirt," said the pin man encouragingly, all traces of his anger fading under his excitement. "When you want to take the picture, just click this little bit here. See the ridge? That detaches the shutter from the lenses, here, here, and here. Then, you've just..."

Hughes changed.

Miss Gleam might have recognized that change. The Scarlet Citadel man he had met on Agorippis Street might have too. But then, they might not have.

Hughes was good at mixing up his Performances.

Fantastic, really.

"That's a nice umbrella," he said, and the pin man started.

His expression spoke volumes. It said, *What happened to your voice? It's different. It was nothing to write home about before, but now, why, you could shave with a voice like that.*

"What?" the pin man managed. "What about my umbrella?"

"It's nice," repeated Hughes. "Lilac is the *sssssweetest* shade of purple." His voice was terribly, sickeningly sharp. So sibilant. So slithery.

Performance Successful!

+3 Experience

The pin man cringed from that voice.

He had dropped his mini button camera yet seemed not to have noticed.

"Funny, I've always had a great fondness for the color purple," Hughes continued. "It evokes all sorts of interesting things. Things you might like too, Mr. Pin Head, if you got to know them more intimately. Things like sunsets. Spring flowers..."

"Bruises?" squeaked the pin man.

Hughes had no intention of hurting this wretched fellow. *But he doesn't know that.* Hughes grinned. "*Bruisssses.* Right."

The pin man paled. He gave his umbrella a mournful look.

It really was a miserably wet day.

"Shit," he said.

***

So it was that Hughes arrived at the cottage. Rills of water trickled from the rearing horses that cornered each section of the rooftop like gargoyles on a cathedral. The carousel that had been demolished and rebuilt into this little abode had been adorned with more than a couple of ponies, mules, and gung-ho stallions. Animals of all sorts preened in plastic from every inch of the cottage, walls to windows. Hughes had a bad moment in which he believed he saw none other than Mr. Glint emerging from the rabble of creatures. But it was only a trick of the light, and his fear was dispelled when the front door opened wide for him.

A girl of perhaps seventeen stood there. Tattoos flowed over her skin like an inky tide over a pale shore.

"I knew you'd come," she told him.

"Did you really?"

She nodded. "I forgot for a bit. But now you're here, I've remembered again."

"Just to be clear, you remembered I was going to come?"

"Uh huh."

"Before it actually happened?"

"Yes."

"Good," said Hughes, amused. "As long as we've got that sorted."

Excited as anything, she went up on the balls of her feet and came down again. Up. Down. Then with two thoroughly inked hands she beckoned him inside.

"I've brought something for you," Hughes said, accepting the invitation and looking forward to bidding the storm farewell for a time.

"I know," said the Painted Girl. "And may I say that is a splendid umbrella."

"Thanks, Krys," said Hughes. He gave her a broad grin as the rain sluiced from its lilac brim. "It was a gift."

***

Hughes stepped over the threshold into the carousel cottage.

But he might as well have stepped back thirteen years.

Molded as it was by the unlikeliest artificers and craftspeople, the cottage made no effort to distinguish its outside from its inside. It was a whole other menagerie of plastic animals inside, all striped hindquarters and spotted limbs and curled tails, furs and fins and muzzles and snouts, tiny quills, huge trunks, and much, much more. A bearded female gnome, also plastic, squatted next to a calliope, her bulky, unmoving fingers poised over the keys that nevertheless thumped up and down. The music was charming and a bit sinister, and hung above the fireplace with its grille made of twisted train tracks was a sign, much less charming and much more sinister than the music fluttering through the cottage like dark birds.

The sign was huge and covered in delicate glass flowers that lit up when you ran electricity through them. There were hundreds of them: daffodils, lotuses, daisies and magnolias, primroses, violets, asters and orchids, and alight they would have bloomed before Hughes' eyes like a meadow in the spring orchards beyond Corinth City's synthetic humdrum colors.

But the flowers lay dark, and so it was by the flickering firelight that Hughes read the sign:

Krys and The Mum Present Their Rotbloom Carnival of
Bright Oddments and Dark Delights.

Hughes gazed at this and at everything else with unabashed wonderment as he did every time he paid his friends a visit.

Even the burning coals in the hearth carried a comfortable, nostalgic smell.

He felt six years old again, and that he was meeting Krys and The Mum for the first time.

Of course to him all those years ago when the carnival tumbled into Symbarr Square, they had been the Painted Girl and the Ringmaster Woman.

Speaking of, the Ringmaster Woman herself sat in an immense chair with upholstery bursting through its emerald green cloth. Its burled walnut could use a dusting. The chair was so immense in fact that it seemed on the verge of swallowing her.

"So it was *you* she meant," the Ringmaster Woman who was called The Mum told Hughes, rather cryptically. "Very well. I suppose you'll be wanting porridge."

"No," said Hughes.

And his stomach growled, *Yes.*

"With jam?" asked Krys, who had sometime in the past few seconds claimed Hughes' hand.

"Really, I'm fine," said Hughes.

His stomach replied, *Blackberry, please.*

Krys giggled at the *squidgy-squeak* sound coming unbidden from Hughes' belly.

"I think your tum has other ideas," she said.

"I think so too," he conceded. "Blackberry jam would be..."

"A stupendous choice!"

In a gale of ratty skirts Krys pirouetted off in the direction of the kitchen, which situated itself through one of three doors exiting this strange, and strangely cozy, sitting room.

"Sit, sit," said The Mum.

There were no other chairs. Hughes elected to obey anyway and hunkered down on the bumpy floor in the aquatic section of the former carousel, surrounded by penguins and eels and a magnificent man o' war jellyfish with yellow-gold tendrils and a clear bell-shaped head filled with valves of frozen blue and veins of pink.

The Mum gave him the once-over, absorbing his features, his weight, his complexion. Hughes had never had a grandmother, but sitting there in front of him, The Mum seemed to be every grandmother in the world fused into a single musty-peppermint-smelling, whey-faced, and shawl-wearing union of grandmotherliness, complete with garters. "How are you then, Gormon?" she rasped.

"Just 'Hughes' is fine, The Mum. No one calls me Gormon."

"It's your name, isn't it?"

"It is," he was forced to agree. "But really it's my dad's name. We share it, but he owns it, if you see what I mean. He calls me 'Junior' and everyone else calls me 'Hughes.' How are you, The Mum?"

"You saw the garden on your way in?"

Hughes said he had indeed seen it.

"How would you describe it?" she asked him.

Hughes wondered how tactful he ought to be. Considering the woman he was speaking to, tact was probably the wrong choice. The Mum viewed delicate, indirect speech the same way Pest Control workers view mouse holes.

"It looks like crap, The Mum," he told her honestly.

"Exactly." She nodded approval. "Not a single peeping poppy or startled sapling of note or merit. Oh, we tried that new fertilizer you brought us last time.

The seeds won't take. This place, Gormon." Her knobbly fingers—twined together—now unwound themselves to snatch a puff of lint from her shawl. "This place, I tell you. Damp and dark and dreary. No good for arthritis; no good for anything! Nothing grows here except weeds and bad habits."

"You could sell this place," he proposed, not for the first time since meeting her. "It's a curiosity if nothing else. Take the metrotram somewhere greener."

"What?" She gave him the sort of look suitable for someone who was a few bananas short of a bunch. "*Sell* the carnival?"

He thought of pointing out they had already sold the carnival, that this cottage, with its beastly walls and dead garden, was the last vestige of the show that had filled a six-year-old Hughes with such awe and joy, the last trace of the show Krys and The Mum had taken to Corinth City, never to leave again.

But while she was a grim, grousy, unpopped boil of a person, Hughes cared very much for The Mum.

So he did not point anything like that out.

Instead he grinned with harmless mischief. "Want to see something?"

"Depends," The Mum replied suspiciously. "Is it a Frank?"

Hughes was taken aback. "A what?"

"A Frank. A trick, you know. You pull one, only it's not a leg, it's roguery of the highest nonsense. Pull a Frank. A shenanigan. Monkey business. A whatsit. 'Gentlemen, gather round, and I'll tell you about this really great Frank I've just done.' You know," she added impatiently. "A Frank."

Understanding dawned.

"Oh," said Hughes with relief. "A *prank*, The Mum. With a P."

"That's what I said," sniffed The Mum. "Well, is it?"

"A Fr—er. A prank?"

"And?"

"No," said Hughes. "It's not a prank, The Mum."

The Mum sighed. "Damn. I could do with one. Never mind." She seemed to get into the spirit of things. With sudden and compelling grace the Ringmaster

Woman drew herself up in her rickety chair. "Unveil your benefaction, noble waymaker," she bid him.

Hughes looked at her blankly. "Sorry?" he said.

"Turn out your pockets you silly man."

"Oh. Right."

He gave her a sheepish grin and obeyed.

"Cor!" The Mum clenched her hands like tree roots gorged on excitement. She leaned forward to look at the thing Hughes held carefully in his palm, her silver-gray eyes as wide as the storm raging over the cottage roof. He could smell her breath from this close, a smell like antique cabinets and fruit'n'nut chocolate—not entirely unpleasant. "Would you look at that," she admired.

In the cup of Hughes' hand was a flower.

The flower was large, its petals ridged and firm and slightly curved to the admiring eye. The Mum took it from him, and with fingers that did not shake or shudder, she stroked those petals from where they edged the flower pinkly to where they bulbed in the middle, lavender and indigo.

Hughes heard a sharp intake of breath from the kitchen door.

Krys was there. A bowl of blotchy blue ceramic steamed in each hand. The smell was wonderful.

"Hughes," she said quietly. "Take these, please."

He took the bowls.

And he watched as the two of them, the young girl who could see the future and the old woman who could see the past, came together to fawn and fuss over the flower he'd brought them, the way relatives will go moonish and starry over a welcome new addition to the family, and they were both absolutely ensconced in the present moment in all its flowery sweetness and porridge warmth.

Hughes could not have resisted smiling even if he had tried.

He'd paid a frankly ridiculous sum for the bloom. In his coat pocket the credit chit his father had given him had been reduced from two-thirds size to a little under a quarter. But this, their reaction, made the cost well worth it.

Later, after the flower had been potted, and porridge (with a generous dollop of blackberry jam) had been eaten, The Mum dabbed at the corners of her mouth with a cloth and said, "On to business, then. Have you come for counsel, Gormon?"

"Hughes, The Mum. But yes," agreed Hughes. "Some advice is exactly what I'm looking for." He set his bowl aside. "The thing is... I need to get my hands on a magic item. That means I've got to either try my luck in a black market (which I can't, since I've got nothing to trade), or join the Scarlet Citadel (which I don't know how to do)... or go to um..."

"Yes?" prodded Krys.

"Or go to... ah..."

"Come along man," snapped The Mum, her glaucous eyes blazing. "Some of us are in our twilight years."

"Iphigenia," said Hughes meekly.

CHAPTER NINE

There was silence for a moment.

Outside a baleful wind began to croon.

"The Wilderness Beyond The Door," said Krys in a strangely distant voice. "The Beastly Continent. *Iphigenia.*" At once she was up off the windowsill she'd been resting on.

Hughes found his hands clutched tight, and the Painted Girl kneeling next to him, staring into his eyes.

"You mustn't go," she said. "No, you mustn't. You could be *hurt.*"

"This one's cute," Hughes said, tapping an octopus swirl of ink on her cheekbone with a finger. He did his best to appear brave. "I'll be fine, Krys. It's very important that I go. And I'm going to have a much better chance of survival if I know what I'm in for. Right?"

She held his gaze a little longer, the tattoos around her eyes a huge assortment of colorful peacock feathers, giving her a fierce and unshakeable look. She might have prevailed too, and cowed him into admitting that, yes, the whole thing was insane and foolish, and then where would Hughes be?

He would have to make a new list, one focused on escaping the city along with his father, charting new lives and...

But no. Hughes held her stare, and without actually engaging his Performance, he willed a look of fantastic determination into his face and felt that resolution burn behind his eyes like the fire warming the coals of the cottage hearth.

A little longer Krys held out... then she gave in.

She looked away sullenly. "All right. We'll help you."

He planted a grateful kiss on her cheektopus. "Thank you, Krys."

"Pish posh," she said, grumpy and pleased all at once. She looked over one shoulder at The Mum. "You start."

"Where?"

"The beginning, naturally."

"Predictable," said The Mum. "Too predictable. How about I start at the end, instead?"

"Um..." said Hughes, too late.

"Oh yes, that's much better!" cried Krys.

"In the end the carnival closed," said The Mum. "And the reason it closed is this: We—that's the girl and I—got too big for our boots. We wanted to run the best show in the world. It would have been easy cobbling together a big top with clowns and creepies and long-leggedy beasties." The old woman vented a tired sigh. "We wanted more."

"Now for the middle," said Krys. "We arrived in Corinth City on a bright sunny afternoon. After our first daytime show, we told the crowd there was more to come. If people returned the following day, they would see wonders as they had never before dreamed!" She stuck out her arm and made a sinuous motion. Before Hughes' eyes, weird shapes flowed and formed. Krys could manipulate the muscles in her body to make her tattoos dance and cavort. Now her arm looked brimmed full of inky krakens and cyclopes and a whole host of other monsters. "So! The crowd left whispering and giggling and keen on seeing these so-called 'wonders.' And under cover of darkness our merry troupe set off with me in the lead and The Mum staying put at the carnival."

Hughes nodded understanding. Krys and her troupe had been up to dangerous business that fateful night. The Painted Girl could glimpse the future only when she was at a distance from The Mum. At the same time, her spinning prophecy meant The Mum was condemned to gaze helplessly into the past. With her eyes blank, her hands fidgeted mightily, and if she had anything crafty nearby like paper, The Mum would fold it into the things she was seeing through a telescope of decades.

The great irony was that when they were reunited, The Mum couldn't seem to recall those events of the past well. Nor could Krys recall the future with any clarity. It was only when they were together, not apart, that they could relax and enjoy the present.

An odd existence, certainly, but at least they were *here*.

"So you snuck off to Iphigenia," Hughes prompted Krys. "You used your powers of divining the future to guide your carnival troupe to the portal."

"The Door," affirmed Krys. She said it with great respect.

"Wasn't it guarded?"

"Oh yes." Krys turned her arm and shifted her muscle so that angry men roared from her elbow. "But my troupe were excellent at taking direction. The shadows were long, and with me reading the future like a script, we slunk and slid and crept, and then we were through The Door and into Iphigenia, lickety-split."

Hughes smiled. "And then what?"

"We captured some beasties for the carnival."

"Just like that?"

"Just like..." Krys reached up and booped Hughes' nose. "That."

"What was it like through the port... through The Door?" he asked, rubbing the tip of his thoroughly booped nose.

"I don't remember," said Krys with a shrug. "Not really."

"I, on the other hand, do," said The Mum. "Mostly because once they'd come back the whole troupe would not shut up about it. Listen here, Gormon. Once you go through The Door, there's hills all around. Floating in the air are these bangly jingly things. Wossname. Bells."

"Bells?" Hughes frowned. "In the air?"

"Don't interrupt. If you walk one way there's a swamp as fetid and rank smelling as... well, as something very fetid and rank smelling indeed, young Gormon Hughes, and no mistake. And if you walk another way there's these big woods all tangled and mossy and full of pygmies."

"Dusty-winged blighters," said Krys.

"And the last way is a desert whose sands are ghostly pale under an eternal night," said The Mum. "But here's the thing, my lad, here's the interesting thing.

No matter which way you go, which way you look, there's always this mountain in the distance."

"A mountain?" said Hughes. "You don't mean... It couldn't be the same mountain, could it?"

"Like it was following us," said Krys. "I remember now. Remember perfectly." She paused and suddenly looked very small. "It was beautiful, but also scary."

"Iphigenia's a funny place, Gormon," The Mum told him, and perhaps it was Hughes' imagination, but all of a sudden the shadows in that sitting room seemed as long as those found in Krys' story. The fire stretched with them from behind its grille, so that all around Hughes the thin orange shadows twitched and contorted and made the plastic animals seem alive.

"A funny place," The Mum repeated. "And if you go there, you be sure and kill a beast from the hills. There are these cow things there and stubborn goaty fellows with horns for hooves and hooves for horns. Kill one of them and you won't get a magic item worth writing home about, but you'll be safe enough. Go to the swamp or the forest or the desert, and you'll meet sterner company than grazers and mixed-up goats. Enter The Door and follow the changing mountain, and you might never return."

With that she grinned humorlessly at him, a death's head expression. Between Krys and The Mum, Hughes considered the former more mystical, as if Krys were a kite with no string or keeper, one you couldn't help but chase after in case it did anything interesting. The Mum was speaking to him like a fortune teller, and not the jaded kind who speak in false Mysicordelian accents either, but the other kind, the kind that seem if not authentic, then at the very least enthralling. Her gaze hypnotized him, and in the cloudy pools of her eyes he saw the past unfold itself. He saw a stage. Spotlights. There was something behind the red curtain. The Mum swept her Ringmaster cane in a wide arc. The crowd baited, biting, waiting. Held breath. A snap! The curtain tumbling in a fanfare of trumpets toot-a-loot! Hughes on his mother's shoulders. He had very few memories of her, but this was one, oh yes.

He watched in slow motion as the curtain crumpled like an inflated crimson cloud someone pricked with a needle, its cabbage rose patterns flattened, as there on the stage, the cage and harness were revealed. From the silent crowd, someone uttered a gasp. Captured by Krys and her troupe and mashing itself mindlessly against the cage, a beast from Iphigenia peered out at them. Here the memory grew indistinct. Hughes hadn't realized how repressed the image was until that moment. Through a fog of forgetfulness, the beast itself was mostly indistinct to him. How much of that was a child preserving his own innocence in the face of the incomprehensible?

No matter the depth of it, Hughes remembered this: as the gasps and murmurs eddied away, no one cheered until the beast stopped charging its cage, swiveled a misty pink-gray eye, unhinged its jaws fantastically wide, and squawked so loudly it seemed as if a cast of hawks were stuffed down its throat and were screaming to be let loose.

As a boy of six, that had seemed jolly amazing.

As a man of nineteen, it frightened Hughes. Frightened him badly.

Because this time, when he met a beast of Iphigenia, not a docile creature chewing cud or tufty hill grass, but an honest-to-God monster, it would be in its own habitat.

There would be no carnival separating its rows of serrated teeth, or its claws, or its long saber-sharp talons from Hughes.

None of childhood's implicit immortality would shield him.

And there would be no cage. No harness.

Nothing.

Enter The Door and follow the changing mountain, and you might never return.

The fine hairs on Hughes' arms and neck stiffened.

"And now, to conclude: the beginning," said Krys sadly, and her voice broke the spell.

Hughes' eyes flickered. The room was normal again.

The Mum was not a dread soothsayer foretelling his doom. She was an old woman. This was her sitting room.

He was safe and he was sound.

Yet somehow this knowledge brought little comfort to wary, agitated Hughes as he listened with intent ears to Krys.

"The beginning is an awfully good place to end, don't you think, Hughes? Well, no sooner had our show started than the Scarlet Citadel stormed the stage. They killed the beast and all the others we'd stowed in the wings." Her small heart-shaped face was stricken, as if she were watching footage of that bloody scene. "One of the Citadel people addressed the crowd. She said The Mum and I were psychotic, we were loony, deranged, demented."

"Which of course is all true," put in The Mum.

"Oh, of course," agreed Krys. "But then she had the gall to say we were planning to unleash the creatures on the city once the show was over. Can you believe such tripe? The Scarlet Citadel told people we were planning some kind of... *murderous encore*."

"Stuff and nonsense," muttered The Mum.

"They had it all wrong." Krys shook her head vehemently. "We were going to *release* the beasts back to their home afterward, back into Iphigenia. Look, we reached too high. We were too ambitious, yes. Fair. But we were not wicked. You believe us, don't you, Hughes?"

Hughes nodded and said he did. He'd heard part of this yarn before, though never the whole thing. He was fascinated.

Krys bunched her skirts (so filthy and encrusted with mud and coffee and fruitcake stains that they emitted a slight *crinkle-crinkle*) and gave them a frustrated yank. "Later we found out we were betrayed by my troupe. They sold us out. And for what? Money, of all things."

"I sympathize," said Hughes.

They both looked at him.

"You do, do you?" said The Mum. "Yes. Yes, now I look at you, I can see it's true. Someone pulled the wool over your eyes, Gormon. Who was it?"

"A woman," he replied darkly. "Kim Kallaimon."

"You love her?"

Hughes hesitated.

I loved her so much I stopped performing and showed myself to her. My true self. And in return she robbed my borrowed credits, stole my car, and left me. He almost said it. But it was too much to admit, even here, even to these two.

So instead he said, "No."

"Good," said The Mum tartly. "You're a bit on the young side for love. For that matter, you're a bit on the alive side to go courting trouble in Iphigenia." She jabbed a hoary finger at him. "But I see you've got the idea stuck in your teeth. There it is then, all we know about the Wilderness Beyond The Door. In short, it's bloody dangerous. And meddling in its affairs only brings about grief and a preponderance of woe."

"I'll be careful," said Hughes.

Cocooned in her chair the retired Ringmaster was unimpressed. "Famous last words. Begone with you. Counsel and porridge have been given. Porridge has been eaten. Counsel has been duly ignored." She fanned both hands, shooing him out. "Begone."

As he left, Hughes turned on impulse and bent his body in a bow. "Thank you for the bright oddments," he said, perfectly serious. "And for the dark delights."

"Away with you," grumbled The Mum.

But the ghost of a smile now haunted her lips. "Scallywag and rogue. Away and bedevil someone else's cottage."

***

Outside the storm spanned the whole sky, from horizon to horizon, and she was a huge gray maid shaking her sheets of rain clean and complaining with her thunder tones.

Hughes propped up his lilac umbrella and considered his next move.

He was mildly distracted by the group of kids graffitiing impractically large breasts on a political poster adorning the concrete face of the nearby datalog building. The poster advocated against the city's rising culture of sexual liberation, and so Hughes thought the enormous breasts (and other assorted graffito bottoms, vaginas, and variously sized willies) could be viewed both as immature pranks and tactical rebuttals.

"Those are very detailed," said Krys next to him.

Hughes jumped. "Not a bother," he said as she laid a hand on his arm. "Just didn't hear you follow me out is all. What are very detailed?"

She pointed at the cornucopia of spray-painted cock.

"Ah," said Hughes.

"Do you reckon it's waterproof paint?" Krys asked.

"I suppose it'd have to be," Hughes said after some consideration. "Wash off in this otherwise."

"True. I wish you weren't doing this."

Her hand was still on his arm. He took it in his own, gave it a squeeze.

"I'm sorry your carnival closed down."

"Sorry this Kim Kallaimon lady hurt you."

He looked down at her upturned face, smutted and dirty and speckled in raindrops.

"Me too," he said eventually.

They walked a short way from the cottage. One of the kids spotted them, waved, and then got back to adding pubic hairs to a particularly veiny penis.

Hughes and Krys waved back.

"What will you do?" she asked him.

Hughes' expression was thoughtful as he scoured the honeycomb of streets ahead of them. "Ironically, in order to get my hands on a magic weapon, I need a mundane one first. Iphigenia is dangerous. More than I realized. I need something sharp, or blunt and heavy, and I'm going to have to steal it or bargain for it at a pawnshop."

He felt something pressed into his hand.

Hughes looked at it. Smooth leather wrapped around a grip lay in his palm, and there was a large knife sprouting from it like a bear's incisor from a gum.

Then Hughes looked at Krys, who was giggling.

"You should see your face," she said. "Be safe, okay?"

"I will." There seemed to be nothing else to say. Other than perhaps, "Thanks, Krys."

"See the patterning on the blade?" she asked him. "Those are folds of iron and nickel. Decorative, naturally. The core is steel. Not Jolene steel, of course, but still strong and..."

"Sharp," he said, admiring the edge.

The Painted Girl nodded eagerly. "Before we brought our carnival here, we traveled all over. In Jaenqui-Across-The-River, they call this sort of short blade a kris knife."

This time it was she who squeezed his hand.

"You keep your Krys knife handy, Hughes," she said. "You hear me?"

"I hear you."

"Good." A puff of breeze blew a tangle of hair across her face. Krys smoothed it back and said, "She's a king's daughter, you know."

After the sweetness of the gift-giving, this statement was entirely unexpected. It set Hughes off balance. "Who's a king's daughter?"

They had come just far enough from the cottage to have triggered her foresight. Her eyes—usually a soft lime green—had deepened to avocado.

Hughes realized he was watching her as she watched the future. He wondered what it looked like. She had never described it, but just then he would have believed her if she'd told him the future was quite similar to the flower he'd delivered to them that day—time like the bee-beckoning center and all possible outcomes blooming outward from that point. A botanical hereafter.

"Did you say something?" Krys asked.

"Me?" Hughes scanned her face. She looked blissful. "No, but you did."

"Did I?"

"You said that she—whoever *she* is—is a king's daughter," said Hughes.

Her dark avocado-colored eyes widened. "Truly? How splendid for her!"

And before he could repeat his question, before he could point out there were no kings in Corinth City, only the government, the Scarlet Citadel, and the many multitudes of gangland lords who might style themselves as kings but were really ruffians in a prolonged knife-waving contest, Krys laughed a merry tinkling laugh and ran back toward the carousel cottage, her skirts like torn messy sails mustered full of blustery wind, her tattoos clinging to her skin despite the best attempts of the cruel June rain.

"Right." Hughes sighed. "I suppose I'll be going then."

He started off toward the Acroppalin Hill, his destination the black slate roofs and stained glass windows of the Polydoros District. There, in a huge, guarded warehouse, he would find the portal to the world of Iphigenia, or as Krys and The Mum called it, The Wilderness Beyond The Door.

His arsenal included: a long moth-gnawed coat the color of soot; pockets full of assorted rubbish, some of which could be useful in a pinch, some of which he'd pinched rather than be useful; a quarter of a credit chit; a set of clothes that would make a beggar appreciate the insulation and fashionability of his disintegrating rags; boots like wet cardboard with laces; and his Krys knife.

All in all, Hughes believed his odds of pulling this whole thing off were, if not good, then at the very least not *completely* hopeless...

ACT THREE

IPHIGENIA

CHAPTER TEN

"Thank you for stopping by," said the guard in a friendly and decidedly pleasant tone of voice. "Be sure to come again, won't you?" And with the practiced aim of a woman who has done this many times in the course of her career as a sentry, and possibly even more during a stint as a professional athlete and martial artist, she planted her foot in Hughes' bottom, hard.

Hughes had been on all fours, the wet street spinning under him, the sounds of rush-hour traffic in his ears, his umbrella upside-down in a deep puddle out of immediate reach, trying without much success to negotiate some air back into his lungs. The kick he was about to receive was a follow-up to the punch this same charming guard had driven into his belly only moments ago. Now he went sprawling. For the second time in as many days, road tarmac flayed the healing skin from his palms, leaving them salmon pink and inflamed and stinging.

Behind him the warehouse door leading to the Iphigenia portal closed. And his chances of crossing the items off his list and saving his life closed with them.

Hughes lay in a sore sodden heap. He waited for someone to see him and rush to his aid, or for a car to come and run him over.

As far as he was concerned, either one would have been completely acceptable.

When neither kind help nor vehicular manslaughter was forthcoming, he grunted a pettish grunt of disappointment and slowly, wincingly got to his feet.

Around him Polydoros District seemed unbothered by the storm—not to mention the unseasonal flooding—that had cleaned out Hughes' own Leonidas District as effectively as the word "rat" will clear most restaurants.

People walked about unruffled and very insouciant altogether, taking important calls and chatting, and the calamitous weather gave them about as much thought as they gave it.

The reasons for this carefree attitude droned above Hughes' head. Clouds of nanites swarming like insects over the runoff and the puddles and the tributaries of rainwater, sucking them up with filament-thin tubes, superheating them in their synthetic stomachs and expunging them through the fine delicate membrane of their wings in clouds. The clouds were colored and scented.

That was why, when Hughes stood up, his nostrils filled with the dizzyingly sweet smell of almond yogurt.

Fending off a sneezing fit (Hughes was not allergic to almonds, but his nose was quite unused to the smell of them and was thus very tickled), he peered out at the late afternoon and saw lightning fork with stark white tines against the slate-black sky. The roofs, building stone, and metal girdings of Polydoros District were almost exactly that color, so richly black as to be almost blue. But the windows lent the District its splendor. Stained-glass they were, and each window showed a different picture. Here a man and a huge cat wrestling together. There a woman seizing a dragon's tail and tearing it clean off. Here a boy with a halo of branded coffee mugs and a beatific smile on his face. There a forest without leaves full of furtive pygmies and strange gaunt wargmen hunched under shaggy pelts.

All family histories, Scarlet Citadel propaganda, and advertisements.

And bang smack in the middle of the District loomed the warehouse.

Hughes turned to look at its huge edifice, his face bleak and long with surliness. Knowing that stealth was not going to be a viable option for him (Hughes recognized his left foot from his right but had often been told by his father that he had the grace of a seagull in a sandwich bin), Hughes had elected to charm his way past the guards and into the Iphigenia portal using his Performance.

This had not gone well.

Now his belly was athrob with pain, not to mention his backside, which felt as if the guard had dipped the sole of her boot in molten iron before searing its imprint on Hughes.

"So much for 'all in all,'" he muttered. "What a mess I'm in."

Adding insult to injury, at the moment of failure, Hughes' Performance had sent him that immensely comforting and not-at-all-infuriating message:

> +1 Experience On A Failed Attempt
> Congratulations!

He fetched his lilac umbrella, shook it off, propped it over his head, and reconsidered his options for a minute or two. The drone of the nanites and the frying-pan hiss of the rain blended together. At length, and with his surly face souring until he wore the bleakest of mopes, Hughes decided that his options were not very promising, and that he was quite fantastically buggered.

He would just have to come up with the money some other way, and only after he'd explained the situation to Miss Gleam and Mr. Glint, who would, Hughes was sure, take the news with generosity and would absolutely not rip his head off and shit down his neck.

He rubbed a hand across his lips. The gesture spoke to great stress.

That damn message kept recurring to him, especially the *Congratulations!*

Hughes grumbled something indecipherable that escaped the notice of the high-heeled women and business-suited men who swept blithely by him, but which could, conceivably, have been an acid-tongued protest against the concept of experience, Performance, all powers like it, their source, and indeed, magic in general, which could piss up a wall for all he cared.

"Excuse me, my guy," said a voice behind him.

Hughes turned to tell them that no, he would not excuse them, whereupon his brain saved him some serious embarrassment by sending his mouth the signal to shut up, which obeyed in the nick of time.

The speaker who had addressed him was a freckled, red-haired woman, perhaps twenty-five. She wore red leather armor. The armor was magnificently tailored, form-fitting, and yes, a rather striking shade of scarlet red.

The letter *J* was stamped on the breastbone.

Which of course meant this was Jolene-crafted armor. The freckled woman wore it, as did her two companions. They loomed enormously at her shoulders, both looking at Hughes with a good deal less patience than the woman was affording him.

"Only we need to get by," the freckled woman explained.

"Er. Right." Hughes' brain was now signaling his legs to move. They wouldn't. "Of course. You're Scarlet Citadel members. Probably on your way through the portal."

The woman smiled kindly. "That's right."

"Sort of a bag and grab endeavor."

Move, his brain commanded his legs.

No, said his legs. *We're fine here, thanks.*

"A bag and grab, yes," said the woman, looking at him in a puzzled way. "Are you all right, my guy?"

"Dandy," said Hughes, who was beginning to sweat. "I've often wondered, do you Scarlet Citadel types have a bar you go to afterward? To celebrate a job well done, I mean."

"Get out of the way," said one of the woman's companions.

"Toast your success sort of thing," said Hughes desperately. "I always like a cup of tea when I've accomplished something. Completed a project I'm proud of. But that's um... that's just me, maybe. Not that I'm suggesting you're anti-tea. Erm. Or purposefully avoidant of caffeinated beverages in general, for that matter." He grinned at their baffled faces. "Most people go for a pint, is all I meant."

"Speaking of pints," said one of the companions, "where the hell's Walter?"

"Search me," replied the other. "He'll turn up, I'm sure."

"Bloody soak," said the first disgustedly.

The freckled woman had clearly decided Hughes was a harmless lunatic. "After a successful mission we usually go for drinks in the *Pear and Princess.*" She gave him a smile that was half pity and half patience. "I'm a Bellini sorta girl."

Move, his brain thundered at his legs just as a bout of actual thunder shuddered in the gloomy skies overhead.

Oh, his legs said glumly. *If you insist.*

Maintaining his slightly manic grin, Hughes finally stepped aside.

"Thank you very much," said the Scarlet Citadel woman with red hair and very lovely freckles. "Have a good one, my guy."

"You too, my girl."

"Don't push it," said one of the companions, jostling Hughes with their shoulder as they passed him.

"Sure," said Hughes, more to the world at large than anyone in particular. He rubbed his shoulder, which was not as uncomfortable as the numb ghost of hurt in his stomach. When he spoke, his voice held something ghostly too, each syllable a minor haunting from the cellar of ghoulish misery that was his present mood. "I won't push. Honestly I'm not sure I could push anything, including my luck. Yeah." He chuckled bitterly. "My stupid luck most of all. Couldn't push it any further if I tried. And I did," he added sadly as the nanite drone and the somber rain and the lonely despair settled over him. "I really did try."

He began to walk. Where to exactly, Hughes himself had no idea.

***

He walked under a billboard. Its inscription (faint on account of the rains) told him he could be fulfilled, mentally and physically, and even spiritually, if only he invested in a bottle of Leopoldo Fernassi Shaving Cream. *Leopoldo Fernassi,* the billboard proclaimed, each letter appearing one after the other as if written by an enormous pen. *Every Man Is A Tiger To Another Man.*

He walked by a retro diner. Inside it looked like the past had been cut out and glued into the present day. Bubblegum popping waitresses rollerskated from table to table. Formica shone from every surface. The cook was a huge man of dark complexion wearing a greasy white vest and an easy "shit man, I only work here" grin. Jukeboxes clicked and ticked. Wall-mounted speakers bounced softly as they sent out their lively bluesy beat. Tap those bongos, Maestro. Pluck those guitar strings. Stroll the bass. Trumpets and clarinets warbled and blasted and blew, and passersby (including Hughes) could hear all that like a slightly muffled invitation, and most could accept it and head inside that diner for a smile and a booty-wiggle and something to eat, but not he.

Not me.

He walked by an overpass roaring and honking with traffic, some commuting into Polydoros and others commuting out and all of them with crap to throw out their car window. There was a dog rooting in this weird pile of migratory junk. Fast food boxes smelling exactly like the diner cook's shirt had looked, oily and somehow comforting, fell apart under her paws. The dog looked better fed than he was. That said, you could beat the straw out of a scarecrow with a golf club and still concede that the result looked considerably less famished than Hughes.

He stopped ten paces from the dog, his hands and most of his arms up to the elbow plunged deep in his pockets.

"Hey pooch," he said.

The dog took no notice of him. She had other concerns on her mind, namely the discarded leavings of those too busy or lazy to find a trashcan. Her white coat was interrupted by a diamond of brown hair that wrapped her hindquarters. The rain had damped it down, plastering every fluffy hair to her body. Half-eaten hamburger clotted her muzzle. Her collar named her: Minny.

Hughes looked around. No nanites patrolled this close to the overpass where there was ample drainage. He could see nearby offices and a nightclub, but the office shutters were drawn and it would be hours before the club opened its doors to the movers and shakers looking for a good drink and a better fuck that Friday night.

It was getting dark.

Hughes looked at the dog again. He wondered whether or not he ought to kill it for supper. He had nothing else to eat, and he was not about to spend the last of his money on a cheap all-you-can-eat Hortesian buffet: one because it would give him the runs, and two because now that his plans had imploded on themselves, he could not afford such an indulgence.

The dog didn't seem particularly edible.

Dogs seldom did.

He supposed most animals belied the serving, at least insofar as a cutlet of meat had no facial features and certainly no soul you could identify, the way eyes were in the habit of guiding you toward the presence of something greater (not good or bad, but greater) somewhere within the owner of those strange, jellified organs absorbing the whole world and everything in it.

What the hell am I thinking about eyes and souls for?

A sudden spell of dizziness took Hughes. He touched his eyelids and applied some pressure, then blinked away the color spots. While he waited for the spell to pass, hunger struck like a spade, digging into him and causing his empty bowels to emit a noise like squittering wet skin on bath tiles. It was a god-awful noise. God-awful feeling. How long had it been since he'd eaten anyway, other than porridge that (though tasty) did not go very far in the long battle against hunger? He thought it had been sometime before his encounter with the dazzling duo.

Now he was thinking about those two. Gleam and Glint. *Such silly names,* he thought. *Such incredibly ridiculous names for such terrifying characters.*

Unknown to Hughes, the Polydoros District overpass was home to a colony of bats adapted to living in the city. In that moment one of them awoke, slid its mousy body from the leathery blanket of its membranous wings, dislodged itself from its inverted perch, and fluttered into the gloom.

Its wings made a papery rustling sound, but addled as his brain was just then, Hughes did not hear: *flutter-flap.*

He heard: *snicker-snick,* the sound of long scissors opening and closing, and he shuddered.

What had he been musing over before this uneasy segue?

Oh yes. To eat dog or not to eat dog?

Well, it was a question.

He looked at Minny sorting through the trash.

On one hand she was rather adorable. On the other, his stomach was twinging with cramp. With little to filter and digest, his bloodstream and stomach were in stasis. His energy flagged. And part of him was still a bit annoyed about the bath thing with Ernie's mutt, Boochums. Maybe this could be a moment of much-needed catharsis.

Maybe my fucking ache of a belly will stop hounding me.

He smiled a wretched smile that did not stick around long after that dreadful pun. He darted a quick look around. Yes, all seemed quiet. Near the nightclub a streetlight was fizzling on, not red like the lamps in Leonidas District but a pretty turquoise green behind its encasing glass. The turquoise light was beautiful in the rain.

Minny finally acknowledged the human cutting in on her chow time.

She gave a desultory warning bark, letting Hughes know he had no business here, and went back to her meal.

Hughes quite liked dogs. Anyway, if he did kill her, he would not be able to bring her body home because his father disapproved of eating domesticated animals. In his heart of hearts Hughes believed his dad would cram pride between two slices of bread and munch that rather than cat, or hamster, or indeed, man's best friend.

"You eat beef," his son had once argued. Hughes hesitated. "I mean, you would if we could afford beef. And cow is domesticated, Dad."

"No, it isn't." His father had picked up a teapot, glared balefully into its dirty depths, and proceeded to give it a thorough clean. "Cow's a butcherblock animal, too dumb to tell its ears from its asshole. Same with goats, pigs, all that bucolic crap. Remember your Mylenia of Lith, son, the great poetess of your grandad's generation: 'Home is the place to hang your hat, warm your feet, and stroke the cat.' There are three kinds of creature, just as there are three kinds of people. Aren't we human beings just animals who've agreed that we ought to wear trousers? Yes, three kinds. Butcherblock, comfortable, and wild. The butcherblock for the slaughter, the wild to do the slaughtering, and the comfortable, who let it all happen while they get on with their lives." His father polished the clean teapot, set it on the countertop, and smiled affectionately when he saw Hughes' expression. "Don't look so peevish, son. You're one of the comfortable ones. So treat your fellows with respect and let the only canines in your mouth be your teeth."

Minny produced another bark. It was no longer a warning. It was heavier, a big smoggy-throated bark that told you this dog did not mess around, collar or no collar. Another bark. Then two more, in quick succession.

Ruff-ruff.

Back off.

Hughes' hand slipped to where the Krys knife rested in his coat... and flinched.

He stepped back, appalled by the thoughts he'd been entertaining. A great soaking shame draped him, nastier than the rains driving in under the lip of the overpass and dripping from his umbrella.

"Easy girl," he said.

Minny glared at him, her eyes hard brown marbles. She barked once more just to make sure they understood one another and then dipped her head back into the mulch of soggy chips, plastic-sheen cheese, moldy burger buns, burnt bacon, and sour-smelling chicken.

Hughes stood there, guilt worming in to join the hunger in his gut. "Sorry. I am a nice person, you know. One wholesome prosōpon. I don't... I didn't *want* to eat you. Not really. I'm just hungry. And tired." His nose was running. Hughes wiped it miserably. "And scared too, I suppose."

Had he read somewhere that dogs understood fear? Could scent it like sleek malicious wolves through the forests of old?

Hughes hung his head. "What am I going to do? What can I do?"

Above him the rest of the bats took wing. They were vampire bats, not rabid but unnerving with their deformed noses, and once more their wings filled the echoey cavernish dark of the overpass with the music of nightmares.

Flutter-flutter-flap.

Snicker-snicker-snick.

Hughes hunched his shoulders, turned to get out of there before he had a heart attack, and jumped when he heard the sound.

***

At first he would have sworn it was his imagination, but one look back at the dog proved whatever he'd heard was as real as the scuffle of bat wings he'd perceived only a second or two before. The white-and-brown-haired scavenger named Minny bristled, craned her neck, took one look at the source of the sound, and bolted.

Hughes' head jerked to follow her flight, then came around again to see for himself. Evening was ready to deepen now. His shadow stretched away from him, his arms and legs tapered into warped claws on the pavement, the umbrella mushrooming oddly in the moist and moonless dusk.

There were a series of pillars here in this underplace, keeping the overpass structure solid and gathering fine street art rather than graffiti. Polydoros District was a far cry from Leonidas, after all.

The sound had come from behind one of the pillars.

Hughes approached. Coming around the pillar, he saw a boot sticking out, and in that moment his hand closed on the smooth leather grip of his Krys knife nestling like a fanged snake in his coat.

He took another tentative step. One more.

The boot had grown a leg. And there was another boot, presumably equipped with a leg of its own.

Anybody lose a mannequin? thought Hughes. He clamped his jaw tight on a convulsion of nervous laughter.

I've got to get ahold of myself. Right now.

He remembered the sound and said, "Hello?"

At least he *meant* to say it. What emerged from his fear-clogged throat was a croak, closer to the word "low" than a greeting.

He swallowed with difficulty and tried again, with more success this time.

"Hello? Are you all right?"

The owner of the two boots (and yes, two legs, he could see that as he continued to draw closer) made no reply.

Hughes wondered if they *could* make a reply.

People did not, after all, wind up under the Polydoros overpass if they were having a good day.

Hughes should know. He was also here.

And there was the sound.

To Hughes' ear it had been deep, and guttural, and there was a touch of the goblin to it, those impish creatures from faerie stories, the ones who stole children and had their dark fun with them, and when they were done they gnawed the little bones and sang their goblin songs, and slept...

Hughes frowned.

Quashing his doubts, he strode around and confirmed his suspicion.

Lying against the pillar was, not a fairytale goblin, but a man.

He was fast asleep.

As Hughes studied him he unleashed a deep and guttural sound. That was the sound that had startled Hughes and Minny. Only snoring.

Hughes did laugh then, a laugh of immense relief.

Below him the man stirred in his sleep. A helmet perched precariously on his head. The straps dangled, and it seemed the man had been trying to get it off with stiff, uncooperative fingers before giving up and packing up sticks for the Land of Nod. As he stirred the helmet fell. Hughes lunged for it, too slow. His fingers barely brushed the cold metal. The helmet clanged so loud Hughes thought the bats might return, thinking war had been declared on their lair.

He scooped the helmet up before it could roll, his eyes flashing to the man in case he'd snapped awake. He needn't have worried.

The fellow was zonked. A fissure to hell could have opened by his crotch and he wouldn't have batted an eyelid.

He went on snoring, fierce intermittent snores that filled the overpass, and Hughes could smell the vodka now.

Hughes froze. He'd smelled it on a man's breath only the night before.

He hunkered down. Slowly his eyes were adjusting to the dark. He examined the drunk in closer detail.

Rat's nest of hair. Squashed, often-broken nose.

No way, thought Hughes. *It can't be.*

Ruddy cheeks crusted with stubble.

Can't be.

But it was. The man was the same one he'd seen leaving the *Pamplona* whorehouse on Agorippis Street, the very same man who'd refused to help him and left him to the questionable mercy of Miss Gleam and Mr. Glint.

Just to be sure, Hughes leaned in closer, breathing through his mouth so as not to inhale that cloying reek of vodka.

Yeah, it was him all right.

If the man had woken up at that moment Hughes would have found himself staring into beady little piggish eyes shot with veins of blood. And his armor. The color, scarlet red, was unmistakable.

With a burst of quick memory born out of memorizing thousands of lines of theatre dialogue, Hughes recalled the freckled woman with red hair and redder armor. She and her companions were Scarlet Citadel. What was it one of them had said?

Something about a missing fourth member of their group.

They were on their way into Iphigenia...

And the three of them were waiting on a fourth member...

Hughes turned the helmet over in his hands. He looked at the scarlet armor. The helmet. The armor again.

Finally Hughes looked at the man's boots. His *dry* boots.

Hughes grinned.

Not a happy-clappy expression, but a real jack-o'-lantern smile. His was a malleable face, as has already been pointed out, and sometimes it lost all its kindness and looked like this: carved and jagged and frightening.

"They'll get their fourth member," he said.

After all, the Scarlet Citadel group would *need* four for their little operation.

Their little... What exactly had he called it?

"A *bag and grab*," he remembered. "Yes, that was it. They're going to need four for the bag and grab, and four is what they'll get."

His mood perking up for the first time in weeks, Hughes turned that terrible smile on the slumbering figure.

"Hello, Walter," he said.

CHAPTER ELEVEN

"There were a number of factors behind his success that odd and fateful night.

First was luck.

In all odd and fateful matters, luck is the paper and the parcel and the colorful ribbon: it contains all other factors like precious Tinfrost gifts inside itself. And, as has been established, Hughes relied very heavily on luck. His Performances lived and died on it, as did the performances of the bygone era of Corinth City plays, in which the toss of a coin determined everything.

One pertinent (and coinish) expression runs like this: actors spin Tails and hope they turn Heads.

There's a lot of old chestnuts like that, and Hughes knew them all. Another thing he knew was this: Theatre is a series of lies sold expensively to the willingly deceived. Miss Gleam might have called them little white lies masking large black truths.

And how willingly is the audience deceived?

Luck decides.

Luck, and the little gifts of preparation and skill and cunning that luck is wrapped around.

Second came those things: preparation, skill, and plain old cunning.

Hughes was desperate but he was not stupid.

It was thirty-five minutes before he returned to the warehouse. In that time he'd done what good actors do. He'd rehearsed. They were rushed, frantic rehearsals, but they served him well that night.

Third was the walk.

It was the plodding, too-slow shuffle of a man who was just sober enough to be embarrassed about the fact he was drunk, and who was too drunk to be able to hide the fact he was a whole lot of fizz and foam away from sober.

The warehouse was huge inside, windowless, and with a massive vaulted ceiling crisscrossed in beams. There was a small foyer area past the door, open topped, and there were trappings of every kind you might expect from a workstation. Water cooler. Coffee machine. Facing the entryway, a vid screen played news footage, mostly stuff about flooding precautions given how the storm was turning out. People milled about, some in white lab coats, others (guards like the one who had given Hughes the boot earlier) wore gray, and even a few in the scarlets of the Citadel. There were no sodium lights in here, or lights of any kind, for the simple reason that there did not have to be. The portal provided all the light you could ask for.

Hughes had only gotten the briefest glimpse of it before and now was not the time for sightseeing. Still, it was hard to ignore.

Three hundred feet of liquid flame, like something had merged a bonfire and a lake, rippled and undulated strangely, without pattern. The fire seemed to snap and tug against the portal's oval frame of smooth black volcanic glass. Like it was testing the edges. Not fighting. Merely trying them out with blazing, groping fingers, the way a baby tries out the bars on its crib.

Weirdly, he felt no heat.

"Walter?" someone called.

He wheeled and saw the freckled woman coming toward him. Her red hair was pinned back now, and her face was a portrait of concern and anger. Her two companions materialized.

"Where have you been, my guy?" she wanted to know.

Hughes approached. On his head sat Walter's helmet. He was dressed in Walter's armor, which was heavy, and which smelled like the sweat inside it had over many moist summer afternoons developed consciousness and was, on the whole, unhappy about this. He carried Walter's enchanted hatchet. He even walked as the man Walter would have walked. From the depths of his helmet he unleashed a grunt so ragged and irritable and mean it could only have belonged to Walter.

His Performance washed over them, quite pungently.

Luck. Rehearsal. The walk.

They combined and Hughes felt a surge of giddy triumph as the two companions exchanged glances, and as the freckled woman sighed, and shook her head, and punched him in the arm.

Performance Successful!

+3 Experience

"Walter, you soak. Couldn't you have held off the bottle until quitting time? No, I guess not. Weather's got us all miserable, and you and Madame Vodka are courting to beat the blues. What am I gonna do with you?" the freckled woman asked him, dealing his arm a second, much harder blow, the kind a big sister might dish out to a younger brother who refuses to learn his lesson.

Following an impulse, Hughes gave the woman a dig in the arm right back and issued another grunt for good measure, this one a trifle friendlier than his last.

For this effort, he was rewarded with a smile that made the freckles on her nose go from full moons to half-moons. "Okay, fella," she said. She jerked a thumb at the Iphigenia portal, beyond which lay the wilderness that Krys and The Mum had warned Hughes about. "Let's go pick a fight."

***

The freckled woman led Scarlet Citadel Unit 45. That Unit (quite a large one for the Citadel, whose members usually worked alone, or in pairs) was made up of four people: the leader; two companions whose names Hughes would learn in due course, but whom he privately referred to as Beard and Nosering; and the drunk named Walter.

The freckled woman's name was Laurana.

Hughes spent about four hours in her company before things went bad, but after a mere four minutes he'd decided he liked her. As the engineers fiddled with their dials and the unit passed through the fire into Iphigenia, Laurana was calm and easygoing, as if she had done this all a thousand times before and would do it a thousand more quite happily so long as she could go for a drink at the *Pear and Princess* afterward and have a nice shower to wash the stink of slain beast off. Hughes liked the smell of spearmint gum that pervaded her, and he liked the way she spoke to her unit with respect, kindness, and a gentle, nudging humor.

She was, in short, a sweet person who did not deserve what happened to her that night.

Unit 45's problems with Iphigenia began the instant they set foot in that other world.

"What is that?" asked Nosering, pointing off into the distance. "That hazy stuff over the trees."

"I'm not sure." Laurana withdrew a little book from her pack and thumbed through it. "Keep an eye on it please while I find out."

In the meantime, Hughes had forgotten to pretend he was drunk. Fortuitously he was so absolutely astonished by the landscape of Iphigenia that he swayed on his feet in a pretty fair approximation of inebriation.

A city boy to his bones, Hughes had often envied country children who grew up on farms beyond the smoke and metal and cars of Corinth. They could roam and adventure in the huge sprawling orchards, pick blossoms, discover bird nests and rabbit dens, hide and seek in the honeysuckle, nibble fruits, and enjoy freshly squeezed juice trickling down their chins at the height of summertime. It never occurred to him they might envy a city boy for his access to schools and hospitals, implant shacks and grotty tattoo parlors, because in his poverty Hughes couldn't go to any of those places.

It did occur to him now that anyone—city born or country bred—would envy the view from this hill where the portal between worlds stood.

Slopes of knee-high grass dipped and rose all around. Beyond them lay the three regions of Iphigenia: a magnificent forest; a forbidding swamp; a cold pale desert. The sky was different over each region. Sunshine bathed the trees and glades of the forest. A pair of suns, noxious green in color, lent their evil light to the swamp. Finally, a cataract-white moon glowed over the desert. And no matter which direction Hughes faced, he saw the mountain looming over the unfamiliar country. Here he turned, and there, and always he beheld the same giant of stone wearing a crown of snow-dusted ice on its high peak.

"What do you think it is, Walter?" said Nosering.

Hughes almost said, "Pardon?" which would have given the whole game away. Instead he gave a questioning grunt.

"See?"

Hughes followed Nosering's gesture toward the forest. At first he thought there was nothing *to* see. A group of birds flitted out of the thicket. His eye was drawn to their flight for a second, he looked back, and then he saw it.

"It's called pygmy dust," said Laurana, saving Hughes from the predicament of answering. She turned a page in her little book.

"Shall I make a wish?" said Beard.

"Not *pixie* dust," Laurana amended without looking up. "*Pygmy* dust."

"What's the difference?"

"One of them exists."

Beard plucked at a clump of his scraggliest facial hairs. "Damn pretty," he said.

Hughes agreed.

The pygmy dust hung suspended in the air over the tops of the trees. At this distance it looked like those tiny motes of dust you might see suspended in shafts of light through windows, only with a blue tinge. That blueness had made the dust hard to pick out at first glance—over the forest the sky was a perfect autumn morning shade of duck-egg blue.

"The pygmies rattle it out of glands in their wings," read Laurana. "The dust takes on different pigments depending on what they want to communicate. Yellow to attract mates. Pink to draw in caedl wasps, which the pygmies prey upon."

"What's blue?" asked Nosering.

"Blue dust means the pygmies are trying to get the attention of dramen, those big gangly guys, remember?"

Hughes recalled the thin, scaly-skinned thing Tommy Fahrenheit had killed down in The Hippodrome's battlefield. He felt a cold razorblade of fear shave up his back.

Laurana continued, "The dramen share a symbiotic relationship with the pygmies, whose mating dust fertilizes the crop they eat every other season."

Nosering was nonplussed. "Which means?"

"Something in the forest just scared the ever-loving shit out of a lot of pygmies." Laurana closed the book with a snap. "They're asking for help."

***

Overhead, a flock of bell-shaped birds soared.

Well I'll be damned, Hughes thought, awestruck and amused. *Bangly jingly things. The Mum did warn me I'd see them.*

She had also warned him about cowlike animals, of which there seemed an endless supply in this hilly region of Iphigenia. As the group headed for the tree line, it seemed they passed at least five hundred of them, huge humpbacked beasts with stubby wet black buffalo noses and liquid-looking marble eyes, who seemed completely untroubled by Laurana and the others, content simply to dip their necks and tug tufts of grass up and chew and chew until the end of all things.

Of The Mum's goatish creatures with horns for hoofs and hoofs for horns, Hughes saw no sign.

Soon they were under the trees, and with that weird omnipresent mountain out of sight and out of mind, Hughes fell in love with the view all over again.

Here in the undergrowth the mossy trees were clustered in flowers that would have lit up the hearts of Krys and The Mum like Halloween bonfires.

The smell inside Walter's armor was unpleasant, as if he were breathing in sour stomach acid and the gassy rich smell of vodka. But now that the forest had welcomed him, much sweeter smells wafted in through the helmet's slitted visor.

No bottle of shampoo could contain a smell that mellow and nourishing. Even the comforting aromas that came when his father cracked open one of his clay tealeaf jars could not compare.

Through the helmet's padding he could hear the muffled sounds of insects and small animals *cheeping* and *chittering* and making a cozy rustling in the bushes and boscage, each plant garlanded with necklaces of berries and unfurling blossoms like a photograph of springtime.

The trees held up shields of leaves against the sky. Here and there the sun pierced those shields with lances of pure gold.

Everything was just... beautiful.

Yet in spite of that beauty, Laurana and her companions were troubled. Hughes could sense it, could *see* it in the way they planted their feet as quietly as they could so as to avoid snapping twigs or eliciting a spooked cry from some roaming critter of the woods.

Something in the forest, Laurana had said.

Something in the forest just scared the ever-loving shit out of a lot of pygmies.

Momentarily forgetting Walter's hatchet at his hip, Hughes' fingers crept up from his sides and touched the hilt of the Krys knife tucked into his belt.

He was just beginning to relax when Beard said in a flat toneless voice, "Oh shit."

The man was staring to the group's left. Afraid to see whatever had elicited this colorful little pronouncement, Hughes nonetheless turned to find out anyway.

A large, wizened tree was there.

Up in the tangled crown of its branches was a pygmy. Hughes had never seen one so close. Now that he had, he was quite unhappy about it.

It was no bigger than a child of three or four. Six-fingered hands hung limply at its sides, and its membranous wings made him think of the bats roosting under the overpass in Polydoros. The pygmy had chubby arms and plump waddly legs.

Its skin might have recently matched the leafy green of the wood, but now there was a gray undercast to it.

The pygmy was dead.

Something had hit it, very hard, and sent it caroming into the treetops. Its chest was one huge bruise. It might have died before the branch skewered it, but the branch had certainly finished it off for good.

"We can't be more than half a mile into the wood," said Nosering. "I've never seen anything like that in these parts. Laurana?"

The freckled woman made no reply. She stepped closer, a spear of sunlight transforming her hair to copper before the canopy dulled it once more, and peered up at the pygmy.

Silence lengthened. For the first time since arriving, Hughes wondered if nightfall was coming. Would it happen slowly, like in his world, or suddenly, as if some strange and menacing hand were sewing the forest up in a bag of darkness?

Nosering shifted uneasily. "Laurana?"

"Uh?" She glanced his way.

"What's going on?"

"I don't know. I say we go a little farther, see if we can find out."

Again that disquieted shuffling of feet. "Sure thing, Laurana. Only... pygmies are dense little guys. Heavier than they look. Whatever hit that thing up into the branches... Well, it must have been mean, you know? Meaner than anything ought to be this close to the hills. Have you seen anything like that?"

"Sure."

This reply caught Nosering off guard. "Yeah?"

Laurana came to him, put a hand on his shoulder, and smiled in a way that would give someone drowning in bad cowardice a lungful of lusty courage. As she smiled that winsome smile, the freckles on her nose did their thing. Full moons to half-moons.

"Not exactly like it, but pretty close," Laurana told Nosering. "Out here we're largely on our own. The book has tips and insights, granted. Not as much as a database—the fact that computers don't work in Iphigenia is a real pain in the butt—and not as much as a bestiary terminal either, but pages will do us just fine for the most part. On occasion, when weirdness strikes out of the blue, much as it's doing today, we need to keep our heads and deal with things as they play out. Right now that involves tracking down what did this and what's causing the pygmies to shoot that blue dust up into the sky."

"And why the hell can't we hear the dramen?" put in Beard. "That's been on my mind since we passed the first berry thicket. Those things are not exactly quiet. If there *is* some threat to the pygmies, some scuffle sorting itself out, we ought to have heard them by now."

"Exactly," said Laurana. She turned her emboldening smile on Nosering again. "Rest assured we *will* get to the bottom of it, and in time for a couple beers at the *Pear and Princess* before closing, okay?"

"Okay." Nosering nodded, her surety fortifying him a little. "You're the boss."

"I'm the boss, old hoss," she agreed. "Now scout ahead and make me happy, huh?"

"You got it."

Nosering set out, Beard close behind him.

Laurana looked at the man she believed to be Walter. Aside from a few animals padding and rustling in the brushwood, they were alone. Hughes watched her smile vanish, listened as she spoke in a voice that was suddenly both restless and secretive.

"Walter," she said. "You don't think this is anything to do with... that stuff Cat was telling us about, do you?"

Um, Hughes thought.

"You didn't tell anyone, did you?"

Hughes shook his head, which seemed to satisfy Laurana.

"But do you?" she murmured eagerly. "You know, think this situation could be related? Be honest with me. I feel like I'm overthinking it."

Hughes was at a complete loss.

Out of desperation he gave an eloquent shrug of his shoulders. The shrug said that, as of yet, he had not considered the applicability of their former and definitely, absolutely real conversation with Cat (whoever she was) upon their current situation (whatever that was).

Then he cleared his throat in a very good approximation of Walter the Drunk clearing his throat, and gestured toward the spot where Nosering and Beard had vanished through a tangle of bougainvillea vines.

Laurana nodded to herself, looking disappointed.

As they drew deeper into the woods, Hughes was sure he heard her say something. At the time he was too focused on not making any undue noise among the fallen twigs and the brittlest branches to think about it. He thought it might have been "hag and grab."

Later, the whole sentence would come to him.

Bag and grab, she'd muttered.

Just another bag and grab.

Less than thirty seconds later they heard Nosering scream.

CHAPTER TWELVE

The imagination is a crooked-minded aunt; she plays tricks on us.

As he and Laurana sprinted toward the sound of those awful screams, Hughes' own imagination—and he had an intensely vivid one—filled his head with such a parlor show of horrors he wished he were anywhere, *anywhere* but in these spectacular and utterly alien woods.

The screams were just too similar, too fucking familiar to the ones he'd heard in the bazaar the night before. It was absurd, but those screams made him quite sure the dazzling duo, Glint and Gleam, were hiding behind every beetle-stuffed tree trunk, every patch of hanging ivy.

The trees. Dear God. The trees tangled closer here in this patch of forest, much, much closer together, forming a kind of gnarled mesh that scraped and scratched against his helmet like the claws of wooden imps.

They could hear something under the screams now.

A growling.

Not from one single throat either.

It sounded to Hughes like Nosering was being torn apart by a pack of wild dogs.

Were there dogs in Iphigenia?

If so, would their appetite include human beings?

Would it include

(*stringy bits*)

Hughes almost moaned at the memory of Mr. Glint's voice.

Farther they ran. Deeper into the woods.

The sun! Where had the sun got to?

Sometime in the past few seconds the canopy had clumped up thickly, bathing the world in shadow.

His imagination showed him a pair of long thin hands stretching out for him from the darkness. Glint's hands, ready to snatch him and smother him and sew him into a bag of nightmares from which there was no waking.

A bag and grab, oh yes.

Foliage rustled all around. *Rustle-rustle.*

Only Hughes heard: *Snicker-snick.*

What am I doing here? he thought. *What the hell am I doing in this place?*

Something about money?

A debt?

A woman?

In his fright he was no longer sure.

Branches snapped, their leaves shredding beneath Hughes' steel-fingered gauntlets. Under the cotton padding he could feel sweat run down his back in rivulets. The flesh on his testicles was crawling avidly. A dizzy, helpless queasiness seized him.

"We're coming!" Laurana shouted to her companions. The screams went on. "We're coming, just hold on!"

Hughes barely heard her and would have felt a surge of admiration for her if he had. His pulse was so heavy in his ears all sound seemed to arrive in his skull through sheets of wool.

The growl ramped up, many-throated.

"What are you?" That was Laurana, pelting past Hughes, her arms and legs pumping. Some part of him recognized she was addressing the source of the growl. "Huh? What the fuck *are* you? Who do you think you are? Doesn't matter. I'm coming for you, and you'll wish you'd stopped at pygmies. Just a little longer, I'm almost there! *Fight, for God's sake! FIGHT!*"

Nosering didn't sound like he could speak, much less fight. He uttered a high, wordless shriek, and fell silent. Terrible quiet crept over the woods.

"God dear God, please be okay," Hughes heard Laurana hiss. "Please."

He knew very little just then, only that this woman—with her freckles that half-mooned sweetly when she smiled—was strong, and that he should stick as close to her as he possibly could. It seemed they had been running a long time, though in reality it could not have been more than thirty-five, perhaps forty seconds.

The exertional heat and nausea were bad, but the fear was worse.

Again he formed the thought, *What am I—*

And there it broke apart as he tripped over an errant root, stumbled, then burst into a clearing in the woods. Off-balance, he just managed to keep his feet.

The clearing was wide and well-lit, and what Hughes saw there made his gorge rise and his heart palpitate in sickening lurches.

The dead lay everywhere, scores of pygmies, as well as a great number of those loping, scaly-skinned creatures called dramen. They'd seen the blue dust and come to help their small-winged friends after all. Now their corpses covered the ground in a mangled carpet.

Sticky, unthinkable smells from their opened bellies insinuated into his helmet like the spells from some aromatic witch brew—the stink punctured his sinuses like a curse.

You won't get sick, he told himself.

You won't because it'll bend you double and strain through the visor, and then you'll be blind on top of everything.

That was when Hughes saw Beard. Half the man's head was intact. The other was a pulpy ruin. Something had excavated his throat and chewed his face until the left cheekbone showed white in the sunshine. By some cruel coincidence his eyes were staring right at Laurana as she emerged into this nightmare, a cold dead stare that seemed to accuse her of turning up too late, too late.

The cause of all this carnage was currently rutting like a truffle pig. Only there were no truffles here. No, it was rutting in Nosering's groin, its muzzle matted in gore.

That day had carried a lot of firsts for Hughes of Leonidas District.

Even so, the monster trumped them all.

At the very sight of it his mean aunt of an imagination retreated, badly frightened by a reality that made fiction seem liverless and chickenshit.

Inflate a timberland wolf until it stands twelve-feet at the shoulder, about as tall as a swing set at your local park. Slap six raven wings on its back. Replace its claws with worms. Break its jaw so it hangs open like a pungent door to hell. Then pump this grotesque sideshow with mustard gas so it seems to be melting from the inside-out.

The monster lifted its head and shifted, revealing a second head almost identical to the first that had been gorging itself on the nearby dead.

The second head had a narrow, crazed look. The first seemed much more alert.

It watched Laurana break the pinkie off her right hand, whisper a word to it, and slip into a stance as the false finger lengthened into a sword.

She charged, her magic item ready to strike this horror down. She uttered no battle cry. What would that have achieved? While Hughes stood paralyzed, she moved with a killer's businesslike silence, the sunbeams turning her hair copper as the smell of blood upon the air.

The monster regarded this display of breakneck speed placidly. Goo dripped from its eyeballs and tongue. A dense mucus had clotted around its flaring nostrils. One of Nosering's balls was hanging by a string of tendon from its lower lip. The monster blinked down at Laurana as she drove the blade up to the hilt into its collarbone. Another blink, a wolf curious about the bee that has just pricked it with its stinger. Otherwise, it gave no other reaction, no inkling the attack had hurt it.

Laurana grunted. "Blink at this, motherfucker."

She bent her wrists at an abominable angle. With a series of pops like snickerdrake firecrackers, her remaining nine fingers severed. Amputated like that, her hands looked like stubby pink lollipops. Snarling, Laurana whispered that same word of activation, and suddenly the clearing was alive with swords.

There were only ten of them, one for each finger and thumb. Yet whirling, cutting, and hewing into the monster they seemed to represent a phalanx of steel.

"Blink at this."

At her telepathic command two of the blades sank into the first head's eyes with a wet *parping* sound. Blooded jelly squirted.

That got the monster going!

It *howled* its astonishment. Its pain. Its *fury.*

With a roll of her wrists, Laurana sent the edge of her blades scraping the walls of its sockets. Meanwhile both eyes ran like poached eggs down the monster's cheeks.

Head number two dove for Laurana, too slow as it turned out.

Evidently as well as being a one-woman armada, she was quick. With a flair for improvisation that made Hughes (stunned stiff but extremely aware of events as they played out) think she would make a decent performer if she had the knack for it, Laurana sent one of her swords between the monster's snapping jaws. They closed just as she pivoted the sword upward, driving the point up through the soft ridged flesh of its palette. Stuff that must have been blood—yet nevertheless had the look and odor of hot tar—steamed and dribbled blackly between its bared teeth.

Hughes realized Laurana was speaking to him. Or rather, to the man he was pretending to be.

"Walter."

Her voice was calm, almost serene, but he sensed a note of desperation under it.

"Walter, get in on this with me, right now."

That note of desperation added, *While we can.*

He went for his Krys knife, felt nothing. Panic skulking up on him, he looked around for it, then remembered the hatchet.

Wrenching it out of its straps, Hughes gave a yelp as a bolt of pain shot up his arm to the elbow. His fingers spasmed and dropped the hatchet. He stared at it dumbly.

The handle shocked me.

He tried again. Same result. He tried gripping it anyway until with a groan of total despair he was forced to let it go, his forearm pulsing. It felt as if someone had packed his hand full of conductor wire and sent wave after wave of nerve-killing volts through it.

"*Walter?*"

His head jerked up at the sheer puzzled anger in her voice.

Laurana had given ground. The monster was falling apart, partly from her onslaught and partly from some internal clock reaching midnight, a death hour oozing from its furry flanks, cracked underflesh, and writhing claws. Yet it was huge, and immensely strong, and whatever she had expected to find here in the forest with her companions of the Scarlet Citadel, Laurana had found something else. Something wicked. Half blind and insane with rage, it lunged for her.

"Wal—no, no get off me get off me DON'T DO THAT—"

While her swords fended off one head, the other (sockets hollow and weeping a noxious mix of yellow pus and brownish blood), brushed across her armored thigh with its hairy chin and bit her leg. It bit to the bone.

Laurana cried out.

Hughes felt something give in him. Hysteria swarmed. And rage. He had never in his life felt such an influx of anger. It boomed up his throat in a red fungal cloud. The world tinged carmine red. He vented a sound closer to a barbarian's wordless yawp than a scream, snatched up the Krys knife (right there useless and sharp by his foot the whole time), and broke into a charge of his own.

Dementedly fast, the monster joggled Laurana back and forth, transforming her for a moment into a bizarre chew toy. Then her ligaments surrendered. With a growl it sent her flying out of the clearing. She struck a tree, and through the red pall of rage, Hughes heard her bones shatter.

Laurana's leg had joined Nosering's scrap of testicle on the monster's muzzle. If he ignored the gristle, blood, and the little jut of bone, it might have only been a discarded part of a mannequin set.

That illusion was dispelled by the monster.

Growling savagely, it sent its tongue questing out, found both testicle and amputated leg, and slurped them greedily into its gullet. With a pang of deep revulsion, Hughes was reminded of Miss Gleam. *Her tongue looked exactly like that. A pink slug tongue oozing over teeth like a basket of needles.*

And then the monster was looking at him, and those scourged black sockets were just like hers.

Just like Gleam's pupils!

Hughes felt—actually *felt*—the courage knocked out of him like breath from his lungs. His tongue tasted bitter bravery and anger as they were expelled through his lips. He locked his knees to keep from trembling. The shakes got him anyway. He quaked like a man five decades his senior shivering in the clutches of pneumonia.

Above him the second head came and lapped at the blood drying under the first head's eyes.

Perhaps if he had been thinking, he would have died there in the woods.

The monster was dying. That much was obvious. Laurana was fierce, and she had given it all she had before its teeth buried themselves to the gums in her body. The thing seemed to be disintegrating, not like the dramen Hughes had seen in The Hippodrome, but like a waxwork puddling under a lamp turned as hot as it could go. Clumps of hair and foul boiled-looking flesh sloughed off its back and shoulders.

Undoubtedly, if he had been thinking, the monster would have finished licking its own waxy gunk and ocular fluid, remembered that Hughes had been there all along, and fallen on him with the last of its strength and teeth hungry for one last bite.

But Hughes was not thinking.

He had entered the strange zeroed-in state he'd experienced on Agorippis Street with Miss Gleam sauntering next to him and Mr. Glint's hand bear-trap tight on his arm.

He saw that Beard had carried cigarettes. Hughes realized he had never smoked one before.

Now seemed as good a time as any.

He picked up the box, flicked the cardboard lid up.

Why, if there isn't one left.

Congratulations were in order.

That sparked something in him, an almost-thought.

But he was busy not entertaining those, so instead of turning that almost-thought into a fully-formed one, Hughes hunted in Beard's pockets. He found a lighter, took off Walter's helmet, stuck the funny little white stick in his mouth, flicked the lighter, and at last inhaled.

It was like tasting the back of a furnace.

Cool air kissed his face. After the sweltering confines of the helmet, it was nice.

The act of rooting about the dead man's body had bloodied Hughes' fingernails. Standing there smoking his first (and quite probably last) cigarette in the crisp autumnal light and the eerie post-massacre quiet, the blood looked like red nail polish. He puffed smoke. His throat felt like a dust-coated chimney. He willed himself not to cough and glanced at the monster.

The oddly tender licking had indeed ceased. Both heads were heavily decayed by now. "Things fall apart" as the old quote ran. Who had written that?

No. He shut his mind.

This house is not open to rogue thoughts just now. Why? Well, because if I start to think, I'm eventually going to have to think about that tongue. That pink slug tongue, and poor Laurana, Miss Gleam and Mr. Glint, not to mention that dark carnival of a dream I had last night, and...

Hughes paused for just a second before taking his second drag.

And if I think about those things, I am going to lose my mind.

He met the monster's gaze. He smoked his cigarette.

I am going to break apart like this monster, only it'll be my sanity crumbling instead of my flesh.

Some dull instinctive part of him thought the monster might be... no, it *was* watching him closely.

Still operating entirely on impulse, Hughes said, "Want to see something?"

He clenched the cigarette between his teeth. He squared his shoulders, which were no longer shaking. He set his feet so the ground was utterly and completely solid beneath him, and he forgot the clearing was now a graveyard for dramen, and pygmies, and two men whose names he did not know, and Laurana, who if there was any justice should be alive, but who was not because there is not.

He cleared his throat.

And with a flourish (because of course there must be a flourish) he reached down, took hold of his Performance, and yanked it up from the reluctant, terrified corners of himself so it shone inside him—*bright!*—brighter than the Iphigenian sun.

The monster leaned closer, both heads slavering and attentive.

Hughes held up the knife Krys the Painted Girl had given him, and doing his best impression of Laurana's mellow voice he spoke the words burning like ashy cigarette flames in his mouth: "Put your heart on my knife."

And saying that, he pushed.

***

Unaccountable as its origin might be (sometimes Hughes wondered just where the power came from, though not today), here was how the magic stood, a representation that he could probe and prod but not understand:

Hughes

<table>
<tr><td colspan="2" align="center">Performance Level: 8</td></tr>
<tr><td colspan="2" align="center">Influence the behavior of others using your physical and vocal performance, as well as your stage presence.

WARNING!

Bad performances result in negative reception.</td></tr>
<tr><td align="center">**Chance of Success: 30%**</td><td align="center">**Next Level:** +3% to Chance of Success
Level 10 Secret Ability: ???</td></tr>
</table>

Surprise and delight thrilled him as the monster's features went slack.

Both heads.

Hughes considered that, his heart rate cogwheeling up a notch. This wouldn't actually work, would it? He inhaled. Blue smoke curled from the sides of his mouth.

You better hope it does, he told himself severely. *You better pray to God it does.*

Because if it doesn't, you are going to die screaming.

<table>
<tr><td align="center">Testing Performance...</td></tr>
</table>

All of a sudden the knife seemed very heavy.

<table>
<tr><td align="center">Testing Performance...</td></tr>
</table>

Sensing those terrible consequences around the corner should he fail, Hughes channeled his physicality: his jaw; chest; and chin gained a certain subtle authority—the effect was almost kingly. Decked out in Walter the Drunk's armor, it was as close to a costume as any powdered wig and silk ensemble.

<table>
<tr><td align="center">Testing Performance...</td></tr>
</table>

With a slight mental shift he found that the surrounding dead did not subtract from his Performance. They *added* to it.

He held this wolfish destroyer in his gaze, held its twitching raven wings, its writhing worm claws, its mad yellow eyes and its empty scooped-out sockets.

He held it with his own dark eyes, dark as his father's best tea, dark as the storm playing its calliope thunder over his home, Corinth City, city of shadows.

He wanted something, was in search of it, hunted for it now.

What? The monster's slack expression seemed to ask that.

What are you hunting, Gormon Hughes Junior, shadowman?

Hughes grinned. It was monstrous.

Why, your heart, my good fellow.

<table>
<tr><td align="center">Registering Result...</td></tr>
</table>

I want your thumping pumping hunter's heart.

<table>
<tr><td align="center">Registering...</td></tr>
</table>

Mine's broken, you see.
So give. Me. YOURS.

<table>
<tr><td align="center">...</td></tr>
</table>

Hughes' concentration snapped in two as the monster's chest ruptured. There was an initial gush of warm blood, some of which joined Beard's blood on Hughes' hand, making it look like a used surgeon's glove rather than a nail-polished affair.

The monster gave an ugly glottal bark of pain. Its back was arching at an impossible angle. The hair tangling its chest was soaked with blood. A whine scurried up its throats. The two eyes Laurana had left it rolled back in its head. Tongues lolled—dead slugs.

Then the breastbone submitted. Bone splintered out, a pale confetti, along with a jetting fountain of rich coffee-dark blood.

Hughes watched in horrific fascination as two slender feminine hands extended from the blasted crater. The cigarette slipped from his mouth, unnoticed as it fell smoldering to the forest floor.

Am I seeing this?

He believed he was.

The arms were coming right out of the monster's chest, *human arms*, blood-streaked but otherwise pristine. Even beautiful in a baffling, macabre way.

The arms reached out, their hands delicate and long, not entirely unlike Mr. Glint's in Hughes' fretful imaginings only a few short minutes ago.

Instead of doing anything dreadful to him though, they placed a...

Hughes swallowed. There was an audible click in his throat.

The hands placed *the monster's large, still-beating heart* on his Krys knife. The point slipped through the heart as effortlessly as a hot knife cutting butter.

The monster slumped. Raggedy wind (not quite breath) sawed out of the hole in its chest. It didn't crash. Didn't make much sound at all. One moment it was upright. The next it slid over, stone dead. The feminine hands lay motionless. Peering into the cavity from which they'd emerged, there was no woman. The hands and the arms that stretched them forth seemed inexplicable.

Speaking of inexplicable, Hughes thought numbly.

His eyes were fixed on the heart.

It beat once-twice.

Once-twice.

Once.

Stilled.

Some part of him expected a comforting green light. That was what happened when creatures from Iphigenia died, after all. He had seen proof of that, most recently in The Hippodrome, watching Tommy Fahrenheit hoist his trophy to a chorus of cheers like some grizzly effigy.

There was no green light. No comfort either.

He set down the knife, and the heart, and went toward the tree line.

***

He found Laurana splayed out among the roots.

Hughes believed that nothing, nothing short of the ground opening up and swallowing him whole, could have surprised him. The ground kept its peace, and nevertheless, Laurana managed to surprise him.

She was still alive.

"I'll get help." He almost said it.

But he looked at her, at the spreading pool of her insides (her leg put him in mind of a wine barrel he'd seen cracked open once in childhood, its cask sloshing, spilling its contents), and he knew help was not going to come.

Not in time.

Not for Laurana.

"Hooyou?" she said.

"Try not to talk," he said, getting down because standing over her felt too much like standing over an open coffin. "It looks like it hurts."

"Hooyou?" she repeated. She grimaced, as if realizing the garbled voice belonged not to some poor invalid at death's door, but her. It was her voice, and she was going to die. He saw her realize that. The impact had crushed her mouth. She spat blood and broken teeth and said, "Who you?"

"My name is Hughes."

"Walt—?"

"Walter's okay. I took his armor. I never meant..."

He stopped. Never meant what?

For this to happen? It would have happened anyway.

Right?

Maybe not, guilt murmured in his ear. *Things might have turned out very differently if Walter had been here.*

"He was drunk," Hughes told Laurana miserably. "He was drunk and a scumbag."

Drunk, sure, guilt continued. *But that hatchet wouldn't let you use it. Walter might have done something...*

Say he had. Well then, as I postulate, things might have wound out a little better for the Scarlet Citadel unit.

And Laurana might not be...

She might not be...

"I want to help you," Hughes said desperately. "There must be a way. You've got to have something, *know* something that can... I mean you Scarlet Citadel people are amazing! Just show me how to make you better and I'll do it, I promise I will. Then everything will be all right again.

"Laurana?"

Her face was a rictus of pain and confusion.

Her eyes opened a little wider as a door might open to let something in. Or out. She stiffened... and then it seemed for all the world as if she were sleeping.

Hughes didn't do or say anything. After a while he bent over her and waited to feel her breath on his cheek.

Nothing.

Earlier he had wondered at the idea of night in Iphigenia. How it came. *If* it came.

Now it did just that, starting with a deepening of the sky, first turning a harder blue, then plum, then a pale green at the very fringes of twilight.

Stars winked overhead.

Hughes touched Laurana's hand, letting his gaze linger on her face.

The freckles there, moonish and pretty, changed to half-moons when she smiled.

Sitting on his haunches, he felt encased in helpless ice.

He had no idea what he ought to do.

His body did.

He looked at this kind, proud woman through a prism of tears, put his head in his hands, and wept.

ACT FOUR

PECULIAR

DEVELOPMENTS

CHAPTER THIRTEEN

Miss Gleam had had just about enough. "Do you go in for punitive realms, Mr. Glint?"

"Nah. My digestion is tickety-boo, Miss Gleam," replied her partner.

This brought Miss Gleam up short.

She took a moment to attune her mental radio to station Glint.

"Yes, I suspect you misheard me, noble fellow," she said slowly. "*Punitive* realms. Not *prune-itive* realms."

"I wondered." Mr. Glint was watching a few bats wheel across the lightning-scorched face of the storm. Those were Corinth City bats up there, evolved to withstand much worse than a little pissant of a tempest such as this. Scenic view, all things considered, yet he wished they would wheel closer. Mr. Glint rather liked bat—their wings were stuffed with the crunchiest of bones. "Depends, then," he said. "What's a punitive realm, Miss Gleam?"

"In this case, my compeer in mutilation, mayhem, and murder, the term 'punitive realms' refers to a place where people who have done naughty things go after they depart this mortal coil. It is their just comeuppance. In other words, it is a place in which the many transgressions of life are met upon death. Met, that is, with the lash, the corkscrew nail, the flaying knife, the fiery tongs, and icy pincers."

"Give us an example."

"With pleasure. The old church's conception of 'Hell' is such a place."

"What?" said Glint. "Pitchforks and that?"

"They certainly feature, old boy. They certainly feature."

Did he go in for such places? Mr. Glint pondered. Given his cognitive faculties, this process took quite some time.

Meanwhile Miss Gleam paced to keep from gnawing the inside of her cheek raw. She'd been pacing for what felt like seventy-four million years (about twenty minutes), and had developed a rhythm, her crocodile leather shoes squeaking and creaking impatiently. No one in the world could pace quite like Miss Gleam.

It was a quarter of one in the morning, the rain was heavier than ever, and the partners were on the wide, wet rooftop of the Leopoldo Fernassi headquarters in Polydoros District. Even though it was shut for the night, the clean smell of men's healthcare products—notes of lavender and oak moss—wafted up from the building's depths.

They were waiting.

Distantly the bats dove under the Polydoros overpass, presumably returning home for a bit of predawn kip. There were fewer cars at this time of night, but now and then the gloom was lit up with their passage like red-orange deck lamps on skiffs in a great strange sea.

"I s'pose," said Mr. Glint speculatively, "that I *do* go in for punitive realms... so long as *I'm* there to have a go at the puning."

"Punishment."

"Punishment, thanks."

A few feet away his partner paced. Slowed.

Stopped.

She looked at him, torn from her reverie, her sparkling blue hair plastered to her cheeks with rain.

"Conflation of the metaphysical and the personal. What use is the trumpeting of clergymen? The exhausting conjecture of kings and court philosophers? Hell is nowhere but here. It goes where we go." Miss Gleam smiled at her sour-mouthed companion with a mixture of awe and approval. "You know, that's rather good, old boy."

"You think so?" said Glint, pleased.

She took three swift steps, lunged around him, and swung her arms about his neck and her legs about his waist in the fashion of a happy koala bear. "I know so! Ask a simple question. Give a simple answer. A simple, shallow answer—with complicated depths, if you can. And you've done exactly that! Now," she said, looking around in bewilderment, "where in God's name are we? Ah. Rooftopped, I see. Did our lofty discussion guide us here? I've quite forgotten."

"Want a reminder?"

"Please."

"We came here to meet with Miss Shimmer," said Mr. Glint dutifully. "This being Saturday's first hour, the silky witching hour what finds itself between twelve o'clock midnight and one ay-em."

He was reciting, of course. Mr. Glint had heard Miss Gleam use those exact words many times.

"Miss Shimmer," echoed Gleam vaguely. "Yes."

The pair were on good terms with Miss Shimmer, who also worked for their employer as part of his special cabal of truly dangerous people. Every Saturday the three met up at a different location to talk shop, exchange pleasantries, and swap ideas for how to handle difficult problems.

Mr. Glint suspected that, on this occasion, his partner was keen to pilfer a job or two from Miss Shimmer, who tended to be busy this time of the month. If there was one thing Miss Gleam despised more than ugly gray ambiguity, it was idleness.

Idle hands make their own trouble, she'd often said, and he believed her.

But then, Mr. Glint believed everything Miss Gleam said.

"Saturday. Naturally. Well said, dear man. Consider my memory jogged. Yet..." Miss Gleam continued to look around with a hopeful expression, as if expecting Miss Shimmer to materialize from thin air, a feat that not even Shimmer (who was sly, and quick, and clever) would have been capable of. When it became apparent that no such appearance would be made, Miss Gleam's normally cheerful mouth twisted unpleasantly. "Yet here we are, punctual as newly wound clocks and not a sign of the woman. Where do you suppose she could be?"

Mr. Glint pondered some more. "Bathing," he said. The answer had been slow coming, but nevertheless it arrived up from the horrible tube of his throat with the surety and finality of a cemetery gate closing for the night.

"Bathing, you say? Yes." Miss Gleam sighed. "That's it, I'm sure. You're two for two tonight, how marvelous. Oh well. Nothing for it." She hopped down from her perch atop him, her shoes making little splashes in the rooftop puddles. "We shall have to put the question to Miss Shimmer."

"Which question would that be?" asked Glint.

"The one," she replied with a big catlike stretch toward the grumbling heavens, "about punitive realms. Hell is where we are, Mr. Glint. I do not like to be kept waiting."

"Right you are, Miss Gleam."

He turned and followed her through the roof-access door, the lock of which Mr. Glint had chewed till it snapped, down the stairs, through a series of corridors like dark intestines perfumed with shaving creams and hair regrowth serum, past the night clerk desk and the night clerk, who Mr. Glint had chewed till the cords in his throat snapped, and through the rotating entrance door of the Leopoldo Fernassi headquarters, two bats who hunted by night and whose skin shone like a diamond-bright sun on a lake's dazzling face.

As they made their way to Miss Shimmer's apartment, people crossed the street to avoid them and walked noticeably quicker until the pair were well out of sight.

Miss Gleam and Mr. Glint.

They had both evolved to suit Corinth City, city of shadows, and wherever they went, Hell went with them.

***

The man was sitting on Miss Shimmer's bed.

He was, not to put too fine a point on it, soaked.

When Miss Gleam and Mr. Glint came in through the apartment's north window, they saw him through the hallway door, drying as he dripped and looking at nothing in particular.

For Mr. Glint that was sufficient.

There, he thought accurately, *is a wet bloke on Miss Shimmer's bed.*

Miss Gleam, on the other hand, was a touch more shrewd than he. She noticed the sitting room carpet and the floorboards in the hallway were quite dry. The man had not come in from the rain.

That was when she began to suspect that Miss Shimmer was dead.

The man heard them approach and looked up. Gleam registered surprise on his face. The emotion seemed to come from somewhere deep within him, as if his brain was a crowded place where lots of things were trying to sort themselves out and not really managing it.

He was in his early thirties, bald, clean-shaven, and dressed in black. Someone—Gleam thought chances were good it was a certain Miss Shimmer— had gouged his chin with something. Not a pen. Not a knife. The wound was shallow, though recent and still bleeding. A fingernail?

It didn't matter.

They stood over the drenched man.

He looked from Glint, to Gleam, then off to one side.

"Fuck." He seemed to exhale the word as if it were a cloud of poison.

"I would wish you good evening," said Miss Gleam, "though in your case, that descriptor would not be fitting. Let us say 'short' instead. Short evening to you. Is she dead?"

"I know you," the man said. "Sparkle and Shitstain."

Miss Gleam smiled, displaying teeth that would make a great white shark reconsider its position in the food chain.

"And yet we are at a loss as to your name. I shall name you for the least likely of animals... how about... rabbit? Yes, that'll do nicely. Wet little rabbit has found his way into the wrong hole." She looked past the bed to the bathroom door. It was open. Wet footprints led out of it, but not in. Curious. Gleam started in that direction. "Hurt him, Mr. Glint. Not too badly."

Mr. Glint stepped forward. With that terrible speed he used for snaring all sorts of agile prey, he knelt, took the man's shoe-clad foot in his hands, and twisted it all the way around as easily as you might turn a doorknob. The man's eyes widened in horror as his ankle joint first splintered, then disintegrated with a sound like pebbles shifting in a sack. He drew in a breath and gave voice to a muffled scream against Glint's hand, which had shot up to clamp over the man's mouth.

"No more hopping for you, little rabbit," said Mr. Glint.

The man had a quick-bolt crossbow in his sleeve. The ownership of such a weapon would have landed its owner in hot water with the streetbeaters, and that was nothing compared to the trouble they'd be in if the Scarlet Citadel found out about it. But the man was a professional, and when you were a professional in Corinth City, you packed for precaution, not pleasure. He flexed his arm (loading the crossbow) and shot Mr. Glint in the belly.

"She's in here," called Miss Gleam from the bathroom. "Drowned as a sack of unwanted wolf cubs. In her own bathtub, no less."

She came out and sat down next to the man, gave him an unnerving little wink, and rooted in her coat for her scissors.

Mr. Glint was staring at the bolt protruding from his abdomen.

"Rabbit shot me," he said.

"Rabbits are tricky vermin at the best of times," said Gleam. "Did you know their teeth never cease growing?"

"Never?"

"Never. Ah, here we are."

Snicker-snick went the scissors.

The man thrashed when he saw them.

Again, monstrously quick, Mr. Glint's hand slid into his mouth and gripped his tongue between forefinger and thumb.

"I'm going to ask you some questions," Miss Gleam told the assassin, for that was what he was. A dirty fetid little assassin, a rabbit who had invaded the wrong hole and drowned its occupant, and who would regret it because while a rabbit's teeth never cease growing, they need only make one mistake before they are outbitten. "I do not truck with ambiguity. I like large black truths and little white lies. This—"

Snicker-snick.

"—makes all the truths and lies apparent. My associate will extricate his hand from your mouth. I ask. You answer. Quietly. Do you understand me?"

The man nodded. His eyes were gray, and his pallor was grayer still. Sweat grimed his skin.

Miss Gleam reached down and patted his hand twice, as if to say, *don't fret.* "Let's begin, shall we?"

The interrogation lasted six minutes on the dot.

The man lasted three hours.

This impressed Mr. Glint, who was not easily impressed.

"Tough bloke," he said later, washing the blood off his hands in the bathtub where Miss Shimmer was floating face down, her body swollen and already bluish-purple with lividity. A few strands of her luminous pale hair wound through his fingers. He disentangled himself, taking care not to tug at her scalp, and dried his hands on a rail-hung towel. "Very tough," he repeated. "Tough as old boots. Do you reckon that's why Miss Shimmer was sweet on him?"

"What's that, old boy?"

"Do you—"

"Yes, yes I expect so."

Miss Gleam, having had time to mull the situation over while she and her partner enjoyed themselves, was eager to get going. Dawn, wet and gray as the pair of wet gray eyeballs placed neatly on one of Miss Shimmer's pillows, was creeping in through the window. It was going to be a busy day.

The man with the gray eyes had been Willard Coosler, a hired killer who Gleam had never heard of, which was always a mark in one's favor. A hired killer who everyone had heard of was not going to be a hired killer for very long.

Over the past six weeks he'd successfully insinuated himself into Miss Shimmer's life. They had been sleeping together for the bulk of a month. Perhaps he was a tough lover. He would need to have been. Sex with Miss Shimmer would not have been for the faint of heart. Tough, certainly, and in Willard Coosler's opinion, Shimmer had grown very sweet on him indeed.

And earlier that night, he had drowned her in her bath.

Why?

Those were his orders.

Who did he take his orders from?

Willard Coosler did not know. He received information from a series of intermediaries.

Who were these intermediaries?

Willard Coosler had not known that either. The unhelpful man described these go-betweens as wearing masks to conceal their identities.

Okay. What masks?

White ones. Cheap plastic.

Gleam frowned, thinking about that. It was a significant detail, but... no. No help there. Costume shops all over the city sold cheap white plastic masks.

Anyway, it seemed that drowning his lover had presented unexpected difficulties for Willard Coosler. Emotional difficulties. He'd developed quite a liking for Shimmer. Killing her had been a real bummer. Evidently he'd been thinking about his life when Miss Gleam and Mr. Glint arrived and found him soaked to the skin on the edge of the bed he'd until recently been welcome in.

Gleam was frowning thoughtfully as Glint came out of the bathroom.

She was thinking about her last question.

What was the killer supposed to do after he'd finished up here?

Willard Coosler had told her that he was supposed to meet one of the intermediaries to collect payment. He was to meet them, "where the bulls go running." The man had no clue what this meant and informed Gleam that the names of his meeting spots were irritating little riddles, probably meant to test his competence. He would receive the second part of the riddle—which would make it a hell of a lot easier to decipher—twenty-four hours after Shimmer's death on his personal wrist communicator.

That communicator was now in Miss Gleam's pocket.

She was interested to see what the second half of this riddle would be.

Yes. A very busy day. No two ways about it. It stretched languidly before her, hour upon delicious hour, ready to be chewed up and swallowed.

In her head she could hear their employer's voice as clear as the torrential hiss of the rains outside. Over the phone, that voice had spoken four clear words to her.

Sometimes you disappoint me.

Gleam wondered how fucking *disappointed* he would be when he learned about the events that had transpired here.

"You all right?"

She looked up sharply. Mr. Glint was there, the morning light brushing his shoulders like crooked gravestones.

"Me, my kind friend? Hedonistic." She slipped through the north window and breathed deep of the thunderous air. "I am feeling everything and everything is feeling me right back."

They had barely begun their return journey to the abandoned leisure center when they spotted Hughes.

He was being escorted through the streets of Polydoros toward nearby Ptolema District. He was naked to the waist, his trousers damp, his feet bare. His face had a dazed, stricken cast, as if he had been jabbed full of a dreamy tranquilizer.

Miss Gleam might have taken a moment from her newly hectic schedule to inquire after Hughes, to remind him of certain obligations on his end, were it not for that escort.

"Seems our brother has a penchant for trouble," she observed quietly. "We shall have to check in on his progress once this other matter is in hand."

Mr. Glint said nothing.

Meanwhile Hughes trudged on, and three units of the Scarlet Citadel marched with him.

CHAPTER FOURTEEN

At nine o'clock sharp a butler walked into Hughes' room.

Room might be something of a misnomer. It was luxurious and downright enormous, about the size of the apartment he'd rented to impress Kim Kallaimon. That apartment's weekly rent had cost him an arm and a leg, and this room was considerably prettier, all polished furniture, fluffy pillows, lamps hooded in scarlet-red glass, even a bathroom. Tiled. His mind couldn't fathom the expense.

There was something missing though. Along with the door that would not open no matter how hard you jangled the knob, it was the only other obvious hint as to the room's real purpose.

Windows.

There were no windows.

Which makes this a cell.

He'd awoken a little after eight (not that he was aware of the time—beautiful though the room surely was, his hosts had not thought to include a clock). After the initial confusion had passed, he'd explored his confinement thoroughly. Satisfied there was nothing to do but wait to see what happened, he had tugged on a pair of trousers (perfect fit, either his hosts were good guessers or they had taken the time to *measure* him) and settled in for what his father called A Hard Think.

He was not particularly afraid. His head was clear, almost clinically so.

The idea that he was in deep shock never occurred to him.

He rifled through the events of the previous evening: stealing Walter's armor; using his Performance to trick Laurana and her unit; the massacre in Iphigenia; his journey back with the monster's heart cradled under his arm; the look of ghoulish fright on the portal operator's face when he'd collapsed through the door between worlds; and... then...

Well, then everything got a little fuzzy, didn't it, detective?

He lowered his head and rubbed his temples. Maybe A Hard Think wasn't such a hot idea.

That was how the butler found him. He walked—no. In his black-and-white regalia, knee-high socks, and gold-buckled shoes, he fairly *swanned* in, trailing a pair of stooped attendants who looked to him for instruction.

"Sir will stand," said the butler.

Hughes did not know for sure that this was his occupation, but come on. You didn't dress like that if you were planning on lion taming.

He stood. "Where am I?"

"Sir is in Redspire. Fourth floor. Guest Wing." Gently but firmly he turned Hughes' face side to side, his expression intent.

"Redspire? You don't mean..."

"Sir's beard is unsightly, and his hair is worse," the butler said. "He will consent to being shaved."

"I will?"

"Yes."

"Oh."

The attendants fell upon him before Hughes could think of a polite way of saying he liked his (admittedly rather shaggy) hair just fine. In a moment his cheeks and chin and throat were lathered in cool, aromatic shaving cream.

"I'm in the Scarlet Citadel?" he asked the butler, who was setting out clothing sets on the bed with neat, fussy little movements.

"Sir was brought here *by* the Scarlet Citadel," the butler corrected crisply. "Sir is in *Redspire*, the Scarlet Citadel's base of operations. Allergies to any fabrics?"

"Sorry? Oh. No. I don't think so," said Hughes. "But, look, I *can't* be in Redspire. That's..." His mind boggled. "That's just not possible. It's the most important building in the city. Tommy Fahrenheit lives there. Lorna Blacktower. Winnifred Dragontail for God's sake! There must be some mistake..."

"Lady Dragontail does indeed live here," said the butler, selecting one of the shirts and primping the cuffs. "On the eighty-eighth floor, in the Lunarlight Wing. It's my understanding that she's looking forward to meeting you."

"Meeting... me?"

One of the attendants rasped a straight razor over his Adam's apple. They finished doing this not a second too soon, for that bundle of cartilage in his throat began to bob crazily as Hughes tried without success to get ahold of himself. He felt as if he were being slowly buried in a grave packed not with earth, but gritty, solid bewilderment.

"Stand aside when you are done," the butler told the attendants.

The attendants dabbed Hughes' shaven, fresh-feeling face with hot towels and obediently stepped aside.

The butler loomed over him, inspecting.

"Better," he said grudgingly. "Pale but without offensive blemish. Sir prefers tea or coffee in the morning time?"

"Sorry, just to be clear," said Hughes. "Winnifred Dragontail—*the* Winnifred Dragontail—wants to meet *me*?"

"Quite so. Tea or—"

"But—"

"—coffee?"

"I don't—"

"Only the kettle is on."

"Sorry?" said Hughes.

"Sir?" said the butler.

They looked at one another, and for a moment they occupied a domain of utter bafflement together.

The butler rallied first.

"Tea it is," he said and went to fetch it.

Hughes sat in stunned silence as the attendants dressed him in shirt, socks, and shoes, all scarlet red as his trousers, and wonderfully comfortable. Not that he was in a position to enjoy this.

Winnifred Dragontail.

The leader of the Scarlet Citadel. The most powerful person in Corinth City, and I'm going to meet her.

The butler had informed him of this as if it were a house party, and Hughes was merely being brought to meet his host.

Why? he asked himself. *What could she possibly want with me?*

Now you mention it, his guilt replied coldly, *there is the matter of the murdered Scarlet Citadel fighters. Remember Laurana, Hughes? Winnifred Dragontail does. Why wouldn't she? Laurana worked for her, after all. Oh, and you'll love this. It's a real treat. They might have even been friends. And now Laurana is dead, and you were the last person who saw her alive. Isn't that a scream?*

Grappling with all sorts of colorful emotions, he looked down at his hands. Someone had put a cup of tea there.

It steamed softly.

Earl Grey.

Maybe it was a form of blasphemy (certainly Gormon Hughes Senior would have thought so), but Hughes had never wanted a cup of tea less in his life.

The butler cleared his throat.

"For his haircut, would sir prefer a kinetic follicle module, an electric razor, or is he inclined toward the old-fashioned barber experience?"

To Hughes' growing alarm the butler produced a pair of scissors and clipped them open and closed.

They went *snicker-snick.*

"Er," said Hughes. "Razor please."

"Very good, sir."

***

Feeling unbelievably fresh (he had never in his life had a hot-towel shave, dear sweet God his chin was *smooth*), and with nerves jitterbugging in his belly, Hughes found himself escorted to an elevator along corridors lined by large pillars, smooth and cream white and veined in gold. It was just shy of half past nine in the morning. The light coming through the tall rain-dappled windows was gray and a trifle uneasy, as if the day to come was frightened of the beastly storm that maintained its grip on the city so fiercely, its thunder a growl, its claws of summer lightning digging deep.

Search as he might, Hughes could see no one about.

"Excuse me?" he asked the butler. "Can I ask, where is everybody?"

"Aside from an ambassador to Hortesia, sir is the only resident of the Guest Wing. The ambassador is fond of a lie-in. I doubt we'll see her."

Hughes believed his question had just been artfully dodged. He decided to press. "And the Scarlet Citadel? What are they up to?"

"Preparations, sir."

Hughes nodded. It made sense. "Places to go, monsters to fight. That sort of thing?"

"Usually sir, usually," replied the butler, not turning around. "Not however, in this case. In this case the preparations are for the funeral. Watch your feet on the step. There we are. Alas, Redspire is a place with more character than a soap opera, and I'm afraid bumped toes and unexpected tumbles are a deplorably common issue. Sir?"

"Hm?"

"Coming?"

"What? Oh yes. Coming."

The elevator was an enormous contraption. Complicated cables snaked up into clunky, noisome darkness. The butler pressed a button and the machine whirred to life. Something bulky began to descend from up there in the black.

Hughes stared up the elevator shaft, not really seeing it. He was listening to the muffled tap of the rains on the nearby window glass, and at the same time, again and again, he felt as if he were listening to the words the butler had just spoken, as if they were droplets of liquid dread tapping somewhere deep inside him.

Tap. Tap-Tap.

For. The-Funeral.

That final word tapped hardest of all.

Funeral.

Preparations for the funeral.

Hughes came back to himself and swallowed. His throat was terribly dry because while he didn't know the names of all three deceased, he did know one.

He had been next to her when she died.

"Will Laurana be buried here in Redspire?" he wondered.

Next to Hughes, his glossy gold-buckled shoes pressed neatly together, the butler's demeanor changed. It was pretty subtle, but Hughes caught it. That mask of fussy "Yes sir, thank you kindly sir" propriety was not without imperfection. There were cracks, and Hughes believed he could see some of them now. The butler looked at him, then returned his gaze to the humming elevator.

"Buried? No. There hasn't been a graveyard in Redspire since the renovations eighteen years ago," said the butler. "The tower is equipped with a crematorium as well as a device that converts decaying tissue into fertilizer for the gardens. There is no shortage of green thumbs among the residents, and some wish to enrich the trees and flowers further, even in death."

Bewildered by this turn in the conversation, Hughes said, "You're telling me people choose to become plant food?"

The butler smiled without humor. "The practice originates in Yi-Shi, I believe. Yes, some members of the Citadel do indeed choose to become, as you say, 'plant food.' Some of them have a little saying about it: 'Arseholes to apples; men to mulch.' In case sir does not grasp the joke, it is a macabre play on, 'ashes to ashes, dust to dust.' Too macabre for me, I think. No, it's my understanding that

Laurie... ah... Miss Laurana's remains will be sent to her family's estate in the countryside."

Laurie, Hughes thought with growing despair. *Short for Laurana. I wonder if this man enjoyed those moon-halfmoon smiles as much as I did.*

Hughes wasn't sure, but he suspected the answer was yes.

Meanwhile silence had fallen in the corridor, not quite tense, but not companionable either.

Hughes got the impression that the subject of funerals was about to be dropped for good, but the butler surprised him. He knocked the heels of his shoes together with a pensive little clicking sound and said, "I'm given to understand Laurana's parents have picked a site for her rest. Cozy spot. Blackberries growing nearby." A pause. And then, softly, "Laurie would have liked that."

"She had a green thumb?"

"Yes."

"Detachable?" Hughes added, remembering the way Laurana fought, each extremity severing to become a blade. He wondered if she'd used them to prune hedges or cut flowers.

That humorless smile reappeared. "Yes," said the butler.

"I only spent a few hours with her," Hughes admitted. "In Iphigenia. She was... well, she was incredibly brave."

No reply.

Sometimes silence said more than words ever could. This one was filled with a mixture of misery and careful restraint. Any doubt in Hughes' mind as to whether the butler really cared for Laurana vanished.

The elevator arrived. They went in. After the press of another button, they felt the platform judder and rise under their feet, climbing toward the eighty-eighth floor.

The butler produced a little handkerchief and dabbed at his eyes.

Hughes pretended not to see.

It seemed the kind thing to do.

***

Gormon Hughes the Performer, son of Gormon Hughes the Teamaster, was not accustomed to meeting important people. He wasn't sure what was required of him. Once, when he was seven, a politician wearing a rust-colored suit had arrived at the door of their shop with a waxy smile and bearing amazing news about the future which (should the politician in the rust-colored suit be voted into office that election season) looked very bright indeed.

Gormon Hughes the Teamaster had listened, politely, as the politician painted a picture of Leonidas District extricated from its junk mound of woes, remodeled, and utterly remade in the image of a place that could not be called *earthly*, but perhaps more accurately, *intergalactic* in its cultural beauty and cosmopolitan largesse.

Meanwhile Gormon Hughes the Performer had listened, become bored, and occupied himself by quietly stealing the politician's equally rust-colored briefcase, emptying it of documents and fliers, and filling it up again with slightly damp tea bags.

Why am I thinking about that now? It hardly seemed the time for reminiscing.

The elevator gave a jerk and stopped at the summit of Redspire tower. As he followed the butler toward the Lunarlight Wing where Winnifred Dragontail kept her appointments, Hughes drew a mental picture of his own. The picture showed the tower looming over Ptolema District. No, over every District. Over the city and the countryside and the whole wide world. Curled around that immense spindle of stone and steel was a dragon. Its eyes were cunning. Its breath rippled like hot air around a furnace grate. Its scales shone rainbow-bright like wicked oil slicks. Its tail... its tail blotted out all earthly understanding, for it was a tail of intergalactic beauty and largesse.

Ridiculous, of course.

The woman he was on his way to meet was just that—a woman, not a dragon.

Still, he could not shake the feeling that with every step, he was marching between a set of hooked claws or closing jaws. That he was going toward judgment and fire. Later, he would understand just how right he had been.

"The Lunarlight Wing," announced the butler, and he wasn't kidding.

Hughes made an involuntary noise of awe.

Moons decorated every feature of the wing. Yellow harvest moons sloped along its arches. Sly orange moons winked from its mantelpieces. Moon-shaped bookcases stood in a craterous library. Moon-curved chandeliers lit each room they walked through. Tapestries of penitent men carrying the moon on their shoulders. Pale, gorgeous light made Hughes' pupils sparkle. Even the fragrance sent out by the perfume processors was *moony*, sort of a cross between sumac and vanilla.

Natural satellites everywhere, thought Hughes. *A hoard of moons. The dragon must have her hoard or she won't be able to sleep.*

Once more the reputation of the woman struck him.

Once more he thought about being seven, about the important quality all adults held at that age, politician or no. Huge and all-knowing, adults had it all under control. They were godlike.

They were dragons.

Such indelible power kids gave them by thinking that way.

And wasn't he doing the same with her? With a woman whose parents had named her *Winnifred* for God's sake?

With a tightening of his fingers into fists, Hughes resolved that even though he did not know what was required of him, he did, in fact, know what was not. He was not (metaphorically speaking) to fill anyone's briefcase with slightly damp tea bags.

He was not to make a complete tit of himself.

They traipsed up a spiral staircase, the rails sculpted to look like dragon heads gushing fire, the banister leather red as if superheated by the flames. No windows had been cut into the walls here, only hammered bookshelves, hung sepia-tinted photographs, as well as portraits commemorating decades of Scarlet Citadel history. Fascinating though these were, Hughes was left to wonder at the glory of the view from this high up.

At the top of the stairs there was a set of double doors flanked by a grandfather clock. The butler flung them wide with what Hughes could not help but recognize as a flourish.

This was the tallest room in the tower—any higher than this and you were kissing roof tiles. A vast domed chamber it was, with comfortable furnishings bathed in the warm glow from a fieldstone fireplace. Six dragons rendered in black stone gazed out at Hughes from the hearth, their hollow sockets aglimmer with flickering flame. He could see a cozy couch, some nice recliner chairs, a dumbwaiter, a bronze astronomy set, and a labeled map of Corinth City. There was a desk with nothing on it but a few notebooks—this detail spoke to either tremendous organization or tremendous disorganization. Hughes was inclined to believe the latter. A single window with frosted glass was set into the east wall. It was open, just a crack, and its shutter rattled now and then as the wind gusted through the blinds. Under the stormy sounds Hughes could hear a velvet-voice singer crooning over a speaker system. The song was an oldie. *An oldie but a goodie*, his father would have said.

A woman and a man rose out of their seats near the fire to greet him.

"Mr. Hughes," said the man. "I'm Doctor John Isherwood. Nice to meet you."

"Pleasure," said Hughes vaguely, shaking the doctor's proffered hand. He was looking at the woman.

"Winnifred Dragontail," she said. "Call me Wendy."

Hughes blinked. "Right. Er. Wendy?"

Don't ask her if she means Winnie or Freddie.

"Are you sure you don't mean Winnie? Or Freddie?"

Damn.

Wendy Dragontail smiled at him. "Pretty sure." The Scarlet Citadel's leader wore slacks, pearl earrings, and the fluffiest sweater Hughes had ever set eyes on. It was pink. Also she was *older* than he'd expected. Maybe seventy. Her hair must have been blonde in her girlhood, a lovely ashen blonde, because now it was white as newly fallen snow, and no less lovely for that. It was pinned up, one big bun and one small, like an oddly glamorous snowman perched on her head. "Have a seat, Gormon."

"Hughes."

"Hughes, quite so. Tea?"

"No, thank you, my Lady."

"How is your father?"

Hughes had to physically restrain himself from blinking at her again. "He's fine, thank you. Um..."

"Excellent. He shall be notified as to your wellbeing, though you may wish to write to him yourself to confirm it. I bet he's an old fuddy-duddy about his teapots, eh?"

This time Hughes did not blink. He gawped. Wendy Dragontail's smile broadened into a grin. "Close your mouth, my lad. You'll catch flies. Well, well, well. Shaved you, did they? Falstaff is also a consummate fuddy-duddy, especially when it comes to the manner in which people are presented to me. Aren't you, Falstaff?"

"Yes, Lady," said the butler. "Only proper."

"Is it not the Lady who should decide what is proper?"

"I shouldn't say so, Lady."

Wendy Dragontail raised an eyebrow. "No? And why not?"

"Because, good Lady," said the butler reverently. "On the one occasion I did not prepare a guest for an audience with you, you gave them what you called a 'once over,' declared that they were 'scruffy as a well-slapped pigeon,' and that they should 'tottle off in a hurry, and if they wanted to speak to you, well, they'd better make a showing of it.' Then, as I recall, you muttered something about how things were in your father's day, how people put in a bit of effort, and other observations of that order. Then you slammed the door."

"Slammed it?"

"Yes. A jolly loud bang."

Wendy Dragontail was frowning mightily. "I did that, did I?"

"Echoed all over the wing," confirmed the butler. "A very good slam, I thought."

"I must have been in foul form."

"Nevertheless, it was the appropriate form at the time, Lady. The *proper* form."

"Ah. Fair enough, Falstaff, fair enough. Point taken. You may go."

The butler sketched a crisp bow and left, closing the doors behind him.

The wind blew, clattering the window shutter. Wendy Dragontail spared it a glance and said, "Sit, Hughes."

Hughes sat, discovering the couch was not as cozy as it looked. It was cozier. Wendy Dragontail joined him, curling her feet up under her bottom. Doctor John Isherwood leaned against a stone dragon. He was portly, thirty-five, thick-jowled, mutton-chopped, and dressed smartly in gray.

He seemed like he was on the verge of posing a question, but Hughes beat him to it.

"Excuse me, your Ladyship, but how do you know my dad?"

"How do you think? I was told," said Wendy Dragontail. She shrugged. "But then, I suppose you're new to all this. Do you know kobolds, Hughes? In my father's time when dragons were a mere rarity rather than an extinct species, dragons had agents called kobolds. I'm given to understand they looked like a cross between a Doberman and an anemic iguana. The point is, the dragons of the past might be gone, but the dragon of today still has need of her kobolds."

There was a pause. Then:

"You're talking about spies," said Hughes, mildly horrified. "You sent spies to find out about me."

Another shrug. She wasn't the least bit embarrassed about it. In fact she looked bemused. "Doctor Isherwood has questions for you. Will you answer?"

Hughes said he would.

It was that or try his luck with the window, and it was a long way down.

Just as he thought of the window, its shutters gave another noisy rattle. Wendy Dragontail shot it a look of sudden irritation. Doctor John seemed unperturbed.

"How well do you remember the last twenty-four hours, son?"

"Pretty well."

Maybe a little too well, Doc.

"Can you take me through it?" Doctor John was watching him closely.

Hughes could, and did.

He omitted a lot of the facts, knowing most of them would not be missed. His trip to The Rotbloom Carnival, or what remained of it. His purloining an umbrella from a streetbeater. His encounter with two of the most dangerous people in the city, their skin glittering subcutaneously.

What he did tell them interested Lady Dragontail and the good doctor very much.

And Hughes was watching his audience closely too.

Because of that, he noticed several things someone else might have missed.

He noticed the way Wendy Dragontail's lips thinned to a white line when Hughes explained how he'd disguised himself in the first place. It made Hughes wonder where the drunk named Walter was now.

Probably preparing, his mind whispered.

Preparing for what?

Nothing much. Just the funeral.

Funerals, he amended bleakly. Nosering and Beard had also died out there in the Wilderness Beyond The Door.

Hughes further noticed the rigidity in Doctor John Isherwood's posture when he described the creature that had slaughtered the Scarlet Citadel unit. That brought a question to Hughes' addled brain: What exactly was John Isherwood a doctor *of?*

Lastly, he noticed the look of whey-faced sadness that passed between his listeners when he spoke of Laurana's death. That look confirmed his suspicions about the dead woman. She had not only been kind to her squad. She had been kind to everyone, her loss was sharply felt, and in his heart Hughes felt the clock springs of shame wind up another few minutes toward some unseen hour of grief. Could he have saved her? *Tap-tap* went the rain on the frosted glass. Could anything have saved her from that grisly end, broken and alone but for a stranger, namely him?

Tick-tock went the clock springs.

Tap-tap.

Tick-tock.

Rattle-stir, and the window shutters were shivering *yessss, yessss, she might have lived.*

When it was over and he'd said his piece, Hughes sat with his head down and his shoulders hunched apishly.

Hooyou? Laurana had asked him in the moments before her life drained away.

Hooyou or who are you?

Well Laurana, sometimes I myself am not sure.

After what felt like a long time, Hughes felt a hand on his arm. His surprise was great and only increased when he saw the hand belonged to Wendy Dragontail. Her eyes were brown, a hearty hazel color that made him think of his own dark eyes during rare spots of Corinth City sunshine. She gave him two brief pats. *There, there.*

She looked past him to the double doors. When Hughes followed her gaze, he saw the butler Falstaff standing to attention. When had he been summoned?

Hughes didn't know—he'd been too engrossed in reliving the dream of yesterday, the nightmare.

"I think young master Hughes will have some tea after all," said Wendy Dragontail. "I'll join him."

CHAPTER FIFTEEN

"How'd you kill it?" Doctor John wanted to know.

It was a few minutes after Hughes' recounting of the previous day. Falstaff had come and gone, dropping off tea like a fussy caffeine dispenser. On the sound system, that crooner was still giving their rendition of sweet romantic songs. Hughes found it an odd choice for background music, both charming and unnerving at the same time.

An oldie but a goodie, he mused. *Wendy Dragontail herself is certainly an oldie, that much is clear, but I'm reserving judgment on whether or not she's—*

"Mr. Hughes?" the doctor said. "You still with us?"

"Yeah."

"I was asking how it was that you managed to kill the creature."

Hughes thought about pushing his Performance, then decided the risk was too great. A white lie would have to do.

"I didn't," said Hughes. "Not really. What you have to understand is that by the time it overpowered her, Laurana had dealt her opponent an astonishing amount of damage. The thing that fell onto my outstretched knife was already dead."

"I believe that," said Doctor John. "At least I *mostly* believe it. Our clean-up crew report the creature's heart was pierced by your knife. That the chest cavity was laid bare, as if pried apart. Practically blasted apart. Based on the tensile strength of the intact dorsal bones, that alone speaks to an act of incredible strength. Yet you, Mr. Hughes, claim to have no combat training."

"The arms," said Hughes, not missing a beat. "The arms opened it from the inside."

"Do you know what those arms are?" asked Wendy Dragontail. "Had you ever seen anything like them?"

"No." Hughes never wanted to again, either. Even the memory of those long slender limbs moving toward him made his mouth fill with bitter stomach acid.

He sipped his tea to wash the taste down his throat. It was good. Not as good as his father made, but then, what tea was?

"What about you?" he couldn't help but ask his audience. "Do you know what they are? Or what that... that *thing* was?"

Doctor John answered. "We've got a fair idea. Right now what we're interested in is what you can remember about it."

Liar, thought Hughes. *I should know. I'm good at those, Doc.*

Out loud he said, "I can't think of anything else, other than what I've told you. It was a massive wolf. It had two heads, black wings, and instead of claws—"

"There were worms," said Wendy Dragontail. "And arms that opened it from the inside." She had been peering at Hughes over her mug. Now she leaned forward ever so slightly. "They put the heart on your knife, didn't they? The hands at the end of the arms."

"They were holding the heart," Hughes admitted. He was alert, hackles raised, but outwardly quite calm. Wendy Dragontail: oldie yes; goodie maybe; but smartie? Absolutely. "Then the creature sort of um... staggered, I suppose you'd say. Fell like a hairy tree trunk. Next thing I know, the heart is beating on my knife. Impaled. Actually it was bloody eerie, now I think about it—"

"Beating?" Doctor John interrupted. If he was stiff before, he was positively taut now. "You never said that it was beating. This is *after* the hands burst from the monster's chest? After they'd lifted the heart out of its body?"

Hughes thought, *Fuck it.* "To be fair, it was only the one beat. Ah. I tell a lie, it was two beats, then one. Is that important? I assumed you knew," he said virtuously. "What with you having a fair idea about the creature's nature and everything."

Doctor John reddened.

Beside Hughes, Wendy Dragontail took a mouthful of tea.

Was that a twinkle in her eye or just Hughes' imagination?

I think so, only not an amused one. This conversation is too severe, too loaded for that. Call it an acknowledgment twinkle then.

Hughes didn't know it, but at that moment the grandfather clock outside Wendy Dragontail's office struck ten o'clock. The storm had gathered itself for another sortie against the city's defenses. Rain swooped and slashed, heavier sheets looking like wide silver arrows fired from the thundercloud ranks advancing across the early June sky.

Inside, meanwhile, Wendy Dragontail's window made a fretful clatter. As Doctor John spoke, Wendy craned over one shoulder and peered irritably at it. No, not irritably. *Loathingly.* Why she didn't just get up and close the troubling thing, Hughes had no clue. She was a little on the rickety side, he supposed. Not quite frail but old enough that leaving the couch might send a bolt of sciatic pain up her leg, or maybe an arthritic convulsion.

"Let me make sure I've got this," said Doctor John, not-so-subtly diverting the topic. "You stole a Scarlet Citadel man's armor, fooled his unit into thinking you were him, and are now the sole survivor of an event that cost the rest of that unit their lives?" The man shook his head. "Sorry, son. I don't buy it. There's got to be some detail you're leaving out. I've seen some decent actors on the vids. Spellbinding, even. No one is that good at imitation. This unit spent years working together. They trained together. Drank together. Something you said, or did, would have given you away."

"They drank together at *The Pear and Princess*," said Hughes. He watched puzzlement cross the good doctor's face. "And I beg your pardon, but you're wrong about imitation. It's like Lady Dragontail's kobolds."

"That so?" Doctor John was nonplussed.

"Spies are just actors that prefer the quiet. Look, I'm not denying it was difficult, but assuming Walter's identity was a mechanical process. It can be broken down. I observed and learned about him. I embodied his movements, found the right pitch for his voice, and reacted as I believed he would to developments in the immediate environment." Hughes made an expansive gesture, and in Walter's slurred tones he said, "An actor prepares, Doc. Prepares and inhabits and improvises."

It was as close to an explanation of Performance as he dared give.

The fact that Wendy Dragontail hadn't said a word on the subject meant one of two things: either she didn't know about it, or she did, and expected Hughes to be ignorant of the power.

Either way, the safest route was secrecy.

"So a combination of research," said Doctor John. "And... what? Natural talent?"

"No," said Hughes patiently because if he had to tread on the doctor's toes, he might as well not make an enemy of the man. "Talent is something you're born with. What I do, I have to work at, or else I start to forget how."

Still, the Doc was unconvinced. "My guess is bribery. Credits changing hands." He hesitated. At some point he'd crossed his ankles and allowed one of the sculpted dragons to take his weight. Turning away from where Hughes sat, the glow of the hearth fire scored his face with harsh orange lines. Fire can lend beauty to lots of people, but for John Isherwood it robbed him of vitality, made him look distant, even a little creepy. "Maybe blackmail," he said.

Hughes was about to protest (namely that he hadn't the funds for bribery, and even the idea of blackmail made his belly do a wobbler), but Wendy Dragontail spoke first.

"When I'm in a muddle," she said, "I always try to sit back and think about the most obvious solution. Not everything has to be convoluted, John. Sometimes, a dessert made of egg whites and sugar is a grand conspiracy with lots of moving parts and complicated twists and turns. But sometimes, it is just a meringue."

"I don't like it," griped Doctor John. "Something about it feels off to me."

She offered him a sympathetic smile. "It might help to leave your doctorate on the sink next to the soap some mornings. I'm all for the spirit of inquiry, so long as paranoia doesn't take over."

Hughes mumbled something.

Wendy Dragontail turned to him. "Pardon?"

"I said, I'm sorry," said Hughes.

"And why should you be sorry?"

He looked at his feet. "For Laurana. For the others too. I can't help but feel responsible for what happened to them. Can't help but wonder if I could have... and Falstaff the butler had a wee cry in the elevator and um... I might have one too, if that's okay."

Wendy Dragontail and Doctor John exchanged a look of astonishment. Hughes didn't catch it. He blinked up at them a moment too late, shocked at how quickly their faces misted up, how fast the tears were coming. What had brought this on? Desserts? The fact Laurana would never enjoy something crunchy-sweet or tartly delicious on her tongue ever again? Or maybe... maybe despair just wanted him for a while. It had business with him. Tapping like poisoned rains. *Tick-tocking* like rotted clock springs. It had business with him.

So that was how Hughes got himself ready for a good old fashioned sob in the sanctum of the most powerful woman in Corinth. He felt the first tear of many slide down his cheek, the treacherous wet bastard. Oh well. No helping it now. Funny how things turned out, eh? Well, not funny exactly. The other one. Dreadful. That was the word. Dreadful how things turned out.

He smiled damply and thought, *Much better.*

What now?

Possibly he would curl up in the fetal position. Actually, not even his current mood could make him ready for the sheer spine-jellifying embarrassment of that. Or could it?

He supposed they would all find out together.

Next to him Wendy Dragontail opened her mouth. What she was going to say Hughes never did find out because it was at that precise moment that the window shutters rattled violently in the biggest gust yet.

The effect on Wendy Dragontail was so unlikely that it startled Hughes out of his present crisis.

She vented a noise of total contempt, a noise of toad-slime revulsion and the last pencil-lead of patience worn away to a nub. She lunged to her feet and advanced with murderous intent on the offending shutters. These she yanked down, crumpled, and dropped to lie on the carpet. With a slam Wendy Dragontail shut the window for good measure, huffed imperiously, and turned back to face them, nostrils flaring.

"I swear, you try to ventilate the place for a few minutes, freshen up and so on, and what do you get? Bebothered by the bloody breeze, that's what you get. Least cooperative of all the elements, I've always thought. Soak up water. Douse fire. Earth... well, you can push it around a bit. But wind? Wind's a pisser. Spend your life chasing its name if you're not wise to the folly of doing so. Isn't that r... is..."

She took a step and shuddered.

She fell.

Not a stumble. Not an elegant faint.

An ugly, deboned-fish kind of a fall, the sort that landed elderly people in cramped hospital beds with shattered hips.

Two things happened:

Doctor John made a strained sound of dismay in his throat, and Hughes acted without thinking.

***

While Hughes was educating Doctor John about the finer points of theatrical research, Miss Gleam was striding across the forsaken bowling alley that occupied the heart of her lair. She hoisted herself up so she was sitting astride the clerk's desk, reached out, grabbed the telephone, and dialed a number.

She listened intently to the burring at the other end of the line, entertaining herself with sweet imaginings of a similar telephone ringing somewhere in Corinth City. She hoped it was delightfully squalid. Given who she was calling, that was almost definitely the case.

There was a scratchy sound and a voice spoke.

"That you Gleamy?"

"Good morning, Mr. Twinkle. I trust that superior example of our ilk, Mr. Glint, is there with you?"

"He's here all right. I wish he'd stop glowering at my cat."

"Mr. Glint has had a run of rather bad luck with cats," said Miss Gleam smoothly. "They play havoc with his digestion. And the others, Mr. Twinkle? They are there also?"

"Sure they are."

"The vivacious Miss Glitter? Misters Glow, Glisten, Flicker, and Flash?"

"All present and accounted for."

"What about Mr. Fulgurate?"

"Funny you mention, I can't see him at present. I'm sure he's around somewhere. He does love a lurk, our Mr. Fulgurate."

"He is there though?"

"Most assuredly."

"Good, now—"

"Here, Gleamy, why couldn't we have held this little get-together in your lodgings instead of mine?"

In the musty dark of the bowling alley her smile was like something profane carved into the face of a saint, all tainted and lawless and sharp.

"I'm afraid our lodgings are quite unsuitable at present, Mr. Twinkle, for there is an amplitude of dust. We would not have been able to hear ourselves think over Mr. Flicker's sneezing."

"Well how considerate of you," said Twinkle, who knew as well as Gleam that she was fibbing quite spectacularly. Mr. Flicker was a devil for a whopping sneeze and could blow his honker nose most gratingly, but that was not why Gleam wanted no visitors.

In truth, she and Mr. Glint knew exactly where the other members of their organization lived. They knew addresses, street numbers, the names of neighbors, known associates, and household pets. Mr. Twinkle's cat was named Lucinda.

And not a one of them knew where Miss Gleam and Mr. Glint lived.

"Anonymity is the best shield," she had once confided to her partner. "Stronger than steel, dear fellow."

Mr. Glint had said, "Right you are, Miss Gleam," and while he understood the concept of anonymity as well as he understood advanced horticultural botany, it was clear over time (when their lair remained a secret) that something akin to the point had been grasped.

Miss Gleam crossed her legs and put the telephone in her lap.

"Mr. Twinkle, place me on loudspeaker if you'd be so kind."

A pause. "Done," he said. "What's the big hubbub?"

"Miss Shimmer is dead. She was killed by an assassin named Willard Coosler last night."

Oh, but the pause was crowded now. Crowded with surprise, fear, anger, and a host of other hot emotions.

"How did he kill her?" This vexingly pretty voice belonged to Miss Glitter.

"He drowned her in the bathtub."

Miss Gleam gave this a moment to (ah ha ha) *sink in.*

Her smile widened hideously. She was in fine fooling today. Murder was afoot, and a mystery, and yummy scrummy vengeance, and wasn't that *grand?*

"But Miss Shimmer was an absolute scragger," said Mr. Flash. "She wouldn't go and get herself scragged without a by-your-leave. Makes no sense."

This pronouncement made them all offer an opinion.

Miss Gleam cut them off mid-tirade. "If you'll allow... ahem. *If you'll allow me to explain.*"

They fell silent, and presently she told them about Willard Coosler, how he'd tricked Shimmer into a romance that ended with her body bloated and her skin sparkling softly under the bathwater. She told them about his communication device and the first half of the riddle he was to solve.

"How's that work then?" said Mr. Twinkle. "Get an incomplete riddle, the rest of it later, and together they should tell you where you ought to go to meet the contact?"

"Together they should be *solvable*, but yes. Succinctly put as always," said Miss Gleam.

"Clever system."

"Mm."

"And no sign of the second part of the riddle?"

"Not until twenty-four hours have passed since the appointed killing time. Midnight tonight."

Mr. Twinkle repeated the riddle's first part to himself, his tone puzzled. "Where the bulls run. Where the bulls run. Haven't the foggiest. You lot?"

There was a chorus of agreement from the others—they hadn't the slimmest inkling.

"Worth a try," said Miss Gleam magnanimously. "Well, I think that about concludes this little pre-noon canoodle, my dulcy darlings. Mr. Glint?"

"Here, Miss Gleam."

Ah. It never failed to hearten her, the way his words fell like cracked stone hammers on the eardrums.

"Return home, please. I'm at my wit's end without you. Tonight we will be on riddle-solving duty, so thinking cap on. The rest of you, vigilance is the watchword. Someone or a group of someones have us in their crosshairs. They are coming for us. Insane? Surely. Yet it's true, and they've already had more success than our employer would believe."

"Yer men... he dersnut knerp?"

Miss Gleam paused.

"Is that you, Mr. Fulgurate?"

"Yers."

"I thought so. No, Mr. Fulgurate. Our employer does not know about Miss Shimmer's untimely demise. Why should he? He has ten thousand concerns to handle on any given day. To be sure, this is a rather pressing matter. But that is *precisely* why we are going to take care of it for him. Quickly. Decisively. And, one hopes, extremely messily when we get our hands on the pustulant miscreant that gave the death order."

"Sounds good to me," said Mr. Twinkle.

A chorus of assent from the others.

"Sublime. Now, BOLO, as the streetbeaters say. Be On The Lookout. When we catch whoever is behind this, I would adore all of you present and unspoiled."

"Take care of yourself, Gleamy," said Mr. Twinkle.

"I'll be in touch," she said and hung up.

***

God, she's so light.

This thought was the first one to cross Hughes' mind since Wendy Dragontail had started to shudder. The intervening time had been erased. His eyes had registered that she was going to fall, and his instincts had taken over.

He helped her to her feet. Out of the corner of his vision, Hughes could see rain rolling down the windowpane in long unbroken streaks.

"There," he told her. "No harm done."

"Thank you, Hughes."

"Don't mention—"

Hughes stopped. Something was happening.

Through her wooly pink jumper, he could feel Wendy Dragontail's arm... he could feel it...

He could not explain what it was doing.

Firming? Hardening? Literally growing?

He cut his gaze to her face to find her looking right back. Those hazel-dark eyes sparkled at him, and with a sudden jolt of confusion Hughes wondered how he could have ever mistaken her for seventy. She straightened, the top of her head rising so she actually stood a hair's breadth taller than Hughes. Her hair was not snow white with age. It was a premature pale.

Hughes' heart was beating quicker now, thumping in his temples. The woman standing in front of him was fifty, if that. And she was fiercely strong. She exuded it. It baked off her like heat from a clay oven.

"Dragon," he heard himself say.

She winked at him. "I'm satisfied. John?"

"He's a good kid," said the doctor. He hadn't moved from his position by the fireplace. There was no trace of panic about him. "I still don't entirely trust that he's been straight with us, but there's no denying what just happened. You were an old lady falling, and he ran to save you. Doesn't get much more Boy Scout than that."

"But..." Hughes stared at Wendy Dragontail. "You *were* old."

She reached into the neck of her jumper and took out a necklace. It was very simple, just an oval of tarnished gold with a dragon's tail curling around the edges.

"Not everything is as it appears," she said. "This is Faethe, Amulet of Dragons. Not gold but magical ore taken from Iphigenia and forged in the bellyfire of its namesake. In that way it is like you, Gormon Hughes."

"Forged in bellyfire?" said Hughes doubtfully.

"No. What? No." She frowned at him. "*Unexpected*, is what I was going to say. Faethe allows me to change my body's density. With it, I can be light as a sack of feathers or heavy as a sack of combine harvesters. My skin is soft as paper one moment and hard as dragon scales the next. I used it for a bit of pageantry just now, Hughes. I hope you don't mind."

"Oh," said Hughes. "I see." His brain caught up with everything that had just taken place. "I was thoroughly tricked, wasn't I?"

"Yes."

"You and Doctor John were testing me to see if I'm a decent person."

"Afraid so."

"And I passed?"

"Mostly."

"Mostly?"

"Mostly."

"Right! Er. Right. So." Hughes was flummoxed. "What now?"

"Now." Wendy Dragontail held up a finger. "We introduce you to your partner. She will keep you safe, and you will do the same for her."

"Partner? Safe from what?"

"Monsters, Hughes. And worse besides."

"I don't understand."

She gave him a pat on the back—*there, there*.

"Sometimes a dessert is just a meringue," she said. "But sometimes things are convoluted. Best to shut up and carry on, eh? Okay, Cate, out you come."

"Sorry?" said Hughes, completely bewildered now.

Wendy Dragontail smiled once more. "Not everything is as it appears."

Out of the corner of his vision, Hughes saw the window grow feet. Two feet. They came right out of the glass. They were in boots, huge fantastic hobnailed boots, and there were legs, and a waist, and a body...

Hughes stepped back, his eyes flung wide, his breath caught in his chest.

The woman emerging from the frosted glass was his age, maybe a little older. Her hair was as red as the fire burning in the hearth, the tattoo of church bells clanging silently on her throat was a lush carmine red, and her clothes were a deeper scarlet red. She was also, incidentally, the most striking looking woman Hughes had ever seen.

"Hughes," said Wendy Dragontail. "Meet Cate Jubilee."

Say something.

"Hello."

Something else.

"Erm. Your boots are enormous."

Amazing, his mind said miserably. *Absolutely amazing.*

A lock of hair like threaded cinders fell across Cate Jubilee's eye.
She stuck out her lower lip and blew it away.
"Welcome to the Scarlet Citadel," she said.

CHAPTER SIXTEEN

Love is tricky.

Back in the time of the very first Gormon Hughes (an avuncular playwright who died seventy-odd years ago of psychedelic jellyfish), it was commonly agreed that love should be about Romance. Not flowers and cakes with decorative icing and a cuddle every other Tuesday. Romance involved big events. Things like the meeting between young star-crossed lovers, serenades on balconies, warring families, and of course, the passionate climax (which usually involve unfortunate misunderstandings about who exactly is drinking the poison—young star-crossed lovers are an endangered species by default).

Later, in the time of the current Hughes' father, theatre, poetry, painting frescoes and all that sort of thing were dead and buried, and love had changed. Now it was about romance. The world was getting bigger, more complicated, and events were getting smaller to compensate. Suddenly a quiet cuddle every other Tuesday seemed fine. Lovely, even.

Nowadays nobody really knows much of anything about love, although most doctors commonly agree that too much of it can kill you.

Before Kim Kallaimon, Hughes had never been in love. She'd come out of the night like something hailing from dreams, or the past, somewhere it was all right to be spectacular all the time. In fact you had to be spectacular, kind, intelligent, carefree, interested, precise, relaxed, and cool. Otherwise you weren't welcome in Kim's world. So Hughes had tried his best to be someone who belonged, and she'd opened her arms to him for the dance and only let go when she realized he was faking the steps.

She'd hurt him, and Hughes had felt his heart encrust itself in a jar of frost, and he was grateful. What else but ice could keep it from falling apart now it was broken?

It said a lot, then, that on first impressions the very sight of Cate Jubilee's nose was enough to thaw that ice even the tiniest bit.

Big. Buttonish. It was a great nose. It had character.

And the way she blew that lock of fiery hair from her eye?

That was a big event in a small moment. That was Romance *and* romance.

Of course no one, not ever, not in all of history, ever believed in love at first sight. That was a simple idea, and love was far too tricky to be caught becoming a simple idea.

Still, that nose...

***

Bidding goodbye for now to Wendy Dragontail and Doctor John Isherwood, Hughes agreed to follow Cate Jubilee for what she called The Grand Tour.

Before they parted company, Doctor John took him aside.

"I hope you'll forgive me playing my part in the deception. You're an unknown quantity. It was important for us to get a handle on who you are."

"It's okay," said Hughes, and he meant it.

"Gracious of you. Listen, son. There's something you'll be called to do later, and I want to be there for it. Tradition demands not, but if you insist, then I'll be brought along. Okay?"

"What is it?"

"The forging of your magic item."

Hughes stared at him, not quite believing what he'd just heard.

"Will you insist I be present?" Doctor John needled. He seemed nervous that Hughes might tell him no.

"Of course," said Hughes. "Sorry, did you say—"

"Thank you." The doctor clasped his hand. "Really, I can't tell you how much I appreciate that. When the time comes for a favor returned, you just ask."

"Oh. Thank you very much. But—"

He felt an arm slip through his.

"Coming?" said Cate Jubilee.

Hughes nodded. All spoken language had been knocked clean out of his skull.

"Don't overwhelm him," warned Doctor John.

Cate Jubilee flapped her hand in a gesture that said, "Yeah, yeah, keep talking."

She steered Hughes out of the private room into the moony warrens of the Lunarium Wing.

Hughes took one last look over his shoulder.

Wendy Dragontail was feeding a length of cut wood to the fire. She stood, took a poker from where it was leaning against the stone, prodded the kindling to get it ablaze, and then she seemed to feel his gaze on her. She met his eye and tipped him a final conspiratorial wink.

Then Cate drew him around the corner, and Hughes was left with his buzzing fizzling flashing thoughts.

"So," he said. "Your name is Jubilee?"

"Uh huh."

"It's an interesting name."

"Interesting like 'nice' or interesting like 'what an interesting collection of rashes'?"

Hughes looked at her to see if she were having him on, but Cate Jubilee's expression betrayed nothing.

"The first one," he said carefully.

"Sweet of you to say. Gormon Hughes is a terrible name."

"Is it?"

She wrinkled her nose. "Hughes is okay. Gormon sounds like a brand of washing detergent."

"It's a family name."

"Sorry."

"Look, Doctor John was saying something about a magic item..."

"Oh, that'll be sorted out this evening," said Cate breezily. "First I've got to show you around. Get your bearings. Have you eaten?"

"No, but let me just—"

"Too late for breakfast. Could you hold out till lunch?"

"Yes, ah, would it be okay to ask you—"

"No time! The elevator's here."

She hurried him inside, flipped a panel, flicked a few switches, shut the panel, and pressed the button next to it to get the mechanism going again. The lift began its clunky descent.

"Listen," Hughes bumbled after a while spent retrieving his courage. "I've got some questions I wouldn't mind firing your way..."

"How are you with armadillos?"

Hughes came up short. "Excuse me?"

"Armadillos," she said. "Allergic to them?"

"I don't think so."

"What about Yi-Shi parrots?"

"Um."

"Any allergies at all?"

Hughes scratched his newly shaven chin. "Dad said the men in our family are a bit weird with shellfish."

"Great. No problem. How do you take your coffee?"

"I've never had it."

"Never had coffee?"

"My dad has very particular views about coffee," said Hughes grimly. Gormon Hughes Senior pronounced the word as if it had ballistic attachments. "Tea for me."

"Each to their own," said Cate with a shrug. "Me, I'm a gallows on legs until I've had my morning latte. Did it really have black wings?"

"Did what have black wings?"

"The creature," said Cat coaxingly. "The one in Iphigenia."

"Oh. Yes." Hughes felt there was more expected of him. "Six of them."

"Did it fly?"

"Not as far as I remember."

"Everyone's talking about it," Cate confided.

"Oh yes?"

"And you, of course."

"Me?"

Cate nodded amiably.

"What are they talking about?"

"They're talking about what's going to happen to you."

"And what's going to happen to me?"

She looked at him as if he had just asked whether or not marmalade was the name of a country or something you put on toast.

"You're being recruited, silly. Why else would I welcome you and show you around?"

He'd been working his way around to this. "The thing is... look, the thing is I *can't* be recruited."

"Why not?"

"Because I'm... well I'm not..."

"It's a bit unusual, true." Cate reached up with her free hand and adjusted the collar of his shirt. "Normally recruits apply through the Ptolemaen Protocol. Or they're scouted from the ranks of the streetbeaters, fighting rings, or... there's other ways I'm forgetting. I was Ptolemaen Protocol."

"What's that?"

"It's like a hereditary system," she explained. "God, this elevator is bumpy. The other ones are much better, you'll see. So if your mum or dad or some other blood relative is in the Scarlet Citadel, you can apply to join via the Ptolemaen Protocol. There's a qualifying tournament and everything."

"So which relative got you in?"

She smiled. She had a wonderful smile, wide and dazzling as a Tinfrost firework display. "My Aunt Trisha Jubilee. I took her name the day she retired and gave me these." She raised one boot and waggled it demonstratively.

"You could use your aunt's magic item?" Hughes was remembering the shock Walter's hatchet had given him in Iphigenia.

"Once they're bonded to you, magic items can be used by everyone you're related to by blood. That's the whole reason behind the Ptolemaen Protocol. You didn't know?"

"We don't really hear much about this place where I come from."

"Huh. You must have heard of Occasional Morphology though."

"Sorry?"

"Ooh, we're here!"

The doors ground apart, and Hughes felt a wall of heat and noise slap him full in the face. Artificial sunlight bathed a jungle of Hortesian palms, Calcifern beeches, hawthorns from Rhönland, maples, oaks, and elms from their own country of Corinthia. To Hughes, whose botanical experience featured weeds and plastic pawnshop blossoms, the sight evoked Iphigenia's forest and more, for these were trees from his own world. Animals of all shapes and sizes cheeped and whickered and garbled and fluttered in this weird thicket.

"This is the global menagerie," Cate said.

"I don't understand. These trees are from all over the world."

"Jolly Winkins, the groundskeeper, uses a special fertilizer, so I'm told. Ingenious, really."

"Is that so?" said Hughes politely. And then, because it was not so much occupying his mind as moving in, refurbishing, and selecting new wallpaper in various shades of worry, he asked, "Erm. What was that about Occasional Morph-something?"

"Hold on. Is that my ickle bickle boo?"

Hughes watched in amusement as she hunkered down, hands on her knees, and made cooing baby noises toward a bush.

His amusement dimmed somewhat as a large inky-furred panther slinked out of the bush. Its eyes were green, and baleful, and yes, it was definitely a great big wild cat. Not that Cate Jubilee seemed to mind.

"There he is! Oosa gooboy? Oosa woosa gooboy?"

The panther padded closer.

"Cate," Hughes hissed through clenched teeth. "It's escaped its cage."

"Cage?"

"On the count of three we run."

"I wouldn't advise it, oh no no no," she warned in that singsong tone, as if everyone around her were a small nappy-bound baby. "That would just pwesent a moving target, wouldn't it my cutie pie?"

"*Cate.*"

Hughes watched helplessly as the panther stalked over and... nuzzled her.

Cate rubbed the predacious thing as if it were a kitten. "See? Hughes has had a twoublesome morning, hasn't he boo boo? He needs to welax and count his wucky stars he isn't being thwown into a wiver with concwete bwocks on his feetses."

"That's not funny."

She pouted prettily. "Don't be narky."

He realized that talking to Cate Jubilee was like those dreams people often had, the ones where you've got the lead role in a play and there's a full house of expectant audience members, only you don't know the script, and you've miraculously forgotten to wear trousers. He tried for rationality again. "That's a bloody panther."

"Nooo, he's just a widdle kitty, isn't he? Isn't dat wight? Wook at his widdle cheekums and teefums!"

She bunched the panther's silky dark muzzle between her hands and rolled it about affectionately. This exposed the sort of teeth Hughes associated with phrases like "rend" and "tear" and "run away very fast." The panther's chest rumbled irritably, but to Hughes' relief and delight it had not, so far, removed Cate Jubilee's arm at the shoulder.

A parrot landed on his head.

"Get off."

Hughes pushed his Performance.

<table>
<tr><td align="center">Performance Failed
No experience awarded.
Hughes did not stand to gain or lose anything.</td></tr>
</table>

"Awesome." Heedless of Hughes' predicament and failed attempts at animal persuasion, Cate stood up, stretched like a lioness, and sighed happily. "Well, that's this floor. Not all of it, obviously. Goes on in all directions. Hither, thither... whatever the last one is."

"Yon."

"I love an educated man. I love it here. Such a rough yet delicate ecosystem. It's a wonder everything doesn't eat everything else. Always pondered how that works. You know, I've heard there's an iceberg lake. With *penguins*. Can you imagine? Maybe next time you come you'll meet Jolly the groundskeeper. Oh well." She reclaimed Hughes' arm. "Shall we go get that coffee?"

"Tea. And yes, I'd like that. First though, could I trouble you for a tissue?"

"Sure. Runny nose?"

"Not particularly," said Hughes pleasantly. "This parrot has just done a formal welcome all over my shoulder."

***

After cleaning himself up and sharing a hot drink with Cate, Hughes found himself whisked up in Hurricane Jubilee. Cate was relentless. She seemed to have boundless reserves of energy. Her excitement didn't grate though. In fact, Hughes discovered it was pretty contagious.

She showed him a great deal of Redspire that first day: sandbox training areas; shooting galleries lined in crossbows and pincushioned dummies; bare-knuckle brawl rings; yards of genuine freshly mown grass hedged into squares for exercise; hangout spots with mezzanine floors and gushing marble fountains; digital archives with cogwheel computers; an artificial lake with a walled promenade circling it; production floors fizzling with advertising ideas, high-heel clicks, telephone chatter, chimes, laughter, spilled ink, and colorful Post-it notes; and it was around then that everything started to blur together for Hughes.

Eventually Cate took mercy on him and declared she would take him to his room for the night. She got him a dinner pastie full of roast potato with rosemary garnish and beef soaked in a tasty brown sauce. Hughes scarfed it down ravenously, and when it was gone he was suddenly very sleepy indeed. Cate took him to the forty-fourth floor where general quarters were located. By then it was closing in on six o'clock in the evening. They passed pipes juddering as they transported hot water up and down the tower, cables bulged with electrical voltage, still more pipes pumping rain down to a sluice at the base of Redspire.

"Some storm," said Cate. "I can't ever remember one like it."

"Oh, I don't know," said Hughes philosophically. "One time I read about one that raged for a year over a cottage in Hortesia."

"Over a village?"

"No. A single cottage. Localized."

"That's weird. Oh! Oh, I've got that beat."

"Go on." Hughes watched her animated expression. He was exhausted, yet listening to Cate seemed to banish the urge to lie down and sleep.

"Jaenqui-Across-The-River had one that rained sausages."

"No."

"Yes!"

"Missiles of pork just pelting down?"

"Talk about meateorology."

Hughes barked a laugh. "Awful." He grinned. "Really, that was so, so bad."

She wriggled her eyebrows like balletic caterpillars. "Zo bed," she agreed in her best impression of the classic cinema vampire. "Zo, zo bed, Meester Hoos. In fect, you veel hev to vork hart to be goot around zees crezy lady. She hez *serious prooblums.*"

"Stop," he begged, giggling.

"I veesh I could," she said dolefully, leading him by the arm into a hallway with closed doors on the right and a balcony overlooking a little grove of orange, white, and blue blossoms on the left. "I really veesh I could, Meester Hoos. But I em commeetted now. Goink to be really awkvard ven it comes to ze ceremony tonight. You'll get your mejic item, ant meanvile I veel be ettached to ze Jolene by ze neck, sucking ant slurping down ze good stuff. *Blut*, Hoos! I'm talkink about varm fresh *blut*!"

"My sides hurt."

She dipped her chin into her neck so that it looked as though she had no chin. "Just vait until I bite zem."

That did it. Hughes had to disentangle himself to lean on the railing. Eventually the laughter subsided. He wiped away a tear. God, it felt wonderful to laugh like that. When was the last time he had?

Hughes couldn't remember.

Fifteen seconds later, Cate, who was admiring the blossom and had not realized their number had grown from two to three, heard Hughes gasp. She spun on her heel, and just as Hughes had, she saw Tommy Fahrenheit standing right behind them like some immense muscular statue. She made a noise like a rhinoceros with sinus trouble.

"Oh, you stealthy bastard. You scared me." On the face of it she was annoyed, though anyone listening could have told you she wasn't really cross with him. "Tommy Fahrenheit, this is Gormon Hughes."

For a moment Hughes was so starstruck that when Tommy stuck out his hand, he merely stared at it as if admiring its size, hairiness, and its striking resemblance to a bear's paw.

"Hughes?" said Cate.

"Eh? Sorry, sorry."

They shook hands.

"Slim," said Tommy Fahrenheit.

"Sorry?"

"You are exceptionally slim." Tommy's arms lay folded across his barrel chest. Veins marbled those arms, and the muscle within rounded out each curve as if the man were stuffed with balls of iron. You could crack stones on Tommy Fahrenheit's calves. He raised a hand and gave a smooth gesture toward Hughes. "You are Corinthian."

"Yes," said Hughes, puzzled.

"Now Tommy..." Cate began.

"Pitiable creature, to be ridiculed by your genetics so."

"By my what?"

"Your genetics." Tommy Fahrenheit indicated Hughes' forehead, chin, and chest. "Your Corinthian heritage. I have seen men of your culture try to achieve a trace of *splendif* by enriching their diet with red meats and by lifting weights at *le gymnase*. This is also pitiable. They grasp at something they will never achieve."

Hughes looked at him blankly. "I'm terribly sorry," he said. "I caught about one word in three there."

"Tommy is a somatist," explained Cate wearily. "An ethno-somatist, actually."

"What's that?" Hughes had never heard of such a thing.

"He's... got a lot of opinions about bodies. Tommy, I'm showing Hughes around. He's new, and he doesn't need you wagging your ethnography at him."

"He is the new recruit?"

"Yes, so perhaps we might—"

"I'm not *that* thin," muttered Hughes.

"You are irrationally thin," said Tommy Fahrenheit flatly. "If you were to stand sideways, it would be as if you had disappeared. Also, your posture is... how do you say..."

"Stooped?"

"*Merde.*"

"Oh? Is that good?"

"In my *langue*, it means *shit.*"

"Oh."

"Yours is the posture of a sexually incompetent lemming," said Tommy Fahrenheit. "I admire that you have accepted your inferior genetic inheritance, but the small details of your body tell me much that is not so admirable about you, like the fact that you are a media fetishist."

Hughes was stunned into consideration. Was he a media fetishist? He did read a lot of theatre, true, but... "I'm definitely not a media fetishist," he said, yet Tommy seemed quite sure on the subject.

"Plainly you are. The slight squint in the eye, the stance, the lemminglike impotency. Gaze upon me, Corinthian. I am the pinnacle of all that you are not." He stood before them, gigantic and... glistening a bit actually. Hughes wondered if that was sweat or oil rolling in beads down Tommy's forearms. "It is in the physiognomy and body structure. It is ethnographic superiority. It is *splendif.*"

He hadn't known her long, but Hughes could sense how rankled Cate was (really pissed now, not playing) when she said, in a low, soft voice, "Tommy..."

That huge hairy hand of his raised again, this time shushing her. To Hughes' astonishment and pleasure, he watched as gently but firmly, Cate reached up and pushed that hand down.

"Now isn't the time," she told the giant.

The famous pageant fighter looked down at her from the upper slopes of Mount Tommy. Then, he shrugged.

"*Bien.* It was nice to meet you, Monsieur Hughes."

"Me? Oh. Right. Yes, um, you too."

They watched him stride away.

"Sorry about that," said Cate. Her smile amplified the apology. It was an exasperated expression, as though she'd had to apologize for Tommy's odd diversions before today, and expected to again.

"Don't be. What was that word he kept using?"

"*Splendif?*"

"Yeah."

They started back down the hallway of closed doors.

"Haven't a clue, really," said Cate. "It sounds like *splendid* but Tommy is Champleurs, and I always make bad guesses at Champleurs. It's a quirky language."

"Quirky people," said Hughes.

"Nah, mostly they're just like everybody else. Tommy's a special case, a pistachio cake with extra nuts, but you get used to him. Don't let him bother you with that whole too-trim business."

"I could stand to gain a few pounds."

"Don't be silly. You're just a bit... bony is all."

"Ribs like xylophone keys, that's me," agreed Hughes. And for no reason he could think of, he asked, "What did he say about your body?"

"Hm?"

"Tommy Fahrenheit. He said I was slim because of genetic inferiority, and you're from Corinth City like me. I was wondering what he said about your body."

"The topic has never come up," Cate Jubilee replied in a light, cheerful voice, and for the second time that day, Hughes knew instinctively that he was being lied to.

"Here we are—your room."

Hughes took in the single bed with scarlet sheets and pillows, the small cogwheel computer ticking softly on the bedside desk, the en suite bathroom (an image of honest-to-God *hot water* filled him when he saw the shower, and he had to struggle to contain his excitement), a tidy kitchen with a small steel-case refrigerator stocked with cheese, pastries, and freshly squeezed juice kept cold, the rich red curtain. There was a window behind that drawn curtain, and opening it he could make out Ptolema District's skyscrapers at eye-level through the haze of rain and early evening mist. Streetlight made a luminous crescent of yellow gold that crept up the window pane. The size of Redspire tower awed him. Better yet, the window opened on a hinge. He could not be expected to escape via spontaneous flight, but he was no longer a prisoner, that much was clear. All in all the room was smaller than the one Hughes had woken up in that morning, but no less grand. In some ways it was more so—for coziness and grandeur could often go hand in hand, and this room on the forty-fourth floor was just about as snug and cozy as he could dream.

Sheets, for God's sake! Warm, fresh-laundered sheets he could snuggle up in when the moon rose behind those massive thunderheads outside. A wild helpless gratitude rose in him. He turned to Cate, who was leaning in the doorway, and smiled.

"Thank you so much for today, Cate."

"You're welcome but it's not over yet," she said. "Take a shower. Should be clothes in the drawer under the bed. Listen to some music if you like. There's a recording program on that wheeler."

"Wheeler?"

"The computer. I'll be back in an hour. Ant ven I return," she added, "you and I veel be goink to see a vooman about a mejik item. Yes?"

"At your command, my dark meestress."

It was her turn to giggle.

"*Veeeeeery goot* Meester Hoos. I see promisink future for you here."

"In your crystal ball?"

"Who has need of such baubles?" Cate Jubilee touched a finger under her eye and tugged it down, exposing the pinkness under the eyeball. "I've got *The Sight.*"

He laughed and she laughed with him.

It seemed to be what he would do with her, and that possibility was grander than the room, the crazy twist of fate in Wendy Dragontail's office, or anything he could think of. Grander than grand was laughing with Cate Jubilee.

When she was gone he wrote a letter to be delivered to his father assuring him that all was well, took a shower, dressed in fresh clothes, and spent three-quarters-of-an-hour trying to get the cogwheel computer to do anything other than sit there, quietly talking to itself in a language of gyros and electricity, which Hughes spoke about as well as he spoke Champleurs, i.e. not at all.

It occurred to him that he had forgotten to follow up on (what had Cate called it?) the Obscure Morphography? Something like that. Well, no wonder. Ideas, no matter how peculiar and arresting, are simply no match for the appearance of a panther. He resolved to ask Cate about it later and returned to the computer, which ignored him.

Now and then his hand went to his rib bones, fingers walking over them absently as if counting them. Other times he would look out the window, his dark eyes not present in this cozy room at all, but some spot ten million miles away, or however long away yesterday might be. In those moments Doctor John Isherwood would have recognized the symptoms of dissociation for what they meant. But the doctor was not there, and after a little while those dark eyes in that crafty, animated face returned from wherever they'd been, and Hughes would frown and grumble over the computer, and it was all okay, all okay...

ACT FIVE

NAMES

CHAPTER SEVENTEEN

True to her word, Cate returned an hour later. Draped over one arm was Hughes' moth-gnawed coat.

Hughes was genuinely thrilled. "I wondered where that had got to!"

"Salvaged it from Falstaff. I couldn't save the rest of your clothes."

"Save them?" He paused with the coat still rucked around his elbows. "Save them from what?"

"Falstaff, the butler," Cate explained. "He was going to incinerate them."

"But those are my things!"

"Ashes now, I'm afraid." She craned out the window, howled like a wolf at the stormy night, seemingly for no reason other than it delighted her, and came back inside, shaking droplets from her fiery hair and latching the window shut. "Had the devil of a time negotiating for the coat. Come along now. Places to be, Jolenes to bother."

Just as they were heading out the door Hughes remembered something, and a good thing too because later events might have turned out very differently if he'd forgotten.

"I'd like Doctor John to be there," he said.

Cate's brows knit together. "Whatever for?"

"He asked. Said he'd owe me a favor if I let him tag along."

"That's interesting. John Isherwood is a night owl. He gets all his best work done after the sun sets. If he's willing to abandon his lab at this nocturnal hour, he must think you and your magic item are more fascinating than his current projects. No mean feat." She set off down the hall, Hughes hurrying to keep up. "That's terribly interesting."

"What's his line of study?"

"I think his background is physics and microbiology. Now he studies the portals."

Portals.

The word was out, and Hughes watched realization pour over Cate's face like ice water.

"Portal. Excuse me." An unruly strand of hair wavered in front of her eyes. She tucked it over one ear. "Forget I said anything."

"About?"

"Exactly. I said portal. Portal, singular. Right?"

"Erm."

"Wonderful."

Hughes got that off-kilter feeling again, like she had all the scripts and he was being forced to improvise. "This portal being Iphigenia?"

"Correct."

"Doctor John's a Portalologist?"

Startlingly lovely, the corners of Cate's eyes crinkled with amusement. "Not exactly catchy, is it? *Portalologist.* No, that would never do. I prefer Dimensional Sawbones."

"And what about the others?"

Her amusement vanished. "Other what?"

"Other... portals?" said Hughes, who was quite lost in the maze of their conversation.

"I'm sure I don't know what you're talking about."

"But you said..."

"I'll just go get the doctor," she said quickly. "Meet you on the bottom floor!"

In the elevator, Hughes took another swing at A Hard Think.

Portals.

So there was more than one.

Where were they located in the city? Where did they lead?

A more pertinent question, he thought, *is why are they secret?*

Cate had only made her mistake because she was comfortable talking about these portals. That led to one simple deduction: within the confines of Redspire those portals were freely discussed. Everyone knew about them. Simple as.

Hughes recalled his most recent trip to The Hippodrome. Watching Tommy Fahrenheit go to work in the bloody arena, he'd come to understand he envied the surety of the people who were working with the full suite of knowledge. These powerful people knew what was going on, and armed like that they made plans and carried out decisions that affected lots of other people. These other people were ignorant that decisions were being made on their behalf. Hughes resented that. He was poor, hounded by rotten people and circumstance, and whatever street smarts he had were worth nothing compared to the common fare here in Redspire. Alone in the noisy dark of the elevator shaft, he grasped that completely. Here, in this tower, people casually dropped that there were not one but *multiple portals* that linked his ordinary world to other, stranger places. The idea exhilarated and disturbed him.

It...

He searched for the right word; thought about the clasps of metal on the computer in his room.

It *riveted* him.

On the way out of Redspire through its busy reception area, gilded doors, and into the classy streets of Ptolema District, he reached deep into his coat, produced the lilac umbrella he'd taken from the streetbeater from his pocket, and thumped it open. He stood out in the rain for ten minutes, watching those same flood-prevention nanite bugs he'd noticed in Polydoros vacuuming up the moisture and smelling the fragrance clouding vaporously from their humming wings. It smelled like jasmine, a tea Hughes liked very much, and he made a mental note to send his father a note explaining the situation. He doubted Gormon Hughes Senior would believe half of what his son had to tell him.

His son was still getting to grips with it himself, truth be told.

Cate arrived, the good Doctor John in tow. It was time for Hughes to get his magic item.

On the way to The Foundry, where the Jolenes worked, Doctor John Isherwood kept his silence while Cate explained that as well as being Hughes' partner, she was first and foremost his patron. In other words, she would sponsor his future.

"Sponsor how?"

"By ensuring that you *have* a future, Hughes," she replied. "To this end I have a lesson for you: do not offend a Jolene."

"Okay," said Hughes. "How does one offend a Jolene? For purposes of avoidance."

"Insult their work. Ask questions. Comment on the preponderance of women working at The Foundry. Ask questions."

"That's not so bad. After all, I've seen their work in action and it's, well, bloody amazing. And women are great too, especially in preponderance."

"Is that so?"

She was looking at him slyly.

Hughes felt hot blood jump to his ears.

"Um... what I meant was..."

"Drone," cut in Doctor John.

As if summoned by his voice, something swooped out of the downpour. It was a metal hummingbird. It hovered over their group on rapidly batting wings of smooth polished steel. Its head twitched side to side, and Hughes could see that both of its eyes were glass beads lit up from within by a yellow glow.

Doctor John held up a plastic card. The creature scanned it, those yellow glows becoming twin cones of light. The scan completed. The eyes blinked green. Then the bird flew away into the night.

"What was that all about?" asked Hughes.

"Ah-ah-ah. Practice makes permanent," scolded his patron. "We're about to be in the company of Jolenes."

"And I gather they're not overly fond of questions?"

"No," said Cate Jubilee accurately. "They are not."

***

There was a ride at The Rotbloom Carnival of Bright Oddments and Dark Delights. "Ride" might be pushing it because that word implied rollercoasters, rollicking carousels, spinning teacups, high highs and low lows, squeals of wonder and fright, and this particular place did not involve any of those.

Call it an exhibit then.

Call it the house of mirrors.

At six years old Hughes had marveled at the way the mirrors slipped and slid together in a huge glass puzzle, the way walking from mirror to mirror changed his reflection. One step and he was an enormous fat Hughes. Two more and he was small and shriveled as a gnome from fairy tales. Half a step left—tall! Diagonal—taller still, and thin as a matchstick!

Hughes strode through Ptolema District with Cate Jubilee and Doctor John Isherwood, and it was like being a boy again, for all about him was glass streaked with rain. No yellows, blues, and greens as in Polydoros. The glass here was the color of Miss Gleam's eyes. With the clouds thick above them and night injecting the storm with an infusion of black ink, each building looked as if God had snapped his fingers at a freshwater lake, raising it in a column and freezing it so that it loomed darkly over the streets. Rain ran in rivulets. Hughes thought, *When I was six the house of mirrors was dry. Now it's weeping.*

Why would a house do a thing like that?

Absurd and terrible, the answer arrived in his head.

It's weeping in preparation for the funeral.

An image of Falstaff came to him—the butler was in the elevator with Hughes, and he was dabbing at his tears with a handkerchief. The handkerchief was lace.

Hughes walked on. The thump of the rains against his umbrella was hypnotic. Absently his fingers brushed his rib bones as if checking that all of them were still there.

When the trio arrived at The Foundry gates and a Jolene came out to meet them, Hughes should have been a bundle of nerves. Instead he felt a surge of great relief.

"Good evening, Jolene," said Cate. "This is Gormon Hughes, the new recruit."

Hughes almost said, "How do you do?" automatically. Thankfully his brain (well-trained in memorizing the lines of kings and killers and all sorts of roles from plays) was quicker than his lips. "Howwww *What* a pleasure to meet you," he amended, just in time.

"And I'm sure you know Doctor John Isherwood," said Cate, sparing Hughes a look that could corrode tungsten. "We're here about Hughes' magic item."

The Jolene regarded them coldly. She was not particularly tall, but her width more than made up for it. Tommy Fahrenheit's muscle had been toned—this woman's muscle was *dense*. Her face was red with exertion, or perhaps general irritation with life and its components. Overall, she gave the impression of a dropped tomato. A message was stitched into her heavy leather work apron. Hughes read it: *My mother-in-law might not be made of metal impurities, but she's still a slag.*

"You can't come in now," said the Jolene. "Now's not a good time. Tomorrow. Come back tomorrow."

"There's been some trouble?"

"Not *trouble* exactly."

Cate straightened. "Explain why we can't come in."

"It isn't possible."

"We have an appointment."

The Jolene shrugged, not denying the existence of such an appointment but not endorsing it either, like some sort of scheduling agnostic.

Hughes watched his partner try a new tack. Cate Jubilee smiled charmingly at the Jolene. "If I return to Redspire without Hughes' magic item, Wendy

Dragontail will want to know why we were turned away. She will also demand to know *who* turned us away."

"Oh, I'm sure she will at that. But I know who you are, Cate Jubilee, and I'll tell you this: nobody threatens a Jolene."

"Quite the contrary. *Lots* of people threaten Jolenes," Cate said. "They only do it once, of course. It's a dangerous business, making threats. Look, I'm merely stating the facts, Jolene. Wendy Dragontail is scrupulous with timekeeping. Hers, and everyone else's. Next to this man's name," she gestured to Hughes, "she has a note that says, 'Acquire magic item.' I don't know about you, but I have no desire to widdle on what is no doubt a very tightly built calendar."

"Can't say I care much about Miss Dragontail's calendar," said the Jolene. "Now, if you'd kindly shag off back to that nice tower of yours, that would be much appreciated."

"If there's trouble, we can help," offered Cate.

"We've got everything handled, thank you."

"Jolene."

"No."

"Jolene."

"Leave."

"Jolene—*Jolene!*" Cate thrust a finger at Hughes. "I'm begging of you, please outfit this man!"

The Jolene glared at her through the rain and the damp clinging mist.

"You're not going to let this go."

"Probably not," said Cate.

"What a busybody." The Jolene threw up her hands. "Yes, very well. I suppose you'd better come along then. Don't say I didn't try and deter you."

CHAPTER EIGHTEEN

Hughes had never seen an old-fashioned forge, and so he had no idea that The Foundry was shaped like a toppled anvil, its horn kissing the ground, its heel perked up like the bum of someone searching their bottom drawer for clean socks, if that someone were three hundred feet tall and fond of iron underthings.

Even if he had been able to recognize its shape, conditions would have made the act of putting two and two together difficult. It was hard to see much of anything. Cold fronts were breathing up from the eastern farmland slope on the heels of the storm, tendrils of mist curled thick as milk, and the rain poured in an almost solid wall.

Radiating reluctance, the Jolene led them inside and up a set of stairs. The stairs were one of the most quietly astounding things Hughes had ever laid eyes on because on first impressions there were no stairs. Just a big ascending chasm climbing up into the rumbling crackling reaches of The Foundry. Yet as the group put one foot in front of the other, a mechanism clicked and began to hum just loud enough to sound like a secret beehive, and one by one the steps rose up vertically from the floor before falling like cut trees, each slotting in a little higher than the last, and lo and behold, there were stairs. Someone had taken the time to polish every single step. For the second time that day, Hughes was confronted by his reflection.

Mirror man, mirror man, fool me, trick me, if you can.

Where had he heard that? At the Rotbloom Carnival all those years ago?

It had the ring of a nursery rhyme.

The Foundry was lit by anbaric lamps set into the distant walls. Orange light flickered and swam, giving the place the feeling of being encased in a hearth of fire and metal. To the left and right of the self-arranging stair Hughes could see areas pocketed here and there like steel caves, and in these caves were workbenches, creaky furnaces, swooping conveyor belts, assembly lines dangling pods of leather like folded-up and slumbering bats, and he could smell foul tannery smells combined oddly with wonderful comforting aromas of scorching wood and chalky minerals and burning coals.

And now he could hear...

"What a hullabaloo," he said.

"Great word," said Cate approvingly. "Yes, those are some agitated voices I can hear, and... yes, that was a shout. Oh my, quite a few shouts. You can confirm, Doctor John."

"Uh huh," said the doctor.

Cate gave the Jolene a meaningful look. "'Not *trouble* exactly,' indeed."

The Jolene grumbled something colorful and turned toward one of the cavernous workstations, mechanized steps clicking into place beneath her boots.

Crammed in there were all of the Jolenes. Every single one. In part they were different. Some wore vests, some wore shirts with their sleeves rolled up to the elbows, and some wore nothing but their work aprons cinched tight at the waist. Some were frazzle-haired like dandelions, some wore ponytails, and some were shaved bald as billiard balls. Every eye color you could imagine was in abundance, and there was a panoply of scars and burns and interesting injuries gained in the process of making beautiful things.

But, mostly, they were the same.

They were all of them fabulously muscular, and they were sisters in bond if not blood, and they were all named Jolene.

"Well, what I call it is a waste of time," said one Jolene.

"She's not a waste of time," said another. "She is, in fact, our sister."

"She's a pot of trouble often brewed."

"You take that back," chimed a loud voice from near the groaning furnace. "You wouldn't trade places with her for a new set of tongs, and it's impossible to say how you'd act even if you did, so you've got no right saying a thing like that."

"I'll not take it back."

"You will, you daft little besom."

"That's enough of that," said a voice, and even though it was a good deal softer than the others, it seemed to carry power among the Jolenes because they all muttered and simmered and went silent. The owner of the voice stepped forward. She was the eldest Jolene, Hughes could identify. She seemed to have gammy knees because she hobbled a bit, and she wore complicated spectacles with lots of interlocking lenses and frames, tinted icy blue.

"I'll not lie, I'm surprised to see you, Cate," said the elderly woman.

"Hello, Jolene. We've come to help with your situation."

"I told them there was no trouble," said the Jolene who had greeted them hurriedly.

"*Trouble?*" Cate looked shocked. If she had worn pearls, she would have clutched them dramatically. "I never said anything about *trouble*. No, I specifically used the word 'situation.' It seems I was right to do so, given the fact that none of you are working. You also tried to turn away members of the Scarlet Citadel on official business. And unless I'm mistaken, that's... yes, that is in fact stifled sobbing I hear from that storage compartment up there near the tanning line. Someone is crying. In distress. So the word 'situation' seems perfectly adequate, I'm sure you'd agree. I'm sure you will because that *is* crying I hear. I'm not mistaken."

"No. Not mistaken," agreed the elderly Jolene. "You are nosy as an anteater and prickly as a hedgehog convention, Cate Jubilee, but you're also correct. I see you've brought company. Doctor John Isherwood." She gave him a gummy smile. "How *nice* of you to take a break from your flasks and philters to join us tonight. This other one is a stranger to me. Introduce yourself, young man."

Hughes suddenly felt hundreds of eyes come to rest on him.

"Meeee." He ended up drawing out the word ridiculously. It had almost sprung past his lips as a question.

Someone giggled.

With his courage jellifying rapidly, he stammered, "Gormon Hughes, at your service." And he bowed, mostly to hide his face.

"Hmm. I see. Well, either he's a simpleton or he's got lovely manners," said the elderly Jolene. "Perhaps both. You are here for your magic item."

"Yes. No. Um. Yes, we are, but first..."

"Firstly, you'll tell us who is up there," said Cate firmly. "And why they're snuffling so mightily the storm outside might consider it a challenge to its honor."

"A sisterly dispute," said the elderly Jolene soothingly. "No great mystery to be uncovered and solved by the tenacious Cate Jubilee. Why don't you wait down in the foyer, and—"

"Hold on, it must be more than that," pointed out Cate. "Otherwise production wouldn't have stopped, and we'd already be performing the ceremony for Hughes."

The elderly Jolene hesitated. Glances passed among the ranks of athletic women. Hughes sensed Cate had scored a point.

By chance, he happened to catch a bit of curious activity as he scanned the crowd. One of the Jolenes who'd been speaking when they arrived—a young girl of eleven or twelve—crossed her arms and huffed. She was ruddy-cheeked, snub-nosed, and looked about as warm and approachable as a battle-axe.

Hughes wondered why she looked so annoyed.

"All right." The elderly Jolene sighed. "So it's a bit more thorny than I'm making it out to be. The truth is, that material you've sent us for Mr. Hughes' magic item is... it's..."

"Outlandish," supplied a Jolene.

A chorus of options followed this, ranging from "mystifying" to "a real chin-scratcher."

"Weird," said the elderly Jolene stiffly. "We can't make head nor tail of it."

"I'd like to see it," said Doctor John.

"You're free to express that," she replied. "Just as we're free to express our refusal."

"With respect, Jolene, this substance is of enormous interest to myself and the other folks back in Redspire." Doctor John gave her a smile of his own. It was thin lipped and more than a little patronizing. "Cards on the table, once Hughes has it, I'm going to make it my business to study the weapon you forge. I'm going to be thorough."

"You're going to run tests."

"Naturally."

"Naturally," she echoed. "And I'm sure us doing the actual forging is only a courtesy. You've probably worked out your own way of doing that, you and these *other folks in Redspire.*"

John's face fell. "I... No, I didn't mean..."

"Never mind what you meant. I don't know what you're doing here, but I've a fair idea. If it were up to me I'd turn you out arse-over-teakettle and let the rain wash away a bit of that smugness you've brought like luggage into our home. But I see that would upset you, and I think Mr. Hughes would rather I not. Still, I don't want to hear another word from you."

Doctor John opened his mouth. Closed it. He nodded.

The elderly Jolene turned her attention back to Cate. "The Jolene in the storage compartment is what you might call our *last resort.* Not so much a straight thinker as a crooked one, and those of us with sense in our heads believe that's exactly what's required to solve our problem. Only she's a bit sensitive."

Hughes had been watching the ruddy-cheeked battle-axe. On the word "sensitive" she'd bristled, and some of the Jolenes around her had given her sharp looks. Something was going on there, something that fit in with the sounds of choked sobbing coming from the storage compartment.

"That sensitivity led to this situation," said Cate, as if reading his mind.

"Yes," said the elderly Jolene.

"This seems simple enough," Cate said with a shrug. "Leave her alone, that's what I say. Stop crowding her. Surely she'll cool off in no time, and we can get on with this."

"She's *very* sensitive," insisted the elderly Jolene. "I take no pleasure in spurning you, young woman, nor you, Mr. Hughes, for that matter. But spurn you I think I shall. Come back tomorrow. Hopefully this will all be a memory by then."

Cate shook her head, much to the older woman's consternation. "You're overcomplicating matters."

"Tomorrow."

"We aren't going anywhere."

Tensions were rising. Hughes could feel it, as if the furnace squatting malignantly in the corner of the room was being turned up hotter and hotter, an unbearable sizzling energy moving between Cate and this matriarch of the Jolenes.

"I'll talk to her," he said.

They all looked at him, their faces incredulous.

"It can't hurt," he added sheepishly.

"You," said the elderly Jolene, "will only make things worse."

"I'll try not to."

And saying that, Hughes began to clamber up assorted shelves and platforms, shuffling and shimmying and pushing aside tools to get closer to the storage compartment.

"I don't suppose you've met many sensitive people," came the voice of the elderly Jolene behind him.

"Why?" said Hughes before he could stop himself, and froze. There were several intakes of breath. That simmering tension increased, wrapping Hughes in a blanket of dread.

What's one way to offend a Jolene?

Ask questions.

He stayed perfectly still, his eyes squeezed shut, waiting for all hell to break loose.

Instead, he heard a chuckle. It was the Jolene matriarch. Whether she was laughing kindly or cruelly, he could not tell.

"No reason," she said. "Good luck, Mr. Hughes."

***

The storage compartment was as big as his father's teashop—bigger, maybe. Hughes scrambled inside, let the shutter close behind him, and peered uncertainly into the darkness.

He heard his dry throat click as he swallowed. "Hello?"

No reply.

Outside the workstation had fallen silent. Threads of light sewed themselves through cracks in the shutter. Hughes' eyes were adjusting. What exactly the Jolenes stored here, he wasn't sure, although it was bulky and lumbery-looking.

"I'm Hughes," he tried.

Nothing.

Hadn't there been sobbing?

Yes. There had been. Cate had twice remarked about it.

So where was it now, and what precisely were these crouched and hulking things before him like...

Wait.

His throat was a parched flute.

That shape, he thought. *That one right there. Sticking out. That looks like...*

Unease crept up his back with stiff, moldering fingers.

In that moment he could almost have convinced himself that in here with him was the two-headed thing. The one that looked like a wolf, inflated and wormy and pumped full of mustard gas.

A wheeze from his windpipe; he had no spit to swallow.

Yeah. It was waiting for him to say just one more thing. Then it would get to its feet and *lunge*. It would come for him as it had come for Laurana, its jaws dripping freely and its eyes rolled to the whites in mad, savage glee.

Maybe its chest would burst again.

Maybe those long, feminine arms would close around him and slowly, so slowly that he could really savor the experience, they would stuff him into the thing's mouth.

Only the top half of him though.

Hughes' lower portions would belong to head number two.

There was no reasonable explanation for this almost-certainty working him over.

But then, reasonable explanations and the dark don't always get along.

The dark and the mean-spirited aunt of the imagination, on the other hand, are best friends.

They team up and then they *fuck* with you.

Hughes' eyes were darting quickly now, swiveling faster than the twitchy head of the bird-drone that had scanned Doctor John's plastic card, and his heart was going like hummingbird wings too, a frantic pace that broke his back and underarms out in a fierce cold sweat.

That was when he heard it. Only a tiny noise. A snuffle.

"Jolene?" he murmured.

Something detached itself from the shadows.

Fright overcame him. Hughes drew a breath to holler (*CATE PLEASE CATE COME NOW!!!*)

... and stopped.

Lurching toward him was not the slavering beast he'd watched die in Iphigenia, but a woman. A big woman, granted. Big as the werewolves out of spooky plays Hughes had read as a boy, and like a werewolf she had hunched shoulders, only hers bristled with benign tumors rather than fur. Swollen lumps of tissue arched her back. Knots of it made her legs ponderous. The knuckles on her hands gave the illusion of having spread, so pervasive were her deformities. Most of her hair was gone (if it had ever been there) but for a single black scrap that wafted with the silent respiration of the filtration system. Unassuming igorish eyes blinked out of sync at Hughes. One of the eyes was green, the other white and mystical as the moon.

"Hullo," she said. "I'd like to borrow your handkerchief, if you have one."

She showed him a sopping rag.

"Only mine's full."

Keeping the newcomer centered in his vision, Hughes fumbled in the deep pockets of his coat, all the while urging his heart to slow down. Luck was on his side. He handed over a blue handkerchief that one of his father's customers had forgotten in the teashop.

"Here you go," he said, pleased his voice held only the faintest tremor. "It's a bit crusty. Sorry."

"That's all right."

There was a blast that would have caused an avalanche in colder climates. The Jolene wiped her nose. "Much better. You can have it back now."

Hughes regarded the handkerchief, which now looked as though it had been dipped in a pond.

"I think I'm okay, thanks."

The woman nodded glumly and wrapped up the handkerchiefs with neat dainty movements, put them in her pocket, locked her fingers together, and looked at her feet as if expecting to be scolded.

Hughes was momentarily baffled.

"You're Jolene," he said, hoping to establish some semblance of common ground.

Another glum nod.

Well, that was a start. What now?

"Well, Jolene, I'm the one who's supposed to get his magic item tonight. I don't know you, but that lot out there seem to, and they think you're the only one for the job. Oh. Um. Oh, hell, do you want me to see if anyone outside has another hankie?"

She snuffled. "Musn't ask questions."

"Sorry. I'm new, if that's any excuse. I'll just go fetch you a..."

"I'm not an ogre."

Hughes blinked. "I never said you were."

"Not you." The Jolene bunched her sleeve in her fingers and dabbed at her eyes. "Jolene calls me that. She says I'm Ogre Jo, and that I steal babbies from cribs and make them into porridge."

"You're saying you were bullied here by Jolene."

"Not Jolene," said Jolene. "I'm talking about *Jolene*."

"Oh, right."

Hughes mused to himself while she continued to snuffle forlornly. Understanding dawned.

"This Jolene who called you... who called you names," he said. "She's got ruddy cheeks."

"Don't know."

"Ruddy means flushed. Um. Red. Really red." He recalled another identifying detail. "She's got a face like a well-slapped ars... like a not very friendly person."

"That's her." The Jolene's nod was glummer than ever. "I wouldn't ever steal a babby. Not in a million yonks. Babbies are for cuddling, not squashing into porridge. I'm thick as clotted cream and even *I* know that."

"I'd love a bowl of porridge."

"Me too."

They stood together in the darkness, sadly bereft of porridge.

"Look," Hughes began. "You really ought to come out of here. Bullies only respond to one thing, and that's confrontation. They just can't cope when one brave person stands up to them. Works every time." Miss Gleam's needle-fang smile loomed in his mind. "With certain exceptions."

"Stand up to Ruddy Jolene. Right. Easy as that." Her sad whuffles cascaded over him. "Thanks very much."

Hughes felt his chances of gaining a magic item slipping through his fingers. "Don't be like that," he coaxed her. "Come on. I need your help."

"Go away. Leave the big stupid ogre alone. Her head's lumpy as her back. She's lumpy all over. *Malformed.*"

Hughes was not sure he'd ever heard a word spoken with such loathing. It occurred to him that she was quoting, that that word (*malformed*) had been used on her the way Tommy Fahrenheit had used the word (*slim*).

No. It was worse.

Hughes was a little on the waifish side, but that was nothing a dietary shift and some exercise couldn't fix. No amount of surgery or skin grafts could help this woman. Yet instead of being approached with sympathy and kind words, some people (people with ruddy cheeks, for example) were in the habit of choosing alternatives. The words sang like dark hymnals in his head. Ogre. Lumpy. Malformed. Ogre. Lumpy.

"No," said Hughes, the tremor in his voice not rising from fear now, hoh no, no fucking way. Anger shot through him in hot red cables. "You don't deserve to be spoken to that way. You've got to listen to me. In fact, let's start over. I'm Gormon Hughes. You're Jolene, although the others called you *last resort* for a damn reason, and that has nothing to do with what you look like. I reckon they called you that because you've got something they value. I'd be surprised if there wasn't a time when you made something, and all the other Jolenes passed it around and muttered to one another, low and quiet so you couldn't hear what they were saying. Only you could see the look in their eyes, and it was a look that made you happy because it meant they liked what you'd made. Adored it. It was really *special.* And I'll bet that it was after that when Ruddy Jolene started saying all those nasty things to you. Almost as if she'd heard about the special work you'd done, and she wished that appreciation belonged to her instead, only it never will because she's a talentless little cow who wouldn't know milk from a bucket. So she took that sorrow out on you. *Takes* it out on you. How am I doing?"

A few desultory sniffles emerged, but no reply, which led Hughes to believe he was doing pretty well. He went on:

"I'm not sure how you became so skilled, Jolene. Whether you were born with it or not, and that doesn't matter. What matters is that your quality is there to be seen, and I want to do just that. I want to see it. No more handkerchiefs. Come out and show me. *I know you are more than the names they call you.*"

She turned from him, letting the shadows swallow her up again.

Before she vanished Hughes caught a few words.

"Then you're thick as clotted cream too."

And as his anger pivoted toward her, Hughes pushed his Performance.

***

Cate Jubilee didn't much care for standing still. It made her unhappy. Movement on the other hand meant action, and that meant life (or at least an approximate semblance of life), and Cate was a woman who loved the little reminders of being alive as much as you might enjoy your own, like a mouthful of chocolate after supper, or a little siesta nap in the middle of a hot day, or birthday surprises, or your mother telling you she loves you very much. Nonetheless, standing still was exactly what Cate was doing. She, Doctor John, and a whole room packed to bursting with Jolenes.

The storage compartment Hughes had entered five minutes ago had very good acoustics. Little sounds became big ones. Hushed voices going back and forth emerged as loud as tennis ball strikes. The crowd outside stood still as statues, hearing everything.

Much as she disliked impersonating a statue, Cate found herself distracted by Hughes. How he listened. What he said.

Ever since she'd observed the conversation play out in Wendy Dragontail's office from her hiding place in the window (Cate was talented with glass and other reflective surfaces, as Hughes would soon learn), she had been watching Gormon Hughes Junior with a growing worry.

What she'd heard him say to that poor wounded Jolene up there in the storage compartment changed things.

Up until now the young man had seemed... well...

She consigned herself to it.

He'd seemed like a lost puppy.

And no wonder, she thought, *given what he's been through.* She'd read the reports coming in from the retrieval party sent to Iphigenia to recover the remains of Laurana and her unit. She had read them twice because the first time her skin had prickled out in gooseflesh, and she'd had to put the report down and sit for a while, listening to the ceaseless chatter of the rains.

In principle Cate understood why Hughes had been tested.

Wendy Dragontail, Doctor John, the whole of the Scarlet Citadel; after the massacre in Iphigenia, seemingly none of them knew what to make of him.

Cate had tested him herself by dropping the word "portals" into the mix. The test was to see if Hughes would explode with questions (which would have revealed him as an eager, excitable man) or keep silent (which would have revealed him as a reserved man, or a man with knowledge he should not have).

But he hadn't done either of those things.

He'd ummed and ahhed and asked a few gentle, oatmealish questions, and then he'd looked at her helplessly with those big dark eyes of his.

A lost puppy hoping the world would make sense soon, scared it would be lost forever.

Cate's right temple itched. She chanced breaking the stillness and gave it a furtive scratch. A Jolene next to her shot her an irritated look. Cate grinned, and the Jolene shook her head and went back to staring fixedly at the storage compartment. It was quiet in there, a deep quiet edged in strangeness.

Only a few seconds ago, Cate had heard Hughes say something that didn't just change her conception of him, it scrambled it.

I know you are more than the names they call you.

He had made a speech (a pretty arresting one) and then he'd finished it with that, the way a fighter might smash their opponent with one final blow, or the way a skilled barista signed the froth on a coffee with a heart or a snowflake.

I know you are more than the names they call you.

Cate didn't think a lost puppy could talk like that.

She didn't think many people could either.

"Look," said one Jolene to the world at large, and Cate did.

The storage compartment door was swinging open.

A twisted colossus of a woman appeared. She looked out at the assembled crowd through a film of tears. Cate recognized her at once. *That's Ogre Jo,* she thought and immediately felt ashamed she had. Up above the assembled masses the Jolene took a deep breath and let it go. Cate thought she looked ready to burst into blubbering ruins, but she didn't. In the firefly-orange glow rising from the room's furnace, the Jolene raised her bulbous head and smiled.

Things happened fast then. Someone in the crowd whooped like a goal had been scored in football, laughter and applause caught like fire in the kindling of good cheer, and now feet were stamping, lips whistling like wild panpipes, and the Jolene came down into a sea of delighted faces and warm embraces, and Cate had the feeling something sisterly and motherly and something else was going on, something wonderful and intimate.

And here came Hughes himself into the happy bedlam.

"You're a one," said Cate Jubilee.

"Sorry?" said Hughes. Jolenes jostled them. "I can't really hear you over"— he gestured vaguely at the hurly-burly surrounding them—"all this."

Cate leaned in, speaking louder. "That was amazing!"

"What was?"

"You!"

"Me?" His brows climbed. They climbed pretty cutely. Not that she took special notice, of course. It was merely an... an observation. *Those are his eyebrows. Just two caterpillars of facial hair. They're going up as his eyes widen in surprise. Perfectly normal. Only slightly adorable,* she concluded. *A smidge at most.*

"It was nothing," Hughes said.

"Hey," said Cate Jubilee giddily. "You, my intrepid partner, are getting *a magic item* tonight."

She expected a big beaming grin. Certainly her comment warranted one. Instead Hughes nodded absently, as if she'd just told him he was going to receive a jam jar rather than the single most important thing he would ever own. If he was smiling, it was a distracted one that never touched those dark eyes of his.

Now she was thinking about his eyes again.

Good grief.

Cate watched as the elderly Jolene pulled Hughes aside to thank him. At least *she* wore a big beaming grin.

A Jolene with ruddy-red cheeks pushed through the crowd. She shouldered Cate Jubilee, hard. "Watch it, bitch," she said.

Cate could only recoil at the sudden sharpness of that. Where had it come from?

"Don't mind her," said a Jolene as the ruddy-cheeked girl vanished into the milling crowd. "That Jolene's popcorn."

"Popcorn?"

The Jolene nodded. One ear was a clot of scar tissue, and she had a tangle of nut-brown curls.

Cate frowned. "I don't understand. Why is she popcorn?"

She saw the Jolene's mouth quirk at the corners. "Simple, salty, and gets stuck in your teeth."

Cate was so tickled by this she threw back her head and laughed like her namesake.

CHAPTER NINETEEN

The Sequins Messenger Club was a strange institution, strange because in a world of telephones and gyroscopic fax machines and even the rare letter, there was still space for a company willing to deliver messages by word of mouth. As their name suggested, they ferried communications between people. As their name also suggested, they wore sequins. Blue sequined tops and blue sequined skirts and shoes practically bathed in bright and boisterous blue sequins. The skeletons of their bicycles were boned in sequins. On wet nights like this one, Sunday June the 11th, they wore raincoats with sequins on the shoulders like blue blossoms speckled with morning dew.

At nine o'clock in the evening, three hours before she and her partner, Mr. Glint, would meet the man she would come to think of as the Archer, Miss Gleam was strolling the Leonidas District bazaar. Her mind was occupied with building a lesson plan for Mr. Glint. The poor dear was having real trouble with conceptualization. He simply couldn't grasp what she was telling him. What she needed was the appropriate metaphor.

Rain muttered on the awnings hauled over the booths and little impermanent shops.

High overhead the thunder gave answer.

Miss Gleam made a little appreciative noise in her mouth. "Mm." It was wonderful background noise, in her opinion.

Although... ridiculous, really... but if she listened to the rains, they did take on a certain ominous quality, like millions of silver taps dripping, dripping...

She shook her head, dispelling the thought.

Let's see. If Mr. Glint doesn't care for explanatory diagrams, maybe I could use hypnopedia, described as the act of learning while under the effects of sleep or hypnosis.

Bemused, she could almost hear his response to the suggestion already.

"What?" he'd say. "Like swinging necklaces and ladies in bangles called something like Madame Fortuna the Omniwossit cooing over crystal balls and going 'ommm' and all that? Sounds dodgy."

One awning—sagged with water—trickled a few heavy drops down her neck, and she winced.

She gave the awning a look of contempt and walked on, avoiding the drips where she could.

Drip-drip went the canvas coverings. *Plip-plip. Trickle-drip.*

She could use somatic learning, learning through motion. Now that was interesting. She pictured Mr. Glint growing to understand conceptualization through dance, for example: waltz, tango, tap...

"I'm sure we turned them off," she said and started at the sound of her own voice.

There were added benefits to lesson planning. Fixating on her syllabus helped her to not think about Willard Coosler, the man who had met, seduced, and then drowned Miss Shimmer in her bathtub (*drip, drip*) the night before.

Miss Gleam didn't want to think about him, or his secretive employers, or his little half-riddle: Meet the assassin's contact "where the bulls run."

She didn't want to think about that purple bloated thing in the bath either. Miss Shimmer. Her flesh pruned and oddly mushy, and the taps, had they dripped?

For the life of her Miss Gleam could not remember.

It was bothering her.

Nearby, a pie seller waved her over to his stall, realized who he was waving at, and promptly did an impression of a snail retreating into its shell.

Never one to pass up an invitation, Miss Gleam sidled up to admire his wares. She inhaled the smell of flaky crust and caramelized pastry, and fillings of apple, plum, and peach, enjoying how much they reminded her of her girlhood when she had first ladled her mouth full of pumpkin pie on All Hallows Eve and when she had flayed the boy who had bought her the slice. Just to see what it was like, you see. The memory brought a smile of great relief to her lips, a smile that made the pie seller cringe even further behind the frame of his stall.

"'Scuse me," said a voice behind her. "You wouldn't be Miss Gleam, would you?"

She turned and saw a young man on a bicycle. He looked about fifteen, and he wore a sulky expression. Both boy and bicycle were awash in blue sequins.

"I am she," agreed Miss Gleam.

The boy gave her a suspicious look. "You got identification?"

Oh, someone's new. "Alas, I find myself bereft of passport, driver's license, or other form of registration. I'm afraid you will just have to take my word that I am she who you have been sent like a knight errant to find. Look no further, sir. Lady Gleam, at your service." She curtsied like a poisonous toad bobbing in a mudslick and tried to look nice. Generally she and her Mr. Glint treated messengers with respect. *Don't punish the postman,* went the old saying.

The sulky boy was unmoved. "Got to have identification, Miss. That's the way it works, Miss."

"Exceptions prove rules," she pointed out.

"No, they don't. Rules prove rules, begging your pardon, Miss."

Of course, *generally* did not mean *always.*

The boy had a cluster of spots on his nose, whiteheads packed with pus. Miss Gleam thought about digging her needle-sharp teeth into those pimples, feeling the gush of blood and warm yellow stuff flow over each gum and all the while watching the boy. Just to see what he would do, you see.

Then that old line about punishing the postman asserted itself, and she decided to be magnanimous and diplomatic.

"Would you like a pie?" she said sweetly.

"Can't eat on the job, Miss. So to be clear you haven't got any proof that you are who you say you are? If not, I'll have to go back and fill out a nondelivery form." Between his blue-sequined shoulders the boy looked more sullen than ever.

"No need for forms, no need for forms." She craned up on her tiptoes. "Yoo-hoo! I say, come here, noble fellow!"

"Who are you talking to?" said the messenger boy.

And a voice like stone coffins cracking together said, "Me."

"How fortunate," said Miss Gleam in a voice like funeral silk as the boy turned to stare at the terrible picture that was Mr. Glint. "Young sir knight, this is my partner. Right now however, you may think of him as my *identification.*"

When the boy was gone (peddling so fast that sequins flew in a confetti from the bike wheels), Miss Gleam reached into her suit pocket. The scissors were there, her old reliable snippers, the blades tucked together cool and smooth.

She hadn't expected to hear from the person who made them tonight.

But then, the universe was like a Tinfrost stocking stuffed with mousetraps instead of presents—full of surprises.

"You remember who made your special ring, oh gallant chum?"

Mr. Glint was scrutinizing the serried rows of pies.

"Yeah. Little dish of strawberry sorbet, she was," he replied. The ring on his finger was as black as the velvet summer dark above the bazaar awnings.

"Indeed. Any guesses as to why she'd like to speak with us?"

Mr. Glint reached into the stall and lifted the pie seller from his hiding spot under the counter.

"You got ankle?" he asked the cowering figure.

"Yes," squeaked the pie seller. "That row there. That's all apple."

"I didn't say apple," said Mr. Glint. "I said ankle."

"Ankle pie?"

"I like ankles."

The pie seller's mouth worked for a moment. Then he said, "We do not stock that particular delicacy."

"We, who?"

"Me. I don't stock it."

"Got any ligament dishes?"

"N-No." The pie seller was beginning to go milk white with fear. "Please don't be upset. I have a family, and..."

"Fair enough," said Mr. Glint. "Two peaches and cream, gov."

The pie seller fainted.

A minute later the two bosom companions were at the fringes of the bazaar, headed uphill toward the meeting spot. They ate their pies. The sky was a meal, feasted on by the storm. Forked tines of lightning stabbed at the dinner plate of bunched black clouds. Even the thunder sounded famished.

Below, in poverty-stricken Leonidas, floodfighters slogged in their galoshes through knee-deep water, calling signals to one another and slinging pumps over their shoulders like the bodies of stunned serpents.

The pair left the chaos behind. Soon it was quiet but for the predictable noises of the rainy city night.

"You never answered my question, Mr. Glint."

"Which one?"

Gleam flicked a crumb off her suit collar. "I asked if you had any guesses as to why the one who made our magic items wants to see us."

"Right."

"And?"

Her partner turned it over. The rain had transformed his face into a gaunt and weeping skull. "Haven't a bettie blue, Miss Gleam."

Bettie blue meaning *Clue*. Goodness. How splendid her companion was!

She considered herself lucky to have found him.

Or maybe he'd found her. Sometimes memory was a gray area for her, and Gleam hated gray areas with an intense passion.

"No matter, valiant comrade. In due course all labyrinths resolve themselves. No maze like the mystery, eh? No matter. We shall find out presently." She glanced at him. "You know, I'm very fond of you, Mr. Glint."

He nodded.

"And you're enthusiastic about me too?"

Another nod.

They walked in silence, one as sour as grave soil, the other as sweet as arsenic.

We found each other, she thought. *That's the truth, bold and black and beautiful.*

***

It took almost a quarter of an hour to clear the majority of the Jolenes out of the workstation. They wanted to see what their sister would make of Hughes' weapon material, how she'd solve its puzzle (if indeed she could), and what shape it might become. In fact they made such a palaver and ballyhoo over it that the Elder Jolene was forced into cursing and corralling them. "Out you stubborn gawkers! Out I say, or I'll clout you in the nose and no mistake!" Grumbling and sending her the filthiest looks, they had skulked off about their business, though not before many of them had shared a final word with Hughes, to whom they were very grateful for his wizardry in coaxing their sister out of the storage compartment.

"I've never been complimented by that many people," he told Cate secretly.

She grinned at him. "Would you call it a preponderance?"

"I'm never going to hear the end of that preponderance line, am I?"

"Heavens no."

"Mm, lucky me."

It was the last bit of earnest conversation they would have that night. Now and then Cate would try to engage him, but Hughes was too absorbed in his own thoughts to be much company. Eventually she took the hint and kept a respectful distance.

Jo (Hughes edited out the "ogre" part of her nickname automatically) stood with her back to the furnace with its eternally smoldering coals so that her enormous body was limned in red light. On the workbench in front of her was the heart of the monster that had killed Laurana and her unit, the same heart that had been offered to Hughes by long, feminine, chest-bursting arms and placed on his Krys knife. Jo had the heart fixed between a pair of calipers. She turned it back and forth, poked and prodded at it, made tiny incisions to look at the intracardiac chambers, and generally seemed to be as perplexed as the other Jolenes had been by it. In one corner of the room sat Doctor John Isherwood, holding quite still with a notebook and pencil at the ready. Cate Jubilee fell asleep. She snored softly.

Hughes couldn't have slept if he tried.

He was thinking about the storage compartment. Alone with Jo he had pushed his Performance and something entirely unexpected had happened. It had worked, sure, but the success itself was nothing to write home about.

The result however, the *feeling*! That had been extraordinary!

Performance Success
Level Up! ***8 → 9*** Congratulations!
The target of your Performance, Jo, was changed by what you said, Hughes. **Experience Boost!**

Chance of Success: 33%	Next Level: +3% to Chance of Success Level 10 Secret Ability: ???

Performance Success
Level Up! ***9 → 10*** Congratulations!
Secret Ability Unlocked: **CHIMERA** Your Performances have the ability to take root in your target's subconscious mind. This can cause profound psychological change, including behavioral adjustment, the development of complexes, or madness.

Chance of Success: 36%	Next Level: +1% to Chance of Success **Level 25 Secret Ability: ???**

Hughes was thunderstruck. Experience boost? Two level-ups in a row? And his new secret power:

CHIMERA.

He had never heard the word before. It had simply arrived in his head along with the swell of emotion that had accompanied leveling up. There was something slightly creepy about it, he thought, and then again something absolutely electrifying.

Not to mention the results of its use.

Behavioral adjustment, the development of complexes, or...

Leaning back in his chair Hughes smiled a grim, private smile.

Yeah. Because you can trigger insanity in other people with nothing but a few words. Magic or no, the human mind doesn't work that way.

Right?

The idea seemed ridiculous to him. Only...

The furnace gave a sputtering cough as it filled its guts with fresh coals. Flame flickered, a dull red luminance like the dreams of dragons. Black smoke belched from the flue. Air filtration sucked it away. The workstation was toasty-warm. No wonder Cate was off in the Land of Nod.

Hughes glanced sidelong at her, then back at the monstrous heart on the workbench. He seemed attentive. But really his mind was off adventuring in the Land of My Life Stopped Making Sense Three Days Ago, Someone Send Help, Chocolates, And Possibly A Cup Of Ginseng And Ginger Tea While You're At It.

Behavioral adjustment, the development of complexes, or madness.
What if...
(CHIMERA)
What if it does work...
(CHIMERA)
The ragged smile twitched on his lips.
Well, if it did work, then with a few words I could drive somebody crazy. I mean completely busted cuckoo clock, round-the-bend craz—
He almost leaped out of his skin when Jo cried, "Ohhh, I see! You poor thing."

Cate grunted. Her lashes fluttered just as Doctor John's fingers stiffened on his pencil. "What?" he demanded. "See what?"

Jo took no notice. She hunted in the cabinets under her workbench. Hughes could hear tinkling sounds. He looked at Cate in case she had some insight as to what was going on. Her eyes were shut.

"Cate?"

She snored like a miniature elephant with a cold. Asleep again.

A *plink* drew his ear.

Jo was arranging little vials on the bench, tall thin ones and stocky round ones, glass skulls, glass pigeons, vials with dragon wings of engraved glass curled up tight around them, and each of them full of what Hughes initially believed to be potions that a hedge witch might use in a children's story, for they were colorful and bubbling concoctions prone to steaming like angry kettles.

"Cate?" said Hughes.

Jo turned a crank on the wall. The furnace grate ground open. She tossed in a vial. Hughes felt his teeth clack together at the shatter it made. But that was nothing. What really got to him was the flames dancing over the fresh coals. They were turning green.

"Umm. Cate?"

"That's a good start," Jo said. "What if I..." Three more vials went in, and with each crunch of cracking glass the fire turned a brighter shade of green.

Hughes glanced at Doctor John. The man was scribbling furiously.

"Cate," said Hughes, who was all for fire changing color in principle, so long as it wasn't happening within detonation range. "I really think it might be a good idea if we—"

Another vial smashed. The flames went yellow.

"Gone too far now." Jo leaped twenty feet into the air without apparent effort, gripped onto a smooth steel handle affixed to the ceiling, and yanked, hard. A shelf slid out of the room's south wall. On it bottles of sparkling dust were stacked neatly together. The Jolene dropped to the floor, selected one bottle from among hundreds, and lobbed that into the yawning mouth of the furnace.

There was a puff, as of trapped wind escaping.

Now the flames were a vivid pink.

"Bugger," said Jo. "That's way off, that is."

Doctor John flipped a page, almost tearing it in his eagerness to note down what he was witnessing.

"What's going on?" said Cate.

Hughes almost fell out of his chair.

Jo unstoppered a diamond-shaped vial and sniffed its contents. She must have heard Cate because she smiled, one of the tumors under her cheek rising into a sort of dimple as she did so. "It doesn't know what it is," she told them.

"Ask her what she's talking about," said Doctor John.

"Why don't you ask her yourself?" said Cate. "She can hear you, you know."

To his credit, John Isherwood had the grace to look abashed. "Can you explain what you mean by that, Jolene?"

"Mustn't ask questions."

A muscle spasmed at the corner of John's mouth. "Okay. You just said, 'It doesn't know what it is,' and I want to know what you mean."

"Easy peasy. When you lot from the Scarlet Citadel bring the wobbly bits from dead monsters, it's up to a Jolene to take those bits and change them. That's craft. That's *forging*. We're good at it," said the Jolene proudly. "We've got secrets."

Doctor John offered no opinion on this, but Hughes was as diligent at spotting nonverbal cues as the Jolenes were at manufacturing. At the mention of secrets, John Isherwood's Adam's apple had bobbed, once, in his throat. That swallow formed a slightly clearer picture of the man in Hughes' mind. For the first time, Hughes wondered if he hadn't made a mistake insisting that the good doctor accompany them tonight. For the first time he wondered if the title he had instinctually assigned John (the good doctor) was accurate or if it wasn't.

Jo spoke again, drawing Hughes back to the workstation where pink fire threw shadows of dark rose everywhere.

"Mostly the forging's simple," Jo said. "Clang, bang, here's your magic item. But sometimes it's tricky. I like those times." Quick as a flash Jo tossed the diamond-shaped vial into the fire. Skirts of flame began to spin slow at first and now faster until all at once they whirled together and roared in their bed of coals. The flames snaked up the throat of the furnace and lapped through the open grate in long licking tongues—pink no longer, instead a terrific shade of green.

The Jolene grinned, wide and waxy. In the cataclysmic light with her single streak of hair plastered to her face with sweat, she really did look like a werewolf.

"Tricky-wicky-dicky times. *Yes. Those* are the times when I get to have fun!" she boomed and closed a huge hand around the heart.

"The fire," breathed Cate.

"I know. I've seen that green before," said Hughes. "In The Hippodrome."

"Will someone explain what the hell is going on here?" snapped Doctor John.

"It's the Iphigenian light," Hughes said, totally unaware of how awestruck he sounded. "The one that sticks around after the monsters from that world die. The one that shines from their remains." After a pause he added, "It's beautiful."

Those last two words seemed to touch Jo. The way she gazed at Hughes then, he could have been her brother. "That's right. Beautiful. But sad too. This heart," she hefted it, showing Hughes and Cate and Doctor John its strange valves and chambers, "doesn't know it comes from Iphigenia. It thinks it comes from somewhere else."

"What does that mean?" said John.

"Mustn't ask—"

"Questions, yeah." John's glasses were steamed. He took them off and began to polish them. "Yeah, I remember." He put them on; they steamed instantly. The room was stiflingly hot. They were all sweating avidly now, the doctor worst of all. He took off his spectacles, scowled at them. "God, I can't believe I've got to explain..." He glanced up at the blurry shape of Jo and back down, and when his words came they had the tired, patient quality of an overworked lecturer on bad overtime. "Look, things don't think. They're inanimate. You understand that as much as I do, Jolene. Surely you do. Consciousness as we understand it is limited to living organisms. I mean"—he chuckled without humor—"you might as well ask whether or not your workbench minds all that crap on it. Not that Jolenes ask anything. The spirit of inquiry is something that happens to other people, as far as they're concerned. Try talking sense, now, or I'll start advocating for the rights of the workbench, who surely does mind."

Much as it must have irritated the good doctor, Jo's grin bloomed into a laugh, the first Hughes or Cate had heard from the woman cruelly nicknamed Ogre Jo. Hughes thought it a very sweet laugh, at that.

She rapped her knuckles on the workbench. "Course it don't mind. It knows what it is. So does the furnace. Matter of fact so do the coals—they *really* know. Metal, wood, leather, stone. They've got as much going on as most people. Maybe a bit *more* than people. But all simple things know what they are, so they don't complain or worry or nothing. They've got *forms* and nothing *mal* about them, for they were made to fit into exactly the right shape, true as true. I'm as thick as clotted cream and *I* know that."

I know something too, Hughes thought, bemused in spite of his misgivings about this whole scene. *I know John Isherwood is seething right now. He's being given the workaround by a woman he believes his intellectual inferior, and good for you, Jo. College education zero, clotted cream one.*

"This heart... is like a person. It's all tumble-jumbled up. Lost. Lumpy like me. It doesn't know what it is," Jo insisted firmly, cutting John Isherwood off as he opened his mouth for another interjection. Her fingers flexed on the heart. The gesture struck Hughes as weirdly tender, almost intimate. "Poor old thing," she murmured. "I will tell you what you are."

Then she raised the heart high above her crooked head and threw it into the flames, which swallowed it with greedy green delight.

CHAPTER TWENTY

Over the months to come the Jolenes would search for their sister, Ruddy Jolene, who went missing that very Sunday in June. They would search high and low, turning over every square inch of The Foundry as they fretted and reassured one another that she was a resourceful young woman and would probably turn up any day now. A Jolene had never left them without saying goodbye before or without a party to mark the occasion. Ruddy Jolene was a rude little besom, but the idea of her going off in such a fashion was unthinkable.

Yes, any day now she'd come back or so they told themselves.

Delusions like that could be comforting, couldn't they?

Two shadows arrived at the dingy bar. The bar had no name, and it was almost impossible to find unless someone who had been there before was willing to guide you. Such places were useful, especially to Miss Gleam and Mr. Glint.

"You're late," Ruddy Jolene told them.

"Our sincerest apologies," said Miss Gleam.

"I *told* you it was urgent. I said so. Didn't I say so?"

"You did. Alas, my associate was feeling peckish. Do express your sorrow at our regrettable tardiness, Mr. Glint."

Mr. Glint wiped something unspeakable from his lips. It was definitely not peaches and cream pie. "Sorry," he said.

Ruddy Jolene huffed. This was not an uncommon occurrence.

She was one of nature's huffers.

They joined her in the dingy bar's only booth.

"What can we do for you, Jolene?"

"I need you to scare someone."

"Scare someone?" There was a hole in the booth partition. A single louse scurried in circles round the hole. Miss Gleam chased it with a shiny fingernail. "Who?"

"Ogre Jo."

"Never heard of her."

"She's a Jolene. She's big and bloated and bulgy, and I want her scared so badly she can never do anything again. Except cry," said Ruddy Jolene, her eyes bright with malice. "She's even uglier when she cries."

"So we frighten this person," said Miss Gleam. "And then what?"

Ruddy Jolene rolled her eyes. "I don't know. Menace her. Make her blubber. You're the professionals."

"No."

For a moment Ruddy Jolene simply sat there. The shock boiled from her face, replaced by outrage. Two button-shaped spots of red appeared on her cheeks (which were plenty red to begin with). "*No*? What do you mean, *no*?"

"We won't do it."

"I *want* you to. And you owe me." She sat up straighter, a red-breasted robin taking charge of the situation. "I designed your magic items. I could have them taken away."

Miss Gleam's finger followed the louse. "Could you really?"

"Of course I could! I'm a Jolene! We are powerful, and praiseworthy, and... and..."

"Prudent?"

"Yes, well, of course we are that too," said Ruddy Jolene, who didn't know that word but wouldn't be caught dead admitting so. Overall, this was not going as planned. She had done them a favor. They were supposed to return it. That was how things worked.

"You are a prudent girl." Miss Gleam teased the tip of her nail over the louse's feelers. They quivered. The bug fled. Her finger gave jolly chase once more. "So prudent that you sent for the finest cutthroats in this fair city..."

"Yes!"

"... who are, immodestly, the best in the whole wide world at hurting people..."

"*Yes!*"

"... you sent for us... to play the part... of schoolyard thugs?"

In the muggy yellow light of the booth lamp, the tiniest flicker of uncertainty crossed Ruddy Jolene's face, but just as quickly it was gone. "You can sneak into The Foundry into Ogre Jo's workstation. There's some secret entrances every Jolene knows about. I can show you."

"I think not." Miss Gleam retracted her finger, leaving the louse to scurry on its way. She stood up and fixed the girl with her rancid milk smile. "After we leave, feel free to approach the bar and enjoy a drink of your choosing, Jolene."

"Leave?" Ruddy Jolene parroted dumbly. "Drink?"

"Our treat. Let it never be said that we are bad friends by imprudent people. Mr. Glint?"

Mr. Glint rose like a waxwork imbued with a dark echo of life. His bald pate shone in the lamplight.

Ruddy Jolene's composure snapped. "You ungrateful shits," she said.

"After you, Mr. Glint."

"You're a toff, Miss Gleam."

"You shits, you shits, you dirty scabby SHITS!"

Miss Gleam unfolded her winter hat, which had a large brim and would suffice to ward off the autumn rains. She tipped the hat at the exploding girl. "Have a charmed evening."

"But you don't *understand*." She meant it to emerge as a command. Instead it warbled up her throat in a pleading whine. Ruddy Jolene hated that. "She's going to forge it for him. I tried. When no one else could figure it out, I thought, 'this is my chance!' My turn!" Here came the tears. She no longer cared. Let them spill, let it all spill forth right now in this stupid bar, into the ears of these stupid, sparkle-skinned shits. "No such luck. I didn't make any headway at all. And everyone was so understanding. Never mind, dear. We're all stumped. Don't be hard on yourself. Bitches."

"Don't call us," said Miss Gleam cheerfully. "We'll call you."

"Daft musty bitches. Nobody expects better of me. But Ogre Jo, those bitches agreed. She'll get it sorted. So I got her good. Called her a lumpy-arse, mushroomhead, called her cancer, leper, loser, which she *is*. I said she squashes babies into porridge just like in fairy tales, only real, and she would if she could. She isn't allowed around the babies, the little Jolenes, in case she squishes their heads with her fat clumsy hands. I got her good. And then..." Her face felt hot as a poker. Her nose was running, eyes streaming. She huffed, a huge petulant huff that she wished would blow away the booth, the bar, the shits, and everything else in one solid gust. "And then that idiot showed up, Hugh-something, and ruined *everything*."

Miss Gleam, who had stopped listening and was holding open the door for Mr. Glint, froze. Slowly, ever so slowly, she shut it.

She came back to the booth, looking for all intents and purposes as casual as a lynx in a quiet wood, sat back down opposite the girl, and said, "Did you say *Hughes*?"

"He talked her out of the storage compartment," said Ruddy Jolene. "I don't know how, but—"

"And when you said, 'Forge it for him,' you meant Ogre Jo is going to forge a magic item for Hughes."

"Crooked thinking, Jolene says." Ruddy Jolene swiped a thumb across her cheek. "Ogre Jo is crooked. Slanty, slumpy, sloped, well I'll show her. Even if you don't help me you ungrateful shits."

Miss Gleam looked at Mr. Glint, who was standing so that he blocked off the booth from any who might glance this way. He needn't have. Except for the barwoman who had no tongue (and who wouldn't have wagged it if she did) there was nobody around. The bar was a blip on the radar of so few, and the storm had kept even the booziest of criminals at home.

Now and then they could hear the *chug* and *rattle* of the metrotram. Other than that, silence. And the rains, of course.

The girl who wanted Ogre Jo to break down blubbering seemed to be doing a good job of displaying misery herself. Her words resounded in Gleam's mind.

Then that idiot Hughes showed up and ruined everything. Hughes, who they had cornered on Agorippis Street not three days ago, and who had spoken about fair compensation, joining the Scarlet Citadel, and other things that should have been impossible, but through his confident voice and shaggy-haired glare seemed somehow plausible, even guaranteed.

Suddenly Gleam was glad they had answered Ruddy Jolene's summons. Very, very glad indeed. She reached over and took the girl's hand.

"A prudent girl might focus herself elsewhere," said Miss Gleam. "A prudent girl might forget all about Ogre Jo and that magic item she's going to make."

"Why should I?" Tears trickled down her chin. A string of snot drew out of one nostril and made a bracelet on one wrist. Despite her despair, Ruddy Jolene's features were crimped in a snarl. She shook Gleam's hand away as if it were full of lice. "Once you go, I'll have no choice."

"But to do what?"

"To beat her, you dumb glittery bimbo. To make that fungusface sorry she was ever born, or hatched, or whatever the fuck she was."

On the word "bimbo" Mr. Glint made to move, but Gleam's raised finger stopped him at the last moment. His mouth was terribly sour. But there was no change there, and if Ruddy Jolene noticed the exchange, she gave no sign of it.

"You wouldn't spoil her work with the magic item," said Miss Gleam in gentle, reasonable tones, the kind a mother might use to a willful child. "After all the item belongs to this Hughes fellow, not Ogre Jo. That wouldn't be fair."

"It's *hers*." The girl's weepy eyes narrowed. "Just like your magic items are *mine*. Will be mine. You'll give them back, but first I'm going to spoil anything she does, anything Ogre Jo does. And yes, you've read my mind, as it happens. I'm going to start with this Hughes guy. His magic item is going to wind up broken. Defective. Let's see how long they all worship Ogre Jo then."

"Even though that isn't fair?"

"Ten years coming second to a deformed ape," said Ruddy Jolene. She pinched one nostril shut and blew hard, sending a gobbet of bloody mucus to quiver like jelly on the stained tabletop. "Longer than that wondering why they didn't just let her die in the fucking crib. My whole life made small by a swollen, smelly monster the others have trained to act like a person. Well, *I'm* a person. I'm a person, and I want—" She cut off abruptly. After a moment of trembling lips and clenching jawbone, the look she leveled at Gleam was pure nasty bile. "Don't you talk to me about what's fair. I don't want to hear it."

Miss Gleam weighed up that bile. It seemed the genuine article.

She sighed.

"Nothing for it, then." Her probing fingernail found the louse and skewered it. "Sorbet's up, Mr. Glint."

The table joggled violently on its stand as Mr. Glint lunged across it. The girl had time to suck in air for a lungful of scream, and then there was something worse than resentment, worse than years of jealousy and hate and huffing.

There was Mr. Glint and his teeth.

Nearby, if you listened, you could hear the metrotram trundling out there in the damp darkness on its overstreet tracks. The night moved on rails of its own, an important evening in which each hour was a carriage, and each carriage packed with minutes for passengers, and all those minutes awake and fluttering with the second-to-second excitement in the lives of likely villains and unlikely heroes far and wide across the soundly sleeping city. Next station: Unclear. Who cared? It was all moving.

Miss Gleam went to the bar and ordered a carpet-nuzzler mojito with extra lime. Behind her thumps and bumps came from the booth, and here, on cue, the pooling blood like melted strawberry sorbet.

And that was what happened to Ruddy Jolene.

***

John Isherwood did not respond in a calm and civilized manner when Jo hurled the heart into the furnace. He acted like a man who was seeing something outrageous and unimaginably cruel unfold, like a child being swept into the path of danger, or an original manuscript being doused in kerosene and set ablaze.

In some ways both metaphors were apt—Hughes had correctly identified something in John Isherwood. Two things, really. A severe dislike for being undermined and an equally powerful desire to take that bolt-cutter brain of his to the padlocked secrets of this world. And other worlds too.

Through partially steamed spectacles the good doctor watched in abject horror as green flames chewed through the nest of muscle surrounding the most intriguing mystery of his life. And by God, was the look of triumph on the Jolene's face *undermining*.

Standing there with that ridiculous grin plastered to her lips, she looked like some half-witted bear who believed she had just won all the honey without realizing she had also disturbed the beehive.

He stared uncomprehendingly at her for a moment, and that was when he smelled the heart. It was cooking. *Charring*.

His fury was so great that his body moved without any thought at all. A red curtain of rage had fallen. He lurched to his feet, notepad and pencil slipping from his fingers as if greased. He bull-rushed the furnace, groaning and thrashing as Jolenes swarmed into the workstation and got ahold of him.

Meanwhile tongues of fire whelmed up from the burning tonsils of the coals. They licked the heart. Tasted it. Devoured it.

Jo seemed oblivious to his pain. The fire ate and she went on grinning.

"What have you done?" he thundered at her. "Damn you. God*damn* you. What the hell have you done?"

***

Hughes felt midnight not as exhaustion but as a slowly mounting excitement. Over an hour had passed since Doctor John's little episode. He was cooling off now, Hughes didn't know where.

Together he and Cate had been escorted away from Jo's workstation. Elderly Jolene led them up the topsy-turvy stairs and then down again at a diagonal, right into the heart of The Foundry.

Here he found himself in a tall room that took his breath away. Its walls teemed with movement. Circuitry wormed here, serpented there. Diodes blinked red and blue and green. Gyros spun. Hydraulic and pneumatic pumps expanded and contracted as if breathing. Pistons worked to the weird clattering cantankerous rhythm of it all, giving Hughes the sense he had just entered the digestive system of an angry metal giant.

The marble floor was white with a ring of platinum silver at the center. An anvil lay at the heart of the ring. Above, the ceiling bore a mural of a hand gripping a simple hammer. Viewed at a distance it seemed the hammer might swing down at any moment, smashing the anvil flat.

"I should like to know what this place is," said Hughes, doing well to remember he ought not to ask questions in the company of Jolenes.

"Mister Hughes, this is the Dynamo," said the elderly Jolene. "A special place to us Jolenes. And to Corinth City in general, I don't mind telling you. It was here that the first Jolene mastered electricity." She bade a group of attendant Jolenes to fetch a few chairs for them. "And spread the word that everyone is to make ready for the ceremony," she commanded them. "Hughes here is to have his magic item. Quite soon I should think."

That set Hughes' excitement leapfrogging, but his mind had grabbed onto what she had said.

"I didn't know Jolenes invented electricity."

"You don't invent things like that," she replied. "You wouldn't look at a man who's had a watermelon land on his head and say, 'he's just invented gravity.' You get curious. How does the watermelon fall? Similarly, why does air get hot and fizzly during a thunderstorm? Why does that lead to lightning? You do experiments. Maybe then you discover some of the invisible components of the world around you, and you decide to take them for yourself. Ah, here come our chairs. Good timing, ladies. My knees are carping fiercely today."

"The first Jolene was a blacksmith's apprentice and one of the earliest scientists of the millennium. After studying carbon and its graphite form, she invented a device for generating static electricity," said Cate, picking up the story as they sat down. "This was long before The Foundry was built, when this was only a little saltbox of a room that the first Jolene rented so she could conduct experiments.

"There were these swings, see. Two of them suspended in the air with silk ropes. And a bowl of gold leaf. The Jolene had someone lie across the swings and had the electricity flow through them with a connecting rod. The charged person reached out their hand and the gold leaf flew up like this." Cate splayed out the fingers of one hand and waggled the fingers of her other one around it, simulating the rush of feathery gold. "But of course the silk wasn't affected. By doing that, Jolene proved electricity flowed through some things and not others. Electric pylons work the same way nowadays." Cate looked at the elderly Jolene for confirmation.

The woman nodded. "Right you are, Miss Jubilee. I see you're a pupil of history as well as being a snoop."

"I don't snoop," Cate protested. "I investigate attractively."

"Eventually the first Jolene got into magnets, and that's when electricity really took off," their elderly host told Hughes, ignoring Cate's pout. "A dynamo is a means of turning mechanical energy into electrical energy. Simply put, it's a machine that makes power."

"You're saying this room powers the whole Foundry," said Hughes.

"Don't be daft," said the Jolene. "It powers the whole city."

"Joking aside, I resent being called a snoop," said Cate. "After all, the situation with Jo wouldn't have been resolved if I hadn't..."

"The... whole city..." Hughes was awestruck.

The elderly Jolene massaged her smarting joints. "There's a whole network of pylons that need upkeep, and Nikandros District is built atop so many focal nodes it might as well be one big battery. Companies take care of that, and maintenance people with toolbelts and hardhats and hungry families to feed, same as every city. But the power comes from here, this room where a woman worked by the glow of a candle and dreamed of lightbulbs."

"*Sleuth*, I can deal with," muttered Cate. "*Snoop* makes me sound like I've got watermarked business cards and a combover."

"I assume the ceremony has more to it than just giving me my magic item," said Hughes.

"Yes," said the elderly Jolene.

"I want to know about it."

"An *oily* combover."

The elderly Jolene put her hand on Hughes' shoulder. It was a large hand, liver-spotted, spidered in fine purple veins. "Give tradition its due, there's a good man."

"But I don't know what those traditions are," he said meekly.

"Look at the mural up there. There's a hammer, and below it an anvil."

"Sure."

"Very symbolic, your basic hammer and anvil."

"Sure..."

"You understand, then."

"No."

The liver-spotted hand gave his shoulder an encouraging pat. "When in doubt, hold your tongue and perk your ears and hope the world doesn't whack you so hard your brain falls out your arsehole." She smiled gummily at him. "Works for me."

CHAPTER TWENTY-ONE

At the instant the clocks struck midnight, Willard Coosler's wrist communicator gave a shrill whistle. Miss Gleam unscrewed the lid. There was a screen set into the device, very small. The screen showed a grainy raven in mid-flight. It dropped a letter that spun, tore open, then burst, filling the screen with text.

Meet where the bulls go running
On the street of born-feet-first

"The street of born-feet-first," said Miss Gleam aloud. "That is not much help. Not much help at all."

"Means Agorippis Street," said Mr. Glint helpfully.

His partner stared at him. It was a rare thing to knock her speechless, but speechless she was.

"Remember the geographer bloke I was telling you about?"

"The one who told you the city was built on loam?"

"Well, he told me that Agorippis Street is named after this other bloke from ages ago named Agrippa," said Mr. Glint. "He was a captain or something."

"A general," murmured Miss Gleam. Wheels of recognition turned behind her eyes.

"Right," agreed Glint. "A general. The geographer told me Agrippa was born wonky. Came out of his mum toes and tiny anklebones first."

"A breech birth!" Gleam raised both hands and fisted them tight with joy. "In which the child is delivered feet first! Agorippis Street, yes. And the place where the bulls go running can be none other than that house of negotiable affection, the one with the buzzing sign—what was the name, what was—*Pamplona!*" She clapped a palm to her brow, her eyes wide black windows of euphoria. "The very name of the general's childhood town. By all the maggoty monarchs in hell, Mr. Glint, you have outdone yourself!"

And so they set off with a spring in their step (Miss Gleam performed the majority of the springing) and a song in their hearts (discordant songs with barbed-wire melodies).

Leonidas District was quiet, its tenement windows dark, and the bazaar packed up for the night. The rain had a muffling effect as if the city were swaddled in damp cotton. Even the floodfighters worked in somber silence. Mist swept the lanes with bone-pale brooms. Little fireflies of red light glowed at the core of the clicked-off sodium lamps. This gave the impression that a hundred-thousand stranded angels were watching the stormy Sunday night unfold through keyholes in some crimson limbo.

They headed up Agorippis Street, and there it was: the sign with the bull goring the matador in grisly neon, and the invitation. *Pamplona*, it read. *All bulls are welcome. The hornier, the better!*

Mr. Glint knocked. A young woman with lollipop-colored hair answered.

"We're closed Sundays."

The two figures did not move. A bizarre thought occurred to the woman, looking at them. *One's a little teapot, short and stout. The other is her handle, thin as a spout.*

She might have giggled, only their exposed skin was twinkling like dead stars, and their combined gaze seemed to burrow through her eyeballs into the wet meat in her skull.

"You can come in for shelter, if you like," she tried.

"Yes," said Miss Gleam.

"Only you'll have to stay in the hall until someone collects you."

"Whose coat is that?"

"I'm sorry?"

"Whose coat is that?" repeated Miss Gleam. "The one hanging on the wall there."

The young woman glanced behind her. Long and chocolate brown, the coat was drying on a peg.

"That's mine," she said.

"Yours?"

"Yes. Look, we really are closed."

"Closed?"

"That's what I'm telling you."

"I believe you are," said Miss Gleam. "Closed, that is. Nevertheless I think that coat belongs to someone. Someone we want to talk to."

"It's my coat."

"Come now, you would not want to make your sign a liar, would you?"

The young woman with the lollipop-colored hair looked at her blankly. "What sign?"

"Your welcome sign. Out here in the street."

And before the young woman could formulate another thought, Mr. Glint stepped forward. "I'm a bull." He stuck out his index fingers and put them to his head, like horns. Then he leaned toward her, so she had the sensation that she was no longer a young woman but a young girl again, and the things other kids whispered about, the things living in the wardrobe and under the bed, those reptilian-pawed boogeymen were real, and here was one of them come for her at last. Mr. Glint's breath crawled up her nostrils like insects exhumed from amber. "See?" he said. "Now you say 'welcome.'"

"Welcome," she squeaked.

"Most kind," said Miss Gleam, and with an air of two cats entering an aviary of soft-throated pigeons lathered in cream, she and Mr. Glint stepped in out of the night.

Pamplona was like most small businesses in Corinth City. Sex work was only recently legal, but Gleam was a great believer in industry, no matter how sticky. Cheap tallow candles burned with a smell that was not lavender, not even close, but was nevertheless giving the whole lavender thing a go. Beaded curtain doorways rattled as the pair pushed through them. Evidently Sundays were open to special bookings because they could hear the sounds of love from all over. The whores who stood at a distance watching them were dressed in furs and frocks that looked almost genuine in the dim candle glow. Their perfumed necks and genitals did little to mask the stink of cleaning fluid and used condoms.

"Remember BOLO, Mr. Glint?"

"Be On The Lookout."

Gleam bared her scalpel teeth to show him how marvelous he was. They looked around and came eventually to a doorway tucked away from all the rest on the third floor of *Pamplona*. The bedroom through this door was remarkably tidy. A large window was set into the north wall, overlooking some rooftops. Inadequately irrigated, the roofs had puddled into enclosed lakes. On occasion, you could see lightning in them, reflected from the roiling sky above.

A man stood looking out at the downpour. He wore a mask. White. Cheap plastic. He saw movement in the glass and was turning to examine the source of light he'd glimpsed (candle fire bouncing off Gleam's gold-enameled incisors) when Mr. Glint jabbed one bony knuckle between his shoulder blades. Wind gushed between the man's lips. By the time he had his breath back he was pinned in place by strong, wiry hands.

"Oh dear," said Miss Gleam, striding up, grasping the man's head and removing his mask. His hair was thinning, shorn in a crewcut. She pursed her lips. "Follicly challenged, Mr. Glint. Nothing for my trusty snippers to work with." The man's eyes bulged as she took out her scissors. He gasped when she cut open his shirt, the steel brushing his bare skin.

"Cuh-cold," he said. Bifurcated, his shirt drifted to the floor. His wallet made a dull thump where it landed.

Miss Gleam eyed the thicket of hair on the man's narrow chest with vast approval. "Much better. How cooperative of you. You know who we are?"

"You're Miss Gleam. And this fine pillar of the community is Mr. Glint."

"Full points, that man. And you know what this does, don't you?"

Snicker-snick.

The man's bladder let go.

"I shall take that as a resounding *yes*," said Miss Gleam happily.

With his free hand, Mr. Glint picked up the wallet and thumbed it open.

"Streetbeater," he said.

"What? Give that here." Miss Gleam snatched it from her partner. Could it be? Yes, that insignia of a boot was their seal of office. "Why would the streetbeaters hire an assassin to kill Miss Shimmer?" she asked the man.

"They didn't," said their captive. His head was disproportionately large compared to his body, giving him an almost pinlike shape. "I mean, ah, I'm sure I don't know what you're talking about."

Snick.

"White blades," said Miss Gleam, studying her scissors and the cut lock of chest hair. "A lie. Mr. Glint."

"No telling porky pies," said Glint, who reached for the man's left eye with long, clutching fingers.

"Wait! Jus-just wait. I'll tell you."

"Why then?"

"I don't know why. I don't. I swear on my mother's life, I don't." His eyes flicked to Glint's hand, which was flexed and ready. "But the streetbeaters aren't involved. Just me, that's the God's honest."

Snick.

The blades turned black. It was true.

"Who then? Who employs you?" Gleam demanded. She came closer. "And before you tell us that you can't say because they will kill you if you do, demonstrate a modicum of courtesy for my associate and I. We are being nothing if not kind to you despite your duplicity and your role in the murder of our kinswoman. Besides, your employer is not here." She seized his hand—which was cold and fishy and scaled with eczema—and teased her filed teeth over the vein in his wrist. "Whereas we are."

The pin man shuddered. Miss Gleam could smell his urine now, sour and yellow and lovely.

"Young man," he said thickly. "Respectable looking. Bow and arrow."

"Bow and arrow?" Bows had gone out of fashion ever since pneumatic bolt throwers had been invented about forty odd years ago. Quick to load, quick to shoot. Who on earth used bows anymore? Miss Gleam had been intrigued before. Now she was fascinated. "This archer paid you to hire Willard Coosler."

The streetbeater nodded. "Coosler was in the clink when I found him. He'd been in hospital before. Attacked one of the nurses. I was put on duty bringing him supper. Talked to him. Seemed a real piece of work in my opinion, Miss. And, well, I had this job the archer gave me. Coosler seemed perfect."

Snick.

Black. True.

"Is he dead?"

"Hm?" said Gleam, who was lost in thought.

"Coosler," said the streetbeater. "Did you kill him?"

"There's a bag under the bed," said Mr. Glint.

"Credits, I imagine," said Miss Gleam absently. "Coosler's payment for our sweet Shimmer." She refocused on the pin man. "Attend, streetbeater. Your assassin is indeed dead, but you might yet feel the rain on your face again if you answer quickly and comprehensively. Did the Archer explain why he wanted Shimmer's life?"

"No, Miss," said the pin man, eager to please. "All he told me was that I should keep an eye out for any rough types who might have a shot at one of you people. Coosler fit the bill, Miss."

"What do you mean, 'you people'?"

"Mr. Shine's crew," said the pin man. "You, Shimmer, Flicker, that creepy one with the speech impediment..."

"Mr. Fulgurate, yes. Hold still."

Snick.

Black went the blades. True and true again.

"You're sure the rest of the streetbeaters aren't involved?" Gleam wanted to know.

"Could be, I suppose. But no one's sidled up to me for a chinwag about it."

Snick.

Black.

"Where did you meet this archer?"

The streetbeater grinned a manic please-don't-slit-me-up-the-middle grin. "That's easy, Miss. Met him at *theuck—*"

An arrow sprouted from the nape of his neck. The heavy bodkin point burst skin, opening his throat. A jet of blood squirted, amazingly hot against Gleam's cool cheek. Shards of broken window played a merry jangling tune. She spied the Archer on the opposite roof just as the second arrow struck the spot where the pin man's blood landed. Gleam's head snapped back. The shaft of the arrow stuck out of her cheek flesh like a pencil rammed into the shiny curve of an apple.

Mr. Glint was moving. He struck the window at speed, caught onto the building's gutter as glass exploded to join the rainfall, swung a great pendulum swoop as it wrenched free of its rivets, and launched himself at the rooftop where the Archer had already begun to flee.

He scaled up, looked around. Lightning shone its palpitating lantern on the scene. The Archer hopped and skipped from roof to roof. His movements were lithe and effortless. The puddles ran deep even up here above the flooded streets, yet the water seemed barely disturbed by his passing.

Glint thought, *I spy with my little eye, something beginning with B,* and took off in pursuit.

If you happened to be out that night (almost no one was) you might have seen them gallivanting up there and believed you were watching a recreation of the old Spring Heeled Jack murders from ye olden times. Ill-favored figures among the water tanks and chimney stacks. Watch the quiver-laden man move like a water dancer in the rain! Watch the gaunt one gaining on him!

Someone had forgotten their washing. Strung out on the line it lashed in the wind, cardigans and shirts and pantyhose, trickling rain and carrying the smell of soaked wool and clean detergent to Glint, who jerked his neck and snapped his jaws like an alligator, biting through the line and not losing a second of time. He could see the Archer's clothes now, form-fitting and dark, as he vaulted a line of tenement chimneys crushed together in a brick sandwich. It was very graceful.

I spy with my rude little eye, something beginning with B.

Glint diverted around the chimneys, caught sight of his quarry against the dirty paneled glass of an abandoned greenhouse, took a running start, and flung himself there with all his strength.

Here it was, a simple sortie across the top of things where too much thinking spelled disaster and where instinct counted double.

The Archer dodged just as Glint landed. Glint felt the glass give. The panel shattered into slivers under his shoes. His legs followed them into a warren of cracked ceramic pots, wilted flowers, rusty water cans, and huge witchy cauldrons of ivy acrawl with beetles and blind white bugs. His torso followed. At the last moment Glint gripped the lattice where one panel met the other, his body swinging, the noxious smells of decaying horticulture gushing up from below. He did not dawdle. In a flash he was back atop the greenhouse, rain rolling down his bald head and sallow cheeks.

But where was the Archer?

There! Glint bent, tested one of the roof panels, and dug in with his horrid fingernails. It came loose.

He lifted it, sighted the Archer, and took careful aim.

I spy with my giddy eye...

As the Archer performed another fabulous vault, this time from one bungalow roof to a much higher one, the panel took him in the back. Glass split and disintegrated. The throw distance was sixty yards. Mr. Glint heard the lovely jubbly smashing sound, even over the thunder rumbling its decibels.

He stalked now, in no hurry.

Struck mid-leap, the Archer had actually cleared the tall lip of the neighboring roof. This square, sensible building was a school just across the border of Leonidas into the wealthier Polydoros District. It was called The Wimples School For Exasperating Young Ladies. A boarding school, Wimples staff had gotten sick of their charges leaving under cover of night to smoke cigarettes and get up to all sorts with boys with names like "Skud." Windows were padlocked, the ground level entrances were patrolled by an uncomplicated security watchman who had little patience for the persuasive power of the fluttering eyelash, and most importantly the roof was blockaded with smooth, uncompromising slabs of granite.

This meant that while Mr. Glint could take his time getting in, the Archer would have a good deal of trouble getting out. The wind had tuckered itself out. It blew gently, tousling the sheeted rain rather than slapping it. Somewhere in the city, a wild dog barked, a nasty bottom-heavy bark clumped with territoriality and hunger.

Glint landed with a squelch in a pile of discarded magazines and dog ends (left by extremely exasperated young ladies who missed Skud). He approached the Archer, who lay in the fetal position with bits of greenhouse panels frosting him.

"Recital's over," said Glint. "Ballerinas can put up their slippers." He stretched forth a killing hand. "I spy with my dancing little ey—"

Quick as a cricket the Archer uncoiled. The lightning uncovered her lantern. By the blue-white shivers of light Glint saw two points like shaved fence boards, and then he saw nothing at all.

He stood there for a moment, his mouth looking for all the world as though the grand opening of a lemon squeezing factory was going on behind his lips.

"B for Blind," he said. "Good one."

Seizing the shafts he yanked both arrows out of his eyes, which ran like bloody egg-yolks down his cheeks. He rubbed his ring with its soot-black stone and waited.

An hour passed.

He could see a faint gray line.

Another hour. Another.

Thin cobwebs traced everything.

Four o'clock now, and he could see the raindrops as well as feel them. Clouds bulked in ghostly wool, endless toys. Dawn bloomed behind them, and he saw that too, just as clearly as he saw the storm wield those wooly toys, cackling its thunder laugh at the futility of June sunshine.

He washed the dried gunk from his face and coat, closed his eyes, and opened them. The school roof was empty. The Archer was half a night and a fraction of morning fled. Scarpered and vamoosed. Flown the coop.

Gone.

Mr. Glint nodded, as one duelist nods to another after they have lost the first round of many, and went home.

CHAPTER TWENTY-TWO

"It's time," said the elderly Jolene.

Cate and Hughes turned to the entryway where two by two the rest of the Jolenes were filing into the Dynamo. They were all in their best dress, which meant that a couple of them had deigned to rinse their armpits. Hughes suppressed a smile. Joking aside, he couldn't help but feel they had a way about them, these craftswomen of The Foundry. A certain gravitas. The Scarlet Citadel had their support, and he wondered who benefited more from that relationship—the Citadel or the Jolenes. What could Wendy Dragontail offer them that they could not simply make themselves?

Whatever the answer, Hughes folded away his curiosity as Jo made her entrance.

She was carrying something under her arm.

"To the ring with you." The elderly Jolene shooed him. "Not you, Miss Jubilee. He's on his own."

Hughes crossed the silver ring and stood behind the anvil. Discontented murmurs broke out among the Jolenes. Startled, Hughes looked to Cate for guidance. She jerked her head forward as subtly as she could. Pulse quickening, Hughes stepped around the anvil so it was behind him. The Jolenes nodded approval.

Hughes exhaled, his relief bizarrely palpable.

It was no penny play, this ceremony business. It was the real show.

He felt unaccountably dizzy. Tension kneaded his upper back and shoulders like a baker kneaded fresh dough.

Jo was there. When had she gotten so close to him?

Hughes tried to smile. It emerged wan, uncertain. Hers didn't. She grinned so wide her eyes became jolly slats. Her wisp of dark hair swayed between them. Under her arm, something new and deadly lay sheathed.

"You mustn't be afraid of changing," she told him.

Cleverly he caught the befuddled question just in time and made it firm and direct with purpose. "Tell me what change you mean."

This earned him a curious look from Jo. "Occasional Morphology," she said, as if it were the name of a common thing all sensible people ought to know about.

Occasional Morphology—that was it! Not Oblong Morphiognomy or whatever it was he'd remembered. Seized by the thrills and the many entanglements of the day, he had entirely forgotten to ask Cate about it.

"I'm really sorry about this, Jo. I don't actually know what Occasional Morphology is," said Hughes.

That stiff-palmed tension in his back pressed all the tighter as all around him the Jolenes broke into uneasy murmurs. He sought Cate's gaze for comfort, could not find her.

Jo came to his rescue.

"No great shakes. So when a magic item and a wielder come together, it's like this big bond, yeah? And when things bond they sort of show one another new ways to be alive." She smoothed her hair back with the flat of her hand. "Mostly that um... communion, right, is small enough it might as well be invisible. But sometimes bonding makes your body change."

"And these changes," said Hughes, "are not so invisible."

"It will be okay for you," said Jo. "No matter what you look like, you will be beautiful."

He looked at her. Malformed, her persecutor had called her. Lumpy. *Anything but,* he thought. *Anything but.* The kindness of what she'd said had struck him with a force that was almost physical. Shocked out of shock. *No matter what you look like, you will be beautiful.* There was really only one thing to say.

"I'm not afraid."

Jo's grin returned, guileless and good, and even wider than before. She hefted her bundle.

"Ready?" she asked him.

Hughes wasn't sure, but he gave her a nod.

All the lights went out.

Hughes looked at the inside of his lids, then at the room. No difference. Panic began to spin its black cycle in him. His misgivings amplified the quiet. He could actually hear his heart horsing from a canter to a gallop, could hear it as hoofbeats thudding against his eardrums. He felt strangely naked in that oppressive darkness. The Dynamo was still, the metal giant's system frozen in an eerie stasis.

And me frozen along with it. Wait...

Something, if he peered closely, something was...

Yes, something was happening.

The ring around him, the platinum silver one that he shared with Jo and the anvil, had begun to send up shoots not dissimilar to bamboo, only these were composed of the most wonderful green light.

He recognized it at once.

Iphigenia light.

The light curved and formed a dome around him. Hughes was struck with the most incredible sensation—he was back in that beautiful landscape in the other world, gazing at the bilious swamp, the moon-bathed desert, the faerie wood. His spine and tongue and fingertips transformed into conductors, Iphigenia flowed through him in a tide of energy somewhere between phototrophic and electrical.

Jo held the new and deadly thing for him to grasp. "This is yours," she said. "Take it. Use it."

"To defend people?"

"And yourself."

"When?"

"When words fail, obviously." Jo gazed into his eyes with her mismatched ones. One was green, the other white and mystical as the moon. "I'm thick as clotted cream..."

"And even you know that," Hughes finished.

Her lupine grin broadened. She joggled the weapon sheath at him.

"Yes. Well. Here goes nothing."

Embarrassed, Hughes curled his fingers round the hilt, and every emotion whisked out of him, leaving behind a shell. He drew the weapon. It filled him full again.

When he was a boy, Hughes had read a play called *A Summer Knights Stroll*. The story followed a hedge knight (poor, nomadic folk not sworn to the service of a Lord or holdfast, forced to sleep under willow trees and wild hedges, hence the name). The knight was called Gwendle of the fallen house of Gardener. On page thirty-one of the play, there was an illustration of Gwendle Gardener. Brigands had waylaid the knight along a forest road, and Gwendle's horse reared back on its legs, front hooves scything the air, and the sword of house Gardener was in its master's grip.

The picture had been deeply evocative for a boy eager to cram his mind to the brim with the extraordinary.

And that sword...

That little jot of ink representing a little wafer of steel...

Fifteen years after he turned that page and saw that sword, Hughes raised his own blade so he could admire it. It was a thing worth admiring.

Thirty-six inches of folded steel shone jade green in the Iphigenian glow. A steel dragon head was affixed at the base of the blade, its maw stretched so that the longsword appeared to flow from its throat. The hilt itself was leather, scarlet red, and swirled in ram horns. At the pommel, a lion of yellow beryl roared.

Without knowing he was doing it, Hughes vented a sound of such childlike happiness, it would have broken and remade his father's heart.

In the span of a few seconds, his list had shrunk appreciatively:

1) ~~Get a magic item.~~

2) ~~Join the Scarlet Citadel.~~

3) Pay back Gleam and Glint's employer.

4)   Have dry feet.

He would reserve judgment on that last one. Having dry feet was not something to mess around about. True, his toes were currently comfy, but dryness had to be a prolonged endeavor.

Whoa. He blinked. There was the dizziness again. Much more pleasant for some reason. A hot air balloon of cresting, chest-expanding joy. *I am a Citadel man.*

And as far as he could tell, he was still Hughes in every way. A quick explorative prod of his face, yes, a glance at his familiar same-old-me body, yes! Occasional Morphology could jog on for all he cared. The only appreciable change was that things were finally looking up. That was excellent. Still, he should probably stop grinning like a complete lunatic. It was probably unseemly. After all, he was *a man of the Citadel.* The adult inside him had a point. On the other hand, as of thirty seconds ago the boy inside not only had a point. It had a whole sword.

God, oh dear God was he *happy.*

"Go on," Jo prompted.

"Pardon?"

"You got to name it."

Hughes glanced around, his eyes piercing the veil of silken green light. The Jolenes. Jo herself. And there, a fiery flake in the throng—there at last he spotted Cate Jubilee. They were all watching him, and that was fine.

The sword drew him back to it. The steel dragon, the leather ram, the gemstone lion. A menagerie that would make Krys and The Mum pass the most lovely compliments. That was a sweet thought, sweet as this thing he was holding that had until recently been a monstrous heart. Its weight felt good in his hand. He had read somewhere that swords were lighter than most people would believe, but Hughes might as well have been holding a starling.

His gladness grew, grew again, and suddenly it reached a crescendo that fireworked him with crackling inspiration. Only the best would do. Well, he had it.

He brought his magic item close and spoke in a voice that would have made Ser Gwendle Gardener draw his own sword forth, kneel, and swear fealty. Everyone heard it and was charmed and heartened for the name he chose, though they had no idea what it could mean. He spoke soft and strong and bright and true.

"Your name is Chimera," he said.

The sword glimmered: *Yes.*

***

That night before the summer wheeled up and got rolling, Hughes had the dream again.

He dreamed of a carousel. This time Mr. Glint's body exploded like a prop in a splatterhouse movie. There was the line of eager carny-goers, and the shapes replaced Krys and The Mum. These new bent, sagging, crooked-limbed shapes took tickets and ushered people onto the ride. The image of them sent heebie-jeebies skittering over his skin like bedbugs. Then there was the figure with the burning yellow eyes. Also the burning yellow headlights of Hughes' *Eschezmont.* Leopard engine yowling. Kim Kallaimon, his (backstabbing) former lover behind the wheel, plowing straight toward him.

At the climax the yellow-eyed figure opened his mouth to speak, and then Hughes sank into deep sleep and knew no more.

Across the city, several otherwise ordinary people dreamed they were in a line for a carousel. The prospect excited them as nothing else had, not for a long time. Come dawn, around the time when a certain Mr. Glint opened his eyes to find himself alone on a school rooftop, most remembered little of the dream itself. They retained only a vague yearning that tugged at their guts like a toddler's pudgy hand tugging at a ball of colored yarn.

Ernie Wilks was one such dreamer. In the mellow gray oblivion of Monday morning he sat on the edge of his bed and stroked his snoring, stinky dog, Boochums. He felt it all right. Felt the tug. Toward what? For a million credits he could not have told you.

By noon the yearning would spool away, though not entirely, an ache of harsh and totally unnamable desire.

Come Monday night more would dream that dream. More on Tuesday. Many more by Friday.

And on and on and on...

ACT SIX

WHICH DOESN'T END WITH A KISS

TWENTY-THREE

Flowers.

They laid bouquet after bouquet on the coffins. There were three there that morning in the Grand Hall of Redspire Tower, each coffin bound for different destinations. Jeroma (Hughes had dubbed him Nosering in Iphigenia) was off to the crematorium. Lyle (aka Beard) was headed for the decomposition machine where everything he was and had been would become fertilizer for fruit trees or perhaps the same kind of flowers adorning his casket. *Larkspur,* thought Hughes, who had a decent knowledge of blooms owing to his friendship with Krys and The Mum. He liked larkspur. Columns of petals, deep purple and white. Would Lyle want that? To bury and regrow as larkspur? Hughes remembered the saying related to him by Falstaff: *Arseholes to apples. Men to mulch.*

It was pretty macabre. *Too macabre for me, today especially.*

The last coffin belonged to Laurana, who would be sent home to sleep forever under a patch of blackberries.

Dressed in a scarlet suit with white flourishes at the cuff and collar, Wendy Dragontail said a few words. Church services hadn't been in fashion for a long time. Hughes thought she spoke kindly enough. He had never been to a funeral before.

The storm mercifully backed off for the time being, but glimpsed through the large Grand Hall windows the thunderheads showed no sign whatsoever of breaking up. No music played. Falstaff cried the whole way through.

Hughes felt a surge of respect and affection for Cate Jubilee as she and a few others offered the butler what comfort they could.

"Lastly, I'll talk about Laurana," said Wendy Dragontail. "A woman who came not last but first in the hearts of anyone who knew her."

Falstaff moaned. Cate held his hand.

Hughes listened along with the rest of them while the head of the Scarlet Citadel talked about a woman he hadn't known long but who rose high in his heart all the same.

The freckles on her nose changed from moons to halfmoons when she smiled, he thought. *Laurana. Laurie. I'm sorry you're not here to see how many people thought the world of you.*

"Beloved friends, we will miss you fiercely."

Undertakers lifted the coffins in a procession.

"Falstaff?"

The butler stood before them all, Wendy Dragontail next to him looking on as the coffins were sent to the fire, the larkspur, the blackberries.

Falstaff read this poem, the words of which inscribed themselves in Hughes' memory, which was not stone, so that was all right:

If I should go before the rest of you
Break not a flower nor inscribe a stone
Nor when I'm gone speak in a Sunday voice
But be the usual selves that I have known

Weep if you must
Parting is hell
But life goes on
So sing as well

Later, an odd thing happened. It happened at the afters, which was a large and superb party the Citadel held to toast and reminisce about the departed.

In the span of the early afternoon the Grand Hall was utterly changed: furniture shifted; curtains swapped; light fixtures adjusted.

Everyone lent a hand, and it was quick work completed with surprisingly nice satisfaction. It was as Cate Jubilee believed—movement was the great consolation prize. Now and then there were even snatches of laughter.

There was nothing like a funeral to remind you that you were still alive.

The odd thing happened while Hughes was taking some time to himself. There was grief involved in his temporary isolation, but for the most part he was simply exhausted. That afternoon in a flurry Cate had introduced him to a whole host of his new peers. Initially he'd relished the opportunity. Then she kept pulling him from group to group. This was Priam King, and Steffan Cerulean, oh, and here were Rosemund Valkyrie and Penelope Auspice, Elena Longfellow, Musif Diamond, and at that point social alarm bells had begun to chime in his head. Hughes had been forced to employ the only technique proven to work in situations of this kind: he had fastened a vague yet friendly smile to his lips, nodded and shaken hands and exchanged how-do-you-dos and listened politely while people told him their names, and he promptly forgot every single one of them.

Hughes was taking a sip of white wine and trying to mentally ready himself for another bout of Whirlwind Jubilee when a well-groomed man joined him on his bench.

"How are you then?" the man asked.

"Me?" Hughes hesitated. He had an acute feeling they'd met before, but where? "Well, I suppose as well as I could be," he said carefully. "Glad to be here. Honored, I mean. Not glad. In the Scarlet Citadel, I mean. Wait. No." Exhaustion gnawed at him, made his tongue feel swollen and stupid. "I *am* glad to be in the... and here, at this, um, occasion. Oh hell." Hughes gave up. "Sorry, Cate has me on the meet-and-greet circuit. I feel like a dishcloth after the Tinfrost banquet cleanup. But I don't think we've met, Mister..."

"Meet-and-greets, eh? Well, it's the day for it. Everyone's here, and those who aren't are on their way. Even those who were abroad, from the countryside all the way to Yi-Shi. Drink?"

"I'm sorted, thanks. People are coming from Yi-Shi?" Yi-Shi was over four-thousand miles away, across a litany of archipelagos and the Spidercrab Sea.

"White wine I see. I'm on the water myself," said the well-groomed man. Ice cubes clinked against the lip of his glass when he lifted it up and rotated it gently with his fingers, as if to reassure Hughes that it was what he claimed it was—only water. "I made a promise about that. Yes, from Yi-Shi, Ikahagua, who knows where else? Not for Jeroma or Lyle, you understand. Those two were okay. Solid. No, everyone is coming here for one person, and one person only."

He looked at Hughes expectantly.

"Laurana," Hughes supplied.

The man nodded, pleased. *I know you,* Hughes thought firmly. *I know those beady eyes, but from where?* He riffled through pages in the book of his memory, pages of faces. Instinct told him he almost had it. Come on. Beady eyes. A pig's small off-putting eyes. He thought it was the man's manner that was confusing him. It upset his kilter. Why should it? No matter. His identity taunted Hughes maddeningly from the tip of his tongue.

"What did you think of Dragontail's speech?" the man asked.

"It was nice. She's very..." He searched for the word, couldn't find it. "Strong, I guess you could say. So much so you feel a bit stronger yourself just being around her. I'm not sure how typical the speech itself was. This is my first funeral. What did you think?"

"I liked it." The man plucked out a small ice cube and crushed it between his back teeth. "All that stuff about hearts. I liked it. You'd know something about hearts, wouldn't you?"

A tiny feather of unease tickled him. "I suppose."

"You know all about them," the man said, his voice low yet totally sure of itself. He was looking at the bench rather than Hughes, or maybe at the condensation beading his glass, beads regarding beads. "That new sword of yours came from a heart. What you don't know—and how could you with the meet-and-greets—is that the gossip wheel is turning. The rumor mill. That's what you and Laurana have in common. Everyone's talking about you. Know what they're saying?"

Hughes wasn't sure he wanted to know. All of a sudden he was not sure whether or not he was safe here at this party, either. The man's small piggish eyes were so familiar, if only he could...

"They're saying you are coping with all of this pretty well. That you must either have your bolts screwed tight or not screwed at all. Courageous or crazy. They're saying that because when they saw those coffins today, paid respects, eulogized, stacked the flowers, all that rigmarole... When they saw that coffin—and I am talking about *her* coffin now—the next logical step for their brains was you. How much pain you must be in. How much guilt you must be choking on. Some people call the phenomenon 'survivor's guilt,' but me? I call it Long Straw Syndrome."

The man's hand closed around his wrist. Hughes couldn't move, could not make a sound. His mind felt blown clear, wall-to-wall, floor-to-ceiling. He sat there manacled by the man's squeezing hand and imprisoned in those beady eyes set into a face that was horribly familiar.

"See, Jeroma and Lyle and Laurie drew the short straws. And you, kid. You drew the long straw. I don't know if you were born with uncommon luck or all too common misfortune, but here you are with your white wine and your heart that gets to beat a little faster every time you meet-and-greet someone new. *As well as you could be?*" The words rasped out of the man's lips, which were peeling over his gums in a rictus. "You say that to me? You're doing *as well as you could be?* You son of a bitch. I should break that wine glass in half and fuck you with both stems."

"Walter," said Hughes. "It's you, isn't it?"

The man he'd stolen armor and a weapon from. The man whose entire unit had died in Iphigenia. How in God's name had he not put it together before? The reason was obvious. Walter looked different. His rat's nest of hair was washed and combed back. He'd taken shaving foam and a razor to the crust of stubble on his cheeks and chin. No vodka breath. Only water on the menu for Walter, who had made a promise (any guesses who to, Hughes? Laurie oh Laurie). Only the squashed often-broken nose might have given him away. And the small black eyes, of course. No bloodshot. The man was not on the wrong side of booze, merely the wrong side of anger. Of fury.

"I'm so sorry, Walter," said Hughes. "Really, I am. You can't know..."

Which were the last three words he should have said.

"I can't *know?*"

Walter's hand shot up. His fingers snarled through Hughes' hair. Short as it was after Falstaff's barber job, there was still plenty to grip.

Walter yanked, and Hughes felt thin filaments of agony plunge into his scalp. He didn't cry out but he did drop his wine glass. It rolled, the shape of the glass making it sketch a circle. Wine rushed for the table edge.

"I know all about it, cocksucker," said Walter. "She's dead and you killed her."

People were starting to look their way.

Hughes barely noticed. "A monster killed her."

"It was a three-strong team. I could have made the difference."

"Then why didn't you?" Hughes' own temper was rising to match his pain, throb for throb. "Why weren't you there?"

From the corner of his eye he saw rage slam into Walter's face, dark red now and getting darker every moment. Hughes wouldn't be deterred.

"I'll tell you where you were," he said. "You were a whole other world away. Naked, drunk, and dreaming of sticking your horn in one of the pretty matadors in *Pamplona.* I'm sorry about Laurana—"

"Don't you say her name."

"But I'm not sorry for you. Not the tiniest jot of pity."

Some part of Hughes flinched from the savagery of that. The rest boiled, simmered, spat with loathing for this man wrenching his hair out by the roots.

You didn't help me, Hughes thought. Gleam and Glint were coming for me and you walked away. You'd just gotten laid and were blasted out of your mind on vodka. Everything was hunky-dory in Walterville.

"You're no kind of person," Hughes told him. And then he said something that made his entire being flinch, even the angry parts. "I reserve my sympathies for your unit. For Jeroma, Lyle, and Laurana. They drew the short straw the day you came into their lives. I am ashamed. So disgustedly ashamed with myself about what happened. But where does that leave you, Walter? You're as alive as I am. A little late to sobriety, but alive. Now how's that Long Straw Syndrome feel, juicehead? You shit-heel barfly *soak*."

Walter's rage was so astounding that his claw-hold on Hughes' hair actually loosened a little. His complexion was livid with blood. The carotid artery in his neck pulsed thick as a shoestring.

"Dead." The man's voice grated up his throat like wind through dead branches. "Dead."

Not an acknowledgment of his loss. Hughes understood that it was in fact a promise. Walter's face was a portrait of murder.

It was in that moment in which the danger seemed greatest that the oddest thing of all happened.

A human hand lanced out of the white wine spill. Before Hughes' unbelieving eyes it rose and kept coming, first wrist, then forearm, extending up from nothing but the tabletop and the alcoholic liquid. Two fingers rammed up into Walter's nostrils.

He uttered an ugly nasal grunt. The thought of untangling himself from his assailant never even occurred to Hughes; the phantom hand was stupefying.

"Joobill," Walter croaked. "Leggo."

Joobill?

What in God's name was he saying?

People were approaching now, curious about the ruckus.

If "leggo" was a corruption of "let go," the hand took no heed. Instead the fingers pushed deeper, almost to the first knuckle. Walter jumped, his disrupted sinuses sending bolts of panic into his spine, thighs, and buttocks. The tips of the fingernails began to stimulate his gag reflex.

It was this that did the trick. Walter released Hughes completely. "*Fugging bitch,*" he retched, close to vomiting, water or no water. "*Leggo of meuck-of meeeeuckk.*"

The fingers gave one final agonizing push that sent convulsions through Walter's whole frame, then slipped roughly out, snot-slick and daubed in blood where veins in his nose had broken.

Hughes watched in stunned silence as the hand slipped back through the white wine. The only evidence that it had come through in the first place was Walter, who tried to stand, toppled on his backside, clawed back to his feet, and staggered off through the small, puzzled crowd forming around them.

"What happened to him?" asked Rosemund Valkyrie. She was from Daethumberland in the cold north, the land where the myth of vampires had originated, and it was her accent of all things that put two and two together in Hughes' mind. He had heard someone parrot that accent with comical exaggeration only yesterday.

Veeeeeery goot meester Hoos. I see promisink future for you here.

"Cate," he said.

He scanned the Grand Hall and spotted her right away.

She was over by the drinks table working a white cloth over her hand. Her index and middle fingers were partially clean. A gloss of snot and streaks of blood could be distinguished. *Rescued me,* he thought. Gratitude and bewilderment warred across his brain. *Rescued me, okay, but how?* When they'd met she'd emerged from Wendy Dragontail's window. Could Cate's body shift between liquids too? He dismissed the idea. It didn't add up. Glass was solid. He looked at the white wine spill and the drinks table, then with widening eyes back at his partner. Reflections! The surface of the liquids were mirrors. Her magic item allowed her to transport her body through those—how *incredible.*

She must have felt his gaze.

As the puzzled onlookers murmured, speculated, shrugged, and rejoined the party, Cate Jubilee winked unsmilingly at him and melted back into the jubilations.

That wink was the little dot under the exclamation point of the whole Walter affair. With its unsmiling sense of dry humor, it said: *Do not vorry, Hoos. I hev got your beck.* It was encouraging and supportive, and almost unthinkably kind.

It was also the single most attractive thing Hughes had ever seen, as emboldening as delicious wine on your tongue, and lovely as fresh cut—

CHAPTER TWENTY-FOUR

"Flowers?" said Hughes.

"Flowers," agreed Hector in his wonderful voice, which was like a slice of carrot cake with cinnamon icing on an autumn day. "What is the matter? Have you some ingrained paranoia of them?"

"No," grumbled Hughes. "I do not have an ingrained paranoia of flowers, Hector. I just don't fancy slashing them to ribbons, that's all."

They were in one of Redspire's training yards. It was the twelfth of June. Over the past few days the storm had redoubled its efforts. Floodfighters worked double shifts and begged for volunteers during sponsored news appeals. Those districts without weather-control nanites were faring poorly. Hughes was constantly worried for his dad. Being dry up here in Redspire was surreal, and more than a little harrowing, given the poverty he had left behind.

Anyway, this particular practice yard was built closest to the eastern elevator, also called the Overgrown Elevator, which led down to the wildest area of the tower's botanical floor. As such the elevator and the yard were host to scores of immigrant ivy, the beginnings of hedges, and little sapling trees with summer flowers budding and opening pinkly on their boughs.

"We waste our time, brother," said Cassandra, who was lying down next to one such tree, her hands behind her head. Her voice was like a slice of lemon tart. Out of convenience so was her general manner. "Have Paris train this boy. Or Creusa and that insufferable husband of hers."

Hector glanced disapprovingly at her. "The fostering of prowess is always worthwhile."

"And what of courage? He won't even hit a flower."

"Wouldn't a training dummy be a bit more... I don't know... conventional?" Hughes asked meekly.

"Your foes will not always be shaped like you are, Gormon Hughes." Hector nodded at one of the trees. "Do as I say."

Feeling ridiculous, Hughes drew Chimera from its scabbard and stepped toward a cluster of flowers.

Hector watched him intently, Cassandra from the corner of one eye as she lay beneath her tree. They were brother and sister, part of Priam King's vast and complicated dynasty. The man seemed to have no end of children. Hughes had learned from Cate that all of them had died during the sack of their home town during the war with Champleurs. Hideously tragic, but life had its strange dovetails. Not long after he buried most of his family, Priam King joined the Scarlet Citadel. Through the power of his newly begotten magic item, a crown of wintry glass as pale as Priam's own beard, he had resurrected his lost children as living ghosts. In almost every category they were as they had been in life, ageing every day, eating when they were hungry, sleeping when fatigue made them cranky. But there were some noticeable changes. There was a spectral quality to them, as though light and shadow were not altogether sure how to treat these unexpected long-term tenants of the living world. And apparently they bled a whitish goo—ectoplasm. Cate admitted there was no proof confirming that last part (it sounded like something out of a ghoulish B movie), but Hughes could tell she believed it.

Another of life's weird dovetails—two of Priam King's children were here now, ordering Hughes to commit plant genocide.

Hughes swung at the flowers...

... and the next moment he was on his back, winded and wheezing while Cassandra gave voice to a loud hyenalike cackle.

"On your feet, friend," said Hector, offering Hughes a hand up.

Hughes made a constricted noise.

"Yes." Hector smiled. "The peonies are very aggressive this time of year."

Out of the corner of his vision, Hughes noticed Cassandra crisscross her legs. On the tree the peony flowers crisscrossed.

"Are you a druid?" he asked her.

"No," Cassandra replied. "I haven't got the facial hair for that. But I do have something of the hermit witch in me. Plants and I get along like old friends."

With a touch as comforting as his voice, Hector adjusted Hughes' stance. "Relax your grip on Chimera. Not so loose as that. Broad shoulders like so. Good." He stood back, satisfied. "The first rule of swordplay is balance. This rule is broken up into composite subrules. Namely: footwork, core strength, and poise."

"The flowers are going to trip me again, aren't they?"

Cassandra spiraled her ankles. The peony spiraled in response.

Hughes sighed. They would trip him all right. And worse.

"Give me what I gave you," said Hector.

"Balance is broken into footwork, core strength, and poise."

"Exquisite." Hector's approval struck bright sparks in Hughes, who in his secret soul was really quite determined to earn the respect of both brother and sister. "There are three of these rules that I have codified over years of killing those who goaded my steel," Hector went on. "Each with their own subset of rules. Learning them will take years, as anything of substance does."

"I want to learn."

Hector inclined his head. "I will teach you. As will Cassandra." Amusement flickered in the fog of his spectral eyes. "And the peony, of course."

That was how Hughes met his sparring partner for the summer—a bunch of no-good rotten bastards masquerading as pretty pink—

CHAPTER TWENTY-FIVE

Flowers decorated the fringes of Wendy Dragontail's notebook, portrait-style.

Her notes themselves were bleak, disconcerting things. Abominations beyond count lay besieged by daffodils and carnations rendered in ink. She found the contrast mildly amusing.

June 21st found her sitting behind the desk in her tower-top office leafing through three specific pages, back-and-forth, occasionally adding annotations to the third page.

If you were looking over her shoulder at that moment, you might have seen certain words cropping up more frequently than others: Cartographer. Castle. Metal chariots. Bonemeal.

She circled *Metal chariots*, turned to the third page, jotted down a new sentence, and circled that too.

What is the fuel?

From her sound system scratched the melodies of piano, strings, and crooner. Her father had worked to music when he sat in this chair. Winnifred Dragontail didn't see the point in breaking tradition. Traditions were important. They were practically gods.

The door to the office whispered open.

"Ah, Falstaff," she said without looking up. "Is it eleven already? My, my. Where does the day go?"

Wearing large blue mittens the butler set down a hot tray of fresh pastries, cup and saucer, and a silver teapot.

"How is our newest recruit faring, Falstaff?"

"Hughes is quite well, my Lady." Falstaff poured the scalding tea. "He has stopped recoiling when I place new flowers in his room."

Wendy's eyes cut to the inky blooms bordering her notebook. They twinkled for a moment. "Hector and Cassandra are treating him... well, I take it?"

"Hector flattens out the kinks in his technique. Cassandra merely flattens him."

"Ah. Well, I'm sure they know best. Now I think I shall help myself to..." She studied the pastries. "Falstaff, am I right in thinking that these are rat droppings?"

"Raisins, my Lady."

"And this filling," continued Wendy Dragontail. "Perhaps the baker's cat is ill?"

"Imitation custard, my Lady."

"*Imitation* custard?"

"All the taste, none of the sugar."

"And none of the need to be pleasing on the eye."

"That's right, my Lady," said Falstaff promptly. "Your dietitian gave very specific instructions."

"Did he? Yes, I suppose he must have." Wendy Dragontail sighed. "Well, well, what a treat I have to look forward to. Thank you, Falstaff. You may go."

Falstaff sketched a tidy little bow and made to leave.

"He seems happy here?"

The butler turned. "Pardon, my Lady?"

"Hughes. He seems happy to you?"

The question took Falstaff aback, though he recovered quickly. "I... should think so. There was that bit of unpleasantness between him and Walter Pillion at the funeral, but that all seems taken care of now."

"Receiving counseling, is he? I should hope so after that business in Iphigenia."

"Counseling? No. Doctor Phelps is on maternity leave until October."

"Can leave a mark, that sort of thing."

"Giving birth? I should say so."

"Hughes, I mean. He witnessed a good deal of strife in Iphigenia. Laurana's death, and so forth. The potential for adverse effects must be considered. Something terrible happens, and in the proceeding days one looks over one's shoulder and finds out that the terrible thing is still very much with them. That it can look back." She perused a section of notes, underlining here and there. "We learned all about that after the war with Champleurs, of course. Soldiers going off to the front and returning home as different people. That sort of thing can leave you feeling isolated, or worse, in your own head."

"Cate Jubilee is his partner," Falstaff pointed out. "I shouldn't think Hughes has a moment to catch his wind, much less dwell on that sort of thing."

"Very good. See that he continues thus, Falstaff. Preserve the happy thoughts."

The butler paused. He had never had a conversation with his mistress like this one. "Are you feeling well, my Lady?"

"Hm?" Wendy looked up from her notes. "What? Yes, fine, Falstaff. Fine. Thank you for tea and the... other things."

"Your humble servant," said Falstaff dutifully and left.

The most powerful woman in the city sipped her tea and got on with work. After a while she tried the raisin and imitation custard pastry, which she regretted.

What felt like a few minutes later (though it was hard to tell, the rain scrunched the daylight hours into a wet tissue paper monotony) there was a tap at the window.

Wendy Dragontail got up and opened it. A figure crouched outside on the sill, thousands of feet above the city streets.

"Knickerbocker, how are you?"

"Just dropping off today's reports, your Ladyship."

Knickerbocker was one of the rare cases of magic item distortion. His item—a little gray sock if memory served—had given him the power to command a legion of rodents from household mice to overpass nocturnal bats. These made excellent spies for Wendy Dragontail, who hadn't been lying to Hughes about her force of informative "kobolds." Unfortunately Knickerbocker's magic item had also turned him into an odd gargoyle creature who slept under bridges and ate bubblegum from the sidewalk. The poor chap didn't seem to mind. In fact, he claimed life was better this way, as he no longer had to worry what people thought about him (since what they almost always thought was "Oh God, oh God, what is that thing?"

"Reports, yes. Thank you." She took the dripping folder from him. "Anything interesting?"

"Bit of rooftop hijinks in Leonidas. That Mr. Glint fellow was involved." Knickerbocker's expression turned nasty. Well, nastier than his usual expression anyway. "That Glint fellow is a rotten piece of work. Always eating my informants."

"I shall read about it with interest, Knickerbocker."

"Good day, Ladyship."

"Knickerbocker?"

"Wossat?"

"You don't happen to like raisins, do you?"

On Wendy's desk a rogue drop fell from the spout of the teapot. It stained the third page of notes she'd been working on.

Cartographer. Castle. Metal chariots. Bonemeal.

Metal chariots was circled.

Written later on and also circled was that question she'd posed herself.

What is the fuel?

Around these mysteries, forming a counterpoint to their grim conjecture, were tangles and thorny bunches of the most beautiful—

CHAPTER TWENTY-SIX

Flowers were important to Krys and The Mum.

Even one was precious. Hughes' gift was the first they'd seen in months. The flower had stood on the mantelpiece in a porridge bowl (full of earth Hughes had arranged to be sent over, dote that he was), and there it had brightened their carousel cottage for days and nights galore. Krys had been more focused and had taken up a project—the sewing and cinching of a new dress. The Mum might have sneered. Instead she had allowed that it was a respectable idea and inquired as to the color and general style. The presence of the flower was a tonic to them.

June went on. The flower began to wilt.

And like a plague that has been staved off though not quite cured, a shadow of discontent returned to the cottage.

The Mum grew grouchy and acidic. For her part, Krys grew distant. She took to the balcony more and more, receiving visions of the future and dashing downstairs to relate them. The Mum was ill pleased. She didn't like being locked into the past, which was what happened when Krys saw the future. She sculpted the past in crêpe paper, a weird trance making her face vacant as she did so. "You never even remember your prophecies, girl," she told Krys.

"I do too."

"Tell me then. You prove it right this moment. And if you can't, you don't go up on that balcony again. I hate being whisked away, girl. *I hate it.*"

"*I can too remember!*"

Doors of twisted plastic were slammed. Sulks stretched. Bitterness began to stew. By early July, the flower had been dead eleven days, and things were very bad between them.

In an effort to improve relations, Krys approached The Mum with a game of Here Comes Princess Partridge.

"I don't like card games," muttered The Mum. "Go on and make us a cup of tea."

"And then we'll play."

"Mmph."

The Mum watched the girl skip into their kitchen, her lips pursed in a way that Hughes would have described as her "lemondrop grandmother pout." The kettle *rumble-rattle-whistled*.

The Mum drew a breath to remind the forgetful little so-and-so to not skimp on the milk when she heard a clatter so loud it made her jump.

"What was that?"

There was a *glup-glup-glup*.

The Mum's face darkened. "Have you dropped the kettle again?"

The girl's voice drifted from the kitchen, soft as a spring breeze, too quiet to hear.

"Lord, give me strength." The Mum's face pinched irritably. She scooted round in her chair. "Speak up!"

"Here comes the Princess," said Krys.

The Mum rolled her eyes. "Rescue the kettle, serve me milky tea, and I'll play a few hands if it will please you."

"No." Krys darted in, her palms pressed together with the tips of her fingers tucked under her chin. Her eyes were wide, her breath coming quick. "No, The Mum. A real Princess."

"What are you talking about you stupid gir—"

Knuckles rapped on the cottage door.

"She's here," said Krys. "They leaf, by the way."

"What?"

"They leaf," the girl repeated and flitted off to welcome their guest before The Mum could voice her bafflement.

Krys opened the door and curtsied. "M'lady. Do come in."

The Princess wasn't dressed like royalty. She wore a pinstripe flannel suit, navy blue and buttoned in brass. Her hair was dark and blue as her suit, cut so it touched the lobe of her ear on one side and the line of her jaw on the other.

Krys peered outside. "Princess, will your other friends not come in out of the rain? Hello! Yes, you under the umbrellas! Won't you come in? No? Very well." She closed the door. "Tea, Princess?"

"No. None for me," said The Princess. She looked at the animals, the gnome playing phantom tunes on the calliope, the deadlight sign, the fire where only a few paltry coals were burning. The only thing she approached was the flower Hughes had brought them. "This was once beautiful," she said.

"Yes." Krys sighed. "It was."

"Not the flower," clarified The Princess. "All of it. I saw your show when it opened in Symbarr Square all those years ago."

"Did you like it?"

"I did." The Princess touched a finger to the Rotbloom Carnival sign. "The big top was especially grand. But you know, I only thought about it in the spring of this year. First time since childhood. Someone I care about reminded me of you." She glanced at The Mum. "Both of you."

"And that's why you've come, is it?" said The Mum. "For a stroll up Memory Lane?"

"May I sit?"

"Do you see any seats here except this one?"

"Hughes sits on the floor when he comes," Krys told The Princess.

"Is that so?"

"Tell us what you want or make like a tree," snapped The Mum.

The Princess traced the long plastic arm of an orang-outan next to the fireplace. "And what does a tree do?"

"It..." The Mum hesitated. She had no idea what trees got up to nowadays. They were probably very different from the trees she remembered. "It pisses off," she said with more conviction than she felt.

Some ghost of emotion moved across the Princess' features. Neither Krys nor The Mum could read that expression. All in all the Princess had a very inanimate face, like dried pottery with little give. It made her quite magnificent, but cold too. "I have an offer for the owners of The Rotbloom Carnival of Bright Oddments and Dark Delights." She told them what she needed. They listened for a while. Soon The Princess fell silent. There was an expectant pause.

"Yes," said Krys at the exact moment The Mum said, "No."

The girl bridled. "You mustn't be so rude, The Mum. She could have us guillotined, drawn, and quartered. Or have our noses lopped off."

"For what it is worth," said The Princess. "I will not have you guillotined."

"I suppose you haven't got one?"

"No."

"What about drawns and quartereds?"

"Organized on arrangement," said the Princess.

Krys grinned at her, though it was not clear whether or not the Princess was joking.

"The whole thing smacks of peril," said The Mum. "We'll have no truck with it. And another thing: you don't look like any princess I've ever heard of. From what you've told us, you seem more like a common thug engaged in commoner thuggery. Do we look like that sort to you?"

"I don't smell peril," Krys protested.

"I do!" The Mum sniffed. "A real pong it is. A peril pong. And now you can make like a tree, young miss princess, *if that's what you are*, and..."

"Spread."

The Mum came up short. "What?"

"Make like a tree," said The Princess, "and spread."

She rolled up a sleeve and typed something into her wrist communicator. "I would never lop off such a reliable nose," she told them. "The Mum smells correctly, Krys. A pong of peril pervades the premises."

Krys giggled. The lean muscles in her shoulders clenched and unclenched, and on her skin jungles of ink rippled with amusement.

"There will be danger," the Princess continued. "Though not at first, and at its worst only a small amount. No greater than the danger of establishing a carnival. Why, no greater than the danger of living in this cottage. After all, most accidents happen in the home."

There was activity going on outside. The Mum tried to meet Krys' gaze in an effort to communicate her apprehension, but the girl was swiftly becoming a monarchist and had eyes only for this strange, blue-suited Princess.

"We've just been sitting around," Krys confided. "Sitting and drinking tea and eating porridge and peppermints all day every day. I don't care about peril pong or menace musk or sinister stink or *anything*. What you're asking us to do, Princess... it will be an adventure."

"You sound like you crave that badly."

"I do, I do, I do!"

"And new dresses."

"She's *got* a new dress," groaned The Mum, who could feel control of matters slipping through her fingers.

"Then she'll have many more." It was the Princess who finally met the old woman's gaze. "And a new chair for you, The Mum. A tree does as a tree does."

The front door opened. Men came in carrying...

Oh, what they were carrying, it took The Mum's musty-grandmother breath and knocked it clean from her lungs and made it gorgeous and pushed it back through her widening eyes and nostrils and her gawping wrinkled mouth.

"See me spread my limbs," said the Princess. "See me shake them. See what comes tumbling to those to whom I am grateful."

Krys' tiny hands covered her mouth. Cyclopes stared in amazement from her thumbs, bodachs and bugbears and bumblebees from her fingers.

"Join me and be beautiful once more," said the Princess.

The men came inside, more and more every moment. They carried wicker baskets, two in each hand. Spilling from the baskets (brimmed up full, how could they be so *full?*) were oodles upon oodles of—

CHAPTER TWENTY-SEVEN

Flowers?
No.
Farmyards?
No.
Ice rinks?
Absolutely not.
Miss Gleam paced her famous pace.
Roving wolves?
No.
Deep fat fryers?
No.

It was a dim and dreary night in the abandoned leisure center, but if you had a torch to shine on her face, you would have seen something before clicking off the torch hurriedly and running for your life.

You would have seen the thin silver line of scarification on her right cheek. Without a good look at him, that scar was all she had to remember the Archer by. That and the anger. The *pique*.

She paced. Her crocodile leather shoes squeaked. Things living in the leisure center peeped out of the holes, watching her with reflective eyes all blue yellow and uncanny in the dark.

Horseshoe fittings?
No.
Tournament games?
No, no, *no*.

Losing the Archer had forced her to give in. She'd telephoned Mr. Twinkle who was to pass on the word to the others, and then with an acute feeling of embarrassment she'd filed a report to their employer's secretary.

Doing the paperwork had been bad. Somehow personal failings looked uglier when they were written down. They confronted you.

Then Mr. Shine himself called her, and that had been worse.

She'd tried to explain the obvious. She believed the matter of Miss Shimmer's assassination could be handled before troubling him with it. As the head of his organization, Mr. Shine was a busy man who *surely* held the delegation of thorny and pestiferous tasks to his best operatives as not merely wise but also necessary. Would he hear about it? Fat chance. His ears and sympathies were closed to her. She'd taken her lumps. "Yes, sir." She listened as he scolded her. "Disappointed. Yes." Her fingernails gouged deep grooves into the countertop of the ruined bowling alley. "Yes, Mr. Shine."

Now it was mid-July. Whelming up from the farmlands into the city on clouds as dense as geography, the storm had finally breached their lair. The basement was a warren of paddling rats. Zero progress toward finding the Archer. Gleam had found herself scanning for plastic white masks in crowds. Ridiculous.

On top of all that she could not find a metaphor to teach Mr. Glint about conceptualization.

That, in many ways, was the worst thing of all.

The rest she could bear.

Letting down her inimitable and sterling partner?

No. That simply would not do.

Her stomach rumbled. Hungry? What sort of time was this to eat? She couldn't remember the last time she'd enjoyed a meal for flavor over fuel. That day in June, maybe. The day they'd gone to *Pamplona*. The streetbeater had been shot. So had she. But before things went screwy, there had been the bazaar, and there had been...

She stopped pacing. Could that be it?

"Mr. Glint!" she called. "Sally in here, dear man!"

He appeared a moment later.

She began to explain her idea to him. Paused. "Mr. Glint?"

"Yeah."

"What have you got behind your back?"

"Nothing."

"Covertness?" Miss Gleam stepped closer. "Secretism? From me? Surely not."

He moved so she couldn't see. "It's not finished."

"*What's* not finished?"

"Hold on a tick."

But she was already behind him, snatching the ragged bit of stationary paper that had once belonged to the owner of the leisure center and now to them.

She stared uncomprehendingly at the page for a moment.

"Mr. Glint, what is this?"

He made a noise so low she felt it rumble in her chest. The grin that tugged her lips then was so enormous you could chart stars across its curve. "Why as I live and decay. This is a poem!"

She thrust it into his hands, scooted herself onto the bowling alley cashier counter, and flung her arms up into the air. "You must read it at once!"

"But..."

"At once, I say!"

His sour mouth worked as he debated. Relenting at last, he smoothed the page as best he could against his birdcage breast, and began to read.

"Sweet Rosy Posey lived in a dozy
Had a nice house all warm and all cozy
Had a nice dog named William Supposy
One winter night a cold wind did blowsey
Got a bad cough and a runny nosy
Sneezed into Saturday, choked into Sunday
Died and was eaten by William Supposy
That was the end of Sweet Rosey Posey"

Mr. Glint's hands fell to his sides. He hung his head.

Miss Gleam slid off the counter. She put her arms around him.

"Very good," she said.

"Really?"

"Excellent." She pulled away, holding him at arm's length and smiling up into his gaunt face. "Really splendid. Want to know about conceptualization?"

"Not good at it."

"You are. You just showed me you are. Attend."

She drew him to the scoreboard where bowlers of yesteryear had tallied their scores. She took a piece of chalk. It crumbled, only a claw remaining.

Mr. Glint watched wordlessly as his partner drew a pie.

"The brain is like a pie. What defines a pie? Lamina."

"Lamina?"

"Layers, Mr. Glint. First, the base." She drew an arrow to the base. "The filling." A second arrow. "The crust." A third arrow. "This is important. Ready?"

He nodded.

"The subconscious." She highlighted the arrow pointing to the base. "The preconscious." A second arrow. "The conscious." A third arrow.

"Subconscious. Preconscious. Conscious. Right." Mr. Glint waited for the lesson to continue.

"Let's start with the conscious mind," said Gleam. "This is where thoughts live when they are immediate and relevant. They are the crust of who we are. What we notice going on. What we think about the things we notice. The bit on the outside.

"The preconscious mind is just underneath. The filling of what we might be. At any moment the filling might be enjoyed, or it might be ignored. It exists by potential. By the principle of 'might.' With me?"

His long-fingered hand rose and went side to side.

"Think so."

She smiled encouragingly. "Stay with me, dear man. This last one might make it clearer. The subconscious mind is the base. This is all the things you've ever done and that have ever happened to you. It's the place where all the information, all the stuff in your life is kept. The foundation of not just who you are now, but what you were before too."

Despite her fizzling energy, her urge to go on, she halted there, not wanting to overwhelm him.

Mr. Glint was terribly silent.

Time stretched agonizingly. Miss Gleam waited, and waited, and when it seemed she could wait no more he opened his mouth to speak.

"When I wrote my poem..." he managed.

"Yes?"

"That was my... my preconstance..."

"Preconscious."

"Preconscious mind... going to..."

"Yes." She came to him, unable to mask her excitement. "You've got it."

'My preconscious mind went to my conscious mind?'

"And before that?"

"The poem... started in my... base bit..."

"Subconscious."

"That, yeah. It started there because it... all starts there." He looked at her. "All of Mr. Glint starts there."

She could have screamed. She did.

"Eeeeeeeeee!"

In a single bound she was atop his shoulders. "What say we head down to the basement? The rats there are water bloated, and you've earned a juicy snack and then some!"

"All right."

"Tally ho! Oh."

The telephone had begun to ring.

"One moment, noble comrade."

She hopped down and whipped it out of its cradle.

"Good evening, sir! How are you this..."

Mr. Shine cut her off. Mr. Glint saw her smile vanish like someone closing a knife drawer.

"When, sir?"

Mr. Shine told her when.

"We shall investigate forthwith."

She hung up.

"Everything okay?" asked Mr. Glint.

"Mr. Flash is dead." Gleam went to him. "Shimmer was not an isolated incident. Someone is killing us."

Mr. Glint shrugged. "We'll kill them."

In his secluded cabin in artistic, musical Cleomenes District, they found Mr. Flash. Mr. Twinkle was already there.

"Ugly sight, Gleamy," he told her.

"You found him?"

"Right enough, I did." Twinkle was uneasy, jumpy, as if he expected the killer to descend out of the bulwark of the storm and take him.

Miss Gleam found Mr. Flash herself where he lay sprawled in his dining room. As with all members of their group, his skin emitted a diamond-dust sparkle. This was a side effect of the process by which they became Mr. Shine's top agents. There were straps involved, and subdermal injections, and pain. Yes. Lots of that last one.

The end result was sparkling skin and a handy capacity for regeneration.

Miss Gleam and Mr. Glint had responded best to the experimental serum. The rest had been less adaptive.

Miss Gleam kneeled down to have a closer look at Mr. Flash.

Ugly sight, Twinkle called it, and he was right.

Mr. Flash was pincushioned with arrows.

They sprouted from him like a field in nurtured springtime sprouts with—

CHAPTER TWENTY-EIGHT

Flowers.

Hughes collapsed into bed. If he never saw another bunch of flowers again, it would be too bloody soon.

He dozed.

"Mmm," he said, rolling over and nestling into the pillows and speaking the burbly language of the immensely tired. "Mmbed. Mmm, yummy bed."

His contented smile changed. Had he seen something on his bedside table?

He opened his eyes, sure that he was mistaken.

There *was* something. A little note.

He reached out and read it through squinty eyes.

Dear Hughes,

I'm going to have a drink at The Pear and Princess *tonight. Would you like to join me? I'll be there from seven o'clock.*

Cate

Hughes looked at the clock. It was six-forty-eight. He was out of bed like debris flung from a catapult.

He telephoned Falstaff.

"Happy thirty-first, sir. How might I be of service?"

"Falstaff... thirty-first?"

"Of July, sir."

Hughes was so addled he had no idea what the butler was talking about.

"Falstaff, Cate just left me a note."

"A note, sir?"

"She wants me to meet her for a drink. I've just spent eleven hours getting my bottom handed to me by a plant. I'm sweaty. If I look down at the phone, I see two receivers. Sheer exhaustion. I'm not at all equipped to deal with this right now."

"What's the venue?"

"*The Pear and Princess.*"

"Yes, that's the usual haunt and will be in fine fettle tonight of all nights. It *is* the thirty-first after all."

"What do I do, Falstaff?"

"Into the shower with you. I'll be down to your room presently. When was the last time you shaved?"

"Shaved?"

"Oh dear."

"I've got nothing to wear!"

"What did the note say?"

Hughes told him.

"This is a serious matter," said Falstaff and hung up.

Hughes entered the bathroom at a dead sprint. The shower was frosty cold, then volcanically hot. The shower gel bottle slipped from his hands. Reclaiming it, it wouldn't open. When he screwed off the entire lid, he dropped it again, slopping his knees in coconut-smelling goo. The rest of the gel went down the sucking drain. A minute later he left the shower with a head full of shampoo, caught a glimpse of himself in the foggy mirror, and dashed back in to finish washing.

"I'm here, sir."

"Falstaff!" Hughes emerged into the bedroom, toweling himself dry. The butler was there.

"Showered, sir?"

"My knees have never been cleaner."

"Here are your clothes."

Hughes dived into the shirt. "God, you're a lifesaver."

"Hold out your neck."

"What?"

Falstaff brandished a straight razor.

"Really?"

"That depends, sir. Would you like to appear before her as the smooth-necked savant or the hairy-necked baboon?"

Hughes stuck out his neck.

"*The Pear and Princess* is located eighteen minutes on foot from the base of Redspire," said Falstaff as he swiped the razor in cool arcs along Hughes' throat.

"Eighteen minutes?"

"I have taken the liberty of telephoning a taxi, sir."

"Oh, you're amazing, Falstaff."

"True. Try not to hop so much as you put on your trousers, sir. This is sharp."

"Sorry."

"Hurt her feelings and you will be."

"Pardon?"

"Sir?"

Hughes blinked at the butler's innocent expression.

"What did you say?"

"That the razor is sharp, sir."

"Ah. Er. Right."

The taxi whizzed him through the rainy night.

"Out to celebrate, gov?" the taxi man asked him.

"Celebrate?"

The man looked at him reproachfully in the rearview. "The thirty-first, gov."

"Oh yeah. Of course."

Would you like to join me? she'd written.

"Celebrate," Hughes breathed, excitement beginning to bubble his gut. "Absolutely."

They arrived at five past seven.

The Pear and Princess was a square building, four stories high and green as a ripe pear. The owners, being fabulously rich, could afford real ivy. It grew so voraciously that it seemed to grasp the building's west and northern walls with huge leafy fingers. The roof was slanted green tile. Four chimneys smoked there, one for each floor below where the fireplaces were strategically placed to give as much heat to the building as possible. Orange light poured from the windows out into the street, warm and inviting. The sign was polished wood brought at great expense from the countryside, a pear-shaped block of chestnut painted with the likeness of a crowned princess at the core in place of seeds.

Inside it was dry and merry with activity. For a moment Hughes felt like Ser Gwendle Gardener heading into the best tavern in a medieval world. He took off his coat, hung it on a peg, and set off to look for Cate.

Mirolaen hung from the rafters. They draped the shelves, the bar, the mantlepieces of the pear-shaped hearths. Hughes recognized the flower and immediately realized how marvelously stupid he had been. Falstaff and the cab driver hadn't been pulling his leg in some sort of weird celebration conspiracy. Today was the thirty-first, and here were the blooms of mirolaen, white as newly fallen snow, to mark the occasion.

It was on this day however many years ago that the war with Champleurs had come to an end on a hill near the town of Origné. Some important people had died, as well as lots of people deemed unimportant. A treaty was signed. Champleurs promised to never start a war again. Mirolaens bloomed on the hill.

"Hughes!"

It was Cate. She beckoned him over.

"Cate, hey."

"How are you?"

"Well, I forgot what day it was if that tells you anything."

She smiled at him. A mirolaen pinned her hair over one ear, delicate and pale against the fierce fire of her locks. The line of her strong jaw uncorked a jar of butterflies in his belly. "Fancy getting drunk with me, Gormon Hughes?"

"Oh yeah."

Round One:

Gorman Hughes	Cate Jubilee
• One pint of brown ale, thick as soup • One shot of Daethumberland tequila	• One pint of Stoving's Apricot Jawglobber • One shot of Daethumberland tequila

"Oh my God," said Hughes.

"Hits like a lawnmower," Cate agreed.

They slid their shot glasses to the end of the table.

"Tell me about your Aunt Trisha."

Her face lit up. "You remembered."

"Course."

"Quite the opening topic. Well, she was vain. Unbelievably, gloriously vain."

"Really? How bad?"

"Woeful. Obsessed with mirrors. Also with self-image. Lavish clothes. Had an implant that kept her voice dainty and free of husk. Regular collagen injections. She dumped her boyfriends like clockwork when they turned thirty."

That got a surprised laugh from Hughes. "Wow."

"Wow is right."

"And is that vanity related to your magic item's ability? Your boots let you teleport between reflective surfaces, right?"

She raised a playful eyebrow. "*Veeeery* perceptive, Meester Hoos. There's been a lot of academic work on magic items. Doctor John Isherwood would gnaw off his own leg to understand them."

"Them and the portals, right?"

"Portals, plural?"

It was Hughes' turn to be playful. "I'm perceptive, right?"

"Mm. Very."

Round Two:

Gorman Hughes	Cate Jubilee
• One pint of Stoving's Apricot Jawglobber • One shot of Missile	• One pint of Stoving's Apple Throatwinkler • One shot of Missile

"Hoh," said Hughes. "Hohhh, no."

"Hoh, yes," said Cate. "Missiles are amaretto liqueur, vermouth, cold-brew coffee, and Windy City whiskey. It's like being punched in the neck by the concept of a good morning."

They slid their shot glasses to the end of the table.

"And sorry, Trisha was your mum's sister?"

"My dad's sister," amended Cate Jubilee. "Mum was an only child."

"Get on well?"

"With Mum? I did."

Did, thought Hughes. *Her mother is either estranged or passed away.* "I'm sorry," he said.

She gave an easy shrug. "Bit of a sad story really. We're not tipsy enough for it."

Hughes suppressed a belch. "I'm getting there." *And if you keep grinning like that, Cate Jubilee, these butterflies are going to set up a flight school.*

"Tell me about your family," she said.

"I don't really remember my mum. Dad runs *The Scriptorium and Flavored Tea Emporium*."

"What?"

"It's a teashop."

"I gathered," she said, giggling. "We should go there."

"Sure," he said, not meaning it. He wanted to get her away from the subject of his life. Her eagerness made defenses rise in him like a phalanx of shields. "Is there a magic item that you envy?"

"What, envy having?"

"Yeah, like want it for yourself."

She thought about it. "I'm not sure about wanting one myself, but I know one I'm scared of."

"That's much more exciting. Oh, sorry."

Hughes crouched to avoid a platter of drinks carried by a server.

"Another round, you two?" the server called.

"Don't you rush us, rascal," cried Cate.

"Wouldn't dream of it, Miss Jubilee."

Cate flicked her tongue like a lizard.

"Where were we?" she asked Hughes. Her inquisitive expression melted into something sly. "What?"

"Um?"

"You're smiling at me."

Hughes realized he was doing just that. "Is it okay?"

"It suits you. Joy is attractive in dark-haired men."

"You're kind," he said, unwilling to admit he was only really like this around her. "So what's the magic item you're scared of?"

"Idris Corlum's Perfect Prison."

"Once more."

"Idris Corlum's Perfect Prison."

They were both laughing.

"And what pray tell," said Hughes, "is Idris Corlum's Perfect Prison?"

"All right. Ready? This absolutely blew me away when I first heard about it." Cate sat forward. "So Idris Corlum got his magic item sixty years ago during the reign of The Old Dragon. That's Winnifred Dragontail's father, Walsingham.

Most people use their magic items to fight, but some... some perform functions in Redspire."

"Like Knickerbocker."

"Yes, exactly. Knickerbocker is a kind of spymaster."

"I like him."

"I do too. From a distance of about ten feet."

Hughes could feel the butterflies fluttering between his ears now. "So Idris Corlum is like a jailer or something?"

"He's a jailer all right. A jailer with only one prisoner."

"Ahhh," intoned Hughes extravagantly. "The thick *plottens.*"

This induced a fit of delighted giggles in his company.

Cate swiped at him good-naturedly. "The plot thickens, you barbarian. So Idris Corlum wears a bracer with three straps on it. If he touches you, he can tear off one of the straps and send you to an inescapable prison."

"How is it inescapable?"

Cate offered him a secret smile. "How indeed. Therein lies one of the Citadel's great mysteries, Hughes. Idris is extremely loyal to Winnifred and her father before her. No one knows how his Perfect Prison works except the Dragontail family and Idris himself of course. The rest of us know only that the Perfect Prison can be used a maximum of three times (one for each strap on his bracer) and that the prisoner..."

He saw something behind her eyes, a mixture of exhilaration and fear.

"The only person deemed dangerous enough to be placed in unbreakable incarceration is Frank Gallant."

"I see," said Hughes. Then he said, "Who's Frank Gallant?"

"Only a name," Cate replied. "A name and another great mystery."

"You're full of intrigue."

"Good point. I should be full of alcohol. Server!"

Round Three:

Gorman Hughes	Cate Jubilee
• One pint of Chickenscratch • One shot of Eggscratch • One pint of Scratchscratch	• One pint of Foxy's Astute Lager • One shot of Henhouse • One shot of Roostercockcrow

"What are these?" said Hughes, looking at the drinks he'd just had on the menu with disbelief. "What am I doing to myself?"

"Why did you pick them?"

"Cate, I liked the names. Thought they were funny. Shared a common wossname... ancestry. Look at this; read the ingredients for Scratchscratch. Is it even legal to have that much alcohol in one place?"

"You've eaten, haven't you?"

"Nope."

Round Four:

Gorman Hughes	Cate Jubilee
• One extra large Improbable Buffalo Wings • Two portions of fries for soakage • One pint of Stoving's Apricot Jawglobber	• One extra large Improbable Buffalo Wings • Six portions of fries for soakage • One pint of Paint Thinner

"Back on the Stoving's?" Cate asked him.

"Yuff," Hughes replied through a mouthful of wing. He swallowed, grinning bashfully and wiping the sauce from his lips with a napkin. "Sorry. Yes, I am. What would be your Perfect Prison?"

"Oh, if Idris Corlum had to jail me? Good one. Ummm. Someplace without reflections, I expect. Whatever the opposite of a house of mirrors at a carnival is."

They slid their plates to the end of the table.

"You like carnivals?" Hughes wondered.

"What's not to like? Interesting too. Interesting history. I've watched a good few documentary vids about them. Speaking of, what's your favorite?"

"My favorite vid? Toughie. What's yours?"

She listed off a few. Hughes hadn't seen any of them. They sounded like cozy crime pictures. He was disappointed he hadn't seen them, they might have formed some more common ground for banter. He needn't have worried. As per usual, Cate Jubilee brought it all off just fine.

"We shall have to watch them together," she announced. "And you'll show me your faves."

"Deal," Hughes replied happily.

"You haven't got a choice."

"I know it."

Laughter flowed between them again.

The butterflies inside him had set up a flight school, a college, and an expert's program. Cate Jubilee snorted when she got a bad case of the giggles. That set those mothlike fellows to fluttering like crazy.

Round Five:

Gorman Hughes	Cate Jubilee
• One Rotund Gin and Wicked Wolf Tonic	• One Hot'n'Baleful Whiskey

Hughes tapped the rim of his glass with a finger. "I think I'm done after this one."

"How responsible. You know what happens to responsible men?"

"What?"

Cate rolled the smoky-smelling whisky at the bottom of her glass and took a sip, her eyes never leaving his. "Someone comes along and makes them irresponsible." The moment crackled, changing every butterfly into a bolt of zigzagging electricity, oozing to warm honey, and then the moment passed and Cate was telling him about so-and-so and such-and-such back at the Citadel. He sat there enjoying the cold courage of his gin and tonic. Enjoying the way she spoke. Enjoying her face as it gave way to emotion after emotion like delightful dominoes falling into place. He wondered if this was what people were talking about when they described his own expressive features. If so, he believed Cate wore those features better. That nose... *God, she's got the loveliest nose...*

Above their heads the lights dimmed and came up.

"Last call," said Cate. "Another, or shall we go?"

He was tempted to stay, but caution counseled that he had never had this much to drink before. "I think I'll quit while I'm ahead."

"Who says you're ahead?"

He felt himself color. "I didn't mean..."

"Hush. Only teasing." She linked his arm. "I've taken care of the bill. No protesting now. You'll take care of it next time. Don't forget your coat. Ready? Into ze vilderness vee go, Meester Hoos."

They hailed a taxi. Rain gushed and guttered and babbled in little brooks. It fell so hard it seemed to slosh across the taxi's windshield in buckets. Hughes barely noticed. There was a mirolaen pinned to his shirt. For the life of him he could not remember how it had gotten there. He and Cate were talking about *The Pear and Princess*, how good a venue it was. There were three seats in the back of the taxi. Hughes sat on the left and Cate sat in the middle. The right was left empty. She was still linking his arm when they pulled up outside Redspire.

"Can I walk you to your room?" she asked.

"I should walk you to yours."

That sly look twinkled in her eyes. "What a lot of walking that would be."

"A preponderance."

"A preponderance!" She slapped her upper thigh, snort-laughing. "Brilliant!"

It was half past eleven, and there were plenty of people out and about in the halls of the tower. Some people wanted to chat with Cate, but she breezed smoothly by, promising to call them tomorrow.

"How tipsy are you?" he asked her.

"*Inebriate of air am I, debauchee of dew.*"

"That's very pretty."

"Ss from a poem," Cate said. "And when Cate Jubilee starts into the poems, you know she's a tipply-wipsy girl."

Hughes debated, then went for it. "That sad story you were going to tell..."

"Not tonight," she said.

They were outside his door. Hughes could hardly believe it. How quickly time whittled away under the paring knife of Cate's company.

She touched the white flower in his breast pocket. "Next time maybe."

He touched the white flower pinning her hair back. "Whatever you're comfortable with."

"I had fun, Gormon Hughes." She pulled back, only a little, but enough to establish distance. "Yet I have notes."

He blinked. "Notes?"

"Write them somewhere you'll remember. You were the spirit of inquisition tonight. Now I appreciate that because it means you want to know about me. But I," she said grandly, "am not without that spirit of inquisition. Next time you do the talking."

He held his hands up. "The Hughes lecture hour."

She laughed. "I mean it."

I know you do, he thought. *Just as firmly as I know that I can never do that, Cate. I showed Kim Kallaimon who I was. My poverty. My love of stories in general and theatre in specific. The worries that gnaw at me. The fact that I get upset and angry sometimes, and I can barely reconcile those feelings, let alone determine their source. You know what Kim did? She... No. No, I can never do it, Cate. But for you, I can fake something wonderful. That way you'll never know. That way you'll never see the face. Masks are better. Masks are safer.*

"Hughes?"

"Hm."

She had reclosed the distance. Her face was tilted up to him. "Nothing. You seemed asleep on your feet for a moment."

"I'm here."

"The thirty-first is hard for me," she admitted. "You made it easier."

Hughes didn't know what to say.

She smiled at his silence. "You had a good time?"

"You were there," he said. "How could I not have?"

He watched her lips curl sweetly. "That," she murmured, "was entirely the right thing to say."

"May I have a kiss goodnight?"

She gave him two.

ACT SEVEN

THE BONEMEAL BOYS

CHAPTER TWENTY-NINE

July finished its shift, punched out, and in came August.

August took one look at muggy, clammy, damp Corinth City, tugged on its bathing suit, and began to swim upstream toward September. At bars like the dingy rathole in which Ruddy Jolene had huffed her last, and at upscale taverns like *The Pear and Princess*, everybody was talking about the same thing—it was the storm of a lifetime. Even those miserly codgers who always felt compelled to point out that everything was fiercer in their day mumbled a grudging agreement. It *was* the worst storm they'd experienced. No arguments here. Only rain.

Which goes to show what some people know.

In fact there had been far worse storms in the past hundred years of Corinth City history. Two of them. They had slammed the streets with a wrath that was somehow old and atavistic. Half the city was underwater in an instant. But they had been short, moving in and out with the speed of insects on the surface of a tropical river. This storm was prolonged.

Floodfighters could keep atop the trouble before it became a disaster, but they were being run ragged. The government discussed emergency measures with their usual toothless fervor. There were rumors of mass evacuations that came to nothing. But the tension left in the wake of such rumor remained like an afterimage of the lightning scorching the perpetual dark of the summer sky, an echo of the thankless thunder. Simply put, people missed blue skies. They ached for sunshine.

In Leonidas District, Gormon Hughes Senior watched the water level rise and fall and rise again, eyeing his teashop's paper walls with a grim solemnity and the quiet resignation of a man who was a little old to be getting worried about anything other than his son, but who would rather his livelihood and house stayed dry while he worried, thank you very much.

Meanwhile in Redspire, Gormon Hughes Junior continued to train. Cassandra despaired of him constantly. It was Hector who saw promise. He told Hughes that meaningful progression was invisible to the participant. "It may feel as though you've accomplished little. Not so. You waste nothing, Hughes. You are young and have good energy to exercise. See your stomach muscles? These lines here tell me you are eating better and putting it to use. A strong core affects the movement of your back. Thus your poise improves every day."

"And my footwork?" said Hughes hopefully.

Hector patted him on the shoulder. "What is the saying? *Two outta three ain't bad.*"

"I suppose I walked into that one. When will I learn the other two rules of swordplay?"

"I surmise that by early October you'll be ready for the second."

"That's amazing."

"Yes. Today Cassandra will throw trees at you."

Hughes grinned. "Oak-kay."

Hector looked puzzled.

"It's a play on words," said Hughes with the sudden acute desperation of those forced to explain their jokes. "Oak tree. Okay."

"Ah."

"She's not... Hector she's not really going to throw trees at me, is she?"

His instructor leaned in, and with an utterly severe expression on his face, he said, "Yew never know. She willow or she won't. Either way there's going to be an aldercation. But her bark is worse than her bite. Branch out. Get to the root of the matter. Or leaf it alone. Either way," he leaned back, imperious as a prince. "Do not be a beech."

Hughes stared, goggle-eyed.

Hector swept away, his ghostly cloak flapping majestically. "Olive these things I do, Hughes, are fir your own good."

Week poured into week. August backstroked on. September drew close.

One point of concern was abilities. No one—not Cate, Hector, even Cassandra—had pulled him aside and explained how they worked. As far as he could tell, Strength, Dexterity, and Intelligence interacted with magic items. The wielder had one focus ability. For example, Cate used Dexterity for her reflection-hopping boots. Priam King used Intelligence for his crown.

But the secrets of how they worked were still incomprehensible to Hughes. There was an assumption that he knew the things he knew, and that was good enough.

In fact he was beginning to suspect there *were* no secret workings. Did Cate and Tommy and the rest of them see and hear the words that appeared when Hughes used his unique Performance ability?

He imagined it had to be so.

But then why not discuss it with him? He'd been afraid of such an interaction since he was more convinced than ever that he was the only person who could use Performance. Now summer was almost over. Those suspicions ballooned in him. Maybe there wouldn't be an interaction. Maybe no one else saw or heard the words except Gormon Hughes.

Which went a long way to explain his reticence in bringing up the subject with Cate or Hector. Hughes had only recently become an insider into this wild and wonderful world of the Scarlet Citadel. The last thing he wanted was to pollute that. Or worse, orchestrate things so he became an outsider once more.

On a sweeter subject, he and Cate were spending more and more time together. However, of a second outing like the night intoxicant with wings, booze, and mirolaen flowers, there was no sign. Hughes got the sense she was waiting for him to take the initiative. Sometimes she got to laughing, and her crinkling eyes invited him to, *Ask me already.*

They said, *Remember, Hughes, this time you do the talking.*

Hughes laughed along and didn't ask her.

One day, the 23rd of August, she never appeared for their scheduled lunch.

Aside from a few pangs of obligatory disappointment, Hughes saw nothing out of the ordinary in this. After all, Cate often was quite late and had in the past canceled altogether. So he was not overly worried, and in any case it meant he had a more ample opportunity to practice his battle steps.

By that evening he was too drained to feel even the teensiest bit aggrieved by the lonely lunch. He could not have known Cate was planning his first foray into the worst danger imaginable.

That night he dreamed the carousel dream again, along with sixty-thousand others across the city. More and more each night shared in the dream. Their versions were different, of course. Hughes was the only one who dreamed of Mr. Glint. And Kim Kallaimon too. But they all—*every single one of the dreamers*— saw the carousel, the three bent, crooked shapes ushering people onto the ride, and the figure with eyes like hellish foglamps.

Most of them also woke restless and frightened.

Practically all of them felt the tug too. The yearning for... for *something*.

Oh well.

Only a case of the moon whispers, right? Right. That's the attitude of a reasonable person. Dreams, even dreams that seem to stalk from brain to brain, feeding on fear and dispensing desire, well... those are just moon whispers received via the cable transmitter of imagination we've all got. We all get a bit funny when we travel to the Land of Nod. Morning brings such reassurances to Corinth City, to the dreamers. You endured the dark. Good job. Naturally, as has been noted, it is easy to be a reasonable person when it's light out.

Then the dark steals back over the world, and you cuddle up and shut your eyes and endure it because you know you can. You've done it before.

It's only moon whispers.

Only the carousel of romping animals.

Only the tarantula-fingered ticket collectors.

Only eyes of terrible burning yellow.

So August swam the last lengths of summer, and the nightmare crept along with it.

***

"Am I intruding?" said Falstaff.

It was Monday morning, August 24th, and Hughes was in tremendous form. That afternoon would bring another bout against his mortal enemy, the peony blossoms, but for now Cassandra was pleased to run him through his paces in the gymnasium. Today she informed him that he was a lump of useless oatmeal and glistening jellyfish vertebrae a total of six times. This figure represented an enormous improvement in their relationship.

"Yes, you are intruding," said Cassandra. "The boy was doing so well that I was merely crushingly disappointed with my life choices."

Hughes sat up smiling. "Don't mind her, Falstaff. How are you?"

"Agreeable enough, sir. Lady Dragontail sends for you."

"Well, I suppose I mustn't keep her waiting then." Hughes stood from the bench and gave a mighty stretch. His back and shoulders sang sweetly aching songs. "See you later, Cassandra?"

"Go on," she said dismissively. "Drag your hapless porridge body from my sight."

Hughes chuckled and fell in step with Falstaff.

"Not going to cut my hair before we visit her Ladyship?"

The tidy little man gave Hughes a look. "Not this time."

They passed a few people in the gymnasium foyer. They were talking in quiet voices. Hughes caught the word "lawless." He felt his happy mood develop a few hairline cracks.

It was an unseasonably bracing morning for late summer. In the empty corridor Hughes felt the mellow air slip through windows left ajar and breathe on his swiftly cooling skin. Shafts of gray storm light made rainy pictograms on the stone floor.

"Any idea what this meeting is about?" he asked the butler carefully.

"Not my place to say, sir."

"So you do know."

"I can neither confirm nor deny."

Hughes' patience thinned. "Falstaff."

"Sir?"

"Has something happened?"

The butler balked at Hughes' tone, it was so forceful and earnest. He halted next to the elevator button, licked his lips (he even did that neatly), and when he did eventually speak he would not meet Hughes' gaze. "Yes. Someone has gone missing. Don't ask me to say more, sir. Lady Dragontail will explain everything as she sees fit."

Missing.

The word clung to Hughes as the elevator rose a hundred floors through sighing darkness.

Someone has gone missing, and Wendy Dragontail wants to see me.

The elevator arrived. When the doors opened, Hughes was surprised to see none other than Hector with his back to them, his gaze fixed on the grandfather clock standing vigil outside the Lady's office.

"Hector. It's good to see you."

"And you, my apt pupil."

The son of Priam King offered his arm.

Hughes grasped it fondly. "Are you here about the missing person?"

Falstaff bristled. "Master Hughes!"

"Oh bugger. Sorry."

"Yes," said Hector. "But if I divulge what I know, our friend here is going to have an embolism."

"It is Lady Dragontail's matter to discuss," fussed Falstaff. He opened the door for Hughes and made to usher him inside.

Before he could follow, Hughes felt Hector's grip on his forearm tighten. His spectral lips moved silently. Hughes read them, though for the moment he couldn't understand what they meant.

Then Hector was gone, the doors were shutting behind him, and Hughes found himself once more within the dragon's lair.

"Hello," he said. Then, because it is the habit of most people to state the absolute obvious when surprised, he also said, "Cate. You're here."

She waved at him from her perch on the windowsill.

"Hughes," said Wendy Dragontail from behind her fastidiously ordered desk. "Do come in. I assume you've heard the news."

"Just that someone's missing."

He heard a groan from Falstaff and had to suppress a grin.

"Missing. Quite so." The leader of the Scarlet Citadel stood and approached a huge board arranged opposite the fireplace. From the mantel the stone dragons seemed to watch that board, and with no fire lit their dull faces seemed locked in expressions of mistrust as though the board was often up to mischief. Hughes peered round to inspect it.

His brow creased.

"Don't keep us in suspense, Hughes," Wendy prompted him. "What do you make of it?"

"Well, it *looks* like a map, my Lady. Here's a town, and then these little bumpy bits are hills. I take it those thin fellows are trees. And this bit up here at the top..." He canted his head to one side. "Some kind of really big house? A manor? I'm not sure what all these numbers mean. I'm trying to see if there's a pattern..."

Next to him Wendy Dragontail stood with her hands behind her back. Faethe, her magical amulet, hung about her neck, golden and intimidating. The effect was rather spoiled by her comfy cotton trousers, her plum-colored sweater, and her socks. There were tiny goblins from fairy stories on those socks. They had speech bubbles. *Scrimbus, scrongus,* said one sock. *Mingus, monglus,* said the other.

It was unclear whether these were the sock goblin names, or if it was how they said, "Good morning."

Sometimes, thought Hughes. *Sometimes I wonder if I amn't dreaming. If the nightmare about the carousel I keep having is actually real life. It'd be a disturbing life, sure, but the socks would be gray.*

"The pattern is a sequence," said Wendy Dragontail. "Note how the numbers go with the tiny symbols here, here, and good gracious, here as well. Together they form equations, but more on that in a moment. Hughes, where do credits come from?"

"Credits?" He stared at her blankly. "From the place that mints them, I suppose."

"Haven't you ever wondered where that is?"

"Nope," he said honestly. "I've often wondered where credits *are*, but not where they come from, if you see what I mean."

"What would you say if I told you that credits came from here?"

"Where?"

"Redspire. The very tower in which you currently lodge."

Hughes said nothing for a moment. "I don't think I'd say anything, my Lady. Something like that is too big to be digested in one sitting."

"A slippery answer, Hughes. But your point is taken. Let me speak plainly. The Scarlet Citadel controls the flow of credits in the city. We are the miners, the mint, and the distribution. But where do they come from, these cubes of pink crystal that people will live, and in some cases, die for?"

Without conscious thought, Hughes looked at the map.

From the corner of his eye, Wendy Dragontail nodded. "Yes. Credits come from that place, and places just like it. From a country you could not hope to find on a map of our continents. Indeed, credits come from another world altogether."

"Eurydice," said Cate, and though her voice was pitched quietly, Hughes heard the word like the toll of some strange sinister bell. Each syllable swept back and forth in the belfry of his mind. *Eur-id-iss-ee.* He felt the patch of skin between his shoulder blades—still damp with sweat from his workout—rash out in gooseflesh.

"Isn't that funny?"

He turned to Wendy Dragontail, who was looking at him with that telltale twinkle in her eye. "Isn't what funny?" he asked her.

"When people hear that name for the first time, they shiver. I have never met someone who hasn't."

That twinkle in her eye told him, *Except you, Hughes. You didn't shiver, and isn't that just a howler?*

"How many other worlds are there?" he asked.

"Two that we know of. Iphigenia, where the creatures die and yield the material for magic items, is common knowledge. And Eurydice, which is secret, and will remain that way." She raised her brows meaningfully.

"Of course," Hughes said. "Mum's the word."

Something was bothering him.

"Iphigenia is full of cow things. Dramen. Pygmies."

"Among other things," said Wendy mildly. He could tell from her expression she knew exactly what he was about to ask.

"Well, on this map you've got here there's a town and a manor house." He indicated lines curling between the trees. "These even look like roads. I was wondering... do *people* live in Eurydice?"

"Falstaff?"

The butler bustled in. "My Lady?"

"Tea, Falstaff. Earl Grey, I think. Hughes will join me. And something soothing for Miss Jubilee, who I suspect is getting a bit restless on her window ledge."

"I am not restless," said Cate. There was a pause. Then she mumbled something that might have been, "*Hot chocolate, please.*"

"And biscuits with chocolate on them. For my guests, of course," Wendy added wearily just as Falstaff made to protest. "Since I would never even think of anything so decadent for myself."

The butler bobbed and went off in search of chocolate biscuits and a teapot.

"Dowdy little fusspot," Wendy grumbled. "Where were we? Ah yes, Eurydice. That realm beyond the second portal. What lives there you ask? Civilization, Hughes. Or whatever the reflection of civilization looks like in a pool of the darkest water on the vilest pavement."

"Sounds cheery," said Hughes.

"Sarcasm is amusing. Eurydice is not. It is, in fact, distinctly uncheery. Do you remember when I told you that nothing is as it appears to be?"

Did he? Yes, now he thought of it. It had been the first time Hughes shuffled his way into this office. She had tricked him using her amulet. "I remember."

"This map shows a region of Eurydice that was mapped by one of our cartographers. These are individuals who have trained their entire lives to scout and take notes in the most perilous conditions. Irreplaceable, or as close to it as makes no difference. One of them drew this map and marked the numbers."

Falstaff returned, doled out delicious drinks, and left them to it. Cate blew the steam off her hot chocolate while Wendy and Hughes took seats by the fireplace.

"Listen to me closely," said Wendy. Hughes needed no instruction. Ancient apish instincts pricked and scraped his nerves. There was something lurking around the corner of this conversation, something to do with what Hector had mouthed to him in the antechamber by the grandfather clock. He sat forward and listened as close as could be.

"Eurydice is not like Iphigenia. The latter is a fixed location. The swamp, the forest, the desert."

"The mountain," said Hughes, remembering its looming craggy face.

Wendy Dragontail gave a curt nod. "The mountain, quite so. These never change. They are always there. Eurydice, on the other hand, is not fixed. It is a place of many parts, a dungeon dimension whose rooms and caverns and corridors shift and meld like beads of mercury on a string."

Hughes understood in a thunderclap. "The numbers on the map. The equations are little algorithms. Your cartographers can map out the place geographically but also mathematically. In other words," he said, unable to control the amazement in his tone, "you can predict the shifts in the dungeon. See what will appear, how it will appear, *when!*"

He gazed at the map, seeing it with fresh eyes.

All those figures. The variation was staggering. And a whole world that could shift and change on a whim? As if it were alive in some totally extraordinary way?

"It's not a manor house, is it?" He looked at her.

"No. It is a castle."

A castle. Internal levers clicked into place. To Hughes the board was not just a board anymore. It was a window into possibility, into the dungeon dimensions of Eurydice where creatures spawned from the plasma into a dark mirroring of civilization built towns, and castles, and who knew what else...

"Nothing is as it appears to be," he concluded, his whole mind feeling zapped with hot laser beams of awe and arrows of cold dread.

"You continue to impress," said Wendy Dragontail. "That's shrewdness, young man. That's wit."

He felt an unexpected rush of pleasure. "Thank you, my Lady. That's... incredibly humbling, especially from you, and you know—"

"Now give me a chocolate biscuit off your plate, there's a good chap."

"Oh, erm. Here you go."

"Well done." She descended upon it greedily.

Hughes sat back in his chair, his vision centered on a point far off in the distance. A whole other world away.

"Why tell me now?" he said.

A gentle *thump* made him glance behind. Cate had slid off the windowsill. She tilted her chin toward Wendy Dragontail as though telling him to focus.

The Lady herself was dunking the remaining halfmoon of biscuit into her tea. "Because it is important that you know, Hughes. Recently the cartographer who made that map went in for one last survey of the areas surrounding the castle."

"Is his name 'Lawless' by any chance?" asked Hughes.

Both women looked at him wonderingly.

Wendy recovered first. "My, my. How the rumor mill churns. Grinding out loaves of secret information instead of bread. No matter. Yes, his name is Isaac Lawless. He holds our highest rank in cartography: Burnished."

"Burnished Isaac Lawless," Hughes said. It was a goddamn fantastic name, in fairness to its owner. "He made this whole map? Alone?"

"And many like it," Wendy replied. "He's quite brilliant."

"That's one word for him," mumbled Cate.

Wendy flashed her a disapproving glare.

"Let me guess," said Hughes. It was one of those moments in which his mouth moved despite the frantic signals his brain was giving it. "He's been captured by whoever owns that castle. You want someone to go fetch him. Namely Cate, and that means me. Us being partners and everything."

"Once again your powers of deduction astonish," said Wendy, and her delivery was so dry Hughes began to redden.

"Sorry," he said.

Wendy popped the sodden biscuit in her mouth, melted chocolate and all, and went back behind her desk. She dabbed at her lips with a handkerchief. "Go to Eurydice. Find the cartographer. Bring him home."

Cate saluted crisply. "Yes, matron. At your command."

Wendy sighed and began to delve through a neat mound of paperwork.

Cate's face was radiant, grinning, but she stopped short when she saw Hughes wasn't coming with her.

"Excuse me?" he said.

The Lady looked up. "Hughes. You are still here."

He steeled his courage. "I was just wondering if Eurydice's shifting, wobbly-wiggly geography had anything to do with Frank Gallant?"

He heard a harsh intake of breath from Cate. There was an icy silence.

"No," said Winnifred Dragontail.

"Right." His brain urged him to run. His traitorous mouth flapped on. "So he's in Idris Corlum's Perfect Prison for some totally unrelated reason then."

"Yes."

"Rrrright. Ahm..."

"That will be all, Hughes."

He left in a hurry, his ears red as strawberries and hot enough to power a Jolene furnace.

Cate was in the lead. He caught up with her.

"I should have warned you," she said.

"Sorry."

"Frank Gallant is not a subject you discuss openly in Redspire."

"Consider me warned."

Her discomfort evaporated. "No harm done."

"Really?"

"No. Just trying to spare your feelings for a moment. That was horrible."

"Oh."

"My cheeks are like smoldering coals."

"My ears get me," said Hughes. "Shall we go save a cartographer?"

She nodded eagerly. They set off to get their things.

"They're nice ears," said Cate.

"I was going to say the same about your cheeks."

"Do not bite zem," she cautioned him. "Zey are too hawt!"

"*Cate.*"

She giggled. The tension of Frank Gallant was fading.

But Hughes could not rid himself of an eerie sense of fear. Hector had meant well, perhaps, but the two words he'd mouthed to Hughes had struck that fear in deep.

Not ready, he'd told Hughes silently.

Cate was talking about provisions. Hughes nodded along dumbly.

Here it was then.

Go to Eurydice. Find the cartographer. Bring him home.

It was his first mission with the Scarlet Citadel. He was going to the place where the organization harvested its money. Hughes could find a way to lay his hands on the credits he needed to pay off Glint and Gleam.

He ought to be electrified with currents of hope.

Instead he felt immersed in gelid water, a lake slowly freezing with wintry terror.

Hector's face was discernible in the murk. No wonderful voice like cinnamon icing on carrot cake. Only the warning articulated from the lips of a dead man.

Not ready.

Not ready.

CHAPTER THIRTY

If you were to open a blueprint of Redspire, you would be struck by the fact that the tower does not have eighty-eight floors as is popularly believed.

For starters, there's an extra bit of space at the top before you reach the roof. It's only titchy, much smaller than the other regions. What could it be, this miniature eighty-ninth floor?

Don't worry. We'll get to it in due time.

For now, let the mind's eye wander to the area below the ground floor. It's far larger than the Lunarlight Wing, or the Grand Hall, or any two floors put together. In these cavernous depths, a door waits to be opened. Through it, evil without scruple does not wait, for it has much to do.

Following Cate's instructions, Hughes rode the elevator to the ground floor. Upon arrival, he opened the handle lid of the elevator crank, exposing a little button he pressed hard with his thumb. The doors shut. Mechanisms clunked into place. Unseen motors hummed. Beneath his feet Hughes felt the unlit box begin to sink. Down and down the lift went, for so long he began to wonder if it would ever stop.

They ought to install lamps, he thought. *You could start to worry. Dark of this kind—blind, helpless dark—sort of hikes up everything bad that might occur to you.*

What bad things? he wondered, annoyed with himself for getting anxious before the adventure had even got going. What are you talking about?

He regretted this line of inquiry. Along the highways of his brain, unlikely roads were seeing a lot of sudden and terrible activity.

Unpleasant recollections drove through him, memories like:

(Hooyou?)

(I know all about it, cocksucker. She's dead and you killed her.)

(Not ready)

"I won't hear you," he told these unexpected visitors from Memory Lane. "I won't."

But he did.

He listened numbly as they hounded him, rode him down. The elevator's motor took on the snarl of freakish engines. He remembered each voice, each harrowing event, with a clarity that was almost supernatural. Maybe it was the dark. Blind. Helpless. Descending.

Leave me alone. He fumbled for the crank and gripped it feverishly as his visitors wheeled round for a second pass at his sanity.

(Hooyou?)

That was Laurana, her freckles spattered with blood.

(Cocksucker. She's dead and you killed her.)

Walter, accusing Hughes of murder on the day they sent Laurana off to be buried under the blackberries.

(Not ready.)

This last from Hector. Wise, patient Hector.

Not ready for what? Why for Eurydice where something worse than harmless elevator-dark brooded. Something that required a robust knowledge of all three rules of swordplay to tackle, not just a cursory grasp of the first. Something that built towns, and castles, and *which Wendy Dragontail believed him ready to fight.*

The breath seized in Hughes' chest. He felt wind blasted by an almost physical relief. His hand gave an involuntary shudder and released the crank. Because that was the crux of the matter, wasn't it? The diversion that cut off the Memory Lane parade, that flicked on a little light no matter how blackly his doubt festered?

Hector the ghost thought he wasn't ready.

Wendy the very-much-alive leader of the Scarlet Citadel thought he was.

He tried a deep breath. It stuttered a little. The second was better.

Along my road—the only road that counts—the lamps glow nice and warm. I keep them going. I am okay and I will be okay.

All that uncertainty had stooped his posture for him.

By the time the floor steadied and the doors opened, Hughes' back was straight. Even a trifle proud.

***

The portal to Eurydice was an exact duplicate of the one that led to Iphigenia. Three hundred feet of flame bordered by black volcanic glass loomed over a similar setup too: office cubicles; air filtration vents; whiteboards covered in yellow post-it notes; water coolers; coffee machines (someone had stuck a paper saying *Out Of Order* to one of these with tape, which was so incredibly mundane it lent the message a kind of weird severity); cogwheel computers and technician boards, not particularly complicated looking, and decorated with an assortment of inkless pens, chip-lipped mugs, and ashtrays apocalyptic with dog-ends and heaped with crumbly gray ash.

Hughes kept his bravado for about ten minutes before admitting he was hopelessly lost in the tangle of officious cubicles. A helpful-looking technician gave him wrong directions. A tired-looking coffee machine repairman gave him the finger.

"Hughes!"

"Cate! Thank goodness. I thought I'd never find you."

"What in God's name are you wearing?"

"My uniform," said Hughes, bewildered. He looked at her. She was wearing a jerkin, breeches, a heavy coat. All were leather and dyed a rich scarlet red. None of them (and this seemed suddenly really pertinent) were her standard issue Citadel uniform. Hughes was nonplussed. "Aren't I supposed to wear the uniform?"

"Didn't the delivery get to you?" Cate asked.

"What delivery?"

She told him to stay put and went off in search of the delivery he didn't know he was supposed to have gotten.

"I know it's your second time going through a portal," said a voice. "But I think I'll treat this as your inaugural trip, if that works."

It was John Isherwood.

"Hello, Doctor."

John's hand, raised in greeting, disappeared to join the other in his white lab coat. He frowned at Hughes' uniform. "What are you wearing?"

"Cate said the same thing."

"I'm sure she's got you covered."

Hughes tried to remember the last time he'd seen the good doctor. He thought it might have been the night he properly joined the Citadel, when he used his Performance to convince a Jolene there was nothing ogrish about her, and in return she forged him the sword he now wore in a scabbard at his hip.

"I wanted to apologize for my behavior that night in The Foundry," said John, as if through his spectacles he could peer directly into Hughes' head. "You probably don't give a flying fuck into a rolling doughnut about this, but I've lost a lot of sleep over the whole thing. I went in with an idea of how things would go. When that idea was challenged, my education and maturity flew out the window. The tantrum hit me, and a night that was your double feature became the Doctor John Conniption Hour. I acted like the part of the horse where the shit leaves."

Hughes grinned. "You weren't that bad."

"I was a terror. When you graduate in my field, the university doesn't hand out oaths of conduct. Good job on the research, now go out and solve the world. The medicinal types swear all right, but not us lab guys. 'Do no harm' covers bedside manner as well as surgery. Makes you think maybe... Well, anyway, I'm sorry."

"You're serious about your work," said Hughes. "That's admirable. And I think the apology ought to go to Jo, not me."

Hughes expected this comment to embitter the tender moment, but once again he misjudged the good doctor.

"Tell you what," said John Isherwood. "I get you in and out of Eurydice today, I'll make her workshop in The Foundry my first destination. Okay?"

"More than okay."

"Here's your partner."

Cate Jubilee joined them. She was carrying a large package ziplocked in plastic.

"How long till we go through?" she asked Doctor John.

John slipped his pocket watch out by its chain. "A little under thirty minutes," he said.

"We'll see you at the entrance." Cate thrust the package into Hughes' arms and began to usher him to an empty cubicle.

Hughes jangled his delivery. "What is this?"

"Your armor. Get it on and meet me outside."

She shut the sliding panel, leaving him alone in the narrow space. There was a computer terminal, a keyboard, and one of the obligatory mugs, its rim filmed in crusted coffee foam. The mug bore the message: *Coffee beans help me through the daily grind.*

Dreadful pun. *Dad would love it.*

Hughes zipped open the package. One by one he laid its contents on the desk. He read the accompanying note with its curvy, careful letters as though it had been written by an unpracticed hand determined to do its best.

to my friend hughes,

i hope this keeps you safe.

come visit me soon and tell me about your adventure.

your prettiest forgelady,
Jo

He looked at the armor, and like a man who enjoys crap puns reading a veritable stinker off a coffee mug, he began to smile.

Twenty minutes later he emerged.

Cate was a portrait of delight. "Look at you!"

"It's a bit loose across the chest," said Hughes.

"If what I've heard about Cassandra's gymnasium routine is true, you'll be filling that breastplate out before you can say 'pectoral muscles.'" She examined him from head to toe as they walked briskly toward the portal. "Mind you, you're filling out the rest fairly well."

Only two months past a diet of tea and starvation, Hughes was not so sure. He *did* feel imposing though, that much was apparent.

Jo had turned him into steel. Gloves and vambraces bled from his hands all the way to his shoulder pauldrons, red as night under a blood moon. His breastplate was an ultralight shell. His greaves and gorget were engraved with flourishes like fire. Hughes' old moth-gnawed coat with its host of clever pockets brushed calves shod in one of the lightest metal alloys in the world. Overall the ensemble weighed less than twenty pounds. In the cubicle he had tested stretching, jumping, even a few fencing positions. The results both pleased and confounded him. For all it inhibited his movement, Hughes might have been wearing pajamas.

They turned a corner, and there it was. The portal to Eurydice—the dungeon dimension, yawned wide and unwelcoming. Whitecoats and attendants and dungareed technicians swarmed at its feet, dwarfed by its sheer immensity.

Doctor John waved them over.

"We're about ready to go on this thing," said John. "Got your logbook, Miss Jubilee?"

She patted her satchel. Both she and Hughes carried one, crammed to the seams with supplies for the journey.

"There should be minimal tread. Isaac... Oh." An attendant scientist handed John Isherwood a clipboard. John scanned it. The way the light from the portal fell, the doctor's glasses seemed to skim and dance with fire. It gave the man a sinister look that Hughes found oddly comical, as if Doctor John were the megalomaniacal villain about to shove two doomed heroes through the jaws of hell.

"Cate?"

"Yes, Hughes?"

"What's tread?"

"Eurydice is always shifting. Remember the numbers on the board in Wendy's office?"

He did.

"John is going to try to get us as close as he can to the spot where Burnished Isaac Lawless arrived," said Cate. "It's almost impossible to be exact, so there's a system that calculates how close or far we might land."

"And that's tread, then?"

"Uh huh."

A horrible idea occurred. "Could we appear inside a wall?"

"Try not to fret," she said, which was very comforting and not panic inducing in the slightest.

"That's fine," said John, handing the clipboard back to the attendant who scurried off. "What was I saying?"

"Something about Isaac," prompted Cate.

"Was it?" John was looking at his pocket watch. "Lost my train of thought. Three minutes until entry. Better get in position."

It was as though a flag had fluttered *GO* over Cate's head. She broke into a run, crowing and laughing and calling for him to come, come quick! Catching her excitement like seasonal flu, Hughes followed.

Technicians looked up at their flight and shook their heads.

Hughes didn't care. Cate was in motion. He would float in her atmosphere.

"Hurry" she cried.

"We have a few minutes," he protested, laughing. "Doctor John..."

"That ditherer would have us dawdle. Blast and blight him thrice over for his sluggerdom."

"Cate!"

"A rescue," she said. "Oh, I've barely been able to contain it, Hughes. I'm so happy. A rescue!"

God she was contagious. "The danger doesn't put you off?" he asked her.

"Garnish for my joy, baby." She leaped, landed in a handstand atop a console (much to the disgruntlement of the people working there), and threw herself forward, a cork exploding from the gladdest champagne. "A rescue! *Yeowowow!*"

Hughes had forgotten his nasty visitors from Memory Lane in the elevator. He'd forgotten his misgivings. He'd forgotten the underground warehouse, Doctor John, the portal now so close its liquid flame seemed to dominate the world. His personal world was the woman yowling as though her whole being demanded it. He could not stop laughing.

Even when Doctor John darted up to where they stood on the entry platform, he was fighting the chuckles bubbling up his throat.

"I've remembered," John said. "He asked me about fuel."

"Who asked you?" said Cate. She was bouncing on the balls of her hobnail boots.

"Isaac. Before he went through that last time a few weeks ago, he asked me about fuel."

"Ten seconds," someone shouted.

"What did he want to know about fuel?" Cate pressed. She wasn't giddy anymore. Her brow was creased with interest.

"He'd been reading about these experiments. Combining electrical energy with magic. Academic stuff. Not actually possible as far as we know."

"Why did he ask you about it?"

John shook his head. "Your guess is as good as—"

"Coordinates aligned."

The portal fluctuated. Wild tendrils of magical fire curled and twisted. No heat baked off the doorway. Only possibility and a formless species of dread.

Through this door another world beckoned.

Let it be different from Iphigenia, he prayed. *Let me be ready.*

Hughes felt Cate's arm snake around him.

They went through together.

***

For a moment the darkness on the other side of the portal was so total he experienced a spell of disorientation. His inner ear rang. Watery bile squirted up from his gut into his mouth. His legs felt rubbery, the bones in his feet melting into clumsy slag.

Click, came a sound in the vertiginous black.

Hughes scrunched his eyes and raised a warding hand as Cate shined her flashlight in his face.

"Sorry."

She swerved it away. Grateful and feeling much more grounded now he could see his boots were firmly beneath him, Hughes took a moment to study their surroundings.

Stone scooped up everywhere he looked. It was granite, hard and lumpy and sensibly gray, the least riveting of rocks. Water trickled in from somewhere above them, forming the natural cavity of space in the rock where they were standing. The torch revealed the cavity moved west in something too narrow to be a tunnel.

They looked at one another.

"Can I fret now?" said Hughes.

They were in a wall.

CHAPTER THIRTY-ONE

They advanced through the tunnel at a snail's pace. Cate examined every inch of the north side of the wall.

"That's our way out," she said cryptically.

Hughes was on lookout duty, prowling the darkness so thick it looked folded with the torch. This was Eurydice, and damp walls mottled in fungus might be popular dining spots for all he knew.

"There we are," said Cate. "That will do nicely."

"You've found a way out?" said Hughes, who was starting to fret about the toxicity of the mushrooms sharing the wall with them.

She nodded cheerfully. Slinging down her satchel, she rooted inside and produced two vials, each about the size of her ring finger. Shouldering her bag once more she approached the north wall, sighted through a crack Hughes hadn't noticed, and pressed on the bottom of one of the vials.

There was a compressed *whumping* sound.

Cate peered through the crack. He heard her make a little sound of satisfaction.

"The stone is loose here," she said, rapping the granite with a knuckle as though it were an oaken door. "See the clusters of mushrooms? Those are all seams weakening the integrity of the structure. Scooch a bit over if you don't mind."

Hughes obeyed, fascinated.

Cate pointed the second vial at the ground and pressed it.

Whump.

Silvery gelatinous goo blasted onto the floor. It was wide and alien-looking, and Hughes grunted in alarm as it congealed. Before his eyes it seemed to harden, and by the light of the torch in no significant time at all the stuff had solidified into a smooth glossy sheet.

It was a mirror.

"See you soon," Cate said and glided into the glass.

Hughes stood alone. Except for the mushrooms. And the damp.

"Somewhere, there's someone just like me in the world," he told this rapt audience. "That man has got his feet up, a book on the go, and a cup of tea within easy reach. Maybe there's a fire. A plate of cakes. The most exciting thing that happens to him is indigestion. Let's call him Hughes 2."

The mushrooms offered no opinion on this fictional doppelganger.

Neither did the damp.

In the resounding silence, it occurred to Hughes that Hughes 2 likely lived the charmed and cozy life of the unbothered. For example, he probably never got transported into walls.

This struck him as cosmically unfair.

He jumped at an unpleasant splitting noise. It was coming from the north wall. Cautious as anything, he laid his ear against the stone. Busy sounds emanated on the other side. Creaking, rattling, rushing.

"Wherever Hughes 2 is," he grumbled, "every sound is identifiable and ordinary."

A few minutes later the wall began to change.

It happened quite suddenly. One moment it was solid and the next some invisible force was acting on it, blowing it down like so many stacked matchsticks. Hughes stepped out of the rubble.

The first thing he saw was the tree. It was an unusual tree, all warped and wicked. Most unusual however, was the mirror on it. Hughes glanced back at the mirror on the stone floor and found his neck craning up and up without conscious effort. Above him rose a small craggy peak, corkscrewed in caves and chimneyed in smoke-colored trees. Tied around a jut of rock was a device of two circles strung with rope.

"Is that a block and tackle?" he said.

'Yes,' said Cate, retrieving it. She was soaked with sweat, and her cheeks were rosy with exertion, but the hint of a smile he spotted on her lips fairly oozed with delight.

Hughes pondered the scene. Ponder might not be entirely accurate, though it was the most grammatically correct way of putting it. Safe to say, if he could have baffled or even flummoxed the scene, he would have.

Cate had squinted through a crack in the wall and seen a tree. Using her vials, she'd made two mirrors and teleported between them. Then using a bloody block and tackle she'd bloody well shifted the loose area of stone and bloody well freed him.

She hopped down from the promontory, tucking everything back into her satchel and offering him a smile that, should their torches die, might well set Eurydice and who knew how many worlds besides to glowing.

"You're incredible," he said.

She poked him hard in the ribs. "Rescue now, flatter later."

"Where could Isaac be?"

She nodded north. "Somewhere in that shambles, I reckon."

He followed her gaze.

The crag they'd escaped was part of a series of little mountains forming a rind-shaped curve, what was sometimes called a "cordillera" of mountains. The cordillera overlooked a valley. Gentle hillocks made a gradual descent into the basin, and all about the valley bustled with a legion of pine trees. Here and there copses of those wicked-warped trees held communion, but for the most part the pines ruled here, carpeting the forest floor with dry brown needles that crunched underfoot. A slice of moon hung in the starry sky. It was the first time Hughes had seen the moon in months. That rush of pleasure soured fast. It was not his moon. Evidence of that presented itself the moment he adjusted his position on the rise and spied the second moon. One was white, the other green. He was reminded of Jo, who had heterochromia in her eyes, two different colors. Green and mystical white. Parallels like that were all around of course. Strange coincidences that might convince the superstitious heart of unseen block and tackles working at the hidden weights of the universe. Who could say? Not he.

In the basin of the valley, hemmed in by pines, Hughes saw the town. And beyond the town, the castle. Spired and vast and slanted with ruination, it squatted malignantly under the moons.

"What are they?" Hughes said, pointing.

Barely visible over the barbican, something was throwing shivering blue shadows against the high walls of the castle bailey.

"Don't know," said a voice at his side. "Shall we find out, Gormon Hughes?"

Hughes said they should. He took courage in that voice.

It belonged to a woman whose name and demeanor stood in defiance of the bleak vista Castle Aldersglen presented. Her hobnail boots squashed drifts of pine needle flat, her hair was a fantail of fire in the night-dark wood, and a warmer woman you could not hope to encounter upon the long road of your life.

Hughes 2 might have peace and quiet, but Hughes 1 had Cate Jubilee.

He knew which he preferred.

Cakes would be welcome though.

***

"That logbook," said Hughes. "Laurana carried one just like it."

"I should hope so. Each unit is issued one." Cate looked up from the logbook and gestured toward a nearby thicket of wicked-looking trees. "Don't walk between two of those. Isaac Lawless calls them 'lynch mob trees.'"

"Why?"

"Because when they get together, somebody is about to get hanged."

Hughes gave the thicket a wide berth. Their mangled trunks seemed to leer at him through the pines.

"So the logbook contains all of the cartographer's notes?"

"As well as the units,'" Cate replied. "I'll tender a report once we're back home. Then everyone can benefit from the things we learned here." She walked quickly, absorbed in the pages. Hughes opened his mouth to warn her she was about to crack her skull off a branch. He shut up when she bent under it, seemingly by instinct.

I wonder if she knows she just does things like that.

He kept apace with her, smiling a private smile despite the claustrophobia worming its way through him. The pines were densely packed. After the hectic forest in Iphigenia, Hughes listened for the furtive noises of creatures in the undergrowth, but there was nothing to hear. Cate's passage sent crunch after crunch echoing through the night. Other than that, nothing.

Sometimes he saw the white moon peeping through the boscage. Other times its green counterpart made an appearance. Hughes misliked that moon. It had a baleful look, a hole cut in the starry plaster of the evening for some perverse intelligence to spy through.

"I thought it was called the dungeon dimension?" he said.

She gave him a quizzical look, but in an instant he could see she understood. "That isn't *the* sky up there," she said. "It's *a* sky. Eurydice's got lots. Countless landscapes. Endless terrains."

"Stars without end?"

"Mm, poetry in the woods. What a thrill."

She grinned impishly at his embarrassment.

"What connects them?" he asked. "The different regions, like. What ties them together, do you know?"

She shrugged. "Ask John Isherwood if you like." Her nose wrinkled. "Though I wouldn't if I were you. Not unless you'd like to spend an afternoon hearing his version of 'we don't know and isn't that interesting?' Some people say Eurydice is the same size as Iphigenia, which isn't any help because they don't know how big Iphigenia is either. Can you hear that?"

"No."

"Listen."

Hughes closed his eyes. A slow, thoughtful frown crimped his features.

"Now you mention it..."

It was very faint. If he had to describe it, Hughes would have struggled. Knife to his throat, he'd have called it a chugging noise. A low guttural chugging, though that wasn't *quite* right...

"The Bonemeal Boys," Cate said suddenly. She turned to face him. "In Isaac's notes he claims the town is abandoned. But the castle *isn't*."

"Bonemeal Boys?" Hughes' frown was very deep now. "What sort of name is that?"

"Presumably the one they gave themselves, Hughes. Isaac wasn't sure who built the community here," she said, holding up her logbook. "Only that the Bonemeal Boys are in charge now. According to him, they ride carriages on two wheels."

"What, like a motorbike?"

"I'm not sure. The big mystery for him is this: what are they burning for..." Her face lit up. "Oh! That's what Doctor John meant!"

"Go on then," said Hughes, lost as per usual in Hurricane Jubilee's gale-force deductions.

"Fuel, Hughes!" She showed him the logbook. "If they're riding wheeled carriages they've got to use *something* for power."

"Or a horse," he suggested. "A horse would do you."

"Yes, I think we can safely discard the idea of horses in the feverish nightmare realm of lynching trees and ghoulish twin moons, thank you very much for that contribution."

Hughes grinned. "Welcome."

She gave him a peck on the cheek, pleased he'd taken her good-natured jibes with grace. "What did John say? He said Isaac was looking into magical fuels. That must be the blue flashing we saw in the castle bailey."

"Why would Isaac care what they're burning to get their carriages going?"

Cate nodded. "Good question. Cartography on behalf of the Scarlet Citadel doesn't just mean mapping the land. Cartographers are expected to map culture too. If the evil here is to be harvested for crystal so we can make credits for the city's economy, then units like us need to know exactly what we're getting into. A topography of threat."

That made sense to Hughes. Something else was troubling him. "Cate, I've been meaning to ask you about that. If the Scarlet Citadel controls the production of credits, why bother making more?"

She looked at him as if he had asked her why goats don't take vacation time or spontaneously combust.

"Look," he said. "If you control the distribution of a currency, then why endanger your people—us—by sending them into places like this? Why not just circulate the existing supply?"

"Expansion, Hughes. Countries use their own currency for now. Little by little that's changing. Look at Champleurs. Since losing the war, they use credits. For God's sake, a century ago Hortesia still used payments in kind. I trade you this milk for that bread." She cocked her head. "Besides, hasn't it occurred to you that if credits can be found here in Eurydice, there might be other things worth discovering?"

"I suppose," he conceded. "But why credits?"

That drew a sweet little chuckle from Cate Jubilee. "They're easily transported, easily atomized into smaller units, and most importantly they make a pretty gleam." She reopened the logbook and started back on the path to Castle Aldersglen. "Most people are magpies. I know I am."

"What shiny thing could distract Cate Jubilee?"

"Why, as of late, you. Now come along." *Crunch-crunch* sang her hobnail boots in the pine needles. "I should like to meet these Bonemeal Boys."

***

The town did not show itself to them all at once.

It revealed itself piecemeal, in stages.

First came the windmill blending in with the pines, its raggedy limbs wheeling gently in a breeze Hughes could not feel. An inspection of its insides revealed only the mill's stony guts stranded in cobweb. No inhabitants.

A quarter of a mile onward they found a steward's house sat on the crest of a hill. The title of its owner was merely a guess from Hughes, but Cate agreed there was definitely something stately in its size and location. Its kitchen, dining room, office, and bedrooms were like something out of a medieval fantasy story, all pinewood cutlery and bowls, cupboards filled with preservative jars (Cate pulled a face seeing these teemed with mold), duck down bedclothes and tallow candles rendered from cream-colored suet. No inhabitants.

Only descending from the steward's house did they find the main glut of town houses. It was a small community, eighty roofs strong, and there were all sorts of facilities that you might expect in an ordinary town, even a school. No inhabitants.

"Who lived here?" said Hughes. "Does the logbook say?"

Riding the same wave of thought, Cate riffled through the pages. "No. Can you hold on here for a while and keep an eye on the castle? I want to check the gardens for corpses."

As she roved away among the overgrown hedgerows, Hughes' face took on the expression of someone who... well, who has just been told their partner is going body searching by the light of two otherworldly moons. It was a sort of peevish grimace. "Check the gardens for corpses? Lovely. Carnations and cadavers. Standard," he said. "Standard Wednesday."

Even that small glimmer of comforting humor chilled and froze stiff after a moment alone. It was almost preternaturally quiet. He watched the castle. No blue shadows. At the very limit of his perception he could hear wind soughing through the pines. He tried to pick them out (they would be the nodding trees), but he couldn't. Feeling suddenly vulnerable in the open air, he took shelter in a hut with a sagging roof. Rats ought to have lived there, leaving tracks in the dust. There was no sign of any or of any opportunistic settlers. It smelled dry and a little like rancid butter. Mr. Glint's tongue smelled like that. Hughes cut his eyes for another scan of the castle barbican. Nothing.

His mean aunt of an imagination began to ruck up on him then. *You just stay out of it,* he commanded. No good. Night yanked the moon on invisible puppet strings toward the western reaches of the valley. Weird greenish glows crept between the rutted roads, lengthening the town into a gaunt caricature of itself traced in shadow. More and more he found himself looking at the windows of houses, convinced he'd just glimpsed something as it slipped furtively out of sight. He started to fixate on an image of a child, a boy strangled by the lynching trees who was buried and woke up, a bonemeal boy who had returned and done away with everyone in the town and retreated into the forest, a boy whose breath reeked of grave earth and who was hurrying through the thickets even now, toward town, gravity working on his decaying limbs until his arms were stretched grotesquely long like the raggedy wings of the mill, the boy's eyes sunken red hollows, canines bared, his jaw swinging on its hinge like the wolf's jaw in Iphigenia, and oh God God God his skinless lips running with spit, slobbering avidly in fact, yes avidly, *hungry for—*

STOP, Hughes shrieked in his own mind. His grip on Chimera's hilt was painfully tight. He relaxed, felt warm blood rush back into his hand, but whatever game his nerves were playing was not over. Through the denuded branches the wind soughed. Moonlight slithered. Movement in the windows. Wasn't there? Wasn't there? In the nearby woods rickles of fallen pine needles looked like piles of fingerbones. Trophies of the bonemeal boy.

I need to get ahold on this fear.

Cate was close by. Carnation and cadaver picking.

Only... he hadn't seen her, had he? How long had it been since she'd gone?

The stillness—draped like a blanket over the waxy pale face of a child—made his mind up for him. He started in the direction he'd seen her take and stopped.

He turned quickly. The woods. What was that sound in the woods?

Whatever it was, it was growing. No wind could sound like that.

In a burst of recognition he knew it. It was the noise he'd heard before they'd descended into the valley. The one he'd foundered in describing, a harsh chest-fuzzing sound. A... He had it now, he thought, turning to face it completely. A... *revving*.

That was when he saw the blue light streaming through the dark railings of the trees. He heard his name whispered.

Cate was in the nearest garden, huddled under untamable hedges. With the revving increasing in volume every second, Hughes went down on his belly and wriggled under the leaves to join her.

And there they waited.

***

It was not a hanged boy. When it came roaring out of the tree line, Hughes could not believe *what* it was.

When Cate related the idea of a two-wheeled carriage, he had pictured something drawn by draft horses out of the preindustrial boom.

The motorcycle (he could only think of it as a motorcycle as that abominable chainsaw growl chewed up from its engine) was made of masonry. Staring at it, you could not help but be confronted by the sheer impossibility of the vehicle. It was blocks of cut flagstone, drawbridge chains, and rampart rock bent and wrenched into shape *around the idea of a motorcycle*. Both wheels—the front hideously larger than the back—blew a constant torrent of smoke over each curve of striated rubber. At the rear, a knobbly cleft of stone that must have been the exhaust pipe belched blue fire. That same sparking sapphire inferno lit the motorcycle from within, a gruesome jack-o'-lantern with handlebars.

At first glance Hughes' eyes convinced him the rider was merely emaciated. Closer inspection revealed the truth. As the motorcycle came to a stop not twenty feet away from where he and Cate lay concealed, Hughes saw the fingers wrapped around both throttles were as naked of flesh as the lynching trees were of foliage. Not a scrap of skin clung to the figure except for one yellow-gray flap hanging from the crooked slats of its ribs. Its vertebrae stood out starkly. Its sockets were hollow tarpits, so black did they seem. The remains of what might once have been a robe pooled at the rider's hipbones like some wretched poncho. At this distance Hughes' nostrils cringed from the smell of putrefaction.

He looked at Cate, wondering what he'd see in her face.

What he saw there wiped the slate of fear completely clean.

Cate Jubilee was not frightened. Cate Jubilee was not somber.

Cate Jubilee was grinning, and it was more roguish and barbaric than the grin worn by the rider, who was, call a pot and kettle black, a skeleton, and thus partial to grins of a roguish and barbaric nature by default.

Despite his complicated affection for her, Hughes was not *completely* decided on the whole Hughes 1 and Hughes 2 thing. Given recent developments here in Eurydice, the idea of somewhere toasty warm and out of danger was beginning to sound increasingly attractive.

He was however, absolutely certain who he did *not* want to be.

He did not want to be the person who made Cate grin like that.

"When the bike tips," she said, producing one of her mirror vials. "Catch it."

Whump.

She was gone—

—and there she was, emerging from the upper window of a house.

She stuffed her fingers in her mouth and gave a shrill whistle.

Hughes watched in a kind of paralysis as the rider jerked in its saddle, rearing its head just in time to acknowledge the existence of Cate's hobnail boots before the law of descending object velocity fed them to it.

He heard kernels of trapped gas in the skeleton's neck pop, and then the rider was rolling in the road.

"Catch it, Hughes!"

His paralysis broke. Scrambling up from beneath the hedge he made a mad dash for the motorcycle. It toppled slowly, as though through treacle. Still, catching it was a close shave, and as he propped it straight again he gained another notch of appreciation for Cassandra and her stringent attitude toward physical fitness. Dear God, but the thing was *heavy*.

Meanwhile Cate was slamming one boot repeatedly on the rider's femur. It lunged for her legs, trying to trip her. Instead of retreating, she let momentum take its course. They rolled, snarling, struggling for supremacy. A dagger of icy dread lodged in Hughes. *Cate, be safe! Those fleshless fingers groping for your throat look as sharp as talons!*

He needn't have worried. When the dust settled Cate lay under the flailing rider, her knee pressed firmly in the curve of its spinal column, her own gloved fingers tangled in its ribs.

"Good evening," she said. "Now what's say you cease wiggling or else I won't stop."

Despite it lacking a voice box, the skeletal rider had no trouble speaking. No compunctions to be polite, either.

"Let me go, pretty petal," it rasped.

"I shall just start then, shall I?" She exerted pressure. The rider's back bowed at an atrocious angle. The creature renewed its writhing. Cate grit her teeth and drove her kneecap deeper among the cords of vertebrae. "More?"

"Petal's got a stinger. Stole that from a wasp, did you?"

"A scorpion." Sweat beaded Cate's temples. A drop rolled down her cheekbone and came to rest on her upper lip, which had drawn back over her teeth. "Give in. Each moment we struggle is a fresh dose of poison for us both. Give in *now*. I don't relish hurting you. Say it."

"Suh-stop," it hissed. "Stoooooop."

"You'll behave yourself?"

"Promisssse."

She eased its suffering, though she didn't go so far as relinquishing her grapple altogether. No fool was Cate Jubilee because this was one of the Bonemeal Boys, and on first impressions even inexperienced Hughes could tell they should take promises and the word of this grim rider with a generous helping of salt. Meanwhile he propped the motorcycle against a nearby house.

By the time he returned, Cate was ready to begin the interrogation.

"Show him Chimera, Hughes."

He drew his sword from its scabbard. The rider went still. This close he could see its eye sockets were not pitch black. Pinpoints of red glinted in there like red dwarf stars viewed through a telescope. They stared fixedly at Chimera.

"You're afraid of this," Hughes said. "Why?"

"Tell him," Cate encouraged her prisoner.

"Sticks and stones don't break our bones," rasped the rider. "But that sticker you've got will cut us plenty."

"Magic items?" Hughes interpreted. "You're vulnerable to those and immune to mundane methods of attack?"

The two red points of lights flicked to his face, then back to Chimera's edge.

That's answer enough.

Hughes turned his hand so the tip of the blade hovered half an inch over the thing's yellowing breastbone.

"See?" murmured Cate. "Two stingers. Who's the petal?"

"I am," said the rider quickly.

"You bet you are. I think you were on patrol. True?"

"Yes."

"On the lookout for what?"

"No one. Ssssk—no! No, I'll tell you. I'll tell you!"

She had worked her knee in again, hard enough for its breastbone to feel Chimera's cold kiss.

"We're keeping our sockets peeled for you. For the Scarlet Citadel."

Cate's eyeballs moved rapidly as she educed the meaning of that. "You've got our cartographer."

"Yes."

"Is he alive?"

"Yes."

"Spoiled?"

No answer.

Hughes saw disquiet pass in a storm cloud across Cate's face.

Spoiled. The word disturbed him as much as Cate's reaction. *The Bonemeal Boys have got Burnished Isaac Lawless in that castle. They're torturing him for information.*

Or because they like it, said some wheedling voice in his subconscious, the voice of his mean aunt of an imagination. *Sticks and stones will break his bones just fine, and the revving of their motors will drown out his screams.*

The cloud had passed from Cate's expression. She was businesslike once more.

"Before I go on," she said briskly. "How many of you Bonemeal Boys patrol this route?"

"Only me."

From where she lay on her back, Cate looked up at Hughes. "Hughes, should you hear an approaching engine, be a good chap and carve a furrow through this fellow's skull."

He gave a stiff nod. Though Chimera's dragon-styled cross guard seemed to breathe fire along the blade, the moonlight transformed it into a length of pale green ice. It was actually rather beautiful.

The wind picked up for a moment. It sent fistfuls of pine needles scureling down the main road of the town where Gormon Hughes and Cate Jubilee and the Bonemeal Boy were locked in a tableau and where they began to speak of sad, strange things.

"I've never seen anything like you," Cate said. "What are the Bonemeal Boys? And don't be glib and say, 'Hell on wheels, baby' or I shall do something horrible to you."

The skeleton hesitated. It had clearly been about to say, "Hell on wheels, baby."

"Not precisely sure where to begin..."

Hughes said, "How do you make 'p' and 'b' sounds?"

Cate and the Bonemeal Boy stared at him.

"You haven't got lips," he explained. "How do you make 'p' and 'b' sounds?"

They continued to stare at him.

Hughes balked but recovered fast. "Erm. Yes. What *are* the Bonemeal Boys, anyway?"

The skeleton resumed its thoughtful silence.

"Like I said, I'm not sure where to begin. Dying, maybe." It seemed to warm to the idea. "Yeah. I'll start with dying."

CHAPTER THIRTY-TWO

The last thought I had was regret. That's how dying works. Your whole mind goes blank. That's the worst part. Not knowing if the feeling is going to come. No matter how bad it is, the absence is worse. Then woopy doo, the feeling comes, splatting down in dollops then gushing over everything you are. We used to tell the kids it was like a paint can tipped over one of them canvasses. The regret I felt was mauve, that nasty color. I welcomed it. About time, I thought. I don't know about you, but that's how it's always been. The dying, the nothing, then the last feeling. And we know about it because we don't stay dead for long.

"This here is Aldersglen, a town of necromancers, and that means the wheel, okay? The wheel of life. Most places life is a straight line. Born and die. Here, and other necromancy places, life keeps going. You die, get the last feeling, sleep, and then somebody—maybe your relatives or your friends or the castle people if you haven't got any—come and wake you up again."

Hughes thought that sounded wretched, even perverse. Death was scary, absolutely, but it was life's natural conclusion. The story had to end sometime. Not today, of course, but sometime. And then he remembered Hector and Cassandra were walking talking spirits. War had put them to sleep, and their grieving father got his magic item to wake them up.

The parallel between those two and this scraped, savage husk harrowed him. It dried his throat out.

"You lived here?" Cate asked their prisoner. "Yes, that makes sense. I wondered why you'd no graveyard. The residents were all raised from the dead. There'd be no point."

"No point in wishing for a grave either. You were getting raised, that was the deal. Why?" The two pinpricks of red in the rider's sockets flared with emotion. "Because the dead are good little workers. We don't eat, sleep, or answer calls of nature on account of not having digestive tracts. Those slop out of your rotting middle parts pretty quick. Novelty of decomposition gets old fast.

"What you've got to understand is this: there were these other folks around. Not necromancers but pyromancers. They had fire instead of entropy. And were they sweet on themselves?" The skeleton's bony fingers twitched. "I guess you could say they were the nobility. Yonder castle? Theirs. The woods? Theirs. The town?"

It fell silent, an ugly sullen silence filled with memories.

"So these pyromancers and necromancers. One ruled over the other, but they both put you to work?" Cate asked. "You being the undead."

"*Yes.*"

Hughes said, "Where are they now?"

The skull grinned at him. It had no choice in the matter.

"Oh, they're still around," it said, and both of them could hear the pleasure in its tone. "Here's the thing. We were happy. Us undead folks. Better to be awake than asleep. Better feeling than nothing. But things change. The wheel keeps on turning. Out of seemingly nowhere this one undead gets to be unhappy. He gets it into that head where his brain turned to mush a long time ago that there's got to be something more, something better than, well, serving. Starts to tell others about it on the quiet. Those pyromancers and necromancers have no right to be the ones in charge, he said. They're riding us! Riding us into nothing but a paste. Into bonemeal.

"So one day us undead turn."

"You killed them?' said Cate.

"We would have died along with them. No. We had them do things to one another. Promised the ones who worked on the others that they'd live. Sort of ironic, huh?"

"Yes," said Cate coldly.

"Sort of funny. We laugh about it all the time. But you want to know what we are, right? Well, what you do is what you are. Here's what we did." The red pinpoints were blazing righteously now. Hughes watched them, almost hypnotized.

"We got our old bosses to figure out how to meld lifeless stone and living fire. And they did! Of course once the living ones had used up all the test subjects, they were real surprised when we got to work on them."

"No," said Cate. "You can't mean..."

"Necromancers make for good engines," said the Bonemeal Boy. "Pyromancers make the prettiest blue fuel."

Realization swept over Hughes. As one, and with a terrible sickening slowness, he and Cate looked at the motorcycle. It was propped where Hughes had left it. Its stone casement. Its purring engine. Its exhaust pipe. There were cylindrical burners at the sides. How had they not noticed those before? Inside, you could just about see the coils of blue fire.

Necromancers make for good engines, Hughes thought, shock numbing him. *Pyromancers make the prettiest blue fuel.*

Heedless of their horror, the motorcycle went on purring.

"Now who rides who?" said the Bonemeal Boy. "Now who the fuck rides who?"

ACT EIGHT

LAWLESS RESCUE

CHAPTER THIRTY-THREE

The door handle to the Dragon's Lair turned.

Wendy was glaring irritably at something under her desk and did not look up. Despite that she still said, "Good morning, Falstaff."

The butler tottled in, folders tucked under one arm.

"New reports for you, my Lady."

"Shouldn't wool insulate heat, Falstaff?"

"My Lady?"

"An envoy from the Marquis de Reon presented me with a gift from his esteemed master. Footwear lovingly crafted from the wool of the famously cold-resistant Champleurs sheep. The latest thing abroad, the envoy called them."

"I can have that checked, my Lady."

"Can you? The trend or the four-legged fabric dispenser?"

"My Lady?"

"Never mind. These... I suppose a charitable soul would call them 'slippers,' are either a joke on behalf of the marquis or proof the Champleurs sheep are one bad winter from extinction. My feet have been chilly all morning."

"I shall have a hot water bottle and your usual shoes brought up at once."

"Thank you, Falstaff. Reports, is it?" Wendy fanned them out on her desk. "Hughes has not returned."

"There was a delay in the drop. Doctor Isherwood is quite swamped," said Falstaff cordially.

"Swamped. Yes." Wendy selected a file. "Unit 31, that is Steffan Cerulean's Unit unless I'm mistaken. Ah. Indeed. Speaking of swamped, he was in Iphigenia's muggier region as of yesterday afternoon." She read in silence. "What is this about 'peculiarities'?"

"According to Steffan, he saw a flock of finchlike birds turn on one another midair."

"Mm. *Blood and Feathers* used to be the motto of the Marquis de Reon's lineage before the war established new traditions. Perhaps today it would be *Bloody*

Cold Toes." Wendy Dragontail made a mark in her notes on Iphigenia. If you looked at them over her shoulder, you would see she was adding to a tally, and you might conclude (accurately) that Steffan's "peculiarities" were not a once-off incident. "When you can extract him from his busy bog of duties, send Doctor Isherwood to me, Falstaff. He and I are overdue for a chat."

"Yes, Lady."

"And make it an extra-toasty hot water bottle, there's a good man."

"Certainly, my Lady."

"Falstaff?"

The butler turned.

"You look weary, Falstaff. Your shoulders slump."

Falstaff straightened with an effort. "Forgive me, Lady. I'm sleeping poorly."

"Nothing to forgive. Is the nattering of this endless storm keeping you up?"

"No, no." For a moment the butler looked unbearably haggard. "A few bad dreams is all." Then the moment passed, he bowed to the dragon herself, and departed about his neat little duties that kept the tower from collapsing in on itself from lack of organization.

***

Bone scraped as Chimera's point swept over a strut of ribcage.

"Hurtsss," hissed the skeletal rider.

"People," said Hughes. "You use people. For fuel."

"Not like you," the creature soothed. "They didn't even look like you. Isn't that what you do? Come here and kill things that don't look like you."

"You, I'm not so sure about. I think you'd muck up any mold you were poured into. Bad, no matter the shape. Maybe the ones that made you and put you to work deserved punishment of some kind, but not this," Hughes said firmly. "Not torment and humiliation."

"Don't you get so high and mighty." That skull grin seemed suddenly taunting. "We know all about you. Agents of the Red Death. You're a plague in our parts. Who are you to judge what we did?"

"You use people," Hughes insisted.

You could fell trees with his tone.

"How many of you are there?" said Cate. "How many riders?"

The creature glared balefully at Hughes. "Plenty more than two."

"Who leads you?"

"Marrow King Maelen.'

The name hung on the air like the cusp of some warlock symphony.

"He's the one who had you kill your former masters," said Cate. "The one who grew unhappy while the rest of the undead were content."

"Yes."

"What does Maelen want with our cartographer?"

"Information."

"What kind of information?"

"I don't know. All I know is your guy won't give us any. You," it said, its voice becoming oily, "you've got a sword, and I see a little knife there in your waistband, but you've never killed anybody."

Hughes made no reply. His face seemed completely devoid of life so that to Cate's eyes, the moonlight showed two skulls gazing at one another.

"The necromancers had this way of thinking about murder," said the rider. "Not the pyromancers, they didn't have two interesting ideas to rub together for kindling. But the necromancers were smart. It was clear they came from somewhere, somewhere outside of this place, far away across the world. They believed that murder took something from the murderer. That it denied them what the dead got. The dying. The nothing. The feelings, even the mauve ones. As soon as you take a life, they said, you were nothing at all." It lowered its jut of jaw, and for a second that fleshless face seemed conspiratorial, as though it knew more than a kid like Hughes would ever want to. "Nothing at all. Just a bag of bones."

Quiet descended on the gutted town. It stretched. And stretched.

And at last, with half of his face sheltered in shadow from the greenish moonglow, Hughes said:

"Cate?"

"Yes?"

"You say the word."

Her expression had been worried. Now it firmed, resolute.

She nodded. "Yes."

As she let go of the rider and rolled aside, Hughes lunged.

Effortlessly, Chimera split the putrid, spongy skull through the middle. Both red pinpoints went out and came back on in its sockets as though the skeleton man had just blinked in puzzlement. The pinpoints dimmed. Faded. Went dark.

Before Hughes' eyes the festersome rider crumpled, bones thinning to papyrus, dusting into puffs, and the puffs themselves that were insubstantial glittered and spontaneously crystallized, the whole thing coming together to form a hunk of pink quartz.

Cate picked up the credit, pleased. When she saw her partner's face, worry overrode her satisfaction.

"Hughes. Are you all right?" She stepped close.

His head was hung. "No," he said after a while. He showed her his dark eyes and gave her a weak smile that made them, if not bright, then at the very least beautifully intent. "Do you fancy taking on a castle with me, Cate Jubilee?"

No verbal reply was forthcoming. Instead she touched his face and gave him that wink of hers, the one that said, *Do not vorry, Hoos. I hev got your beck.*

***

They had very little trouble approaching Castle Aldersglen.

Once Cate stopped them, and as they crouched, keeping ever so still amidst the pines, Hughes thought he heard the rumble of a motorcycle pass by.

Sheathed at his side, Chimera was a great comfort to him. It helps alleviate fear when you carry terror with you as an ally.

The pines clumped thick and then gradually dissipated as they drew near to the walls surrounding the bailey. They couldn't see the drawbridge or the barbican from here, and a good thing too, since they both reckoned that part of the castle would see lots of activity and would have the most guards stationed there. Visible over the ramparts, the castle looked exactly as it ought to.

If by "ought to" you meant partially demolished, slouched with neglect, and festooned in cobwebs so long they billowed like curtains of rotted silk through glassless windows.

But there was a grandness to it that remained. Where glass had not been smashed, windows shone green in the moonlight, a nice emerald green that Hughes couldn't help but find lovely. Blocks of granite hauled from the mountains held fast against rigorous time. And there, among the crumbling castle turrets, he spied a banner flapping softly, red and gold mixed in a likeness of fire.

"What now?" said Hughes.

"I'm going to find Isaac," said Cate.

"What? Alone?"

"I'll be back soon." She fished a vial from her satchel and squeezed it. *Whump.*

Hughes stepped back as a new mirror covered the tufty grass.

"How often can you do that?"

"Sorry?"

"The mirror," said Hughes. "How often can you traverse the glass?"

"As often as I like." Cate took out three more vials and stuffed them in her shirt pocket. "I carry the vials in case there's no reflective surfaces nearby. Could you hold this?"

He took her satchel. "Can you bring people with you?"

"What, through the looking glass? Not unless I want them to die."

"It kills them?"

"Oh yes." She tapped the heels of her boots together. "But these keep me safe."

Hughes watched her gauging the windows of the castle, picking the likeliest spot to begin her search. He supposed it made sense. When they'd been trapped in the mountainside she had teleported without him. "Deadly mirrors," he said. "Spooky."

"There's always danger in vanity." She stepped onto the pane of glass. "Stay safe, handsome."

A moment later, alone with two satchels and the gossiping pines, he heard another ghoulish roar.

He thought there was more than one motorcycle this time.

It was hard to tell.

Minutes ticked by. Now and then he would hear revving engines, some distant, some far closer, and for one awful moment he thought he glimpsed blue fire. For the most part the seconds rolled by in comparative silence, punctuated by the wind sighing as it got on with the task of dequilling the pines one needle at a time.

Hughes debated running swordplay drills with Chimera but decided against it. When danger reared its gnarled head, common sense dictated you must not be caught with your metaphorical trousers down.

He sat with his back to the bailey wall and thought about the Bonemeal Boy, about the light dimming in the creature's eyes. It had been justified, of course. That was what you told yourself. *I'm sure it's what the soldiers from Champleurs told themselves when they killed Hector and Cassandra and the rest of their family.* How did the mantra go? For King and for Country.

Motivations were funny old things. As he'd told John Isherwood, they were central to an actor's preparation. *This thing I'm doing, this gesture I'm making, this word about to trip off my tongue: why, why, why.*

He watched the red pinpoints snuff out in the skull through the binoculars of recent memory.

It had been justified, of course.

For Dragontail and for Citadel.

For Cate and for Cake.

Hughes smiled. He was glad he could smile, even a rueful one.

"Has something tickled you, Hughes?"

His reverie snapped. "Cate. How are you?"

"Only you looked happy as a box of frogs just now."

"Did I?"

"Lies elongate the nose. Has mine grown?" She crossed her eyes to check. "No, same as ever." Silhouetted by the trees Cate was down on one knee, hiking a sock over a bare calf. "Odd as expressions go, really. Surely the frogs would be better off leaping through some swamp rather than whacking their heads off the lid and croaking dolorously. You know a better one?"

"A swamp or a box?"

"A *saying*," she clarified "Here's one: strike while the iron is hot." She stood. "Isaac is being held in a room up there."

Hughes followed her finger to one of the more decrepit castle towers.

"There are guards posted, but I should be able to take care of them without too much trouble. Escaping, now there's the tricky part. The portcullis is open and the drawbridge lowered, but the courtyard is infested with those skeleton men. No luck there. But around the wall, northwest of where we're standing, I thought I saw an old porter's entrance half swallowed in gorse. I imagine it's been bricked up on this side of the wall, but if there's a way out, it's there."

"What can I do?" said Hughes.

She was rooting in her satchel. "Take my block and tackle. Go to the porter's entrance. Get it open fast as you can."

Hughes took what he needed from her. "And meanwhile you'll rescue the cartographer."

"Incisiveness like that will get you far in the modern Citadel."

She stretched, her body moving through the forms with a businesslike aura. *An actor prepares*, thought Hughes. *And so does a fighter.*

"Take care," he said. And then, because he was worried it sounded a bit too doom-and-gloom, he added, "A preponderance of care."

Cate paused in the act of rolling her neck and shot him a look that, against all probability in these hostile environs, fluttered his chest full of butterflies. "A preponderance," she agreed. "If you can't get the porter entrance open, try to winnow a crawl space below it with the block and tackle. If I'm nowhere to be seen for ten minutes, go back to the drop site. The portal reopens every hour for a quarter of a minute. Report what you've learned. Miss me while we're apart. All that malarkey."

She was gone before he could tell her that he'd only ever used a block and tackle once before, and that it hadn't gone well. His father still didn't have full mobility in his left knee.

***

She slipped between reflections with the ease of an art student slipping between waitress jobs. And like a waitress awaiting her big break as one of film's famous ingénues, she was almost insufferably excited.

She thought it had been a good idea, keeping the extent of her giddiness from Hughes. If he found out, he might start to cool on her. Then again, if he found out about the other thing, the thing that absolutely no one else knew about (except for Auntie Trisha, who was dead), cool was the best she could hope for. More likely there'd be frostbite and inevitably a kind of emotional ice age, after which they'd never speak to one another again.

Oh, but what was she doing entertaining glum thoughts?

Where was that bounding joy?

Through a net of mirrors like the faceted eyes of an insect, she could see Burnished Isaac Lawless. The cartographer was naked. He'd been tied to an interrogation chair with frayed ropes. Someone had tried to gnaw through them. Evidence pointed to Isaac himself, though the gnawing couldn't have been recent. Welts lumped his face into a swollen mask. One nostril was torn. His mouth was encrusted with blood. Handfuls of his hair had been ripped out at the root, leaving his scalp to bleed so the remaining clumps were wine-dark and stiff as straw. Bruises purpled his chest and arms, and they spread in wide yellow-black puddles on his upper thighs.

He looked flat unconscious.

The door opened and a guard came in. Another joined it. Aside from differences in height and a few distinct bone cavities, they looked much the same as the skeleton she and Hughes had taken prisoner. There wasn't much room for custom features when you hadn't any to start with.

They started toward Isaac, not with the intent of questioning him. It seemed they'd tried questioning and were now attempting the stewing technique of interrogation, i.e. allow the captee to stew upon how all this unpleasantness could end if only they cooperated, and more poignantly, beat them until they resembled stew.

Both skeleton men closed on the inert cartographer.

This new development caused a change in Cate, who had, for a disturbing moment, not been enjoying herself. Her knuckles began to itch. A grisly smile capered along the curve of her mouth. They were nasty pieces of work, these Bonemeal Boys. Now she would show them what that was like on the receiving end. In the great highway of motion that was her life, no roadblock (no matter how steep) could resist being overcome by her enthusiasm for a good brawl.

From her hiding place in the room's cracked window, joy bounded through Cate Jubilee, bright and sweet and pure. *There you are,* she thought. *I was almost worried.*

Boots first she passed into a world where all problems could be reduced to their simplest elements. You try to kill me while I try to kill you.

Bliss.

Before they knew what was happening she had swept the knobbly legs from under one guard and was crushing its pelvic floor under her boot. The other she pushed toward the recumbent Isaac.

You might fool them, Lawless, she thought wryly. *But you don't fool me.*

The skeleton stumbled, regained its balance and looked up. It was eye level with the mapmaker they'd beaten until he conked out. Only he wasn't conked out.

He was staring at the skeleton with the look a feral donkey gives the callous handler once the bridle comes off.

"Hey. Pal. Does your da do roofs, pal?" said Burnished Isaac Lawless. "We'll get him to mend this."

His forehead caromed into the cleft of bone where once the creature's nose had been. In accordance with all laws of barroom disagreements, the skull snapped back, and in the hollow sockets both pinpoints of light swiveled erratically.

Cate's skeleton unlatched its piano-key teeth and vented a muffled cry—muffled because her other boot was now lodged in the hinge of its jaw. She ground the heel. Necromancy had hardened the bone. She'd felt that unnatural strength from the ribs of her first Bonemeal Boy. Time dimpled it, sucked the marrow from the osteal tubes until they were dust flutes, but the bone itself was tough and unyielding as wood. Nevertheless her boot—fortified by magic—proved too much for Eurydice's black magic. There was a revolting crunch that reminded her of those mounds of pine needles out in the woods. The skeleton's jaw fell away like an unscrewed luggage clasp.

"Over here, gorgeous."

She jerked and saw Isaac motioning to the thoroughly-nutted skeleton. It was getting up. One pair of Jolene-enchanted hobnail boots later, and it was over.

"All right, Isaac?"

"Come to me rescue, have you love?"

"Hughes and I."

"The skinny bugger?"

"He's filling out." She brushed the bone fragments off the heels of her boots. "Let me have a look at those restraints." She bent to the knots. Up close the cartographer smelled horrible. *They didn't take him to the toilet. Just left him here between bouts of questioning.* "Why did they hurt you so badly, Isaac?"

"First day their king come up to me, very friendly like. Said he'd had a geg through me logbook. I got 'em encoded. He asks me to translate."

"What did you say?"

"Said there was a passcode, secret like. Could only be given with a whisper."

"Oh dear."

"Gullible bugger leaned in."

She knew what he'd done but didn't want to believe it. "You didn't."

He snickered. "See that door? See it's got new hinges? That's cause I sent him through it like crap through a cat's woggler. That king don't know shite, but he knows how to fall, I'll give him that. Tumbled six flights before the others could stop him. Rest of the bony buggers had to piece him back together with glue they found in t' cellar."

"There's one hand free," said Cate, moving to untie the other. She could hear engines purring, a chugging jagged purr that brought to mind not the adorable kittens of bookshops or cozy kitchens but rather the mutated jaguars of the last jungle in hell.

"They're working for someone," said Isaac. His voice had lost any trace of his usual crazed joviality. He sounded serious.

"Oh yes?" Cate glanced at him distractedly. "Who?"

"Dunno. Someone who knew what questions to ask."

"What did they ask you?" The rope was really annoying her.

"Stuff about the Citadel and that. Stuff they'd no right knowing."

"Almost got it now. Stuff who had no right knowing?" said Cate. "The Bonemeal Boys or their mysterious benefactor?"

"Both," said Isaac grimly. His mirth came back with a vengeance when she finally got him loose. "You're a toff. Now, there wouldn't be a pair of kecks about, would there?" He grinned at her. His teeth were like cracked pavement. "Only I'm feeling a draft on me John Thomas."

"I'm afraid I don't have any trousers for you."

"How about a sock, then?"

"Mine are on my feet. Sorry."

"Suppose I'll have to make do."

He nabbed the scraps of rotted clothing from the dead—*correction, unalive* skeletons and fashioned them into what could charitably be called a skirt, or more truthfully, a codpiece.

"What do you think?" he asked.

"You might have been better off in restraints."

He ignored her. "Where's the skinny bugger, then?"

"He's filling out," she said automatically. "Hughes is waiting for us by the porter entrance. Can you walk?"

He nodded, and she believed him.

Isaac Lawless was an unusually compact man, about four feet tall and about as wide. Still, what the cartographer lacked in verticality he made up for in sheer mania, like a Jack Russell Terrier with mapping skills.

It was a wonder he'd been captured in the first place. But that was unfair, wasn't it? Isaac had no magic item. Still, it hadn't stopped him from being a thorn in the side of the Bonemeal Boys. From all accounts he'd given them no end of trouble.

She held the door open for him and paused. "What's that sound?"

"Just the engines," grumbled Isaac. "They're always going around here. Drive you mad."

"No, it's not them."

Or was it? It sounded like them all right, only... *thinner* somehow. A growl from a parched tiger, yes and much more *sinuous* than the rumble of the heavy pyromantic engines, and...

And it was...

Cate's heart skipped a beat.

"Isaac, *hurry!*"

He frowned at her mid-hobble, and that was when the floor erupted under their feet.

CHAPTER THIRTY-FOUR

They drill holes in the surfaces of frozen lakes in Daethumberland. They do it for fishing. Here's how it works: they take this thing that looks like a giant wine bottle opener called a hand auger, and they plant the tip on the ice, grip the sides, and turn. It's easy to fuck up (ice is famously uncooperative), but if you do it right you get a nice peephole boring down and down until it reaches water so cold it'd stop your heart. Into this hole the fisherfolk lower their jigging rods baited with snake-tongued minnow, whipworm, and wishbone.

As he watched the tower collapse, Hughes felt as though he were being lowered into one such hole. He had no conscious thoughts. No tangible worry for Cate or even Isaac who he did not know. Simply that feeling of cold, claustrophobic descent.

The pane from the tower's surviving window blew out as the structure gave up the long fight against gravity. Slivers of superheated glass plunged into the battlements as easily as spoons through warm honey. Velocity pried off roof tiles, and they rained down on the courtyard. Smoke rose biliously, choking the night. Blocks of mountain stone fractured and split, crumbling into clouds of chalky debris.

"Oh my God," he said, ignorant that his mouth was moving at all. "Holy God."

The crash, when it came, combined with the bellow of motorcycle engines. The mixture was so catastrophic it thawed him out of shock.

Hughes ran.

He left the block and tackle next to the porter's door, which was very much still bricked-up and impenetrable. He would have to get a lesson on how the damn thing worked from Cate.

That was presuming she was...

Now look, he told himself. *Don't be ridiculous. She's* got *to still be...*

I mean yes, the tower fell, and there's evidence of an explosion, but she couldn't actually be...

Hughes ran harder.

Following the bend of the castle wall, he soon came to the drawbridge. There were three skeletal riders there, all of them gazing at the courtyard carnage. Chimera hewed off one cadaverous head, and by the time the third was reaching for his weapon, Hughes had struck the second down.

The Bonemeal Boys had stubbed their masters' staffs into crude batons. The third rider brandished its club in one hand and steered with the other. It spurred forward, Hughes slipped into a stance, Chimera pale green in the moonlight like a spike of malice, and at that crucial moment the dust cloud from the ruination of the tower spilled out through the gate and covered them.

Thinking quickly, Hughes pressed his advantage. He could hear his opponent's engine. If he trod lightly, the rider would have no such luck. He stalked forward, his sword at the ready.

A shape insinuated itself from the murk. He closed on it, and almost at once he recognized the motorcycle. He aimed for where he believed the saddle must be and swung. Chimera carved through thin air.

Another shape rose up and Hughes understood too late. The cunning rider had dismounted and crouched near the large front wheel, obscuring it from view while with a bony-fingered hand it had continued to rev the engine. Now the skeleton grinned up out of the clearing cloud, its socketed pinpoint eyes like red candles ahead of some funeral procession, a death march.

The baton took Hughes in the belly. Jolene's armor displaced the force of the attack. Still, those undead bones carried phenomenal strength. The breath gushed out of him in a wheeze.

As he bent double at the waist, the rider's backswing crushed his cheekbone. The pain was both immediate and incredible. Hughes staggered back, willing himself to keep his footing. As he flailed something stiff dug under his armpit— a section of the drawbridge rope. He gave it his weight. The baton had broken skin. His cheek felt sticky and warm. Across the bridge his opponent had abandoned the ruse. Back on its motorcycle, it lurched forward in a rush of blue fire, intent on riding Hughes down.

Hector's training would do Hughes credit in battles to come, but with the motorcycle bearing down on him it was Cassandra's exacting exercise regimen that saved him.

He whirled and hacked at the corded rope. At the steel's bite the rope sponged out in curling strands. Another cut pared it thinner still. Hughes could hear the growing crescendo of the bike's engine, closing, closing, closing.

With a wordless cry he raised Chimera over his head and brought it down in a vicious arc, cleaving the rope in two. His hand closed on the barbican-anchored portion of rope just as certain forces of pressure yanked it. His other hand—the one clutching Chimera—shot out. Impact sang a jolting song up his arm and into his shoulder joint as he was propelled into the air. The results were more than worth it.

As the motorcycle went careening into the ditch, its rider stayed very much aloft. Chimera had rammed it through the eye.

They fell together, skeleton and man.

Half a minute later, Hughes' eyes fluttered open. He groaned. The agony in his cheek reminded him of hand augers again, only instead of boring into a frozen lake, the point was being trammeled into his head. On the bright side, the fall seemed to have popped his shoulder back into place. That was merely excruciating.

Also, there was some sort of invisible acupuncture happening along his arm.

Distressing words like "fracture" and "tear" occurred to Hughes.

With a concerted effort he got up.

Retrieving his sword took more effort than he'd anticipated. In the end he had to apply pressure with his boot before—with a sound like crunching breakfast cereal—Chimera came free.

It took half the creature's skull with it. Bone fragments scattered. The sockets lay dark. No red pinpoints. No death march.

Out, out, brief candle, he thought.

Getting the motorcycle out of the ditch would have presented a problem had the other two riders not so obligingly left theirs around for the taking.

Hughes rammed Chimera back into its scabbard and slid onto an unoccupied saddle.

He grasped the handlebars.

So far, so good.

Mimicking the gestures he'd observed (as has been established, Hughes had a very good memory for vocal intonation and physical gesture—an actor prepares and so forth), he pressed the ignition with his foot and gave the left handlebar a twist.

The engine guttered to life.

O-kay. So the block and tackle had been a nonstarter.

He would have better luck this time.

The dust cloud had dissolved a bit by then, and he could see the courtyard, the fallen tower, and beyond that Castle Aldersglen. There seemed to be no one about. Which meant Cate was either underneath the rubble, or she'd escaped with Burnished Isaac Lawless. Or the Bonemeal Boys had one more prisoner to add to their collection.

Or (and this was the option that had him really, really worried) none of those were right. Cate could hop into reflective surfaces. A window was a reflective surface, right? Which meant that, in theory, those slivers of white-hot glass that had exploded from the tower and peppered the castle walls...

Well, there was the possibility that if the window was destroyed while Cate was inside...

A skeletal rider came crashing through the door to the old scullery. It attempted to rise from its tangle of degraded limbs, but someone had crammed both of its arms through the gap in its pelvic floor.

"Cate's alive," murmured Hughes. And then, much louder, "*You're alive!*"

If his partner heard him, she gave no indication of it.

He could hear her though, could hear the *rumble-scuffle-smash* of out-and-out warfare braving the bowels of Castle Aldersglen.

Emboldened, Hughes ratcheted up the engine till it droned like a wasp nest with a chest infection. That drowned out his worries. For added benefit, something in that noise actually increased the anger he hadn't known he was fostering until this very moment.

They drill holes in the surfaces of frozen lakes in Daethumberland.

It's only afterward when they've caught dinner that they stoke up the cook fires.

Cold and warmth are inter-reliant; you can't understand one without experiencing the other. Nerve endings also hint at their closeness. While shivering in the icy tongs of hypothermia, the dying person actually experiences the nonsensical sensation of being baked alive.

Similarly, Hughes' system was sick of fright. There'd been too much of it to stomach in Eurydice, or to lung or liver for that matter. He was done with it. On the other hand, his system had enjoyed short, turbulent affairs with fury in the past. Take the case of Walter at the funeral, for example. That was pretty bad. How about the first Bonemeal Boy's attitude to using people for fuel? That had riled him (Hughes was terribly conscious of the ancient stone and living fire trembling beneath him). The cold touch of alarm gave way to the hot passion of anger.

Sometimes it went the other way.

But not today.

The knowledge that Cate was alive brought immense, almost desperate relief, true. However, it came packaged with the understanding that someone had tried to drop a tower on her. Hughes' heart was eyeing up that most wildly rambunctious of emotions across the dancefloor. There was only one thing for it.

A tango of sizzling rage was in store.

***

He rode into bedlam on vulcanizing rubber.

There was little time to register his surroundings—a motorcycle was rocketing right for him, smoke threading its rider's collarbone and skull so it had the look of a chimney fashioned from bones. Of course, little time was not no time. Recalling the first rule of swordplay

(*balance*)

he hoisted himself in the saddle and snared hold of a dangling chandelier.

His bike hurtled on without him. Calamitous sounds leaped to his ears as the bikes collided, all bursting tire and screeching metal and detonating engine. Waves of heat pushed first his coat, then Hughes himself, and lastly the chandelier. Its remaining crystal fixtures shattered. He barely noticed a hot line of pain trace itself from the ball of his Adam's apple to the lobe of his right ear. His attention was riveted by the rider. Formerly enveloped in smoke, it was thrown forward only to be snatched mid-flight by none other than Cate Jubilee.

Whump.

She and the rider vanished into a fresh mirror.

A moment later Cate emerged from a window overlooking the hall, for yes, indeed, this was the castle's main hall. Hughes' frantic mind absorbed that information as well as the fact that although Cate and the rider had entered the mirror together, only she had reappeared. The rider was simply gone.

Deadly mirrors, he'd said to her before this madness had unfolded. *Spooky.*

Had that really been less than an hour ago?

Below him the hall was chaos.

Riders wheeled and strobed in crazed figure eights. Fire bucked and spat from the wooden furnishings. Black-tracked carpets curled in at the corners with the rising heat. Wisps of curtain as thin as butterfly wings smoldered. The enormous room was a carton holding ugly smells inside it: cooking lice eggs; noxious worm rot; burning hair and animal hide; melting metal from every mangled wreck. It made him dizzy, but that was all right. Hughes was already lightheaded on account of the blinding anger.

Even the sight of Marrow King Maelen didn't do a thing to douse that unquenchable brutality searing through him.

In life, Maelen was an inordinately large man. Stripped of skin and muscle, his skeleton was no less gigantic, which lent a certain amount of credence to that age-old excuse of some people not being fat exactly, only a tad expansive in the bone department. Maelen's wrath was no less corpulent, for when he'd led the usurpation against Castle Aldersglen and won, he'd lopped off the heads of the leading pyromancers, dipped them in tar carted in barrels from the pits hidden amongst the nearby mountains, and hung the shrunken black trophies with string so they dangled from the bones of his ribs like the baubles of a nightmarish dreamcatcher. That hardly summarized his decoration. Floating several feet off the ground, he glared up at Hughes, and Hughes saw that Maelen had in fact removed his legs and grafted dual engines in their place. They were cylindrical, warped, and chunky. Six exhaust vents jutted from each appendage, bathing the king in blue flame from beneath and casting his grotesque shadow on the defaced tapestries and crooked thrones of the pyromancers who even now thumped together in Maelen's ribcage like moldy walnuts in a spoiled sack.

Some part of Hughes understood this monstrous flying apparition must have brought down the tower, which had only needed a bit of encouragement to fall in the first place. Those leggy engines certainly explained the burst of superheated glass and the pall of rising smoke he'd watched blot out the paler of Eurydice's moons. Maelen must have thwarted Cate right when she was about to pull off her rescue.

Speaking of rescue, Maelen couldn't attend to Hughes personally. He had his hands full with a nude figure who was trying to impale the king with a bit of broken column.

"Here. Skinny," the naked man called to Hughes. "Come down here and help me with this divvy bastard."

Hughes swung the chandelier, judged the distance between himself and the floor (poorly, as it turned out), and landed squarely atop Marrow King Maelen's shoulders.

"Oh shit," he said.

A fist with knuckles like billiard balls clouted him from his perch.

Hughes was up a moment later. His mouth was full of warmth. He spat it out. *Red*, he thought. *My spit is red.*

He remembered he wasn't alone.

"Isaac Lawless, I take it."

"That's me. Bleeding all over the shop."

"You're hurt?"

"Not me," said the cartographer. "You."

Hughes looked down. He wore a bib of blood. "Ah. I suppose this is a bad time to tell you I think my arm is broken."

"Noticed it were sort of floppy," said Isaac charitably, fending off a pair of Bonemeal Boys with his column.

A gaseous growl rolled out of Marrow King Maelen. "Me, oh my, you got yourself a whole crop of friends, huh Isaac? They're springing outta the woodwork. Boys! Form a ring!" He leered over the pair, severed tar-dipped heads knocking against the line of his breastbone. "We got new recruits to induct."

The hectic patterns of the motorcycles began to form up, assembling in a deadly circle.

"Shite," muttered Isaac. "Was hoping they wouldn't do that. We've got to take Maelen. Give him a go over. Are you left-handed, pal?"

"No."

"This should be a doddle then."

They charged. Hughes feinted low while Isaac lashed high. Maelen made no effort to avoid either blow. He let Chimera rake his shin and a pillar explode into smithereens against his chest. This taught Hughes something about their foe.

Here was a person who had been denied the grave. He had grown resentful of the servitude imposed on him by the masters amongst whom he'd once counted himself. He had led an uprising. Which was really rather impressive, come to think about it.

But taking the hits like this also told Hughes one vitally important thing. While Maelen might have overthrown his oppressors for freedom, he had also done it out of hatred. Pure vitriolic loathing, cared for, developed, and delivered upon with interest. He didn't hate Hughes and Isaac and Cate because they were invaders in his world. He didn't hate them because the feeling was mutual.

He hated them because they were *alive*.

So he took some pain (and it *did* hurt, particularly Chimera's slash, Hughes knew that for certain by the grunt that escaped the king). What was a little pain when weighed against the chance to inflict some of his own?

Engines blasting, the Marrow King reigning over the husk called Aldersglen snatched up Isaac and kicked Hughes in his injured arm.

Hughes had never felt anything like it.

He screamed.

Vaguely he heard Cate, her voice raised. She was waylaying the motorcycles as they drew in around them. Mirrors materialized everywhere. Riders and vehicles vanished into them at an astonishing rate, but there were always more of the smoke-laced gang, gung-ho emaciations refused the dignity of rest, who followed Maelen when he made them aware of that dignity denied, this band whose pact was signed in bonemeal.

A few creatures launched themselves from their rides before Cate's mirrors could swallow them. Hughes fought them. The wounds on his cheek and neck were bleeding freely. On his armor the bloody bib was widening into an apron.

Meanwhile Maelen held the squirming Isaac high, looking absurdly like a father raising his newborn son. This illusion vanished as Maelen laid his great bony thumbs on Isaac's eyelids and began to press.

"We gonna hang you up by your heels, make a slit, and bleed you dry," bellowed Maelen happily as he felt the eyeballs integrity begin to give. Soon blood would squirt as vessels in the eyeball burst, then the squishy white sclera, then both in a nice pink mix. "I took it easy on you even after you sent me down the stairs and took my legs from me. Disassembled my ride and made me some new legs. I thought, 'Shit, it turned out okay.' And I *need* Isaac. Hold still, hold still. Wriggly little bug, aintchya? No more, I say. We got us new prisoners, and I bet they'll talk much more than you. So we gonna hang you up, Isaac. We gonna slit you from crotch to crack. Then when you're chalky white and numbed up and you thinking, 'Thank you Poppa Maelen for your mercy, here comes an end to the aching'—*Hah!* *Then* we gonna bring out the peeling knives. Us Bonemeal Boys are dishes served without meat. To join you got to lose yours. That'll wake you up, thinking 'bout that." He laughed and it was viler than the rumble of the ghoulish engines he'd forced his enemies to build. "That'll make you wish you never slithered out your mama's slimer. And when it's over you'll be mine."

Isaac Lawless was weeping blood by now.

"If you could crush me ears while you're at it," he said. "Only I'd rather die listening to me own thoughts if it's all the same to you."

Maelen's sockets blazed purple red. Indignation hissed through his clenched teeth. It was clear that of all the living beings he had grown to despise in his undeath, the cartographer was swiftly becoming his least favorite.

Too late the king caught the flash of movement.

There was a chorus of amazed revulsion from the Bonemeal Boys accompanying the brief chopping sound, which was not dissimilar to the sound a lovingly honed axe blade makes passing through diseased, rain-softened wood.

The Marrow King's hiss broke off.

Isaac fell, which might have pulled some critical muscle, had Hughes not lessened the cartographer's impact with his own body.

"Thanks," said Isaac, wiping the gore from under his eyes with a casualness that was terrifying. "That really gave me a hand, that did."

"Don't mention it," said Hughes.

They scrambled up and backed away from Marrow King Maelen, who was gawking down at his arm. With one smooth swing of Chimera, Hughes had just cut it off.

"Get it?" said Isaac, wiggling his bruised eyebrows. "A *hand*? Gave me *a hand*?"

"Where are your trousers, Mr. Lawless?"

"Me kecks? These thieving shites nicked them. Here, you all right, pal?"

"Yeah." Hughes was swaying on his feet. Sweat ran down his face in rivers. "The pain bill for my injuries has turned up. Costs an arm and a leg."

"Heh, good one."

Hughes smiled weakly and flexed his good fingers on Chimera. "I'm not in the least bit scared though, which I don't mind telling you is refreshing for me."

"Scared? Not of this lot."

"Right," Hughes agreed. "You know Miss Gleam and Mr. Glint?"

"Yeah, I've heard of them."

Hughes measured Marrow King Maelen, his smile growing a little stronger despite the agony working in his arm. "Compared to those two, this guy's a pussycat."

***

On and on the tango went, flame and fury transforming Castle Aldersglen into a lantern held against the rustling dark of the valley. A bird came to watch the dance unfold. The woods were as surprised as anything to see it. There hadn't been a bird in these parts in, well, longer than even the roots could remember. On December-cold wings it glided betwixt the pines and swerved to avoid the groping limbs of the lynchwood trees. Following the raucous sounds through spotlights of moon it flapped above the three riders Hughes had struck down, through the gate, and over the tumbledown tower. There was a little lattice overlooking the castle hall. The bird perched, nudged aside shards of glass with its beak, and settled in to watch.

There was a good deal of smoke polluting the air.

The bird did not mind.

It could see just fine.

To-and-fro its velvet head twitched. Tick-and-tock. The very motion of despair.

It was a spy, that bird from elsewhere.

If Hughes could pierce the fug of thick eye-watering smoke himself, seeing the bird's eyes would have taken him right back to square one. It would have whisked him out of anger and put him right back in the icy fishing hole.

To-and-fro.

Tick-and-tock.

He would have seen it and been reminded of the quick, unnerving motion of crooked hands collecting tickets for a dream carousel. The very motion of despair.

But of course Hughes could not see. He was demonstrating the first rule of swordplay. His arm hung limp at his side, the other was compensating as best it could, and he was angry, and dangerous, and secretly quite sure that he was going to die at any moment.

The bird watched him with interest through those eyes, those lambent slitted lumps of burning yellow.

***

Having successfully sewn disarray through the ranks of the Bonemeal Boys, Cate Jubilee had joined the fight against their king. His bulk prevented her from dragging him through one of her impromptu mirrors to his doom, so she was making do with her boots.

"Why," she grunted from her position atop his shoulders and between each stomp upon the unyielding centipede of his spine. "Why. Must. You. Be. So. *Difficult.*"

"That's the business, pet!" Isaac Lawless declared in the brief period connecting headbutts. Beaten to a pulp and ready to exact vengeance he was latched like a kind of demonic warthog onto Maelen's clavicles, and had been nutting the skeleton king repeatedly.

Hughes, for his part, had his still-functioning hand completely full keeping Maelen's legs at bay. The engines holding the king aloft seemed a blur to him. It was all he could do to parry the logs of solid metal, dodging incoming blasts of blue fire in an effort to avoid becoming a human cigar.

"Boys!" cried Maelen. "Can't you see them whipping on me? These assassins all softness and sinew? Don't you care?"

His plea asserted some control. They stopped searching the mirrors for their fallen brothers in bone, gathered themselves up with the parts Chimera had left them, shook their skulls and gave voice to their fealty.

"Barrow Lord, we truly do!"

"We'll save you!"

"Tear them down!"

"Slit them!"

"Flay them!"

"Gut them!"

"Slay them!"

In a tide of screeching wheels and maggoty grins, the Bonemeal Boys came to the aid of their king.

"My cavalry!" Maelen crooned. "Let's oust this pestilence of flesh. No prisoners."

He closed a huge hand round Cate's boot, flung her forcefully at Isaac, and staggered Hughes with skin-boiling heat that pulsed from his exhaust pipes. "Full throttle."

CHAPTER THIRTY-FIVE

Ever observant, he took in the scene. Cate and Isaac lay momentarily stunned. Maelen and the surviving Bonemeal Boys converged upon them.

All about the hall burned blue and tangerine. Shadows romped and rollicked like a festival of imps across the walls. In his ears the engines chugged and growled so loudly he would have sworn someone was juggling chainsaws.

Here they came, the enemy of the hour, closer every moment. Not Miss Gleam or Mr. Glint yet despicable all the same.

Hughes made to raise his sword arm and found he couldn't.

He blinked at it dumbly. *Up*, he commanded. *Up. Up.*

The word moved sludgily from his brain to his lips.

"Lup," he mumbled thickly. It was only then that he realized the extent of his exhaustion. He must have bitten his tongue earlier. Against the back of his teeth it felt twice its normal size. *Lup.* What sort of slurred attempt was that? It was a drunk's word.

He turned with a detached curiosity as a thrown baton dislodged itself from the smoke. Luck (or misfortune, depending on who you asked) guided it true. It knocked Chimera from his hand and crushed both phalanges in his thumb. By this time a cut on his scalp he did not remember getting had bled as heartily as the wounds at his cheek and throat, closing one eye for him.

And then luck (or misfortune, again depending on who you asked) bade him look one final time at those wall-mounted tapestries he'd noticed when he'd been hanging from the chandelier earlier. When they were made the tapestries showed groups of people—or things that looked very much like people, only stranger in some unaccountable way—huddled around fires for warmth. Toasting their hands over the crackling pine logs, they seemed to be telling stories. Big folk were present, and small ones. Children. Cozy scenes of fellowship. Even the twin moons of Aldersglen looked wholesome and comfortable, sweet white and gentle green.

And the Bonemeal Boys had vandalized these images. Scratched and scrawled and hoodlumed them until they were perverse scraggly things barely clinging to the stone. They had taken even these, the woven memories of this community, and at their Marrow King's order they had sabotaged them. Demolished them with *gusto*.

Hughes' face changed. It returned from the faraway exhaustion. Convulsions passed over the muscles in his cheeks and beneath his eyes. Chimera lay at his feet, forgotten. The vanguard of motorcycles was right on him. He could pick out the grooves in the forerunner's front tire. His nose was filled with the sickly sweet smell of them. Their grins stretched in a discolored panorama. Snarling through a wet red mask, Hughes pushed his Performance.

Hughes
Performance Level: 10

Influence the behavior of others using your physical and vocal performance, as well as your stage presence. **WARNING!** *Bad performances result in negative reception.*

Chance of Success: 36%	Next Level: +1% to Chance of Success **Level 25 Secret Ability:** ???

"Necromancers and pyromancers of Aldersglen," he called. "I am Gormon Hughes—wielder of Chimera, scarlet agent of the Last Dragon of Redspire, mirror man, shadow player. If fiery fate has not robbed you of your ears, I *beg* you lend them to me now."

His heart leaped as the closest motorcycle slalomed violently, the front wheel missing him by less than six inches. Much to the disgruntlement of the Bonemeal Boys, the rest of their rides were also misbehaving. Blue fire gushed out of exhausts, preventing the skeletons from reaching Hughes... for the moment.

Thank you, he thought, and in a rich, clear voice that filled the hall he said, "For too long have you languished in cells of steel and stone. Perhaps you showed cruelty in those days of yesteryear when you were masters of this country and its castle. But is your current torment just? How apt can the caress of endless flame be when it sears sanity and chars hope? How much probity and fairness presents itself in the inferno?"

With a roar, Marrow King Maelen lunged for him. He would put an end to this speech-slinging meat. To his utter astonishment the king found himself hauled back. Not by Cate or Isaac, but by the very engines keeping him aloft.

Thank you, thank you, Hughes wanted to shout. But he must go on at once, while he had momentum, while the Performance was alive and building.

"Whatever his intentions in the beginning, this Marrow King is no monarch, unless a slug can rule anything. A viper. A leech suckled fat on the blood of former victories.

"For God's sake, to this day he parades your heads before my eyes! That is not justice. It is cruelty that you might rectify."

Swirling eagerly the blue fires battened away the skeleton horde. The Marrow King clawed at his legs, craving to be free so he could squash Hughes' head in his paw. Meanwhile the rapt audience wanted more, more, more! He sensed they wanted to know: how could they rectify Maelen's evil?

With a flourish Hughes told them.

"Friends, I call for one last bonfire. Let the offense and the wrongdoer burn together. Melt and conquer. And then, when all lies incinerated, learn of life beyond the windblown ashes. It must be sweeter than this. Kinder. Quiet and distant from the rattle of this mortal contraption, this dark machine outpacing peace. Now, to your kindling! One last blaze will crown you sovereigns once more! Catch! Catch!"

Heart pounding, he first predicted, then experienced the push.
He felt the familiar words pour over him.

Testing Performance...

Thirty-six percent represented good odds. In more than a third of probable outcomes, this worked. He held onto that.

Catch.

Testing Performance...

To your kindling, he prayed.

Catch.

***

Cate came to as Hughes made his plea to the necromancers and pyromancers of Aldersglen. Her head throbbed steadily. It was nauseating. Isaac's brow was notoriously hard, and now she had firsthand experience of that.

She closed her eyes and listened to Hughes. He was making a speech. She hadn't heard him deliver one of those since that time in The Foundry.

This one was pretty good.

That seemed woefully inadequate, but right now she was having trouble thinking about anything other than her headache, which was splitting. Another thing, it was too hot in here. Too stifling. When she baked (infrequently but enthusiastically), she always enjoyed the part where you put on your mittens and opened the oven, only to receive a faceful of heat. She pictured a wide, warm mouth somewhere deep inside the oven blowing heat across her cheeks, leaving them to tingle for minutes after. This room was hotter than that by a long shot, an immobile blanket of clamminess that bit the skin rather than kissed it.

Hughes had stopped talking. That was nice of him. Usually she found his voice soothing as a puppy's soft fur, but a moment ago it fairly boomed, almost unrecognizable.

Where was Hughes? Cate looked for him and saw Burnished Isaac Lawless instead. Surprise, surprise, the cartographer was on his feet and gazing all around them. She wished she could read his expression. The swelling hid his feelings completely.

Her eyelids were heavy.

I'll look for Hughes later, she told herself and lapsed into darkness.

***

"Catch! Catch!" he implored them, and catch they most certainly did.

Blending and fusing into pillars of fire the victims of the Bonemeal Boys caught in the motors and the machinery, liquefying their prisons. Stone sundered. Metal oozed. Burning tires bounced.

Next they caught in the underlings. Skeletal riders threw up their hands to protect themselves. Fire seeped through the narrow shutters of their wasted fingers, and like fists from vengeful hell the pyromancers and necromancers punched up through the frightful grins and out the skullcaps. Crowded and crowned in blue fire, they became living wicks.

Out, out, brief candle, Hughes thought for the second time that night. He didn't know it, but watching the results of his Performance he looked rather daunting. Half blinded by blood, there was something of Krys' tattooed cyclops about him. He was still angry. He wanted to suck down the streams of fire and exhale them over the valley. The pines. The town. The castle. All of it. One huge tallow drum.

"I hope it shows up," he murmured. "I could beat it now if only it came."

Some part of him wondered what he was talking about and was stunned to realize he meant the two-headed wolf creature from Iphigenia.

Show up? It couldn't. It was dead. In a burst of gore two feminine hands had slipped out of its monstrous chest. They placed its heart on his Krys knife, which was forged into the sword he nursed now with a trembling arm.

Must be the heat, he rationalized. *It's making my brain sweat.*

The hot air baking off the columns of fire *was* overpowering, certainly. It rippled over him in sheets, rashing his exposed skin in red bands of superficial burn. It wrung tears from him and dried them into his pores before they could trickle as far as his chin.

At last, in a single unified stanchion, the former residents of Castle Aldersglen came for Maelen. The Marrow King made no effort to shield himself. He flailed and clawed, fighting the unconquerable.

"Away!" he screamed. "Away from me. You're propellant. Combustables. *Fuel,* I say, only fuel for my Boys, my dear ones, myyyyYY *YYYAAAAAAAAHHHHH–*"

His protests melted into wordless howls along with his legs. Steel dribbled and hissed. Maelen went over, raking himself madly with his hands. The flames flew up, painting the castle's core a vibrant and exquisite blue, and crashed down to swallow his writhing form. In their rib-bone casement the tarred heads vaporized. The torso, limbs, and skull seemed to distend, and with an expulsion of flagitious gasses, they exploded. The king's grin—lunatic with agony in those final moments—disintegrated into a clump of mealy ash.

Hughes could scarcely see. He was balancing on the treacherous edge of unconsciousness. With grim determination, he forced himself to look as the fire skimmed over Maelen's ashes as though confirming the king's death for themselves.

A good thing he'd kept his wits about him because at that moment the pillars spiraled around him. Hughes heard whispers like the *furdle-snip* of wildfire in dry moss. He couldn't understand them; there were too many.

Taking a stab in the dark, he said, "Erm. Yes, well, you're most welcome. And thank you for your help."

The fire nuzzled him. No burn.

Hughes couldn't suppress a smile. Something simmered inside him, a bright conflagration that the strange tenderness of the moment had quelled. Had he been angry? Furious?

Maybe.

He squeezed his eyelids with the pads of his fingers, took a deep breath, and let it go.

Well, he was himself again. Dog tired, but not unpleasantly so.

"What comes next for you?" he asked the fire.

In answer, blue tendrils of warmth shot up, split the castle open with a hatchet's precision, and pulled the living flame up into the night.

"I see," said Hughes. "Good stuff."

He sat down heavily.

"How'd you do that?"

Hughes looked up into the apocalyptic face of Isaac Lawless.

"You just let the knees drop," he replied. "It's not difficult."

"I'm not talking about *sitting*, you daftie," said Isaac. "I'm talking about you cooking that lot like a Sunday roast."

"The fire did that."

"Yeah. Right." Isaac jabbed a finger under Hughes' nose. "But you put them up to it."

"How about I tell you when we're not flies in the proverbial ointment?"

"Over a bevvy?"

"A what?"

"A bevvy," said Isaac, exasperated. "Drinks like."

"Oh. Yes, all right."

"Your treat?"

"I don't think so," said Hughes. He chanced a look at Cate. She was snoring, adrift in The Land of Nod, presumably dreaming about a round of bevvies at *The Pear and Princess*. With her oblivious to this conversation, honesty became available to him like a seldom-used pen in the stationary of communication. "You see Isaac, the truth is, I haven't actually got any money."

The cartographer grinned.

"The only thing you're short of, pal, is observation."

"Pardon?"

Isaac looked around them. "Have a goggle yourself."

Hughes obeyed.

"Good grief," he said. "Is that..."

"You bet your skinny tush it is," said Isaac.

"He's filling out," said a groggy voice.

"Cate." Hughes was on his feet in a moment.

"What happened?"

"We won. The rest can wait," said Hughes, although he had no intention of telling her anything about his Performance. Invention would have to fill out the gaps in her memory. He was already troubled by Isaac's knowledge of it, though the man seemed more interested in alcohol than answers.

Moonlight poured in through the open castle roof. There was something different about that light. Hughes put it out of mind, and much more besides.

He smiled, warm and glad.

Worry could wait. As could the pain lurking at the edges of his perception. His arm. The wounds on his face and scalp. That splinter of ache in his chest that drove deeper every time he lied to Cate, or hid the truth from her, which was as good as lying when you got right down to it.

It could all wait just a little while longer. At least until he'd properly treasured what he was seeing here and now in the aftermath of battle and the sensations it nurtured and fastened in him like pendants of hope, yes, irresistible, beguiling HOPE.

"Cate."

"Yes, Hughes?"

"Cate, there's so *much.*"

***

Searching the castle's cluttered storehouse, they turned up an unlikely species of spider, an ungovernable growth of mold, assorted sundries, and an old cart. Cate tested the cart. This involved rolling it for a time and acquainting its general structure with her hobnail boots. Afterward she pronounced it sturdy. "Hell on wheels," Hughes said drily, and was rewarded with a bout of Jubilee giggles. So they loaded the cart with the credits that had spawned from the corpses of the Bonemeal Boys and began to make their way back toward the drop.

The plan was that Cate would head into the mountainside, go through the portal, and have Doctor John shift the coordinates so they could get the cart through, not to mention Isaac, who was not in prime condition to go spelunking (though he was highly amused by this particular word when Hughes mentioned it, Isaac being living proof that just because you have a mind of iron, it doesn't mean you are not, on occasion, an absolute horseshoe).

It was still dark. Night never seemed to end in Aldersglen. But their spirits were high. Isaac speculated on his next mission, and Hughes and Cate kept catching one another smiling. The catching made them smile all the wider. *It wouldn't ache at all to tell her she's beautiful,* Hughes thought.

"Cate," he said. "You're beautiful."

She didn't look surprised, only happy. "Thank you, Hughes. So are you."

"Suit yourselves. I'll take maps any day," said Isaac Lawless. "Better curves."

Cate's laughter seemed to fill the whole valley. Their path guided them back toward the cordillera. They stuck to the pines and found them good company. Time passed quickly as it always did when things were at their calmest and best, and with an eagerness for home quaking sweetly in their bones they rolled the cart to a stop just outside the drop zone.

Isaac settled down against the trunk of a lynchwood tree, which behaved itself after he bit it.

A little ways off, on the jut of land overlooking the valley, Cate approached Hughes.

"Ready to get back to civilization?" she asked him.

"Definitely." They were standing close together. Hughes' index finger brushed the knuckles of her hand. They were bruised, swollen, grouted in blood. "Cate..."

"I hope you're ready for the pandemonium," she overrode him excitedly. "You'd better be. There's going to be a rumpus. A brouhaha. A kerfuffle."

"Sorry?"

"A *party.*" She hugged him, tightly and briefly, and then stood back, holding him by the forearms. "Your first foray into the dungeon dimension of Eurydice was a smashing success, don't you think?"

Hughes snuck a glance at the cart, laden to the brim with credits. Their pinkness sparkled gloriously. Every facet, every feature—they were flawless. Most of them had solidified from the desiccated remains of Marrow King Maelen, who was evidently well-endowed in bounty if not in survivability. The cartload represented a small fortune, and apparently for his share Hughes was entitled to a tenth of it. Cate received fifteen percent. The rest went to the Citadel. Hughes wasn't bothered. A tenth of that hoard might not pay off much of his enormous debt to Mr. Shine, but it would surely mollify Gleam and Glint for a while.

Cate was looking at him expectantly.

"Self-praise is no praise," he said. "That being said, I was amazing."

"Careful." She poked his sides good-naturedly. "The portal is only a hundred feet wide."

"Mm, and we want my fat head to fit through?"

"Not fat," she said crossly and kissed him. "Just filling out."

While he tried to organize a jar to control the internal butterflies, she turned for a parting look at the valley. Her face tilted skyward.

"Is that beautiful too?" she asked him.

Hughes looked at the starless heavens over Aldersglen. The two moons were gone. In their place was a single moon, round and smooth as a new cup.

It was blue.

"It's certainly an improvement," said Hughes.

ACT NINE

AUTUMN WALTZ

CHAPTER THIRTY-SIX

In his spare time (of which there was gradually less and less nowadays) Doctor John Isherwood sketched birds.

It was evening, the 25th of August. Hughes and Cate had returned with Isaac in the predawn hours of the morning. They had caught up on sleep, woken to a feast, and now as far as John understood, the kid was being honored with his first Triumph.

At a little after eight o'clock sounds of mingled revelry came to the doctor's door, but not a one passed through. Inside his study on the eighty-second floor of Redspire, John Isherwood enjoyed the sort of quiet you might find in a hermit's hovel or at the bottom of a lake.

Stepping in, a newcomer would be struck by the frankly deplorable state of its cleanliness. A lifelong bachelor with an evolved sense of privacy, John Isherwood often listened politely to Falstaff's hand-wringing offers to spruce up the place—listened, that was, with the bullnecked understanding that no such sprucing would ever occur. Doctor John's study was his church, a sacred vestibule for he and he alone. If the butler didn't like it, he could take it up with Winnifred Dragontail.

Down in the subsection of the tower, as well as in a privately funded floor of Corinth University, he conducted experiments. Those were clean, sterile, bunkerlike places for him. Okay for the kinetic portions of the job. Here in this jumble of rattle-belly-empty thermoses, scattered notebooks, textbooks, academic treatises, vases bursting with poorly pruned devil's ivy, dumb cane, and Horstesian geraniums, the good doctor mused. He *planned.*

That was a thing worth savoring in solitude.

Little enough blueprinting tonight though. He was tired. Tomorrow afternoon he was to meet with Doctor Amelia Dean. The pair would discuss Hughes' sword, which the kid chose to call Chimera. John wondered where Hughes had learned the word. It wasn't exactly common.

John himself had learned the word earlier that year, in spring he thought, or late winter. He'd read it in a book about ancient Corinth City theatre. According to the book, the Chimera was a character who featured in a lot of plays like the Narrator, the Harlequin Fool, the Judge, or the Chorus. This Chimera played the part of the dramatic catalyst. In other words, the one who stirred the pot and got the action cooking.

Later on, or so the text vouchsafed, the Chimera went on to symbolize the death of a maternal figure at the hands of her son. That day in her office, Winnifred had asked Hughes about his father. There'd been no mention of a mother. John wondered where the woman was, or indeed if she were anywhere. *Maybe he killed her in childbirth.* Normally a superstitious thought like that would never even cross his mind, but John had some cause for a little mystical thinking.

Because what was the symbol of the Chimera? Why, if it wasn't a three-headed beast: lion, dragon, and ramhorn goat. The same beasts Ogre Jo had fashioned into Hughes' sword.

This seeming coincidence rankled John.

Either the idiot savant was a student of classical Corinthian theatre, or something else was going on here.

He slipped a finger under his spectacles and scratched an eyelid. The gesture took him back to university in a time when glasses were things his father wore, not prim spry medical student John.

Not as young as I used to be, he thought. Again that word intoned itself in the belfry of his bones. *Tired.*

You'll be right as rain in the morning. His mother's voice, kind and reassuring. *A spell of sleep works magic, Johnny. Besides, forty-three isn't old.*

"No. But it's when you died, Mom," he said aloud.

To that, her voice had no rejoinder. *My voice*, he thought. In his opinion the dead only spoke through that which outlived them: art, scientific discovery, and of course the children who remembered them while doodling birds on a windy Tuesday night.

At least the rain had quit.

He sat in a large, cushioned chair of white and red before a pair of stately glass doors, his legs crossed, his sketchbook nestled in his lap.

Outside the doors lay a balcony he rarely used, and there, hung above the railing was a birdfeeder. Gripping one of its perches by the talons and pecking vigorously at the seeds was a little summer woodlark. No, the crest on the head was too pronounced.

A skylark.

John had welcomed it with a nod as though inviting a dance partner to the floor and set about capturing the bird in image. Now he was almost finished, and the skylark looked plump and content.

"Hold that pose a second longer, okay?"

The bird didn't move.

"Much obliged. Want to hear what the brilliant poet says about Chimeras?"

The bird ate a seed and resumed its perfect pose.

"You got it. Thinking about mothers put me in mind of it. I only read the poem once so forgive me if I royally fuck it up. Here goes: *But up from my wounds/ from this goat's body/ up from my wood-smoke lungs/ from the milk of me/ comes a song/ a melody/ to open yours/ then lick them clean.*

"What do you think of that?"

John put the last lines on the sketch and looked up to see what his model thought of the poem.

The skylark was gone.

In its place roosted a new bird. Against a backdrop of moonless night, its plumage was tarmac-dark and speckled white. Oily eyes peered in at the man with his pencil still hovering above his drawing. Pinned by those oddly penetrative eyes, John Isherwood recognized the bird's species. *A nightjar.*

He had not seen one of those since his uncle's house. How long had it been? Twenty-five, no, thirty years? Richard Isherwood was, like his nephew after him, a devoted ornithologist. He had also been a taxidermist. Stuffed birds nailed onto plastic logs lined his entry hall. Richard had called it his "feathered welcome mat,", as in, "Come inside my child. I've rolled out the feathered welcome mat just for you."

One of the prized fixtures was the nightjar collection: somber, pygmy; spotted nightjars; three lesser nighthawks; ocellated; tawny-collared; whippoorwills; and so on.

John had always found his Uncle Richard's view on domestic decor a trifle suspect and his collection of crossbows outright menacing. When it came to capturing birds, he preferred the pencil.

Still, as he sat there staring at the feeder's newest occupant, Doctor John Isherwood (forty-three years young and still capable of recognizing fear when he felt it) had to suppress the urge to lunge from his chair, throw the balcony doors open, and send the bird flapping with a swing of his arm.

It was the *size* of the thing.

Did nightjars usually grow that big?

He didn't think so. Even with its wings folded, this one more closely resembled the Harvest Owl Uncle Richard had shot down in Daethumberland in dimension, and that thing had weighed almost a full five kilograms.

He watched it through the paneled glass. The bird was motionless.

Stuffed, he thought, and felt his blood run just a little colder.

It occurred to him that if it wasn't stuffed like one of Uncle Richard's birds, then at the very least it hadn't shown a lick of interest in the feeder itself. If not in seeds, then where did its appetite lie?

That was when he saw its beak drip.

Rainwater, he rationalized. *Just a couple drops of rainwater is all.*

But it wasn't raining. It hadn't been for hours.

Some voice in him, not at all like his mother's, but rather an echo of childhood terror whispered, *It's blood.*

"It can't be." His lips barely moved.

Through solid glass the bird could not have heard him. It simply could not have. Nevertheless, roosting there on the feeder, it gave a kind of ugly twitch. John's college educated mind would have called it a *spasm*.

How does the feeder not tip? he wondered. *That thing looks ungodly heavy.* Unbidden, the fact rose in him that five kilograms was about the average weight of a human head.

The bird ruffled and went still. For the briefest instant, he glimpsed something under it, something long and sharp as the knives taxidermists used to open the bird before the insides were spooled out and the sawdust was crammed in.

They were too crooked to be talons. Too long. Too sharp.

I'm not safe here. I really am not safe here anymore.

Which was patently ridiculous. Even if it had wanted to come inside

(inside, inside the house to stuff the people living there)

it could not. Doors barred its way.

Another drip fastened his gaze on the beak.

Blood. This time the word had an edge of hysteria to it. *It's blood all right. Where did the skylark go? Where did it go?*

It was a good question.

That thing killed it. His mother again, and in life she had never sounded so frightened, not even when the doctors had diagnosed her with liver failure. *It killed that skylark, Johnny. And it wants you. You see that, don't you my sweet boy?*

John Isherwood experienced a spasm himself then, a shiver that went from the vulnerable soft patch of flesh beneath his groin to his throat by way of his bowels, which were becoming loose with fright.

He had to see the bird for himself.

A little light would dispel the illusion, surely.

There was a switch that lit up the anbaric lamp on the balcony. He didn't use it much. He had no reason to. Yet right now turning on that lamp seemed utterly essential. From the corner of his eye he could just barely make out the switch on the nearest wall. It was perhaps six feet away. Two quick strides and he'd be there.

Of course the moment I snap the switch and the light comes on there will be no bird.

Could that be possible? He had never suffered from sleep paralysis, which was a common cause of nighttime hallucination. And besides, he had never felt so awake in his life.

Yet the idea that the thing outside was not real granted him a distinct flavor of courage. It was only the dripping that stopped him rushing to his feet. It was too irregular, only happening twice since he'd first looked up and seen his peculiar visitor. Blood coagulated pretty fast outside the body, and it began to dry even faster. But if there was enough of it...

If there's enough of it, that scared childish voice whispered inside him. *Enough of it to form rubies of red plasma, then it drips.*

They'd buried his mother in her rubies—a whole necklace of them.

"What a waste," said Uncle Richard.

John hadn't known whether or not he meant the gemstones or his sister-in-law.

A third drip, thicker this time. He could almost hear the sickening *plop* it made as it hit the tilework.

He didn't go for the switch. Instead he sat in his chair like a museum waxwork. He could feel sweat prickle his underarms. One warm bead slid down his side.

Out in the stillness and the dark the nightjar squatted, watching him as he watched it.

I've got to go for it. Any more of this and if I'm not already crazy then I will be.

Here it was, another gush of bravery.

Two paces.

That's all it'll take.

Wait for it, Johnny, whispered Ella Isherwood, his mother who'd died of liver failure and been buried in her red, red rubies. *Wait for it, my dear one...*

NOW!

He sprang for the wall-mounted switch with a speed that would have humbled (or scared the shit out of) the medical student he'd been. His fingers fumbled, found nothing.

He couldn't look, but he was positive he had seen movement on the balcony. It was coming for him.

The switch was gone.

John gave an animalistic grunt of dread.

Something was scrabbling at the glass. Or was that his fingernails on the plaster?

"Please," he croaked. "Please."

His fingers found purchase. Whatever it was he jerked at it with crazed desperation.

Harsh light flooded the balcony. John stood back for a look, his sides heaving and slick, expecting to see nothing at all out there.

The bird hadn't moved.

Its beak—which was long and tapered and built for rending flesh—was gobbeted with gore. Crumpled on the balcony tiles like something discarded was the skylark. It had no throat.

Understanding chilled him to the marrow.

That was what he'd seen dripping from the nightjar's beak.

The skylark's torn throat.

He raised widening eyes to the intruder still balanced impossibly on his feeder.

The nightjar opened its mouth, a round pink hole lined in red, shrieked, and took wing.

John Isherwood collapsed back into his chair.

An hour later he rose, shaking, and called Wendy.

CHAPTER THIRTY-SEVEN

About an hour before Doctor John received his unexpected guest, Cate escorted Hughes all the way up to the eighty-eighth floor of the tower.

"Don't dawdle," she said. "We're late enough as it is."

"Cate?"

"What is it, Hughes?"

"I don't know what we're late *for*."

They finally found an elevator that wasn't in use. Cate ushered him in. "For your Triumph. I tried telephoning you," she said.

"I was with Hector on the fifty-first. What's a Triumph?"

"The fifty-first? Not the sauna, I hope. You need to keep your cast dry."

Hughes glanced down at the heavy plaster molded around his arm. Not broken, thankfully, but their scuffle with Maelen had earned him a torn ligament, superficial burns, and exactly thirty-one stitches. His dad would pitch a fit. Hughes reminded himself to send another letter home, maybe obscuring some of the more colorful details of his adventure, as well as the location of that adventure, which was tippity top secret...

On second thought, maybe he'd just write to him about the weather.

"Hughes?"

"Hmph? Oh. Um. Sorry, Cate. I was miles away. Once again?"

"I was asking whether or not Hector had the forethought to keep you well away from the sauna."

She needn't have worried. Hector had taken him for a few circuits round the hairpin-shaped athletics field.

"Was he terribly angry that you accepted the mission to Eurydice?" Cate asked.

Hughes considered. "I don't think Hector knows how to be angry," he said. "I think he lacks the necessary glands, to be honest."

His ghostly mentor had been displeased though.

That much was abundantly clear in the way he refused to meet Hughes' eye, in the stiffness of his congratulations.

Not ready, he'd mouthed before the mission began, and in some ways he'd been right and in others, wrong. Evidently the spoonful of right didn't help the wrong go down, but Hector was more complicated than that.

His teacher's coldness confronted Hughes with the idea that here was someone who cared about him in a different way than he was used to, a care of wellbeing from circumstantial friend to circumstantial friend that said: You've just come into my life, don't go, don't go. Hector felt that for him, and to no one's surprise it was extremely mutual. Hughes wanted to learn more about Hector's family, about swordplay, about battle and strategy.

He wanted to listen to it all couched in that voice like cinnamon carrot cake enjoyed on a crisp autumn day.

"One more question?" said Cate hopefully.

"Not until you tell me what a Triumph is."

"Too late. It's a surprise now."

"Not really," said Hughes, perfectly accurately. "I know it's happening. I just don't know what it is."

"You fidget when you're nervous."

"I do not."

"You do." She gave him a sage look. "Like a sort of internal wiggle. Did Hector ask how you defeated Marrow King Maelen?"

"Yeah."

"And you told him?"

"No."

"I bet he adored that."

"Mm, really inked me back into the pages of his good books." The elevator clunked and rattled, carrying them up the gullet of Redspire. Hughes shuffled his feet awkwardly. "I said I had to talk to you about it first."

"Thoughtful."

"You think so?"

"I think it's thoughtful."

"Ah, I thought so too."

They both stared straight ahead, their faces as serious as marble statues carved in the likeness of extremely important and equally serious people.

Cate broke first.

"*Pfffff.*"

She keeled over, laughing.

Hughes' composure fled. He covered his face with a hand, his shoulders trembling.

That was why, when the elevator doors opened, those members of the Scarlet Citadel gathered to celebrate their new recruit's Triumph found Gormon Hughes chuckling helplessly and Cate Jubilee a riot of giggles with one arm and a large tumble of her furnace-colored hair slung around his shoulders.

Of course the two of them went from the frying pan of elevator shenanigans into the fire of a swinging, swaggering, lollygagging, fanfaronading party.

Here comes the Citadel's mobile brass band with tuba, trumpet, thumping drum, hear the horns and the crooner hello!

A one.

A two.

A one, two, three, four—

The idea of a Triumph came from those early days of Corinth City when it was just a paltry little hodgepodge place somebody built on a hill near the sea. There was a throne. A king sat there, mostly for fear of what would happen if he didn't. On one occasion, after winning a war of no particular importance, but whose victory was quite flashy and impressive, the king held this big march that wound and ribboned through every roof-templed street and tree-lined avenue. So was born the tradition of the Triumph.

There hadn't been kings in a long time, but as has been established Wendy Dragontail's family found traditions to be important things. Belief was like the essence of pyromancers—it was fuel, and fuel had to power something or else what would be the point?

Hughes found himself positioned as the central float in a fantastic parade that started in the Lunarlight Wing and ended at the base of Redspire. Every floor featured. Every wing and most of the rooms too, most of which he'd never seen before, and all passing in a blur of whistlers and streamers, scarlet skirts, suit jackets, dresses, heels, boots, belt buckles, wristwatches, monocles, spectacles, and what a spectacle the booze was!

The cocktail list at *The Pear and Princess* seemed small time compared to the galactic avalanche of alcohol that night. Fluted glasses bubbled clear and sweet, slices of apricot on the rim and other rims dusted in sugar. Tankards. Steins. Sublime ciders and ales and barley beers.

At one point as the band moved smoothly from one jazzy number to another, Hughes caught sight of Cate. She was boogying. There was no other word for it. Sometimes a dance is just a bop, but on rare, beautiful occasions you boogie. Hughes knew himself as more of a flailer, so he restricted himself to drinking, which was much safer.

"We should go somewhere later," he said.

Cate whirled and came to rest. She blew a few strands of tickling hair from her nose, lowered her arms, and then seemed to hear him properly. "Yes!"

"You'd like to?"

"Love to!"

He fairly beamed. This woman. You could forge magic boots. Beat them into shape. But you couldn't forge that contagious energy.

"I'll find you," he said.

Cate opened her mouth to reply.

"Ah, if it is not the media fetishist with arms like the socks of famine-stricken infants," came a deep voice from somewhere in the region of the ceiling. "*Bonsoir, Monsieur Hughes.*"

Hughes sighed inwardly and braced himself for what was about to happen. "Hello, Tommy."

Tommy Fahrenheit loomed over him. Hughes looked to Cate for support and discovered she'd abandoned him, the impish fiend.

"I hear that you faced *une armée de squelletes*," said Tommy.

Hughes rapidly translated "army of skeletons."

"Cate and I, yes."

"I admit," Tommy continued without waiting for a reply. "I am surprised that you did not find common ground with them, given you are, in effect, a variety of ghoul."

"I'm quite convinced I'm not a ghoul."

"You have the unappealing complexion of a ghoul." Tommy cocked his head. "Or perhaps you are a coatrack that has developed a perverse form of life."

"I always have to check in on my self-confidence after I talk to you, Tommy," said Hughes. "Just to make sure it hasn't thrown in the towel."

"Ah, good!" A hand like a shovel with five small handles attached clapped him hard on the back. "A towel rack. The Corinthian heritage has often been compared to it in ethnographic somatism, just as the Mysicordelian heritage has been compared to the open-toed sandal or the crocodile-ravaged hammock."

"I think Falstaff is calling me over," said Hughes, desperation shading his tone.

"*Bien.* I will wait."

"No, please, mingle away."

The giant from Champleurs shook his head. "Together we must convince Cassandra that she must pull you out of *le gymnase*. Her attempts to shape you into something approaching *splendif* are extremely offensive."

"Falstaff, there you are."

Hughes disentangled himself from Tommy Fahrenheit.

The butler was holding a tray stacked with dirty glasses and clean glasses, and there was a clever plastic partition keeping them separate. "Good evening, sir," he said. "Brandy? Beer? Apricot fizz?"

"What's the beer?"

"I believe it's something called Scratchscratch, sir."

Hughes was sorely tempted but settled for a fluted glass of fizz. It was not yet a Scratchscratch point in the festivities, otherwise known as the "let's all just have a quick nap on any available surface and possibly do mushrooms" stage.

"How are you, Falstaff?"

"Busy. Interminably so."

You wouldn't have it any other way, Hughes thought.

"I fear the party isn't moving at the speed my Lady predicted it would." The butler examined his watch. "Nine-thirty and we've only covered floors eighty-eight through sixty-four. Not even a *third*, sir."

Hughes surveyed the party as they walked together. It was all in motion, dizzying and delightful and so wonderfully *fun*. He saw a figure approach Tommy, and with a spark of amusement mixed with horror he realized it was, speak of the demoness, Cassandra. He imagined he was in for quite the lecture from her once Tommy unveiled their secret plans to keep him as scrawny as possible for the sake of being true to culture.

Hughes made an irritable sound in his mouth. "Tommy's a lot, isn't he?"

Falstaff turned to him. "A lot of man, sir?"

"That too." He sipped his drink. The bubbles tingled with a summery sweetness on his tongue. "Is this champagne?"

"No, sir." The butler's hand darted out, steadying someone before they could topple down a flight of stairs. "Champagne comes from the capital region of Champleurs, southwest of the L'Aguilaume Mountains."

"I wonder does Tommy come from there."

"I think not, sir." The butler produced a handkerchief and wiped a spot of foam from Hughes' collar. "Tommy comes from outside that particular region.

Îles de Geuroigne, I believe." The butler leaned in conspiratorially. "Which makes him not champagne but rather a sparkling white windbag."

Hughes' eyebrows shuttled up. "Was that a joke?"

"Try and enjoy the evening, Master Hughes. The Lady Dragontail does not call for a Triumph often. Incidentally, should you wish to avoid unpleasantries with a certain Walter tonight, I advise keeping toward the front of this lot." He gestured to the rambling train of confetti-flecked partygoers behind them. "Is that helpful, sir?"

Hughes wore an awed expression. "Falstaff, what was Redspire like before you?"

Without apparent effort, the butler shimmied under a wildly swaying trombone.

He seemed to muse on the question for a moment.

Then he said, "There's a saying: *When in Ikahagua, do as the Ikahaguans do.* It is a strict culture, even now in our modern times, full of customs and rituals. The saying is logical. If I might amend it slightly to suit my own circumstances: *When in Redspire, dust as the residents refuse to.*"

"Ah."

The butler took the fluted glass from Hughes' unresisting fingers and gave him another, topped up and sparkling in the golden glow of the corridor. With a wave of his white-gloved hand, Falstaff vanished into the throng. Probably to glue on broken heels, mend clothing, establish a judicial parity in the city, and solve world hunger. God, the man was a powerhouse.

"Hughes!"

He spun. A woman with sable-colored hair and one ear beckoned him over.

"Hello, Elena."

Elena Longfellow made space for him in their group. "Stroll with us," she said. "We can't wrangle Cate, and Isaac's as reliable as a chocolate kettle for stories. Tell it true. Skeletons? Not really, right?"

"They rode motorcycles," he supplied helpfully. The ensuing amazement on their faces gave him an acute case of embarrassment. To allay its symptoms, he said, "I'm not sure if that makes it more or less believable."

"No, you're soooo fine," said Penelope Auspice. Her accent made the last word "foyne." "Only the other day Colin Wildheart and I fought a flying zeppelin."

"No way."

"Way!"

"What was in the zeppelin?" asked Hughes.

"Yeah, do you know, it was a bit weird." Penelope twiddled the straw of her daiquiri. Where she had gotten a daiquiri was anyone's guess. "We never actually found out *who was in it* if that makes sense?"

"Colin's magic item is volatile," Elena Longfellow explained when she saw Hughes' puzzlement. "His slippers twirl him into pirouettes of lightning. Sometimes he can't control it."

"I've told him just to wear the one slipper," said Penelope. "Would he hear it? Fashion-conscious arsehole."

Her accent made this "orsehole."

She looked suddenly alert. "OhmyGodohmyGod, here he comes. Quick, Hughes, talk about something else."

"Um." The group's eyes (except the newly arrived Colin's, which were fixed angrily on Penelope, who spoke in the kind of stage whisper that shattered windows) were on him. With no recourse, he was forced to go for the first subject that sailed into his head.

"So, ehm, Elena," he said. "Why do they call you 'Longfellow'?"

A chorus of groans greeted this.

Elena Longfellow puffed out her chest. She grinned like a pirate who has just been asked how exactly she got that hook and the wooden leg. Also the eyepatch. Also the monkey that does interesting tricks with sawblades. Also the scurvy.

"*Well*," she began.

"Oh for fock's sake," said Penelope.

"WELL," shouted Elena Longfellow over the din of music and any further protests. "You know the way our sister nation is called Jaenqui-Across-The-River? Well there's this bridge, see. Or rather, there *was* a bridge..."

***

Remember the carousel?

Not the one smelted down from the Rotbloom Carnival of Bright Oddments and Dark Delights. That one's a cottage for the Ringmaster Woman and the Painted Girl. Forget them, huh? They're busy just now anyway.

And forget about the storm too. That vagrant circus is on the way out. September has that taken care of.

The dream carousel. Yes, you've got it.

That one hasn't worn out its welcome. Quite the contrary—people love it!

Here's Sheila Kofatch, the one-time frazzled schoolteacher who let a younger Hughes use her shower out of nothing but run-of-the-mill kindness. Sheila's a kind lady. It sits like an oven-warmed pastry in her heart. Sheila lives with her husband and two lil'uns in Nikandros District. Nice apartment. Hubby's a property realtor, after all. Sheila has been dreaming about the carousel since July. Lil'un number one (their eldest, Carrie-Anne) began envisioning those pretty ponies and happy hamsters and elegiac elephants at the onset of August. Hubby and lil'un number two aren't going to have the dream. There's no particular reason for this. Imagination might play a factor. A certain *openness* between the ears. Regardless, when what happens, happens, hubby and lil'un number two will be spared the immediate effects. What they will not be spared is the nightmare.

Here's Ernie Wilks, owner of the biggest, stinkiest dog in the city. He was one of the first to have the dream. Like Sheila (who once lived within whistling distance of Ernie) and her daughter Carrie-Anne, he awakens every morning with a feeling—more and more insistent each time—that he wants something. Lately for

Ernie, that want has begun to morph into a need. The fact that he can't reconcile just what he needs is maddening. He's started losing time. Whole tracts of the day disappear down the gullet of his absentmindedness. Tomorrow, Wednesday August 26th, he will think of nothing else all afternoon. He will even forget to feed his best friend. Boochums will whine, will go so far as to nudge his feeding bowl toward Ernie to get his master's attention, but to no avail. As far as these foggy spells go, Sheila and Carrie-Anne are not far behind.

Here is Falstaff. The dreams are pretty recent for him, yet already he can feel thin tendrils of mist creeping over his awareness. He covers it well, but on the night of Hughes' Triumph he drops six glasses, each one stuffing shards of fear inside him. This bout of uncharacteristic clumsiness is actually the best he could hope for. By early September things are worse. He is worried he's got a brain tumor. Irrational, of course, given his age, but in his defense there's a family history of it. His grandfather developed a mass of cancerous cells on his brain. Malignant, of course. He was dead at thirty-six. Thirty-*six*. Falstaff himself is thirty-eight. Thirty-eight, clumsier by the day, full of a desire he doesn't understand, and terrified.

Here are two-hundred thousand other people who have had the dream.

Here they are dreaming. Waking up. Wanting. Needing.

More and more every night.

Round and round it goes.

Against a backdrop of evening, the nightjar flies. Where the moon dares to touch it (the moon is on its way back to Corinth City, you'll see) the bird casts three shadows.

It's almost time.

Round and round. More and more every night.

Remember the carousel.

It remembers you.

CHAPTER THIRTY-EIGHT

August 25th, twelve o'clock midnight.

Hughes had been toasted half to death by people keen to honor him. He needed to get out of here. He told Cate as much.

She took immediate action, flitting between groups and getting everyone interested in an impromptu karaoke session. While people decided where the hell they were going to get a karaoke machine from at this hour, she and Hughes made their escape.

"You're a genius," he said.

"The drunk are easily hoodwinked. Look, no rain!"

She slipped into a puddle and appeared atop a building two hundred yards away. This astounded Hughes. Not the magic but the fact he could make her out up there, hear her whooping at the thimble of starlight visible through a gap in the cloud cover. There was no fog to dampen the sound, no silvery rain to draw the curtain on this sight.

"Where shall we go?" said Cate, reappearing beside him.

"I don't know."

"Oh."

"But I know who does."

"*Ooooh*." She jigged on her bootheels. "This is *exciting*."

Taking a few shortcuts to the metrotram station, they left Ptolema District's superstructures behind. Hughes could see the dual carriageways like heart valves from his seat on the train. Twenty minutes later they were in the tangle of roads between Leonidas and the wealthier Districts. Puddles grew large in these parts. Some were the size of duck ponds, but one or two were as wide as swimming pools, and near enough as deep, their oily surfaces reflecting the washing lines and telephone cables strewn above. Cars and lorries cast up feathers of water.

Passing a florist called *Amontillado's* where not long ago Hughes had haggled over the price of a flower, they came to a long street full of animated posters.

"Young man!" proclaimed the late William Keatons. "Great to be out late, eh? And on a date no less."

"Who is this?" Cate asked Hughes, but the posters answered her before he could.

"William Keaton, ma'am. Pleasure to toll in the witching hour with you. You know who you remind me of? Ginger Dujour, my co-star in *Springtime For The Winterhat.* Wonderful picture. You know, Ginger wasn't just beautiful. She was pretty too."

Cate spread her hands and bowed elaborately. "Hughes," she said, dipping her head. "What's happening?"

Hughes explained the corporate ownership of the late actor's likeness.

"I thought we left the necromancers behind in Eurydice," she said. It was clear she found the display as macabre as he did.

"I want to show Miss Jubilee a great time, Billy K," said Hughes, unable to soften the hope in his voice. It made him croaky and ridiculous, all this passion working away in him. "Better than great. Good too. I thought you might have some suggestions."

"Oh-ho-hoozah! Do I ever?" Behind a street of two-dimensional smiles, circuitry tapped into an index of sponsored events. A thousand Willian Keatons gave the young couple a foxy old gentleman's wink.

"That cast of yours has your arm crooked just right," they told Hughes. "Have either of you seen my movie *Masquerade?*"

A minute later they were off toward the center of Nikandros District. They found its square athrob with activity. Unlike the bazaar at the heart of Leonidas, Nikandros had a large statue at its core. It was a statue of the last King of Corinth, more commonly known as the Tyrant. It always struck Hughes as odd that there was a statue to him and none to the people who'd ousted him and broken his throne. Or to the gallowman, for that matter. The one who'd fixed the noose around the Tyrant's throat and pulled the lever. Hundreds of years later and here the Tyrant still presided, in a way, over a court of lilac lamps, street theatre, nightclubs, vanilla-vodka-scented alleys and cigarette-clogged gutters. Funny old world.

"Busy, isn't it?" he said to Cate.

"Yes," she said. "I was talking to Lorna Blacktower, and she said that the storm was like an angry farmer keeping everyone's jolly summer spirits penned up. Now the farmer's leaving, and the pens are swinging open."

"The animals can rule the farm."

"As nature intended."

A clown figure advertising a circus-themed nightclub offered his hand to Cate. She took it, gasped at the electrical shock, and pinched the clown's nose in retribution. The nose honked dejectedly.

They went on, keeping an eye out for the place William Keaton described.

"Tell me about your victory," said Cate. "How did you do it?"

Hughes took a deep breath, and consoling himself that this probably wasn't going to upset or distance her, he told Cate Jubilee about his Performance. Some details he considered a little too much to go into at the moment, in the bustling Nikandros square, such as the percentage chance of success his ability gave him, or the secret power he still had yet to use: CHIMERA. The rest he gave her, unedited.

Cate listened attentively. Ahead, a crowd was assembled outside one particular club. The pair curved around it. It was quieter on the other side, and that was where she stopped him.

"That's how you beat Maelen and the Bonemeal Boys?"

Hughes nodded.

"You *persuaded* them to death?" She looked horrified.

"No," said Hughes quickly. "No, it wasn't like that. I convinced the pyromancers and necromancers in their engines to um... well, to explode in these columns of fire and ahm... burn our enemy to a... crisp."

Cate's stare bored into him. She still looked horrified.

"I take it you've never heard of someone else doing anything like that?" said Hughes.

"No."

"No documented cases within the lore of the Scarlet Citadel?"

"No."

"I see." Hughes rubbed the back of his neck sheepishly. "Look, I've been able to do it ever since I can remember. I've wondered where it comes from, what its limits are, what it *means*."

"You," said Cate, "are going to speak to Doctor John and Wendy Dragontail about this."

"You think I should?"

"I know you should. Is that how you survived the attack in Iphigenia? The one that killed Laurana's unit?"

He averted his eyes. A moment later her finger guided him softly back so he was looking at her. Her face was bathed in purple light from the streetlamps. *Not just beautiful,* he thought. *Pretty too. A prettiness that goes under the skin and into the luminous stuff of the soul.* "Yes," he said. "And how I got Jo to come out of the storage compartment in the Foundry."

He watched her expression darken. "You didn't do that, did you?"

"Yes. Why?"

"Because while using a power like that on someone who means you harm is one thing," said Cate Jubilee, her tone icy. "Using it on someone just because you can is another."

He sensed he'd lost footing along the slopes of her good opinion.

"But it helped her," he said. "I thought because she was in such a state... And she came out of the whole thing much more confident."

"Yes," she said, and the ice had deepened dangerously. "But it still benefited you, didn't it?"

Hughes thought for a moment. He breathed in and out, long and slow. "Yeah," he said. "Yeah, it did. I'm sorry, Cate. I'll apologize to Jo. Tell her about what happened. Hopefully she'll forgive me. And I'll speak to Wendy and Doctor John," he added. "Maybe they can help me come to grips with the whole thing."

"Good." She smiled, and the tension thawed. "It's an incredible thing, Hughes."

"What, the Performance?" He raised his brows. "Really?"

"Extraordinary. I have never heard of anything like it."

"You looked..." *Horrified.* "Taken aback," he said lamely.

"See it from my perspective," she said, taking his hand and leading him back into the throng of people. "The man you're interested in tells you he can reach into minds with all the difficulty of combing warm honey. I *was* taken aback. I still am. Wouldn't you be?"

Hughes supposed he would.

The building opposite the Sequins Messenger Club headquarters in Nikandros square. That was what Billy K said. There was the headquarters across the way, its sign as gaudy as its employees' costumes, so their target must be...

Cate spotted it before he did. *The Coconut* was a three-story dance house. There was a marquee overhanging the entrance. Mounted spotlights shone on twelve sculptures foxtrotting across the marquee. Music that made a rebel of sensibility wound out of its windows. Masked shapes cavorted up there.

Needless to say they rushed inside.

There were no elaborate masks left behind the counter. Luckily the attendant had a box of cheap white plastics. Hughes paid for two with a full credit chit.

"Are you sure?" said Cate while the attendant gave him his change.

"My turn to treat you, remember?"

"Thank you, Hughes."

He smiled magnanimously, although just stepping past the cloakroom and the bouncers, a deep disquiet traipsed through him. And no wonder. His entire share of the Bonemeal Boy job was sequestered in the deepest pockets of his moth-gnawed coat, and it was not there to ensure Cate's good time. Rather, it was an insurance policy.

Unlike Doctor John (who was still awake at this unlikely hour and would be for the foreseeable future), Hughes was expecting guests.

He wasn't sure when exactly they'd come. Maybe tonight. Maybe a month from now. The one thing he knew for certain was that it wasn't a case of *if*. It was a case of *when*. He had a debt.

That music they'd heard from the street wasn't coming from a recorder. There was a live band in here, their instruments hooked into *The Coconut's* gyrosonic system. They wore wolf masks and bore the slightly goofy, slightly wonderful name of *Rufus and the Pack Tactics*.

It was tricky in the crowded space, but the pair eventually found a spot in a corner where Hughes could dance without walloping someone with his cast, which was cumbersome, and unwieldy, and in Cate's estimation utterly adorable.

They danced, and it was about what you might expect from a lissome woman in hobnail boots and a young man with an arm like a boomerang. They got a lot more laughing done than hip thrusts. Although maybe there were a couple hip thrusts in there.

"Don't overexert me," said Hughes. "I've got to keep my cast dry."

"*Hughes!*"

"Sweat." He laughed. "I was talking about sweat."

"No dirty mindedness."

"I would never."

She gave him a look that would have driven a nun from piety. "You mustn't corrupt impressionable young ladies with your frankly abominable vulgarity."

"Me?" he chuckled. "Corrupt you?"

"Fanning the flames of existing corruption then. Don't be pedantic, Hughes. It's unseemly. Sweat is right though. It *is* hot in here."

There was a decorative mirror nearby. Cate peered around. Nodding to herself she reached into her pocket and took out a little nametag. Pinning it to her shirt, she vanished into the glass and returned to him a moment later with two glasses full of crystal-clear water packed with ice cubes.

She handed one to Hughes and grinned at his flummoxed expression.

"I absolutely hate dithering about at bar counters waiting to be served. It's one of my pet peeves. About a year ago I devised the most brilliant plan." She tapped the nametag before slipping it out of sight. Hughes read it. It told anyone who cared to look that her name was Catherine and that she was pleased to help them. "My great-uncle Montgomery Jubilee runs a chain of bars in Polydoros. I had him spread word throughout the popular taverns and clubs that his grandniece—a member of the Scarlet Citadel—likes to do part time bar work."

Now Hughes was starting to grin. "So when you randomly appear through the glass overlooking a bar and nab a few drinks..."

"No one questions anything."

"You could be the best thief in Corinth City."

She wrinkled her nose and smirked around a mouthful of water like the goblin of mischief she was. "Don't let it deter you from buying me things."

What could he do but burst out laughing?

Sweeter than sweet was shooting the shit with cheeky, devilish, delightful Cate Jubilee.

Things took a turn later on. From seemingly nowhere the music softened. The jitterbug liveliness ebbed out of it, and something sultry drew in. Romantic patches began to form throughout the dance house, one big river of charming guitar pluckings and piano notes that gave rise to longing and little estuaries and ponds of intimacy everywhere you looked.

Hughes wasn't caught up in it. He was wary. Now and then Cate would try to get him talking about himself, and he would divert as gracefully as he could manage. It occurred to him that he'd been wrong to tell her about his Performance.

No, he thought firmly. *I wanted to tell her, and I'm glad after the fact. It felt good sharing a secret.*

But it felt vulnerable too. Almost *incriminating*. As though giving over a little ground meant sacrificing a lot of safety. Hadn't Kim Kallaimon taught him anything? He had told her about his life, and her response was desolation. Exposure, no matter how well-justified, meant a direct increase in the odds that Cate would learn something about him she didn't like. So he had to be careful.

It was like this waltz they were dancing now, with music wrapping them like autumn leaves wrapping a meadow.

He had to watch where he stepped.

"Um with ee," she said.

The music had swelled just as she spoke. Hughes leaned in. "Sorry?"

"*Come with me.*"

He nodded. She took his hand and led him up to the third-floor balcony. With no rain to ward off, the awning had been rolled in, so there was a panoramic view. The statue of The Tyrant showed his profile. There were a few people enjoying the open air up here, but they had their own thoughts or conversations to nibble away at, so Hughes and Cate might as well have been alone. They removed their masks. Hughes stowed his in one of his coat's many pockets. Below them the square was still buzzing with life. It was three o'clock in the morning, stars melted through the clouds, and soon the sun would rise like an old friend who had not been seen in a long time, and who had many a golden story to tell now he was back.

Cate Jubilee had a story of her own to tell Hughes, though it was far from a golden tale as he would soon find out.

"She was tall," she said softly.

"Who was tall?"

"My mum."

Hughes understood almost at once. Cate was ready to talk about her family, a subject she'd avoided on their first date at *The Pear and Princess*. He leaned on the cool, smooth balustrade, his ears pricked up and alert as she said:

"A remarkably tall woman, and this was pre-war Corinth where it was unfashionable for a woman to be taller than her husband."

"And was she?"

Cate waggled two fingers. "By almost two inches."

"That isn't very much."

"Dad was six-foot-four."

"Oh. *Oh.*"

She nodded. "That was *out* of heels, mind. Really trim too. And glamorous. Like a movie ingénue."

"Ginger Dujour," said Hughes.

Cate smiled. "When William Keaton said that earlier it knocked the wind out of me."

"I didn't notice."

"I em *veeeeeery* subtle," she wheedled. In her ordinary voice she continued. "Everyone always used to say Mum was a ringer for Ginger Dujour. 'You know, you look just like that actress.' I used to devour vids when I was small. After what happened to Mum, I thought I might never watch one again, in case it featured Ginger Dujour. I didn't know what that would do to me. Silly really. Nowadays I can watch one of Ginger's pictures and it doesn't bother me at all." She paused. "Or so I tell myself."

Silence fell. Hughes made no move to fill it.

Cate crossed one boot over the other, set her elbows on the rail, and tilted her face up so she could watch the last march of the summer storm clouds and the advent of autumn.

"When Marshal Francoise Villefort was assassinated during his visit to Mysicordelia and Champleurs declared war on the world, Dad was one of the first to volunteer for the trenches. He'd fought in the War of Greens and Grays when he was only fifteen. He lied on his enrollment form, said he was twenty. Ended up a decorated veteran with a special commendation for bravery.

"I don't actually remember this, but I've talked to people about it, and apparently Dad missed fighting. He felt uneasy as a civilian. Bloodthirst had its hooks in him even then, I suppose. There was this one time at a dinner party. Someone asked him how he could stand trench warfare where you contracted diseases easily and were forced to eat your boots for lack of supper. Dad's famous line was: 'Well, I never contracted disease. And as for boots, they were never as tough as this beef.'

"Anyway, he signed up, was handed an Easy Knock'n'Stock crossbow plus a fistful of bolts, and got carted off with thirty-thousand other people to the front lines to die."

"And did he?"

"Die?" She shook her head. "No. He was there at Origné though. He was there on the hilltop battle that decided whether or not Champleurs would be defeated or the war would rage on another year. No medals for Dad that day. Instead a soldier thumped him in the temple with the pommel of their axe. By the time Dad woke up the battle and the war were over. Flowers grew on the hill."

Hughes remembered the mirolaen in Cate's hair, white on red.

"He came back changed," she said, shifting around so she could fold her arms on the railing and rest her chin against them. "It wasn't post-traumatic stress or anything. It was the thump. It scrambled his brains. At least I think so. One morning he went out and bought a workman's mallet. About this big. He rode the train home and chased us around the house with it, Mum and I. I hid under my bed. He didn't find me. Mum, he did find."

Hughes felt his mouth go dry. The urge to fold her up in his arms was strong, but he resisted. He sensed she wasn't finished, and he was right.

"He killed her in my room," said Cate. "When he was done he tried to find me again. I remember getting this glimpse of him and thinking, 'There is nothing of my father in that thing.' He had this glazed look on his face, like there was nothing going on behind it. The only sign that his brain was telling him anything was the spittle collecting at the side of his mouth and these sort of grunts he was making. The state he was in, he never even checked under the bed. So yeah, he didn't get me. Sometimes I think I looked at Mum's body, and other times I'm convinced I was too smart to. Like I knew that image would knock the life from me the way the mallet never did. I don't think I would have recognized her either—Dad hit her in the face and head. Hearing this doesn't upset you, does it?"

He put a hand on hers. She didn't look at him.

"My Aunt Trisha was scheduled to visit that day. I never asked her about it, but now I think I should have: just what she felt when she came out of a sane world into an insane one. In one moment, her sister-in-law is alive and her brother is a normal—slightly absent but by and large normal—man. In the next, her brother has killed his wife and is actively hunting his daughter with a workman's mallet, and there's a clump of blood and hair stuck to the mallet. Shards of bone. It must have been terrible for her."

What about you? Hughes thought. *You were only tiny and you had to see all that happen.*

The sky was almost completely clear now. The moon was a no-show, but the stars made up for it. For another hour or so they'd put on a glittering cabaret. Gazing at them Cate gave a sniffle. She wasn't crying. This was an old story. Even so, her composure amazed Hughes. "Aunt Trisha took Dad away and had him institutionalized and then took me to live with her. I got these when she died." She kicked a leg up behind her, showing one of her hobnail boots. "You know what's funny? Even in hobnail boots I'm *still* not as tall as Mum."

There it was. One tear. No fuss. Just one. It rolled down her cheek, and it told Hughes in no uncertain terms: *Now.*

He came behind her and slipped his good arm around her waist. She hugged him back, her head nestling into the curve of his neck and jaw.

"Is this a new tattoo?" said Hughes.

He felt Cate stiffen against him. Before he could ask if she was all right she had relaxed again.

"Yes," said Cate. "It's new."

It was a motorcycle with a skull-and-crossbones motif. A translucent Saniderm bandage covered where the needle had suffused her skin with ink. Cate's hair was so thick it was a wonder he'd spotted it at all.

"Do you get tattoos every time you win a fight?"

She nodded and said nothing. Hughes had the impression he wasn't supposed to have seen that tattoo. Or that the subject of her tattoos was one Cate didn't like broaching. More steps to watch in this dance of theirs.

Hughes offered to buy her a drink. When he came back with it, they talked about small, inconsequential things until at last Cate said, "Tell me something about yourself. What's your favorite book?"

Ah. Here was motive then. That story about her family had been an act of vulnerability and trust. But it had also been intended to elicit the same thing from Hughes. Tit for tat. *You give me, I give you.*

Tell me something about yourself. A phrase as refreshing as a glass of water for some people. For Hughes, it was poison on ice cubes.

Tell me something about yourself. Something bitter and unpleasantly warm flowed over his tongue. It took him a moment to recognize it for what it was, and when he did, the taste got worse. *Resentment.*

"Cate."

"Please. I want to know."

This is ridiculous, he thought. *I can't keep stuff like that from her.*

You've got to, some part of him insisted. *Remember Kim.*

Maybe it was the booze, but for once he ignored the voice of caution.

"Do plays count?" he wondered.

"What do you mean?"

"Like theatre."

Holding her at this angle, he could only see a little of her face. Even so there was no mistaking what he saw there. Bewilderment, stark and disquieting.

"Plays," she said as if the word had never crossed her lips before. "Do they still make those?"

"No."

"Sorry," she said, and the baffled amusement he heard in her tone sounded to Hughes just a little too close to condescension. "It's just... Plays. Wow. They're a bit... old hat, aren't they?"

"I like them," said Hughes stiffly. "Tell you what, come and dance with me."

"Wait, hold on."

She turned, laying her hands flat on his chest. "Don't close up now. What's the play called?"

'Cate, I really—"

"Is it a rollicking title?" she pressed, her voice going goofy. "Romping? Rrrrrrubinesque?"

"It's called *A Summer Knight's Stroll*. Come inside."

"No," she said firmly, and now there was no humor in her. "How would you read a play?"

"One word at a time."

She flicked his ear.

"Ouch!"

"That was glib, Hughes. Glib and rude. I meant in what setting do you read them? Do you use a page emulator or your computer? Do you have little rituals you do beforehand? Cozy cup of tea? Biscuits? Nice roaring hot fire?"

It sounded wonderful. *But here's the thing, Cate. We could rarely afford biscuits, let alone a computer or an emulator. And with its paper furnishings the teashop I grew up in is a fire hazard with extra steps.*

Aloud, he said, "Mostly just the tea." In the spirit of things, he added, "Cardamom and fennel, if I get my way."

"Yes, that makes sense. Your dad owns the *Scriptorium and Flavored Tea Emporium*," she said. "Such a gallopingly good name for a caffeine house. Does he do coffee?"

Wrong again, Miss Jubilee. Coffee is, you guessed it, too expensive.

"Dad doesn't go in for coffee," said Hughes. "He says it gives him wind."

"What District is it in?"

Hughes frowned. "My dad's wind?"

"No." Cate's grin was earnest and bright as a new moon. "The Emporium. Is it nearby? Can we go?"

"Cate, it's almost sunrise."

"True, true. Hm." She tapped her chin with a finger. "Foiled by the only decent weather to show its face in months, how typical. Tomorrow then, after you apologize to Jo in the Foundry."

"I don't think that's—"

"Is Gormon Hughes Senior as big a fusspot about his teas as Wendy Dragontail said? Of course he is, the man owns an Emporium. No exotic teabag parcel then. Drat. There go my gift plans. What shall I bring instead? Wine? Wine's traditional, I suppose. Don't worry about a thing, I am *excellent* with parents. My ex's mother still sends me a card every Tinfrost, and he is *not* a fan of that, let me tell you."

"Don't bring anything," Hughes said. "I mean, you won't need to. Won't be able to." His frown deepened. "Look, what I'm trying to say is that I'm not going, so why would you?"

"Oh, but you haven't visited home in ages."

It was like grappling the wind. Hurricane Jubilee was approaching full bluster.

"You'll be playing the dutiful son and the sweet suitor, all in one fell swoop. *Two birds, one teashop* and so on."

"But I don't—"

"We are going," she said primly. "And I won't hear another word about it."

And with that said she hugged him tight. "Thank you for opening up with me. And for listening. And for being a puppy with a rottweiler inside."

Tomorrow, Hughes thought, dread creeping over him. *Tomorrow after I apologize to Jo in the Foundry.*

"Do I get a say in any of this?" he asked her.

"Afraid not," Cate replied. "Goodnight, Hughes." She kissed him. "Thank you for the lovely evening." She kissed him again, deep and slow. "Performance or no, you earned your Triumph."

"Goodnight?" He blinked. "But aren't we going to..."

In a single smooth movement she tipped over the railing.

Whump.

"... dance?"

Hughes stared down at the marquee and the new sheet of mirror glass hardening on it.

He could taste her lip gloss—almond and apricot. They were sweet but no match for the bitter thing still coating his tongue like lacquer.

The resentment.

He finished his drink and left *The Coconut*, his hands deep in his coat pockets.

On a street whose name he didn't know, he looked down a slope of road at the clipped hedges nuzzling the red brick of the train station. The station had one window below its clock, and it turned out that this was a morning for small miracles wrought in glass. The station faced the east, and in that circle of glass set into the brick Hughes saw dawn break. Out of a horizon of indigo and carmine rose an egg of molten gold. The stars blew out like cold barnyard candles. Those few lingering clouds, feathery and pale, turned a gentle canary yellow. Birds twittered. The air, mild under the auspice of evening, seemed abruptly mellow with the promise of a warm morning and a hot afternoon. Here he was then, appearing in the eye of the train station. That old golden friend with stories to tell. Well, Hughes had heard quite enough stories for the time being. He was not immune to the beauty of it though. No, not immune at all. He walked a little farther, a sensation of blissful solitude settling on his shoulders as though daylight itself was being constructed for his benefit. Feeling an odd yet superbly welcome surge of confidence, he packaged his worries about Cate, wrapped them with a bow, and set them aside to be opened on the train, or bed.

In a pot on his left were some false roses. Someone must have set them out when the storm threw its last thunderbolt. Hughes approached them.

They weren't false—they were real!

He inhaled their musk and felt a tingle somewhere deep in his sinuses. Hughes sneezed. "Hoh, goodness gracious," he said and smiled the toothsome smile of someone who has just done an absolute trumpeter on a quiet street and who has against all common decency uttered the phrase "goodness gracious" while not being a dowdy upper-class maid in her middle-nineties.

Then he sneezed again.

Long, cadaverous fingers closed around the cast on his arm. The plaster fissured and cracked. A shadow blotted the sun.

"Gesundheit," said Mr. Glint.

CHAPTER THIRTY-NINE

You," said Hughes.

"*Us*," oozed Miss Gleam, who had set the toes of her shoes on the lower lip of someone's veranda and was hanging upside down over the street like the most glittery and grotesque bat you daren't even imagine. "Lady Fortune shows us her favor, Mr. Glint. Hello, brother Hughes. How are you at this hour in which mother moon gathers her star children and flees the vicious consuming fires of father sun?"

"I know what 'favor' means," said Glint.

"Yes?"

"Means bosoms."

"In certain contexts," his partner allowed. "Here though, it is merely luck, a substance which always seems to elude our poor brother's grasp, like ambrosia denied to an unfit God."

There was a scrambling, a sinuous crawling, and then she was in front of Hughes.

"You didn't answer my question," she said. "How are you?"

"Peachy," he said.

She tutted. "Do I need to produce my snickling scissors? No, there's no need for us to take our roles in that particular pantomime again. Not when we are such bosom compatriots."

"I thought you said..." began Mr. Glint.

"A figure of speech, dear man," said Gleam promptly.

"Your clothes," said Hughes, his voice thin with horror. "What's wrong with your clothes?'

Miss Gleam looked first at him, her mouth crimped with one canine exposed, and then down at her suit as though confirming it were still there. It was, or a fetid ghost of it at least. Her tie was rumpled and blotched with spots of silken decay. Lining burst through her collar. One cufflink was gone, and the sleeve was worn and ragged. The other sleeve wasn't much better, this one dyed a grisly brick color like the train station walls—old blood on older fabric. Larvae from the wormy things that lived in her lair had hatched and begun to chew everything from the inside out. The ensemble was all coming apart at the seams, a vast disintegration. It looked like the sort of suit someone had been buried in, exhumed and shaken out and slipped into like a tomb spun from the darkest of looms.

Bad as hers was, Mr. Glint's looked as though wild dogs had been at it.

Gleam's lips twitched in a scowl. She fixed Hughes with a look that could curl tin. "Our apparel is none of your concern. The money, Hughes. Where is it?"

"I have it."

"You do?" said Glint.

Hughes nodded. Mr. Glint looked disappointed. "Shame," he said.

"Well," said Hughes. "I have a bit of it. A down payment."

"Hughes," said Gleam. "While it is most certainly true that I find your snatchings at control and self-assurance hilarious to the point of outright whimsy, my patience is at an all-time low. I do believe it is building a cellar to accommodate even more agitation. We will have the sum in full now or Mr. Glint and I are going to show you what we did to the last person who tried to make a down payment. As I recall he was a magician."

Mr. Glint brightened considerably. "He had a rabbit in his hat."

Gleam cocked her head to one side. "He did, didn't he?"

"The doves flew away," said Glint. "But I got the rabbit by the ears. Then I said, 'Would you like a rabbit in your head instead Mr. Magician?' What with his top hat being squashed and all."

"How considerate of you. What became of that hapless hopper?"

"It disappeared," said Mr. Glint. "Alakazam." He looked at Hughes with a face like death carved into hard white wax. "Did you know that rabbit's teeth never stop growing?"

"I didn't," said Hughes.

He had been right in Eurydice. The Bonemeal Boys were horrid. Marrow King Maelen was worse—a sagging, clacking monstrosity fueled by the ghosts of his own people. But nothing, not *anything*, could be as wretched nor as frightening as Miss Gleam and Mr. Glint.

What should I do?

It was a stupid, childish question. There was only one thing he *could* do. Watch his footing. Tread softly. None of Cate's boogying here. This was the *danse macabre*, where your partners will hurt you for each mistake.

Hurt you and make you disappear, Hughes thought. *Alakazam.*

"Mr. Glint," said Hughes. "Would you kindly let my arm go so I can get your money?"

"You got two."

"Yes. I do have two arms," Hughes said, his voice patient and betraying not the slightest hint he would like to continue having two arms for as long as humanly possible, and failing that, inhumanly probable. "Only my pockets are very deep in this coat, and I'd like to use my cast arm for purchase."

"Which pocket?"

"Inside, third from the left."

Mr. Glint fished in the pocket. The closeness of those long fingers to his flesh made Hughes wish for Chimera. Not that the sword would have done him any good. Mr. Glint would likely take it from him, eat Hughes whole, and then use the blade as a toothpick before yawning his jaw wide and sliding it down his gullet as if it were a snake stiff with rigor mortis.

Mr. Glint took out Hughes' credits and piled them one by one in Miss Gleam's hand. She looked at them critically.

"Those credits represent my share of a job," Hughes told her. "A job I was sent on by Winnifred Dragontail. I'm in the Scarlet Citadel now. I've even got a magic item, a sword that is, I dare say, almost if not as sharp as your scissors, Miss Gleam.

"This haul is only the start. A... An appetizer," he corrected himself. He had almost said 'down payment' again. Outwardly he was quite calm. Inside his pulse cantered in his veins and tore up clods of dry crumbly dread. "Look, I've already done the impossible. All I've got to do now is a few more things for the Citadel and you'll have everything I owe and more, *much* more."

Miss Gleam was looking at him with the glossy black gaze of a shark considering an intelligent species of clam.

He had no idea what she might have replied because at that moment Mr. Glint removed the last credit from Hughes' pocket. Something came out with the credit, snagged on Glint's fingers. It made a thin warbling clatter on the pavement stones.

Miss Gleam looked at it, and Hughes watched the shark of ravenous cruelty retreat and the octopus of extreme curiosity swim into her expression. As she picked the object up, this was replaced by the squid of disbelief, the manatee of rapid deduction, and finally, the kraken of anger.

The thing that had dropped from Hughes' pocket was something he had stowed there earlier that evening. He had forgotten it was there.

For some reason it was having a palpable effect on Miss Gleam.

Hughes could not think why. It was only a mask. A cheap white plastic mask.

"Hold our brother still, Mr. Glint."

Hughes felt Glint's other hand—the one not gripping his plaster-encased arm— lock around his neck.

Sunlight found the street they were on. It gleamed on a pair of scissors, denticulated all over with sawtooth-shaped points.

Snicker-snick.

The sound sent his pulse *whickering* and *thudding* crazily into his temples. Hughes groaned miserably. The thumps resounded in his ears.

"Where did you get this?" Gleam demanded, shaking the mask in Hughes' face.

"At a dancehall. *The Coconut*," said Hughes, remembering the name just in time. "Earlier tonight."

Snick.

The scissor blades turned black: truth.

Gleam glared at them. Standing so close he could smell the reek of her, like a pan of oily sausages left to congeal and develop maggots.

"Who gave it to you?"

"A man, just... just some man behind a counter."

Snick.

Black: truth.

"This man, what did he tell you? Was there a bow? A bag of arrows?"

"What?"

"Arrows." Her eyes were wide and skittish. Frustration had pulled her sparkling lips into a bloodless hyphen. "Thin shafts of wood. Fletched and barbed or bodkinned. You shoot them."

"No," he said, scared and confused beyond measure. "I don't know what you're talking about."

Snick.

Black went the blades. A pure, jet black without ambiguity.

Gleam growled at them, actually growled like the dark wood denizens in a fairy story, and turned to Hughes.

"Tell the truth," she snapped.

"I am. I promise I am, I swear it swear it *swear it.*"

It was too much. The stink. Mr. Glint's elongated hands. Gleam's bizarre questions. Starkest of all, the gorgeous morning contrasted with this gruesome scene he had been yanked into against his will.

Better attempted control than none.

Hughes pushed his Performance.

And as he did that, he dredged himself to the core, seized hold of his new ability

(CHIMERA)

and sent it lancing into Miss Gleam's head. Her features—pinched with growing viciousness—suddenly slackened.

CHIMERA

Your Performances have the ability to take root in your target's subconscious mind. This can cause profound psychological change, including behavioral adjustment, the development of complexes, or madness.

Time seemed to slow as it always did when he used the power.

Hughes' pulse beat double-time. Unspeakable instincts murmured to him. It would work. It wouldn't. It must. It might never again.

He was aware of the sunshine continuing to spill its warm syrup over the streets. Past the train station it touched a beautician's shop. There was a poster on its side wall, partially torn and speckled in pigeon droppings. The poster showed a hand teased over a cigarette, maybe a partnership between the tobacco company and the people selling the red polish that lent the hand a certain allure. It was damn early and damn late at the same time (such was the curse of half past four in the morning), but nevertheless somebody on this street had their fire going. Smoke poured from their chimney and over the poster, so it looked as though the red-lacquered nails were poised around a lit cigarette.

The sight of that was strangely familiar to Hughes.

For the life of him he could not place it.

Well, he had larger concerns at present.

Words sizzled across his mind in huge synaptic parabolas. He shut his eyes against them. They buzzed in fantastic neon letters behind his lids.

Performance Successful!

Warning: CHIMERA has lodged in the target's barbershop brain. It is not a welcome tenant there. The mind's landlady will not accept payment. The debt remains due.

Hughes opened his eyes.

He was looking into two pools of liquid shadow. Against all laws of anatomy there was a nose below them and a mouth below that, which began to spread in a grin like cyanide jam over arsenic toast.

"Brother dearest. My most sorrowful and woebegone apologies," said Miss Gleam. "These are trying times, but it is no excuse to treat our comrades and compatriots with disdain. Watch." She put away her scissors and made a flourish with her hand to show there were no surprises in store. "No more threats. Only promises of our own. I solemnly and with no ill-favored feelings toward you vow that no harm will come to you if you will simply give us the remaining balance that you owe our employer." Her grin widened, as trustworthy as a cliff edge. "Render unto Shine what is Shine's, noble countryman. And that little bit extra for myself and my associate, if you'd be so good."

"I told you," Hughes said. "I don't have it now. You can search me."

"Yes," she agreed. "We can. But we won't. Instead we will go for a drink. Are you thirsty, Mr. Glint?"

"Could go for a tipple, Miss Gleam."

"Marvelous. I was thinking..." she leered at Hughes, "*tea*. Can you recommend anywhere in particular?"

They're going to the Scriptorium and Flavored Tea Emporium.

"No," he said. "Wait, I'll... I'll get the money for you this afternoon. Right now in fact," he amended desperately.

Miss Gleam shook her scintillating head. "Now is much too late."

"Please. I'm begging you not to." Hughes gave her an imploring look. "He's my dad."

"We shall be sure to give him your regards," said Gleam cheerfully. "And after that, we shall also inform him why he is being abused so slowly and so rigorously by Mr. Glint and I, both of whom are lifelong students and connoisseurs in the art of nerve endings and their manipulation." She gestured, and Glint let Hughes go. "I'm sure that will be a comfort to him. Knowing his son sent us to him."

"Please don't," said Hughes. Images of his father hearing a knock at their door came to him. Gormon Hughes Senior rising from his theatre-book chair, opening the door, and the look on his face seeing these two there. "Don't hurt him."

He pushed his Performance again.

Nothing happened. But of course nothing happened, he had never been able to use the power again so fast.

This time counts for all, he thought. *I've got to keep my dad safe.*

He strained and thrashed in the inner reaches of himself.

Nothing.

Gleam regarded her partner. "I think we've tarried long enough. The early worm throttles the bird, as they say. Shall we depart, my excellent fellow?"

Glint nodded. "Right." He hooked a finger at Hughes. "Hurt him?"

Gleam's grin sliced deeper into her cheeks. "I intend to, Mr. Glint. Indeed I intend t—" She froze. "Did you hear that?"

"What?" said Glint, looking up and down the street.

It was empty. Nothing moved except the smoke curling from the chimney.

"It sounded like..." Gleam swallowed. "A bowstring creaking."

Hughes was too busy trying to get his Performance to cooperate to pay close attention. He was vaguely aware of the popping sounds of released nitrogen from Mr. Glint's neck bones as the tall figure craned to examine the rooftops. "No archer," he said.

Miss Gleam visibly relaxed. "Where was I?"

"Going to the teashop," said Mr. Glint.

"Teashop? Why would we go to a teashop?"

Mr. Glint shrugged. "Scrag someone's dad."

"Yes. Yes, that sounds right." Gleam covered her sparkling face with a hand that looked dipped in the dust of crushed opals. She seemed about to speak when her whole body seized up. "There it is again!"

"There what is?"

"Can't you hear it?"

She looked up wild-eyed into Glint's face. The streets lay quiet as tombs.

"Well, can't you?" she asked him.

"Don't hear nothing."

She seemed to lose interest in him, baring her gums at the surrounding streets as though daring them to action.

"Home," she said. "We must go home at once."

"What about the teashop?"

"Who cares about caffeine at a time like this, when danger's quiver is full?"

She pocketed Hughes' credits, paused, and peered down at the mask in her other hand. Eyeless, lipless white plastic stared back at her. Miss Gleam's expression wilted. She dropped it, her fingers trembling, and stalked off without another word.

From his sunken sockets Mr. Glint scanned the chimney stacks.

His gaze came to rest on Hughes. "You hear a bowstring?"

Hughes didn't trust himself to speak, so he shook his head.

Mr. Glint made a thoughtful noise. It sounded like a blender being fed into a slightly larger blender.

For reasons Hughes did not entirely understand, he cleared his own throat and said, "Excuse me. I'm not sure if this is a personal question or not, but do you like carousels?"

"Dunno," said Mr. Glint. "What's a carousel?"

"Ah. In that case, never mind."

The eyes in that bald, forbidding head lingered on him.

Why did I say that? Why did I say anything?

"Do you like conceptualization?" said Mr. Glint.

"Sorry?"

"Conceptualization. It's like a pie, only in your head."

"I don't really know what you mean," said Hughes. "Sorry."

"Better go now." Mr. Glint reached into the calamitous thing he called a suit, took out a fist-sized beetle, and set it scurrying over his knuckles. "Be seeing you," he told Hughes (who felt as though he'd just been in a car accident involving whiplash and possibly cranial trauma).

With the birds chirping, the violet sky lightening to blue, and the real honest-to-God roses sending out their perfume, Mr. Glint lumbered after his partner toward home, or wherever nightmares went at break of day.

CHAPTER FORTY

Problems are pretty similar to that ever-apparent mountain Hughes saw in Iphigenia—everywhere you look, there they are looking right back. While their scale can be daunting, people inevitably find ways to overcome their problem mountain. Sometimes this involves one big leap, or as is the case with certain resourceful people, mining equipment. More often than not the process involves little steps. You hack away at it. The crags become mounds. Mounds become scree. Scree becomes dust. Vacuum up the dust, and hey presto. No more problem mountain. Take that, ya monolithic fuck.

On the first clear bright day of summer (and really, by then August was prepared to hand everything over to September and the rolling autumn season, which had driven the storm off like some wrathful God) Gormon Hughes Junior went about turning crags into dust.

Paying a visit to the old teashop in Leonidas District, Hughes endured his dad's fretting over his sprained arm. When he eventually managed to get a word in edgeways, he attempted to convince his dad that maybe he ought to come to Redspire for a while. It'd be no trouble. Hughes would arrange all the details.

This went down like something that goes down very badly indeed.

"Why would I do that?" said Gormon Hughes Senior. "The academic year is starting in five days, lad. I don't claim to know any students personally, but I do know what they like. They like feeling immortal as all young people do, and they like delicious tea at reasonable prices. I've got to prepare for the crowds."

His son took umbrage. "People in Redspire drink tea. I bet you could set up a roving stall or something."

"Who would mind the shop?"

"The shop would mind itself, Dad. The storm's over. No chance of damp creeping in. Extra damp," he amended, spying something spongy and greenish-purple in one corner. "Look, I'd like you there. I miss you."

His dad made a little sound. He went back to fussing over something or other on his pristine countertops. "Son, parents don't follow their children out into the world." His smile was lopsided. "You raise them up and send them out, and if you're lucky they remember you and if you're not they don't. The only thing that's certain is change. Constant transformation. Ruby-cheeked babas blink and suddenly they're schooled and ready for the first of many journeys. They blink again, they're married, partnership for the next adventure. Once more, they're old, and all their journeys are closed books, annotated with regrets and cherished things. It's what my old man—your grandfather—used to call the Autumn Waltz."

"I could never forget you, Dad."

"I know."

Hughes watched his father finish up at the counter, approach, and felt something toasty-hot pushed into his hands.

"Could I have a telephone installed here?" said Hughes, staring into his cup of honey-ginger-and-vanilla chamomile. "It's for security, Dad. I'm in the Citadel now. That sort of courts danger. For me and those around me."

"A telephone?"

"Yes."

Gormon nodded. "If it'll sate you, sure. I'll keep a telephone. Maybe I can look up some old friends of mine."

"I'll bring you a telephone book."

"Good lad."

Hughes sipped his tea. It was exceptional, sweet and delicate as springtime on the tongue. "I'll come home more often."

Gormon nodded again. This time he grinned, and for a moment he looked closer to forty than sixty. "I'll keep the kettle on for you," he said.

After that Hughes stopped by the Foundry. Jo was pleased to see him.

"Are you working on anything interesting?"

"One or two things," she said vaguely. "Maybe. Could be for you."

"Me?"

She wiggled her eyebrows.

"What's happening with your eyebrows?"

"I'm wiggling them," she said. "That sort of builds up the mystery, don't it?"

Hughes agreed that it did. He got into the meat of things. After he was done remonstrating himself she accepted his apology. He could tell she didn't fully understand the idea of Performance. Maybe it would have troubled her more if she did. Cate's dark expression the night before told Hughes all he needed to know about the subject. He had interfered in a good person's mind. Had wrapped it in strings and yanked like some crackpot puppeteer. It disturbed Cate. Thinking about it in those terms, Hughes wasn't exactly proud of himself either.

"It won't happen again," he told Jo. "Truth be told I'm sorry it ever happened in the first place."

"That's all right," she said graciously. "Now, you better scarper. I'm about to work with salamander iron and that stuff's piping hot."

Hughes left her to it.

Back in Redspire he spoke to Falstaff about arranging a telephone delivery to his father. The butler seemed distracted. There were purple pouches under his eyes and a haggard quality under layers of politeness. He brushed off Hughes' concern, noted the delivery on a neat little notepad, and bustled off in the direction of the next crisis.

"Okay," said Hughes.

It was a few minutes later. He was alone outside Wendy Dragontail's office. Doctor John was in there with her. He could hear them talking, their voices muffled through the paneled wooden door.

"Okay," he said again, knocked, and went in.

"Hughes. Do come in." The Dragon herself stood examining another map of Eurydice. John Isherwood was there, as was, much to Hughes' surprise, Cate. They were all in casual clothes (with the possible exception of Doctor John, who seemed permanently ready to deliver a lecture, although today he looked as frazzled as Falstaff). Cate's cream-colored t-shirt showed off the muscles like cables in her arms. Wendy Dragontail's forest-green cardigan showed off the fact she had arms, and that was about it.

"We were just discussing your patron's next mission," said Wendy Dragontail.

"Right. Well, there's something I need to speak to you about," said Hughes. "There's this thing that happens to me sometimes. No, that's not right. I happen to it, and it happens to other people. Damn. Hold on, I wrote it down on a piece of paper somewhere..." He fumbled in his coat pockets for a moment. Slowed. Stopped. He looked at them. "What next mission?"

"I'm going into Eurydice with Isaac Lawless," said Cate Jubilee.

"Isaac?" Hughes was caught completely off guard. "But he's injured."

"Expected to make a full recovery," said Wendy Dragontail. "Cate will make the initial foray into Eurydice. Isaac will catch up when he can."

"You can't send her there alone," said Hughes. "There's... well there's no more lunatics on motorcycles, I'll grant you. But the place is mean as a bag of porcupines. She'll be killed."

Cate smiled to herself.

"Your loyalty does you credit, Hughes," said Wendy. "Rest assured that all necessary precautions will be taken. Besides, before I partnered you together, Cate operated entirely on her own."

"She... Oh." Hughes frowned. "She did?"

"Indeed." A small twinkle entered Wendy's eye. "She was what you might call a 'lone wolf.' Although I think a more appropriate term in Cate Jubilee's case might be 'lone firing squad' or perhaps 'lone red panda on bad acid.' Surely you yourself can attest to her prowess on the battlefield?"

"Well, yes. Of course. But..."

"Very good. Cate, you may begin preparations to leave."

Cate uncrossed her arms and nodded. "I'll be ready in an hour, my Lady."

"Excellent. John, does that give you time to orchestrate the drop?"

"Should do." Doctor John looked uncomfortable. "I'll speak to you later about... that other matter."

"Pardon? Ah, yes. Capital idea." Wendy went to her desk and sat down. "Now, I'm sure both of you are eager to be about your business."

The pair left, Cate shooting Hughes an apologetic smile.

The door clicked shut.

Hughes strode up and laid his hand on Wendy Dragontail's desk.

"Where is she going?" he demanded. "Right into the lion's mouth, I'll bet. You don't waste any time, do you? We're only back twenty-four hours and already you've cooked some other caper. You'd send me too if I had both arms."

Wendy looked at Hughes' hand until he took it off the desk.

"I would send you since you proved yourself up to the challenge. I'm given to understand that Castle Aldersglen has significantly fewer inhabitants." She opened a drawer and plucked out a file. "Isaac's report," she explained. "An enlightening read. I particularly like this section here toward the end: The wee scrawny bugger—his codename for you, Hughes—had a chinwag with the engines. Got them so fired up they burst their cylinders. Burned the bony bastards something fierce. Maelen got his, all right. And then there is a good deal of colorful language describing the inferno, with special attention paid to how nice a candle the Marrow King made in his final moments."

Wendy set the file aside and steepled her fingers.

"I'm glad you came," she said. "It saved me the trouble of sending for you. Explain."

"May I ask where you're sending Cate?"

"If I answer, will you tell me everything?"

"Yes."

She watched him over the tips of manicured fingernails.

"Cate is going to track the origins of the necromancers. Some force guided Maelen. Planted the seed of rebellion in him, so to speak. It told him what to ask Isaac during his internment at the castle. Questions about Corinth City. About the Scarlet Citadel. Maelen was an unimaginative skeleton. That being the case I agree with Isaac—something else is at work here. Isaac himself suspects that force can be found in whatever country the necromancers hail from. The place must exist. They did not materialize in Aldersglen in a puff of unfortunate-smelling smoke. Between them, Cate and Isaac stand a fair chance at discovering the truth."

"There's something you're leaving out," said Hughes. "Something you won't tell me."

That twinkle again, her hazel eyes crinkling up at the corners. "Your turn."

Hughes considered holding out for everything, then relented.

"You should be a politician," he said.

She gave a languid shrug. "I lack the oily handshake, not to mention the stomach. Remind me to tell you about The-Two-For-One-Tuesday-Vindaloo incident."

So Hughes told her about his Performance. With Cate the words had flowed naturally. She was easy to talk to. He assumed it would be like that now, but he was wrong.

He talked about his childhood, about how he had discovered the power one night when a drunk wouldn't pay his tea bill. The cheapskate prick had wheeled angrily from father to son, and things might have gone south quickly had his face not gone vacant as a pit. A second passed, maybe two, and all of a sudden he was telling them that he was awfully sorry for the trouble. He'd pay for the tea. Nice tea too. Hughes talked about experimenting with Performance. Finding out he couldn't use it twice on someone, not unless some time had elapsed. Learning what the percentages signified. He talked about success and failures. There had been plenty of both, though more often than not the scales tipped against him.

And all the while Hughes waited for that same straightforwardness he'd had with Cate to arrive. He waited... and waited...

It never came.

In this office with its coiled stone dragons and its window overlooking the whole city, the words were hard.

"I'm not sure where it comes from," he concluded after what seemed like an eternity. "I can feel the Performance moving in me the same way you might feel joy or sorrow or any strong emotion. When I told her, Cate said she'd never heard of anything like it. Have you?"

"Magic abilities generally work that way. Strength, Dexterity, and Intelligence are the key attributes of the Scarlet Citadel. They are how we connect with our magic items. For example, my amulet Faethe uses Intelligence as the root of its power."

While he'd spoken Wendy Dragontail had leafed through the pages of a book. It looked like a personal diary. Now she began scribbling in it. "As to where these things come from, I'm afraid your guess is as good as mine. John Isherwood believes it is something to do with the portals, but for all the evidence he has, it is equally likely the magic comes from sea turtles or a healthy diet." She glanced up at him. "But I have avoided your question." She returned to her notes. "The answer is 'no,' Hughes. A resounding 'no.' I have never heard of someone who can do what you do."

"What does that mean?"

"It means I made a mistake sending you to Eurydice." She underlined a few words she'd written and laid her pen aside. "You are too valuable to risk."

"Valuable?"

"Naturally." She sat back, stitching her fingers together across her belly. "From this moment on, you are my personal inquisitor."

"Personal..." He mustn't have heard her right. "Sorry, what did you say?"

"A personal inquisitor."

Ah. He had heard her right. A sinking sensation compressed his stomach.

"I've always wanted one," continued Wendy Dragontail. "I'll put you in touch with Knickerbocker, my spymaster. Together you'll form a new branch of the Citadel. Call it, oh, Research and Sanitation. Discovering problems." She brushed her diary and pen into an open drawer. "Washing them away." She shut the drawer and peered at him, her face expectant.

"What sort of problems?" said Hughes.

"The Citadel has enemies," said Wendy Dragontail. "In this city and beyond. In the kitchen sink of modern conflict, the dishes pile up quickly. They require attention, if order is to be maintained. Let me give you an example. Say someone on my staff is contacted by a member of the Mysicordelian foreign consulate. The staff member is greedy and accepts a bribe to spy on me. They are discovered by one of Knickerbocker's rodents, and they are brought in for questioning. They deny the charges. This is where you come in."

Realization struck him in a thunderclap.

"No," he said. "No, I... couldn't do that, my Lady."

"It would be for the good of the Citadel," said Wendy Dragontail, her tone the very spirit of reason. "The dirty dishes pile up, Hughes. They pile up as you would not *believe*."

"That might very well be true," he said. "Even so, you'll have to clean them yourself."

"It is a direct order, Hughes."

"You can put that order *ubi sol non lucet*. With respect, Your Worship."

She looked at him seriously. "You realize you'll be expelled from the Citadel? Your sword—Chimera, isn't it?—confiscated. Insubordination has no home here."

He nodded stiffly.

"You'll never have the chance to follow Cate into the jaws of the proverbial lion, even when you recover. Indeed, seeing her again will be quite impossible."

Hughes' expression twisted as a wave of unnamable anger swept over him. He felt like leaning over that fancy desk and testing that amulet of hers. He mastered himself. "Will that be all, my Lady?"

"Indeed, Hughes. You disappoint me. I had thought you a man to watch. Alas, it seems I need only watch you as far as the door."

He stood. "Can I say something?"

"Kindly vent your frustrations elsewhere," she said, perusing a fresh file on her desk. "Goodbye."

By the time he reached the door the initial shock had worn off. His fingers closed on the knob. Its hard, smooth solidity brought home the reality of the situation.

"You're very like your father," said Wendy Dragontail.

"Pardon?"

He whirled.

"What did you say?"

"Your father," she repeated casually. "A marvelous judge of character, yet utterly incapable of concealing his own feelings. You also have a vein that pulses here when you're upset." She indicated her temple.

"You've never met my father."

She looked at him sympathetically. "I hope you'll forgive me the deceptions. I'm a cautious woman but there's no malice in it. Honest."

"Deceptions?" Hughes almost lost his footing.

What was she talking about?

The second thunderclap of the afternoon hit.

No, he thought. *Not again.*

She'd tricked him. Tugged the wool over his eyes for a second time. She didn't want him to set up a new branch of the Citadel with Knickerbocker. She wanted to see what Hughes would do when confronted, how much of himself he'd compromise to please and obey her. This time he did lose his footing.

"Sorry," said Wendy. She was supporting him. Later, he would wonder how she had crossed the distance so quickly. The desk was at least forty feet from the door. "Truly I am."

"Don't be," he said. "I'm just... Can someone die of relief?"

"Lean on me."

Hughes obeyed while his balance returned. There was no give there. Wendy Dragontail's amulet was exerting its power, and she was solid and firm as oak.

"How do you know my dad?"

"I lived in Leonidas District."

"You?" The idea of this woman living in the chaos of Leonidas threatened to dizzy him all over again. "When?"

"In my twenties." She smiled. "So sometime around the dawn of civilization."

"Come on," he said. "You're not a day over thirty."

This morsel of trite flattery earned him a toothy grin from the most powerful woman in the city. "Can you stand?" she asked him.

"Yeah. Think so."

His legs were only moderately jellified. Seeing he was okay she let him go. The grin softened. "Fancy a cup of tea?"

He gave her a grave look. "I would murder one."

"Or me, perhaps, given how I've treated you."

Hughes was inclined to agree but found he couldn't. He had not realized how crushing the weight of worry had been until it was lifted. He felt light all over. Lightheaded, hearted, lungfuls of light, gusts of breath as delicate as thin ceramic and intoxicating as gin.

Over by the desk again he sipped his mug of Earl Grey and thought how strange a parallel this was.

First tea with his father, and now tea with Wendy Dragontail.

Down in the gutter, now up in the tower.

Weird old world.

"Needless to say, the use of this Performance of yours will be restricted to enemies of the Citadel," said Wendy.

"I used it on Walter," said Hughes.

She waved this away. "I expect you had your reasons. But this persuasion of yours is a loaded crossbow. I trust you'll aim its bolt in the right direction."

"I'll use my best judgment, my Lady."

"Yes, I rather think that's a slippery way of saying, 'I'll decide which direction is right,' Hughes."

"Is it, my Lady? I hadn't noticed." Hughes swirled his tea and took another sip. "Spoiled for targets, I reckon."

He felt her stare like two solar beams.

"The creature in Iphigenia," said Wendy Dragontail. "The one with the two heads. You used your Performance to kill it, didn't you?"

"Yeah."

"You made it put its heart on your knife."

A brief pause. Hughes drank his tea. Then he said, "Yes."

"I have your word you will not abuse this power, and you'll report any developments to me at once?"

"You have my word."

Wendy sat back in her chair. "Very well, Hughes. I am satisfied."

He set the mug on the silver tray Falstaff had brought them and stood.

"Thank you for the tea, my Lady."

"Why don't we try 'Wendy'?"

He pursed his lips and nodded. "Thank you for everything, Wendy."

She raised a hand as he left. He didn't notice. Picking up the telephone, she dialed for the nurses' station on one of the lower floors.

"Good afternoon. Could you make a call on Gormon Hughes this evening? His cast is cracked. Thank you so much."

Hours winnowed away. Note page followed note page. Report after report. The lemon-yellow light coming through the window went pink and deep with dusk. Wendy went on working. But her mind was elsewhere. Her heart too, if she were being halfway honest with herself. It didn't seem the day for honesty. Hell. She could have honesty file a report, maybe she'd get to it later.

There was the moon. She could see it fetching west on invisible strands of night.

She got up and walked to her window. The view was crystal clear. Corinth City spread out below her, a radiant kitchen stacked with plates and cutlery, spotless and filthy, and very few clever enough to tell which was which.

She grinned enormously.

"Put it where the sun doesn't shine. Ha!"

***

Dear Meester Hoos,

read the note on his bedside table.

Sorry to creep and sneak and scurry and snoop into your room without your permission. I want you to know that I hummed spy-vid music the entire time. This means you cannot be annoyed with me—it would be superbly unsporting and grouchy of you.

Also sorry about how I acted yesterday. Insisting we visit your father was bad of me. I was pushy. No excuses.

Thank you for telling me about your fondness for plays.

A Summer Knight's Hole *sounds scrumptious!*

All jokes aside, hearing that made me realize how starved I am for details about your life. You've been closed with me, and while mystique can be attractive in someone I've only just met, it isn't something I want in a prospective partner.

Therein lies quandary number one: how do I ask you to open up while not being a busybody?

Quel dommage! as the Champleurs say.

And there are things about me you don't know yet. Of course there are. Mostly small and silly, but not all. Some are important. I think of them as intimacies. In my defense we've only just started growing close, and while I certainly guard those intimacies, I have talked about myself. Lots. It's been amazing—I'm extremely articulate and almost painfully adorable (no more jokes, I swear).

You, on the other hand, only gave a snippet of a glimpse into yourself last night. Still, that's quandary number two: how do I ask you to open up while not being a hypocrite?

I'm off to Eurydice for a while.
Maybe when I'm back I'll be quandary-less, and you'll be insight-full.

I care about you very much.
I wouldn't write this letter if I didn't.

See you soon, handsome.
C. Jubilee Esquire

P.S. Why do you have a blanket made of pages on your bed?

***

September cartwheeled over the city, her stockings blue and her hair trussed in horsetails of gold. Meanwhile the carousel dream skimmed under her, a dark sister for a bright month.

One Sunday morning Gormon Hughes Senior was reading a charming little play about a girl escaping city life to start up a farm in the countryside. The majority of his concentration was reserved for the story, which was really getting rolling, but a little of it circled around the idea of breakfast. Normally he skipped that most important of meals since there was nothing that could accommodate it in the cupboard, only some lunchly and dinnerly grub.

Still, it was Sunday, the nine o'clock sunbeams pierced his window like pretty firebolts, and his till had a modest taking from the day before when a troupe of college students wandered in for the rustic teashop experience.

Against all habit his stomach rumbled.

He frowned down at it, then up at the play. He put the story down.

"Gormon," he said. "You're right on the cusp of your own winter. Let's spend autumn credits while they're there to spend, huh?"

"Good idea," he answered himself.

He got dressed.

"Thanks."

He donned his coat and doffed it again; it looked warm out.

"Don't mention it."

And he shut the door behind him.

On the zigzagging stair that led down to the street, he paused, cocking one ear.

Dogs. One barking, one whining piteously.

He knew of only one dog in this building, and that was Ernie Wilks' Saint Bernard, Boochums. The whining was Boochums, no question. The barking... He listened. It sounded like a smaller dog, maybe a border collie. The barks were lusty enough. The dog was hitching them up from the depths of its throat.

His belly gave a groan, and for a moment he could think of nothing but scrambled eggs with cheddar cheese, luscious strips of bacon, pancakes, Daethumberland syrup, and orange juice so cold it perspired through the cloudy glass.

He took a step toward the street where people were going to and fro and stopped when the barking started up again. He looked up and down the stairwell. None of his neighbors seemed curious about this little canine symphony.

So why am I? he thought.

Because you know Ernie. The man has barely enough to look after Boochums, much less himself. No way he would take in another dog.

It occurred to him that the dog was in another apartment. Or Ernie was watching a very loud vid, although this seemed unlikely. Anyway, what vid? Pissed-off dog showreel? Plus, there was the whining. Hearing that goofy giant Boochums emit a sound so plaintive moved him. He pressed a hand to his stomach and took it away. Breakfast could wait a little longer.

He lurched up the way he'd come, the steps sighing their metallic sigh under him.

Outside the door there could be no doubt. The barking was coming from Ernie's place.

Gormon knocked.

The sounds went on.

He knocked again. "Ernie?"

He heard toenails click against floorboards. They approached the door. A simpering sound came from the other side.

"Boochums? That you, boy?"

The sound went on. But the barking had stopped, and despite the warmth of the morning Gormon felt apprehension form a chilly fist around his small intestine.

"Ernie?" he said. His friend's name came out dry and raspy. With an effort he swallowed and tried again, louder this time. "Ernie, are you in there?"

Nothing. Not even the whine.

Gormon looked at the doorknob. It would joggle in his hand, but it wouldn't turn.

He touched it, very tentatively, listening for a noise that might halt him from within. Silence.

The knob turned.

Without knowing he was doing it, Gormon slid his tongue over his upper lip and brought his teeth together in a thorny grimace.

All thought of breakfast was forgotten now.

He pushed open the door and went in.

The mild shock Boochums gave him as the big dog scrabbled back from the opening door was nothing compared to the fright he got when the other dog barreled toward him.

It was a wolfhound, lean and rangy. Its coat was iron gray, and as Gormon recoiled against the wall it went up on its hind legs and planted both forepaws on his shoulders. His knees buckled. Lean and rangy, sure, but the dog was easily a hundred-and-twenty pounds. How had he reckoned it small? It must have been on the other side of Ernie's apartment, distance dampening the sound. It barked, that low guttural bark thrusting up from old vocal cords. Its breath gushed warm and acrid smelling over his cheeks.

Gormon stared into the brown eyes darting wildly under the dog's shaggy brows. So Ernie had taken in a stray. Here was the evidence wrinkling its muzzle before him. Why then did he feel that hand of cold apprehension kneading his guts?

Because Ernie couldn't afford to keep this dog.

There must have been a windfall in his life. But from where?

The dog was giving him the creeps. He half expected it to begin slobbering (Dear God don't let it have rabies) and lunge for the soft flesh under his chin.

The hound barked and barked. Its head swooped this way, that way. Its tail was a stiff rod.

Where *was* Ernie?

That was when Gormon noticed the dog's arm. It was severed at the shoulder. In its place was a metal prosthetic. He gazed at that prosthetic for a long time.

It looked a lot like Ernie's.

Boochums lay down, his jowls settling on the floor, and gave a whimper of despair.

CHAPTER FORTY-ONE

Mr. Glint entered the pharmacy and coincidentally every other customer decided their various medical needs were not *that* pressing. They hurried out as fast as they could without actually running.

The girl behind the counter was a chirpy young woman with a septum piercing.

Every shop had at least one chirpy young woman with a septum piercing. It must be in a guidebook somewhere.

Mr. Glint stood opposite her.

"Hello!" she said. "How can I help you today?"

"Need something for worry," he said.

"I beg your pardon?"

"Worry," said Mr. Glint. "It's like rotten eggshells going crunch. Up here." He pointed to his head.

The young woman with the septum piercing did some mental gymnastics. "Ohhh. You mean anxiety medication." She smiled. "Have you a prescription?"

"No," said Mr. Glint. "I just say what comes next."

She blinked at him, her positive consumer dynamic balking in the face of something she struggled to understand.

"Not a 'script,'" she said, trying to regain her balance. "A prescription. The piece of paper saying which medication you should be on. Doctors give them out."

Mr. Glint nodded. He reached over the counter and took a roll of receipts and a pen.

She watched him slowly and carefully draw an X. He handed it back to her. "There," said Mr. Glint.

"I'm sorry. This won't do. It has to come from a doctor."

"I am a doctor."

"What's your field?"

He looked at her. "Improvised surgery."

She gave him every pill he could carry.

Mr. Glint went home.

The leisure center looked no more hospitable in fair weather than it had in foul. Autumn sunlight gathered in the crooked shards and disintegrating boards populating the windows. Where it shone inside, it revealed the grime on the bowling pins, the thick coating of hairlike dust on the laser-tag beamers and green baize tables and billiard balls of numbered resin, and it also revealed Miss Gleam. She was curled up like an evil-minded cat in a broom closet. Spindled cobweb was already being strung over her face by the inhabitants of the closet. Mr. Glint brushed these away.

He stood over her for a moment, his face a portrait of sour-mouthed musings. Then he fetched a chair and set the bottles of medication on it. They formed nice, neat rows. There was no water in the rusty taps, but the basement was still blanketed in eight-inches of rat-flavored rainwater. So he filled a glass with that and put it on the chair too.

After an hour of consideration and hunting slippery mandibled things he'd heard swimming in the basement darkness, he settled down to some revision. Miss Gleam said the key to retaining information was going over it again and again until it stuck, and she was always right.

Conceptualization, then. He wiped the bowling alley blackboard, and taking up the chalk, drew the pie. He wrote the words, which took him a long time.

Crust. Filling. Base.

Conscious. Preconscious. Subconscious.

He looked at the squiggly letters.

"I get an idea," he said and drew a line up the diagram. The line ended in an arrow at the top of the pie, the conscious crust. "It comes up to me."

Then he drew another line, this one sloping down the diagram from the conscious crust to the subconscious base of the pie. "I go down to the idea," he said.

He was not altogether sure about this second bit, but it sounded right.

Mr. Glint unhanded the chalk and stood back to study his work.

It struck him that the arrows on the ends of the lines should go in case Miss Gleam woke up. Arrows were not a welcome topic in their lair. Nor were bows, nor those who fired them. He erased the arrows, and not a second too soon.

"What was that?"

He turned and saw Gleam crouched in the doorway. The doors themselves had rotten hinges. They stood splayed and lice-chewed and mottled in flaking paint. One of them sheltered his partner from a bar of revealing sunshine. Her skin was bright nonetheless, and her agitated eyes brighter still.

"That... sound," she said. "What was it?"

"Chalk," said Glint. "I put medicine out. And water."

"Chalk?" She straightened and came in to join him, but her eyes kept flickering to the windows and entrances. "Yes. It was soft. He'll tread softly when he comes, noble chum. That's how he got the better of Flash. Fleet feet, and ever so discreet."

"Did you not see it? I put it on the chair."

She gave him an absent smile that showed off every single fang in her gob but failed entirely to reach her eyes. Mr. Glint didn't think she'd heard him at all.

"Here's what peels my peach and plucks my pentatonics," she said, pacing the length of a bowling aisle before slamming the recall button to summon a ball. "Why was our brother Hughes wearing a mask in the first place?"

A lime-green ball spat up from the long-unused track system.

"Now you might point out that the white plastic mask is as common as crumbs in a tramp's beard, astute man that you are Mr. Glint. But these are extraordinary days we find ourselves in. They require exploration with a willing hand." She slid two fingers and a thumb into the ball to demonstrate. Something spongy and damp inside gave under the pressure of her touch. Sighting along the lane of unpolished pine, she plunged her hand deeper, crouched, swung back, and let fly. The ball plunked. It rolled. It veered for the gutter, then at the last moment spun true. Pins clattered in a spectacular burst of dust.

Miss Gleam stood, her head ever so slightly canted to one side, her scalpel-smile crooked as the bends of bad country roads. "I have been thinking about my questions, Mr. Glint. The ones I posed to Hughes." The pins were reset. She hit the recall button. Her lime-green ball shuttled up the conveyor belt. The track complained loudly but held fast. "Indeed I have pondered them in sleeping and waking. And it is with no doubt whatsoever that I tell you this—I bungled them."

She squished her fingers into the pliant spongy grooves and lifted the ball.

"Did I ask him what he intended to do with the mask? Certainly not. Don't you see, oh kindred in sadism? This all began after we became involved with the boy. After we followed him through the bazaar." She toyed with the ball, letting it pendulum her arm back and forth. "A counter-plucking in my mind tells me I am grasping at thin air. But the major chords play a sinister melody. Hughes dancing around us at every turn. Is he the one behind the murders? I hear you. He is poor as the crumbs even the tramp will discard when his moustache yields them. How could he afford assassins of the Archer's caliber? Brace yourself, my dear. I have an answer for that too. You see borrowing is a habit hard broken. Other creditors are not so skilled in collecting as we are. I think it's very possible that once we get a look at the center of the spiderweb, we will find Hughes or someone close to him there, manipulating the strands."

"No mask."

She hesitated mid-roll. The ball plunked. It rolled. It veered into the gutter.

"Forgive me," she said, turning to face him. "I didn't catch that."

"No mask," repeated Mr. Glint. "On his boat race."

"Who wasn't wearing a mask?"

"Hughes."

Gleam's brows came together. "Of course he was. I saw him."

"I found it in his pocket," Glint persisted.

"Did you? Yes. I surmise you did at that. That organ between your ears is growing very detail oriented, Mr. Glint, you mark my words."

Her partner grunted like a string instrument breaking over a slightly sturdier string instrument. Reaching up, he hoisted himself into the sill of a window and peered out at the abandoned area around the leisure center. It was quiet. Their lair squatted in that quiet, keeping itself to itself, never disturbing or being disturbed. Distantly he could see a tree. It was rich and green and lively. Not for long. This was autumn, and that meant entropy, a word he was most proud to know. Entropy meant death of every kind. You could keep winter. That was the end result. But autumn? Autumn was the season that killed the year. Mr. Glint was looking forward to it.

"No mask, you say?" Miss Gleam murmured. "I would have sworn on my father's flagellated bones he was in a mask."

"You haven't got a father."

"True, true. Bah! Nary we mind." She flung up her hands and let them come to rest on her hips. She was feeling vastly better. Clearer somehow. "How long have I been cooped up in that closet, Mr. Glint?"

"Not long."

"Not long is too long by half! Come down at once. We must go out, for there's culling and cruelty to deliver in spades. Our employer has debtors. Grudges. Ingresses and extrications in need of our attention." She grinned up at Glint, who landed next to her and adjusted his suit. "All rather messy, I'm afraid."

"Don't be afraid," he said. "It's only stringy bits."

"Quite so. Our primary concern however, is new apparel. Our *suits*, Mr. Glint. I am referring to our *suits*, which are in a deplorable state."

"Bit manky, yeah."

"Literally worse for wear." She gestured widely. "Will you not offer your arm, noble fellow?"

"No."

She deflated. "Oh."

He held out both arms. "Shall we go?"

Her laughter struck each pin of silence like a bowling ball.

"Let's!"

The telephone rang.

"Never a dull moment. Hold that stance, Mr. Glint." She lifted the phone out of its cradle. "Good morning, sir," she trilled. "Mr. Glint and I were just about to—"

"Gleamy," the caller bleated. "It's me."

She felt the good humor pour out of her like water from a pail.

"Mr. Twinkle, your timing is appalling. This had better be urgent, since I gave the strictest instruction that this number only be dialed in an emerg—"

"He scragged them. All of them. Oh fuck me, this is horrible..."

"Stop it at once," she said bitingly. "Show some self-possession, man. A little sangfroid."

"Sorry." She heard the click in his throat as he swallowed. "Sorry."

"Now, who precisely scragged who?"

"Miss Glitter. Mister Glow. Mr. Glisten. And I think Flicker. I-I'm not sure."

The list of names gave her such a start that—for a brief and merciful minute—dread had no hold on her. Only bewilderment and a peculiar sense of that darker thing skirting her defenses, looking for chinks in her armor.

"You must be mistaken, Mr. Twinkle," she said. "Our friends are more than capable of looking out for themselves. BOLO, remember? Be On The—"

"But I saw them, Gleamy!"

'What do you mean, saw them?'

"They were *in my house*. He... Oh *ffffffuck*."

"They're alive," she hissed over his whimpers. "Don't speak to me this way. I won't stand for it."

"Oh, Gleamy. Gleamy he... he stuck them up. On the walls, like. They were opposite the door, so when I... when I came in... Gleamy, I think he wanted me to find them there. Like a pinup show in hell. The blood..."

Dread slithered over her nerves then, an anaconda of disbelief and horror. Soon it would coil around her, a sickly smothering.

"He told us no one would ever scrag us," Twinkle complained. "Mr. Shine. He promised. He promised, Gleamy..."

"Shall I take my scissors to you, Mr. Twinkle? I bet every word you've said would turn my blades as white as snow."

"I got out of there. Nabbed my cat, Lucinda, and scarpered. Now I'm in a safehouse I keep for emergencies. Never thought I'd need it." He laughed, a ghoulish sound crackling over the telephone line. "Shows what I know. Fuck me. Fuck *meeee*."

Here it was.

The serpent of dread had its coils round her. They squeezed.

"Who killed them?" she said.

Mr. Glint was next to her. She hadn't noticed him till now. She cut her eyes to his and back to the phone cradle. Really she was picturing Twinkle in his safehouse, skin glimmering with their shiny injection fluid and a concoction of sweats both hot and cold.

"Say again, Gleamy?" said Mr. Twinkle. "Line's dog-eared."

"Who killed them?"

"Who do you think? The Archer. On my wall, my wall, he fucked them to death with arrows and they were *on my wall*—"

"What about Fulgurate?" she cried. "You didn't mention him? Is he safe?"

"Who knows? I called Shine before you. Got his secretary. Sniveling bitch wouldn't put me through to him. 'He's completely tied up,' she said. Told her I'd tie her up like a Tinfrost roast if she didn't put me on." She heard him snigger. It was worse than the laugh he'd given before, a slender lunatic amusement. "Hung up on me. Reckoned I'd try you instead."

"We'll come to you at once," she said promptly. "Where's this hidey-hole of yours?"

"You mean it?" He sounded stunned and almost sane for the first time since calling her. "Thanks, Gleamy. You're a kind soul. I always said so, even when—"

"Yes, yes. Swiftly now."

"Right. Right. Course. The safehouse is in Cleomenes, little spot on a perch near the... Hold on."

His voice was fainter. She pressed the phone close, hoping the connection wouldn't fail them in the crucial moment. "Mr. Twinkle?"

There was a crash on the other end of the line.

"Oh... No. No *No NO!*"

"What is it?"

"Mr. Fulgurate." Mad fright made Twinkle's voice high and keening. "He just came through the solar. Thought for a moment he was having a lurk, but there's steel points through his head. Shot him from behind, the blighter. Gleamy, I don't want to die."

"Where are you? You must tell me."

"Look after Lucinda, all right? She's a lovely pussycat."

"*Where are you?*" she thundered.

"All purrs and lapping at her milk bowl. Beautiful creature." Sobs stuffed his throat. She could hear him weeping. "Raised her from a kitten, I did. She—"

Miss Gleam heard the arrow before Mr. Twinkle himself felt it. It was the thinnest sound she had ever listened to, thinner and stranger than the last death rattle of the most decrepit invalid.

There was a gurgling, a heavy thud as of a powerfully built body going down like a chainsawed tree, and then silence.

Miss Gleam stood there with the phone pressed to her ear. No breath passed her pallid lips. Her lungs and heart were fixed in total stasis. In that moment her entire self funneled into the act of listening.

She heard them. Footsteps. They were dancer-graceful, and they were velvet-soft. Just as she'd known they would be.

She heard an untangling clatter and then silence returned. Only it was different now.

In her chest, her heart gave a single juddering beat and went still once more. The Archer. It was him. He was on the line.

She could picture him standing over Mr. Twinkle's body as Twinkle thrashed with his legs and lashed with his arms, his mouth full of his own blood, drowning on dry land and in impossible times.

"Who are you?" she said. She had intended it as a demand, forceful and strong. Instead her voice emerged as a clogged whisper.

The Archer made no reply.

Threaten me. Menace me. Be minacious, foreboding, cruel, she thought desperately. *Do anything. Say anything. Show me you are a man and not...*

Not what? She had no clue.

Then the line went dead. She looked at the receiver. Eventually she put the phone down.

Mr. Glint asked her something. She didn't hear what. Her feet were bringing her somewhere. She let them, feeling as though she were passing through a gauze, or a dream world of arrows and white masks and sparkling skin made stiff and bluish-purple with the lividity of death.

In the broom closet half a mirror hung from the wall. The glass was cracked. That felt appropriate. She was cracking, after all. Coming apart.

Admitting that to herself brought no comfort. Only a strange emotion that bordered on panic but never quite crossed over.

Things fall apart. The center cannot hold.

Who had written that? Right now she simply could not recall.

She tilted her head this way, then that way, watching her segmented reflection monkey each movement. When she stopped, she focused on one of her eyes. It was black as a bowl of pitch. That was okay. Normal.

But her cheek—iridescent as ever—had developed a small yet noticeable convulsion. It was the first physical tick of her life, and it was centered on her silvery scar.

He shot me there, she thought, outrage beginning to boil in her belly. *He shot me right there, and now the flesh is working like he's tugging on it with a cord.*

An urge to claw at the spot overwhelmed her. She'd scratch until traitor skin and turncoat muscle dangled from her face in flaps and strings. Before she knew what was happening her fingernails were hooked inches from the convulsion, the infuriating fucking *twitch.* It was like a parasite, a snakeshape writhing inside her.

Gleam thought, *But I already have things inside me. Our employer's needles made me hollow as a drum, but other things have made me full.*

She thought of Mr. Glint's poem about Rosey Posey, who had died of a respiratory illness and been devoured by her loyal dog. It comforted her. A bit.

Shuddering, she lowered her hands.

In her scarred cheek the tick went on ticking. Not a snake, a clock. A clock that had worked well until recently. Now her springs were coming loose because things fell apart and the center couldn't hold.

Gently, she soothed herself. *Easy does it, cunningest of clevers. Never mind that rogue convulsion. It's only a cramp or a collection of motor nerves misbehaving. Only that and nothing more.*

Nothing more, except... except she did mind. She needed to relax but that was unthinkable.

Not with what she'd just heard on the phone.

She paced awhile to keep from rending herself to pieces. Glancing at her reflection was no help. The spasm hadn't improved. If anything, it actually looked a little worse.

She might have to cover it. With her hands? No. Her hands were less scrupulous than the dirty rotten twitch.

A mask then.

Maybe Hughes can lend me his, she thought. This struck her as absurdly funny. She threw back her head and laughed, wicked, and woeful, and mad.

Something touched her. She reeled, her laugh becoming a shriek.

But it was only Glint. Brave, brilliant Mr. Glint, the fondest friend a woman could ask for. She offered him her glossiest smile. From the corner of her eye she saw her reflection. Its expression—anemic and stricken—seemed to *accuse* her.

"Me?" she whispered. "But I'm quite innocent, judge. I assure you. Ask your son. He brought me a slice of pumpkin pie on All Hallow's Eve. Missing, you say? Send the bailiff. Actually, don't bother. I have your boy here in this jar."

She looked with a sudden sad clarity at Mr. Glint. "I rather think I'm coming undone, old chap."

Her partner held out a bottle. She took it and read the label.

Sertraline.

"But these are for people," she said. "I don't... I've never..."

"Got some water here."

She accepted the fetid glass.

Glint said, "If they don't work, say the word. Got lots of bottles."

"And if none of those help?"

Mr. Glint shrugged his shoulders. "Could always kill you," he said.

She touched his arm. "Promise?"

When he was gone she swallowed a handful of pills and checked the mirror. No jerks or spasms. Her face was without fault or flaw.

But it had been there. No stray imaginings on this ride. It would return quickly or it would bide its time. The shortening autumn hours would tell. That it *would* return wasn't up for debate. Of that she was quite sure.

White masks. Arrows. Mr. Shine's employees being hunted. Small questions, comparatively. The big question, when it came, reached over her mind like the cobwebs wafting stickily from the closet corners and the handles of the brooms. *What is happening to me?*

She would have reason to ask it again before her business with Hughes was done.

Too late, as it happened.

***

"Is that a deer?" said Hughes. He was supposed to be concentrating on his training, but he'd happened to glance out the window and what he'd seen there had him transfixed. It was eight o'clock in the morning, and ten floors below them the Ptolemaen street had two occupants. One of them was an irritable looking man with a pencil moustache. He was in a telephone box and seemed to be on an important call. The other street occupant was...

"A doe," said Hector beside him.

"A deer," Hughes marveled.

"A female deer," Hector clarified.

"Ray," said Cassandra.

"Would anyone like tea?" someone said, popping their head in. Hughes didn't recognize them. "Oh, hello all. Um."

The two living ghosts regarded them coolly.

The kindly stranger paled. Hughes came to their rescue. "Just a drop of."

They nodded and fled gratefully.

"Ray?" said Hector.

Cassandra pointed. "Golden sun."

"I see."

They looked out at the scene together. The deer was trying to come into the telephone box. The man with the pencil moustache was putting up a valiant effort to keep it out.

"I've never seen a deer in the city before," said Hughes. "Have either of you?"

"We don't get out much," said Cassandra.

"Oh." Hughes went back to looking. The deer was in the box now, snuffling at the receiver. The man was doing his best to ignore it. "A deer. That's wild."

"Perhaps," said Hector, watching the deer curiously, "not in this case."

"There you are," said Cassandra. "What kept you?"

Hughes turned to the private training room's door, expecting to see a person with a teapot. Instead he got his second surprise of the morning because it was another living ghost. He had the look of Hector and Cassandra, but where they were sturdy and broad he was willowy. His face was sweet, but Hughes detected a wiliness under it. It was the sort of face that said, "Thank you so much for welcoming me, King of somewhere-or-other. This really is a splendid castle. Incidentally, do any of your daughters bar their windows at night?"

"Gormon Hughes," said Hector. "Our youngest brother, Paris."

"The apt pupil," said the newcomer, gripping Hughes' arm. "Good to meet you, Hughes. Your name is a popular one in my family of late."

"My name?"

"Oh yes."

Hughes didn't know what to make of that, though some small corner of him registered flattery and commenced to glow.

"October lies a full fortnight from now," said Hector. "I intended to forestall this until then. Cassandra convinced me otherwise. Make ready, Hughes. Today we begin instilling rules two and three of swordplay into your body."

That internal glow struck up sparks. Hughes beamed. "Are you serious?"

"Deeply. Your performance in Eurydice was a thing worth admiring."

For a moment Hughes thought he meant Performance with a capital P. He dismissed the idea. Hector couldn't know about his secret ability. The only people who did were Wendy Dragontail, Cate, Jo, and Burnished Isaac Lawless. Before he'd gone off through the portal to join Cate, Isaac had (between a cocktail of insults and frankly bizarre anecdotes) confided to Hughes that he'd been sworn to secrecy about the whole Performance thing.

Hector was saying something, and Hughes made a quick return from the world of speculation.

"Rule two of swordplay is defense."

"What are the composite subrules?" Hughes asked dutifully.

Cassandra rolled her eyes but the question pleased Hector. "You have an enviable memory, Hughes. The composite subrules of defense are assessment, parrying, and riposting."

"May I hazard a guess at the third rule of swordplay?"

"By all means."

"Offense," said Hughes. "With one composite subrule—stick them with the pointy end."

Cassandra grumbled inaudibly. Over her shoulder Hughes saw Paris grin impishly.

Hector's impassive expression didn't budge. But his eyes held a grudging amusement that made Hughes glad he was growing the courage to make little jokes like that in the company of such important and respectable people. "Not untrue," said Hector. "Offense has more than one subrule though, and none of them involve sticking your opponent with anything."

"Not unless they ask nicely," said Paris.

Hector ignored him much more effectively than the pencil mustachioed man had ignored the deer invasion. "The subrules are attacking, feinting, and the Trojan Imperative."

"What's the Trojan Imperative?" said Hughes.

Hector gestured to his siblings. "You are aware of how we died?"

Hughes admitted he wasn't. "I thought it might be rude to ask."

"Some might say trickery killed us. Me, I blame folly." Hector sat on a supply box next to a pair of training dummies. His elbows rested on his knees. His spectral fingers laced together. "Our hometown of Troy held under siege for nineteen months. General Ulyssé led the Champleurs force hemming us in. One night I led a sortie that should have been suicide. Instead we destroyed their supply wagons, leaving Ulyssé's troops starved as well as weary, and returned safe behind our well-stocked walls. In a stroke of savage genius, Ulyssé ordered her force to build a bull from planks of wood. They left it as an offering of defeat and retreated beyond the far-off hills. Thinking the day won, I had the bull brought within the walls. Little did I know the bull was hollow, and inside lay a contingent of Champleurs assassins."

"Oh God," said Hughes.

"Under cover of night they crept out, slit my throat and all the members of my family they could find. Then they opened the gates. Ulyssé led her force in effortlessly. Nineteen months. My last nineteen months. Ours," he said, glancing at Cassandra who had come to lay a hand on his shoulder.

Hughes could guess the rest. Troy fell. General Ulyssé left a garrison and headed onward to join up with the rest of her king's armies. A month later the ferocious counter-offensive from the allied forces smashed those armies. The Champleurs were cowed into a retreat. At length the fate of the continent played out at the hilltop battle near the town of Origné. Mirolaens grew on the hill while history danced on the head of a pin.

Hector got to his feet and approached his student. There was none of his usual comfort on display. His gaze was not gentle or kind.

"Listen to me. You will learn how to avoid death and mete it out in dark abundance. That is the Trojan Imperative. To this end I have enlisted Paris to spar with you for he is a dangerous man."

"Come, brother. He survived Cassandra's peony." Paris took a practice sword from the supply box. "Consider me the shrinking violet."

Hector and Cassandra gave them space.

Hughes drew Chimera.

Paris sketched a mocking bow and came for him.

Each clash and bout was punctuated by a steady stream of instruction from Hector, and the occasional hyenalike laugh from Cassandra as Paris gave Hughes the thrashing of a lifetime.

After an hour Hughes begged a break. Paris relented.

"You're worse than the Bonemeal Boys," said Hughes between labored gasps. He was encased in sweat. Bruises were already blooming under his shirt and trousers. He was sore, all of his conditioning with Cassandra was abandoning him in the face of exhaustion, and moreover he was pretty sure Paris was going easy on him.

"Sorry for the delay," said the stranger, poking their head in again. "Falstaff's laid up in bed with a head cold or something. The kitchen staff are in disarray. Here's your tea, sir."

"Oh! I forgot about this. Thank you very much." He sipped and regretted it. It was cold coffee. The kitchen must really have been in a state. Falstaff would be mortified. Hughes did his best to pass it off. "Good, very good. Thank you. You know, Hector wasn't joking," he said, turning to his new sparring partner as the helpful person tottled off. "I can see I've got an uphill struggle ahead of me. You're a terror with a blade, Paris."

The youngest son of Priam King inclined his head, smiling roguishly. "Thanks," he said. "But really I'm much better with a bow."

ACT TEN

DREAM WARRIOR

CHAPTER FORTY-TWO

It happened in stages, or possibly all at once.

As with any crisis event, it depended on where you were standing.

For Sheila Kofatch's property realtor hubby, it was the latter. On October 4th he returned home after what Sheila referred to as a "washcloth day" (i.e. any day that left you feeling like you'd been wrung out) and was alarmed to find his apartment full of smoke and his youngest daughter howling herself hoarse from the bathroom. She had locked herself in there to hide from the two beetles—each as big as her fist—that she'd seen skittering over the kitchen cupboards. Sheila's hubby turned off the pan, feeling a stir of queasiness when he smelled the blackened lumps of burger mince, and went in to see what the matter with his little girl was. The problem identified, he asked her where Mommy and Carrie-Anne were. She didn't know. Had they gone out? She didn't know that either, though she hadn't heard the front door open or close before the attack of the killer beetles. Thinking that he'd call Sheila's sister the moment his immediate issue was taken care of, hubby began a valiant bug hunt, a decision that would haunt him for the rest of his life.

Three days later, when most people were worried that the rain was back (it was in fact a light shower, no great worry), a college student named Olivia Peters suffered a mental breakdown. On the evening of the 6th she left a party with a nice boy named Bevin Wyatt. He'd offered his place. Olivia agreed. Bev had been a good lay, and the cuddles hadn't been half bad either. The morning after, October 7th, Olivia woke to a disturbing sensation like she had been folded in a cocoon of slippery wet stockings. She turned and looked into the slitted eyes of a seventy-pound octopus. Its gelatinous head moved and for a fleeting moment, she saw the protrusion of its beak. Her screams woke Bevin's roommate and their neighbors, who would never forget that morning, though many tried.

That day of the 7th was a precursor to real trouble.

On the 8th, the news reported three people killed by a bear in a dress shop in Cleomenes District. The bear had proceeded to mangle a streetbeater who tried to intervene, and the copper would likely have died had she not been saved by none other than Tommy Fahrenheit of the Scarlet Citadel, who happened to be nearby.

On the 9th, the news ran for an extra hour. There were simply that many incidents—wild animals appearing and people vanishing into thin air. In smooth, untroubled tones, the news anchor announced the government had declared a state of emergency. Over that same broadcast, a rogue member of staff changed the subtitle reel. The new reel told audiences at home that the people were not going missing, but rather that they *were* the animals.

The culprit responsible for the switcheroo was identified. He had a history of conspiracy theorism and was sacked on the spot. Too late, of course. The idea was out there, and while healthy skepticism put up its shield to protect the public consciousness, mass hysteria slowly put up its arms and began to flail them.

Rumor and gossip made the rounds.

It was a hoax.

A political stunt.

A sham.

But for some, like the sulky-faced boy who had delivered Ruddy Jolene's message to Glint and Gleam that summer and who woke one morning to a lynx scrabbling at his bedroom door and no sign of his mother, it was terribly real. Their number grew and grew.

Nevertheless most people got up every morning on the normal number of legs. They ate breakfast. They drove to work. They watched vids, tucked the kids in, and kissed their partners goodnight.

It's the way of cities.

For its part, the Scarlet Citadel paid this strange series of events with the same attitude as the summer flooding. Life went on inside the tower. Of course Knickerbocker reported to Wendy Dragontail. Evidently the mice, rats, bats, and other vermin weren't happy about these changes in their ecosystem. Wendy added the matter to a long and complicated list, and that was that.

Gormon Hughes Senior, who didn't own a television, only heard about the "people transforming into animals" panic from a couple of elderly women who visited the teashop. After they left he checked up on Boochums and the mystery dog. He'd asked around about Ernie without a sliver of success. The old codger could be anywhere. But there was the matter of the arm. Ernie's arm had been amputated in a workplace accident, and he'd spent a chunk of the insurance payout on a newfangled metal limb powered by cogwheel hardware. The mystery wolfhound was also missing an arm. A metal one was socketed in its place. Tiny cogs spun at the wrist and tricep. Feeling ridiculous, Gormon said the name Ernie, only to have his horror crystalize when the dog yapped happily and wagged its tail as though the name delighted it. Or perhaps gave it relief because someone had finally recognized it...

That was October 16th. It was, by anyone's metric, a gorgeous day. The sun shone on car windshields, the air was crisp enough for cardigans if not fur coats, and the whole world seemed covered with a bowl of lovely blue. Broadly speaking the city was treeless, but in Redspire there were hornbeams, cherry dogwood, buckeye, weeping birch, locust, oak, and maple, and all flamed red and ochre and gold with the turn of the season. On the botanic floor imported animals were getting their artificial homes ready for hibernation. It ought to have been a reposeful time, but the tower was always busy with one thing or another. Eurydice's credits and Iphigenia's magical items beckoned constantly, not to mention press tours, Hippodrome events, and the trappings of corporate social responsibility— all these went hand in hand with crisis management, of which there might be several on any given day.

Hughes, fresh from another round against the devilishly skilled Paris, listened to his dad on the telephone. He was glad he'd convinced him to have it installed. What he heard bothered him deeply. Word of these alleged transformations had of course reached him, but it was strange how life in the tower detached you from the immediacy of city trouble. That trouble had been his whole life. Now he was embroiled in a new rigmarole, and it took real concern in his father's voice to yank Hughes out of it.

"Let's say the dog is Ernie," said Hughes. "God, I can't believe I just said that."

"Doesn't feel real," affirmed Gormon.

"Right. Um. Okay, okay. Let's say Ernie has morphed somehow. These other people in the city have too. There must be some commonality linking them. Was Ernie behaving oddly?"

His father thought about it. "The last time I spoke to him he seemed okay. A little washclothed, maybe."

"You mean tired?"

"Tired, yeah. Our old neighbor Sheila used to say that. Wonder what became of her."

"She got married," said Hughes absently.

Ernie had been showing signs of fatigue.

Not much to go on, but it was a start.

"I'll ask around about it, Dad." As an afterthought, he said, "I'll have some kibble sent over too."

"Thanks, son."

He hung up, wondering if he should contact Wendy Dragontail or John Isherwood first. *Neither,* he decided. *Wendy's probably got a dozen irons in the fire, some of them likely to do with the state of emergency around these beastly appearances. And there are three drops to Eurydice this afternoon, which means Doctor John is going to be neck-deep in data. No, my best bet for the moment is Falstaff.*

The butler had his powdered, carefully manicured finger on the pulse of Redspire.

He dialed the number for the administration office on the first floor. Falstaff wouldn't be there, but the office kept a copy of his daily planner in case of emergencies.

Hughes recalled his father's description of the dog. A gray-whiskered wolfhound with one metal limb. *Seems like an emergency,* he thought and pushed the call button.

Instead of the normal one-two chime, the connection gave an odd staccato sound, and then a monotone note hummed into his ear.

He was sitting on the edge of his bed, the fabric of his shirt stuck to the small of his back with rapidly drying sweat. The note went on droning. There was a thin quality to it. Waspish. Slowly, Hughes' face crimped in a frown. Like his dad, he was a newbie to the wonderful world of telecommunication. By luck he'd never encountered a busy line before. He didn't know it *was* busy, only that the sound was different than usual.

His dad's controlled anxiety had spooked him, and this only increased his tension. He took the phone from his ear with an uncomprehending look that verged on irritation and listened again. Now the drone was gone. There was nothing to hear.

One speedy rinse in the shower later he was toweled, dressed, coated, and ready to find out what was going on. He opened his door and came face to face with Tommy Fahrenheit. The curly-haired man's head almost brushed the lintel of Hughes' door. The corridor's pillars framed him on either side, their columns encircled by maple leaves like bloody handprints. Tommy handed him a cup and saucer. "*Une tasse du café.*"

"*Merci,*" said Hughes in Champleurs.

"Walk with me."

"Actually, Tommy, I've got to..."

"It will only take a moment."

They fell into step together, the best pageant fighter in Corinth City and, well, the other one. Hughes had to jog to keep up with his companion's long-legged strides.

"I have spoken to Hector," Tommy said. "He believes that the rumors are true."

Hughes' mind was full of rumors about people turning into animals, so the look he gave Tommy was perplexed, as you might have guessed.

"I am referring to the tales of your exploits in Eurydice," said Tommy. "They are numerous and full of compliments."

"Are they?"

"Drink your *café.*"

Hughes sniffed suspiciously. "It smells like wet dog."

"It does not smell like wet dog. Your Corinthian heritage has given you nostrils that revel in soup made from potatoes and other such prosaic aromas."

Hughes sipped his coffee. It didn't taste like wet dog. It tasted like several dogs dipped in dirty rainwater.

Or several damp wolfhounds. I've got to hurry this along. "What did you want to talk about, Tommy?"

"Hector is South Corinthian, but before it was sacked his town of Troy carried the heritage of ancient Champleurs. Thus the dominant alleles in his body are the same as mine, and I must respect his attempts at *splendif.*"

"I still don't know what *splendif* is," Hughes admitted.

"Nor will you ever," said Tommy Fahrenheit candidly. "You are honored."

"I am?"

"*Certainement.* By speaking on your behalf Hector has afforded you status in my eyes. Are you aware of the drops today?"

"To Eurydice, yeah."

"There is also one scheduled for Iphigenia. A retrieval team. They will return with two monsters from the swamps of that other world." Hughes followed him round a bend in the corridor leading to the elevator. "I will fight the greater monster at The Hippodrome. You will fight the lesser, stimulating the crowd for the main event. In your Corinthian blues *musique*, this is called the Warmup Act."

Hughes was flabbergasted. "You want me to open for you?"

"*Oui.*"

"At The Hippodrome?"

"You will be introduced as a promising new talent. A prodigy, perhaps." Tommy flattened his hand and screwed it side to side in a gesture of uncertainty. "It is lies, this marketing speech, but to the audience it is delicious as bread to the starving pauper, or wine to the parched alcoholic."

"Does this mean you don't think I'm a sexually incompetent lemming?"

Tommy took his mostly full coffee. "I would not say this," he said, and drank. "The second thing is this: have you spare linens I might borrow?"

Hughes was starting to feel like he might need a lie down. "Linens?"

"For my bed," Tommy explained. "Mine have not been changed in five days. The man who comes with fresh ones did not come on Tuesday."

Today was Thursday. Hughes supposed his linens were changed sometimes, but he'd requested his newspaper blanket. Falstaff hadn't even questioned him about it.

"I might have some tucked away under the bed," he told Tommy. "I'll take a look later."

"*Merci beaucoup.* I am told some Corinthians do not change their bedclothes for weeks at a time. Such a flaccid approach to hygiene surprises even me, a scholar of your limp and spiritless culture."

"You must really put a lot of trust in Hector," Hughes said drily. "Partnering up with a member of a limp and spiritless culture just because he thinks I'm halfway decent at hitting things with my sword."

"Hector is formidable," said Tommy Fahrenheit. "Killing him was hard."

Hughes froze. "What?"

"He made it very difficult, is what I'm saying."

"You..." He felt as though the wind had been driven out of him. "You killed Hector?"

Tommy turned around and looked at him. He finished the coffee and set it down on the balustrade. "You did not know?" He sounded genuinely curious.

"Of course I didn't know." Anger rose from some grouty corner of his guts, a dark red mist of it. "And I certainly won't be fighting alongside you or before you or anywhere near you. I'd rather bite down on broken glass and hiccup than, well, than... so don't ask me about it again. How can you even be here?" he snapped. "How has no one done something about you, you racist—you *murderous* bastard?"

"Race is merely a symptom whereby the effects of culture can be diagnosed," said Tommy evenly. "But this is no time to debate ethnographic somatism, when you are so incensed. Do you call all soldiers murderers?"

A shiver ran through the sizzling fog of rage. Hughes hesitated. "You were a soldier in the war with Champleurs? That can't be right. You would have only been..."

"Nine years old," said Tommy Fahrenheit. "Almost ten, which made me one of the oldest in my troop. General Ulysse took Troy with her wooden bull trap seven months before the war ended. I was conscripted along with other children three months before that. Later, by the time Origné's people evacuated their town, while the blood soaked their hill and gave rise to the blooms of mirolaen, our king was more desperate than ever. A decree was sent early on the day of defeat conscripting children as young as five. I do not doubt that should we have won at Origné, the king would have pushed knives into the hands of babes still sticky with amniotic fluid from their mother's wombs." He shrugged his enormous shoulders, then grew stern when he saw Hughes' expression. "Do not make this face. This one." His eyes bulged. His mouth slung open. He held it for demonstration, then let the mask of horror fall away. "It is offensive to regard."

Hughes felt his ears heat up. "Were you inside the wooden bull? The one General Ulysse used to ambush the people of Troy."

Tommy nodded.

"I got it wrong before," said Hughes. "You're not a racist murderous bastard. You're a racist murderous bastard who used to be a racist murderous bastard kid."

"It was war." Tommy seemed unphased by Hughes' barbs. He gazed out over the balustrade at the midfloor garden flowers, perhaps replacing each blossom mentally with snow-white mirolaen. "If it comforts you, Hector forgave me."

"I find that hard to believe."

"Scratch at reality all you like, Monsieur Hughes. Your beliefs make no mark on it. Ah." He brightened. "Perhaps you may keep your spare linens in reserve after all."

Two members of tower staff came out of the elevator. One of them riffled through a daily planner. The other carried a mound of bedclothes so wide and tall it obscured their whole head.

Hughes and Tommy caught their conversation mid-tirade.

"—least he could have done," said the daily planner. "Even so, look at this list! The specifications are intolerable."

"They can't be that bad," said the mound of bedclothes. "Read me a random one."

The daily planner read aloud. "Lorna Blacktower: full arrangement; lavender scented sheets; frumped pillows; room to be aired during turnover; one copy of this week's *Neglectigée* to be placed on her bedside table... For God's sake, now I need *magazines*?"

"It does seem overwhelming," soothed the mound of bedclothes. Something shifted in the pile. "Oh dear. I think I'm about to tip over."

"It's so unfair," complained the daily planner. "How can one person keep so many uniquely shaped plates spinning?"

"Really, I'm beginning to teeter here."

"It's intolerable."

"Help."

The bedclothes began to cascade, only to land like wounded birds in the arms of Tommy Fahrenheit. He sniffed the sheets. "These linens have the consistency and smell of horsehair."

"That's because they're for Elena Longfellow," said the daily planner, snatching back the linens and restacking them on the poor obscured fellow. "We haven't got your things, Mister Fahrenheit. Your bedclothes are part of load six-through-eight, which we should deliver..." He consulted some notes. "Oh, at this rate, next Wednesday."

"Can you tell me where Falstaff is?" said Hughes.

The staff members opened their mouths to reply.

"I will lend a hand to room turnovers," cut in Tommy. "It is imperative that I have fresh linen for my slumber."

"It can't happen," said the daily planner. "We're way behind on everything today because..."

Tommy Fahrenheit leaned over them like a steel wrecking ball over a to-be-demolished zone. "It *will* happen, little Corinthian. I will fetch my gloves of alacrity." He turned to Hughes. "We will discuss The Hippodrome when the retrieval team returns. You will need a new coat. The one you wear is a dismal flap of fabric. Donning it will tell audiences you are poverty-stricken or a lackadaisy whore who prostitutes his psyche to underground fashion on behalf of the pimp called Transgression. I would not want the crowd to jeer at you. *Au revoir.*"

"Bloody Champleurs," muttered the daily planner as Tommy vanished into the elevator. "Come along, we must get a head start on these rooms before he returns to muck it all up."

"Wait," said Hughes. "I need a word with Falstaff."

"Don't we all," said the mound of bedclothes.

"What, he's not around?"

"He's around all right," said the daily planner. "We're just not sure which one he is. Haven't you heard?"

No. But then I hadn't heard that it was Tommy Fahrenheit who killed Hector either.

"I'm out of the loop here," Hughes told them. "What do you mean, *we're not sure which one Falstaff is?*"

"Which penguin," came the muffled voice from behind the mound of bedclothes. "We're not sure which penguin he is."

CHAPTER FORTY-THREE

"Far as I can tell he was down here supervising a delivery of food. We have over a thousand clients here in the global menagerie. I looks after them best I can, and I'm the best at it, but in a pinch on busy days like today I likes to call down Falstaff. He's a prissy so-and-so, but he's good with the clients, I'll give him that."

Thin and grumpy, groundskeeper Jolly Winkins was a man with the look and general temperament of a rake. A walrus was eating sea cucumbers out of his hand.

Hughes rucked his coat tighter about himself and mused on what the groundskeeper had said. They were in the coldest part of the menagerie. "When did Falstaff transform into a penguin?" he asked Jolly.

"Not sure exactly. I went away to feed the turtles at half past seven. They get uppity when they ain't 'et breakfast. I come back, and Falstaff wasn't anywhere to be found. I look around for him anyway, and it's only when I cross the icebowl—that's what we call yonder frozen bit on the lake—that I copped we'd one extra penguin."

"Couldn't you have miscounted?"

Jolly's lips twisted. "Miscount the clients? Don't be daft. So I sees the penguins have sprouted a new member, and since they ain't worms what grow other worms if you cut them in half, and since there's talk of transmogrificationalwossit going on at the moment, I made what you might call an informed bit of logical reasoning." Jolly shook his head. "Miscount the clients. *Tsk.* Never heard the like."

Hughes eyed the penguins. They were loafing around, although he was given to understand that standing about looking aloof was the default state for penguins.

"They do look a bit like butlers," he said.

"Bit of natural irony, that," Jolly agreed grudgingly. "Hard to tell which is which, though I think that one's him."

"Which?"

"That one."

"I see."

The penguin looked identical to the others.

"Was Falstaff acting strangely?" asked Hughes, amateur sleuth.

"No more strange'n usual."

"Did he seem tired?"

Jolly thought about it. "Now you mention, I suppose he did, at that. Usually spritely as anything, our Falstaff. This morning he came in looking prickly and mopey, like he wanted some pointers on hibernation from the hedgehogs."

Visible exhaustion. If Dad's right about Ernie then that's a shared symptom. Hughes wondered if there was anything blatant he was missing.

"No other odd behavior that you could see?"

"Nah," said Jolly, giving the walrus beside him a friendly pat. "But he was tired, true enough. How'd you know to ask me that?"

"I made what you might call an informed bit of logical reasoning."

The groundskeeper snorted.

In their black and white suits the penguins were getting lively. Some lifted their wings a bit. Others chattered, their drooping beaks full of gossip, most likely about their newest member. Hughes looked past them, deep in thought.

"Jolly?"

"Nngh?"

"Have you ever heard of people turning into animals?"

Jolly scratched the thicket of stubble under his chin. "Knickerbocker count?"

"I don't think so."

"Then no. Good thing too." Jolly shook the cucumber bits off his hand, took out a box of cigarettes, and offered one to Hughes, who took it and put it in his pocket in case things somehow managed to get even more stressful. "Some people reckon we're still monkeys picking nits out of one another's hair. Reading and writing and 'rithmetic, that's all for show. And some people don't just thinks it. They likes it. Want to be apes getting up to all sorts. No more worries about school lunches or mortgage repayments. Back to the base apes, they say. Back to knuckling our way round the place. Who needs philosophy when you got bananas?" Jolly lit up, inhaled, and blew a devious little smoke ring. He looked at Hughes from the side of his face. "Rubbish. People wouldn't have a clue how to be animals. It's all in the head. Like how dogs used to be wolves in the forests a long time ago. Still gnawing on bones, but now it's master or mistress what forks up the treat. They got civilization. We got it too. No use wishing it wasn't because it is." Another smoke ring dissolved over the gelid waters. "Be hell in a handbasket, people turning into things they don't know how to be."

"Does Lady Dragontail know?" said Hughes. "About Falstaff?"

"Reckon so. Whole tower knows, on account of it falling to pieces."

Hughes understood what he meant. On his way to see Jolly in the menagerie he'd overheard cooks squalling at porter staff, porter staff griping to maids, and the telltale snip of lighters. Maids chain smoke because as the last unappreciated link in the complaint chain they are forced to take up vices. Most maids have livers and lungs that would shock you. Hughes had noticed meals burned. Dust accumulated. Deliveries were missed. Potted coffee went cold. Requests and tasks stacked in a pancake tower of unhappiness. Everything was going higgledy-piggledy, and everyone cursed Falstaff with one breath and wished he were there with the next.

"Things fall apart," said Hughes.

"The center cannot hold," Jolly said, completing the quote. "Where you off to?"

"I've got to go see a woman about a dog."

Jolly tamped the end of his smoke, sending up a mosaic of embers, and put it in a baggie. "You do that."

***

The elevator wouldn't budge.

Hughes thought, *First the telephone, now this.*

He pressed the button for the eighty-eighth floor again. No dice. He pressed it and held it down. Nada.

Redspire didn't have stairs. Was he trapped in the global menagerie? On any other day that would be an excuse to ramble and pet the cootsie-wootsie widdle panthers, as Cate called them. Today it was a problem, and a big one at that.

Reason shoved claustrophobia aside. He would try another button. Failing that, another elevator. There were at least three on every floor of the tower.

He thumbed the eighty-seventh floor (some part of him recalling its pomegranate decor from the evening of his Triumph, though for a fistful of credits he couldn't tell you what business was carried out there), and wonder of wonders, the cranks began to spin, cables spooled, and the elevator began to climb.

Hughes was puzzled. The eighty-seventh was fine, so what about the floor above that? The eighty-eighth was the Lunarlight Wing. At its heart, the Dragon's Lair where stone dragons curled around a fireplace and the last living drake herself sat behind her desk of burled walnut, her hoard invisible because every coin and jewel was knowledge, and that meant sovereignty.

He wondered if Wendy was okay.

He wondered if the same magic that had transformed Falstaff and Ernie and who knew who else into animals had got its scale on. Could the eighty-eighth be blocked for safety? Was a dragon up there, her breath melting the top of the tower like an ice-cream cone on a hot June afternoon?

As he passed the eighty-sixth, his thoughts full of tile and glass and stone dribbling in rivers on molten slag down the face of Redspire, he became aware of a mounting sound. *The gurgle and rush of dragonfire.* He quailed. His fingers crept unconsciously to the emergency stop button. The elevator juddered, the doors slid open, and the caterwaul of a full-blown mob rode over him in disorienting waves.

Pomegranates were certainly prominent in the design of the eighty-seventh floor. But there were other things too, things that told a story. There were frescoes and tapestries and carpets and statues. They told the story of a young woman beckoned out of the safety of her garden by an older man with a disturbingly long face. There was a grim, forbidding world under the sweet beauty of the garden. There stood the young woman and the older man arm in arm, his head crowned in fire of purple and gold and her hand clutching a half-eaten pomegranate, its seeds spilling. Spring and summer showed the woman back in her garden, surrounded by comfort while autumn and winter snatched her back into that bleak undercroft. The young woman didn't look happy about this arrangement. Lamps of blown glass shaped into plump fruit blushed with a ripe red-pink light. A plaque called this the Proserpina Wing, though a more appropriate inscription might have been "asylum" or perhaps "run."

It was a wall-to-wall kerfuffle and no mistake. People gesticulated and shouted, shoulders jostling, shoes scuffing carpet, mashed toes, veins popping in temples, spittle flecking and foaming, calls for calm, calls for order, calls for explanations, someone ringing a lunchtime bell senselessly, tinkling a glass with a spoon, rabbles rowing and ruckus-thumping in the tight-thronged crush.

Hughes cast about for anyone who looked like they were taking charge, but it was impossible. Someone backed into him. He stumbled, only for hard-knuckled hands to steady him.

"Hello, Rosemund," he said.

"Good morning, Hughes. Looking for her Ladyship?"

"I am. What's going on with the eighty-eighth floor?"

"No one's sure. There's been no communication. Coupled with Falstaff's enpenguining, people are getting upset. I need to send a sensitive parcel to my family in Daethumberland, and no one I've spoken to has the first inklings of how that might work. I shouldn't have relied on Falstaff. I'm a grown woman in a dangerous job, but..." She scrubbed a palm over her jaw awkwardly. "He's just always there to help, right?"

Hughes thought of the time he'd telephoned the butler before his first date with Cate Jubilee. Falstaff hadn't hesitated. What had he said? Something so serious it was almost comical. Oh, yes! Falstaff had listened to Hughes' romantic plight, and then said in his clipped, fastidious tones, *This is a serious matter.* "Always there to help," Hughes parroted. "That's Falstaff. A miracle worker in gold-buckled shoes."

"It's all very muddled at the moment." Rosemund Valkyrie looked around, clearly as unsure of who was in charge around here as Hughes was. Her blonde hair stuck out in corkscrews.

"Sleeping poorly?" he asked her, trying to keep his tone casual.

"Bad dreams," she replied. "I usually don't." She flashed him a brief, perfunctory smile. "Dream, that is. One of the cleaning staff told me I was sleepwalking in the night too. Haven't done that since I was in ladybug-spotted dungarees."

Bad dreams, Hughes thought. Neurons began to fire at the back of his brain. *Bad dreams...*

"Hughes," a voice whispered.

He looked up. Rosemund was up on her tiptoes. She wasn't paying him any attention. *Then who...*

"*Hughes.*"

He turned, slowly and cautiously in case it was someone unpleasant.

It was quite the reverse!

From a pomegranate seed-shaped mirror, Cate grinned at him.

You're back! he wanted to shout it. That would make the fact of her return realer than real. The words fizzed through him, champagne-hissing joy. *Cate's back! Check the meteorology report, gentlemen! Hurricane Jubilee's a'blowin! Lock up your spouses and nail down your houses. It'll all work out in the end.*

"But I never asked why you're up here," said Rosemund.

Behind her, Hughes spied Cate raising a finger to her lips.

"It's Tommy," he improvised. "He needs bedclothes."

Rosemund's fair-colored brows rose like feathered wings. "Is it for his *splendif?*"

"Yes. No. Um." Hughes watched those brows rise a little higher. "I didn't ask."

Cate was pointing to a narrow hallway leading off from this central area of the wing.

"I'm stifled," Hughes told Rosemund. "Aren't you stifled?"

"No, not really."

"Must be your outfit. Very good airflow in... erm..." He faltered, then soldiered on. "In fur. Well known fact."

"Is it?"

"Absolutely," he said, sending his legs frantic signals to start moving toward the narrow hall. "Why I was only saying recently that it really is the best for sweltering, ah, conditions. Yes. In fur you cannot err." He gave her a cheerful smile. "I'll just go and source some, shall I?" he said and ran for it.

Rosemund stared after him bewilderedly.

Cate led him through the wing, a compass glimpsed through mirrors. Pointing where? He couldn't say. He followed anyway.

Cate's grin never wavered. It was wide and bright and full of girlish mischief. *Come, come, Proserpina,* that grin said. *Gardens are sweet, but my world is sweeter still.*

After losing track entirely of where he was, Hughes hurried by a cabinet full of books, cowspotted with age and encased in glass, through an arched door and at last found himself in a small, uncomplicated office with a computer set on a tidy desk. Its hardware was the only source of convolution in the room. Spiraled in toothy cogs, the keyboard and screen were both spotlessly clean.

There was a soft sound. The air changed. Hughes stepped back as a door swung open where before there was only smooth wall. Cate emerged.

It's been five weeks, he told himself. *She left me a letter that spoke to incredible vulnerability. Whatever I do, I mustn't trivialize that by being obvious.*

Cate came close and stopped, her chin jutting.

There was an expectant pause.

"You're back then," said Hughes.

Damn damn damn.

She gave him a sardonic look and went back through the secret door.

On reflection, a hello kiss had probably been too much to hope for.

Hughes caught up with her. "Was that Falstaff's room back there?"

"Yes."

He waited for more. More didn't arrive.

Uncertainty sent up a warning flare. *Hm.*

Hughes looked around. They were in a tunnel. Tiny clawed things like the hands of baby dragons held lanterns that guttered to life as they passed. The tunnel coiled round and round, ascending like a snake slithering unseen inside the walls of the tower. At one point, so faint it might have been his ears playing tricks on him, he thought he heard raised voices. Were they passing the outraged crowd?

He had a misty recollection of Falstaff telling him about renovations in the tower years ago. Had this tunnel been built then, or back when the Scarlet Citadel was finding its feet? Were there more like it? There was a pleasant thought. A whole network of hidden passages leading who knew where. Spies and assassins and... other sordid types would just adore a feature like that.

He cleared his throat and gave Cate a quizzical look in an attempt to draw her into conversation. When that didn't work, he did his best to look like someone who really wanted to get something important off their chest. Hughes was a specialist at conveying stuff like that. His face became the very portrait of divulgement.

This however, did not have the desired effect. Cate ignored him.

Hmm.

Warning flares burst in his head, one after the other. This was bad. Hughes was no expert on young women, but you'd have to be thick as clotted cream to not recognize the silent treatment. The only question was: Why was she angry?

Asking her would probably make things worse.

No, it was obviously something... well, obvious.

He had read her parting letter so many times he'd ended up committing it to memory. In the increasingly frosty silence, he was reminded of one of its closing remarks. *I'm off to Eurydice for a while. Maybe when I'm back I'll be quandary-less, and you'll be insight-full.*

I've disappointed her, he realized. *Just now, a few moments ago while she hopped from mirror to mirror, she looked happy, right? That's because she was hoping I'd resolved things on my end. Turned the shortcomings into long-goings, so to speak. She believed she would open the secret door in Falstaff's room and there I'd be—insight-full and ready for the next step in our relationship. Possibly with roses and a box of chocolates for good measure.*

But if that was the case, did that mean she'd refused to make up her own mind about the whole thing? Was she foisting the decision making onto him?

Hughes doubted it. Foisting wasn't Cate's style. The more likely scenario was this: Sometime during her adventure she had weighed up the cost of being a hypocrite and decided she could foot the bill. She wanted him to open up. No bullshit. No excuses. *Tell me who you are, Gormon Hughes.*

That had to be it. It explained the grin. The prospect had excited her.

And then she'd opened the door, and stuck out her chin, and let the expectant silence pour out behind her and over him, and then he'd said...

Oh God, *he'd* said...

He smothered a groan.

It's funny how quickly one emotion gives way to the other.

No. Not funny.

The other one.

Terrifying.

On the heels of his embarrassment, right on cue, Hughes felt *it* arrive. That nasty bitterness furring his tongue. Resentment. *You're no angel,* he wanted to tell her. *Your wings aren't open to anyone who wants to look. When I saw your newest tattoo, you went stiff as a board. Why? See, you've got secret doors too, Cate. Ones I can't open. Maybe you're willing to pay the cost of being a hypocrite, but who says I'll charge? No angel.* That fantastic gladness at seeing her was now a crumpled wreck. When his mind looked for them, all of the questions he'd been intending to ask her had vanished. Just like that. Wonder of wonders.

Their feet followed a steady incline. Ahead the tunnel split, the stone snake becoming a hydra. Without hesitation Cate sallied down one of these, and less than a minute later she opened a door. Hughes stepped through.

He blinked.

They were in the antechamber outside the Dragon's Lair.

Suddenly Falstaff's ability to appear from nowhere and at exactly the right time made much more sense.

"Ah, Hughes."

Aside from a sweater enameled in a scale pattern, Wendy seemed to have avoided the inconvenience of becoming a dragon. A spike of jade fastened her bone-pale hair in a bun. On its plinth, the room's record player made no music. Its stylus was still, a hobbled crane unable to lift the mood.

"Do sit down." Wendy waved her hand at a young man in the corner. He was tapping frantically away at a computer. "This is Montcrieff. With the telephones jammed up, he's become my personal dispatcher in this trying time. Speak freely around him. I have a strong suspicion that if the roof were to cave in, he would only notice if a piece of debris cracked his screen. Cate, thank you for coming so quickly. Isaac's report tells me it was a lamentably unproductive trip."

"Maelen and the Bonemeal Boys burned most of the necromancer's writings when they took control of Aldersglen. We salvaged what we could and followed up. One lead looked promising for a while. Turned out to be a wild goose chase." Cate raised herself into the windowsill, one leg wedged against the glass, the other dangling its hobnailed boot over the floor. "All in all, a complete bust."

Wendy Dragontail jotted something in her notes. "How is the atmosphere on the eighty-seventh?"

"Firework powder, your Ladyship."

Wendy looked up. "Explain."

"One struck match and it'll all go boom," said Cate.

"I see. Hughes, I trust you are aware of our present situation?"

"People are being transmogrified," said Hughes. He chewed his cheek. *Oh hell, nothing ventured and all that.* "I think it's because of a dream."

That snared their attention.

"What makes you say that, Hughes?" said Wendy Dragontail sharply.

"Just a hunch, my Lady. That and some of what Jolly Winkins calls logical reasoning." His brow creased. "In so far as anything can be logical when butlers start belly-sliding on ice, I suppose."

Hughes looked between them. Both Cate and Wendy were watching him intently.

"It all started earlier this summer," he began.

He told them about his dream, only omitting Mr. Glint and Kim Kallaimon. Unlike other gauzy phantasmagoria strewn across his life, he could picture this one with a vividness that was almost supernatural. He described the carousel, the sinister ticket sellers, and the figure with burning yellow eyes.

"Yellow eyes?"

Wendy's voice was so jagged it made Hughes jump.

"Yeah. Really bright like torches."

"You're quite sure?" she pressed him.

"Yes, my Lady."

He heard a small noise under Wendy's desk. At first Hughes thought it was her playing a pensive game of kick-the-slippers. It was soft enough to pass for slippers, that was true. But there was an organic quality to it that made him think of cats curling their tails around your leg.

"Were there nightjars in this dream?" said Wendy, rerouting his train of thought.

"Nightjars?"

"Caprimulgus Mysicordelianos. Birds, Hughes. Small nocturnal birds that migrate to Corinth in the spring and leave in early September in search of warmer climates."

"I wouldn't know," Hughes replied honestly. "I'm not very good at recognizing birds. I used to think crows were eagles that had fallen into a chimney."

"Never mind. Do continue."

"My dad said Ernie Wilks looked dead tired. Jolly Winkins said Falstaff was looking pretty peaky too. I'm sure you'd have noticed if that were true or not, my Lady."

"I can do better than that," she said. "What if I told you that Falstaff has been plagued by dreams very much like the one you describe?"

"I'd be both vindicated and terrified, Your Worship," said Hughes. "Rosemund Valkyrie mentioned bad dreams to me only fifteen minutes ago. It would imply black magic, the kind you read about in fairy stories. The ones that aren't quite evil enough to keep kids up at night but scary enough that they remember them for the rest of their lives. I'd say we're up a certain creek without a certain paddle, in other words." He swallowed. "*Is* that what you're telling me?"

Wendy leaned over her desk. "*I say, Montcrieff! Can you hear me?*"

The young man grunted something like, "Urk."

"*Could you get in touch with Knickerbocker please? He's to ask any people who were turned into rodents if they had worrisome dreams about a carousel before they transformed.*"

"Curk?"

"*Yes, a car-ou-sel, Montcrieff. Knickerbocker will know what you mean.*"

"Urk."

"*Similarly, I'd like you to send a message to our contacts at the various media agencies. The approved list should be in the files you've got somewhere. Tell them to conduct interviews with traceable links to the affected people. Family, friends, and suchlike. The focus of the interview will be those dreams I just mentioned, and they are to send their transcripts to us before submitting to their editors. Have you got that, Montcrieff?*"

"Urk."

"*Thank you.*" Wendy leaned back, then seemed to remember something and leaned forward again. "*And another thing, Montcrieff!*"

"Urk?"

"*Inform Doctor John Isherwood I have an update for him, and he is to make his way to me using the Proserpina tunnel.*"

"Urk."

"*Thank you.*" She leaned back, massaging her throat. "I ought to have gotten you to bring me a pot of tea from the kitchen, Cate. Without Falstaff's regular doses, I seem to be going into withdrawal."

There was that noise again. It was sinuous, just like a cat's brushing tail.

"What is that?" said Hughes.

"What is what?" Wendy checked an earmark and flicked to that page in her notes. "Quite recently Doctor Isherwood had a frightening experience in his study. A large nightjar killed a starling on his balcony and perched on his feeder. It watched him for an indeterminate period of time, quite motionless."

"Sounds unnerving," said Cate.

"The following day I had him check his readings from both portals. Iphigenia was stable. Eurydice was not. Evidently there was some sort of fluctuation. I believe graphs are involved. Rather above my head, you understand. In consultation with a few trusted graduates from the University, John has concluded that something came through the portal on the night you both returned from your battle in Castle Aldersglen."

"The nightjar," murmured Hughes.

On the windowsill, Cate drew a deep breath and let it go. Her face was pinched with disquiet. Hughes imagined he looked about the same.

"Allow me to string these beads into a coherent necklace." Wendy steepled her fingers. "Several months ago Hughes began to dream of a carousel, a device that is constructed from the likenesses of animals. At the same time, a creature of presently unknown origin appears in Iphigenia and kills Laurana's unit. Hughes is the only survivor. Time passes. The dream inflicts itself on other people. In Eurydice, Isaac Lawless is captured and questioned. Something I kept private, for it held no bearing on either of you, was this: One line of questioning concerned a prisoner we have here at the tower. Frank Gallant, otherwise known as the Dream Warrior. He is the figure you've described from your dream, Hughes. Frank Gallant's eyes burn like yellow torches."

Hughes and Cate both exploded with questions. Wendy raised two fingers and quieted them.

"Upon your return from Aldersglen, an unwelcome visitor to our world visits John Isherwood. John admits that he has, since childhood, had recurring nightmares about his uncle's collection of stuffed nightjars. Behold, the beads connect. Some a bit more wonkily than the others, perhaps. I still have to uncover the meaning behind the two-headed wolf with its heart-laden arms. What role it plays in all this. And Hughes' Performance ability remains a complete mystery. Nevertheless, when viewed from this cold vantage point, a theme emerges."

"Dreams," said Cate. "Whoever is behind this is turning people into animals via their dreams."

"Who is Frank Gallant?" Hughes demanded. "It's about time I knew."

Wendy's fingers drummed together. Once. Twice. She regarded him over the crescent moon-shaped nails. "The nightjar is not the first thing to cross over from Eurydice. Frank came first. My father, Walsingham, the Old Dragon, led the Citadel then. There was no prelude to what happened. It simply occurred. On All Hallow's Eve, October the 30th, Frank Gallant came crashing through the portal.

Chaos ensued. Around him people fell instantly asleep. Hallucinations seized a few. One woman bit her own tongue into two pink pieces. My father attempted to subdue Frank while Idris Corlum set up the Perfect Prison. The Old Dragon fell into a deep sleep. Unlike the others afflicted by Frank's slumbering curse, he stayed that way until he died."

"I'm sorry," said Hughes.

Wendy Dragontail's expression did not change. "Thank you," she said eventually. "We know nothing about Frank. The term Dream Warrior was given to him by the rumor mill, which grinds out the most tenacious and long-lasting loaves, I find."

"We've got to let him out of the Perfect Prison," said Hughes. "He's been trying to speak to me. Warn me, maybe."

"You can't be sure of that," said Cate. "He might have been about to undo whatever is protecting you from the spell. If we let him go, he might turn you into a puppy, and we'd be no closer to solving all this."

"Or a rottweiler," he muttered.

The ghost of a smile touched Cate's lips. It told him he was still high in her estimation, that she still cared for him very much. It also told him that clever inside jokes would not thaw the layer of frost between them. Only one thing would, and if he could pull his head out of his bottom and recognize a good thing for what it was, she might consider resurrecting her smile from ghost to grin.

All of that in the tug of several facial muscles. He wished he were crapper at reading them. What was the use in noticing things like that when you couldn't act on them?

"Cate has the right of it," said Wendy. "We can only be sure that Frank is not responsible for our current predicament. Why else would he remain quiet for so long? The prison has him sealed. I admit, given my family history with him, the idea of allowing him out of the Perfect Prison strikes me as either desperate or stupid. Possibly both." She sighed. "Alas, with things degrading rapidly it seems we are left with no alternative."

"Wait," said Hughes. "Before we go on, we should do something about the people who've been changed."

"Ah, yes. A sterling point." Wendy leaned forward in her chair. *"I say, Montcrieff! Can you hear me?"*

"Urk."

"We must ensure that those who have been turned into animals do not come to harm. Correction, any more harm. Contact veterinary groups and other animal rights organizations. Not pest control. Under no circumstances are you to contact pest control. In fact, notify our production team here in the Citadel that all pest controllers and zookeepers are to be placed on administrative leave. With pay, naturally. Let production know that secrecy is of the utmost importance. We cannot allow rumor to spread like fire through dry moss. Is that understood?"

"Urk."

"Thank you."

She leaned back. "Satisfied, Hughes?"

"More than, my Lady."

"Very well. Where was I?"

"Desperation and stupidity," supplied Cate helpfully.

"Indeed. The last refuge, one might call it." Morning was traipsing toward afternoon. Judging from the view through the office window it was still lovely outside. A block of sunshine had been moving slowly up from the carpet onto the desk. Now it touched Wendy's steepled fingers. Dust motes danced in the light. Wendy Dragontail's eyes lingered on their spirals and curlicues. When she spoke, it was in a voice free from all fire and mettle. "Egg whites and sugar."

Then the bravado of command seemed to brim her full again. She straightened.

"We shall free Frank Gallant from his Perfect Prison." She must have seen the look of delight on Hughes' face. She quickly added, "I should note that doing so presents certain difficulties."

"No problem, Your Worship," said Hughes. Tingles of anticipation bolted up his back. He was going to meet the figure from his dreams. Finally, he would hear what Frank Gallant had to tell him. "Where is the Perfect Prison?"

"On the eighty-ninth floor," said Wendy. "But..."

"Eighty-ninth?" Hughes couldn't help but grin a rueful grin. "I'm learning all sorts of things today. A whole extra floor? Well, you live, you learn. Shall we go, Cate?"

"While your aplomb is commendable, Hughes, you will soon find you are understating matters." Wendy laid her forearms on her desk. Her gimlet gaze withered the grapes of his enthusiasm to raisins of doubt. "A more accurate summation would be 'some' problem."

"What more could there be?" Cate said. "Aren't the nuisances piled high enough already?"

"Certainly. I fear however, that the mountain of our predicaments has gained another significant slope."

They frowned at her.

"How so?" said Cate.

"During my daily visit to the eighty-ninth floor, I discovered the turnkey of the Perfect Prison in an... unseemly state."

"I don't understand," said Hughes. "What kind of unseemly state?"

"This one." Needing both hands for it, the leader of the Scarlet Citadel lifted something out from under her desk, whereupon it proceeded to stare at Hughes and Cate. They stared back, their mouths forming perfect 'o' shapes. Those soft sounds Hughes had been hearing suddenly made horrifying sense.

Oh no, he thought.

"Cate Jubilee, Gormon Hughes," said Wendy Dragontail formally. "Let me introduce you to what I have reason to believe is currently Idris Corlum."

Idris Corlum churtled a greeting.

He was a stoat.

CHAPTER FORTY-FOUR

Afterward, Hughes was never quite sure how it had all been decided. There were some disagreements about the particulars, a bit of repartee and verbal jousting (mostly for the look of the thing), but in the end it was all set out in the proper order like silver soup spoons at a fancy supper.

"Marvelous," said Wendy Dragontail with a clap for emphasis. "I'll contact Desdemona Cauldronpot."

"Who?" said Hughes before Wendy could attract the attention of the eloquent Montcrieff.

"You haven't met her? Charming woman," said Wendy blithely. "A few spanners short of a toolbox but a consummate professional."

"That's good," said Hughes. "Um. A professional what?"

"Her magic item lets her put people to sleep," said Cate. "Her real name's Denise Caldwell, but she discovered occultism recently."

"Occultism?"

"You know. Auras and oozing candles. Ravens on skulls. Poetry that makes your eyeballs itch."

"Bangles?"

"Bangles often feature," agreed Cate. "You know. Occultism."

"So she discovered that and changed her name to Desdemona Cauldronpot?"

"Precisely."

The woman sounded a few spanners, wrenches, screwdrivers, and nails short of a toolbox to Hughes. He was a few pieces short of a jigsaw right now himself. When was the last time he'd eaten anything? Come to think of it, when was the last time he'd had a proper night's sleep? Could have been last night, could have been the dawn of the industrial era.

"And sorry," he said. "What exactly is Desdemona Cauldronpot going to do?"

"We were only saying," said Wendy. "Didn't you hear? *I say, Montcrieff!*"

"We're going to put you to sleep," said Cate under the hubbub of Wendy's instructions. "Since you seem to be protected from the dream curse, it makes sense."

Hughes remembered now. "Sorry. Got a bit lost in the conversational weeds there. So while I sleep I'm going to speak to the ticket collectors."

"How are you feeling about it?"

A picture of hands like misshapen spiders drew itself in his head. They plucked up tickets with a skittery speed, unhooked the partition rope, and ushered people onto the carousel with a welcoming gesture that made his stomach clench into a tight greasy ball.

"Remind me why I agreed to this?"

"You projected an agreeable air," said Cate, turning round so she could swing both legs over the floor.

"Haven't I got a choice?"

"Always." She looked at him. "But we don't." And while butterflies did indeed begin to flutter around his clenched belly, it was a greenish swarm, their wings dusted with the pollen of suspense and conviction.

Reluctant conviction, maybe.

But conviction nonetheless.

After all, how could a person receive a look like that and turn away?

Not even the insincerity forming a carapace around his broken heart could cope with that.

That was how he ended up sitting across from a woman who smelled like pervasive cat and jangled even when motionless.

"How does this work?" he asked her.

"You might try relaxing for a start," said the occultist formerly known as Denise. "Inhale of the incense. Feel the cosmic eccentricities as they inform your body."

"Inform my body of what?"

"That it is... very relaxed," said Desdemona. "Also you must practice the tranquility of soundless meditation."

"You mean shut up?"

"Yes."

Hughes shut up.

They were in a little alcove in the Lunarlight Wing. Cate and Wendy stood unobtrusively to one side. The alcove was lined with bookshelves. On Desdemona née Denise's orders a blackout curtain that deterred all external light and sound had been erected around them. Candlelight flickered on book bindings and suffused the smoke curling from the incense burner. Inexplicably, that also smelled of cat.

"I've had a word with the crowd on the eighty-seventh," Cate told Wendy in a hushed voice. "They're going to help gather those affected by the curse."

"Jolly good."

"It was really sweet actually," said Cate. "The moment I explained things it was as though all of their problems were whisked away. They filed into the elevator in one determined stream of bodies. I've never seen some of them look so... galvanized." Her tone was rich with pride. "Every single one of them was ready to... well, not kick arse perhaps, but definitely assist in the safeguarding of transmogrified buttock."

"The tower is not the city," said Wendy sagely. "But one is part of the other."

"I will now light the ceremonial candle," announced Desdemona. "By its flame the pathway to the dreamworld shall be illuminated."

"What are all these other ones doing?" said Hughes, forgetting the tranquility of soundless meditation.

"Helping me to see where the ceremonial wick is," she replied tartly. "So I can light it, all right? Does that work for you?"

"Sorry."

She gave him a piercing look and resumed her attempts to locate an unburned candidate in her box of matches.

"Speaking of streams," said Wendy. "The tide of incidents has thickened considerably. The city is quickly becoming a carnival with no ringmaster."

"I should go and help where I can," said Cate, compassionate patriot.

"No. There's no telling how long Hughes will be in the dream," dissuaded Wendy. "He could be in and out in the blink of an eye, and where would you be? Gallivanting heroically no doubt and quite useless in the grand scheme of things. Stay and be ready to lead Hughes wherever this business takes the pair of you. Indeed, take Denise's—ah—*Desdemona's* advice. Relax. Partake of the strangely feline-scented air."

"There we are," said Desdemona Cauldronpot. She held an unstruck match aloft in triumph. There was a sandy scratch, a *fizzle-puff* of igniting sulfur, and the ceremonial candle was lit. "Spirits," she intoned. "Convoke! Harken to my voice!"

Hughes wondered how she went grocery shopping.

Amalgams of flour, salt, and yeast! Fall into my consecrated basket from thy breadbound sepulchers! No, not seeded. It must be wholegrain, or it must not be, so sayeth the voices in my head, amen.

He suppressed a burst of laughter in the sufficiently harmonious dark.

He was mildly startled when the pillar of incense tipped against its iron casing. Smoke shivered. Had the candles dimmed too?

"The spirits are present," said Desdemona. "They touch our auras, make them incandescent. Our third eyes are about to open."

"Good luck," whispered Cate.

He shot her a grateful smile. She really was wonderful. Aggrieved as a bag of scorpions and still willing to wish him well. He really ought to consider unshelling this thing around his heart and letting her in. Later, of course. That was the thing about later. It was never "now."

"Now." Wicks blazed. They lit Desdemona from below, the lines of her face scored in otherworldly orange. The effect was rather persuasive. The best

Mysicordelian sibyls could learn a thing or two from her about stage lighting. "Gaze upon my brow, Gormon Bruise."

"Hughes."

"Whatever."

He gazed upon her brow. There was a circlet clasped around it. It must have been her magic item. At the center of the circlet was a sunset-colored tourmaline. Hughes squinted in the dimness. Had she... she hadn't drawn a dot in the middle of it, had she?

She had. During her costuming as Desdemona Cauldronpot, Denise Caldwell had taken a marker to her magic item. Now the stone stared at Hughes, a third eye open to the world of the mystical, earrings made of resin, and pets with names like Nightshade or Phantom.

He looked into it, aware his eyelids were trying to slam closed like lead curtains. He yawned a huge jaw-creaking yawn.

When had he gotten so...

***

... sleepy?

Hughes opened his eyes and thought, *Chalk.*

When he was six, the day before the Rotbloom Carnival arrived, he'd met a boy tattooing a wall with a fistful of chalk he'd nicked from school. The boy had invited him to join in. It was only when he found out Hughes didn't go to school that the name-calling started. Performance was off the table. Pudgy fists flew. Hughes had moped home afterward, his puffy cheeks and sniffling nose lathered in chalk. The sky above him now was exactly that shade of color.

He sat up and had a look round.

Charcoal buildings hemmed him in everywhere he looked. The brickwork was nonexistent. Gray-and-black smears narrowed and lightened into streaks of yellow.

He supposed those were meant to be windows. Some buildings were slopey. Others slanty. None stood straight.

This is Symbarr Square, he thought and reconsidered. *It's how a child would draw it on crêpe paper.*

He peered at the sky. Initially he'd believed it was chalk-colored, but that wasn't quite right. It *was* chalk. The whole sky was scrawled and smudged. Distantly, he could make out the slender lowercase m's meant to signify a flock of birds. And there! If he scrunched his eyes he could see the bits where the chalker's hand had slipped. White for sky. Black for birds. These other bits were... nothing. Implacable nothing. Looking at them made his head throb and his eyes feel soaked in bleach.

A bird detached itself from the immobile flock.

It crested down, becoming three-dimensional in a way nothing else here seemed to be. It closed the distance between them. It got bigger. Bigger. Bigger still.

By the time it landed on the building in front of him, it was the size of a car.

Hughes counted a total of twelve talons gripping the splotched lip of the roof. Each one was as long as a grown man and as curved and sharp as a scimitar. The massive flyer was black all over, except its beak, which was a deep, unsettling red. *Gorged on blood*, Hughes' mind speculated. *So often steeped in viscera that the rending parts of the bird has forever been dyed red. Just look at the talons.*

He knew what he'd see, but he looked anyway. The tips of those scimitars were red and glossy wet.

To his astonishment the beak dripped. Something splatted on the chunky cobbled street. *Blood.* Ridiculous, of course, but there it was. Its coppery tang flooded his nostrils, stimulating his gag reflex. He thought he was going to puke.

Then the blood began to move.

It slipped between the cobbles, scrolling in crooked symbols until at length words began to form.

With steadily mounting dread, Hughes read them.

STEP

RIGHT

UP

With a gargantuan *snap,* the bird's wing spread wide.

Hughes brought up his hands to ward it away. His breath caught. His hands, once lithe and clever from years of helping his dad brew tea and perfecting physical gestures for his Performance, were pudgy. Stuffed with puppy fat.

He looked down at himself and moaned.

Small shoes. Wrinkly blue socks. Kneeless trousers stranding with tufts of fabric. One of his father's shirts tugged over his head, drooping as low as his upper thighs. Of his Scarlet Citadel attire and his moth-gnawed coat, there was no sign.

He looked up. Rows of charcoal buildings had dissolved while he was distracted. Ahead, beneath the great bird that rowed the pale sky on dark oarlike wings, was the carousel. Animals of all shapes and sizes were trapped inside. Absent was the playfulness of most carny rides. The animals were not posed as if they were baying, or cheeping, or bleating, or making any pleasant natural noise. They were poised as though they were screaming. No child's hand had rendered that thing.

This is a dream. A figment of the mean aunt imagination blown up into something that looks real.

To prove it he leaned down and touched a cobble. It was icy cold against his palm and solid as a gravestone.

Sick with fear his eyes returned to that macabre invitation.

STEP
RIGHT
UP

Groping for courage that would not come, Hughes obeyed.

His body belonged to himself, to another Hughes, from a long time ago.

It was the body of a six-year-old boy.

***

As he neared it, he found it more and more difficult to look directly at the carousel. It was nothing like those spots of nothing above him. Those were merely impossible.

The thing that made the ride so upsetting to regard for longer than a few seconds was the fact that it was real. That octopus was a person. Those beetles were people. That bear too. They all were.

Laced into often-mended, round-toed shoes and the same wrinkly blue socks he'd worn on and off for three years, Gormon Hughes stopped with his fingers balled into chubby fists before the dream curse. That was what the carousel was, after all. An embodiment of the spell. A totem of black magic.

A flicker in his peripheral vision. He waited a moment, and there it was again. Amongst the silently screaming animals, something moved.

He darted a look. It was only a cockroach on a tomcat's back.

Unwilling to dare actually speaking, his lips formed the words, "I'm here."

Up in the cavernous reaches of the carousel, something large skittered.

~*Welcome Gormon Hughes* ~

The voice arrived in his head without bothering to involve his ears. There was a wicked texture to it, like the sound of a baby crying, or the sound its mother's footsteps make as they stalk toward its crib, or the sound of the knife, a lipless steel song in her hand. That triangle of ugly images paraded through him, and beholding their contours he understood what he was being shown. The voice he heard did not belong to one single source. The squalling baby, the footsteps, the knife. Three wicked things equaled three equally wicked voices.

"Thank you for having me," he said, not surprised to hear the voice of a six-year-old come out of his mouth. "I dreamed of you."

They spoke to him, the three conjoined into one.

~ *And we of you* ~

Another flash of movement. His head jerked. A simeon face, fiberglass, its teeth exposed in a soundless cry for help.

~ *It was a mistake coming here* ~

Two more sinewy scuttlings. He tried to isolate them, to see what he was dealing with. It was like trying to glimpse the wind.

~ *Here we are strong* ~

The voice that was three voices sounded smug.

~ *Here we are mighty* ~

~ *Here we are master* ~

They sounded pompous.

To Hughes, who felt that ball in his bowel lengthen into a nerve-pricking needle of dread, they sounded ready to spring a trap that had been on the cook and hob and boil for ages.

And I marched right into it, he thought numbly. *Oh my God.*

Overhead the titanic bird began to disassemble. The nightjar arched its body and *shrieked.* Vibrations rippled through the dream world. Blood and tissue pulped the bones and sucked the marrow greedily. The bastard concoction seeped. Feathers drooled a briny slop of death mucus. The carousel was spinning now, faster than lightning bolts thrown by a summer storm, and the feathers spun with it. As a vortex they spiraled down toward Hughes. Any moment they would engulf him.

~ *We are the Nightjar Coven* ~

~ *Witches of Eurydice* ~

~ *You will not change* ~

~ *You defy us* ~

Hughes threw up his arms for all the good it would do him. Through the mesh of his crisscrossed fingers he watched the spiral's point grow and grow.

~ *So we shall make an example of you* ~

The first feather brushed his cheek, which opened instantly. Blood splattered (*step right up and ride the meat train*). A hot stinging line of pain lit up his face. He felt as though he'd been kissed by a straight razor.

~ *We shall make a chimera of your flesh* ~

~ *A beautiful and squalid dream* ~

~ *All shall look upon you and despair* ~

~ *Sleep now* ~

Wind whipped savagely. The vortex howled. It made him think of hurricanes. How many hurricanes had he seen before now? "Only you, Cate," he said.

Then the chalk sky, and the charcoal structures, and all that he was, went dark.

CHAPTER FORTY-FIVE

The Archer slunk into the abandoned leisure center.

It took a rare Dexterity with a capital D to slink. Most people could only manage a light prowl. Possibly a skulk, if they had the bone structure.

The foyer was empty except for a couple of canvas-draped mannequins. Just to be safe he shot both of these in the head. When they didn't charge him, the Archer gave a contemptuously attractive smile that Hughes would have recognized in an instant, should he have been there to see it, and moved on.

Keeping to the oppressive shadows that seemed to pool here in spite of the glorious sunshine outside, he made his way to the bowling alley. His footfalls were preternaturally quiet. Rodents who had evolved to survive the many chemical and predaceous hazards of the leisure center (even the worst predator of all) barely glanced up from their chittering conversations at his passage.

The alley was empty—pins bunched in their stalls like rotting bananas. Cracked glass overheads stared with sightless eyes matted in dust. Dirty windows fouled the light coming into the place, but the quality of the air was worse. Something had died in here. Lots of somethings. There were no carcasses, but that mealy whiff like the smell humming off a gravedigger's tools was everywhere. The ceiling was a study in water stains, interesting hairy molds, and disrepair. Pipe leaks *plipped* and *dripped.* Unseen insects clicked their mandibles and *tick-tick-tapped* along the rusting gutters. All of this the Archer absorbed in the time it would take you to tug on a shoe.

On that note, under the racks of decaying bowling shoes, a telephone crouched.

Slipping effortlessly over the countertop, the Archer picked up the telephone and listened to the drone. The Bakelite transmitter was cool against his ear. No one had used it recently. He laid the phone back in its cradle, his eyes roving the dark for signs of his quarry. Nothing.

No joy in the restaurant either. The Formica tables were split with fungus, underbellied in old bubblegum. The grubby deep fat fryers hunkered like crusty wardens of the dead kitchen. The waterlogged basement turned up only chunky floating things that revealed themselves to be severed rat tails. Based on their size they had belonged to very big rats indeed. The stub of the tails were all the same. They'd been bitten clean in two.

Management office, no. Bathrooms, no. Laser tag field, no. Giftshop full of amusing little postcards and t-shirts with things like "I'm a woman of p-leisure" on them, no.

The Archer went back to the foyer. That was it, then. The foxes had moved into the ruined henhouse and had flown the coop before he—the wolf—could come and add to his cabinet of foxtails.

He stretched languidly and walked past the mannequins he'd shot earlier. He was looking forward to getting out of this place. It didn't frighten him, nothing so common as that. It was the air. It made him want to rinse out his sinuses and sneeze himself clean. Really, he was better than all this. Urban hunting was so... pedestrian. So unexciting. Oh, some of his targets had been trickier than others, but where were they now? Wolves and foxtails. It made him nostalgic for the woods. There'd been a meadow growing near Troy. He'd taken girls there to dance, and on occasion, do the old horizontal waltz.

He was only a few steps from the filthy main door. First chance he got, he was going to petition his father to go for an adventure. He was ready to see forests again. Hunting good times. Those were worthy quarry.

He paused.

Hold on. Mannequins?

He hadn't questioned their presence at first, but this was the foyer of a leisure center. What were mannequins even doing here?

He turned, meaning to investigate.

Miss Gleam punched him in the belly. After their first meeting that summer, she had removed the arrowheads from the one he'd loosed into her cheek and the two he'd used to puncture her partner's eyes. With a little adhesive tape and an old glove she'd found in the management office, she had fashioned a weapon that was not so much a knuckle-duster as a knuckle-impaler.

"Well, flay my fingers and excoriate my rummy-tum-tum," cooed Miss Gleam, yanking the arrow out of her head and driving deeper into the Archer's guts with her knuckles. "And stone the crows while you are at it. I cannot believe I ever doubted this would work."

"Told you," said Mr. Glint, stripping off the canvas and brushing down his new suit. She'd told him to keep it clean and clean he would keep it.

"First poems, now plans. Is there anything you cannot do?"

Mr. Glint thought about it. "Fast," he said at last.

The Archer looked down unbelievingly at his stomach. Jets of milky ectoplasm squirted from the wound.

"What?" Miss Gleam frowned over her shoulder. It cleared and she gave voice to a laugh like the catcalls of incubi in hell. "*Fast* as in *forego breakfast, luncheon, dinner, and supper.* Indeed, never be satiated if you can help it—that's the motto of the true hedonist. Your loquacity, garrulity, and esurience never fail to amaze, old chap."

The Archer couldn't take his eyes off the flow of ectoplasm. He was a living ghost, emphasis on *living*. Which did not mean he was immune to death. It merely meant he'd cheated it, and then only the once.

Then there was pain. He hadn't felt that, not since the Champleurs assassins had detached from their wooden bull and grabbed a handful of his hair and cut his throat from ear to ear. Apparently he could still feel it.

"Get it out of me," the Archer said. Whether he meant the agony or the arrowheads was anyone's guess.

"What? This?" said Miss Gleam sweetly, and with the arrow in her free hand she skewered his balls.

For a second it felt like someone was holding an ice cube against the soft scrotal bag. Then both testicles popped with faint wet squishing sounds, and he wished for the knives in the Trojan dark, wished someone would cut his throat for him. Son-of-a-bitch it *hurt*.

The excruciating quality was so great it went through his paralysis and drove him to action.

He clicked one of several buttons on his quiver. An arrow slid out the bottom instead of out the top. He gripped it and gave Miss Gleam some of what she'd just given him.

Bellowing her surprise, she clutched her ear, which now sprouted an arrow shaft complete with delicate scarlet fletching.

Mr. Glint bullrushed him. Reflex squeezed his leg and lower back muscles. He flipped and heard the shatter of glass as Glint went through the main door.

Escape, that was what mattered now.

He broke into a run.

Mr. Glint got to his feet, again taking the time to pick studs of broken glass off his nice new suit, and fell into step with Miss Gleam who was holding the freshly removed arrow. A gory bit of her ear clung to the point.

They started after him, two foxes who had tricked the wolf into the ruined henhouse, only to reveal they had been disguised wolfskinners all along.

"Scarlet-fledged arrows," said Gleam. "Scarlet red for Scarlet Citadel. Adds up. Calculates correctly. Hughes must have sent him to scrag us. Our brother's got new friends, new friends intent on removing his old enemies. Well, well, we'll just see about *that*, won't we?"

Mr. Glint looked at her. The medication hadn't worked. She was a glittering yarn of perissology (which means someone who uses ribboned packages of words instead of plain unadorned boxes, at least that was how she described it), and now that yarn was being unspooled. Not just one thread at a time. Lots of them and going in different directions. Her cheek spasmed constantly.

And he had so looked forward to spending the end of autumn with her. He'd been convinced she'd get better. She was Miss Gleam, the smartest woman in the world. Now he wasn't so sure.

"I think we've misjudged our bow-wielding foe. He seems like an obliging soul. See the droplets?" Gleam pointed. "He's leaving a trail for us to follow."

Mr. Glint let the hunt take over.

Fleeing as though his life depended on it (which was in a way quite true) the Archer wasn't making an effort at stealth anymore. *I hear with my little ear something beginning with B.*

"What's that stuff oozing out of him?" wondered Miss Gleam. "It's not blood. We've seen enough of that to know for sure. But then what?"

"Haven't the foggiest," said Mr. Glint. "It looks tasty."

***

The roar of the maelstrom hadn't stopped. This was a sticking point. It ought to have stopped the moment that column of blood and bone and black feathers hit him.

Which meant it hadn't hit him.

Sometime in the past few seconds he'd scrunched his eyes shut.

Hughes opened them.

He was still in the dream world. The vortex still raged above him. His small six-year-old chest was open. There were no ribs on display. It was a tunnel into darkness, like a hole in a hollow tree trunk. Two long arms extended from the hole in his chest. Red fingernailed and feminine, they were raised protectively in front of him. The palms were cupped around something small. Was it beating?

My heart, he thought. *It's my heart.*

Green light poured out of the ladylike hands, or his heart, or both. It was sweet as spring flowers and at the same time as poisonous as the stingers of February wasps. Dark feathers sizzled to smoke the instant they touched it.

Awed and dumbstruck, Hughes looked at the carousel. And only for a moment before they scurried out of sight, he saw the Nightjar Coven. He *saw* them, the three witches of Eurydice, though the glamour they wove about them like strands of midnight meant he could never quite remember just what he'd seen. They seemed composed of animals, or the essence of animals.

Humped gorilla backs. Crooked cranelike shoulders. Goiter-lumped throats like toads, warts filled with marsh gas, and webbed gout-swollen toes. Grasshopper legs supporting bloated hippopotamus bellies. Twitchy spiderlimb fingers. Their heads twitched from side to side like the birds from which they drew their Coven's name.

And their eyes. Their eyes were snake's eyes, slitted and yellow.

Even when they were gone he could feel those eyes on him.

He sensed their surprise, a tincture spiced with no small amount of disgust and fury. A dream this might very well be, but that was their preferred terrain. *Sleep now*, they'd commanded him, and there was no doubt in his mind it would be murder.

An idea came to him. It was irresistible. The green light. The hole in his chest. The arms. His heart. It was simply too theatrical to waste. He couldn't help himself. He was, after all, a performer. *Let's see.* Words wouldn't do, not now. Sometimes only a gesture could do the talking.

He spread his arms, curled his hands so the palms pointed to the sky, and gave the cowering Nightjar Coven the most taunting of bows.

Bizarrely, under the bellow of the hurricane he thought he heard the grinding of train wheels coming to a halt. Giving it a second, he understood. It was the witches. They were *rasping* at him. Dry throaty rasps that said, *You arrogant little fuck.*

Hughes relished that. Relished it *deeply.*

The vortex throbbed, engorging as energy passed through it. Its insane wheeling slowed. Invisible fingers plucked the feathers until they were bare, and then even these remnants faded. It seemed the witches were calling off the attack for now. With nothing to shield him from, the arms drew back into Hughes' chest. Flesh knit itself closed. Before he knew it the green light and the hole disappeared without ceremony. His heart was beating inside him. He had not realized how much he'd missed it until the moment it was returned.

God, that felt wonderful. He could have wept for joy, but for now he had a job to finish.

He let his bow deepen a bit, saying nothing, a goading smile on his lips.

~ *You're a cheeky child* ~

said the witches as one.

~ *Truculent* ~

~ *Just like our precious honey boy* ~

Hughes straightened up. *Our precious honey boy.* He remembered their eyes, snakish and burning yellow.

"Frank's your son," he said.

~ *That is what he calls himself* ~

~ *We gave him a better name* ~

~ *Would you like to hear it* ~

Hughes had the feeling he really didn't. "No, thank you."

~ *How we miss him* ~

His mind leaped to a conclusion. A good one, as it turned out.

"You're the ones who gave the orders to Maelen and the Bonemeal Boys. You put the dream of rebellion in his head. That was why he killed the people in Aldersglen and settled in to wait for a cartographer to show up. It was only a matter of time. The Citadel explores voraciously. And that's why Maelen questioned Isaac about the Citadel," he said. "You told him to because..." His eyes widened. "Because you want your son back." His voice sounded different. Riper. He looked down at himself. Normal shoes. Scarlet shirt. Moth-chewed coat. He was himself again, even here in the dream. Emboldened, he asked the largest of the many questions vying in his mind. "Why did Frank leave you in the first place?"

~ *He was willful* ~

"You mean stubborn?"

No reply, which meant stubborn barely covered it.

"And that's all?" said Hughes. "Just a bit of family strife? Why the curse, then? Why turn everyone into animals?"

~ *We had to come in* ~

"Into my world?"

~ *Yes* ~

~ *The curse is a door* ~

~ *When enough have become beasts we can reach out* ~

~ *And touch the dreams of our honey boy* ~

~ *And bring him home* ~

Hughes mulled this over. Layers of mystery peeled back under his scrutiny.

"Can Frank stay awake as long as he wants to?"

~ *Yes* ~

"That's what you mean then," he said. "The transformations make you powerful, and with enough power you can force your son to sleep. To dream. Then he's yours again."

~ *Shrewd as well as cheeky* ~

~ *You remind us of him very much* ~

~ *You must forgive us* ~

~ *The feathers were only meant to frighten you* ~

Yes, frighten me to death, he thought. *And you can ubi sol non lucet that apology, okay?*

Aloud he said, "If someone got Frank to go to sleep for you right away, you'd have no need for the door."

Silence.

"You could change everyone back."

Silence.

"I could help you."

~ *YES* ~

He staggered. The word had torn through his thoughts like claws through paper.

"On you go, then," he managed. "Change them back and you've got a deal."

~ *We are not fools Gormon Hughes* ~

~ *We are the Nightjar Coven* ~

~ *As old as the black hourglass sands* ~

~ *As wise as the deepest river stones* ~

~ *As cunning as the thorniest woods* ~

"But they're people," he said, unable to keep the anger from leeching into his voice. "They don't deserve what you're doing to them. They're just trying to put one foot in front of the other, but no, you've got to have them do it on unfamiliar paws."

He knew it wouldn't work, not when he couldn't perceive his targets completely, but he pushed his Performance.

He felt it begin to enfold the carousel, then falter. The animals screamed their soundless screams, and in his head the three witches laughed.

~ *Shrewd and cheeky and quick-tempered* ~

~ *Our honey boy will like you* ~

~ *Listen closely* ~

~ *We shall lift the dreaming curse* ~

~ *When he is home with his mothers who love him so* ~

Up through the cobbly ground into the soles of his feet, Hughes felt himself begin to wake up.

"*Wait*," he implored them. "You've turned Idris Corlum into a stoat. We can't open the Perfect Prison."

~ *Idris has his own honey girl* ~

~ *He dreams of her* ~

~ *His bluntest joy and sharpest shame* ~

~ *She's the spit and polish of her daddy* ~

The chalk and charcoal faded. Hughes had never been scuba diving. If he had, he would have compared the rise toward the surface to this. Only much less pleasant. Dizzying absence swarmed over him, and as he looked at the carousel he saw the animals were gone, and the carny ride was crammed with people. They were frozen in statues, the monkeys and manatees all changed to lanky boys and big-boned men, the jackdaws and carnivorous ants and elephants changed to girls and women, large and small. Where two beetles had been, he spotted his former neighbor, Sheila Kofatch, and a girl who looked just like her, only little.

He wanted to thrust his arm out, to save her and all the rest by pulling them out of this nightmare in a linked chain, a conga line of rescue and awakening. He tried and was thwarted. The current of consciousness pulled him with hands as strong as Mr. Glint's.

But the thought of outstretched limbs wrenched a final question from him.

"Please. Those arms that came out of me," he said. "What are they?"

~ *A gift for a willful boy* ~

~ *Tatty bye Gormon Hughes* ~

~ *We will meet again* ~

~ *Where the roads meet* ~

He opened his mouth.

A nightjar flew out.

Then he woke up.

***

They followed the pearly dribblous goo that was not quite blood.

It led them to a ventilation chute. The Archer had unscrewed the grate, probably using one of his arrowheads, and scrambled inside.

"Resourceful little coxcomb," said Miss Gleam. She could see herself admiring him, though truth be told, she'd prefer to eat his tongue.

Mr. Glint lifted himself up and into the chute without a word.

By chance, one of the leisure center sables (a cousin to the weasel with the same needle-tip teeth) hopped onto the bowling console. Only a few rooms from the alley, Miss Gleam heard the thumping roll of the ball as it came up through the system, and went to investigate. The culprit behind the disturbance was gone by the time she arrived, but the ball was there. It was scarlet red.

With her scarred cheek jerking wildly, Miss Gleam picked it up.

***

"How do you feel?" Cate asked.

"He's got a daughter," Hughes said, trying to breathe himself out of nausea. Reentry into the waking world had happened all at once. It had not been a smooth landing. "And Frank's their son."

"Do not mind his gobbledygook," said Desdemona née Denise. "A bit of cosmogonic bewilderment is quite normal." She stood and began to blow out the ceremonial candle as well as the other much less ceremonial ones.

Hughes glanced around. With the blackout curtains up it was hard to tell how much time had passed.

Cate knelt beside him and took his fingers. "Sticks of ice," she said. "Brow."

He bent forward obediently. She laid a hand to his forehead.

"Slightly elevated temperature. Shall I get you a hot water bottle?"

"No," he said. "I feel better. Really." It was true. The warmth of her touch grounded him. In his head the events of the dream were sorting themselves into orders of importance. "Where's Wendy?"

"Here, Hughes." She stepped into his field of view. "You were gone twenty minutes on the dot. And with the last candle extinguished, allow me to pull back this curtain. There we are. Thank you Deni... Miss Cauldronpot. Your assistance in this grave time shall be remembered."

"The spirits and I are at your service."

"Are they? I shall bear it in mind."

Shawl drawn about her like a moony cloak, bangles rattling like a cutlery box, and leaving behind a smell like a lost cat shelter with no population control, Desdemona Cauldronpot swept out of the alcove.

"What a strange person." Wendy turned back to Hughes. "Well, my lad. Tell us what you've learned."

Hughes filled them in, sparing no detail.

When he was done there was a heavy, pondering silence.

"Leaving aside the madness of the arms staving off the blood-feather vortex," said Cate, crafting possibly the oddest sentence Hughes had ever heard, "we can't give them what they want. Bad as our situation is, these witches are going to use Frank to pollute it even further. It's a dream curse. He's the Dream Warrior."

"Yes, but we've got to try something," Hughes protested. "You didn't see the carousel, Cate."

"It was part of the dream."

"Right now that dream is a reality," said Hughes. "It's out there in the streets playing with innocent people. Treating them like carnival exhibits. You should have heard their voice. One voice, three unbelievably evil ladies. I thought witches in fairy tales were nasty." He looked at her. "Before they tried to kill me, I think I heard the real them. The honest, unedited version of the Nightjar Coven. I was already as good as dead in their eyes. Why bother hiding their true selves? They're enjoying this, Cate. That's the real Coven. The carnage. The misery. It's all a fairground ride to them. Giving them Frank might not solve things outright, but we don't lose a thing by speaking to him. And that means setting him free."

"Quite so," said Wendy Dragontail. "Unfortunately, our path to doing so remains obscured."

"What do you mean?" said Hughes.

He worried he'd drawn the wrong conclusion. Hadn't Cate's aunt passed down the hobnail boots to her? If magic items were hereditary, that meant Idris Corlum's daughter could activate the Perfect Prison.

A terrible idea struck him. "Is Idris' daughter also an animal?"

"That I cannot say. As far as I'm aware Idris Corlum—while happily married—has no children."

"What?" Hughes gawped uncomprehendingly. "That can't be right."

"I'm afraid so. She cannot be his bluntest joy because she does not exist."

Standing beneath one of the alcove bookshelves, Cate Jubilee's arms were crossed, her body still. As Hughes and Wendy bandied back and forth, her expression had firmed with realization. She grasped the truth before either of them.

"The Coven also said his daughter was his sharpest shame. Perhaps he's not so happily married." She smiled without humor.

Wendy bridled. "Idris Corlum is a man with more loyalty in his little finger than most have in their whole bodies."

"To you, Your Worship? And to his job? Absolutely."

"Explain yourself."

"All I'm saying is that the Perfect Prison isn't the only lock he's capable of keying. He might have quite a few of them on the go."

"I'm sure I don't appreciate your insinuations," said Wendy Dragontail.

Cate shrugged. "I shall steer clear of them going forward, my Lady. Here's a statement: It's not going to be easy, but there *is* a daughter to find." She unfolded her arms and rested her hands on her hips. "As long as we don't ask his wife, we should be off to a good start."

CHAPTER FORTY-SIX

Paris of Troy—living ghost, son of Priam King, scaler of ivy trellises to the balconies of courtly women, and the Archer who shot Mr. Twinkle through the throat while he was on the phone to Miss Gleam—was in a tight spot.

About four feet wide and two feet high, to be precise.

He was also trapped.

The ventilation chute had come to an abrupt and rather inconvenient end. During the leisure center's heyday, air was propelled down the chute and into the bowling alley, the restaurant, the pool table corner, and the manager's office by means of nine-bladed fans arranged in rows of six. When the electric company killed the power, the blades flickered, slowed, and came to an eternal stop like teeth in the skull of a stunned eel.

Less than a minute ago he had crawled around the corner, gasping at the sharp pins of pain rooting in his groin, and been confronted by fifty-four rotatory blades caught in a standstill. He could reach an arm through them without danger of having it scythed off. But even if he had a year to measure the curves and angles and a block of butter to grease himself with, he could not fit through.

Now, awash with sweat, sticky with ectoplasm, and squatting back on his haunches, he considered his next move. There wasn't enough room to turn. Going back would involve shuffling his hips, stopping on occasion to crane his head and make sure the way was clear, but what good would that do? The chute was one long tube paneled in sheets of corrugated steel. There were no divergent paths.

So if he went back, it would have to be all the way to the opening of the chute itself. If he made it okay, he could shimmy down beside the grate he'd unscrewed, take stock, and look for an alternative route of escape. His mind went to the signal arrow stuffed in his quiver. To say he'd never expected to use it was an understatement. Indeed, quite a large part of him was struggling to cope with the fact that this was happening. That part—a craven, boyish part that in the past had feared the retribution of jilted husbands and outraged fathers—advised him to curl up and send out a kind of psychic hope of rescue. He could nurse his popped testicles. Wouldn't that be nice?

With one last rueful look at the blades, he started to shuffle back.

He was going to get out of this.

He *had* to.

That was when he heard a voice issuing from somewhere behind him like November wind soughing through drifts of twigs and dead autumn leaves. If the oldest, bleakest cemeteries could speak they would do so with that voice.

It said, "Sweet Rosy Posey lived in a dozy. Had a nice house all warm and all cozy."

I am going to die in here, he thought. He was still as a woodcut, his whole body lacquered with fear. *But before I do I'm going to howl my lungs out. That voice will draw sounds out of me I've never imagined. Maybe that'll get the fan blades going again. Maybe it'll wake me from death, the sheer torment. Hey, third time's the charm, right?*

"Had a nice dog named William Supposy." Paris could hear the *crump, crump* of long-fingered hands pressing down on the thin metal sheets of the chute. The voice was closer. "One winter night a cold wind did blowsey. Got a bad cough and a runny nosy. Sneezed into Saturday, choked into Sunday."

No. I died helpless once. Not again.

It hurt, and hurt badly, but he turned around. He even managed to nock an arrow in his bow. Firing it would be impossible in such cramped quarters. Still, God loved a trier. He glanced down at himself for the first time since Gleam had stuck him with his own arrow.

What he saw did not exactly inspire confidence.

His shirt and pants looked as though someone had emptied a bottle of creamy liqueur over them. Through the fabric a pouch of warm wetness kissed his right thigh. Despite an empty bladder, he seemed to be pissing himself. Not a continuous stream, mind. Quick warm squirts. With an effort he smiled his roguish smile. *That's your heartbeat, you damn fool. Each arterial thump pumps blood through the hole she made in you.*

Ahead in the dark, a smooth, bulbous thing rounded the corner.

Paris felt his smile fall away.

The thing revealed itself to be the cap of a bald head. "Died and was eaten by William Supposy. That was the end of Sweet Rosey Posey."

Mr. Glint looked up.

Their eyes met.

"I hope it hurt," said Paris. "When I shot you before. I hope it hurt."

The sour-mouthed man (although Mr. Glint stretched the definition of man to breaking point) made no reply. He just came onward.

Paris backed up until he felt the dull edge of a blade nudge his spine.

How would his brother, Hector, react to all this?

Likely the noble bastard would bear it all with dignity.

Paris didn't think he could. Knew it, in fact.

The best he could offer was hate.

"Choke," he whispered harshly. "Eat away, monster. But I'll throttle you from the inside, I swear."

No reply.

"And haunt you. I am a ghost, after all."

No reply.

Paris tried to think of fitting last words. None occurred. The only thing he could think was *Hector, Cassandra, father, someone help me,* and then Mr. Glint's long-fingered hand enfolded his ankle like a signed letter from hell.

The chute, not designed to hold the weight of one person, much less two, collapsed.

They landed on one of the pool tables. Paris hit the dusty green baize. He was lucky, losing the wind from his lungs in a gust and that was all. Mr. Glint was not so fortunate. His outstretched arm struck the hardwood table edge. There was a sickening snap as his ulna burst through the skin of his elbow, fouling his brand-new suit and jutting up like a pale finger.

Mr. Glint stared at it the way a child might stare at a new family pet. That "how did you get here?" expression did not change one iota when Paris drew back, loosed, and pinned the tall, gaunt horror to the floor through his foot.

High windows cast dirty sunbeams on the room. Assessing the thickness of the glass in a flash, Paris selected his signal arrow, brought his shoulders to the draw, and let fly. Three-quarters of an inch of glass spidered with cracks, bowed outward, and exploded out onto the street. Inside the arrowhead, a cartridge of magnesium crackled and ate through the thin shell of casing steel. Blinding light went up hissing and spitting white fire into the endless blue afternoon.

Mr. Glint broke the arrow shaft and slid his foot free, but by then the Archer was already halfway to the foyer, his gait somewhere between a limp and a sprint, his breath a rattling wheeze, warmth seeping down his belly and legs, unspeakable pain threading his body, and that heart-melting smile plastered from cheek to cheek.

Life, life, life. What a woman she was.

He would scale anything for her.

Even ivy.

***

Alcoholics don't really sleep. In a giant constellation of binges, passing out is the black space between cold rest-stop stars.

Walter Pillion, who as a boy swore off booze (especially vodka) after what it did to his father, and who was now one of the most avid drunks in the entire city, awoke to a feeling like someone was plunging his head in a bucket of water packed with ice shavings.

Which turned out to be an accurate summary of the situation.

The familiar violence of waking up (headaches, bowel and liver cramp, slow, painful urination, the hairy-tongued mouth rinse of vomit, the creeping guilt, and the knowledge that he would never, ever drink again) quailed in comparison to the unbearable displeasure of this wet welcome back into reality. Crystal-clear ache daggered through his pupils and enveloped his brain. And, oh dear God. The *chill*. It was fucking *freezing*.

There must have been light above him because he could see his hair wafting in oily strands before his eyes and the grouted bottom of the bucket.

He fumbled. There was a hard, smooth surface under his hands. He flattened his palms and gave an almighty heave. He rose, lashing and sputtering.

The dazzling light that sunspotted his eyes was actually just an overhead anbaric lamp. It gave a gentle sea green light and showed the other people in the room a man undergoing slow corrosion. Walter's hair was not a rat's nest so much as a warren. He had cleaned up for the funeral in June, it was the least he could do for poor Laurana before she was trundled off to sleep forever under her family farm's blackberries. But now it was October and he wore a tangled beard, a scowl that seemed nailed under his nose, and a yellow jaundiced look around his blood-scored eyes, which any doctor will tell you means the liver is packing its bags for a long, rather deadly vacation.

"Walter," said Wendy.

He spat a mouthful of ice water. "Lady Dragontail." His gaze swiveled, taking in Cate Jubilee with mild rancor before fixing Hughes with a look of naked loathing. "I see the hot air balloon has touched down after his Triumph."

Wendy cut in quickly. "Did you recommend a brothel to Idris Corlum?"

He jumped.

"I beg your pardon, good Lady?"

"Don't you 'good Lady' me, Walter Pillion."

He shrank as The Last Dragon bore down on him.

"Did you recommend a brothel to Idris Corlum—he of the Perfect Prison— yes or no?"

"I might have," he said, "but I..."

"Quickly man, before you congeal."

"Noble Lady, I was going to say that while he did, ah, approach me, it was because of my patrol route in Leonidas District," oozed Walter, who looked as though he'd like to go back to the bucket. "Idris knew I was familiar with the reputation of several houses of negotiable intimacy, and though I myself would never stoop to engage in... um..."

"Yes, yes. You are the soul of purity," snapped Wendy Dragontail. "What was the name of the brothel?"

"*Pamplona*," said Walter.

"Can you take us there?"

"No need," said Hughes. "I know where it is."

An hour later they stepped out of Wendy Dragontail's car into a pedestrianized zone.

"That truck almost hit us," said Hughes. "Did he crash?"

He had. People were gathering around, peering anxiously at the wreck through the fug of smoke.

"I'm going to see if the driver's okay," said Cate, tying her hair up in a fiery bun to match Wendy's. Hughes wondered if there was some unspoken feminine code about stressful situations requiring buns. He gave Cate quick instructions on how to reach *Pamplona*. She scanned around for reflective surfaces near the crash site, nodded to herself, and vanished into a glass storefront.

As with the brutal summer storm, Hughes' home District of Leonidas seemed the worst affected by the dream curse. In Ptolema the wheels of action turned quickly with animal rights groups, veterinary leagues, and common pavement-jockey streetbeaters rising admirably to the occasion. Impromptu preservation sites were being coordinated, including cages, saltwater tanks, thermal chambers for warm climate creatures, and boreal cubicles for cold ones. Amazing, sure. But the streets outside Ptolema told a different story.

Ignorant bliss had disintegrated. Panic spread under the city's skin like a new bruise.

The car had passed through Polydoros, and Hughes saw animals hopping, dashing, flopping, and slithering with unchecked abandon. Broadsheets and tabloids swerved in the breeze, sensationalizing madness. People were holed up inside their homes. Curtains twitched. Children and older folk alike peeped out as the oddness unfolded. Some people tried to flag down their car as though it were a taxi. Some looked confused, others hurt. Mostly they seemed terrified.

Leonidas was a darker tale even than that. The vulnerable knew they were at the bottom of the list to receive help, so they had started helping themselves. Word was only just now reaching them of the curse, and then only in trickles and rivulets of information. As Hughes and Wendy hurried toward *Pamplona* and saw the electric billboards go live, informing the public not to hurt any animals, they ran into a man ordering several workers to break the necks of any small critters they came across. Rabbits or hares were best, but he'd take all comers. The man wore a shirt that said *Gordon Gorgeous Goods: If You Want Meat Mine Can't Be Beat!*

Gordon was all gorgeous, good smiles when Wendy Dragontail approached him. He wasn't smiling by the time she'd finished speaking. He pelted off toward his employees, his face stark white and his Adam's apple bobbing crazily.

"Stop!" he roared. "They're people, goddamnit! *Stop, stop, STOP!*"

One worker paused in the act of swinging a chinchilla by its fluffy tail. The chinchilla was missing two fingers, which had been bitten off by Mr. Glint earlier that year during Hughes' caper through the Leonidas bazaar.

"Agorippis Street," said Wendy when they reached it. "Has it been so long?"

"Was it different when you lived here?" asked Hughes.

"To put it mildly," she said. "This is a molted snakeskin of a street. A dead husk where once something lived. Ah. But here is our destination." She rapped on the door.

Hughes glanced at the neon sign, turned off in the daylight. The gored matador seemed like a bad omen.

The door opened. "Yes 'm," said a deep voice.

"You are the owner of this establishment?"

"No, 'm."

"Fetch them, please."

"Yes, 'm."

The door closed.

"Seemed a polite fellow," said Wendy.

Hughes was impressed, though not altogether surprised. Wendy projected an aura that Desdemona Cauldronpot would have called "enthralling" or something, but which he thought of as plain-old-fashioned entitlement. She sounded like she belonged right where she was, doing exactly what she was doing. Hughes wondered what would have happened if she'd been turned into an animal. He suspected he and Cate would now be taking orders from a gibbon.

"Don't leave me in suspense," she said.

"Sorry?"

"You're grinning, Hughes."

He looked at her, this titan of rulership with sunshine soaking in her white hair, billions of invisible atoms of power bouncing under her sweatpants and cardigan, and that twinkle in her eye that said so little, and withheld so much.

"In my dream, the witches seemed totally confident," he told her. "At least at first. When things didn't go their way, it aggravated them. If they're capable of arrogance and rage, that means they've got the whole human suite of emotion. If they can inspire fear, maybe they can feel it too." Hughes glanced up the street toward the frantic sound of bicycle bells, the bleat and whuffle of transformed people on the loose, and someone weeping softly. Leonidas was alive, but it was hard to believe on Agorippis Street. *A dead husk*, Wendy had called it. Well, Agorippis Street wasn't going to become his home, all condemned and flaking and forlorn. He wouldn't allow it. "Frank has been trying to contact me," said Hughes. "He's embroiled in the witches' plot somehow. His mothers, they might very well be, but do we really want to bet they'll give up their stranglehold on the city if we hand back their son? No, they'll keep their spoils and spread the curse until the whole city is one big jungle. Come to think of it, Frank might be the key to them doing that. He comes out of the Perfect Prison, and we all end up going in, in a manner of speaking." He broke off, listening. The city seemed loud to him just now, an orchestra reminding him it was still playing, that it *needed* to go on playing. "I know it sounds crazy, but I can't shake the certainty that Frank was trying to warn me. I'm talking about a strong conviction here. What he did to your father was horrible, your Ladyship. But I'm convinced it was... well, that the act of him coming to our world was the same as someone waking up in an animal's body. Alien. Terrifying. Now he's had time to cool off, *years* to acclimatize, and he's reaching out. I think we can set about turning this nightmare on its head, him and I. And Cate, of course. I expect we wouldn't get very far without her."

Wendy patted his shoulder. "We shall see."

The door opened. A young woman in a backless dress, winged eyeliner, and laddered stockings appeared. She reminded Hughes of Krys, who had given him the knife he wore at his hip, though this girl had none of Krys' vibrancy. She twiddled her feet and smiled sadly at them.

"You must be here about my daddy," she said.

Back in the thoroughfare, Cate Jubilee was finishing up with the driver (the man's brother-in-law had nodded off in the passenger seat, and to the driver's horror he was suddenly sharing his truck with a duck-billed platypus), when through the hectic bustle of Leonidas she heard a peculiar fizzling noise. Craning her neck, she spied a chemical sparkling over the tenement rooftops and thought two words: *Magnesium flare.*

She wondered who needed help.

***

He thought he was home free until Miss Gleam leaped over a decommissioned pinball machine and charged him. Over her head she held a bowling ball the way ancient shamans held sacrificial knives in paintings where the artist is generous with the color red.

As if the scene couldn't grow any madder, a fancy car finished what Mr. Glint had started earlier and ruptured the main doors.

It tore in Paris' direction at full speed.

Miss Gleam was almost on him, so he shot her twice, once for each knee. The arrows were perfectly aimed, splitting her kneecaps like hatchets bisecting overripe pumpkins.

Miss Gleam did not seem to notice.

"Catch," she crowed, and with a smile that displayed all her teeth like a surgeon displaying her cutting kit, she threw the bowling ball at his head.

Wheels screeched.

The bowling ball bounced off the car's rear door. It did not make so much as a dent. The passenger door opened. Paris felt himself being yanked into the car and pulled unceremoniously to rest his head on someone's lap.

He grinned weakly at his rescuer. "I thought Cassandra would come."

"Wrong sister," the Princess replied. To her driver she said, "In your own time."

The car whipped around, throwing off Miss Gleam who was attacking the dense material encasing the windshield with her fangs and fists and glittering claws.

"I should have listened to your Painted Girl," said Paris as they sped away from the leisure center. His vision was darkening. The pain swallowing him had abated. He felt injected with a relief like Novocain. "And that Ringmaster Woman," he added. "They told me I'd be hurt."

"Yes," said the Princess. "They did."

"Are you angry with me, sister?"

She stroked his hair. "No one could be angry with you for long, Paris."

"Glint and Gleam will give it a try."

"No," she said, and though her calm, reasonable face remained strenuously calm and utterly reasonable, the Princess' voice was more barbed and sharp than any arrow in her brother's quiver. "They won't. The reason being that before the sun sets, Miss Gleam and Mr. Glint will both be as good as dead."

CHAPTER FORTY-SEVEN

Her name was Estelle, and she'd been waiting for them.

"Magic item inheritance is amazing, really. It's like a witch's magic wand," she explained as only a thirteen-year-old could explain. "When the witch dies she doesn't want just anyone waving it willy-nilly-hilabaroo. She's got to have a successor lined up, right?"

"Indeed," said Wendy Dragontail. "Indeed, Hughes?"

"Absolutely," he said. "You know, Cate?"

"I know."

"Right," said Estelle. "So how did Daddy die? Was he hit by a metrotram and it disemboweled him?"

"Estelle!"

They were in the parlor of *Pamplona*. Sex workers were getting ready for the evening, though a bit hesitantly, given the general uproar in the city and the specific presence of Wendy Dragontail in their house of hanky-panky.

The woman who'd called Estelle's name in a tone that didn't say "mother" so much as yawp it from the rooftops was Gwendolyn Gardener.

"Like the knight in that story," she'd informed them. "Don't pretend like you know it. No one does."

"I do actually," Hughes had said, and he had given her a bow that raised everyone's eyebrows as if via strings. "Blessings and fair tidings, Dame Gardener."

Of course Gwendolyn had been taken with Hughes from that moment on, offering him all sorts of nibbles and treats, coffee and cake and suchlike while her daughter, Estelle, told them all about Idris Corlum's secret life.

It should be mentioned that they had been wrong to worry about Idris' marriage. Mrs. Corlum was in on the whole thing. Since she couldn't have children and Idris had no other family, the couple mutually decided he ought to pass on the vambrace that contained the magic of the Perfect Prison to an heir. It was simply too useful to waste in a museum display case. Guided by Walter the Drunk, Idris had disguised himself and sneaked out of Redspire. He'd met Gwendolyn by special arrangement, explained his desire, and offered her a substantial investment in her business for her trouble. Gwendolyn Gardener, owner of *Pamplona*, took one look at swiftly decaying Agorippis Street and agreed. He was fifty-seven and embarrassed. She was thirty-seven and industrious.

Estelle was the result.

She was a bizarrely tired looking girl, as though she and the concept of sleep were acquainted but only at a distance of several continents. Hughes found himself liking her, and her mother. And the staff of *Pamplona*, now he considered it. They were reading folk, a rare breed. Books were tucked between provocative watercolor paintings and bottles of massage oil. He wondered idly if he should tell his dad about this discovery, maybe send some of *Pamplona's* employees toward the *Scriptorium and Flavored Tea Emporium*. Then he thought about his father's expression should he happen to mention how the workers earned their wage between bouts of skimming fiction and decided it was probably not a wise idea.

"Idris isn't dead," said Gwendolyn Gardener. "If he was, he'd have had the decency to send one of them sequined lads with word of it."

"Your mother is correct," said Wendy. "Idris is not dead. He is, in fact, a stoat."

"See?" said Gwendolyn smugly. "I told you."

Estelle had the wherewithal to look admonished. "I was only asking."

"Have your employees been transmogrifying?" Cate asked Gwendolyn.

The brothel owner puffed out her cheeks and blew a thoughtful raspberry. "Our Naomi turned into a lizard at about two o'clock today. That anything to do with transmoggything?"

"It might just be related," said Cate, her expression deadpan.

"So Idris is a gerbil..."

"Stoat."

"Right, and you need my Estelle to use the Perfect Prison, yeah? Oh, don't go gawking at me. Course Idris told me all about it. You're secretive up in Redspire, but there aren't many hidden things in *Pamplona*, not unless it's an extra credit or two tucked in your knickers for safekeeping." Gwendolyn pinched her daughter's cheek. "Well, you can take her, as long as she's happy to go."

Estelle attempted an earnest smile, which emerged as a kind of pained grimace.

"Daddy's vambrace is a *bit* like a magic wand, I suppose," she said. "I always wanted to be a witch."

Hughes, Cate, and Wendy Dragontail exchanged a grave look.

Somewhere out in Leonidas an elephant trumpeted, and as if that preposterous sound were in fact a starting flag waved to commence a race, there came the rhythmic sound of hoofbeats. It was too heavy to be horses. As they rushed back to Redspire and the prisoner ensconced on the eighty-ninth floor, Hughes spotted the source of the ruckus. Following some unspoken herd instinct, those who had transformed into bulls had found one another. Over the course of mere minutes, what had begun as a trot had escalated into a mindless stampede. Nostrils flared. Damp fresh laundry smelling clothes snagged on flailing horns. Bovine muscle rolled under taut October-prickled flesh. Those still occupying human skin had the good sense to stay inside, but how long before more danger presented itself behind the supposedly safe walls of the homestead? It occurred to Hughes that sooner rather than later, unless the matadors were quick as August lightning, there would be a goring. And blood, waves and waves of it in astounding quantities.

The floodfighters shouldn't have hung up their galoshes. He flinched inwardly at the grimness of the thought, and how its very lack of warmth felt so appropriate.

Later, the fact that he had been wrong about all this would hit him, and hit him hard.

Things in Corinth City were not on the verge of tipping over into tragedy.

They were already there.

***

"Estelle?" said Cate in the elevator as Wendy inserted a unique key above the floor buttons. "Are you ever in your mum's work when she and her staff are..." She seemed to deliberate, then gave up. "When they're working?"

"Sometimes." Estelle looked furtive, more than a little cautious.

"Have you ever had anyone say anything to you?"

"Like what?"

"Something that made you uncomfy, like."

"Oh, that." The girl's tension unraveled. "No, not since Mum signed a protection deal with Mr. Shine."

Hughes' heart missed a beat. Mr. Shine. The name sent tendrils of unease curling around his spinal cord. Cate and Estelle carried on, oblivious to his trip down Memory Lane.

"Who's Mr. Shine?"

"He's the boss of Miss Gleam and Mr. Glint."

Cate nodded. "Oh, *them* I know. A protection deal, you said?"

"Lots of people have one." Estelle sighed. It was clear the topic didn't interest her much. As Wendy pressed the elusive button for the eighty-ninth floor, the girl brightened suddenly. "Did he disembowel anyone?"

"Who?"

"The man in the Perfect Prison. Or maybe he hangs his victims up and goes *medieval* on their bottoms."

Cate frowned. "What sort of vids has your mother been letting you watch?"

Estelle wrinkled her nose. "I don't watch vids. Mum says they make the jelly in your eyeballs grow legs."

Cate wasn't much for maintaining a frown, especially in the face of such charming savagery. She grinned instead, and to his exceeding gladness Hughes felt the tendrils loosen their grip on him. He listened to Cate play the all-knowing adult with charm and style. "Frank Gallant isn't a serial killer from a crime story, Estelle. He is a man who steps from dream to dream. His mothers are three witches, who in their dark collaboration form the Nightjar Coven. To mark him as their own, he has inherited their eyes, just like you've inherited your dad's magic item for a little while. You must be courageous as anything when those eyes fix on you."

"What color are they?"

"Good question. Burning yellow. Isn't that so, Hughes?"

"Like foglamps on a night of mist," he agreed.

Estelle was suitably pleased. "Ooh! Well that's all right then."

As the elevator climbed, she said in a hopeful voice, "And he tortures people in their heads, then? Psychologically?"

"I suppose he could do," Cate admitted. "If he were so inclined."

"*Brilliant.*"

The floor gave a lurch that sent their stomachs rolling. *Clunks* echoed around them. Stillness. The doors did not open.

Hughes was nonplussed. What was going on?

Into the silence, Wendy Dragontail's voice streamed clear and strong. "Scarlet brother be my shield."

A recorded voice answered. If pressed to describe it, Hughes would have called it gentlemanly, a warm, whiskey-sipping, bushy-browed sort of voice.

"Be the weapon that I wield," said the voice.

"I will be your courage true," said Wendy.

"I will burn like fire for you."

"If I'm laid eternal low."

"We pray that it shall not be so."

"Yes, but if it comes to be?"

"We will carry on for thee."

A final *clunk* resounded, and the doors parted. Hughes stepped out, his mouth slinging open. He didn't bother to disguise his wonderment. If the Lunarlight

Wing was rife with moons, then this must surely have been the wing of the Dragonlords.

A carpeted hallway ballooned into a grand foyer framed by scaly balustrades and a stairwell wrapped by three dragons carved from golden-brown citrine, rainbow opal, and alexandrite that seemed purple one moment, twilight blue the next. The stairs themselves were pine, their edges curled as though wreathed in fire. To the left, an arch led to a room of armor stands. Hughes saw ornate suits aligned in a phalanx of steel. To the left, a second arch gave way to a high-ceilinged room where the bones of a great drake hung suspended by wire.

"Is that real?" asked Estelle in a tiny voice.

"Of course not," said Wendy. "Everyone knows the dragons disappeared long ago."

"But..."

"And that their bones were never recovered."

"Yes, only..."

"It's wonderful to see that you've inherited Idris' capacity for taking a hint," Wendy said smoothly.

The girl slumped, defeated. "Thank you, Lady."

They took the stairs, close enough to trace the slender scales of each gemstone dragon if they'd a mind to.

"Whose voice was that?" Hughes asked. "In the elevator."

"My father, Walsingham," Wendy replied with affection. "Terribly prudent man. He commissioned the eighty-ninth floor as the site for the Perfect Prison." He watched her expression sober. "Little did he know its first and only occupant would be his doom."

Eager to get her mind off that harrowing subject, Hughes said quickly, "And that chorus? Did Walsingham invent that?"

It was Cate who answered him. "*Scarlet brother be my shield!* That was the old battle chant of the Citadel."

"A relic of drearier days," said Wendy. "And before my father's time. But this is hardly the appropriate time to reminisce. The Perfect Prison is quite close. Which reminds me..."

She withdrew a vambrace from her pocket. It was plain, the leather tawny brown and supple. There, in the groove of the wrist, he made out the small *J* of the Jolenes. Hughes counted two straps wrapped around the vambrace's forearm. He recalled Cate's giddy words from the thirty-first of July, the evening they got sozzled on beer with names that didn't sound like the names of beer at all.

The Perfect Prison can be used a maximum of three times. The only person deemed dangerous enough to be placed in unbreakable incarceration is...

"Through here," Wendy ushered them as Estelle tightened her new brace.

At the top of the stair a chandeliered chamber unwound into nine corridors. Wendy brought the company down the fourth. Given the security measures in place so far, Hughes wondered what fate awaited those who took their chances with any of the other eight.

Ahead lay a crooked door.

"And now I must defer to our turnkey," said Wendy Dragontail. She looked at their puzzled expressions. "Is there a problem?"

Estelle pointed at the crooked door. "This is it?"

"Yes."

"But it's... it's, um..."

"Understated," Cate supplied.

"Is it?" Wendy regarded the door. Paneled boards. Handle. Lintel. Frame. It was just a door. Crooked though, and Hughes was mystified and a little creeped out to discover it was hard to look at for very long, similar to the carousel or those illogical scrawls of nothingness in his dream.

"No," Wendy mused after a moment. "I think it states things quite clearly. Cate, you will accompany Hughes into the Perfect Prison."

"No, my Lady."

"No?"

"Wouldn't be right, your Ladyship."

The leader of the Citadel's face was impassive. "And why not?"

"I sleep like a kitten, your Ladyship."

"Meaning?"

"No one insinuates themselves into my head. That goes for you, me, and the girl."

Only for me, thought Hughes. *She thinks Frank and I need to meet face-to-face with no one else around to spoil it.*

"And should things go bad, and Frank Gallant attacks Hughes?" Wendy demanded. "What then?"

"Then Frank had best avoid dreaming of mirrors," said Cate.

They stared at one another. Cate won.

"Oh very well," said Wendy, looking away. "Estelle, if you please."

Estelle looked back and forth between Hughes and the door. "So what, I just turn the handle?"

"That is generally the order of operation," said Wendy.

"Oh."

Estelle stepped forward with the pomp and circumstance of a girl who is thirteen-going-on-fifty-seven, and who has read a lot of books about this sort of thing and wasn't about to let a stupid crooked door ruin it for her.

Standing next to Cate, Hughes performed a quick mental inventory and was pleasantly surprised to find himself both calm and focused. He had expected the mean aunt imagination to be up to her old tricks, but the contrary turned out to be true. He was excited. No two ways about it. Thrilled as a boy climbing aboard his first carousel ride.

Beyond that crooked door was a figure of indescribable origin. A man the rumor mill had dubbed the Dream Warrior. And weren't the connotations of that as dark and juicy as a pomegranate?

That conviction that the figure with the yellow eyes blazing through the sepia-tinted world of dreams was captivating. He hadn't been lying to Wendy before, he couldn't shake it if he tried. It was marrow deep. A goddamn *certainty.*

He wanted to meet Frank Gallant.

Was desperate to, in fact.

A hand squeezed his arm. He didn't look to see the source of that encouragement. He didn't have to.

Estelle turned the handle. The crooked door opened.

Snick.

Feeling Cate's eyes on him, Hughes entered the Perfect Prison.

***

It was dark inside. Not the pitiless dark of Miss Gleam's eyes. A light allowed him to distinguish the details of the Perfect Prison, wan and gray, although later Hughes was hard pressed to recall if there had been windows, or lamps, or even candles. The dry air smelled of woodchips, lacquer, old cloth, glue, and must, like the inside of an old toy box you might happen upon in the attic of your childhood home. Shelves lined the walls. Rows and rows of them climbed from floor to ceiling. They were full of limp, lifeless child-shapes.

Hundreds of sewn-button eyes stared sightlessly at Hughes.

Yes. Darkness blanketed this place. It was a puppet workshop, snug and sinister and charming and evil all at once.

The only wall bare of puppets was the one across from where he'd come in, the one he was facing now. Hughes had no idea what to make of it. It was a stage.

He was aware of something changing. His fingers brushed Chimera's hilt. Shadows lengthened. Spotlights clicked on. Now there *were* puppets onstage. But how had they gotten there? No strings tugged them. He counted three, and with a growing curiosity Hughes recognized them at once. Bent and beastly, he was looking at wood carvings of the Nightjar Coven.

Another puppet appeared, holding of all things a small lovingly crafted violin.

Before his widening eyes this new arrival tapped its bow and began to saw at the instrument's fretboard, which against all rationality sent up a lively tune. The Nightjar Coven responded, the music animating them.

Flawlessly synchronized, the three witches put their gnarled hands over their faces: *les femmes sont triste*, as Tommy Fahrenheit would say. After this little display of despair, they each raised a finger: *an idea has struck!* One by one they began to cavort, a weird loping dance that raised the hairs on Hughes' arms.

It culminated in them removing something from themselves. At first it was hard to tell what exactly, but Hughes prided himself on his perception.

Unless he was mistaken, through a kind of surgical voodoo, the Coven had just removed their wombs.

He watched avidly as the wooden lumps meant to represent uterine tissue fused together. The lights and the music struck out, leaving him blind. With an uproar of melody, they came back on. Where the witches' wombs had been, there now stood a puppet. A girl.

To the merry sawing of the violinist, the witches coddled and fawned over their little one. They formed a ring encircling her with their bandy, sinuous arms, their heads thrown back in silent cackles: *the Coven has grown, joy of joys!*

The lights dimmed. The music took on a somber, almost malevolent tone.

Hughes watched as the girl puppet escaped the ring while the witches laughed obliviously. And she wasn't a girl but a boy, and here he was growing tall, and the witches hunting high and low for him, and the man was always the slimmest hair's breadth beyond their reach.

Then the witch puppets turned to Hughes. Up to then his engagement in the production was strong. He'd been rooting for the hero. *Escape!* his heart crooned. *Go, go. Leave these old battleaxes behind and don't look back!*

Now in the hunt for their boy, the Coven were looking beyond the bounds of the stage. Hughes felt fear gush through him as they lunged like jackals.

The spotlights went out, and that drab gray color returned to the room. No music came to him, only the rapid thumping in his chest. The stage was gone too.

Hughes gazed at the far wall, as fascinated as he had ever been.

A bed was there. Impossibly, it clung to the wall by its legs, floating twenty inches above the floor. Lying there on its sheetless mattress, upside down and covered in what Hughes thought might be cobwebs but were in fact severed puppet strings, was a man.

The man was as dark as Hughes was pallid. Fanned out on the bed, his locks were woven in braids. Aurora borealis, the same sort of northern lights Hughes had marveled at in vids of far-off Daethumberland, strobed and wound through those braids.

Frank Gallant was as beautiful as a dream.

In this Perfect Prison he slept amongst the cut strings.

Awed and feeling flickers of trepidation, Hughes took a moment to check that he was not trapped in here (odd how intuition casts shadows on our courage when we least expect it) and was both alarmed and relieved to see no door behind him. Only a handle set into a shelf of stitched, button-eyed faces.

He turned back.

Frank's eyes were open.

For a moment Hughes could almost have believed he felt their blazing yellow glow pour over him like liquid fire. He didn't speak. He couldn't have if he had tried. He stood there like a hare in headlights.

Gracefully, in one exquisite motion, the Dream Warrior flowed down from his bed of incarceration. The strings accompanied him, clinging to his form in a gauze. Before his feet touched the ground, the strings had begun to change. They coursed over his heels and ankles, forming shoes of brick-colored leather. Now he wore a white shirt, trousers and a jacket of deep blue corduroy, and a tie that elegantly matched his shoes. Cufflinks were the final touch, chains of silver Zs used in animations to signify sleep. With that the strings were gone.

Frank Gallant approached, his hands submerged in the pockets of his suit.

"I'm sorry," said Hughes before he could stop himself.

Frank's head tilted ever-so-slightly to one side.

"About your mothers."

Frank nodded understanding. "Don't be."

Only he didn't say it because his lips never moved.

Frank's voice was as somnolently beautiful as his looks, and it spoke directly into Hughes' head.

"It's a day for people inheriting things," said Hughes.

Another head tilt from the Dream Warrior.

"In order to get you out of here, I needed to dream. Your mothers helped me. They spoke into my head as you do."

"In that case I'll give my tongue a workout," said Frank. *Really* said, this time. "And I assure you, man, those wily old hags only help themselves."

"I believe it."

"You know, I'd like to give it a try."

"Helping me?"

"Sure," said Frank. "Peace and goodwill. Nectar to the needy. All that shit."

He offered Hughes a hand.

Hughes took it, anticipating that his fingers would pass through Frank's like mist and oddly grateful when they gripped solid flesh. "I get the sense there's something in it for you," he said. "Well? What's your nectar of choice?"

Frank Gallant laughed, a rich, musical laugh. "Why, vengeance, of course. Finest ambrosia around."

ACT ELEVEN

IN A SLANTING WISE

CHAPTER FORTY-EIGHT

Somewhere wicked, a telephone began to ring.

It rang once. Twice. Before the trill of the third ring, glittering fingers plucked it up.

"Salutations and good morrow, sir," said Miss Gleam. "I've been meaning to call you about Lucinda. Mr. Twinkle's cat? Never found, the poor thing. Sorrowful is the detritus of war. Lost but not forgotten, etcetera. But listen to me blathering. Dear sir, how *are* you faring on this—"

The voice on the other end of the line told her to shut her mouth if she knew what was good for her. It told her to listen closely, for there was an emergency, and she and her associate were needed posthaste.

As the voice laid all of this out, Miss Gleam's lips curled at the corners. She listened as Mr. Shine, criminal mastermind, corrupting financier, and runner of so many rackets throughout the city, he might as well set up a mobile tennis court, explained that he was in danger. The people who organized the killing of Mr. Twinkle, and Miss Shimmer, and all the rest, had found him. They were coming.

Mr. Shine told Gleam that despite the grim prospect of this news, he wasn't worried. Gleam would hang up the phone, and she would get her dimwitted glutton of a partner, and together they would make their way to Mr. Shine's lair as quickly as possible.

"Sincerest apologies, sir. I seem not to have heard you correctly. What was that you called Mr. Glint?"

A dimwitted glutton, repeated Mr. Shine. *A gorging ignoramus who was damn lucky he was useful.* Testily, impatiently, Mr. Shine asked Gleam why she was still talking to him when she ought to be moving?

There was a brief silence. Then:

"We are, as ever, at your beck and call, sir," said Miss Gleam cheerfully.

Mr. Shine said he was glad to hear it.

"There is one small matter, sir."

Mr. Shine asked if it couldn't wait.

"I'm afraid not, sir."

Mr. Shine said if it was so fucking important, why didn't she spit it out?

Miss Gleam held the receiver closer to her mouth, making sure he would not miss a single word she said.

"I really do hope you win, sir. The enemy is at your gates, true, but such battles have often been won by the defenders. In fact history favors those who begin a siege enclosed by stone walls, rather than those outside them. Fight robustly, sir. Trounce them well. Live another day." She leered then, her eyes bulging, and her grin like something carved in crumbling marble. "Because tomorrow I am going to find you, and I am going to cut you into shiny little pieces for the magpies. Isn't that disappointing?"

She hung up the phone. Then, thinking better of it, she picked it up, cradle and all, and *squeezed*. The phone broke into smithereens. She savored the word. "Smithereens. Oh, I feel so much better."

Mr. Glint grunted. "What will we do for work?"

"My indefatigable friend, we have entered the rank and file of the self-employed. Thus," she said, rubbing her hands together, "we shall do as the market dictates. Buy. Sell. Name your preference."

Mr. Glint gave this due consideration. "Slit," he said. "And pull out the market's insides."

"Spoken like a true capitalist," said Miss Gleam. She hugged him tight, donned her hat, and then turned toward the horizon. She could see it through their broken foyer door. It was blood red, a promising sign. "I suggest that for our first job we mix business and pleasure." Her cheek gave a single ugly twitch. "Say, a family visit."

***

As Frank shook hands with Estelle ("Guess you're my new warden, little lady. You don't mind hobnobbing with the riffraff, do you? No you do not. Estelle, right? I'm Frank Gallant. Hey, that's some grip. I better watch my P's and Q's.") Hughes made the arguably brave and possibly risky decision to speak to Cate.

"Where's Wendy?"

"Whisked away by production to draw up a broadcast plan. Communication is a shambles in the tower and Falstaff is a penguin."

Hughes doubted Wendy had put up much of a struggle when production had come sniffing around. Standing here in corduroy and leather with an easy smile and hair rippling with polar lights was the man who'd killed her father. Yeah, indirectly maybe, but it didn't change the fact the voice coming over the elevator recorder belonged to someone currently lodging in a coffin. Knowing Wendy Dragontail (and Hughes didn't think he did, not really, only those scales she decided people had business seeing), he thought that if things worked out in the end, Frank would meet the Last Dragon on a field of her choosing. Or he'd wind up back in the prison if he wanted to keep his shins intact.

"Any word on how the city's doing?" Hughes asked Cate.

She gave him a sidelong look that told him everything he needed to know.

"We'd better hurry," he said. "Frank?"

"Hughes, my man. The last time you went into the dream world, you used hypnosis, right?" said Frank,

"An enbangled woman lulled me to sleep with a magic item."

"Same pot, different kettle. Okay. Consider that the front door approach. I can take you round the back."

"An ambush," said Estelle.

Frank Gallant grinned. "Got it in one, sugarplum. Hughes, we're going to need somewhere quiet to do this thing."

With a compulsive rub of his neck, Hughes weighed potential options. "I suppose my room would do?"

"Splen-*didly.*"

"Can you take more than one person, Frank?" Cate wanted to know.

"Sure I can. Let's walk and talk. What's your name, red?"

"Cate Jubilee."

"Cate short for Catherine or Catelyn?"

"Catherine."

"Okay, Catherine, nice to meet you. Sure I can take more than one person. They'd want to be sure themselves about going. My mothers are as cruel as they are smart, and they are devilishly smart. They root around in dreams because all the wards you've got up when you're awake slide down when you're snoozing. And there's no guarantee I could keep anyone other than Hughes from slipping into their nightmare realm unnoticed. So," he said, measuring her with those burning yellow eyes, "you sure?"

She nodded. "Double sure."

"You needn't worry about Cate Jubilee," Estelle barged in. "Daddy tells me about everyone in the Citadel, and *he* says Cate's an absolute terror."

Frank Gallant chuckled. "If you say so, little lady, who am I to deny it."

With Cate sending a crestfallen Estelle to the global menagerie for safety (a sentiment Hughes didn't entirely share as he still wasn't sure about the panthers), they set their sights on Hughes' room.

"What tincture do I smell upon the air?" said Frank.

"Crude oil and galvanized rubber," said Cate. They were in the elevator.

"Wonderful." Frank breathed deep and sighed happily. "Wonderful."

Evidently lots of things were wonderful in Frank Gallant's book. He mooned over the pillars in the corridors, the little midfloor garden blooming with autumn crocuses, the way the sunshine rushed in through windows as if there was some urgency behind it. "Every fingertip a coin," he said, turning his hand to see. "I feel wealthier for this warm October gold."

"He's enjoying himself," murmured Hughes.

"He's free," said Cate with mild reproval. "How would you be?"

They ran in silence for a bit. Time was ticking on.

Don't even think about it, said the wounded, mistrustful part of him. *You know what'll happen. Kim showed you. So don't you even think about it.*

Hughes shoved it down where its muffled cries couldn't delay him.

"Cate. There's something I want to talk to you about..."

"This must be the place!" bellowed Frank from up the corridor. "Hughes, this has you written all over it. And papered all over it, I see. Is this some bohemian blanket, or what?"

Out of the corner of his eye, Hughes noticed the ghost of a smile curving Cate's mouth. *All right,* he told the wounded internal voice. *You win this time. But she has a right to know.*

Even if she won't tell you certain things? the voice that was really a part of himself retorted. *Remember the tattoo on her neck? She's keeping secrets, there's two of you in it. And you want to be honest with her, even when she might go off you?*

Yes, he sizzled. *Even then. Besides, she's off me now. If being honest has the slimmest chance of resurrecting that ghost smile into something living and staggeringly lovely, then that's what has to be done.*

The pieces of his broken heart shuffled off dejectedly to have a sulk.

"How will this work?" said Cate as they gathered in Hughes' room.

"Here's how. To get to my mothers' dream realm in Eurydice in a way they don't notice, we've got to visit Mole, Badger, and Toad."

"Not more animals," groaned Hughes.

"Don't bust your wimple, man. Mole, Badger, and Toad are stand-up guys. They kept me company when I was a kid. The only friends I ever had." Frank Gallant's face grew conspiratorial. "But they are mischievous fellows. All dream folk are. They entertain themselves with games. We want to go through them in order to ambush my mothers, we've got to play."

"How?" said Cate.

"The only game in town, red. Language. Words have as much power in dreams as they do in the waking world. Mole, Badger, and Toad have their own bailiwick, namely truth and lies."

A group of overworked servants bustled past Hughes' door. They all looked up, and with the sun from Hughes' window backlighting them, they looked like assassins meeting in a bright hovel to discuss dark work.

Frank brought them back to business. "When you go dreamstrutting, the guys will appear one by one to you. There'll be something in the way, some obstacle you'll have to deal with. Mole, Badger, and Toad will tell you what to do."

"Won't you be there to guide us?" Hughes asked.

"In a way. To keep us as stealthy as can be, I'm going to go in disguise. Sorry to say it Hughes, but it'll be in the form of different animals."

They shared a smile, Hughes' rueful and Frank's charming.

"Listen up. This next part is important. If the guys are telling the truth about how to overcome the obstacle, I'll behave just as that animal should," said Frank. "If they're lying, I'll behave as that animal shouldn't. So say Mole tries to sell you a lie and I'm a rooster. I might hiss like a snake or lay an egg that dissolves into snowflakes."

"Whereas if you cock-a-doodle-dooed, we'd know Mole was telling the truth," said Cate.

"Right as rain."

"Seems simple enough." Cate unfastened her bun, shook her hair out, bent double, combed her fingers through it like a rake combing through fire, and stood up again, a phoenix rising to the occasion. "Have you something in mind for when we get the drop on the Coven?"

"I'm glad you asked me that," said Frank Gallant. "The answer is yes. I do."

On this he would elaborate no further.

Instead he gazed out the window at the ebbing daylight. "Morning, afternoon, twilight, dusk," he said. "Last comes evening in her plunge-line dress. Revenge is sweet, but your world's clock time is sweeter. Iron hands pulling along sacks of seconds, mounds of minutes, and with a surety that cannot be bargained with, only understood, evening gathers every hour in her purse and sets off toward whatever morning holds. Maybe she has a little fun along the way." He looked at them. "I'd like to stay here in your world, outside the bonds of the Perfect Prison. When this is over, will you vouch to Wendy on my account?"

"No," said Cate. She must have registered their surprise at her quickness because she continued. "We could. But it would only be words. Those might be good enough to entertain dream badgers and the like, but here in the waking world it's actions that do the real convincing. Often those involve words, true, but action is about the thing itself. The resolve and motivation and wondering if it was all worth it and doing it anyway." She gave him an encouraging look. "If it helps, you're off to a healthy start."

Frank regarded her in goading silence, but trying to outstare Cate Jubilee was like trying to bring down a wall with withering insults.

He sighed. "Only one thing to do then."

He lay down on Hughes' bed.

"I knocked the pillows off last night," said Hughes. "Are those necessary for... whatever it is you're doing?"

Frank's closed eyes crinkled with amusement. "I think we'll get by."

From the ceiling, the floor, the furniture, even the windowpane, emerged thousands upon thousands of strings.

"Wait for me, evening lady," said Frank in the whispering din that dragged Hughes and Cate into the arms of sleep. "You just hang on tight. I'll be back in no time."

CHAPTER FORTY-NINE

There were hyenas outside the *Scriptorium and Flavored Tea Emporium*. Before the transformation they had been basically good people. A college student. A plumber having a nap in his car between jobs. Several members of the All Girls National Poker Club, who coincidentally boarded at The Wimples School For Exasperating Young Ladies, where gambling was as rife as the practice of rolling a report card into a marijuana spliff.

None of which would have been any comfort to Gormon Hughes, who was eyeing the pack from the narrowing safety of his teashop. He wasn't too keen on the bristles spiking up from their spotted fur, and he really wasn't pleased about their teeth, which were yellow brown as old book pages, and though they weren't particularly sharp, seemed to be built for the gamey fare of the savannah rather than the soft pickings of the city.

By his foot, Boochums gave a hopeless whine.

Gormon watched one of the hyena's ears perk up and decided he didn't much care for that facet of their anatomy either. That particular hyena looked up at the building, and then at the zigzagging stair climbing it as though wondering how this strange device worked.

Over by the kettle, the wolfhound that was probably Ernie Wilks gave two throaty barks.

"Hush, boy," said Gormon calmly, and the dog did, but too late.

Down in the deserted street, more hyenas were alerted, their ears flared. The one who'd been studying the building yawned, exposing far too many of those disquieting teeth. A long pink tongue lolled out and slipped back into the gummy threat that was its mouth.

It padded forward.

Wet warmth as Boochums licked his hand plaintively.

Son, thought Gormon as he stroked the dog's head. *Whatever it is you've got on the brew, make it fast.*

The hyena stepped onto the bottom stair.

***

Thwack.

Hughes sat up sharply, his eyes flashing open.

Establish your surroundings, he thought. *Then find one of these dream gentlemen Frank was talking about.*

He got to his feet and looked around. Hillocks rolled for miles in every direction. There was no sign of Cate. He hoped she was all right. Time enough to worry later. For now...

Atop one of the hillocks, only six hundred yards away, stood a house. The house made no sense. To begin with it was a sort of squashed igloo-shape. The bricks were red, the shutters white, and the front door... completely absent, actually. There was a chimney though. It was under the house, supporting it against all laws of weight distribution. Holes had been made in it at regular intervals, and from these billowed a clean wintry-smelling smoke, the sort that means a fire to snuggle beside and warm your brandy over.

In the yard was a mole. He was chopping logs into kindling with an axe that was twice-and-three-quarters the size of him.

Thwack.

Hughes approached. "Erm. Hello, am I speaking to the Mole?"

"*The?*" The mole peered squintily, as moles do. "I don't know about *the.* I'm *a* mole."

"And your name is?"

"Mole, of course."

"R-right," said Hughes, trying to get a grip on things. "I'm trying to get to the Nightjar Coven in Eurydice."

"You've no business being there," said Mole.

"I've got plenty."

"Well then there has no business with you." *Thwack.* "Only trouble."

Hughes watched two perfectly split logs tumble to the ground. Mole set another log on the block and hefted his axe.

"Mind if I help you?" said Hughes.

The Mole squinted up at him. "That would be very nice," he admitted. "My sciatica is murder in this weather."

You mean in pleasant rural coziness? thought Hughes, but he took the axe and raised his eyebrows.

"Light," he said.

"It's as heavy as it needs to be," said Mole, sitting on a nearby stump.

Hughes took a swing.

Wh—

The axe hadn't managed to bisect the log.

"Just bring it down hard on the block," said Mole, taking out a jar that couldn't possibly have fitted in his waistcoat and trousers and rubbing a balming lotion into his aching back.

Hughes obeyed.

—ack.

"Good," said Mole. "And again, squire."

Hughes fetched another log. In his peripheral vision, he saw a grasshopper leap onto Mole's shoulder. Mole seemed not to notice.

That must be Frank.

"Can I get to Eurydice from your property?" he asked in a casual voice.

"Sure enough you can. But take your mind from that and put it on your swing."

The grasshopper's mandibles moved. That seemed pretty normal. So Mole was telling the truth.

"How do I get there?"

"You're a tenacious bugger," said Mole, wincing as he worked the lotion in. "Suit yourself. If you want to go in the direction of the witches, what you do is, you take the axe, right? And you chop my head off."

Hughes froze in the act of chopping.

He looked at the Mole, then at the grasshopper. It was glowing orange.

"I don't believe you," said Hughes carefully. "How do I make progress, really?"

"I wasn't lying about the axe," said Mole.

The grasshopper stopped glowing.

"That I do believe," said Hughes, getting into the swing of things so to speak. "So I take the axe, and I cut you more wood for a nice huge fire?"

"No," said Mole.

The grasshopper's spindly legs moved, so that was true.

Hughes didn't understand. If the axe was definitely involved, then what...

His throat dried up.

"*You* have to cut *my* head off," Hughes said.

Mole squinted at him knowingly.

A minute later, a noise tumbled over the hills.

Thwack.

***

Miss Gleam and Mr. Glint strode into Redspire as twilight quilted the sky with indigo. On an ordinary day this would have been impossible. There were safeguards. First, Ptolema District itself was patrolled by mechanical birds who scanned a small pass that was sent by the government to each person in residence. Should someone unwelcome fail to present a pass, the streetbeaters would be notified. This, according to those who worked in Ptolema District's glass superstructures, kept the lower classes from causing any high-grade fuss. Second, the Scarlet Citadel was filled to the brim with capable fighters imbued with magical abilities, a compelling deterrent to any would-be-infiltrators.

However, it was not an ordinary day. The mechanical birds were busy scanning rogue otters in the District fountains, and the Citadel was empty except for a skeleton crew of staff, one of whom was unfortunate enough to be womaning the front desk at reception.

"Excuse me," she said. "You can't be in... here..."

"Really?" said Miss Gleam. "Well, that's no great shakes. As chance would have it, we have no intention of lingering but are hoping to find the room belonging to our fond and fabulous brother." She leaned over the desk, grinning in a way that would have made the hyenas outside the *Flavored Tea Emporium* wish for the intervention of tigers. "Perhaps you can point us toward it."

The receptionist subtracted her duty to the Citadel from the sum total of Miss Gleam's request, factoring in a few fanglike decimal points. The result didn't seem worth finding out what would happen if she refused.

Scrolling with her mouse, she opened a file on her cogwheel computer.

"What's the name, please?" she said.

***

She woke looking at herself.

Clambering off the slippery floor, Cate took in the realistic quality of the image. They'd even gotten her bells right, the tattoos chiming forever against the belfry of her throat. She looked around, and there she was again. A regiment of Cate Jubilees furrowed their brows. The effect reminded her of that poor screen actor Hughes had introduced her to, the one who'd died and had his likeness propped up for companies to advertise things. What was his name again...

Hughes.

She cast about for him and came up short. Hughes wasn't here, which meant he was either close by or they'd been separated. Cate however, was not lacking for company. She was also in the ceiling, and yes, the floor too now she peered down for a gander.

Unlike her partner, she had not visited every exhibit The Rotbloom Carnival of Bright Oddments and Dark Delights had as a child, but she recognized a house of mirrors when she was cordoned inside its glass heart.

She began exploring her space. She discovered quickly it was not a small claustrophobic gazebo but rather a huge labyrinth with ramps, boulevards lined in reflective strips, and even strange caves with uneven floors that clicked under the soles of her hobnail boots.

The idea that she might want to hop inside a mirror and gain a deeper understanding of the place crossed her mind, but she cast it aside pretty quickly. There was something oddly disturbing about all those versions of herself splayed out like light through a diamond. Usually Cate took solace in her reflection. Its two-dimensionality actually bolstered her sense that here, on this side of the looking glass, she possessed a strong sense of personal depth. She was a woman who prided herself on ability to confront the things in her life that other people might find uncomfortable, distasteful, or even a little spooky. Hell, who was she kidding? Some facets of who she was—and facets was the word—were downright terrifying.

But by and large mirrors helped. Even the grimy ones.

Maybe those ones most of all.

That reassurance was not present here in this house that seemed melted out of one huge berg of glass. The fact that it *was* a house seemed totally clear to her, the reason being that images had lived here before and would live on after she was gone, reflecting nothing but themselves on and on and on, picture without end, amen.

And him, she thought. *He lives here too.*

"Who?" she said. The sound of her own voice startled her. It wasn't ownership (the voice belonged to her), but something else. The *pitch*.

She gazed at herself in one of countless surfaces and had to cram her hand into her mouth to keep from screaming.

In a watercolor-design blouse, skirt, and small derby boots, the regiment of Cate Jubilees stared wide-eyed at her. She was eight years old, and she was wearing the outfit she'd worn on the day that... Oh dear God, it *was* that day, wasn't it?

"He lives here too," she said in a hoarse whisper.

And as if summoned by that she heard it. It came from somewhere deep in the maze. Not right here, but not far away either.

A grunting sound.

Cate ran.

This is a dream, she thought, willing her pitter-patter heartbeat to slow. *These reflections of me are false faces. Smoke and mirrors, right? Any moment now I'll run across Badger or Mole, and then Frank will be there, or even Hughes, God I hope so HughesHughesHughes be somewhere safe and take me there.*

Only, I am there. She thought this firmly, suppressing her panic. She had tricked herself, thinking she'd heard that grunting sound. It was the outfit, and besides, it was disorienting being surrounded in a ceaseless barrage of yourself from every angle.

She listened. Nothing.

She slowed to a jog, grinning self-consciously. Now, hadn't that been silly?

Still, it was clear this place was just as dangerous as Frank had claimed. An inhuman intelligence moved behind the mirrors. It was messing with her. She wondered again where Hughes and Frank were. She labeled that a secondary concern. Primary was her need to find one of the dream animals.

By now she had slowed to a brisk walk, and her head was bundled up with the acute embarrassment of those who think they hear something large shambling and rasping around their backyard, only to find a plastic bin liner snagged on the shed's padlock. Noises could be uncanny like that.

In the war against Champleurs, there had been cavalry charges. Some soldiers went home and became writers and vidmakers. In a documentary she'd seen, one man said that horses sounded like people when they screamed.

Why was she thinking about the war?

Because of the grunt, she answered herself. *I heard that sound on the day I wore these clothes.*

Across a million surfaces, Cate Jubilee began to speed up once more. The skin on her arms had pimpled in gooseflesh. And then, quite abruptly, she stopped.

Less than thirty feet away, from behind a carton-shaped tower of glass, stepped her father. He was bare-chested, his pants stained with old urine and fresh orange juice. A film of spittle had formed at the corners of his mouth. In his left hand he held a workman's mallet. Its head was clotted with blood and human hair.

"Cathy," he said. "I finally found you."

***

Rolling intolerably fast like a well-kicked football was not, in Hughes' opinion, an experience worth recommending. He rolled and spun, and with a gooey *splodging* sound, he landed knee-deep in a white wood. The realization that he still had knees, as well as a stomach, chest, and a neck that had not been shorn in two with an axe, was a most welcome one.

Candlewax trees loomed all around him, dribbling from their upturned branches that were leafed with merry dancing flames. Ten inches of wax covered the forest floor. Here and there he could see tin apples painted green and red poking through the oozy mess. They were the kind you might hang on your tree at Tinfrost in December, though Hughes was estranged to them, having never possessed the funds for holiday celebration.

For some reason the ground held a warm thermoslike heat, keeping the wax nice and warm and globulous.

In the flickering gloom, he could make out a figure shuffling toward him on bandy legs. Hughes squinted, looking a good deal like the mole who'd just cut his head off a few moments ago.

"As I live and breathe, there he is!"

It was Badger. He was negotiating the morass on tall stilts that carved through the wax like a knife through cold butter.

"What spiffing luck!"

"Hello, Badger. I'm sorry I haven't got much time for pleasantries, but..."

"You're on your way to the Nightjar Coven," said Badger. "I've just come from Mole's. He's told me all about it."

Hughes wasn't sure how this was technically possible but then remembered he was talking to a badger on stilts in a candlewax wood, and thus technical possibility could stuff it.

"It's my pleasure to be a guide to you," Badger said. "There, beside you, is your basket."

Hughes glanced down. There was a woven basket by his left leg. It had not been there before. He picked it up anyway, and that was when he saw the wolf.

It was very close, only a stone's throw away, but Badger seemed as oblivious to it as Mole had been to the grasshopper.

Frank.

"Thank you, Badger," said Hughes, his voice as confident as it could be given the fact that it was a very large wolf. "Um. It's a good basket. What next?"

"It's quite simple. Fill that basket with red apples."

The wolf raised its hind legs up and up until it was doing a handstand.

That was definitely not included in the suite of normal wolf behavior.

"Are the apples relevant?"

"Certainly," said Badger, offended.

The wolf set its legs down and squatted on its haunches. That looked okay.

Hughes nodded. "How about just the green ones, then?"

"No, no, no," insisted Badger. "Don't be ridiculous. They've absolutely got to be red!"

The wolf whistled.

"Can wolves whistle?" said Hughes.

"What?" said Badger.

"Nothing. I think I'll stick with these green fellows if it's all the same to you."

"This is highly unorthodox," steamed Badger from atop his stilts while Hughes set about filling the basket.

The wolf placed one in his hand.

"Thanks, Frank."

It blinked yellowly at him and padded off.

In no time at all the basket was brimmed up full.

Wax plipped and puddled around them.

"Nothing happening," said Hughes.

Badger rolled his eyes. "I suppose you'd better eat one, since you've gone to all that trouble."

The wolf did nothing but stare with a faint air of menace, which Hughes took to mean that Badger's exasperation was a mask for the truth.

He selected an apple, brushed a bit of wax off out of general principle, and sank his teeth into wafer-thin metal.

It crunched.

***

"Have you ever seen the like?"

"Nope."

The freshly self-employed duo stood outside Hughes' room. The door was open. Inside, a blockade of strings prohibited entry.

Miss Gleam examined them up close. "Nylon," she said. "I've always had a preference for catgut."

"Me too," said Mr. Glint, who was hungry.

Through crowding thunderheads of madness, faint rays of the old Miss Gleam emerged. She chuckled fondly. "Not for cleaning your molars with, my exemplar in hygienic practice. Or for slurping out of things with a fork and spoon, for that matter."

"You said 'cat guts.'"

"Cat*gut*, Mr. Glint. For instruments, fishing rods, and marionettes. Though I have seen puppets maneuvered in that delightful herky-jerky way by all sorts, including piano wire, trimmed sailor rope, or garroting string."

Mr. Glint nodded. It was good to hear Miss Gleam talk like that. Her stream of consciousness meant the rivers of life were running as they should.

"Why should Hughes' room be contaminated by a sudden case of nylon strings?" Miss Gleam said. "Truly it is a quandary for the ages."

"Haven't got ages."

"Mr. Glint, you are the very apogee of veracity today."

"Thanks."

"Indeed!" she cried. "Let us espouse the ideals of instrumentalist, the fisher, and the puppeteer, whose combined artistry topples nations and delights even the most bumptious of hobbyists. Without further ado."

She went to cut the strings with her sparkling fingernails. The instant they made contact with the nylon, her fingernails unwound, stranding and fusing into the blockade. Next went her fingers. Then her hand. Then her arm.

"Oh," she said.

Mr. Glint grabbed for her. She slipped through his fingers, thinner than thin. He was alone in the corridor.

A clatter drew his attention. A portly man in muttonchops stood stock still. A clipboard was on the floor, the source of the noise. The man must have been immersed in his reading because he'd walked right up to Mr. Glint, glancing up just in time to avoid bouncing into him.

Mr. Glint picked up the clipboard and looked at what was written there.

"What's this?"

"What's... Findings. Research findings," stammered the man.

"All argle-bargle to me." Mr. Glint handed him back the clipboard. "Where do these strings go?"

"Strings?"

"These ones."

"I... I don't know."

Mr. Glint nodded. "Well, toodle-pip," he said and touched the wall of nylon. In a moment he was gone, leaving Doctor John Isherwood to faint dead away.

***

"Come here and give us a kiss."

Cate recoiled.

That was not her dad. It only looked like him, spoke like him, stood with his hunched posture, and even smelled like him, a pungent aroma of pan oil, cigars, bitty orange juice, and sweat.

Then again, her dad hadn't been her dad either. Not on that day.

Most mystifying of all was the apparition's reflection. It didn't have one. Endless Cates studied him unbelievingly. *But he has eyes for me, only me.*

"Your mum's gone for a lie down," he told her. "What do you say we look for your kite in the cupboard and lose it up a tree? Would you like that?"

He had often brought that up when he came back from the trenches, despite his wife and daughter reminding him—gently at first, then with growing impatience—that little Cathy had never owned a kite.

As for Mum having a lie down...

Cate found her eyes drawn to the mallet head in his hand. The hairy gore was still wet. A revulsion verging on primal horror closed her throat. She took a few quick steps back, a child retreating from something that has come to her from that place where things that go bump in the night are all too real.

Her father's face darkened. "Who told you you could move? Did I tell you? I didn't tell you." He began to advance. "You move when I say so, my girl. *Has your mum spoiled you while I was away?*"

That did it. That raised, paternal voice edged in the mudslime of trench warfare.

Cate turned on her heel and bolted.

"There she goes. Proof in the pudding. Well I'll *fix* you, Cathy." His footsteps thundered behind her. "I'll fix you like I fixed *her.*"

Only a dream, she thought frantically. *Pale masks in the dark. Falsefalsefalse!*

"Come here you little shit! I'm going to crack your head like an egg and scramble your brains!"

She dared not dive into the glass.

Whatever was showing her that *thing* behind her was not something she wanted to be closer to.

The maze whirred by on all sides, distortions of glass showing the daughter in flight, yet nothing of the hulking shadow trailing her and closing in, yes, closing steadily in...

CHAPTER FIFTY

Hurtling through a darkness full of tinny rattles and metallic knocks like a can of spray paint being shaken with gusto, Hughes took a moment to congratulate himself. He thought he was doing rather well. Of course, this opened up the possibility of the midden hitting the propeller. But with Frank as the director of this dreamy play, Hughes felt that he was, at the very least, in capable hands.

Instead of hissing out in a spray of colored particles, he felt himself poured into the next portion of the dream realm. He was in a hall fashioned out of long, soft brushstrokes. A watercolor. Hughes had read a whole host of illustrated books that came with watercolors. The fluid style soothed him, especially ones set in a pastoral scene, which were inevitably, achingly beautiful.

He did not find this hall beautiful.

Gassy green light filtered through the drawn curtains. Chopped wood burned with a similar swampy glow from jagged, spiky stone hearths. The carpet, which fuzzed its way from one corner of the hall to the other, showed armies of toads, frogs, newts, salamanders, and engorged wormy caecilians. They were fighting on a red hill, though it was unclear whether or not the hill had been red before the battle began or if it was a pigment defined by the entrails of which there was no shortage. At the summit of the hill loomed a manor house. It was much more sensibly built than Mole's chimney-supported cottage, but the more he looked at it the less Hughes liked the manor.

This time Frank appeared before the host of the dream.

A dark bird flitted down from the eaves and fluttered around Hughes' knuckles until he held his hand flat. He smiled when it perched there, its tiny claws solid, unpainted, and oddly comforting for that in this weird watery den.

"I'm no expert on birds," said Hughes. "I told Wendy and Cate that I used to think crows were eagles that had fallen into chimneys. Between you and I, Frank, I also used to think red-breasted robins were red because they suffered from serial embarrassment."

The bird on his hand twittered.

Hughes remembered Frank's rich bellyful laughter and smiled.

"I'd be willing to bet that for this last leg of the journey, you've taken the shape of your mothers' Coven," he said. "A nightjar."

"So here you are then."

The voice whelmed up the hall and over Hughes in a warbly blast. Vibrations trembled up through his boots. Rumbling down the hall on two huge, webbed toes was an absolute zeppelin of a toad. Stooped over his cane he was easily two-stories tall. Clusters of warts clung like milky fungus to his greenish-gray skin. His throat sagged damply over his collar. He wore a soldier's uniform, red as the bloody hill depicted on the hall's carpet. His epaulettes were of frayed gold, his cuffs laced, and his silver buttons tarnished or missing entirely.

He came to a halt in front of Hughes, lording over his guest with his slimy fingers gripped tight about the head of his cane.

"I had hoped Mole and Badger were fibbing. Evidently they were not, more's the pity. Where is Frank? I know he's hiding somewhere."

"You mean you can't see him?" Hughes said innocently.

"*Brrrrrhuh*, indeed I cannot!"

"More's the pity. How do I get to the Nightjar Coven?"

Toad blinked. It was a slow process. "Not much heat in those fires," he declared, moving to a hearth and rapping it with his cane. "Mole's been neglecting his axe I wager. Spare the whetstone, spoil the blade. That's what I used to tell my men in the war."

The nightjar flitted to Hughes' wrist, exactly at the spot where a watch would be.

Hughes nodded understanding.

"Look, I'm in a bit of a rush," he told Toad. "Would you mind skipping the cantankerous sergeant bit, please?"

"*Sergeant?*" Toad blustered. "*Sergeant?* I was a *general*, boy! I've a mind to grind you up and put you in a saltshaker. Sergeant indeed!"

The nightjar darted off Hughes' wrist and began to circle the manor house on the rug.

Trying to tell me something.

He studied the battle on the carpet again as Toad muttered to himself. There was a force led by a massive toad—he assumed it was this very creature—and it was charging up the hill toward the manor. The artist had rendered the massive toad's face with the most avid greed Hughes had ever seen.

"You were fighting for the manor," he said.

Now that Hughes' eyes were adjusting to the miserable gloom, he could make out shades of vaporous green light surrounding the house.

"And this hall is inside it!"

Toad turned. "What's that you're saying? Speak up, you insectile little twerp."

The toads won the battle, and as a reward for commanding his force, Toad got to claim this manor as his own. "I was just admiring your abode, Toad."

"I despise rhymes."

"Unintentional, unintentional," Hughes soothed, assuming the role of the excellent guest. "I think you've really, ah, spruced the place. Am I detecting a reek of *eau du lilypad?*"

Toad ribbited grotesquely. The sound of it shuddered through Hughes' chest.

"Notice that, did you? *Brrrrrhuh.* Well, you have a modicum of taste, I suppose. I don't suppose you've enlisted?"

"In the army, sir? No, sir," said Hughes, taking his cue to address the former general with respect. "Though someday I might be brave enough to join, sir."

"It's about common decency, not bravery, boy. Warfare is morality. The two are interchangeable."

"Yes, sir."

"The only way to show your fellow man you love him is by ramming something sharp into his belly and giving a twist. You release him from his mortal coil with honor. There is no kiss like the kiss of death, isn't that so?"

"Yes, sir."

Words are just air with a few extra bells and whistles, he told himself. *Blow them out for this despicable windbag and maybe you can get out of here.*

Toad blinked his chrysoberyl eyes. "The Nightjar Coven, eh?"

"That's where I'm headed, sir," said Hughes. Frank flitted back to his hand.

"The way might be opened," allowed Toad. "First, you must convince me that you have understood what I've told you about love."

That wasn't right. It wasn't a statement that could be interpreted as a lie or the truth. Hughes looked to Frank for help. The bird's head twitched back and forth as birds' heads are wont to do.

"Well?" Toad demanded.

"You spoke to Mole and Badger?" Hughes asked desperately, hoping this would jog the old bastard's memory and let him know he was doing this all wrong.

"Yes, yes. *Brrrrrhuh,* I spoke to those two fools. What of it?"

I don't have time for this.

He hadn't asked Frank if he could use his Performance on the dream folk. Some part of him must have assumed he wouldn't need to, and thus far it had been proved right. What would happen if he failed?

"I can see you've no interest in going any further," said Toad. "It mustn't be important to you."

Hughes took three crisp strides, raised his free hand, and jabbed a finger into his host's sloshy bloated stomach.

"Let." Jab. "Me." Jab. "Through." Jab.

And with that he hauled up every dreg of his power and unleashed it on Toad.

Soon after, echoing through the hall was a loud clear pop.

***

No place is truly empty. You might have the sense they are, especially if that place is usually stuffed with people like breadcrumbs and herbs into a Tinfrost turkey. Hospitals, schools, leisure centers. In the absence of human beings, such locations cry out for something, and something answers.

Silences seem deeper there, and the rodents and bugs that burst through widening cracks in the plaster, tiles, and moldy wood fixtures seem only to accentuate the feeling that any who tread there are likewise as abandoned as their immediate environment. Loneliness gathers flies. It starts to stink.

But while that feeling exists, it is only that—a sensation.

Even the most decrepit wreck of a leisure center where once life exploded in twizzlers, snickerdrakes, and other sundry fireworks, teems with life.

No place is really, truly empty.

Some version of this idea moved like a glacier in the cold arctic of Mr. Glint's mind. Still, what he was seeing now was as close to empty as possible.

He was standing on a featureless gray plate. No, not gray. Sapped. Leeched. Colorless.

Beside him, Miss Gleam gave a low whistle of appreciation.

"Sumptuous toxin-fueled air," she said. "Gaze upon pollution's bounty, noble comrade."

Mr. Glint looked doubtfully at the vacuous plane. It went on and on.

"Don't see nothing," he said.

His partner frowned at him as though he had sprouted a tail. "What are you talking about? Look at that!" She swept her arm, encompassing absolutely bugger all in a big gesture. "A lake fetid and rainbow-slick with the fossil fuels of the pre-radium age! A church whose gables, steeple, and belfry tower fairly weep with the blood of holocausted masses, all mulched in the name of Mother Faith, the fickle creature. Not our cup of tea, Mr. Glint, but delicious nonetheless."

"Don't see a lake," he said. "Don't see a church neither."

She ignored him, listening intently. "That voice," she said.

Mr. Glint turned his head back and forth in vain. There was nothing to hear.

She hopped excitedly. "It's Hughes! He's saying... hold on... Axe... apples... lilypad..." She sombered. "Headed? Headed where?"

She set off after the voice.

Mr. Glint made to follow. Despite his turn of speed (which few ever expected, not until it was too late), he had to hurry to keep up with her. Then he couldn't keep up.

"Miss Gleam," he said.

Every step took her yards away from him. "Headed where?" The margin grew. She took three strides and a football field separated them.

"Miss Gleam. I'm here."

She was a speck.

"Can't you see I'm here?"

A mote.

He slowed, stopped, and watched her vanish completely.

Alone in the anemic wasteland, Mr. Glint hung his head.

He was not morose, or commiserating with himself. In her chocolate box of compliments that she reserved for him, one of his favorites was "professional." That translated to no messing about. Plus he liked the way it sounded in his head. Thinking of heads, what did this place remind him of?

He settled in for a bit of what Miss Gleam called "cogitation." No time passed. Seconds were strangers here.

Eventually he reached a one man consensus. Best not to worry over where Miss Gleam had gone. Best instead to worry where he was now and how he might be elsewhere.

He looked down at the bland flat plate.

It *did* remind him of something, something he'd learned about during conceptualization classes.

He pictured the board, the chalk. Slow images began to form and the words that accompanied them.

Conscious. Preconscious. Subconscious.

Crust. Filling. Base.

"The pie," he said. "I remember."

He could almost sense Miss Gleam's pride in him.

He was still staring at the ground, if you could call it ground. He hunkered down, his long legs sticking out like clothes hangers. He scraped a nail over the stuff beneath him and examined it.

Flaky.

"Found you, Mr. Crusty Conscious."

With a bone-chilling *crrrrrrack*, Mr. Glint unhinged his jaw, bent low, and began to eat.

***

First one hyena crested the stair. Two more followed. The rest of the pack were idling around, but none could resist noticing their companions' interest in the building.

This was it. The crucial moment in which the one in front would investigate what it had heard or continue up the zigzagging stairwell.

It yawned laconically, exposing that nasty mouth in all its snaggle-toothed glory.

Keep going, Gormon Hughes urged it as he peered out the window. His body was filmed in sweat. Warm beads rolled down his sides from the drenched hair under his arms. *You keep climbing. You've got wanderlust for the plains of Ikahagua, so follow your paws. See if they take you there.*

To his despair the leader approached the door on which was hung the sign for the *Scriptorium and Flavored Tea Emporium*. The hyena's head duked side to side like a boxer's. This close he could make out the glossy pinkness of its gums. Suddenly it came to a halt and snapped its gaze to the window. Gormon slipped out of sight, flattening himself against the wall.

A moment later, claws began to scratch at his door.

"Get out!" he roared at the top of his lungs, hoping to scare it away. "Get out of here!"

Eerie silence greeted this, then the scratching resumed, a touch more insistently he thought.

This was crazy. What in God's name was he worried about? Unless hyenas had developed opposable thumbs during today's unlikely events, he and the dogs were quite safe. Even if by some horrible turn of fate the beasts jumped up and spun the doorknob just right (even the idea of that was so ludicrous it heartened him), then the latch would thwart their bristly advance.

A frightful thought occurred.

Had he closed the latch?

Terror seized him as he craned around to check, but the rising warmth of panic was cooled right down once he laid eyes on it. The latch was in place all right, good little latch that it was.

More claws joined those scratching at the strawberry-colored wood of the door.

From beneath a chair cobbled together out of manuscripts, the wolfhound began to growl.

Ernie Wilks, you shut your yapper.

Latch or no latch, this was as grim as he'd ever felt. The telephone lines were gummed up, and without that he had no means to signal for help.

The wolfhound's growls crackled into loud mean-blooded barks.

"Ernie!"

He whirled, intending to scold the mutt that was in the normal course of things twenty-odd years his senior and felt the chiding words break apart in his throat.

Ernie wasn't barking at their would-be-company on the other side of the door. His ire was focused on something inside the apartment.

Against all probability, Boochums the Saint Bernard had managed to catch a few winks during the excitement. Now he raised his head, giving the wolfhound that canine look of total puzzlement. Over him, on the countertop, was the biggest fucking bird Gormon Hughes had ever seen.

In a blur of speed it rended a wad of fur and flesh from Boochums' hindquarters. The dog yelped, bolting to its feet and dashing toward Gormon, almost bowling him over. Not a brave dog but a big one.

The bird regarded the dogs and the man with a slender avian evil Gormon didn't care for in the slightest. Its beak dripped.

The wolfhound barked, Boochums licked his wound, whining softly, and outside the rest of the pack began to crowd the door like gawkers at a public hanging.

***

While Mr. Glint was chewing his way through the crust and filling on his way to the promised base, Miss Gleam was thinking about sanity.

She had always been mad and pleased about it. Yet under the lunatic tangle of piano wire, nylon, and catgut ran a few threads of perfect coherence. Up until recently she could have stranded them out for you. One was a love of those sounds that trip off the tongue, sesquipedalian (which is a long word that means long word—language is odd) and brief. Then came her career, from the misadventures of childhood to the tortures of Mr. Shine's injections, to her own rather more elective procedures, to her present circumstances as a self-employed woman who would not so much take on the world as throttle it black and blue. Last was Mr. Glint, who completed her.

Pelting hell-for-leather after Hughes' voice, which she could snatch at but never fully grasp, she would not have been able to tell you any of this.

Visions threatened to drown her like a dazzling blue-haired kitten. She saw grinning masks of cheap white plastic; a monster that combined a lion, a ram, and a dragon; arrows loosed in a volley that blotted out the lightning-wracked face of a storm.

Even the landscape she'd initially admired was turning traitor. Pollution plants smogged their last and were devoured in gorse and creeper ivy. Corrupt churches crumbled. Implements of torture rusted. Before her eyes her precious leisure center was demolished, rebuilt, and reopened. She could hear games, music, teasing, and shouting and laughter. It made her sick.

In short the threads were falling apart. The center could not hold.

The one sure thing was Hughes.

His voice was a beacon, one she followed eagerly, no, *needfully*.

Somewhere deep, deeper than the unraveling threads that were Miss Gleam, she *knew*.

Dark hair dark eyes black truths white lies.

HughesHughesHughesHughesHughesHughesHughesohdearestbrotherHughes.

It was all his fault.

As she ran, the scissors around which she had built much of her professional ethos and moral predilection poked out of, and then slipped from, her pocket. They were gone almost instantly, sucked up in the mutating abyss.

She would never think on their whereabouts, not even in the seconds before the calliope would begin its dark, lilting tune and things would be at their most extreme. She was simply too far gone. The era of little white lies and large black truths was over. Only ambiguity remained, loathsome and spread out in a kaleidoscope of gray.

***

Cate was by no means immune to the rigors of fear. As far as she was concerned, fear was a most useful thing. Without it, bravery would just be arrogance in a ballgown.

During dangerous missions, and particularly in the throes of battle, she would face death with bravery smoldering in her chest like a red-rimmed furnace coal.

At age fourteen, during a long and painful conversation with her Aunt Trisha, Cate had decided this was thanks in no small part to her dad, though it would be pushing the truth to say she was grateful about it. Witnessing her mother's murder had exposed Cate to the disease of mortality with the unintended consequence of inoculating her to the dread that consumed many when confronted by the fact that, yes, like those who came before and those who would come after, you were only around enough to sample the wares before closing time. And sample she did, delighting in the details in spite of (or maybe because of) the fact that tomorrow might never come.

The world was great, so why wait?

Now it seemed her medicine was turning to poison.

She was running for her life, and she was scared so bad she knew the moment she stopped, her stomach would give a lurch and she would vomit.

She could hear her father lumbering after her, could picture the spit trickling down his chin, and his lips pulled back in a slobbery smile that would have indicated a rabies infection in an animal. In a human being, it indicated an even greater danger.

Scooting as fast as she could through the hole in a doughnut ring of glass, she made to broaden the gap between her and her pursuer... and found to her dismay she couldn't.

Crystalline thorns and delicate glass-petalled roses formed an impassable thicket to her front and right. To her left a fallen obelisk mirror blocked her path.

"Peekaboo," said a voice.

He was looking at her through the doughnut ring. As he spoke he moved his face so different parts of it were visible. One eye. His grin with the bottom row of teeth jutting forward apishly. His flaring nostrils. The other eye. Cate had thought her fear couldn't sink any deeper into the queasy acidic pond of her gut. She was wrong. She pressed her back to the thorns as far as she could without them breaking the skin through her blouse and watched the nightmarish pantomime play out.

"What's this?" he cooed. "Is it a naughty girl? Is it... a vampire? I've got my trusty hammer, but I left my wooden stake at Origné. You always could do the accent. *Veeeeeery charmed to meet you. I em Catherine, end you are most velcome to my home.* A real crowd tickler at parties."

They looked at one another, her two eyes perfectly mapping onto the one visible through the glass ring. "Cathy," he said, and his voice was normal. "Sweetie. Come back through. I was only goosing. Just pulling your leg, see? Your Aunt Trisha locked me up in a loony bin. The nurses are never around, and the orderlies do things to us. Pick on us and worse if we put up a fight. They hurt me bad, Cathy. I hurt. I need my little girl. Won't you come here and give your old dad a hug and a peck on the cheek?"

She was four steps from the hole before she realized what she was doing. It had been his voice, paternal and coaxing, with none of the awful post-war languor in it. He'd sounded so miserable. Every muscle in her body had answered his call. She backed away again, shaking her head, her eyes riveted on that one glaring eye.

"Cathy?" He shifted so she could see him pronounce her name. "Cathy baby?" His tongue pushed over his upper lip, wetting it. "Do you remember the one about the little girl and big bad wolf? No vampires in that one, but I bet you can do all the voices. Want to tell Dad?"

A spindle of thorn sliced her palm. Cate hardly noticed.

"No? Well, cometh the hour, cometh the iceman."

He slid the head of the mallet through the ring and waggled it in a jaunty fashion. Strands of her mum's hair wafted, and then the mallet was going back through the hole.

"There was this wolf, you see. He had a family and friends, and when the time came to do his thing for his lupine country, he signed up. No problem."

Swish. Cate gasped as the mallet bit into the doughnut shape. Slivers tinkled.

"In the woods where the wolf and his people lived, there lived an old biddy named Grandma. She was a greasy-fingered, wrinkly-mouthed old biddy, and she wanted the whole wood for herself."

Swish.

Tinkle-tinkle.

"She had the means as well, don't you think she didn't, Cathy! So what could the wolf do? He ate the old bitch up! Ipso facto. Gone and gobbled. The woods are safe to thrive and grow."

Swish.

Tinkle-tinkle.

"Here's the bit where things go awry for our wolf. Word reaches Grandma's daughter, and her daughter, who wears a red hood and knows a bloke with a hatchet and a spare bag of stones."

Swish.

Tinkle-tinkle.

Beads of blood welled and ran down Cate's bare calves. Her blouse was stained crimson where the thorns dug deep.

"The wolf gets taken in by the red hooded girl and ends up cut and sewn up for dead. Hngh."

Swish.

The brittle remainder of the ring shattered.

"There we are."

He stepped over the debris. "I came home and you were all different. You and your mum and everyone else were the red hood and the hatchet man, Cathy. You cut me and sewed me up for the grave."

"You came back different," she said through tears she hadn't known were coming until they spilled over her cheeks. "A crossbow stock hit you in the head."

"The woods have got to get better. They've got to be fixed." He smiled, adjusting his grip on the mallet handle. "It takes work. You stopped me from doing my work all those years ago when you hid under the bed. Let's finish it together."

Cate sobbed, once. It was the bitterest sound she'd ever given voice to.

"Hush, love. Aren't you dead already?" he said, his tone still even and coaxing. "You might hide the truth with tattoos and hide the dying with movement and life. Who are you fooling?"

"You don't know a thing about that."

"Yes, I do."

"No." She rubbed her damp eight-year-old nose, and with a warmth that stunned her as much as it did him, she smiled. "You don't. You're not even here."

He closed in and touched the sodden mallet head to her cheek. "You sure about that?"

"Pretty sure. You never left the trenches, Dad. Moving, yes, but only in a straight line and never getting anywhere." Cate brushed the mallet aside without resistance. "And while I may hide some things and hide from others, I relish the moving. Because what there's no hiding from is the fact that when you go, you must take things with you. There's a reason you've taken this form. It's how I've chosen to leave you. Stuck in that one horrible day. Languishing, and left to rot. But her," she said, her smile widening into the patented Jubilee grin. "Her, I take with me always."

The lines in her father's expression deepened. "Who?"

Cate was eye-level with him now. Gone were the blouse and skirt and boots that couldn't stomp a fly. She could feel tough fabric wrapping her tight and more importantly heavy hobnails in her boots. Herself once more, she tilted her chin over his shoulder. "Her."

Her dad turned.

A full two inches taller than her husband-turned-murderer, glamorous as the movie actress, Ginger Dujour, stood Cate's mother. Poised in her fingers like those elegant cigarette holders from opera houses, glinted two shards of broken mirror.

Pop.

Cate's dad lost both his eyes.

Crunch.

He lost the mallet as the glass bit deep.

Thwack.

And off went his head.

Cate closed her eyes. Loving arms enfolded her.

She hugged her mum for the last time.

CHAPTER FIFTY-ONE

Something was happening to Mr. Glint.

He remembered... And that was already a stumbling block.

He remembered things Miss Gleam had told him, and how to hoover up squirmy things into his gob, and how to hurt people, but he never remembered the bits.

What bits? he asked, swallowing another mouthful of the subconscious.

The bits of the jigsaw, he answered himself. The jigsaw that, when put together, made Mr. Glint. He had never considered that before. He'd never had a reason to.

Miss Gleam's voice came to him from the past. *The subconscious is the place where all the information, all the stuff in your life is kept. The foundation of not just who you are now, but what you were before too.*

He bit off more, masticated, and gulped it down.

Deeper he delved, and deeper still.

There was something inching through the oozy ichor of his memory, something about...

Mr. Glint paused mid-chew.

A book. There were pictures of animals on its pages, yes, and words, and the words were brand new and exciting because he was only just old enough to realize that words were important if you had a chance of being understood.

Here was a bath popped full of flowery-smelling bubbles and sailed by scores of rubber ducks. And here was... a woman and a man, and they both looked like Mr. Glint only with most of their jigsaws filled in, the parts that made her Mum and him Dad.

He remembered their gentle urgings. He mustn't pull girls' hair, or poke other boys in the shnozz, or pick fights against those who were smaller than him, for he was big for his age, and size in the body was only as good as size in the head.

Then the woman and the man were gone, and there was only Mr. Shine's vein-nicking needles.

Mr. Glint didn't care to remember that.

Yet something compelled him to go deeper. Maybe it was the subconscious itself.

Eat, it bade him. *Eat and be filled up.*

Complete the jigsaw.

Dormant emotions inside him shook off the cobwebs, coughed dust, and puttered to life.

Mr. Glint ate on.

***

When she opened her eyes she was somewhere new.

It looked like a city, only drawn with charcoal under a chalk sky.

"Cate!"

She spun and saw Hughes hurrying to her, his open, expressive face pulled into a smile. As they embraced, he opened his mouth to speak, so she shut him up.

He made a little sound of surprise, then another one of pleasure. After a moment he pulled away. "Aren't we in a rough patch at the moment?"

"Don't overthink it."

"Yep. Okay."

After a luxuriantly long kiss, she disentangled herself from him and looked around. "Chalk and charcoal, just like you described."

"Yeah."

"Where's Frank?"

"I'm not sure. He guided me through the dream folk."

"Lucky."

She saw worry creep over his face. "Did something happen?"

"Yes, but for now we must..." She gave him a smile that mixed resolve and grief. "We must keep moving, eh?"

He brushed a thumb over her cheekbone. "Whatever you like," he said. He had such control over his voice. Inquisitive one moment, soothing as a hot water bottle held against her aching soul the next. She saw something catch his eye behind her. He slipped his hand in hers, and they headed for a closer look.

On one black-and-gray corner smelling of grainy, smoky charcoal were two buildings like any other. At the mouth of the alley between the buildings, a stringless wooden puppet lay in a boneless heap. Its dead face told them nothing, but its finger did. That wooden digit pointed down the alley and into shadow.

"Step right up," Hughes muttered darkly.

Cate gave him a puzzled glance, but he only shook his head and followed the puppet's pointing finger.

Frank was here all right, and he was guiding them both.

"There are empty patches in the sky," said Cate wonderingly.

"Did you never leave blank spots when you drew as a kid?"

She had. "I never imagined myself walking in a child's rendition of a city. But there must be some mistake. Frank told us we were going to the Nightjar Coven's home."

Hughes was quiet for a moment. He drank in the smears forming rows of buildings, the tall poles sketched matte black with their heads smeared in white meant to look like streetlamps. "I think this is their home," he said. "This area looks just like Symbarr Square in our world. The only strong memory I have from there is the Rotbloom Carnival when I was six. I've been nursing a suspicion for a while now. You remember I told you about Krys and The Mum?"

"One can see the future, but it locks the other in visions of the past."

"They also make great porridge."

"Honey?"

"Blackberry jam."

"Oh my."

"Anyway," he said as they found another puppet guiding them toward their destination, wherever that was. "Something I haven't told you is that Krys snuck a team of carnies into Iphigenia. They were there to collect otherworldly creatures to really wow the audience." Hughes' brow was tightly knit, one long dark line. "I'm wondering if she left something behind for the Coven to find. To... I don't know... consume and become a part of. A melding of ideas, the way dreams meld memories into..."

"A soup of strangeness?" Cate supplied.

"You're an impish little so-and-so, you know that?"

She laid a finger on the tip of her nose, a gesture that said, *Me, good sir? Oh, but there must be some mistake!*

Another puppet pointed them through an arch of scribble-scratch black.

They walked under it, Cate with her fingers snarled thoughtfully in her hair, Hughes with his hands plunged ponderously in his pockets.

"It would explain the carousel," Cate allowed. "Say the Coven are as evil and intelligent as Frank proposes. They've lost their son and they need a way to get him back. They set one plan in motion, Marrow King Maelen and the Bonemeal Boys. Then, when Krys comes through, her magic draws the Nightjar Coven. Their nasty prying witchy minds track Krys back to Symbarr Square and the carnival. The things they see in our world give them an idea. So begins the slow process of invading our dreams. Only a few pebbles at first, but gradually their power builds to the avalanche that Corinth is currently being buried under. Transforming into animals and all that malarky. That would make whoever is in charge desperate enough to bow to the Coven's demands and free Frank Gallant back into the clutches of his mothers."

"There's a science to portals," said Hughes, fitting his theory with support beams. "Krys couldn't know it. It makes sense that she went in without the proper safety measures. And yes, as you say, a person with her power might very well attract the Coven's attention. Oh God, she'd be miserable if she heard me talking this way. She's got a sensitive heart."

You mean entirely unlike your own? Cate thought wryly. Out loud she said, "There's a flaw in your logic." She held up one fist, then the other, and knocked them together. "Portal science tells us Iphigenia and Eurydice are two entirely different worlds. Not even a hint of conjunction."

"What's that?"

"Crossover."

"No hint of it? And those people turning into alligators in our world would agree with you, would they?"

She hesitated. It was a good point.

"Well, I hope you're right," said Hughes. "Because if witches can jostle their way into our dreams, who can say what's next? And if there *is* crossover between the worlds, a conjunction of the, ah, *physical* variety, then we're in real trouble." His voice was steady as a rock, but a different stoniness showed on his face. In that moment Cat thought he looked like a walking epitaph. "As much trouble as Laurana and her unit got into."

He's talking about the wolf with two heads. Cate understood. Like Wendy, John Isherwood, and anyone else who knew about it, she had puzzled over the monster's appearance herself. It was utterly alien, especially in the pygmy forest slaughtering the dramen wholesale. But to suggest the creature came into Iphigenia from Eurydice...

Even the *notion* of that was...

Hughes picked up the pace. "There."

Cate refocused. Ahead of them lumping the dream like a pustule was the carousel.

She caught up with him. Hughes had one hand tight as an angry crab's claw around Chimera's hilt. For her part Cate adjusted her satchel full of instant mirrors. Hughes erroneously thought that any creature too large to fit into her mirrors couldn't be dragged into one. Not so. The creature had to be the same weight as Cate, although there was a large enough margin for error that animated skeletons and rather heavy opponents often spent their last moments wondering why it felt like they were being lowered into a cold bath. She wondered how rakish or how fat the witches of the Coven were.

She supposed there was only one surefire way to find out.

Her arms and legs pumped. Her heart thudded her arteries which spurred the blood which fueled the brain which invoked the glands which dumped adrenaline into the blood, and HERE at last was the comet sensation, the burst of pre-fight bravery before the scything gaze of autumnal death, a harvest time of rippling corn and wheat and barley, clanging funereal bells, ask not for whom THEY toll, and the sizzling blood fording capillaries like bridges, punching through yesterday and heedless of tomorrow because TODAY, yes, today—

She would fight again.

Red hair streamed behind her like a comet's burning tail.

Cate Jubilee laughed a high, euphoric laugh and put one hobnail boot in front of the other.

***

The Nightjar Coven took umbrage at that laugh. From the depths of the carousel they watched the pair draw near. The plan—so cunning of them to have devised it!—was for the first time showing hairline cracks.

They had expected Hughes to come at once with their honey boy in tow. Instead there had been a delay, and while Hughes had indeed eventually arrived, that giggling harlequin he'd brought with him was not Frank.

The witches were fuddled. And because they were unused to that feeling, they were off guard. And because no one except their son had ever caught them off guard, they were suspicious.

~ By congregation of nightpriest, nightgroom, and scabrous nightbride ~

~ We welcome you back Gormon Hughes ~

greeted the witches, their three voices merged into one brain-worming whole. Their tone, polite and agreeable, did not change as they said:

~ *We cannot fail to notice* ~

~ *You have failed to bring us what was promised* ~

Hughes gave the carousel a frosty stare and exchanged a moment of mutual decision with Cate. Together they stepped onto the ride. Hughes drew his sword.

~ *You dare draw steel on witches* ~

~ *We who are as old as the black hourglass sands* ~

~ *As wise as the deepest river stones* ~

~ *As cunning as the thorniest woods* ~

"And as blind as bats," said Frank Gallant. "Long time no see you ragtime crones."

Before Hughes' eyes spindles of string surrounded three almost invisible shapes. The witches *shrieked.* The sound of it exploded in Hughes' head.

"I've got them!" hooted Frank. "Cate! Hughes! Give them all you've got *NOW!*"

Crooked and hideous, the witches shrank from them. Invincible as a nightmare they had been, now suddenly vulnerable. All three of them might have recovered in time for a counteroffensive, but Hughes and Cate were partners, and the spirit of combat moved in them effortlessly.

Chimera parried ten raking claws.

Poise, counseled Hector's voice across months of training, and Hughes' back became firm and flawless. He slipped inside the closest witch's flailing limbs and lay Chimera's edge to the back of her grasshopper-thin thighs. The blade's steel—forged from a monstrous heart in Jolene fire—sliced, met resistance, and sliced some more. Legless, the witch toppled. Slitted yellow eyes flew wide.

Hughes wondered idly if they'd ever experienced pain before.

He doubted it.

The Coven meted it out in spades, but outside the maternal ache of turning their child against them, they'd never contended with it themselves.

"I hope it stings," he told her. "I hope it feels like your stumps are full of wasps."

The witch opened her mouth—to vent her agony or her rage, Hughes never found out which—and Cate's boot squashed her goiter-swollen throat.

An earthquake's force shuddered the carousel. It began to spin, the transformed people banking up and down at crazed intervals.

~ *FIE* ~

~ *MURDERERS* ~

~ *OUR SISTER DEAD* ~

~ *A GALLOWS GRIEF ABOUT OUR NECKS* ~

Two voices howled, conjoined in hate.

Cate and Hughes pushed their advantage, but the ride bucked beneath them and the witches were relentless.

Cate built a mirror trap, and instead of felling another witch found herself seized between spidery fingers that skittered over her head and squeezed. The bones in her jaw ground at the hinge. She kicked against the witch's chest, strong at first, then more and more feebly as her vision clumped in sooty black spots.

~ *WE SHALL VENGEANCE OURSELVES* ~

~ *YOUR FATHER WILL BE FEASTED ON HUGHES* ~

~ *NO HELP WILL COME TO HIM* ~

~ *ONLY PAIN* ~

~ *AND WHEN HE IS ONE BREATH FROM DEATH* ~

~ *WE SHALL TELL HIM HIS SON RANG THE VERY BELLS OF SUPPER* ~

~ *LET THAT NOOSE YOU AS YOU HAVE HANGED US* ~

Dad, thought Hughes.

***

The bird took wing.

Before Gormon Hughes Senior knew what was happening, it had flown to the latch on his door and was nudging it with its beak.

A wordless grunt of horror escaped him. He lunged, hoping to grapple its wings closed and bear it to the floor.

The latch came loose. In slow motion he saw the chain dangling like a hangman's rope. Outside the scrabbling intensified. With a white ball of fear whacking off the edges of his brain, Gormon heard the knob turn.

The wolfhound leaped, took the bird's wing in his mouth, and brought his teeth together. There was an audible crunch. At the same time, Gormon brought his shoulder to the door just as the hyenas nosed it open. One had its head through. The impact fractured something crucial in its throat. Hughes felt a bizarre surge of pity for it as the door swung back, but there was no time to question it. He put his whole weight to the door. It wasn't enough. The pack was simply too strong.

To one side of the room pages scattered from clipped furniture as the bird tried to peck out Ernie's eyes.

Gormon felt something give in his shoulder. It hurt, and worse, he gave ground. They would be inside any moment.

"Oh God," he wailed. "Oh God please, *please!*"

He had no sense of what he was saying, and if he did he wouldn't have known what he was begging for. Relief, maybe. Or his son. Right now, they both meant the same thing.

Suddenly, inexplicably, the pressure eased.

Gormon grinned manically as relief flooded him. But what had caused it?

He looked down and saw Boochums—cowardly, stinky Boochums—holding his side to the door.

"Good dog," he gushed through his teeth. "Holy fucking God, good boy Boochums."

Through the strawberry-colored wood, he heard one of the hyenas begin to laugh.

***

Strings came out from under the witches' nails like thin maggots. They prized the fingers crushing Cate's head loose.

~ *Frank* ~

~ *Oh honey boy* ~

~ *Can't you see they're killing us* ~

"Someone has to." His voice boomed in all directions. It seemed to cloak the world. Instead of further upsetting the carousel, the wild bucking actually smoothed out.

Cate grit her teeth against the hurt singing through her skull. Together she and Hughes mounted an assault. The witches met them among the animals, a rising/dipping battleground. Teleportation glass hardened. Fists and booted feet flew. Steel hacked through hagflesh.

~ *Frank please* ~

They cursed as Cate stamped on a set of lobsterish mandibles.

~ *Having you was the sweetest thing* ~

~ *We ever did* ~

~ *Sweet and good as warm honey to the sorest throat* ~

~ *We only wanted you to come home* ~

Frank's laughter rolled over that sketched country. "You think I'm stupid? I wasn't made yesterday, you fabulists. Every night outside the thing you called home was the happiest of my life."

~ *Ungrateful* ~

"On the contrary."

~ *Confused* ~

"Never been surer of anything."

~ *Disobedient little shit* ~

Hughes and Cate felt Frank Gallant's smile. It seemed to suffuse the very air.

"You loved me as a girl, and then as a boy. But you never cultivated my love so I could give it back. Reciprocity's a two-way street, Mommas. I turn out my pockets and find I've got no affection to give. But disobedience?"

Strings noosed both witches, choking their breath into whistling clucks and garbles.

"Disobedience I can *deliver.*"

The nooses tightened.

"Now," said Cate.

Hughes readied Chimera for a killing thrust.

Something sharp caressed the nape of his neck. He stiffened.

"Brother," a voice whispered into his ear.

"No," moaned Hughes. "Not you. Anything but you."

"You've slung quite the load of slurry at me and mine," the voice said. "But sling as you might, you cannot dull that which gleams eternal. Drop it."

His sword clattered.

"Hughes?"

Cate.

He raised his hands, he wasn't entirely sure why. Perhaps to keep her away, stop her from doing something that might get her hurt.

"Kill her!" Frank said. "Her mind is coming apart! There's blank spots, and they can fill those up!"

"It was your car," Gleam told Hughes. "I *knew* I recognized it when it came to save your bowman. To think you were probably inside. Close enough to bite." She made a noise that sent shivers up each node of his spine. Was that supposed to be a chuckle? It sounded closer to a dry retch. He wished he could turn around and see her. "The Escateline *Eschezmont,*" muttered Gleam. "Wasted on the likes of you."

"Kill her, Cate, there's no time!"

"I can't." Cate sidestepped, trying to keep both the witches and Gleam in her sight. "She's got a knife."

Hughes realized the sheaf on his hip was empty. *My Krys knife.* Gleam must have snatched it in the chaos.

"Too long," said Miss Gleam. "Too long have you been ointment in my flies, a lion's paw in my splinter, an impediment of the most nettling species." The knife's cold kiss drew a warm reply. He felt blood run down his neck, sticking his shirt to his skin. Miss Gleam heaved a long, contented sigh. "At last our merry chase is truly over. I must ask you, dear brother, now we are at the finish line. Has that handsome weathercock throat of yours any burst of jocularity? Any jape? A joke? You have been funny since the first. Troublesome. But ever so amusing."

"You're making a mistake."

"Mm. A cliché. Not your best effort."

Hughes felt the knife retract.

"Wait," Cate said. "Please. No, no *DON'T!*"

Hughes felt the knife part skin and thoracic muscles. By the time it scraped his ribs (which seemed to take a long time, though it all happened in a fraction of a second) all his air was gone. He staggered, the hilt standing out of his back like something malformed.

~ *YES* ~

exulted the witches.

Wrestling free of Frank, they got to Miss Gleam one-third of a second before Cate. Sometimes that's all it takes. Knife edge. Pin head. Whatever. On the most delicate of ballrooms, angels and devils dance the autumn waltz of death.

The witches crawled into Miss Gleam like you might crawl into bed after one of those days that knocks you around. The difference being she was not a willing host. Beds seldom protest. It would be an ugly thing if they did.

So it was with Miss Gleam, who was already a striking ruin to behold.

As Cate's boots took her full in the chest, Gleam was pleased to discover that pain, like her treasured threads of sanity and her employment to Mr. Shine, seemed to be a thing of the recent past. A storm had blown inside her just now, but that was no great worry. She rather liked thunder. Didn't she?

Didn't she what?

Didn't who what?

Didn't...

(...)

She managed eight words. "One winter night a cold wind did blowsey."

Inside her head the last fibers of thread joined the clot of untamable madness yarn. The two were indistinguishable. Language vaporized. History obliterated. All traces of humanity pulverized.

Lights out.

Terrible silence stretched, broken only by the metallic cranking of the carousel.

Surrounded by an assortment of hooves, tails, pincers, knuckles, paws, talons, fins, and every kind of foot from the ordinary to amphibious, Hughes touched Cate's hand. She was kneeling next to him, and though she could only stare at the figure before them, at his touch her fingers responded. They wound through his, held them just gently enough to be tender and just strong enough to comfort him. Hughes needed comforting.

Breathing had suddenly become a little trickier. Hot hooks of pain dug through his back on every inhale. Exhaling was okay, but you could only do it for so long before you needed a gulp of air.

There was also a rusty quality to his breathing he didn't much like.

She pierced a lung, he thought. *That's why it hurts so badly. Every time I inhale, I collapse it a little further and fill what's left of it with blood.*

Too late he remembered a trick of his own, one he'd had up his sleeve since that night he'd been cornered by her in Agorippis Street.

Oh well. It wasn't as though things could get any worse.

Of course, being a man well-versed in the drama of stories, this was the part where things would get much worse. Out of the frying pan, into the fire sort of thing. But this was real life, which only became a story when you least expected it to, such as on dream carousels after you've been stabbed. *Oh crap*, he thought. No need to panic. Not yet. Perhaps the tale of the Nightjar Coven would be an exception. After all, he *had* been stabbed. Surely it wasn't too much to hope for.

The carousel's speed increased. Somewhere close by, a calliope began to play. To its darkly jaunty tune, the thing that had once been Miss Gleam raised its head, and with two voices concocted into one single bugle of malice, it said:

~ *Frank's on a time out* ~

~ *We've decided to let him watch* ~

~ *And watch he will* ~

~ *While we rip you to ribbons* ~

~ *And from ribbons to the finest strings* ~

~ *You will not be beasts* ~

said the witches wearing Miss Gleam like a suit of sparkling skin.

~ *We shall make puppets out of you* ~

~ *A homecoming gift for our honey boy* ~

"Just once," Hughes wheezed to the universe at large. "Couldn't it have been out of the frying pan into a nice relax and a cup of tea? Just *once...*"

CHAPTER FIFTY-TWO

Cate reached into her satchel and came out with her four last instant mirrors, one capsule between each finger.

~ *One mortal woman against us* ~

~ *How plucky* ~

Cate rolled her shoulders, her neck, her ankles. Little pops and crackles emerged from each, discordant with the calliope.

She touched the bells tattooed at her throat. "See these?"

~ *We are going to gobble you up like a wayward girl in a fairy tale* ~

"See them?"

~ *Yes* ~

chuckled the witches.

~ *We see your puerile bells* ~

"Ask not for whom they toll," said Cate Jubilee. "They toll for thee."

The thing that had been Miss Gleam scowled.

Gripped by desperation, Hughes pushed his Performance. Nothing happened. He could only target Miss Gleam, and she wasn't here anymore.

Cate and the Coven closed till they were only a few feet apart. They circled one another, the cornucopia of the Coven's bestial victims forming a strange arena around them.

It began. Who moved first, Hughes could not say.

Cate was quicker, but Miss Gleam was no slouch before, and now a pair of homicidal witches were in the driver's seat. They refused to let Cate drag them into the mirrors she created. Every time she tried they grasped a carousel pole or a handy mahogany animal. A devil in a close-quarters brawl, Cate landed almost every strike while the Coven landed nearly none. But Miss Gleam's body was durable. Worse, she seemed to heal slowly but surely, and her nails were as razor-sharp as her teeth. In order to win, Cate had to be lucky many times. The Coven only had to be lucky once.

As Hughes negotiated air into his lungs, the coppery tang of blood filling his mouth, they pinned Cate to the central ballast of the carousel and slashed at her carotid artery.

Planting her boots on Miss Gleam's upper thighs, Cate pushed herself high, turning something fatal into a nasty cut. A freshet of blood dappled Gleam's cheeks and chin. Spasms wracked that stolen face. Her eyes showed almost no whites. They were deep and black as wells without end.

Thunking her boots on the ballast, Cate ran up it, flipping to land behind her opponent and putting the Coven in a stranglehold.

The hold was broken, renewed, and broken again.

On raced the calliope! On the rise and fall of the animals! In another world, Corinth City was falling apart because the center could not hold, and Cate was flagging. Hughes could see that plain enough. Her sides heaved. One of Miss Gleam's nails had shorn one of her nostrils. Blood ran freely, lipsticking and contouring her in a ghoulish halfmask. The problem was Hughes couldn't raise both arms above his head at the moment, much less help the woman he adored.

~ Tolls for who ~

the Coven mocked her.

~ Jingle jangle ring and chime ~

~ Tolls for you ~

~ Watch us gut her honey boy ~

~ See what being bold gets you ~

Just then, Hughes thought he heard something under the carousel hydraulics and the lilt of the calliope. He wasn't sure, but it sounded like footsteps.

Cate misjudged a kick. She slipped in her own blood. The Coven were on her in a moment, rending and slitting and lacerating and cuttingcuttingcutting.

Hughes stiffened. A wordless shout of rue crashed over his tongue, but he could not have let it out if it meant his life. A tall, gaunt shadow cast itself over the Coven. Unaware of it, they raised a hand and narrowed it into a trowel. Intent on scooping out Cate's insides, the hand plunged toward her belly.

Long fingers smothered it at the wrist.

The Coven snapped their head around, fangs gnashing their frustration.

Mr. Glint regarded them dispassionately.

The change was as fast as it was astonishing. All of the malevolence poured from the stolen face, and something surfaced. It was not the witches, nor was it their Dream Warrior son. It was a little fragment of something that had been and was now gone forever. Just a gleam, but there it was.

The calliope stopped. The carousel pitched violently and came to a jarring halt.

Mr. Glint opened his arms wide—a question.

Gleam responded at once, pressing her body to his. Their suits, both fashioned out of dark material, lent them the look of two halves of the same whole, finally reunited.

"Mr. Glint," she said in a small voice. "I don't want to go."

"That's all right. I'll come visit."

"Promise?"

He nodded and held her while she shuddered.

"I'm not myself," she said. "Do you... remember that other promise you made me?"

"Yes."

"Keep it, would you?"

"You sure?"

She smiled. "Scared, but sure."

And with his sour-mouth, Mr. Glint smiled back. "Gleam on, you crazy diamond."

Then he took her head between his hands, and twisted.

***

When Hughes saw Mr. Glint break Miss Gleam's neck, the impossible happened.

He found he could not only move but was, in fact, obliged to. Rolling onto his front he dragged himself to Cate. Air hissed through his teeth, but his progress was admirable considering he had a lung-deep hole in his back.

Meanwhile, with Miss Gleam dead, the witches were being forced out of their vessel, and Frank Gallant with them. The Nightjar Coven emerged first. Their slitted eyes were narrowed in concentration. They had been foiled, perhaps, but to them a hitch in execution did not mean an end to festivities. Here was another vessel to yank open and bloat with their unique strain of poison.

But when they made to do just that, they found Mr. Glint's mind unyielding.

As though sensing their intent, Glint said, "Sorry. Full up."

He grabbed them both. *Crrrrrack* went his widening jaws. And that was how the two remaining members of the Coven learned that a little of Frank's solidifying magic persisted. For untold years they had strung their boy along, letting him fulfill them while leaving him hollow and deprived in some vital yet intangible way.

Now they wore the strings, and Mr. Glint's grip was adamantine.

He began to eat them, tearing out huge chunks of flesh with his tombstone teeth, mincing it up, and going in for seconds, thirds, and fourths as they writhed and wriggled. He didn't mind. He was used to his meals putting up a fight.

Ribboned in gashes that wept blood, Hughes and Cate looked on in amazement.

In Corinth City, hundreds of thousands of transmogrifications began to undergo a rapid rewind. For some the process was merely unpleasant, mostly in the case of those who had become apes and monkeys, but for the vast majority it hurt like hell. Some felt nothing at all, and those were the instances that would accrue the most sorrow in the days to come. Sheila Kofatch and her daughter Carrie-Anne for instance. Investigating an odd clanging sound he'd heard from his kitchen, Sheila's anxiety-racked hubby saw their mangled bodies half-stuffed into the garbage can (where recently the corpses of two giant beetles had been deposited) and felt something irreplaceable snap inside him.

Hardship of this nature was in ample supply as the reversions swept over every District, but here and there genuine instances of hope lit up the stewing dark.

Gormon Hughes Senior, for example, found his attention drawn to Ernie Wilks. No longer a wolfhound, the old codger was lying in a state of exhaustion, feathers in his mouth. Boochums padded over and settled down next to his master, his doggie tongue lolled out and his sides heaving happily. That vile black bird had vanished into thin air, as had the hyenas outside his door, thank God. In the place of the latter were nine extremely disoriented people, including a plumber whose neck would need a brace and a lot of salve, it was that badly bruised from Gormon slamming the door on it.

Back in Eurydice, Mr. Glint's feast was over. There were a few jiggly bits left. These he chewed slowly, savoring, filling in the corners.

Where it lay on the carousel, Miss Gleam's body quivered and expelled a torrent of strings. From these a man grew defined. Frank Gallant had hardly appeared when Mr. Glint seized him.

"Stop!" Hughes shouted. "Mr. Glint, that's Frank Gallant you're holding. He didn't have any part in what happened to Miss Gleam."

Mr. Glint did not seem convinced. "He was in her. Means he's got to die."

"Hold on a moment." Hughes propped himself up, wincing. God, but it hurt to breathe. A broken arm seemed a doddle compared to this. "That man is the enemy of the witches you just... ingested."

"What?"

"You just ate my mothers," said Frank. "Thanks, by the way."

"Don't mention it," said Mr. Glint. "Still got to kill you though."

"Any chance we might talk this out?"

"No."

Frank Gallant shrugged. "Can't blame a guy for trying. Chomp away."

Mr. Glint said nothing. Then he said, "Really?"

"Yup. Reckon you earned it. Those crones were bad news."

"Frank, what are you doing?" Hughes stage-whispered. "He's going to eat you."

"Looks like it," Frank agreed. He gave Mr. Glint's stomach a friendly pat. "But at the end of the day, I got mine. Consider me satiated."

"What about living in our world?" Hughes demanded. "Courting the lady of evening? Ring any bells?"

"Shit, Hughes. That was just a dream. Don't sweat it. I knew I wasn't coming back to enjoy your world. Frivolity like that? Joy that makes the heart flutter and the whole soul sing?" Frank laughed, and this time it spread around the empty carousel where no animals existed, only the bewitching amusement of the Dream Warrior. "That could never be for me. I don't deserve it. That's for heroes like you and that lady there, the one you're lucky to love. Not me," he said, shaking his head and letting his laugh mellow into a honey-sweet smile. "I got to live pulling my own strings. That's enough." He looked up at Mr. Glint. "Hope you enjoyed the appetizer. You're about to enjoy the main course."

Mr. Glint grunted. He clapped hold of Frank, lifted him up, and brought Frank's smiling face toward his mouth.

Crrrrack.

Cate, barely conscious, mumbled something incoherent.

Hughes couldn't let this happen. He couldn't rely on the percentages of Performance either. The risk was too high.

Tapping into his natural talent, he spoke with vim and vigor.

"Look at me, Mr. Glint."

When both Glint and Frank did so, Hughes reached back through months of experience, all the way to the outset of summer when he had gained a little chicanery for just such an occasion.

Perk Activated: Criminal Eloquence

Instead of using a Performance, you can force a criminal to reconsider

their actions.

This Perk can only be used **once**.

Mr. Glint's face did not go slack.

To Hughes' distress there was no marked change whatsoever. He wondered if Mr. Glint had done something that had altered the way Hughes' power viewed him. Was the man no longer a criminal? Surely he was. Anyway, even if he wasn't, criminally terrifying must count.

Mr. Glint unhanded Frank.

"What gives?" Frank asked him.

"Dunno," said Glint.

Frank looked at Hughes, then Glint, and back at Hughes. He jerked a thumb.

"He did something to you?"

Mr. Glint scratched his bald head. "Couldn't tell you, Mr. Gallant."

"Hughes, you did something to him?"

Hughes wasn't completely sure himself. "Mr. Glint. Are you still of a mind to eat Frank?"

"Nope."

Hughes slumped. "Then yes. I did something." He laughed. "Oh, it hurts to laugh."

Despite having been stabbed, and probably emotionally traumatized beyond repair now he thought about it, Hughes was indescribably happy. Now all that was left was to go back to Corinth City to tell them the good news. He would just rest his eyes for a moment.

Nearby, Frank Gallant's head hung low. His face was hidden from view to all. "I get to go back?" he asked softly. "Me?"

When he received no reply, he turned. His expression was radiant with hope. The aurora in his braided hair shone turquoise blue, and his eyes were orbs of golden fire.

"Hughes?"

He approached his friend. Out for the count. Cate too.

"Hey, Glint?"

"Yeah?"

"Hypothetically speaking, how many people could you carry?"

Mr. Glint counted on his fingers. After a moment he said, "Lots."

Frank Gallant nodded. "Correct."

As they walked back toward the waking world, Mr. Glint carrying Hughes over one shoulder and Cate over the other, and Frank carrying Miss Gleam, the gaunt man wanted to know something.

"Mr. Gallant?"

"Hit me, Mr. Glint. *Yeoch!*"

"But you said..."

"It was an expression, man." Frank hopped on one leg, trying not to drop Miss Gleam. "That's some kick. Steel toed? Never mind." He shook his leg to try and get feeling back into it and limped on. "What were you going to say?"

Mr. Glint was silent for a time, as if slotting each piece of his question so that it left nothing out that needed asking.

"When someone dies, can you visit them? Even if you're still alive?"

Frank Gallant glanced at Miss Gleam. Back at the carousel she'd ranted and raved. Now she seemed peaceful. She might have been asleep and dreaming, if you didn't know better.

Frank looked at the far horizon. Chalk and charcoal were melting away. Firmer earth shaped underfoot. A brighter land. A prettier sky. No blank spots.

"There's some would say no," he told Mr. Glint. "And some who would say yes. Death is the only story we're sure to tell, and it's the one we know the least about. Who knows what doors we'll cross, what the mirror will show once it comes time to know ourselves in the last looking glass, or if there is such a thing as a human being that can understand and relate what they see, that those who come after might recall the revenant teachings and live fuller, truer, better days."

They left the dream behind. The real world took shape around them.

It was full dark. Lady Evening was out in her full splendor. Frank felt her dance toward morning. But not too fast. Time enough for a little fun.

She had waited for him after all.

"Me?" he said. "I believe that this life we lead is a slanting wise. Who knows what might happen?"

Mr. Glint turned his face to the full October moon.

Against a backdrop of stars it gleamed like a promise.

EPILOGUE

He really had to start keeping a diary.

"I'm sorry, Hector," he said, looking at his new pocket watch. "I'm late already."

"Make it up to me." Hector's cinnamon-carrot-cake voice seemed to summarize the day. It was half past one in the afternoon of November 1st. They were in the overgrown area of the training yard with its enormous windows offering their view. The sun was a big juicy apricot in the fruit bowl-blue sky, and the weather was clear and cheerful. Any day now it would turn (if you listened quietly, you could almost hear winter swearing cold oaths), but for now it was excellent, and oh God he'd thought it was half past twelve not one!

"Hughes?" said Hector, his voice part stern, part bemused.

"Make it up to you. Yes," Hughes blabbered. "Anything, but I've..."

"You will put in more time with Cassandra. I understand you've been busy of late. But swordplay makes demands of us that our stamina and muscle must meet, else we mummify our technique and inhume our skills in shallow graves."

"Of course, Hector, I will. I mean I won't. Er." Hughes couldn't get his shirt over his head. He realized it was partially inside-out. "Now, I really should..."

"It would not do to have to rest upon your laurels," said Hector sagely. "Success is a fine thing, but it should not betoken repose. Repose is for obese tomcats and elderly people addicted to chocolate digestive biscuits and vids about ripped bodices and murdered spouses."

"Yes, Hector."

"I have a gift for you."

Hughes paused mid-dress. "Say again?"

"It is underneath the table you laid your coat on earlier."

Hughes had wondered what that was. A gift from his instructor, whom he admired so deeply? He retrieved it right away. It was a rectangular box.

Momentarily forgetting his lateness, Hughes unstuck the lid and opened it.

"We will have frost this year," said Hector. "My brother, Paris, predicts it, and he is seldom wrong about such things. I make no secret of this, Hughes. You are an apt pupil. Likely my best. I display something, and without delay you have internalized it. When I train you I feel I possess a second shadow, one whose presence warms me, and that is no small matter for a ghost such as I." Hector offered one of his rare smiles. "Similarly, I hope this token of my approval warms you, should the need arise."

Hughes didn't know what to say. He removed the crinkling wrapper and took out his gift. It was a scarf, hand-knitted and wonderfully soft. Flowers were embroidered on it.

Peonies.

Soon thereafter, grabbing a takeaway lunch to eat on the way, Hughes was waylaid in the reception area at the base of Redspire by none other than Jo.

"Hullo, Hughes," she said, her mismatched eyes lighting up. "I was wondering when you'd turn up."

"Hello, Jolene. Listen, I wish I could chat, but..."

"How's Chimera doing?"

"Fine," he said, thrown by the question. "My sword? Fine. It's in my room at the moment. Why?"

"Just some idea I've been sinking my teeth into," said Jo. "Like one of them *innovations*. You know?"

"Sounds exciting. Um... Jolene, could this possibly..."

"This idea, right, it's called adaptive metallurgic folding. And what *that* means is..."

"Jo, I've really got to run."

She gave him a bewildered look from beneath her bushy brows, like a huge shaggy-haired fuzzy-armed werewolf who was very bewildered indeed. "You forget about our lunch plans?"

He *really* had to start keeping a diary.

Evidently his silence spoke volumes.

"You did," she said. She looked at her feet. Her fingers wound together like thick bashful sausages. "That's all right. I forget me too, now and then."

His heart melted. "Hey. You mustn't speak about yourself that way. Here." He handed her his lunch. "The first of my three-part apology."

She accepted it daintily. "What are parts two and three?"

"I'll think of something."

She nodded, her disappointment outpaced by curiosity and the prospect of a yummy lunch. She opened the bag. "I love toasties."

Me too, grumbled his stomach.

"Enjoy," he said.

"And what's this?" Brown paper rustled as she rooted about. "A bun!"

He grinned. "Clotted cream."

Her cheeks went rosy. She smiled, looking away. "Even I know that."

He hadn't gone ten paces outside the tower when someone called his name. He spun to give whoever it was guff and immediately felt his seething frustration cool.

"Falstaff!"

The butler swanned up to him, coattails and neat polished buttons and politeness abounding. "I thought you might need a lunch," he said, handing Hughes two bags. "The second is for your appointment. I've included a packet of kibble in that one, a brand called Mutt's Best Friend. Most amusing, I'm sure, if one has the sense of humor of a dead pigeon."

"You," said Hughes, "are without doubt the greatest butler who has ever taken up the arms of dustpan and brush."

"So they tell me, sir." Falstaff reached up, undoing Hughes' scarf and retying it expertly. "I never pay much heed. The work needs doing. Wear your scarf like this from now on. See the way I loop it?"

Hughes confirmed that he did.

"It is the height of fashion in Jaenqui-Across-The-River, and what kindles fashionable there catches here, if you take my meaning. Incidentally," Falstaff continued smartly, "your special package has been arranged for five o'clock."

"Special package?"

"Yes."

"Right," said Hughes, totally lost. Various lightbulbs fizzled on in his head. "Ohhhh! *That* special package."

"Quite so. There we are." The butler stepped back, tucking his arms tidily behind his back and appraising his handiwork. "Will you head straight to her after your appointment?"

"I've got to catch the three-thirty-five to my dad first."

That perturbed Falstaff. "Will you have enough time?"

"He will if he is not reliant on the metrotram," said a new voice.

They both looked around in time to see Wendy Dragontail murmur something to her driver. She was in the company of several hand-wringing people who were, in Hughes' opinion, either ambassadors or moneylenders. Possibly both.

Wendy Dragontail slid off her elkskin gloves. "Falstaff, be a lamb and see to these ambassadors and moneylenders, would you?"

"With pleasure, my Lady."

The butler gave Hughes a small bow that managed to contain a large plentitude of fondness and pottered off to keep the Citadel's center held, so things would not fall apart.

"Despite much adversity, October has recouped in time for the changing of the guard," said Wendy, standing next to Hughes. "Let us hope November has no odd surprises in store."

"Paris King says there's frost on the way," Hughes said helpfully.

"Did he? He's seldom wrong about such things."

"That's just what Hector said."

"You look harried as anything, Hughes. Take my car." Wendy's expression changed. "Fair warning upon your return—Doctor John has been asking after you."

Hughes just bet he had. Ever since the Nightjar Coven's defeat, John Isherwood had been trying to corner him. The good doctor's hunger to research Performance and the sword called Chimera verged on ravenous. In time Hughes would be keener to help. For now, he was content to sidestep John for as long as he could.

"How's Estelle?" said Hughes. "I haven't seen her around."

"The Perfect Prison is one of the most powerful magic items in the world," replied Wendy. "I understand Estelle is... how would you put it? *Acquainting* herself with it. Her father, Idris, has elected to teach her as part of his retirement. Regardless of how events have..." The Last Dragon's lips thinned. "Transpired... there may be cause to use the Prison sooner than we think."

She still doesn't trust Frank. Hughes wished he could sway her on the subject, but he was the newest recruit to the Scarlet Citadel, and she was the woman at its summit. He held out hope though. If an October like the one they'd just had could recoup for the changing of the guard, anything could happen.

"Oh shite," he said, clapping a hand to his forehead. Fumbling in his pocket, he remembered who he was next to. "Sorry, your Ladyship. Damn watch is stuck in my coat lining. You wouldn't have the time, would you?"

She rolled up her sleeve. "Almost two."

There was a blur of movement. Wendy Dragontail observed from a distance as Hughes launched himself through the passenger window of her car, calling instructions to her driver as he wrenched on his seatbelt. Her eyes twinkled for a moment, then the moment was gone. "Ah, Madam Ambassador. Do come this way..."

***

Traffic was blessedly light, and Hughes arrived at the house in Ptolema District's gorgeous suburbs exactly eleven seconds before Ernie Wilks.

"Did you walk all the way here from Leonidas?" he asked.

"Sure did."

"But I sent a cab for you."

Ernie cackled his witchy laugh. Even with the nightmare of the carousel and its engineers fresh in his mind, Hughes could not help but find the sound heartening.

"Like I'd put some poor slob through a whole car ride with Boochums smelling up the backseat," said Ernie.

Boochums barked as though to confirm this would have been the case. Hughes wasn't sure how the dog did it, but Boochums actually managed to bark pungently.

One fist couched in the small of his back and the other hanging by his side, Ernie looked around at the houses. "Would you have a goose and gander at these? Who knew they built them so big. I could adopt twenty kids and still leave the saran wrap on half the beds."

"Hm? Oh, right," said Hughes, riffling through his coat. "Almost forgot. Here you go."

"What's this?"

"Your key."

Ernie took it, rubbed a thumb over the brass teeth, and peered up at Hughes with curmudgeonly suspicion. "Key to what?"

"Let me show you."

They walked up the drive of a sprawling estate, Hughes in the lead and Ernie in a state of mounting unease.

Inserting the key and turning it in the lock, Hughes pushed the front door open.

"After you," he said.

"I don't think so. Whose house is this?"

"It's yours, Ernie."

The codger gave him the wary, studious look of someone who has not fully registered what has been said.

"I was offered it as part of my Second Triumph in the Citadel, so I said yes. But the truth is I like living in Redspire. I asked my dad if he'd like to come be your housemate, but you know how he is. The man would rather drink paint thinner and tell you it tasted like Earl Grey than leave the teashop. You don't have to live alone though," Hughes added hastily. "You could invite people to live with you. Whoever you like."

Ernie's face was still a mask of doubt. "Kid, I don't understand what you're talking about. How can this be mine?"

"Because the owner—me—says it is."

With obvious qualms, the old grouch agreed to be given the tour, nodding disinterestedly and muttering the occasional word of reluctant appreciation as Hughes showed him the estate's numerous comforts.

It was only when they reached the bathrooms on the second floor that Ernie underwent his second and final transformation of the autumn. It was as though someone had wadded him with cynicism, and now, quite suddenly, he came unblocked. Emotions gushed over his wrinkled, peevish face.

"Like it?" said Hughes.

Ernie stepped forward, his shoes making a light *tepping* sound on the plum-colored tile. The bathroom was nothing especially fancy—just a sink, a toilet, and a few racks for towels and lavatory paper within easy reach of both. Except, that was, for the bath. It was fantastically large, its surface grainy and skin-tingling with a mix of polymer resin and crushed stones. Clawed feet held it aloft. Soaps, bath salts, scented candles and other fragrant things lined up in rows on a stand hammered next to the bath for the comfort of its occupant. The taps fairly sparkled in the afternoon glow.

"This for Boochums, kid?' Ernie asked him. 'This for my doggie?"

Hughes' perplexity at this statement gave way to a goofy grin. He chuckled. "No, Ernie. This one's for you." His delight only increased as the old man looked at him incredulously. "Ernie, Boochums' bath is upstairs. It's *much* bigger than this one."

Ernie Wilks began to cry.

***

Four o'clock and he was cutting it very fine.

He took the steps wending up to the *Scriptorium and Flavored Tea Emporium* three-at-a-time. A parcel was tucked in the crook of his arm. It contained an antique stoneware teapot from Mysicordelia as well as several aromatic boxes of that country's darker, sweeter tea. Hughes, keen to surprise Gormon Hughes Senior on his birthday, had not dropped any clue about this gift during their telephone call the previous evening.

He hoped it would convey thoughtfulness and gratitude, but some part of him worried his dad would make contented rumblings, set the teapot aside, and simply erase its nuisance from his memory. He could be a stickler about anything to do with his work.

Hughes arrived at the strawberry door. An unconscious snarl curled his upper lip when he saw the scratches the hyenas had left. The Coven were gone, but less than a fortnight had passed since the witches had sprung their fatal trap. The tally of the dead and injured had only begun to plateau over the weekend. Gouges like the ones in his father's door were present all over. It would be a long time before those marks faded, even after repairs. Maybe they never would.

Turning both the knob and his mood in a roundabout circle, Hughes went in and was not at all prepared for what awaited him on the other side.

"Oh. Good afternoon."

Two bullnecked men with faces riddled in scars loomed over him. As Hughes grinned sheepishly, they looked at one another before shooting inquisitive looks to the room's largest table. Sitting around it in a mist of mint and jasmine tea steam were Gormon, Krys, The Mum, and...

"Kim?" he blurted.

Kim Kallaimon stood. She was wearing a suit that would assassinate and take the place of any alternative at the height of fashion. It was mango. She looked stunning.

"Ah," said Gormon. He brought his hands down on his thighs and kneaded them awkwardly. "Krys. The Mum," he said. "Would either of you fancy an ice cream?"

"Yes please!" said Krys, at exactly the same time as The Mum said, "Banoffee."

The three of them filtered out, each one pausing by Hughes. His father gave him a sheepish grin of his own. Krys hugged him. The Mum, cryptic as was her nature, simply looked deep into his eyes, and shook her venerable head, and left on a personal quest for the sacred treasure known as banoffee ice cream.

"Leave us," Kim told the two bullnecked men.

They nodded. One of them said, "Yes, Miss Shine."

The door shut. They were left alone.

Kim resumed her seat. "Hello Hughes."

"Why," said Hughes, his tone coating every word in lead, "did that man call you Miss Shine?"

"Because that's who I am. Please."

She gestured to the seat facing her.

Hughes put down his parcel and took it. His face was carefully blank, his posture guarded.

"You look good," she told him.

Hughes said nothing.

"And you're furious. You wear your whole self on both sleeves. It's quite amazing."

Hughes said nothing.

"Those men called me Miss Shine because I have taken over the *former* Mr. Shine's business. His assets are now mine, including the revenue of all outstanding debts. That is what I want to tell you up front, Hughes. Your debt has been eradicated. You are a free man."

Hughes said nothing.

"The second thing I want to tell you is that I lied to you. This was during our time together. I'm going to tell you the truth now, rough and unvarnished. I'm only sorry that it took me this long to do so."

Hughes poured himself a cup of tea.

"My name is not Kim Kallaimon," said not Kim Kallaimon. "I was born in Troy. During its sack by General Ulyssé, I was the town nobility's only survivor. My name is Creusa King. I am the daughter of Priam, sister to Hector, Cassandra, and Paris. And, until recently, the wife of Aeneas."

A tremble ran through the hand holding the teapot. Even so, Hughes did not spill a drop.

"In the spring of this year I left my husband. I left clues indicating that I'd fled the city for Jaenqui-Across-The-River. Aeneas is still there, I believe. For this, I am not sorry. He is an... unworthy man."

Hughes set the teapot down. Jasmine-scented steam billowed from his cup.

"I moved about aimlessly for a while, and one night I met you. I was smitten at once. You were too, naturally. Don't bother denying it because I see your agreement writ in undeniable letters behind your eyes."

Hughes said nothing.

"So you see. The night you confessed that you were not the affluent, successful man you'd led me to believe you were, you confronted me not only with your deceit but also my own. Two people fascinated by one another, both embodying illusions, and both unwilling to deal with our rightful circumstances. Isn't that extraordinary?"

Hughes drank his tea. Jasmine filled his senses. He neither confirmed nor denied the extraordinary parallels between them. He did not even acknowledge them, for doing so might establish a blueprint foundation for her to build upon as the conversation progressed. So he said nothing.

"That night I left you. I took your car and what money you had because by depriving you of those things I made you as naked as you had made me. For this, I couldn't be more sorry.

"Spring became summer. Guilt gnawed at me. I kept picturing you waking up, visualizing you as you realized what I'd done to you in the most vivid technicolor. Eventually I couldn't bear it. I had to make things right. Approaching you would be impossible. Instead I would circumnavigate, as my brother Hector circumnavigated the defenses of his enemies in war.

"Mr. Shine was a wretched caterpillar who dreamed of becoming a golden moth. He kidnapped children and through a science whose nature is not yet clear to me, he created Miss Gleam and Mr. Glint and others like them. After that, Shine's coronation as the king of Corinth's underworld was a matter of apathy. Who could stand against his glittering vanguard? Who would even try?"

Kim leaned forward. This room, a room he had grown up in and always considered vast for its papery ups and downs and edges, felt small with her here. Dwarfed. Shrunken. Hughes said nothing.

"At first I engaged a number of independent killers. When this ultimately failed, I turned to Paris. He became my right hand. He has always loved me dearly. I think he even enjoyed himself up until the moment where Miss Gleam punctured his testicles with one of his own arrows."

Hughes watched the clouds of steam curl and waft with Kim's breath.

"Also essential to my success were Krys and The Mum. You had told me about their cottage forged out of the wreck of a carousel. It seemed fitting that I enlist them in this... call it a mission. A mission to free you of debt and to show you how much I care about you."

Hughes said nothing.

"Krys' power to gauge the future proved invaluable. We wiped away all of Shine's top brass. His hegemony was crumbling. It was time. On the day people transformed into animals, my forces stormed his lair and bashed in his head. I'm told he wept before Hector killed him. I wasn't sure whether or not to tell you that part, but from that tiny flicker at the corners of your mouth, I'm glad I did.

"By the way, you mustn't be angry with my siblings for keeping my identity a secret from you. I asked them to because it was important that I tell you everything face-to-face."

Your name is a popular one in my family of late, Paris had told him.

And months before that, Krys the Painted Girl, had looked him in the face and said, *She's a king's daughter, you know.*

Hughes drank his tea.

Kim sat back in her chair. "The reason I came here today was this: I wanted my final act before speaking to you like this to be one that would reveal my commitment to your happiness. Earlier this afternoon with Krys and The Mum as witnesses, I invested in the *Scriptorium and Flavored Tea Emporium.* There is no partnership. Your father retains complete control. Ah. I see you're surprised that a prideful man such as he would stoop to allow a criminal's funds to fuel the development of his livelihood. Clearly your father is not opposed to criminality, as long as it is honest. I have the documents he signed to prove it. Would you like to see?"

Hughes said nothing.

"Besides, I intend to clean up much of Mr. Shine's organization in the coming weeks. I have improved not only your circumstances but your father's as well. Why did I do this?"

She smiled. A smile like Kim's could enslave you. Hughes would know.

He said nothing.

"Isn't it obvious? It's because what I did to you... it destroyed me. More importantly, I did it because I still care about you."

This time the tremble tinkled the bottom of his teacup against its saucer.

Your name is a popular one in my family of late.

She's a king's daughter, you know.

He didn't know she'd come around the table until her finger traced a gentle path over the line of his jaw. Her manicured nail rasped over his stubble. When it came to his chin, she applied the softest pressure, tilting his face up to hers.

"Your car is parked nearby. Your *Eschezmont*."

It was your car, Gleam had told him in Eurydice. *I knew I recognized it when it came to save your bowman. To think you were probably inside. Close enough to bite.*

She's a king's daughter, you know.

"I've got the keys, Hughes. We can drive somewhere. Don't you understand? All of this, everything I've done, has been one big offer. And that offer... is me. Creusa King. Kim Kallaimon. Me, Hughes. I want you to be with me. Your heart's newly mended, I can see that. Mine's brittle too. Will you not give them the chance to grow strong together?"

They looked at one another, her hand on his cheek.

"Will you say nothing?"

***

It was ten-to-six in the evening, a sickle moon cleaved the November sky, and Cate Jubilee sat alone on a bench in a park in quiet Nikandros District. She was inventing excuses.

"Cate, look, I went to visit my dad and got roped into a debate about whether it's called regular tea or orange pekoe. That's why I'm late. I'm so sorry."

It was, all things considered, an unbelievable impression of Hughes.

The park had these artificial trees. They had been commissioned by the government as part of a community-building exercise after Nikandros' industrial sector had shut down during the post-wartime recession. Most of the initiatives had turned out very poorly, but these trees had turned out beautifully. Widely spaced and spiraling around themselves the way asteroid belts spiral around some planets, the trees were weird and avant-garde and totally, completely useless. They also looked nothing like the real thing. That was the point.

"Cate, listen, I ran into Burnished Isaac Lawless and he was out of his brains on a cocktail of red hawk, blue swallow, and other narcotics. I had some, one thing led to another, and he and I are now husband and wife. Guess which is which. I'm so bloody sorry."

Beside her was a package. It had been waiting for her when she'd arrived, tucked surreptitiously under the bench with a little card:

G. Hughes

Cate had been pleased as punch. In her mind the dots aligned into a clear and charming image. This was the situation: Hughes had ordered something for the two of them to enjoy, and in a further act of loveliness, he had it delivered so it would be there when they arrived. Some part of her giggled, knowing Falstaff had undoubtedly had a hand in the smoothness of the whole thing, but hey. It was the thought that counted.

And with Hughes arranging this cute get-together with the phrase, "I've got some things I want to tell you," thought counted for a lot.

Now it was five-to-six, he was almost an hour late, and whatever goodwill he'd earned was quickly dwindling.

"Cate," she said glumly. "Don't laugh. The Nightjar Coven are back, only they're clowns now. They honk your nose and you turn into a croissant for exactly fifty-five minutes. Anyway, I got here as fast as I could. It's imperative that we make up and kiss. I think the all-butter pastry flavor is almost gone. Oh, and by the way I'm the sorriest ickle bickle panther in the menagerie. Mwwwwwah."

Someone cleared their throat.

She jumped.

Hughes was standing ten feet away, hands submerged in his pockets, brows raised in amusement.

Cate's eyes flickered. "How much of that did you hear?"

"A fair bit. For what it's worth, I'm the sorriest ickle bickle panther in the menagerie."

"We never speak of this again."

"Which part?"

"Exactly. Sit down before I happen to you."

"I'll stand then."

"*Hughes.*"

He joined her on the bench, suppressing laughter.

"You didn't open it."

She glanced at the package. She opened her mouth to say that no, she had waited for him like the adorable paragon of chivalry that she was, and then she saw his face. "What's wrong?"

"It's beer. I thought about wine but it just didn't feel very *you*."

"Hey." She scooted so they were close. "Did something happen?"

"Stoving's Apple Throatwinkler. What a name for a drink. This place is pretty at night, isn't it?" He peered out over the slope of the park. "Funny trees, mind you."

His thighs were clamped on his hands as if keeping them warm. Cate tugged one out by his sleeve and held it.

"Won't you talk to me, Gormon Hughes?"

He looked at her. Her eyes held him. Her hands too. Her red hair was a portrait frame around her face, and that face held him closest of all. Especially her nose, which was an adorable paragon of nasalness.

He smiled a smile as brittle as he felt all over, and nodded.

"Well," she prompted sweetly. "Go on then."

So he did.

***

After ten minutes of unbroken monologue, Cate opened the package, fished out two cans of still-cold beer, cracked one for him and two for her.

Hughes sipped between each island of speech.

He spoke about himself, beginning at the end and working backward. His rock-solid passions. His vague hopes. His deepest dreads. He spoke about his feelings of being othered for his poverty, his interests. He raked the coals of his resentments. He laid himself bare to her.

Cate cracked a third beer and listened, her legs crossed under her and her expression as intent as anything he'd ever seen.

He told her about Kim, about the heartbreak, and about what had just transpired in his father's teashop. He spoke until he could speak no more, and when all was said and done and he had wept and chuckled in equal measure, he let the still November eve steal over him. He sat motionless, awaiting her judgment.

For what seemed a long time, Cate Jubilee did not say or do anything.

She leaned back against the bench, put out her legs and arms, and stretched a huge feline stretch. She stood. "Up," she told him.

Hesitantly, not at all sure what was going to happen, Hughes obeyed.

She stood chest-to-chest with him. "Arms raised."

What on earth was she talking about?

"Trust me," she said.

And he did trust her. Whatever came around the corner, that much was certain. Hughes raised his arms to Cate's satisfaction.

"Good," she said and sprang.

He was laughing even before he grasped the full extent of her evil genius. One of the things he had not admitted to that night was being ticklish. Cate had simply known, the wily she-devil.

They struggled, her tickling relentlessly and him trying (and failing) to ward off her fingers. They seemed to be everywhere at once. He was tempted to check himself for mirrors, and the thought of that only hiked up his giddiness.

The bench overlooked a slope that started gentle but grew steep fast.

Hughes lost his footing and took her with him. They rolled together, both now hysterical with laughter. An onlooker would probably have thought them escaped loons fighting over an imaginary treasure, but aside from the peculiar trees and that curve of moon peeking through their branches, they were alone.

Momentum slowed them. Cate ended up on top.

"*That* was it?" she roared. "*That* was the big secret?"

"Can't breathe," he giggled. "Oh God."

"I cannot believe you. Give me your cheeks. *Give me them I say!*"

She smooshed his cheeks with her fingers and nibbled them, going, "Ang, ang, ang, ang!"

Which did not make breathing easier.

"I've never laughed so much," he managed.

"You absolute idiot."

"Hey now, easy."

"You've got some eclectic tastes and one bad breakup! Why didn't you tell me? What did you imagine I'd say?" Cate arched her back and laid a hand against her brow theatrically. "Oh Hughes, you gormless, gutless Gormon. It was not meant to be."

He bolted up, going for her underarms and delicious revenge.

She was too quick!

With a muffled *thump* she pinned his hands with her elbows, leaned down, and began nuzzling his collarbone. This was surprisingly similar to tickling and started Hughes off again.

"End you've gut ay leedle beet hoff resentment inside you," she teased over his pleas for mercy. "My Gott, Hughes. Eets like you are ay hooman beink vit *emotions!*"

"I'm dying!"

"You are crezy, crezy man."

Finally she relented, slinking off him. They lay next to one another, panting and grinning wide, stupid grins to match the moon.

"Thank you," he said, turning to look at her. "You don't know how happy that makes me."

"Ridiculous," she chided him. "We're going to your dad's teashop tomorrow."

"You'd like to?"

"Love to."

"Well then it's settled."

She propped herself onto one elbow, resting her chin in the cup of her palm. "I'm sorry about Kim. Creusa, I mean. You must have been so hurt for all of that to be pent up inside you. And for so long too."

"Pretty hurt," he admitted. "Hard to feel hurt now though. Want to head back to the bench?"

"No," she said primly and proceeded to snuggle into him right there on the ground.

Hughes put his arms around her. A wisp of cloud tried to steal the moon's show, but the sickle blushed it full of pale and sent it on its way.

He felt... something...

It rose without further warning. Incandescent, it shot through his whole being.

<table>
<tr><td align="center">Hughes</td></tr>
<tr><td align="center">Honesty Level: ?</td></tr>
<tr><td align="center">While Performance influences those around you by force, its results are
ultimately hollow victories secured by manipulation.
You chose Honesty tonight. It guarantees nothing. It secures nothing.
But it is not hollow.
It is the elixir of hope.
Drink, then, and be made whole.</td></tr>
</table>

He waited for more. When it became clear there wouldn't be any—no percentage bonus, no secret abilities—he took a deep breath. Let it go.

The elixir of hope, huh?

He liked the sound of that.

They lay together under the broad stars.

"I wonder if this is what Frank and Mr. Glint do every night," Cate said.

Hughes chuckled. "They do seem pretty inseparable recently, it's true."

"The two most unlikely friends the universe has ever thrown together. Move your arm a bit. Oh perfect. I'll tell you one thing: Mr. Glint doesn't live up to his reputation."

"No?"

"No," she said. "He's worse."

A light breeze flowed over them. Neither of them minded. They were toasty warm.

After a while, Cate said, "I have something I need to tell you."

"About your tattoos?"

A pause. "Yes."

"In that case no need," said Hughes. "I knew as soon as I brought it up that night in *The Coconut*—it's a touchy subject. Take your time. When you're ready, we'll talk about it."

"Hughes, you've just been more vulnerable with me than anyone has ever been. It wouldn't be fair."

"Maybe not," he said firmly. "But it'd be right."

To that she had no reply.

No verbal one at least.

A whisper of fabric signaled her head moving from his chest. Her face tilted up to him. Their eyes met, bright and dark. Hughes offered. She took him up on it.

It was without question the best kiss of his life.

"Love you, Cate."

"That won't do."

"What?"

"It's quite simple. You see, I'm absolutely head over heels for you too. Utterly doo-lally in love. Arse over teakettle." She sighed. "There's only one thing for it. We're going to have to see who loves who more."

"Cate..."

"Stop grinning. I'm seriousness incarnate."

"You're mad."

"And?"

"Fair enough."

She flipped over, kicking her heels in the air and sizing him up through narrowed eyes. "Tell me, Gormon Hughes, how much do you love me?"

Hughes looked at her.

Cate looked back.

They said it at exactly the same time. The P word.

Maybe it wouldn't work. Complications would arise. It was inevitable. Trouble seemed to orbit both of them like astral debris.

Then again, maybe it would. Like all important things that wobble on the knife edge of truth (the real truth, the kind that doesn't need percentages to matter), only tomorrow would tell.

For now there was laughter.

It might just be enough.

<u>END OF BOOK ONE</u>

<u>A NOTE OF THANKS</u>

With a glad heart, I'd like to take this opportunity to thank you, reader. The transportive qualities of a novel are pretty undisputed; certainly my favorites have taken me places I could never have dreamed of. I hope this tale was a journey that pleased you as much as it excited (and delighted!) me.
Now, if you like, rant and rave about this book to your friends! Leave a review on the platform of your choosing!
Your support means the world.
As a certain forgemistress is wont to say: I'm as thick as clotted cream, and even I know that.

Jack Fields
March, 2024

ARISE ALPHA

By Jez Cajiao

When you steal a hundred grand from some very bad people, the best way to survive is to stay small and quiet...

Possibly its not to save a pair of drowning girls, not go 'viral' on social media and certainly not to let the local police take your passport, trapping you on a small 'party' island in the middle of the Mediterranean Sea.

But Steve isn't the average guy, he's ex-military, ex-enforcer and ex-human. He's a one-man nanite fueled nightmare for those that cross the line, and he's decided that it's time to clean up his act. He's going to make up for the things he's done, and save 'the little guys'.

It's a nice fantasy, but even he has to admit, it's really just a justification, because he's a very bad man, with horrifying abilities, and he's only just learning what he's capable of. He needs a reason to not go to the dark, and if that's hunting down the creatures of the night and beating them to death with their own femurs?

Well, he's just the man for the job.

Stolen money. Greek Islands. Werewolves and Enforcers...
What could possibly go wrong?

https://www.amazon.com/Arise-Alpha-Dark-LitRPG-Adventure-ebook

THEFT OF DECKS : BOOK ONE

By Lars Machmüller
When the deck is stacked against you? Change the game!

In the frontier town of Isarn, Chase will never be more than the lowly Darkborn thief he is. Banned from training, banned from acquiring better cards, if the Lightborn had their way, he'd be banned from life itself.

He's not alone though, and the one thing he and his friends have is determination. Losing a hand to a brutal punishment only fueled his obsession to get access to his own amazing, reality-bending cards.

That is the path to power and a future for them all. Nobody cares where you came from when you're rich enough. For now, though, they're facing both established powers, churches and age-old prejudices. It's time to get to work, and if the Lightborn won't share and play nice?

Sometimes the only way to get dealt a better hand is to steal the whole damn deck!

D&D meets Magic the Gathering in this epic fantasy deckbuilding LitRPG

https://mybook.to/TheftofDecksbook1

QUEST ACADEMY

By Brian J. Nordon

A world infested by demons.
An Academy designed to train Heroes to save humanity from annihilation.
A new student's power could make all the difference.

Humans have been pushed to the brink of extinction by an ever-evolving demonic threat. Portals are opening faster than ever, Towers bursting into the skies and Dungeons being mined below the last safe havens of society. The demons are winning.

Quest Academy stands defiantly against them, as a place to train the next generation of Heroes. The Guild Association is holding the line, but are in dire need of new blood and the powerful abilities they could bring to the battlefront. To be the saviors that humanity needs, they need to surpass the limits of those that came before them.

In a war with everything on the line, every power matters. With an adaptive enemy, comes the need for a constant shift in tactics. A new age of strategy is emerging, with even the unlikeliest of Heroes making an impact.

Salvatore Argento has never seen a demon.
He has never aspired to become a Hero.
Yet his power might be the one to tip the odds in humanity's favor.

Buy on Amazon

WANDERING WARRIOR

By Michael Head

A divine quest to deliver justice.
One year to accomplish his mission.
After nineteen planets, there's something different about this one.

James Holden has reached the maximum level there is for a human. That's perfect, since he's the only one of his kind. A wandering warrior, without control of his destination, tossed between universes by gods who've failed to tell him why. James is the lone Judge on a new world in need of someone to balance the scales. He isn't afraid to do so with extreme prejudice. As the Chief Justice, he has to right the wrongs the innocent can't fix themselves.

As James quickly discovers, the roots of corruption run deep. Guilds choose to protect themselves rather than the people. Monsters roam the wilderness unchecked. Judgment is usually a decision between right and wrong, but nothing is ever that simple. This time, being the strongest human won't be enough to punish the guilty. James might have to recruit some new blood, even if he prefers to work alone.

On his twentieth world, he is going to win, no matter the cost. James will have to find a way to break past the limits of the system if he's going to have a chance at making a difference.

Buy on Amazon

KNIGHTS OF ETERNITY

By Rachel Ní Chuirc

When Zara awoke in chains she thought she'd gone mad.

She was Zara the Fury - mistress of flame and fear. Her name was whispered across the land, from ramshackle taverns to the royal court. Even the heroic Gilded Knights thought twice before crossing her path.
She was feared—*respected.*
Now she was curled up on a dirt floor on her fiancé's orders. Valerius, leader of the Gilded, mocks her cries for help. And the kingdom is on the brink of war over the missing Lady Eternity...
But that wasn't why Zara thought she had gone mad.
The reason why is that the last thing she remembered was blood, an arcade screen, and the gun that changed everything.

But no chains can hold the Fury, and when she gets out?
The world is going to *burn*.

SOCIAL MEDIA

Jack Fields Author Page
https://www.facebook.com/JackFieldsAuthor

LitRPG Legion Page
https://www.facebook.com/groups/litrpglegion

LITRPG!

To learn more about LitRPG, talk to authors, and have an awesome time, please join the LitRPG Group.

https://www.facebook.com/groups/LitRPGGroup

FACEBOOK

Here's a few wonderfully active Facebook groups I'd recommend, as you'll get to hear about great new books and new releases.

https://www.facebook.com/groups/LitRPGlegion/

https://www.facebook.com/groups/GamelitSociety

https://www.facebook.com/groups

https://www.facebook.com/groups/LitRPGforum/

RECOMMENDATIONS

If you liked this novel, you might also like...

Creation's Bane by Kevin Sinclair

Knights of Eternity by Rachel Ní Chuirc

Quest Academy by Brian J. Nordon

Somnia Online by K.T. Hanna

The Good Guys by Eric Ugland

The Ten Realms by Michael Chatfield

UnderVerse by Jez Cajiao

Wandering Warrior by Michael Head

World of Chains by Lars Machmüller

Jack
Fields
20

www.ingramcontent.com/pod-product-compliance
Lightning Source LLC
Chambersburg PA
CBHW070333170726
48291CB00001B/39